MW00629650

FIC Saramago
Saramago, Jose.
Blindness
PLAINFIELD PUBLIC LIBRARY, 1120 STAFFORD ROAD

BLINDNESS

———

SEEING

Blindness

Translated from the Portuguese
by Giovanni Pontiero

Seeing

Translated from the Portuguese
by Margaret Jull Costa

JOSÉ SARAMAGO

Houghton Mifflin Harcourt

BOSTON · NEW YORK

2011

Blindness, Copyright © José Saramago and Editorial Caminho, 1995,
English translation copyright © Professor Juan Sager, 1997

Seeing, Copyright © José Saramago and Editorial Caminho SA, Lisbon,
2004, English translation copyright © 2006 by Margaret Jull Costa

ALL RIGHTS RESERVED

For information about permission to reproduce selections from this book,
write to Permissions, Houghton Mifflin Harcourt Publishing Company,
215 Park Avenue South, New York, New York 10003.

www.hmhbooks.com

Blindness was first published in English in Great Britain in 1997 by The
Harvill Press. *Blindness* is a translation of *Ensaio sobre a Cegueira* and is
published with the financial assistance of the Instituto Português do
Livro e das Bibliotecas, Lisbon, which is gratefully acknowledged.

Seeing is a translation of *Ensaio sobre a Lucidez*.
TRANSLATOR'S ACKNOWLEDGMENTS
I would like to thank José Saramago, Manucha Lisboa, Ben Sherriff, and
Sílvia Morim for all their help and advice, and, in particular, my fellow
Saramago translator Maartje de Kort.

Library of Congress Cataloging-in-Publication Data
Saramago, José.
[Ensaio sobre a cegueira. English]
Blindness / José Saramago ; translated from the Portuguese
by Giovanni Pontiero. Seeing / translated from the Portuguese
by Margaret Jull Costa.
p. cm.
ISBN 978-0-547-55488-4
1. Blind—Fiction. 2. Blindness—Fiction. I. Pontiero, Giovanni.
II. Costa, Margaret Jull. III. Saramago, José. Ensaio sobre a
lucidez. English. IV. Title.
PQ9281.A66E6813 2011
869.3'42—dc22   2010052587

Book design by Melissa Lotfy

Printed in the United States of America

DOC 10 9 8 7 6 5 4 3 2 1

Blindness

PUBLISHERS' NOTE

The translator died before completing his revision of
this translation. The Publishers acknowledge the help
of Margaret Jull Costa in fulfilling this task.

For Pilar
For my daughter Violante

IN MEMORIAM

Giovanni Pontiero

If you can see, look.
If you can look, observe.

—*Book of Exhortations*

THE amber light came on. Two of the cars ahead accelerated before the red light appeared. At the pedestrian crossing the sign of a green man lit up. The people who were waiting began to cross the road, stepping on the white stripes painted on the black surface of the asphalt, there is nothing less like a zebra, however, that is what it is called. The motorists kept an impatient foot on the clutch, leaving their cars at the ready, advancing, retreating like nervous horses that can sense the whiplash about to be inflicted. The pedestrians have just finished crossing but the sign allowing the cars to go will be delayed for some seconds, some people maintain that this delay, while apparently so insignificant, has only to be multiplied by the thousands of traffic lights that exist in the city and by the successive changes of their three colours to produce one of the most serious causes of traffic jams or bottlenecks, to use the more current term.

The green light came on at last, the cars moved off briskly, but then it became clear that not all of them were equally quick off the mark. The car at the head of the middle lane has stopped, there must be some mechanical fault, a loose accelerator pedal, a gear lever that has stuck, problem with the suspension, jammed brakes, breakdown in the electric circuit, unless he has simply run out of gas, it would not be the first time such a thing has happened. The next group of pedestrians to gather at the crossing see the driver of the stationary car wave his arms behind the windshield, while the cars behind him frantically sound their horns. Some drivers have already got out of their cars, prepared to push the stranded vehicle to a spot where it will not hold up the traffic, they beat furiously on the closed windows, the man inside turns his head in their direction, first to one side then the other, he is clearly shouting something, to judge by the movements of his mouth he appears to be repeating some words, not one word but three, as turns out to be the case when someone finally manages to open the door, I am blind.

Who would have believed it. Seen merely at a glance, the man's eyes seem healthy, the iris looks bright, luminous, the sclera white, as compact as porcelain. The eyes wide open, the wrinkled skin of the face, his eyebrows suddenly screwed up, all this, as anyone can see, signifies that he is distraught with anguish. With a rapid movement, what was in sight has disappeared behind the man's clenched fists, as if he were still trying to retain inside his mind the final image captured, a round red light at the traffic lights. I am blind, I am blind, he repeated in despair as they helped him to get out of the car, and the tears welling up made those eyes which he claimed were dead, shine even more. These things happen, it will pass you'll see, sometimes it's nerves, said a woman. The lights had already changed again, some inquisitive passersby had gathered around the group, and the drivers further back who did not know what was going on, protested at what they thought was some common accident, a smashed headlight, a dented fender, nothing to justify this upheaval, Call the police, they shouted and get that old wreck out of the way. The blind man pleaded, Please, will someone take me home. The woman who had suggested a case of nerves was of the opinion that an ambulance should be summoned to transport the poor man to the hospital, but the blind man refused to hear of it, quite unnecessary, all he wanted was that someone might accompany him to the entrance of the building where he lived. It's close by and you could do me no greater favour. And what about the car, asked someone. Another voice replied, The key is in the ignition, drive the car onto the pavement. No need, intervened a third voice, I'll take charge of the car and accompany this man home. There were murmurs of approval. The blind man felt himself being taken by the arm, Come, come with me, the same voice was saying to him. They eased him into the front passenger seat, and secured the safety belt. I can't see, I can't see, he murmured, still weeping. Tell me where you live, the man asked him. Through the car windows voracious faces spied, avid for some news. The blind man raised his hands to his eyes and gestured, Nothing, it's as if I were caught in a mist or had fallen into a milky sea. But blindness isn't like that, said the other fellow, they say that blindness is black, Well I see everything white, That little woman was probably right, it could be a matter of nerves, nerves are the very devil, No need to talk to me about it, it's a disaster, yes a disaster, Tell me where you live please, and at the same time the engine started up. Faltering, as if his lack of sight had weakened his memory, the blind man gave his address, then he said, I have no words to thank you, and the other replied, Now then, don't give it another thought, today it's your turn, tomorrow it will be mine, we never know what might lie in store for us, You're right, who would have thought, when I left the house this morning, that something as dreadful as this was about to happen. He was puzzled that they should still be at a standstill, Why aren't we moving, he asked, The light is on red, replied the other. From now on he would no longer know when the light was red.

As the blind man had said, his home was nearby. But the pavements were crammed with vehicles, they could not find a space to park and were obliged to look for a spot in one of the side streets. There, because of the narrowness of the pavement, the door on the passenger's side would have been little more than a hand's-breadth from the wall, so in order to avoid the discomfort of dragging himself from one seat to the other with the brake and steering wheel in the way, the blind man had to get out before the car was parked. Abandoned in the middle of the road, feeling the ground shifting under his feet, he tried to suppress the sense of panic that welled up inside him. He waved his hands in front of his face, nervously, as if he were swimming in what he had described as a milky sea, but his mouth was already opening to let out a cry for help when at the last minute he felt the other's hand gently touch him on the arm, Calm down, I've got you. They proceeded very slowly, afraid of falling, the blind man dragged his feet, but this caused him to stumble on the uneven pavement, Be patient, we're almost there, the other murmured, and a little further ahead, he asked, Is there anyone at home to look after you, and the blind man replied, I don't know, my wife won't be back from work yet, to-day it so happened that I left earlier only to have this hit me. You'll see, it isn't anything serious, I've never heard of anyone suddenly going blind, And to think I used to boast that I didn't even need glasses, Well it just goes to show. They had arrived at the entrance to the building, two women from the neighbour-hood looked on inquisitively at the sight of their neighbour be-ing led by the arm but neither of them thought of asking, Have you got something in your eye, it never occurred to them nor would he have been able to reply, Yes, a milky sea. Once inside the building, the blind man said, Many thanks, I'm sorry for all the trouble I've caused you, I can manage on my own now, No need to apologise, I'll come up with you, I wouldn't be easy in my mind if I were to leave you here. They got into the narrow elevator with some difficulty, What floor do you live on, On the third, you cannot imagine how grateful I am, Don't thank me, today it's you, Yes, you're right, tomorrow it might be you. The elevator came to a halt, they stepped out onto the landing, Would you like me to help you open the door, Thanks, that's something I think I can do for myself. He took from his pocket a small bunch of keys, felt them one by one along the serrated edge, and said, It must be this one, and feeling for the keyhole with the fingertips of his left hand, he tried to open the door. It isn't this one, Let me have a look, I'll help you. The door opened at the third attempt. Then the blind man called inside, Are you there, no one replied, and he remarked, Just as I was saying, she still hasn't come back. Stretching out his hands, he groped his way along the corridor, then he came back cautiously, turning his head in the direction where he calculated the other fellow would be, How can I thank you, he said, It was the least I could do, said the good Samaritan, no need to thank me, and added, Do you want me to help you to get settled and keep you company until your wife arrives. This zeal suddenly struck the blind man as being suspect, obviously he would not invite a complete stranger to come in who, after all, might well be plotting at that very moment how to overcome, tie up and gag the poor defenceless blind man, and then lay hands on anything of value. There's no need, please don't bother, he said, I'm fine, and as he slowly began closing the door, he repeated, There's no need, there's no need.

Hearing the sound of the elevator descending he gave a sigh of relief. With a mechanical gesture, forgetting the state in which he found himself, he drew back the lid of the peephole and looked outside. It was as if there were a white wall on the other side. He could feel the contact of the metallic frame on his eyebrow, his eyelashes brushed against the tiny lens, but he could not see out, an impenetrable whiteness covered everything. He knew he was in his own home, he recognised the smell, the atmosphere, the silence, he could make out the items of furniture and objects simply by touching them, lightly running his fingers over them, but at the same time it was as if all of this were already dissolving into a kind of strange dimension, without direction or reference points, with neither north nor south, below nor above. Like most people, he had often played as a child at pretending to be blind, and, after keeping his eyes closed for five minutes, he had reached the conclusion that blindness, undoubtedly a terrible affliction, might still be relatively bearable if the unfortunate victim had retained sufficient memory, not just of the colours, but also of forms and planes, surfaces and shapes, assuming of course, that this one was not born blind. He had even reached the point of thinking that the darkness in which the blind live was nothing other than the simple absence of light, that what we call blindness was something that simply covered the appearance of beings and things, leaving them intact behind their black veil. Now, on the contrary, here he was, plunged into a whiteness so luminous, so total, that it swallowed up rather than absorbed, not just the colours, but the very things and beings, thus making them twice as invisible.

As he moved in the direction of the sitting-room, despite the caution with which he advanced, running a hesitant hand along the wall and not anticipating any obstacles, he sent a vase of flowers crashing to the floor. He had forgotten about any such vase, or perhaps his wife had put it there when she left for work with the intention of later finding some more suitable place. He bent down to appraise the damage. The water had spread over the polished floor. He tried to gather up the flowers, never thinking of the broken glass, a long sharp splinter pricked his finger and, at the pain, childish tears of helplessness sprang to his eyes, blind with whiteness in the middle of his flat, which was turning dark as evening fell. Still clutching the flowers and feeling the blood running down, he twisted round to get the handkerchief from his pocket and wrapped it round his finger as best he could. Then, fumbling, stumbling, skirting the furniture, treading warily so as not to trip on the rugs, he reached the sofa where he and his wife watched television. He sat down, rested the flowers on his lap, and, with the utmost care, unrolled the handkerchief. The blood, sticky to the touch, worried him, he thought it must be because he could not see it, his blood had turned into a viscous substance without colour, into something rather alien which nevertheless belonged to him, but like a self-inflicted threat directed at himself. Very slowly, gently probing with his good hand, he tried to locate the splinter of glass, as sharp as a tiny dagger, and, by bringing the nails of his thumb and forefinger together, he managed to extract all of it. He wrapped the handkerchief round the injured finger once more, this time tightly to stop the bleeding, and, weak and exhausted, he leaned back on the sofa. A minute later, because of one of those all too common abdications of the body, that chooses to give up in certain moments of anguish or despair, when, if it were guided by logic alone, all its nerves should be alert and tense, a kind of weariness crept over him, more drowsiness than real fatigue, but just as heavy. He dreamt at once that he was pretending to be blind, he dreamt that he was forever closing and opening his eyes, and that, on each occasion, as if he were returning from a journey, he found waiting for him, firm and unaltered, all the forms and colours of the world as he knew it. Beneath this reassuring certainty, he perceived nevertheless, the dull nagging of uncertainty, perhaps it was a deceptive dream, a dream from which he would have to emerge sooner or later, without knowing at this moment what reality awaited him. Then, if such a word has any meaning when applied to a weariness that lasted for only a few seconds, and already in that semi-vigilant state that prepares one for awakening, he seriously considered that it was unwise to remain in this state of indecision, shall I wake up, shall I not wake up, shall I wake up, shall I not wake up, there always comes a moment when one has no option but to take a risk, What am I doing here with these flowers on my lap and my eyes closed as if I were afraid of opening them, What are you doing there, sleeping with those flowers on your lap, his wife was asking him.

She did not wait for a reply. Pointedly, she set about gathering up the fragments of the vase and drying the floor, muttering all the while with an irritation she made no attempt to disguise, You might have cleaned up this mess yourself, instead of settling down to sleep as if it were no concern of yours. He said nothing, protecting his eyes behind tightly closed lids, suddenly agitated by a thought, And if I were to open my eyes and see, he asked himself, gripped by anxious hope. The woman drew near, noticed the bloodstained handkerchief, her vexation gone in an instant, Poor man, how did this happen, she asked compassionately as she undid the improvised bandage. Then he wanted with all his strength to see his wife kneeling at his feet, right there, where he knew she was, and then, certain that he would not see her, he opened his eyes, So you've wakened up at last, my sleepyhead, she said smiling. There was silence, and he said, I'm blind, I can't see. The woman lost her patience, Stop playing silly games, there are certain things we must not joke about, How I wish it were a joke, the truth is that I really am blind, I can't see anything, Please, don't frighten me, look at me, here, I'm here, the light is on, I know you're there, I can hear you, touch you, I can imagine you've switched on the light, but I am blind. She began to weep, clung to him, It isn't true, tell me that it isn't true. The flowers had slipped onto the floor, onto the bloodstained handkerchief, the blood had started to trickle again from the injured finger, and he, as if wanting to say with other words, That's the least of my worries, murmured, I see everything white, and he gave a sad smile. The woman sat down beside him, embraced him tightly, kissed him gently on the forehead, on the face, softly on the eyes, You'll see that this will pass, you haven't been ill, no one goes blind from one minute to the next, Perhaps, Tell me how it happened, what did you feel, when, where, no, not yet, wait, the first thing we must do is to consult an eye specialist, can you think of one, I'm afraid not, neither of us wears glasses, And if I were to take you to the hospital, There isn't likely to be any emergency service for eyes that cannot see, You're right, better that we should go straight to a doctor, I'll look in the telephone directory and locate a doctor who practises nearby. She got up, still questioning him, Do you notice any difference, None, he replied, Pay attention, I'm going to switch off the light and you can tell me, now, Nothing, What do you mean nothing, Nothing, I always see the same white, it's as if there were no night.

He could hear his wife rapidly leaf through the pages of the telephone directory, sniffling to hold back her tears, sighing, and finally saying, This one will do, let's hope he can see us. She dialled a number, asked if that was the surgery, if the doctor was there, if she could speak to him, No, no the doctor doesn't know me, the matter is extremely urgent, yes, please, I understand, then I'll explain the situation to you, but I beg of you to pass on what I have to say to the doctor, the fact is that my husband has suddenly gone blind, yes, yes, all of a sudden, no, no he is not one of the doctor's patients, my husband does not wear glasses and never has, yes, he has excellent eyesight, just like me, I also see perfectly well, ah, many thanks, I'll wait, I'll wait, yes, doctor, all of a sudden, he says he sees everything white, I have no idea what happened, I haven't had time to ask him, I've just arrived home to find him in this state, would you like me to ask him, ah, I'm so grateful to you doctor, we'll come right away, right away. The blind man rose to his feet, Wait, his wife said, first let me attend to this finger, she disappeared for several moments, came back with a bottle of peroxide, another of iodine, cotton wool, a box of bandages. As she dressed the wound, she asked him, Where did you leave the car, and suddenly confronted him, But in your condition you couldn't have driven the car, or you were already at home when it happened, No, it was on the street when I was stationary at a red light, some person brought me home, the car was left in the next street, Fine, let's go down, wait at the door while I go to find it, where did you put the keys, I don't know, he never gave them back to me, Who's he, The man who brought me home, it was a man, He must have left them somewhere, I'll have a look round, It's pointless searching, he didn't enter the flat, But the keys have to be somewhere, Most likely he forgot, inadvertently took them with him, This was all we needed, Use your keys, then we'll sort it out, Right, let's go, take my hand. The blind man said, If I have to stay like this, I'd rather be dead, Please, don't talk nonsense, things are bad enough, I'm the one who's blind, not you, you cannot imagine what it's like, The doctor will come up with some remedy, you'll see, I shall see.

They left. Below, in the lobby, his wife switched on the light and whispered in his ear. Wait for me here, if any neighbours should appear speak to them naturally, say you're waiting for me, no one looking at you would ever suspect that you cannot see and besides we don't have to tell people all our business, Yes, but don't be long. His wife went rushing off. No neighbour entered or left. The blind man knew from experience that the stairway would only be lit so long as he could hear the mechanism of the automatic switch, therefore he went on pressing the button whenever there was silence. The light, this light, had been transformed into noise for him. He could not understand why his wife was taking so long to return, the street was nearby, some eighty or a hundred metres, If we delay any longer, the doctor will be gone, he thought to himself. He could not avoid a mechanical gesture, raising his left wrist and lowering his eyes to look at his watch. He pursed his lips as if in sudden pain, and felt deeply grateful that there were no neighbours around at that moment, for there and then, were anyone to have spoken to him, he would have burst into tears. A car stopped in the street, At last, he thought, but then realised that it was not the sound of his car engine, This is a diesel engine, it must be a taxi, he said, pressing once more on the button for the light. His wife came back, flustered and upset, that good Samaritan of yours, that good soul, has taken our car, It isn't possible, you can't have looked properly, Of course I looked properly, there's nothing wrong with my eyesight, these last words came out inadvertently, You told me the car was in the next street, she corrected herself, and it isn't, unless they've left it in some other street, No, no, I'm certain it was left in this street, Well then it has disappeared, In that case, what about the keys, He took advantage of your confusion and distress and robbed us, And to think I didn't want him in the flat for fear he might steal something yet if he had kept me company until you arrived home, he could not have stolen our car, Let's go, we have a taxi waiting, I swear to you that I'd give a year of my life to see this rogue go blind as well. Don't speak so loud, And that they rob him of everything he possesses, He might turn up, Ah, so you think he'll knock on the door tomorrow and say he took the car in a moment of distraction, that he is sorry and inquire if you're feeling better.

They remained silent until they reached the doctor's surgery. She tried not to think about the stolen car, squeezed her husband's hand affectionately, while he, his head lowered so

that the driver would not see his eyes through the rear-view
mirror, could not stop asking himself how it was possible that
such a terrible tragedy should have befallen him, Why me. He
could hear the noise of the traffic, the odd loud voice whenever
the taxi stopped, it often happens, we are still asleep and external sounds are already penetrating the veil of unconscious-
ness in which we are still wrapped up, as in a white sheet. As
in a white sheet. He shook his head, sighing, his wife gently
stroked his cheek, her way of saying, Keep calm, I'm here, and
he leaned his head on her shoulder, indifferent to what the
driver might think, If you were in my situation and unable to
drive anymore, he thought childishly, and oblivious of the absurdity of that remark, he congratulated himself amidst his despair that he was still capable of formulating a rational thought.
On leaving the taxi, discreetly assisted by his wife, he seemed
calm, but on entering the surgery where he was about to learn
his fate, he asked his wife in a tremulous whisper, What will I
be like when I get out of this place, and he shook his head as if
he had given up all hope.

His wife informed the receptionist, I'm the person who rang
half an hour ago because of my husband, and the receptionist showed them into a small room where other patients were
waiting. There was an old man with a black patch over one eye,
a young lad who looked cross-eyed, accompanied by a woman
who must be his mother, a girl with dark glasses, two other
people without any apparent distinguishing features, but no
one who was blind, blind people do not consult an ophthalmologist. The woman guided her husband to an empty chair, and
since all the other chairs were occupied, she remained standing beside him, We'll have to wait, she whispered in his ear.
He realised why, he had heard the voices of those who were
in the waiting-room, now he was assailed by another worry,
thinking that the longer the doctor took to examine him, the

worse his blindness would become to the point of being incur-
able. He fidgeted in his chair, restless, he was about to con-
fide his worries to his wife, but just then the door opened and
the receptionist said, Will you both come this way, and turning to the other patients, Doctor's orders, this man is an urgent
case. The mother of the cross-eyed boy protested that her right
was her right, and that she was first and had been waiting for
more than an hour. The other patients supported her in a low
voice, but not one of them, nor the woman herself, thought it
wise to carry on complaining, in case the doctor should take offence and repay their impertinence by making them wait even
longer, as has occurred. The old man with the patch over one
eye was magnanimous, Let the poor man go ahead, he's in a
much worse state than we are. The blind man did not hear him,
they were already going into the doctor's consulting room, and
the wife was saying, Many thanks for being so kind, doctor, it's
just that my husband, and that said, she paused, because frankly
she did not know what had really happened, she only knew that
her husband was blind and that their car had been stolen. The
doctor said, Please, be seated, and he himself went to help the
patient into the chair, and then, touching him on the hand, he
spoke to him directly, Now then, tell me what is wrong. The
blind man explained that he was in his car, waiting for the red
light to change when suddenly he could no longer see, that several people had rushed to his assistance, that an elderly woman,
judging from her voice, had said that it was probably a case of
nerves, and then a man had accompanied him home because he
could not manage on his own, I see everything white, doctor.
He said nothing about the stolen car.

The doctor asked him, Has anything like this ever happened
to you before, or something similar, No, doctor, I don't even
use glasses. And you say it came on all of a sudden, Yes, doctor,
Like a light going out, More like a light going on, During the

last few days have you felt any difference in your eyesight, No, doctor, Is there, or has there ever been any case of blindness in your family, Among the relatives I've known or have heard discussed, no one, Do you suffer from diabetes, No, doctor, From syphilis, No, doctor. From hypertension of the arteries or the brain cells, I'm not sure about the brain cells, but none of these other things, we have regular medical checkups at work. Have you taken a sharp knock on the head, today or yesterday, No, doctor, How old are you, Thirty-eight, Fine, let's take a look at these eyes. The blind man opened them wide, as if to facilitate the examination, but the doctor took him by the arm and installed him behind a scanner which anyone with imagination might see as a new version of the confessional, eyes replacing words, and the confessor looking directly into the sinner's soul, Rest your chin here, he advised him, keep your eyes open, and don't move. The woman drew close to her husband, put her hand on his shoulder, and said, This will be sorted out, you'll see. The doctor raised and lowered the binocular system at his side, turned finely adjusted knobs, and began his examination. He could find nothing in the cornea, nothing in the sclera, nothing in the iris, nothing in the retina, nothing in the lens of the eye, nothing in the luteous macula, nothing in the optic nerve, nothing elsewhere. He pushed the apparatus aside, rubbed his eyes, then carried out a second examination from the start, without speaking, and when he had finished there was a puzzled expression on his face, I cannot find any lesion, your eyes are perfect. The woman joined her hands in a gesture of happiness and exclaimed, Didn't I tell you, didn't I tell you, this can be resolved. Ignoring her, the blind man asked, May I remove my chin, doctor, Of course, forgive me, If my eyes are perfect as you say, why am I blind, For the moment I cannot say, we shall have to carry out more detailed tests, analyses, an ecography, an encephalogram, Do you think it has

anything to do with the brain, It's a possibility, but I doubt it.
Yet you say you can find nothing wrong with my eyes, That's
right, How strange, What I'm trying to say is that if, in fact,
you are blind, your blindness at this moment defies explanation, Do you doubt that I am blind, Not at all, the problem is
the unusual nature of your case, personally, in all my years in
practice, I've never come across anything like it, and I daresay
no such case has ever been known in the entire history of ophthalmology, Do you think there is a cure, In principle, since I
cannot find lesions of any kind or any congenital malforma-
tions, my reply should be in the affirmative, But apparently it
is not in the affirmative, Only out of caution, only because I do
not want to build up hopes that may turn out to be unjustified,
I understand, That's the situation, And is there any treatment
I should follow, some remedy or other, For the moment I prefer not to prescribe anything, for it would be like prescribing
in the dark. There's an apt expression, observed the blind man.
The doctor pretended not to hear, got off the revolving stool
on which he had been seated to carry out the examination, and,
standing up, he wrote out on his prescription pad the tests and
analyses he judged to be necessary. He handed the sheet of paper to the wife, Take this and come back with your husband
once you have the results, meanwhile if there should be any
change in his condition, telephone me, How much do we owe
you, doctor, Pay in reception. He accompanied them to the
door, murmured words of reassurance, Let's wait and see, let's
wait and see, you mustn't despair, and once they had gone he
went into the small bathroom adjoining the consulting room
and stared at length into the mirror, What can this be, he murmured. Then he returned to the consulting room, called out to
the receptionist, Send in the next patient. That night the blind
man dreamt that he was blind.

ON OFFERING to help the blind man, the man who then stole his car, had not, at that precise moment, had any evil intention, quite the contrary, what he did was nothing more than to obey those feelings of generosity and altruism which, as everyone knows, are the two best traits of human nature and to be found in much more hardened criminals than this one, a simple car-thief without any hope of advancing in his profession, exploited by the real owners of this enterprise, for it is they who take advantage of the needs of the poor. When all is said and done, there is not all that much difference between helping a blind man only to rob him afterwards and looking after some tottering and stammering old person with one eye on the inheritance. It was only when he got close to the blind man's home that the idea came to him quite naturally, precisely, one might say, as if he had decided to buy a lottery ticket on catching sight of a ticket-vendor, he had no hunch, he bought the ticket to see what might come of it, resigned in advance to whatever capricious fortune might bring, something or nothing, others would say that he acted according to a conditioned reflex of his personality. The sceptics, who are many and stubborn, claim that, when it comes to human nature, if it is true that the opportunity does not always make the thief, it is also true that it helps a lot. As for us, we should like to think that if the blind man had accepted the second offer of this false Samaritan, at that final moment generosity might still have prevailed, we refer to his offer to keep the blind man company until his wife should arrive, who knows whether the moral responsibility, resulting from the trust thus bestowed, might not have inhibited the criminal temptation and caused the victory of those shining and noble sentiments which it is always possible to find even in the most depraved souls. To finish on a plebeian note, as the old proverb never tires of teaching us, while trying to cross himself the blind man only succeeded in breaking his own nose.

The moral conscience that so many thoughtless people have offended against and many more have rejected, is something that exists and has always existed, it was not an invention of the philosophers of the Quaternary, when the soul was little more than a muddled proposition. With the passing of time, as well as the social evolution and genetic exchange, we ended up putting our conscience in the colour of blood and in the salt of tears, and, as if that were not enough, we made our eyes into a kind of mirror turned inwards, with the result that they often show without reserve what we are verbally trying to deny. Add to this general observation, the particular circumstance that in simple spirits, the remorse caused by committing some evil act often becomes confused with ancestral fears of every kind, and the result will be that the punishment of the prevaricator ends up being, without mercy or pity, twice what he deserved. In this case it is, therefore, impossible to unravel what proportion of fear and what proportion of the afflicted conscience began to harass the thief the moment he started up the engine of the car and drove off. No doubt he could never feel tranquil sitting in the place of someone who was holding this same steering wheel when he suddenly turned blind, who looked through this windshield and suddenly could no longer see, it does not take much imagination for such thoughts to rouse the foul and insidious monster of fear, there it is already raising its head. But it was also remorse, the aggrieved expression of one's conscience, as already stated, or, if we prefer to describe it in suggestive terms, a conscience with teeth to bite, that was about to put before his eyes the forlorn image of the blind man as he was closing the door, There's no need, there's no need, the poor fellow had said, and from then on he would not be capable of taking a step without assistance.

The thief concentrated twice as hard on the traffic to prevent such terrifying thoughts from fully occupying his mind, he knew full well that he could not permit himself the smallest error, the tiniest distraction. There were always police around and it would only need one of them to stop him, May I see your identity card and driving licence, back to prison, what a hard life. He was most careful to obey the traffic lights, under no circumstances to go when the light was red, to respect the amber light, to wait patiently for the green light to come on. At a certain point, he realised that he had started to look at the lights in a way that was becoming obsessive. He then started to regulate the speed of the car to ensure that he always had a green light before him, even if, in order to ensure this, he had to increase the speed or, on the contrary, to reduce it to the extent of irritating the drivers behind him. In the end, disoriented as he was, tense beyond endurance, he drove the car into a minor road where he knew there were no traffic lights, and parked almost without looking, he was such a good driver. He felt as if his nerves were about to explode, these were the very words that crossed his mind. My nerves are about to explode. It was stifling inside the car. He lowered the windows on either side, but the air outside, if it was moving, did nothing to freshen the atmosphere inside. What am I going to do, he asked himself. The shed where he had to take the car was far away, in a village outside the city, and in his present frame of mind, he would never get there. Either the police will arrest me or, worse still, I'll have an accident, he muttered. It then occurred to him that it would be best to get out of the car for a bit and try to clear his thoughts, Perhaps the fresh air will blow the cobwebs away, just because that poor wretch turned blind is no reason why the same should happen to me, this is not some cold one catches, I'll take a turn round the block and it will pass. He got out and did not bother to lock the car, he would be back in a minute, and walked off. He had gone no more than thirty paces when he went blind.

In the surgery, the last patient to be seen was the good-natured old man, the one who had spoken so kindly about the poor man who had suddenly turned blind. He was there just to arrange a date for an operation on a cataract that had appeared in his one remaining eye, the black patch was covering a void, and had nothing to do with the matter in hand, These are ailments that come with old age, the doctor had said some time ago, when it matures we shall remove it, then you won't recognise the place you've been living in. When the old man with the black eyepatch left and the nurse said there were no more patients in the waiting-room, the doctor took out the file of the man who had turned up blind, he read it once, twice, reflected for several minutes and finally rang a colleague with whom he held the following conversation: I must tell you, today I dealt with the strangest case, a man who totally lost his sight from one instant to the next, the examination revealed no perceptible lesion or signs of any malformation from birth, he says he sees everything white, a kind of thick, milky whiteness that clings to his eyes, I'm trying to explain as best I can how he described it, yes, of course it's subjective, no, the man is relatively young, thirty-eight years old, have you ever heard of such a case, or read about it, or heard it mentioned, I thought as much, for the moment I cannot think of any solution, to gain time I've recommended some tests, yes, we could examine him together one of these days, after dinner I shall check some books, take another look at the bibliography, perhaps I'll find some clue, yes, I'm familiar with agnosia, it could be psychic blindness, but then it would be the first case with these characteristics, because there is no doubt that the man is really blind, and as we know, agnosia is the inability to recognise familiar objects, because it also occurred to me that this might be a case of amaurosis, but remember what I started to tell you, this blindness is white, precisely the opposite of amaurosis which is total darkness unless there is some form of white amaurosis, a white darkness, as it were, yes, I know, something unheard of, agreed, I'll call him tomorrow, explain that we should like to examine him together. Having ended his conversation, the doctor leaned back in his chair, remained there for a few minutes, then rose to his feet, removed his white coat with slow, weary movements. He went to the bathroom to wash his hands, but this time he did not ask the mirror, metaphysically, What can this be, he had recovered his scientific outlook, the fact that agnosia and amaurosis are identified and defined with great precision in books and in practice, did not preclude the appearance of variations, mutations, if the word is appropriate, and that day seemed to have arrived. There are a thousand reasons why the brain should close up, just this, and nothing else, like a late visitor arriving to find his own door shut. The ophthalmologist was a man with a taste for literature and a flair for coming up with the right quotation.

That evening, after dinner, he told his wife, A strange case turned up at the surgery today, it might be a variant of psychic blindness or amaurosis, but there appears to be no evidence of any such symptoms ever having been established, What are these illnesses, amaurosis and that other thing, his wife asked him. The doctor gave an explanation within the grasp of a layman and capable of satisfying her curiosity, then he went to the bookcase where he kept his medical books, some dating back to his university years, others more recent and some just published which he still had not had time to study. He checked the indexes and methodically began reading everything he could find about agnosia and amaurosis, with the uncomfortable impression of being an intruder in a field beyond his competence, the mysterious terrain of neurosurgery, about which he only had the vaguest notion. Late that night, he laid aside the books he had been studying, rubbed his weary eyes and leaned back in his chair. At that moment the alternative presented itself as clear as could be. If it were a case of agnosia, the patient would now be seeing what he had always seen, that is to say, there would have been no diminution of his visual powers, his brain would simply have been incapable of recognising a chair wherever there happened to be a chair, in other words, he would continue to react correctly to the luminous stimuli leading to the optic nerve, but, to use simple terms within the grasp of the layman, he would have lost the capacity to know what he knew and, moreover, to express it. As for amaurosis, here there was no doubt. For this to be effectively the case, the patient would have to see everything black, if you'll excuse the use of the verb to see, when this was a case of total darkness. The blind man had categorically stated that he could see, if you'll excuse that verb again, a thick, uniform white colour as if he had plunged with open eyes into a milky sea. A white amaurosis, apart from being etymologically a contradiction, would also be a neurological impossibility, since the brain, which would be unable to perceive the images, forms and colours of reality, would likewise be incapable, in a manner of speaking, of being covered

in white, a continuous white, like a white painting without to-
nalities, the colours, forms and images that reality itself might
present to someone with normal vision, however difficult it
may be to speak, with any accuracy, of normal vision. With the
clear conscience of having fetched up in a dead end, the doctor shook his head despondently and looked around him. His
wife had already gone off to bed, he vaguely remembered her
coming up to him for a moment and kissing him on the head,
I'm off to bed, she must have told him, the flat was now silent,
books scattered on the table, What's this, he thought to himself, and suddenly he felt afraid, as if he himself were about to
turn blind any minute now and he already knew it. He held his
breath and waited. Nothing happened. It happened a minute
later as he was gathering up the books to return them to the
bookshelf. First he perceived that he could no longer see his
hands, then he knew he was blind.

   The ailment of the girl with dark glasses was not serious,
she was suffering from a mild form of conjunctivitis which the
drops prescribed by the doctor would clear up in no time, You
know what to do, for the next few days you should remove
your glasses only when you sleep, he had told her. He had been
cracking the same joke for years, we might even assume that it
had been handed down from one generation of ophthalmologists to another, but it never failed, the doctor was smiling as
he spoke, the patient smiled as she listened, and on this occasion it was worthwhile, because the girl had nice teeth and
knew how to show them. Out of natural misanthropy or because of too many disappointments in life, any ordinary sceptic, familiar with the details of this woman's life, would insinuate that the prettiness of her smile was no more than a trick of
the trade, a wicked and gratuitous assertion, because she had
the same smile even as a toddler, a word no longer much in use,
when her future was a closed book and the curiosity of opening

it had not yet been born. To put it simply, this woman could be classed as a prostitute, but the complexity in the web of social relationships, whether by day or night, vertical or horizontal, of the period here described cautions us to avoid a tendency to make hasty and definitive judgments, a mania which, owing to our exaggerated self-confidence, we shall perhaps never be rid of. Although it may be evident just how much cloud there is in Juno, it is not entirely licit, to insist on confusing with a Greek goddess what is no more than an ordinary concentration of drops of water hovering in the atmosphere. Without any doubt, this woman goes to bed with men in exchange for money, a fact that might allow us to classify her without further consideration as a prostitute, but, since it is also true that she goes with a man only when she feels like it and with whom she wants to, we cannot dismiss the possibility that such a factual difference, must as a precaution determine her exclusion from the club as a whole. She has, like ordinary people, a profession, and, also like ordinary people, she takes advantage of any free time to indulge her body and satisfy needs, both individual and general. Were we not trying to reduce her to some primary definition, we should finally say of her, in the broad sense, that she lives as she pleases and moreover gets all the pleasure she can from life.

It was already dark when she left the surgery. She did not remove her glasses, the street lighting disturbed her, especially the illuminated ads. She went into a chemist to buy the drops the doctor had prescribed, decided to pay no attention when the man who served her commented how unfair it was that certain eyes should be covered by dark glasses, an observation that be-sides being impertinent in itself, and coming from a pharma-cist's assistant if you please, went against her belief that dark glasses gave her an air of alluring mystery, capable of arousing the interest of men who were passing, to which she might reciprocate, were it not for the fact that today she had someone waiting for her, an encounter she had every reason to expect would lead to something good, as much in terms of material as in terms of other satisfactions. The man she was about to meet was an old acquaintance, he did not mind when she warned him she could not remove her glasses, an order, moreover, the doctor had not as yet given, and the man even found it amusing, something different. On leaving the pharmacy the girl hailed a taxi, gave the name of a hotel. Reclining on the seat, she was already savouring, if the term is appropriate, the various and multiple sensations of sensuous pleasure, from that first, knowing contact of lips, from that first intimate caress, to the successive explosions of an orgasm that would leave her exhausted and happy, as if she were about to be crucified, heaven protect us, in a dazzling and vertiginous firework. So we have every reason to conclude that the girl with dark glasses, if her partner has known how to fulfill his obligation, in terms of perfect timing and technique, always pays in advance and twice as much as she later charges. Lost in these thoughts, no doubt because she had just paid for a consultation, she asked herself whether it would not be a good idea to raise, starting from today, what, with cheerful euphemism, she was wont to describe as her just level of compensation.

She ordered the taxi-driver to stop one block before her destination, mingled with the people who were following in the same direction, as if allowing herself to be carried along by them, anonymous and without any outward sign of guilt or shame. She entered the hotel with a natural air, crossed the vestibule in the direction of the bar. She had arrived a few minutes early, therefore she had to wait, the hour of their meeting had been arranged with precision. She asked for a soft drink, which she drank at her leisure, without looking at anyone for she did not wish to be mistaken for a common whore in pursuit of men. A little later, like a tourist going up to her room to rest after having spent the afternoon in the museums, she headed for the elevator. Virtue, should there be anyone who still ignores the fact, always finds pitfalls on the extremely difficult path of perfection, but sin and vice are so favoured by fortune that no sooner did she get there than the elevator door opened. Two guests got out, an elderly couple, she stepped inside, pressed the button for the third floor, three hundred and twelve was the number awaiting her, it is here, she discreetly knocked on the door, ten minutes later she was naked, fifteen minutes later she was moaning, eighteen minutes later she was whispering words of love that she no longer needed to feign, after twenty minutes she began to lose her head, after twenty-one minutes she felt that her body was being lacerated with pleasure, after twenty-two minutes she called out, Now, now, and when she regained consciousness she said, exhausted and happy, I can still see everything white.

A POLICEMAN took the car-thief home. It would never have occurred to the circumspect and compassionate agent of authority that he was leading a hardened delinquent by the arm, not to prevent him from escaping, as might have happened on another occasion, but simply so that the poor man should not stumble and fall. In recompense, we can easily imagine the fright it gave the thief's wife, when, on opening the door, she came face to face with a policeman in uniform who had in tow, or so it seemed, a forlorn prisoner, to whom, judging from his miserable expression, something more awful must have happened than simply to find himself under arrest. The woman's first thought was that her husband had been caught in the act of stealing and the policeman had come to search the house, this idea, on the other hand, and however paradoxical it may seem, was somewhat reassuring, considering that her husband only stole cars, goods which on account of their size cannot be hidden under the bed. She was not left in doubt for long, the policeman informed her, This man is blind, look after him, and the woman who should have been relieved because the officer, after all, had simply accompanied her husband to his home, perceived the seriousness of the disaster that was to blight their lives when her husband, weeping his heart out, fell into her arms and told her what we already know.

The girl with the dark glasses was also accompanied to her parents' house by a policeman, but the piquancy of the circumstances in which blindness had manifested itself in her case, a naked woman screaming in a hotel and alarming the other guests, while the man who was with her tried to escape, pulling on his trousers in haste, somehow mitigated the obvious drama of the situation. Overcome with embarrassment, a feeling entirely compatible, for all the mutterings of hypocritical prudes and the would-be virtuous, with the mercenary rituals of love to which she dedicated herself, after the piercing shrieks she let out on realising that her loss of vision was not some new and unforeseen consequence of pleasure, the blind girl hardly dared to weep and lament her fate when unceremoniously, without giving her time to dress properly, and almost by force, she was evicted from the hotel. In a tone of voice that would have been sarcastic had it not been simply ill-mannered, the policeman wanted to know, after asking her where she lived, if she had the money for the taxi, in these cases, the State doesn't pay, he warned her, a procedure which, let us note in passing, is not without a certain logic, insofar as these women belong to that considerable number who pay no taxes on their immoral earnings. She gave an affirmative nod, but, being blind, just imagine, she thought the policeman might not have noticed her gesture and she murmured, Yes, I have the money, and then under her breath, added, If only I didn't, words that might strike us as being odd, but which, if we consider the circumvolutions of the human mind, where no short or direct routes exist, these same words end up by being absolutely clear, what she meant to say was that she had been punished because of her disreputable conduct, for her immorality, and this was the outcome. She had told her mother she would not be home for dinner, and in the end she was home early, even before her father.

The ophthalmologist's situation was different, not only because he happened to be at home when he was struck by blindness, but because, being a doctor, he was not going to surrender helplessly to despair, like those who only take note of their body when it hurts them. Even in the anguish of a situation like this, with a night of anxiety ahead of him, he was still capable of remembering what Homer wrote in the *Iliad*, the greatest poem about death and suffering ever written, A doctor is worth several men, words we should not accept as a straightforward expression of quantity, but above all, of quality, as we shall soon see. He summoned the courage to go to bed without disturbing his wife, not even when, muttering and half asleep, she stirred in the bed and snuggled up to him. He lay awake for hours on end, the little sleep he managed to snatch was from pure exhaustion. He hoped the night would never end rather than have to announce, he whose profession was to cure ailments in the eyes of others, I'm blind, but, at the same time, he was anxiously waiting for the light of day, and these are the exact words that came into his mind, The light of day, knowing that he would not see it. In fact, a blind ophthalmologist is not much good to anyone, but it was up to him to inform the health authorities, to warn them of this situation which might turn into a national catastrophe, nothing more nor less, of a form of blindness hitherto unknown, with every appearance of being highly contagious, and which, to all appearances, manifested itself without the previous existence of earlier pathological symptoms of an inflammatory, infectious or degenerative nature, as he was able to verify in the blind man who had come to consult him in his surgery, or as had been confirmed in his own case, a touch of myopia, a slight astigmatism, all so mild that he had decided, in the meantime, not to use corrective lenses. Eyes that had stopped seeing, eyes that were totally blind, yet meanwhile were in perfect condition, without any lesions, recent or old, acquired or innate. He recalled the detailed examination he had carried out on the blind man, how the various parts of the eye accessible to the ophthalmoscope appeared to be perfectly healthy, without any trace of morbid changes, a most rare situation in a man who claimed to be thirty-eight years old, and even in anyone younger. That man could not be blind, he thought, momentarily forgetting that he himself was blind, it's extraordinary how selfless some people can be, and this is not something new, let us remember what Homer said, although in apparently different words.

He pretended to be asleep when his wife got up. He felt the kiss she placed on the forehead, so gentle, as if she did not wish to rouse him from what she imagined to be a deep sleep, perhaps she thought, Poor man, he came to bed late after sitting up to study the extraordinary case of that poor blind man. Alone, as if he were about to be slowly garrotted by a thick cloud weighing on his chest and entering his nostrils, blinding him inside, the doctor let out a brief moan, and allowed two tears, They're probably white, he thought, to well up in his eyes and run over his temples, on either side of his face, now he could understand the fears of his patients, when they told him, Doctor, I think I'm losing my sight. Small domestic noises reached the bedroom, his wife would appear any minute now to see if he was still sleeping, it was almost time for them to go to the hospital. He got up cautiously, fumbled for his dressing-gown and slipped it on, then he went into the bathroom to pee. He turned to where he knew a mirror was, and this time he did not wonder, What's going on, he did not say, There are a thousand reasons why the human brain should close down, he simply stretched out his hands to touch the glass, he knew that his image was there watching him, his image could see

him, he could not see his image. He heard his wife enter the
bedroom, Ah, you're up already, and he replied, I am. He felt
her by his side, Good morning, my love, they still greeted each
other with words of affection after all these years of marriage,
and then he said, as if both of them were acting in a play and
this was his cue, I doubt whether it will be all that good, there's
something wrong with my sight. She only took in the last part
of the sentence, Let me take a look, she asked, and examined
his eyes attentively, I can't see anything, the sentence was obviously borrowed, it was not in her script, he was the one who
should have spoken those words, but he simply said, I can't see,
and added, I suppose I must have been infected by the patient
I saw yesterday.

With time and intimacy, doctors' wives also end up knowing
something about medicine, and this one, so close to her husband in everything, had learned enough to know that blindness
does not spread through contagion like an epidemic, blindness
isn't something that can be caught just by a blind man looking
at someone who is not, blindness is a private matter between
a person and the eyes with which he or she was born. In any
case, a doctor has an obligation to know what he is saying, that
is why he is professionally trained at medical school, and if this
doctor here, apart from having declared himself blind, openly
admits that he has been infected, who is his wife to doubt him,
however much she may know about medicine. It is understandable, therefore, that the poor woman, confronted by this irrefutable evidence, should react like any ordinary spouse, two of
them we know already, clinging to her husband and showing
natural signs of distress, And what are we going to do now, she
asked amid tears, Advise the health authorities, the Ministry,
that's the first thing to do, if it should turn out to be an epidemic, measures must be taken, But no one has ever heard of
an epidemic of blindness, his wife insisted, anxious to hold on

to this last shred of hope, Nor has anyone ever come across a blind man without any apparent reasons for his condition, and at this very moment there are at least two of them. No sooner had he uttered this last word than his expression changed. He pushed his wife away almost violently, he himself drew back, Keep away, don't come near me, I might infect you, and then beating on his forehead with clenched fists, What a fool, what a fool, what an idiot of a doctor, why did I not think of it before, we've spent the entire night together, I should have slept in the study with the door shut, and even so, Please, don't say such things, what has to be will be, come, let me get you some breakfast, Leave me, leave me, No, I won't leave you, shouted his wife, what do you want, to go stumbling around bumping into the furniture, searching for the telephone without eyes to find the numbers you need in the telephone directory, while I calmly observe this spectacle, stuck inside a bell-jar to avoid contamination. She took him firmly by the arm and said, Come along, love.

It was still early when the doctor had, we can imagine with what pleasure, finished the cup of coffee and toast his wife had insisted on preparing for him, much too early to find the people whom he had to inform at their desks. Logic and efficacy demanded that his report about what was happening should be made directly and as soon as possible to someone in authority at the Ministry of Health, but he soon changed his mind when he realised that to present himself simply as a doctor who had some important and urgent information to communicate, was not enough to convince the less exalted civil servant to whom, after much pleading, the telephone operator had agreed to put him through. The man wanted to know more details before passing him on to his immediate superior, and it was clear that a doctor with any sense of responsibility was not going to declare the outbreak of an epidemic of blindness to the first minor functionary who appeared before him, it would cause immediate panic. The functionary at the other end of the line replied, You tell me you're a doctor, if you want me to believe you, then, of course, I believe you, but I have my orders, unless you tell me what you want to discuss I can take this matter no further, It's confidential, Confidential matters are not dealt with over the telephone, you'd better come here in person. I cannot leave the house, Do you mean you're ill, Yes, I'm ill, the blind man said after a pause. In that case you ought to call a doctor, a real doctor, quipped the functionary, and, delighted with his own wit, he hung up.

The man's insolence was like a slap in the face. Only after some minutes had passed, had he regained enough composure to tell his wife how rudely he had been treated. Then, as if he had just discovered something that he should have known a long time ago, he murmured sadly, This is the stuff we're made of, half indifference and half malice. He was about to ask mistrustfully, What now, when he realised that he had been wasting his time, that the only way of getting the information to the right quarters by a safe route would be to speak to the medical director of his own hospital service, doctor to doctor, without any civil servants in the middle, let him assume responsibility for making the bureaucratic system do its work. His wife dialled the number, she knew the hospital number by heart. The doctor identified himself when they replied, then said rapidly, I'm fine, thank you, no doubt the receptionist had inquired, How are you, doctor, that is what we say when we do not wish to play the weakling, we say Fine, even though we may be dying, and this is commonly known as taking one's courage in both hands, a phenomenon that has only been observed in the human species. When the director came to the telephone, Now then, what's all this about, the doctor asked if he was alone, if there was anyone within earshot, no need to worry about the receptionist, she had better things to do than listen in to conversations about ophthalmology, besides she was only interested in gynaecology. The doctor's account was brief but full, with no circumlocutions, no superfluous words, with no redundancies, and expressed with a clinical dryness which, taking into account the situation, caused the director some surprise, But are you really blind, he asked, Totally blind, In any case, it might be a coincidence, there might not really have been, in the strict sense of the word, any contagion whatsoever, Agreed there is no proof of contagion, but this was not just a case of his turning blind and my turning blind, each of us in our own home, without our having seen each other, the man turned up blind at the surgery and I went blind a few hours later, How can we trace this man, I have his name and address on file in the surgery, I'll send someone there immediately, A doctor, Yes, of course, a colleague, Don't you think we ought to inform the Ministry about what is happening, For the moment that would be premature, think of the public alarm news of this kind would provoke, good grief, blindness isn't catching, Death isn't catching either, yet nevertheless we all die, Well, you stay at home while I deal with the matter, then I'll send someone to fetch you, I want to examine you, Don't forget that the fact that I am now blind is because I examined a blind man, You can't be sure of that, At least there is every indication here of cause and effect, Undoubtedly, yet it is still too early to draw any conclusions, two isolated cases have no statistical relevance, Unless, at this point, there are more than two of us, I can understand your state of mind but we must avoid any gloomy speculations that might turn out to be groundless, Many thanks, You'll be hearing from me soon, Goodbye.

Half an hour later, after he had managed, rather awkwardly, to shave, with some assistance from his wife, the telephone rang. It was the director again, but this time his voice sounded different, We have a boy here who has also suddenly gone blind, he sees everything white, his mother tells me he visited your surgery yesterday, Am I correct in thinking that this child has a divergent squint in the left eye, Yes, Then there's no doubt, it's him, I'm starting to get worried, the situation is becoming really serious, What about informing the Ministry, Yes, of course, I'll get on to the hospital management right away. After about three hours, when the doctor and his wife were having their lunch in silence, he toying with the bits of meat she had cut up for him, the telephone rang again. His wife went to answer, came back at once, You'll have to take the call, it's from the Ministry. She helped him to his feet, guided him into the study and handed him the telephone. The conversation was brief. The Ministry wanted to know the identity of the patients who had been at his surgery the previous day, the doctor replied that the clinical files contained all the relevant details, name, age, marital status, profession, home address, and he ended up offering to accompany the person or persons entrusted with rounding them up. At the other end of the line, the tone was curt, That won't be necessary. The telephone was passed on to someone else, a different voice came through, Good afternoon, this is the Minister speaking, on behalf of the Government I wish to thank you for your zeal, I'm certain that thanks to your prompt action we shall be able to limit and control the situation, meanwhile would you please do us the favour of remaining indoors. The closing words were spoken with courteous formality, but left him in no doubt that he was being given an order. The doctor replied, Yes, Minister, but the person at the other end had already put the phone down.

A few minutes later, the telephone rang yet again. It was the medical director, nervous, jumbling his words, I've just been told that the police have been informed of two cases of sudden blindness, Are they policemen, No, a man and a woman, they found him in the street screaming that he was blind, and the woman was in a hotel when she became blind, it seems she was in bed with someone, We need to check if they, too, are patients of mine, do you know their names, No names were mentioned, They have rung me from the Ministry, they're going to the surgery to collect the files, What a complicated business, You're telling me. The doctor replaced the receiver, raised his hands to his eyes and kept them there as if trying to defend his eyes from anything worse happening, then he said faintly, I'm so tired, Try to get some sleep, I'll take you to your bed, his wife said, It's pointless, I wouldn't be able to sleep, besides the day isn't over yet, something could still happen.

It was almost six o'clock when the telephone rang for the last time. The doctor, who was sitting beside it, picked up the receiver, Yes, speaking, he said, listened attentively to what he was being told and merely nodded his head slightly before ringing off, Who was that, his wife asked, The Ministry, an ambulance is coming to fetch me within the next half hour, Is that what you expected to happen, Yes, more or less, Where are they taking you, I don't know, presumably to a hospital, I'll pack a suitcase, sort out some clothes, the usual things, I'm not going on a trip, We don't know what it is. She led him gently into the bedroom, made him sit on the bed, You sit here quietly, I'll deal with everything. He could hear her going back and forth, opening and closing drawers and cupboards, removing clothes and then packing them into the suitcase on the floor, but what he could not see was that in addition to his own clothes, she had packed a number of blouses and skirts, a pair of slacks, a dress, some shoes that could only belong to a woman. It vaguely crossed his mind that he would not need so many clothes, but said nothing for this was not the moment to be worrying about such trivialities. He heard the locks click, then his wife said, Done, we're ready for the ambulance now. She carried the suitcase to the door leading to the stairs, refusing her husband's help when he said, Let me help you, that's something I can do, after all, I'm not an invalid. Then they went to sit on the sofa in the sitting-room and waited. They were holding hands, and he said, Who knows how long we shall be separated, and she replied, Don't let it worry you.

They waited for almost an hour. When the doorbell rang, she got up and went to open the door, but there was no one on the landing. She tried the internal telephone, Very well, he'll be right down, she said. She turned to her husband and told him, They're waiting downstairs, they have strict orders not to come up to the flat, It would appear the Ministry is really alarmed. Let's go. They went down in the elevator, she helped her husband to negotiate the last few steps and to get into the ambulance, then went back to the steps to fetch the suitcase, she lifted it up on her own and pushed it inside. At last she climbed in and sat beside her husband. The driver of the am-bulance turned round to protest, I can only take him, those are my orders, I must ask you to get down. The woman calmly re-plied, You'll have to take me as well, I've just gone blind this very minute.

THE suggestion had come from the Minister himself. It was, whichever way one looked at it, a fortunate not to say perfect idea, both from the point of view of the merely sanitary aspects of the case and from that of the social implications and their political consequences. Until the causes were established, or, to use the appropriate terms, the etiology of the white evil, as, thanks to the inspiration of an imaginative assessor, this unpleasant-sounding blindness came to be called, until such time as treatment and a cure might be found, and perhaps a vaccine that might prevent the appearance of any cases in the future, all the people who had turned blind, as well as those who had been in physical contact or in any way close to these patients, should be rounded up and isolated so as to avoid any further cases of contagion, which, once confirmed, would multiply more or less according to what is mathematically referred to as a compound ratio. Quod erat demonstrandum, concluded the Minister. According to the ancient practice, inherited from the time of cholera and yellow fever, when ships that were contaminated or suspected of carrying infection had to remain out at sea for forty days, and in words within the grasp of the general public, it was a matter of putting all these people into quarantine, until further notice. These very words, Until further notice, apparently deliberate, but, in fact, enigmatic since he could not think of any others, were pronounced by the Minister, who later clarified his thinking, I meant that this could as easily mean forty days as forty weeks, or forty months, or forty years, the important thing is that they should stay in quarantine. Now we have to decide where we are going to put them, Minister, said the President of the Commission of Logistics and Security set up rapidly for the purpose and responsible for the transportation, isolation and supervision of the patients, What immediate facilities are available, the Minister wanted to know, We have a mental hospital standing empty until we decide what to do with it, several military installations which are no longer being used because of the recent restructuring of the army, a building designed for a trade fair that is nearing completion, and there is even, although no one has been able to explain why, a supermarket about to go into liquidation, In your opinion, which of these buildings would best suit our purpose, The barracks offer the greatest security, Naturally, There is, however, one drawback, the size of the place is likely to make it both difficult and costly to keep an eye on those interned, Yes, I can see that, As for the supermarket, we would probably run up against various legal obstacles, legal matters that would have to be taken into account, And what about the building for the trade fair, That's the one site I think we should ignore, Minister, Why, Industry wouldn't like it, millions have been invested in the project, So that leaves the mental hospital, Yes, Minister, the mental hospital, Well then, let's opt for the mental hospital, Besides, to all appearances, it's the place that offers the best facilities because not only does it have a perimeter wall, it also has the advantage of having two separate wings, one to be used for those who are actually blind, the other for those suspected of having the disease, as well as a central area which will serve, as it were, as a no man's land, through which those who turn blind will pass to join those who are already blind, There might be a problem, What is that, Minister, We shall find ourselves obliged to put staff there to supervise the transfers, and I doubt whether we will be able to count on volunteers, I doubt whether that will be necessary, Minister, Why, Should anyone suspected of infection turn blind, as will naturally happen sooner or later, you may be sure, Minister, that the others who still have their sight, will turn him out at once, You're right, Just as they would not allow in any blind person who suddenly felt like changing places, Good thinking, Thank you, Minister, may I give orders to proceed, Yes, you have carte blanche.

The Commission acted with speed and efficiency. Before nightfall, everyone who was known to be blind had been rounded up, as well as a considerable number of people who were assumed to be affected, at least those whom it had been possible to identify and locate in a rapid search operation carried out above all in the domestic and professional circles of those stricken with loss of vision. The first to be taken to the empty mental hospital were the doctor and his wife. There were soldiers on guard. The main gate was opened just enough to allow them to pass through, and then closed at once. Serving as a handrail, a thick rope stretched from the entrance to the main door of the building, Move a little to the right, there you will find a rope, grab it with your hand and go straight on, straight on until you come to some steps, there are six steps in all, the sergeant warned them. Once inside, the rope divided into two, one strand going to the left, the other to the right, the sergeant shouted, Keep to the right. As she dragged the suitcase along, the woman guided her husband to the ward that was nearest to the entrance. It was a long room, like a ward in an old-fashioned hospital, with two rows of beds that had been painted grey, although the paint had been peeling off for quite some time. The covers, the sheets and the blankets were of the same colour. The woman guided her husband to the far end of the ward, made him sit on one of the beds, and told him, Stay here, I'm going to look around. There were more wards, long and narrow corridors, rooms that must have been the doctors' offices, dingy latrines, a kitchen that still reeked of bad cooking, a vast refectory with zinc-topped tables, three padded cells in which the bottom six feet of the walls had padding and the rest was lined with cork. Behind the building there was an abandoned yard, with neglected trees, their trunks looking as if they had been flayed. There was litter everywhere. The doctor's wife went back inside. In a half-open cupboard she found straitjackets. When she rejoined her husband, she asked him, Can you imagine where they've brought us, No, she was about to add, To a mental asylum, but he anticipated her, You're not blind, I cannot allow you to stay here, Yes, you're right, I'm not blind, Then I'm going to ask them to take you home, to tell them that you told a lie in order to remain with me, There's no point, they cannot hear you through there, and even if they could, they would pay no attention, But you can see, For the moment, I shall almost certainly turn blind myself one of these days, or any minute now, Please, go home, Don't insist, besides, I'll bet the soldiers would not let me get as far as the stairs, I cannot force you, No, my love, you can't, I'm staying to help you and the others who may come here, but don't tell them I can see, What others, You surely don't think we shall be here on our own, This is madness, What did you expect, we're in a mental asylum.

The other blind people arrived together. One after another, they had been apprehended at home, first of all the man driving the car, then the man who had stolen it, the girl with dark glasses, the boy with the squint whom they traced to the hospital where his mother had taken him. His mother did not come

with him, she lacked the ingenuity of the doctor's wife who declared herself blind when there was nothing wrong with her
eyesight, she is a simple soul, incapable of lying, even when it is
for her own good. They came stumbling into the ward, clutching at the air, here there was no rope to guide them, they would
have to learn from painful experience, the boy was weeping,
calling out for his mother, and it was the girl with dark glasses
who tried to console him, She's coming, she's coming, she told
him, and since she was wearing her dark glasses she could just
as well have been blind as not, the others moved their eyes
from one side to another, and could see nothing, while because
the girl was wearing those glasses, and saying, She's coming,
she's corning, it was as if she really could see the boy's desperate mother coming in through the door. The doctor's wife
leaned over and whispered into her husband's ear, Four more
have arrived, a woman, two men and a boy, What do the men
look like, asked the doctor in a low voice, She described them,
and he told her, The latter I don't know, the other, from your
description, might well be the blind man who came to see me
at the surgery. The child has a squint and the girl is wearing
dark glasses, she seems attractive, Both of them came to the
surgery. Because of the din they were making as they searched
for a place where they might feel safe, the new arrivals did not
hear this conversation, they must have thought that there was
no one else like themselves there, and they had not been without their sight long enough for their sense of hearing to have
become keener than normal. At last, as if they had reached the
conclusion that it was not worthwhile exchanging certainty for
doubt, each of them sat on the first bed they had stumbled
upon, so to speak, the two men ending up beside each other,
without their knowing. In a low voice, the girl continued to
console the boy, Don't cry, you'll see that your mother won't
be long. There was silence, then the doctor's wife said so that

she could be heard all the way down the ward as far as the door, There are two of us here, how many are you. The unexpected voice startled the new arrivals, but the two men remained silent, and it was the girl who replied, I think there are four of us, myself and this little boy, Who else, why don't the others speak up, asked the doctor's wife, I'm here, murmured a man's voice, as if he could only pronounce the words with difficulty, And so am I, growled in turn another masculine voice with obvious displeasure. The doctor's wife thought to herself, They're behaving as if they were afraid of getting to know each other. She watched them twitching, tense, their necks craned as if they were sniffing at something, yet curiously, their expressions were all the same, threatening and at the same time afraid, but the fear of one was not the fear of the other, and this was no less true of the threats they offered. What could be going on between them, she wondered.

At that moment, a loud, gruff voice was raised, by someone whose tone suggested he was used to giving orders. It came from a loudspeaker fixed above the door by which they had entered. The word Attention was uttered three times, then the voice began, the Government regrets having been forced to exercise with all urgency what it considers to be its rightful duty, to protect the population by all possible means in this present crisis, when something with all the appearance of an epidemic of blindness has broken out, provisionally known as the white sickness, and we are relying on the public spirit and cooperation of all citizens to stem any further contagion, assuming that we are dealing with a contagious disease and that we are not simply witnessing a series of as yet inexplicable coincidences. The decision to gather together in one place all those infected, and, in adjacent but separate quarters all those who have had any kind of contact with them, was not taken without careful consideration. The Government is fully aware of its

responsibilities and hopes that those to whom this message is
directed will, as the upright citizens they doubtless are, also assume their responsibilities, bearing in mind that the isolation
in which they now find themselves will represent, above any
personal considerations, an act of solidarity with the rest of the
nation's community. That said, we ask everyone to listen attentively to the following instructions, first, the lights will be kept
on at all times, any attempt to tamper with the switches will
be useless, they don't work, second, leaving the building without authorisation will mean instant death, third, in each ward
there is a telephone that can be used only to requisition from
outside fresh supplies for purposes of hygiene and cleanliness,
fourth, the internees will be responsible for washing their own
clothes by hand, fifth, it is recommended that ward representatives should be elected, this is a recommendation rather than
an order, the internees must organise themselves as they see
fit, provided they comply with the aforesaid rules and those we
are about to announce, sixth, three times daily containers with
food will be deposited at the main door, on the right and on the
left, destined respectively for the patients and those suspected
of being contaminated, seventh, all the leftovers must be burnt,
and this includes not only any food, but also the containers,
plates and cutlery which are all made of combustible material,
eighth, the burning should be done in the inner courtyards of
the building or in the exercise yard, ninth, the internees are responsible for any damage caused by these fires, tenth, in the
event of a fire getting out of control, whether accidentally or
on purpose, the firemen will not intervene, eleventh, equally,
the internees cannot count on any outside intervention should
there be any outbreaks of illnesses, nor in the event of any disorder or aggression, twelfth, in the case of death, whatever the
cause, the internees will bury the corpse in the yard without
any formalities, thirteenth, contact between the wing of the

patients and that of the people suspected of being contagious must be made in the central hall of the building by which they entered, fourteenth, should those suspected of being infected suddenly go blind, they will be transferred immediately to the other wing, fifteenth, this communication will be relayed daily at the same time for the benefit of all new arrivals. The Government and Nation expect every man and woman to do their duty. Good night.

In the silence that followed, the boy's voice could be clearly heard, I want my mummy, but the words were articulated without expression, like some automatic and repeater mechanism that had previously left a phrase suspended and was blurting it out now, at the wrong time. The doctor said, The orders we have just been given leave no room for doubt, we're isolated, probably more isolated than anyone has ever been and without any hope of getting out of this place until a cure is found for this disease, I recognise your voice, said the girl with dark glasses, I'm a doctor, an ophthalmologist, You must be the doctor I consulted yesterday, I recognise your voice, Yes, and who are you, I've been suffering from conjunctivitis and I assume it hasn't cleared up, but now, since I'm completely blind, it's of no importance, And the child who's with you, He's not mine, I have no children, Yesterday I examined a boy with a squint, was that you, the doctor asked, Yes, that was me, the boy's reply came out with the resentful tone of someone who prefers people not to mention his physical defect, and with good reason, for such defects, these as much as any others, are no sooner mentioned than they pass from being barely perceptible to being all too obvious. Is there anyone else here I know, the doctor asked, could the man who came to see me at the surgery yesterday accompanied by his wife be here by any chance, the man who suddenly went blind when out driving his car, That's me, replied the first blind man, Is there anyone else, please speak up, we are obliged to live here together for who knows how long, therefore it is essential that we should get to know each other. The car-thief muttered between his teeth, Yes, yes, he thought this would be sufficient to confirm his presence, but the doctor insisted, The voice is that of someone who is relatively young, you're not the elderly patient with the cataract, No doctor, that's not me, How did you go blind, I was walking along the street, And what else, Nothing else, I was walking along the street and I suddenly went blind. The doctor was about to ask if his blindness was also white, but stopped himself in time, why bother, whatever his reply, no matter whether his blindness was white or black, they would not get out of this place. He stretched out a hesitant hand to his wife and met her hand on the way. She kissed him on the cheek, no one else could see that wrinkled forehead, that tight mouth, those dead eyes, like glass, terrifying because they appeared to see and did not see, My time will come too, she thought, perhaps even at this very instant, not allowing me to finish what I am saying, at any moment, just as happened to them, or perhaps I'll wake up blind, or go blind as I close my eyes to sleep, thinking I've just dozed off.

She looked at the four blind people, they were sitting on their beds, the little luggage they had been able to bring at their feet, the boy with his school satchel, the others with suitcases, small, as if they had packed for the weekend. The girl with dark glasses was conversing in a low voice with the boy, on the row opposite, close to each other, with only an empty bed between them, the first blind man and the car-thief were, without realising it, sitting face to face. The doctor said, We all heard the orders, whatever happens now, one thing we can be sure of, no one will come to our assistance, therefore we ought to start getting organised without delay, because it won't be long before this ward fills up with people, this one and the oth-

ers, How do you know there are more wards here, asked the
girl, We went around the place before deciding on this ward
which is closer to the main entrance, explained the doctor's
wife, as she squeezed her husband's arm as if warning him to be
cautious. The girl said, it would be better, doctor, if you were to
take charge of the ward, after all, you are a doctor. What good
is a doctor without eyes or medicines, But you have some authority. The doctor's wife smiled, I think you should accept, if
the others are in agreement, of course, I don't think it's such a
good idea, Why not, For the moment there are only six of us
here, but by tomorrow we shall certainly be more, people will
start arriving every day, it would be too much to expect that
they should be prepared to accept the authority of someone
they have not chosen and who, moreover, would have nothing
to offer them in exchange for their respect, always assuming
they were willing to accept my authority and my rules, Then
it's going to be difficult to live here, We'll be very fortunate if
it turns out to be only difficult. The girl with dark glasses said,
I meant well, but frankly, doctor, you are right, it will be a case
of everyone for himself.

Either because he was moved by these words or because he
could no longer contain his fury one of the men got abruptly
to his feet, This fellow is to blame for our misfortune, if I had
my eyesight now, I'd do him in, he bellowed, while pointing in
the direction where he thought the other man to be. He was
not all that far off, but his dramatic gesture was comical because his jabbing, accusing finger was pointing at an innocent
bedside table. Keep calm, said the doctor, no one's to blame in
an epidemic, everyone's a victim, If I hadn't been the decent
fellow I am, if I hadn't helped him to find his way home, I'd
still have my precious eyes, Who are you, asked the doctor, but
the complainant did not reply and now seemed annoyed that
he had said anything. Then the other man spoke, He took me

home, it's true, but then took advantage of my condition to steal my car, That's a lie, I didn't steal anything, You most certainly did, If anyone nicked your car, it wasn't me, my reward for carrying out a kind action was to lose my sight, besides, where are the witnesses, that's what I'd like to know. This argument won't solve anything, said the doctor's wife, the car is outside, the two of you are in here, better to make your peace, don't forget we are going to have to live here together, You can count me out, said the first blind man, I'm off to another ward, as far away as possible from this crook who was capable of robbing a blind man, he claims that he turned blind because of me, well let him stay blind, at least it shows there is still some justice in this world. He picked up his suitcase and, shuffling his feet so as not to trip and groping with his free hand, he went along the aisle separating the two rows of beds, Where are the other wards, he asked, but did not hear the reply if there was one, because suddenly he found himself beneath an onslaught of arms and legs, the car-thief was carrying out as best he could his threat to take his revenge on this man who had caused all his misfortunes. One minute on top, the next underneath, they rolled about in the confined space, colliding now and then with the legs of the beds, while, terrified once more, the boy with the squint started crying again and calling out for his mother. The doctor's wife took her husband by the arm, she knew that alone she would never be able to persuade them to stop quarrelling, she led him along the passageway to the spot where the enraged opponents were panting for breath as they struggled on the ground. She guided her husband's hands, she herself took charge of the blind man whom she found more manageable, and with much effort, they managed to separate them. You're behaving foolishly, said the doctor angrily, if your idea is to turn this place into a hell, then you're going about it in the right way, but remember we're on our own here, we can expect no outside help, do you hear, He stole my car, whimpered the first blind man who had come off worst in the exchange of blows, Forget it, what does it matter, said the doctor's wife, you were no longer in a condition to drive the car when it disappeared, That's all very well, but it was mine, and this villain took it and left it who knows where, Most likely, said the doctor, the car is to be found at the spot where this man turned blind, You're an astute fellow, doctor, yes sir, no doubt about that, piped up the thief. The first blind man made a gesture as if to escape from the hands holding him, but without really trying, as if aware that not even his sense of outrage, however justified, would bring back his car, nor would the car restore his sight. But the thief threatened, If you think you're going to get away with this, then you're very much mistaken, all right, I stole your car, but you stole my eyesight, so who's the bigger thief, That's enough, the doctor protested, we're all blind here and we're not accusing or pointing the finger at anyone, I'm not interested in other people's misfortunes, the thief replied contemptuously, If you want to go to another ward, said the doctor to the first blind man, my wife will guide you there, she knows her way around better than me, No thanks, I've changed my mind, I prefer to stay in this one. The thief mocked him, The little boy is afraid of being on his own in case a certain bogeyman gets him, That's enough, shouted the doctor, losing his patience, Now listen to me, doctor, snarled the thief, we're all equal here and you don't give me any orders, No one is giving orders, I'm simply asking you to leave this poor fellow in peace, Fine, fine, but watch your step when you're dealing with me, I'm not easy to handle when somebody gets up my nose, otherwise I'm as good a friend as you're likely to meet, but the worst enemy you could possibly have. With aggressive movements and gestures, the thief fumbled for the bed where he had been sitting, pushed his suitcase underneath, then announced, I'm going to get some sleep, as if warning them, You'd better look the other way, I'm going to take my clothes off. The girl with dark glasses said to the boy with the squint, And you'd better get into bed as well, stay on this side and if you need anything during the night, call me, I want to do a wee-wee, the boy said. On hearing him, all of them felt a sudden and urgent desire to urinate, and their thoughts were more or less as follows, Now how are we going to cope with this problem, the first blind man groped under the bed to see if there was a chamber pot, yet at the same time hoping he would not find one for he would be embarrassed if he had to urinate in the presence of other people, not that they could see him, of course, but the noise of someone peeing is indiscreet, unmistakable, men at least can use a strategy denied women, in this they are more fortunate. The thief had sat down on the bed and was now saying, Shit, where do you have to go to piss in this place, Watch your language, there's a child here, protested the girl with dark glasses, Certainly, sweetheart, but unless you can find a lavatory, it won't be long before your little boy has pee running down his legs. The doctor's wife intervened, Perhaps I can locate the toilets, I can remember having smelt them, I'll come with you, said the girl with dark glasses, taking the boy by the hand, I think it best that we should all go, the doctor observed, then we shall know the way whenever we need to go, I know what's on your mind, the car-thief thought to himself without daring to say it aloud, what you don't want is that your little wife should have to take me to pee every time I feel the urge. The implication behind that thought gave him a small erection that surprised him, as if the fact of being blind should have as a consequence, the loss or diminution of sexual desire. Good, he thought, all is not lost, after all, among the dead and the wounded someone will escape, and, drifting away from the conversation, he began to daydream. He didn't get very far, the doctor was already saying, Let's form a line, my wife will lead the way, everyone put their hand on the shoulder of the person in front, then there will be no danger of our getting lost. The first blind man spoke up, I'm not going anywhere with him, obviously referring to the crook who had robbed him.

Whether to look for each other or to avoid each other, they could scarcely move in the narrow aisle, all the more so since the doctor's wife had to proceed as if she were blind. At last, they were all in line, the girl with dark glasses led the boy with the squint by the hand, then the thief in underpants and a vest, the doctor behind him, and last of all, safe for the moment from any physical attack, the first blind man. They advanced very slowly, as if mistrustful of the person guiding them, groping in vain with their free hand, searching for the support of something solid, a wall, a door frame. Placed behind the girl with dark glasses, the thief, aroused by the perfume she exuded and by the memory of his recent erection, decided to put his hands to better use, the one caressing the nape of her neck beneath her hair, the other, openly and unceremoniously fondling her breast. She wriggled to shake him off, but he was grabbing her firmly. Then the girl gave a backward kick as hard as she could. The heel of her shoe, sharp as a stiletto, pierced the flesh of the thief's bare thigh causing him to give a cry of surprise and pain. What's going on, asked the doctor's wife, looking back, I tripped, the girl with dark glasses replied, I seem to have injured the person behind me. Blood was already seeping out between the thief's fingers who, moaning and cursing, was trying to ascertain the consequences of her aggression, I'm injured, this bitch doesn't look where she's putting her feet, And you don't look where you're putting your hands, the girl replied curtly. The doctor's wife understood what had happened, at first she smiled, but then she saw how nasty the wound looked, blood was trickling down the poor devil's leg, and they had

no peroxide, no iodine, no plasters, no bandages, no disinfectant, nothing. The line was now in disarray, the doctor was asking, Where is the wound, Here, Here, where, On my leg, can't
you see, this bitch stuck the heel of her shoe in me, I tripped,
I couldn't help it, repeated the girl before blurting out in exasperation, The bastard was touching me up, what sort of woman
does he think I am. The doctor's wife intervened, This wound
should be washed and dressed at once, And where is there any
water, asked the thief, In the kitchen, in the kitchen there is
water, but we don't all have to go, my husband and I will take
him there, you others wait here, we'll be back soon, I want to
do weewee, said the boy, Hold it in a bit longer, we'll be right
back. The doctor's wife knew that she had to turn once to the
right, and once to the left, then follow a narrow corridor that
formed a right angle, the kitchen was at the far end. After a few
paces she pretended that she was mistaken, stopped, retraced
her footsteps, then said, Ah, now I remember, and from there
they headed straight for the kitchen, there was no more time
to be lost, the wound was bleeding profusely. At first, the water from the tap was dirty, it took some time for it to become
clear. It was lukewarm and stale, as if it had been putrefying inside the pipes, but the wounded man received it with a sigh of
relief. The wound looked ugly. And now, how are we going to
bandage his leg, asked the doctor's wife. Beneath a table there
were some filthy rags which must have been used as floor cloths,
but it would be most unwise to use them to make a bandage,
There doesn't appear to be anything here, she said, while pretending to keep up the search, But I can't be left like this, doctor, the bleeding won't stop, please help me, and forgive me if I
was rude to you a short time ago, moaned the thief, We are trying to help you, otherwise we wouldn't be here, said the doctor
and then he ordered him, Take off your vest, there's no other
option. The wounded man mumbled that he needed his vest,

but took it off. The doctor's wife lost no time in improvising a
bandage which she wrapped round his thigh, pulled tight and
managed to use the shoulder straps and the tail of the vest to tie
a rough knot. These were not movements a blind person could
easily execute, but she was in no mood to waste time with any
more pretence, it was enough to have pretended that she was
lost. The thief sensed that there was something unusual here,
logically it was the doctor who, although no more than an ophthalmologist, should have bandaged the wound, but the consolation of knowing that something was being done outweighed
the doubts, vague as they were, that had momentarily crossed
his mind. With him limping along, they went back to rejoin the
others, and once there, the doctor's wife spotted immediately
that the boy with the squint had not been able to hold out any
longer and had wet his trousers. Neither the first blind man
nor the girl with glasses had realised what had happened. At
the boy's feet spread a puddle of urine, the hem of his trousers
still dripping wet. But as if nothing had happened, the doctor's
wife said, Let's go and find these lavatories. The blind stretched
out their arms, looking for each other, though not the girl with
dark glasses who made it quite clear that she had no intention
of walking in front of that shameless creature who had touched
her up, at last the line was formed, the thief changing places
with the first blind man, with the doctor between them. The
thief's limp was getting worse and he was dragging his leg. The
tight bandage was bothering him and the wound was throb-
bing so badly that it was as if his heart had changed position
and was lying at the bottom of some hole. The girl with dark
glasses was once again leading the boy by the hand, but he kept
his distance as much as possible, afraid that someone might discover his accident, such as the doctor, who muttered, There's
a smell of urine here, and his wife felt she should confirm his
impression, Yes, there is a smell, she could not say that it was

coming from the lavatories because they were still some distance away, and, being obliged to behave as if she were blind, she could not reveal that the stench was coming from the boy's wet trousers.

They were agreed, both men and women, when they arrived at the lavatories, that the boy should be the first to relieve himself, but the men ended up going in together, without any distinction of urgency or age, the urinal was communal, it would have to be in a place like this, even the toilets. The women remained at the door, they are said to have more resistance, but there's a limit to everything, and the doctor's wife was soon suggesting, Perhaps there are other lavatories, but the girl with dark glasses said, Speaking for myself, I can wait, So can I, said the other woman, then there was a silence, then they began to speak, How did you come to lose your sight, Like everyone else, suddenly I could no longer see, Were you at home, No, So it happened when you left my husband's surgery, More or less, What do you mean by more or less, That it didn't happen right away, Did you feel any pain, No, there was no pain but when I opened my eyes I was blind, With me it was different, What do you mean by different, My eyes weren't closed, I went blind the moment my husband got into the ambulance, Fortunate, For whom, Your husband, this way you can be together, In that case I was also fortunate, You were, Are you married, No, no I'm not, and I don't think there will be any more marriages now, But this blindness is so abnormal, so alien to scientific knowledge that it cannot last forever. And suppose we were to stay like this for the rest of our lives, Us, Everyone, That would be horrible, a world full of blind people, It doesn't bear thinking about.

The boy with the squint was the first to emerge from the lavatory, he didn't even need to have gone in there. He had rolled his trousers halfway up his legs and removed his socks.

He said, I'm back, whereupon the girl with dark glasses moved in the direction of the voice, did not succeed the first or second time, but at a third attempt found the boy's vacillating hand. Shortly afterwards, the doctor appeared, then the first blind man, one of them asked, Where are the rest of you, the doctor's wife was already holding her husband's arm, his other arm was touched and grabbed by the girl with dark glasses. For several moments the first blind man had no one to protect him, then someone placed a hand on his shoulder. Are we all here, asked the doctor's wife, The fellow with the injured leg has stayed behind to satisfy another need, her husband replied. Then the girl with dark glasses said, Perhaps there are other toilets, I'm getting desperate, forgive me, Let's go and find out, said the doctor's wife, and they went off hand in hand. Within ten minutes they were back, they had found a consulting room which had its own toilet. The thief had already reappeared, complaining about the cold and the pain in his leg. They re-formed the line in the same order by which they had come and, with less effort than before and without incident, they returned to the ward. Adroitly, without appearing to do so, the doctor's wife helped each of them to reach the bed they had previously occupied. Before entering the ward, as if it were self-evident to everyone, she suggested that the easiest way for each of them to find their place was to count the beds from the entrance, Ours, she said, are the last ones on the right-hand side, beds nineteen and twenty. The first to proceed down the aisle was the thief. Almost naked, he was shivering from head to foot and anxious to alleviate the pain in his leg, reason enough for him to be given priority. He went from bed to bed, fumbling on the floor in search of his suitcase, and when he recognised it, he said aloud, It's here, then added, Fourteen, On which side, asked the doctor's wife, On the left, he replied, once again vaguely surprised, as if she ought to know it without having to ask. The first blind

man went next. He knew his bed was next but one to the thief's
and on the same side. He was no longer afraid of sleeping near
him, his leg was in such a dreadful state, and judging from his
groans and sighs, he would find it hard to move. On arriving
there, he said, Sixteen, on the left, and lay down fully dressed.
Then the girl with dark glasses pleaded in a low voice, Can we
stay close to you on the other side, we shall feel safer there. The
four of them advanced together and lost no time in getting
settled. After a few minutes, the boy with the squint said, I'm
hungry, and the girl with dark glasses murmured, Tomorrow,
tomorrow we'll find something to eat, now go to sleep. Then
she opened her handbag, searched for the tiny bottle she had
bought in the chemist's. She removed her glasses, threw back
her head and, keeping her eyes wide open, guiding one hand
with the other, she applied the eye-drops. Not all of the drops
went into her eyes, but conjunctivitis, given such careful treatment, soon clears up.

I MUST open my eyes, thought the doctor's wife. Through closed eyelids, when she woke up at various times during the night, she had perceived the dim light of the lamps that barely illuminated the ward, but now she seemed to notice a difference, another luminous presence, it could be the effect of the first glimmer of dawn, it could be that milky sea already drowning her eyes. She told herself that she would count up to ten and then open her eyelids, she said it twice, counted twice, failed to open them twice. She could hear her husband breathing deeply in the next bed and someone snoring, I wonder how the wound on that fellow's leg is doing, she asked herself, but knew at that moment that she felt no real compassion, what she wanted was to pretend that she was worried about something else, what she wanted was not to have to open her eyes. She opened them the following instant, just like that, not because of any conscious decision. Through the windows that began halfway up the wall and ended up a mere hand's-breadth from the ceiling, entered the dull, bluish light of dawn. I'm not blind, she murmured, and suddenly panicking, she raised herself on the bed, the girl with dark glasses, who was occupying a bed opposite, might have heard her. She was asleep. On the next bed, the one up against the wall, the boy was also sleeping, She did the same as me, the doctor's wife thought, she gave him the safest place, what fragile walls we'd make, a mere stone in the middle of the road without any hope other than to see the enemy trip over it, enemy, what enemy, no one will attack us here, even if we'd stolen and killed outside, no one is likely to come here to arrest us, that man who stole the car has never been so sure of his freedom, we're so remote from the world that any day now, we shall no longer know who we are, or even remember our names, and besides, what use would names be to us, no dog recognises another dog or knows the others by the names they have been given, a dog is identified by its scent and that is how it identifies others, here we are like another breed of dogs, we know each other's bark or speech, as for the rest, features, colour of eyes or hair, they are of no importance, it is as if they did not exist, I can still see but for how long, The light changed a little, it could not be night coming back, it had to be the sky clouding over, delaying the morning. A groan came from the thief's bed, If the wound has become infected, thought the doctor's wife, we have nothing to treat it with, no remedy, in these conditions the tiniest accident can become a tragedy, perhaps that is what they are waiting for, that we perish here, one after the other, when the beast dies, the poison dies with it. The doctor's wife rose from her bed, leaned over her husband, was about to wake him, but did not have the courage to drag him from his sleep and know that he continued to be blind. Barefoot, one step at a time, she went to the thief's bed. His eyes were open and unmoving. How are you feeling, whispered the doctor's wife. The thief turned his head in the direction of the voice and said, Bad, my leg is very painful, she was about to say to him, Let me see, but held back just in time, such imprudence, it was he who did not remember that there were only blind people there, he acted without thinking, as he would have done

several hours ago, there outside, if a doctor had said to him,
Let's have a look at this wound, and he raised the blanket. Even
in the half-light, anyone capable of seeing would have noticed
the mattress soaked in blood, the black hole of the wound with
its swollen edges. The bandage had come undone. The doctor's
wife carefully lowered the blanket, then with a rapid, delicate
gesture, passed her hand over the man's forehead. His skin felt
dry and burning hot. The light changed again, the clouds were
drifting away. The doctor's wife returned to her bed, but this
time did not lie down. She was watching her husband who was
murmuring in his sleep, the shadowy forms of the others beneath the grey blankets, the grimy walls, the empty beds waiting to be occupied, and she serenely wished that she, too, could
turn blind, penetrate the visible skin of things and pass to their
inner side, to their dazzling and irremediable blindness.

Suddenly, from outside the ward, probably from the hallway separating the two wings of the building, came the sound
of angry voices, Out, out, Get out, away with you, You cannot
stay here, Orders have to be obeyed. The din got louder, then
quietened down, a door slammed shut, all that could be heard
now was a distressed sobbing, the unmistakable clatter made
by someone who had just fallen over. In the ward they were all
awake. They turned their heads towards the entrance, they did
not need to be able to see to know that these were blind people
who were arriving. The doctor's wife got up, how she would
have liked to help the new arrivals, to say a kind word, to guide
them to their beds, inform them, Take note, this is bed seven on
the left-hand side, this is number four on the right, you can't go
wrong, yes, there are six of us here, we came yesterday, yes, we
were the first, our names, what do names matter, I believe one of
the men has stolen a car, then there is the man who was robbed,
there's a mysterious girl with dark glasses who puts drops in for
her conjunctivitis, how do I know, being blind, that she wears

dark glasses, well as it happens, my husband is an ophthalmologist and she went to consult him at his surgery, yes, he's also
here, blindness struck all of us, ah, of course, there's also the
boy with the squint. She did not move, she simply said to her
husband, They're arriving. The doctor got out of bed, his wife
helped him into his trousers, it didn't matter, no one could see,
just then the blind internees came into the ward, there were
five of them, three men and two women. The doctor said, raising his voice, Keep calm, no need to rush, there are six of us
here, how many are you, there's room for everyone. They did
not know how many they were, true they had come into contact with each other, sometimes even bumped into each other,
as they were pushed from the wing on the left to this one, but
they did not know how many they were. And they were carrying no luggage. When they woke up in their ward and found
they were blind and started bemoaning their fate, the others
put them out without a moment's hesitation, without even giving them time to take their leave of any relatives or friends
who might be with them. The doctor's wife remarked, It would
be best if they could be counted and each person gave their
name. Motionless, the blind internees hesitated, but someone
had to make a start, two of the men spoke at once, it always
happens, both then fell silent, and it was the third man who began, Number one, he paused, it seemed he was about to give his
name, but what he said was, I'm a policeman, and the doctor's
wife thought to herself, He didn't give his name, he too knows
that names are of no importance here. Another man was introducing himself, Number two, and he followed the example of
the first man, I'm a taxi-driver. The third man said, Number
three, I'm a pharmacist's assistant. Then a woman spoke up,
Number four, I'm a hotel maid, and the last one of all, Number
five, I work in an office. That's my wife, my wife, where are you,
tell me where you are, Here, I'm here, she said bursting into

tears and walking unsteadily along the aisle with her eyes wide open, her hands struggling against the milky sea flooding into them. More confident, he advanced towards her, Where are you, where are you, he was now murmuring as if in prayer. One hand found another, the next moment they were embracing, a single body, kisses in search of kisses, at times lost in mid-air for they could not see each other's cheeks, eyes, lips. Sobbing, the doctor's wife clung to her husband, as if she, too, had just been reunited, but what she was saying was, This is terrible, a real disaster. Then the voice of the boy with the squint could be heard asking, Is my mummy here as well. Seated on his bed, the girl with dark glasses murmured, She'll come, don't worry, she'll come.

Here, each person's real home is the place where they sleep, therefore little wonder that the first concern of the new arrivals should be to choose a bed, just as they had done in the other ward, when they still had eyes to see. In the case of the wife of the first blind man there could be no doubt, her rightful and natural place was beside her husband, in bed seventeen, leaving number eighteen in the middle, like an empty space separating her from the girl with dark glasses. Nor is it surprising that they should try as far as possible to stay close together, there are many affinities here, some already known, others that are about to be revealed, for example, it was the pharmacist's assistant who sold eye-drops to the girl with dark glasses, this was the taxi-driver who took the first blind man to the doctor, this fellow who has identified himself as being a policeman found the blind thief weeping like a lost child, and as for the hotel maid, she was the first person to enter the room when the girl with dark glasses had a screaming fit. It is nevertheless certain that not all of these affinities will become explicit and known, either because of a lack of opportunity, or because no one so much as imagined that they could possibly exist, or because of a simple question of sensibility and tact. The hotel maid would never dream that the woman she saw naked is here, we know that the pharmacist's assistant served other customers wearing dark glasses who came to purchase eye-drops, no one would be imprudent enough to denounce to the policeman the presence of someone who stole a car, the taxi-driver would swear that during the last few days he had no blind man as a passenger. Naturally, the first blind man told his wife in a low voice that one of the internees is the scoundrel who went off with their car, What a coincidence, eh, but, since in the meantime, he knew that the poor devil was badly injured in one leg, he was generous enough to add, He's been punished enough. And she, because of her deep distress at being blind and her great joy on regaining her husband, joy and sorrow can go together, not like oil and water, she no longer remembered what she had said two days before, that she would give a year of her life if this rogue, her word, were to go blind. And if there was some last shadow of resentment still troubling her spirit, it certainly blew over when the wounded man moaned pitifully, Doctor, please help me. Allowing himself to be guided by his wife, the doctor gently probed the edges of his wound, he could do nothing more, nor was there any point in trying to bathe it, the infection might have been caused by the deep penetration of a shoe heel that had been in contact with the surface of the streets and the floors here in the building, or equally by pathogenic agents in all probability to be found in the contaminated almost stagnant water, coming from antiquated pipes in appalling condition. The girl with dark glasses who had got up on hearing his moan, began approaching slowly, counting the beds. She leaned forward, stretched out her hand, which brushed against the face of the doctor's wife, and then, having reached, who knows how, the wounded man's hand, which was burning hot, she said sadly, Please, forgive me, it was entirely my fault, there was no need for me to do what I did, Forget it, replied the man, these things happen in life, I shouldn't have done what I did either.

Almost covering these last words, the harsh voice from the loudspeaker came booming out, Attention, attention, your food has been left at the entrance as well as supplies for your hygiene and cleanliness, the blind should go first to collect their food, those in the wing for the contaminated will be informed when it's their turn, attention, attention, your food has been left at the entrance, the blind should make their way there first, the blind first. Dazed by fever, the wounded man did not grasp all the words, he thought they were being told to leave, that their detention was over, and he made as if to get up, but the doctor's wife held him back, Where are you going, Didn't you hear, he asked, they said the blind should leave, Yes, but only to go and collect our food. The wounded man gave a despondent sigh, and once more could feel the pain piercing through his flesh. The doctor said, Stay here, I'll go, I'm coming with you, said his wife. Just as they were about to leave the ward, a man who had come from the other wing, inquired, Who is this fellow, the reply came from the first blind man, He's a doctor, an eye-specialist, That's a good one, said the taxi-driver, just our luck to end up with the one doctor who can do nothing for us, We're also landed with a taxi-driver who can't take us anywhere, replied the girl with dark glasses sarcastically.

The container with the food was in the hallway. The doctor asked his wife, Guide me to the main door, Why, I'm going to tell them that there is someone here with a serious infection and that we have no medicines, Remember the warning, Yes, but perhaps when confronted with a concrete case, I doubt it, Me, too, but we ought to try. At the top of the steps leading to the forecourt, the daylight dazzled his wife, and not because it was too intense, there were dark clouds passing across the sky, and it looked as if it might rain, In such a short time I've become unused to bright light, she thought. Just at that moment, a soldier shouted from the gate, Stop, turn back, I have orders to shoot, and then, in the same tone of voice, pointing his gun, Sergeant, there are some people here trying to leave, We have no wish to leave, the doctor protested, In my opinion that is not what they want, said the sergeant as he approached, and, looking through the bars of the main gate, he asked, What's going on, A person who has injured his leg has an infected wound, we urgently need antibiotics and other medicines, My orders are crystal-clear, no one is to be allowed to leave, and the only thing we can allow in is food, If the infection should get worse which looks all too certain, it could soon prove fatal, That isn't my affair, Then contact your superiors, Look here, blind man, let me tell you something, either the two of you get back to where you came from, or you'll be shot, Let's go, said the wife, there's nothing to be done, they're not to blame, they're terrified and are only obeying orders, I can't believe that this is happening, it's against all the rules of humanity, You'd better believe it, because the truth couldn't be clearer, Are you two still there, I'm going to count up to three and if they're not out of my sight by then, they can be sure they won't get back, ooone, twooo, threee, that's it, he was as good as his word, and turning to the soldiers, Even if it were my own brother, he did not explain to whom he was referring, whether it was to the man who had come to request medicines or to the other fellow with the infected leg. Inside, the wounded man wanted to know if they were going to supply them with medicines, How do you know I went to ask for supplies, asked the doctor, I guessed as much, after all, you are a doctor, I'm very sorry, Does that mean there will be no medicines, Yes, So, that's that.

The food had been carefully calculated for five people. There were bottles of milk and biscuits, but whoever had pre-

pared their rations had forgotten to provide any glasses, nor
were there any plates, or cutlery, these would probably come
with the lunch. The doctor's wife went to give the wounded
man something to drink, but he vomited. The taxi-driver complained that he did not like milk, he asked if he could have coffee. Some, after having eaten, went back to bed, the first blind
man took his wife to visit the various places, they were the only
two to leave the ward. The pharmacist's assistant asked to be
allowed to speak to the doctor, he wanted the doctor to tell
him if he had formed any opinion about their illness, I don't
believe this can strictly be called an illness, the doctor started
to explain, and then with much simplification, he summed up
what he had researched in his reference books before becoming blind. Several beds further on, the taxi-driver was listening attentively, and when the doctor had finished his report, he
shouted down the ward, I'll bet what happened is that the channels that go from the eyes to the brain got congested, Stupid
fool, growled the pharmacist's assistant with indignation, Who
knows, the doctor could not resist a smile, in truth the eyes are
nothing more than lenses, it is the brain that actually does the
seeing, just as an image appears on the film, and if the channels
did get blocked up, as that man suggested, it's the same as a car-
buretor, if the fuel can't reach it, the engine does not work and
the car won't go, as simple as that, as you can see, the doctor
told the pharmacist's assistant, And how much longer, doctor,
do you think we're going to be kept here, asked the hotel maid,
At least for as long as we are unable to see, And how long will
that be, Frankly, I don't think anyone knows, it's either something that will pass or it might go on forever, How I'd love
to know. The maid sighed and after several moments, I'd also
like to know what happened to that girl, What girl, asked the
pharmacist's assistant, That girl from the hotel, what a shock
she gave me, there in the middle of the room, as naked as the

day she was born, wearing nothing but a pair of dark glasses, and screaming that she was blind, she's probably the one who infected me. The doctor's wife looked, saw the girl slowly remove her dark glasses, hiding her movements, then put them under her pillow, while asking the boy with the squint, Would you like another biscuit, For the first time since she had arrived there, the doctor's wife felt as if she were behind a microscope and observing the behaviour of a number of human beings who did not even suspect her presence, and this suddenly struck her as being contemptible and obscene. I have no right to look if the others cannot see me, she thought to herself. With a shaky hand, the girl applied a few eye-drops. This would always allow her to say that these were not tears running from her eyes.

Hours later, when the loudspeaker announced that they should come and collect their lunch, the first blind man and the taxi-driver offered to go on this mission for which eyes were not essential, it was enough to be able to touch. The containers were some distance from the door that connected the hallway to the corridors, to find them they had to go down on all fours, sweeping the floor ahead with one arm outstretched, while the other served as a third paw, and if they had no difficulty in returning to the ward, it was because the doctor's wife had come up with the idea, which she was at pains to justify from personal experience, of tearing a blanket into strips, and using these to make an improvised rope, one end of which would remain attached to the outside handle of the door of the ward, while the other end would be tied in turn to the ankle of whoever had to go to fetch their food. The two men went off, the plates and cutlery arrived, but the portions were still only for five, in all likelihood the sergeant in charge of the patrol was unaware that there were six more blind people there, since once outside the entrance, even when paying attention to what might be happening behind the main door, in the shadows of the hallway, it was only by chance that anyone could be seen passing from one wing to another. The taxi-driver offered to go and demand the missing portions of food, and he went alone, he had no wish to be accompanied, We're not five, there are eleven of us, he shouted at the soldiers, and the same sergeant replied from the other side, Save your breath, there are many more to come yet, he said it in a tone of voice that must have seemed derisive to the taxi-driver, if we take into account the words spoken by the latter when he returned to the ward, It was as if he were making fun of me. They shared out the food, five portions divided by ten, since the wounded man was still refusing to eat, all he asked for was some water, and he begged them to moisten his lips. His skin was burning hot. And since he could not bear the contact and weight of the blanket on the wound for very long, he uncovered his leg from time to time, but the cold air in the ward soon obliged him to cover up again, and this went on for hours. He would moan at regular intervals with what sounded like a stifled gasp, as if the constant and persistent pain had suddenly got worse before he could get it under control.

In the middle of the afternoon, three more blind people arrived, expelled from the other wing. One was an employee from the surgery, whom the doctor's wife recognised at once, and the others, as destiny had decreed, were the man who had been with the girl with dark glasses in the hotel and the ill-mannered policeman who had taken her home. No sooner had they reached their beds and seated themselves, than the employee from the surgery began weeping in despair, the two men said nothing, as if still unable to grasp what had happened to them. Suddenly, from the street, came the cries of people shouting, orders being given in a booming voice, a rebellious uproar. The blind internees all turned their heads in the direction of the door and waited. They could not see, but knew what was about to happen within the next few minutes. The doctor's

wife, seated on the bed beside her husband, said in a low voice,
It had to be, the promised hell is about to begin. He squeezed
her hand and murmured, Don't move, from now on there is
nothing you can do. The shouting had died down, now a confusion of sounds was coming from the hallway, these were the
blind, driven like sheep, bumping into each other, crammed together in the doorways, some lost their sense of direction and
ended up in other wards, but the majority, stumbling along,
huddled into groups or dispersed one by one, desperately waving their hands in the air like people drowning, burst into the
ward in a whirlwind, as if being pushed from the outside by a
bulldozer. A number of them fell and were trampled underfoot.
Confined in the narrow aisles, the new arrivals gradually began
filling the spaces between the beds, and here, like a ship caught
in a storm that has finally managed to reach port, they took
possession of their berths, in this case their beds, insisting that
there was no room for anyone else, and that latecomers should
find themselves a place elsewhere. From the far end, the doctor
shouted that there were other wards, but the few who remained
without a bed were frightened of getting lost in the labyrinth of
rooms, corridors, closed doors, stairways they might only discover at the last minute. Finally they realised they could not
stay there and, struggling to find the door by which they had
entered, they ventured forth into the unknown. As if searching
for one last safe refuge, the five blind internees in the second
group had managed to occupy the beds, which, between them
and those in the first group, had remained empty. Only the
wounded man remained isolated, without protection, on bed
fourteen on the left-hand side.

A quarter of an hour later, apart from some weeping and wailing, the discreet sounds of people settling down, calm rather
than peace of mind was restored in the ward. All the beds were
now occupied. The evening was drawing in, the dim lamps

seemed to gain strength. Then they heard the abrupt voice of the loudspeaker. As on the first day, instructions were repeated as to how the wards should be maintained and the rules the internees should obey, the Government regrets having to enforce to the letter what it considers its right and duty, to protect the population with all the means at its disposal during this present crisis, etc., etc. When the voice stopped, an indignant chorus of protests broke out, We're locked up here, We're all going to die in here, This isn't right, Where are the doctors we were promised, this was something new, the authorities had promised doctors, medical assistance, perhaps even a complete cure. The doctor did not say that if they were in need of a doctor he was there at their disposal. He would never say that again. His hands alone are not enough for a doctor, a doctor cures with medicines, drugs, chemical compounds and combinations of this and that, and here there is no trace of any such materials, nor any hope of getting them. He did not even have the sight of his eyes to notice any sickly pallor, to observe any reddening of the peripheric circulation, how often, without any need for closer examination, these external signs proved to be as useful as an entire clinical history, or the colouring of mucus and pigmentation, with every probability of coming up with the right diagnosis, You won't escape this one. Since the nearby beds were all occupied, his wife could no longer keep him informed of what was happening, but he sensed the tense, uneasy atmosphere, bordering on open conflict, that had been created with the arrival of the latest group of internees. The very air in the ward seemed to have become heavier, emitting strong lingering odours, with sudden wafts that were simply nauseating, What will this place be like within a week, he asked himself, and it horrified him to think that in a week's time, they would still be confined here, Assuming there won't be any problems with food supplies, and who can be sure there isn't already a shortage, I doubt, for example, whether those outside have any idea from one minute to the next, how many of us are interned here, the question is how they will solve the matter of hygiene, I'm not referring to how we shall keep ourselves clean, struck blind only a few days ago and without anyone to help us, or whether the showers will work and for how long, I'm referring to the rest, to all the other likely problems, for if the lavatories should get blocked, even one of them, this place would be transformed into a sewer. He rubbed his face with his hands, he could feel the roughness of his beard after three days without shaving, It's preferable like this, I hope they won't have the unfortunate idea of sending us razor blades and scissors. He had everything necessary for shaving in his suitcase, but was conscious of the fact that it would be a mistake to try, And where, where, not here in the ward, among all these people, true my wife could shave me, but it would not be long before the others got wind of it and expressed surprise that there should be someone here capable of offering these services, and there inside, in the showers, such confusion, dear God, how we miss having our sight, to be able to see, to see, even if they were only faint shadows, to stand before the mirror, see a dark diffused patch and be able to say, That's my face, anything that has light does not belong to me.

The complaints subsided little by little, someone from one of the other wards came to ask if there was any food left over and the taxi-driver was quick to reply, Not a crumb, and the pharmacist's assistant to show some good will, mitigated the peremptory refusal, There might be more to come. But nothing would come. Darkness fell. From outside came neither food nor words. Cries could be heard coming from the adjoining ward, then there was silence, if anyone was weeping they did so very quietly, the weeping did not penetrate the walls. The doctor's wife went to see how the injured man was faring,

It's me, she said, carefully raising the blanket. His leg presented a terrifying sight, completely swollen from the thigh down, and the wound, a black circle with bloody purplish blotches, had got much larger, as if the flesh had been stretched from inside. It gave off a stench that was both fetid and slightly sweet. How are you feeling, the doctor's wife asked him, Thanks for coming, Tell me how you're feeling, Bad, Are you in pain, Yes and no, What do you mean, It hurts, but it's as if the leg were no longer mine, as if it were separated from my body, I can't explain, it's a strange feeling, as if I were lying here watching my leg hurt me, That's because you're feverish, Probably, Now try to get some sleep. The doctor's wife placed her hand on his forehead, then made to withdraw, but before she could even wish him good night, the invalid grabbed her by the arm and drew her towards him obliging her to get close to his face, I know you can see, he said in a low voice. The doctor's wife trembled with surprise and murmured, You're wrong, whatever put such an idea into your head, I see as much as anybody here, Don't try to deceive me, I know very well that you can see, but don't worry, I won't breathe a word to anyone, Sleep, sleep, Don't you trust me, Of course, I do, Don't you trust the word of a thief, I said I trusted you. Then why don't you tell me the truth, We'll talk tomorrow, now go to sleep, Yes, tomorrow, if I get that far, We mustn't think the worst, I do, or perhaps it's the fever thinking for me. The doctor's wife rejoined her husband and whispered in his ear, the wound looks awful, could it be gangrene, It seems unlikely in such a short time, Whatever it is, he's in a bad way, And those of us who are cooped up here, said the doctor in a deliberately loud voice, as if being struck blind were not enough, we might just as well have our hands and feet tied. From bed fourteen, left-hand side, the invalid replied, No one is going to tie me up, doctor.

The hours passed, one by one, the blind internees had fallen asleep. Some had covered their heads with a blanket, as if anxious that a pitch-black darkness, a real one, might extinguish once and for all the dim suns that their eyes had become. The three lamps suspended from the high ceiling, out of arm's reach, cast a dull, yellowish light over the beds, a light incapable of even creating shadows. Forty persons were sleeping or desperately trying to get to sleep, some were sighing and murmuring in their dreams, perhaps in their dreams they could see what they were dreaming, perhaps they were saying to themselves, If this is a dream, I don't want to wake up. All their watches had stopped, either they had forgotten to wind them or had decided it was pointless, only that of the doctor's wife was still working. It was after three in the morning. Further along, very slowly, resting on his elbows, the thief raised his body into a sitting position. He had no feeling in his leg, nothing except the pain, the rest had ceased to belong to him. His knee was quite stiff. He rolled his body over onto the side of his healthy leg, which he allowed to hang out of the bed, then with both hands under his thigh, he tried to move his injured leg in the same direction. Like a pack of wolves suddenly roused, the pain went through his entire body, before returning to the dark crater from which it came. Resting on his hands, he gradually dragged his body across the mattress in the direction of the aisle. When he reached the rail at the foot of the bed, he had to rest. He was gasping for breath as if he were suffering from asthma, his head swayed on his shoulders, he could barely keep it upright. After several minutes, his breathing became more regular and he got slowly to his feet, putting his weight on his good leg. He knew that the other one would be no good to him, that he would have to drag it behind him wherever he went. He suddenly felt dizzy, an irrepressible shiver went through his body, the cold and fever made his teeth chatter. Supporting himself on the metal frames of the beds, passing

from one to the other as if along a chain, he slowly advanced
between the sleeping bodies. He dragged his injured leg like a
bag. No one noticed him, no one asked, Where are you going
at this hour, had anyone done so, he knew what he would reply, I'm off for a pee, he would say, he didn't want the doctor's
wife to call out to him, she was someone he could not deceive
or lie to, he would have to tell her what was on his mind, I can't
go on rotting away in this hole, I realise that your husband has
done everything he could to help me, but when I had to steal
a car I wouldn't go and ask someone else to steal it for me, this
is much the same, I'm the one who has to go, when they see
me in this state they'll recognise at once that I'm in a bad way,
put me in an ambulance and take me to a hospital, there must
be hospitals just for the blind, one more won't make any difference, they'll treat my wound, cure me, I've heard that's what
they do to those condemned to death, if they've got appen-
dicitis they operate first and execute them afterwards, so that
they die healthy, as far as I'm concerned, if they want, they can
bring me back here, I don't mind. He advanced further, clench-
ing his teeth to suppress any moaning, but he could not resist
an anguished sob when, on reaching the end of the row, he
lost his balance. He had miscounted the beds, he thought there
was one more and came up against a void. Lying on the floor,
he did not stir until he was certain that no one had woken up
with the din made by his fall. Then he realised that this position was perfect for a blind person, if he were to advance on all
fours he would find the way more easily. He dragged himself
along until he reached the hallway, there he paused to consider
how he should proceed, whether it would be better to call from
the door or go up to the gate, taking advantage of the rope that
had served as a handrail and almost certainly was still there. He
knew full well that if he were to call for help from there, they
would immediately order him to go back, but the alternative

of having only a swaying rope as his support, after what he had
suffered, notwithstanding the solid support of the beds, made
him somewhat hesitant. After some minutes, he thought he had
found the solution. I'll go on all fours, he thought, keeping under the rope, and from time to time I'll raise my hand to see
whether I'm on the right track, this is just like stealing a car,
ways and means can always be found. Suddenly, taking him by
surprise, his conscience awoke and censured him bitterly for
having allowed himself to steal a car from an unfortunate blind
man. The fact that I'm in this situation now, he reasoned, isn't
because I stole his car, it's because I accompanied him home,
that was my big mistake. His conscience was in no mood for
casuistic discussions, his reasons were simple and clear, A blind
man is sacred, you don't steal from a blind man. Technically
speaking, I didn't rob him, he wasn't carrying the car in his
pocket, nor did I hold a gun to his head, the accused protested
in his defence, Forget the sophisms, muttered his conscience,
and get on your way.

The cold dawn air cooled his face. How well one breathes
out here, he thought to himself. He had the impression that
his leg was much less painful, but this did not surprise him,
sometime before, and more than once, the same thing had happened. He was now outside the main door, he would soon be at
the steps, That's going to be the most awkward bit, he thought,
going down the steps headfirst. He raised one arm to check
that the rope was there, and continued on. Just as he had foreseen, it was not easy to get from one step to the next, especially
because of his leg which was no help to him, and the proof
was not long in coming, when, in the middle of the steps, one
of his hands having slipped, his body lurched to one side and
was dragged along by the dead weight of his wretched leg. The
pain came back instantly, as if someone were sawing, drilling,
and hammering the wound, and even he was at a loss to explain

how he prevented himself from crying out. For several long minutes, he remained prostrate, face down on the ground. A rapid gust of wind at ground level, left him shivering. He was wearing nothing but a shirt and his underpants. The wound was pressed against the ground, and he thought, It might get infected, a foolish thought, he was forgetting that he had been dragging his leg along the ground all the way from the ward, Well, it doesn't matter, they'll treat it before it turns infectious, he thought afterwards, to put his mind at rest, and he turned sideways to reach the rope more easily. He did not find it right away. He forgot that he had ended up in a vertical position in relation to the rope when he had rolled down the steps, but instinct told him that he should stay put. Then his reasoning guided him as he moved into a sitting position and then slowly back until his haunches made contact with the first step, and with a triumphant sense of victory he clutched the rough cord in his raised hand. Probably it was this same feeling that led him to discover almost immediately, a way of moving without his wound rubbing on the ground, by turning his back towards the main gate and sitting up and using his arms like crutches, as cripples used to do, he eased his seated body along in tiny stages. Backwards, yes, because in this case as in others, pulling was much easier than pushing. In this way, his leg suffered less, besides which the gentle slope of the forecourt going down towards the gate was a great help. As for the rope, he was in no danger of losing it, he was almost touching it with his head. He wondered whether he would have much further to go before reaching the main gate, getting there on foot, better still on two feet was not the same as advancing backwards half a hand's-breadth inch by inch. Forgetting for an instant that he was blind, he turned his head as if to confirm how far he still had to go and found himself confronted by the same impenetrable whiteness. Could it be night, could it be day, he asked himself, well if it were day they would already have spotted me, besides, they had only delivered breakfast and that was many hours ago. He was surprised to discover the speed and accuracy of his reasoning and how logical he could be, he saw himself in a different light, a new man, and were it not for this damn leg he would swear he had never felt so well in his entire life. His lower back came up against the metal plate at the bottom of the main gate. He had arrived. Huddled inside the sentry box to protect himself from the cold, the guard on duty thought he had heard faint noises he could not identify, in any case he did not think they could have come from inside, it must have been a sudden rustling of the trees, a branch the wind had caused to brush against the railings. These were followed by another noise, but this time it was different, a bang, the sound of crashing to be more precise, which could not have been caused by the wind. Nervously the guard came out of his sentry box, his finger on the trigger of his automatic rifle, and looked towards the main gate. He could not see anything. The noise, however, was back, louder, as if someone were scratching their fingernails on a rough surface. The metal plate on the gate, he thought to himself. He was about to head for the field tent where the sergeant was sleeping, but held back at the thought that if he raised a false alarm he would be given an earful, sergeants do not like being disturbed when they are sleeping, even when there is some good reason. He looked back at the main gate and waited in a state of tension. Very slowly, between two vertical iron bars, like a ghost, a white face began to appear. The face of a blind man. Fear made the soldier's blood freeze, and fear drove him to aim his weapon and release a blast of gunfire at close range.

The noise of the blast immediately brought the soldiers, half dressed, from their tents. These were the soldiers from the detachment entrusted with guarding the mental asylum and its inmates. The sergeant was already on the scene, What the hell is going on, A blind man, a blind man, stuttered the soldier, Where, He was there and he pointed at the main gate with the butt of his weapon, I can see nothing there, He was there, I saw him. The soldiers had finished getting into their gear and were waiting in line, their rifles at the ready. Switch on the floodlight, the sergeant ordered. One of the soldiers got up onto the platform of the vehicle. Seconds later the blinding rays lit up the main gate and the front of the building. There's no one there, you fool, said the sergeant, and he was just about to deliver a few more choice insults in the same vein when he saw spreading out from under the gate, in that dazzling glare, a black puddle. You've finished him off, he said. Then, remembering the strict orders they had been given, he yelled, Get back, this is infectious. The soldiers drew back, terrified, but continued to watch the pool of blood that was slowly spreading in the gaps between the small cobblestones in the path. Do you think the man's dead, asked the sergeant, He must be, the shot struck him right in the face, replied the soldier, now pleased with the obvious demonstration of the accuracy of his aim. At that moment, another soldier shouted nervously, Sergeant, sergeant, look over there. Standing at the top of the steps, lit up by the white light coming from the searchlight, a number of blind internees could be seen, more than ten of them, Stay where you are, bellowed the sergeant, if you take another step, I'll blast the lot of you. At the windows of the buildings opposite, several people, woken up by the noise of gunshots, were looking out in terror. Then the sergeant shouted, Four of you come and fetch the body. Because they could neither see nor count, six blind men came forward. I said four, the sergeant bawled hysterically. The blind internees touched each other, then touched again, and two of them stayed behind. Holding on to the rope, the others began moving forward.

WE MUST see if there's a spade or shovel or whatever around, something that can be used to dig, said the doctor. It was morning, with much effort they had brought the corpse into the inner courtyard, placed it on the ground amongst the litter and the dead leaves from the trees. Now they had to bury it. Only the doctor's wife knew the hideous state of the dead man's body, the face and skull blown to smithereens by the gunshots, three holes where bullets had penetrated the neck and the region of the breastbone. She also knew that in the entire building there was nothing that could be used to dig a grave. She had searched the parts of the asylum to which they had been confined and had found nothing apart from an iron bar. It would help but was not enough. And through the closed windows of the corridor that ran the full length of the wing reserved for those suspected of being infected, lower down on this side of the wall, she had seen the terrified faces of the people awaiting their turn, that inevitable moment when they would have to say to the others, I've gone blind, or when, if they were to try to conceal what had happened, some clumsy gesture might betray them, a movement of their head in search of shade, an unjustified stumble into someone sighted. All this the doctor also knew, what he had said was part of the deception they had both concocted, so that now his wife could say, And suppose we were to ask the soldiers to throw a shovel over the wall. A good idea, let's try, and everyone was agreed, only the girl with dark glasses expressed no opinion about this question of finding a spade or shovel, the only sounds coming from her meanwhile were tears and wailing, It was my fault, she sobbed, and it was true, no one could deny it, but it is also true, if this brings her any consolation, that if, before every action, we were to begin by weighing up the consequences, thinking about them in earnest, first the immediate consequences, then the probable, then the possible, then the imaginable ones, we should never move beyond the point where our first thought brought us to a halt. The good and the evil resulting from our words and deeds go on apportioning themselves, one assumes in a reasonably uniform and balanced way, throughout all the days to follow, including those endless days, when we shall not be here to find out, to congratulate ourselves or ask for pardon, indeed there are those who claim that this is the much-talked-of immortality, Possibly, but this man is dead and must be buried. Therefore the doctor and his wife went off to parley, the disconsolate girl with dark glasses said she was coming with them. Pricked by her conscience. No sooner did they appear at the main entrance than a soldier shouted, Halt, and as if afraid that this verbal command, however vigorous, might not be heeded, he fired into the air. Terrified, they retreated into the shadows of the hallway, behind the thick wooden panels of the open door. Then the doctor's wife advanced alone, from where she was standing she could watch the soldier's movements and take refuge in time, if necessary. We have nothing with which to bury the dead man, she said, we need a spade. At the main gate, but on the other side from where the blind man had fallen, another soldier appeared. He was a sergeant, but not the same one as before, What do you want, he shouted, We need a shovel or spade. There is no such thing here, on your way. We must bury the corpse, Don't bother about any burial, leave it there to rot, If we simply leave it lying there, the air will be infected, Then let it be infected and much good may it do you, Air circulates and moves around as much here as there. The relevance of her argument forced the soldier to reflect. He had come to replace the other sergeant, who had gone blind and been taken without delay to the quarters where the sick belonging to the army were interned. Needless to say, the air force and navy also had their own installations, but less extensive or important, the personnel of both forces being less numerous. The woman is right, reflected the sergeant, in a situation like this there is no doubt that one cannot be careful enough. As a safety measure, two soldiers equipped with gas masks, had already poured two large bottles of ammonia over the pool of blood, and the lingering fumes still brought tears to the soldiers' eyes and a stinging sensation to their throats and nostrils. The sergeant finally declared, I'll see what can be done, And what about our food, asked the doctor's wife, taking advantage of this opportunity to remind him, The food still hasn't arrived, In our wing alone there are more than fifty people, we're hungry, what you're sending us simply isn't enough, Supplying food is not the army's responsibility, Someone ought to be dealing with this problem, the Government undertook to feed us, Get back inside, I don't want to see anyone at this door, What about the spade, the doctor's wife insisted, but the sergeant had already gone. It was mid-morning when a voice came over the loudspeaker in the ward, Attention, attention, the internees brightened up, they thought this was an announcement about their food, but no, it was about the spade, Someone should come and fetch it, but not in a group, one person only should come forward, I'll go, for I've already spoken to them, said the doctor's wife. The moment she went through the main entrance door, she saw the spade. From the position and distance to where it had landed, closer to the gate than the steps, it must have been thrown over the fence, I mustn't forget that I'm supposed to be blind, the doctor's wife thought, Where is it, she asked, Go down the stairs and I'll guide you, replied the sergeant, you're doing fine, now keep going in the same direction, like so, like so, stop, turn slightly to the right, no, to the left, less, less than that, now forward, so long as you keep going, you'll come right up against it, shit, I told you not to change direction, cold, cold, you're getting warmer again, warmer still, right, now take a half turn and I'll guide you from there, I don't want you going round and round in circles and ending up at the gate, Don't you worry, she thought, from here I'll make straight for the door, after all, what does it matter, even if you were to suspect that I'm not blind, what do I care, you won't be coming in here to take me away. She slung the spade over her shoulder like a gravedigger on his way to work, and walked in the direction of the door without faltering for a moment, Did you see that, sergeant, exclaimed one of the soldiers, you would think she could see. The blind learn quickly how to find their way around, the sergeant explained confidently.

It was hard work digging a grave. The soil was hard, trampled down, there were tree roots just below the surface. The taxi-driver, the two policemen and the first blind man took it in turns to dig. Confronted by death, what is expected of nature is that rancour should lose its force and poison, it is true that people say that past hatreds die hard, and of this there is ample proof in literature and life, but the feeling here, deep down, as it were, was not hatred and, in no sense old, for how does the theft of a car compare with the life of the man who stole it, and especially given the miserable state of his corpse, for one does not need eyes to know that this face has neither nose nor mouth. They were unable to dig any deeper than about three feet. Had the dead man been fat, his belly would have been sticking out above ground level, but the thief was skinny, a real bag of bones, even skinnier after the fasting of recent days, the grave was big enough for two corpses his size. There were no prayers for the dead. We could have put a cross there, the girl with dark glasses reminded them, she spoke from remorse, but as far as anyone there was aware while alive, the deceased had never given a thought to God or religion, best to say nothing, if any other attitude is justified in the face of death, besides, bear in mind that making a cross is much less easy than it may seem, not to mention the little time it would last with all these blind people around who cannot see where they are treading. They returned to the ward. In the busier places, so long as it is not completely open, like the yard, the blind no longer lose their way, with one arm held out in front and several fingers moving like the antennae of insects, they can find their way everywhere, it is even probable that in the more gifted of the blind there soon develops what is referred to as frontal vision. Take the doctor's wife, for example, it is quite extraordinary how she manages to get around and orient herself through this veritable maze of rooms, nooks and corridors, how she knows precisely where to turn the corner, how she can come to a halt before a door and open it without a moment's hesitation, how she has no need to count the beds before reaching her own. At this moment she is seated on her husband's bed, she is talking to him, as usual in a low voice, one can see these are educated people, and they always have something to say to each other, they are not like the other married couple, the first blind man and his wife, after those first emotional moments on being reunited, they have scarcely spoken, in all probability, their present unhappiness outweighs their past love, with time they will get used to this situation. The one person who is forever complaining of feeling hungry is the boy with the squint, despite the fact that the girl with the dark glasses has practically taken the food from her own mouth to give him. Many hours have passed since he last asked about his mummy, but no doubt he will start to miss her again after having eaten, when his body finds itself released from the brute selfishness that stems from the simple, but pressing need to sustain itself. Whether because of what happened early that morning, or for reasons beyond our ken, the sad truth is that no containers were delivered at breakfast time. It is nearly time for lunch, almost one o'clock on the watch the doctor's wife has just furtively consulted, therefore it is not surprising that the impatience of their gastric juices has driven some of the blind internees, both from this wing and from the other, to go and wait in the hallway for the food to arrive, and this for two excellent reasons, the public one, on the part of some, because in this way they would gain time, the private one, on the part of others, because, as everyone knows, first come first served. In all, there were about ten blind internees listening for the noise of the outer gate when it was opened, for the footsteps of the soldiers who would deliver those blessed containers. In their turn, fearful of suddenly being stricken by blindness if they were to come into close contact with the blind waiting in the hallway, the contaminated internees from the left wing dare not leave, but several of them are peering through a gap in the door, anxiously awaiting their turn. Time passed. Tired of waiting, some of the blind internees had sat down on the ground, later two or three of them returned to their wards. Shortly afterwards, the unmistakable metallic creaking of the gate could be heard. In their excitement, the blind internees, pushing each other, began moving in the direction where, judging from the sounds outside, they imagined the door to be, but suddenly, overcome

by a vague sense of disquiet that they would not have time to
define or explain, they came to a halt and retreated in confusion, while the footsteps of the soldiers bringing their food and
those of the armed escort accompanying them could already be
heard quite clearly.

Still suffering from the shock of the tragic episode of the
previous night, the soldiers who delivered the containers had
agreed that they would not leave them within reach of the
doors leading to the wings, as they had more or less done before, they would just dump them in the hallway, and retreat.
Let them sort it out for themselves. The dazzle of the strong
light from outside and the abrupt transition into the shadows
of the hallway prevented them at first from seeing the group of
blind internees. But they soon spotted them. Howling in terror, they dropped the containers on the ground and fled like
madmen straight out of the door. The two soldiers forming the
escort, who were waiting outside, reacted admirably in the face
of danger. Mastering, God alone knows how and why, their legitimate fear, they advanced to the threshold of the door and
emptied their magazines. The blind internees fell one on top
of the other, and, as they fell, their bodies were still being rid-
dled with bullets which was a sheer waste of ammunition, it
all happened so incredibly slowly, one body, then another, it
seemed they would never stop falling, as you sometimes see in
films and on television. If we are still in an age when a soldier
has to account for the bullets fired, they will swear on the flag
that they acted in legitimate defence, as well as in defence of
their unarmed comrades who were on a humanitarian mission
and suddenly found themselves threatened and outnumbered
by a group of blind internees. In a mad rush they retreated to
the gate, covered by the rifles which the soldiers on patrol were
pointing unsteadily between the railings as if the blind internees who had survived, were about to make a retaliatory attack.

His face drained of colour, one of the soldiers who had fired, said nervously, You won't get me going back in there at any price. From one moment to the next, on this same day, when evening was falling, at the hour of changing guard, he became one more blind man among the other blind men, what saved him was that he belonged to the army, otherwise he would have remained there along with the blind internees, the companions of those whom he had shot dead, and God knows what they might have done to him. The sergeant's only comment was, It would have been better to let them die of hunger, when the beast dies, the poison dies with it. As we know, others had often said and thought the same, happily, some precious remnant of concern for humanity prompted him to add, From now on, we shall leave the containers at the halfway point, let them come and fetch them, we'll keep them under surveillance, and at the slightest suspicious movement, we fire. He headed for the command post, switched on the microphone and, putting the words together as best he could, calling to mind words he remembered hearing on vaguely comparable occasions, he announced, The army regrets having been forced to repress with weapons a seditious movement responsible for creating a situation of imminent risk, for which the army was neither directly nor indirectly to blame, and you are advised that from now on the internees will collect their food outside the building, and will suffer the consequences should there be any attempt to repeat the disruption that took place now and last night. He paused, uncertain how he should finish, he had forgotten his own words, he certainly had them, but could only repeat, We were not to blame, we were not to blame.

Inside the building, the blast of gunfire deafeningly echoing in the confined space of the hallway, had caused the utmost panic. At first it was thought that the soldiers were about to burst into the wards and shoot everything in sight, that the

Government had changed its tactics, had opted for the wholesale liquidation of the internees, some crawled under their beds,
others, in sheer terror, did not move, some might have thought
it was better so, better no health than too little, if a person
has to go, let it be quick. The first to react were the contaminated internees. They had started to flee when the shooting
broke out, but then the silence encouraged them to go back,
and once again they headed for the door leading into the hallway. They saw the bodies lying in a heap, the blood wending
its way sinuously on the tiled floor where it slowly spread, as if
it were a living thing, and then the containers with food. Hunger drove them on, there stood that much desired sustenance,
true it was intended for the blind, their own food was still
on its way, in accordance with the regulations, but who cares
about the regulations, no one can see us, the candle that lights
the way burns brightest, as the ancients have continuously reminded us throughout the ages, and the ancients know about
these things. Their hunger, however, had the strength only to
take them three steps forward, reason intervened and warned
them that for anybody imprudent enough to advance there was
danger lurking in those lifeless bodies, above all, in that blood,
who could tell what vapours, what emanations, what poison-
ous miasmas might not already be oozing forth from the open
wounds of the corpses. They're dead, they can't do any harm,
someone remarked, the intention was to reassure himself and
others, but his words made matters worse, it was true that these
blind internees were dead, that they could not move, see, could
neither stir nor breathe, but who can say that this white blindness is not some spiritual malaise, and if we assume this to be
the case, then the spirits of those blind casualties have never
been as free as they are now, released from their bodies, and
therefore free to do whatever they like, above all, to do evil,
which, as everyone knows, has always been the easiest thing

to do. But the containers of food, standing there exposed, immediately attracted their attention, such are the demands of the stomach, they heed nothing even when it is for their own good. From one of the containers leaked a white liquid which was slowly spreading towards the pool of blood, to all appearances it was milk, the colour unmistakable. More courageous, or simply more fatalistic, the distinction is not always easy to make, two of the contaminated internees stepped forward, and they were just about to lay their greedy hands on the first container when a group of blind internees appeared in the doorway leading to the other wing. The imagination can play such tricks, especially in morbid circumstances such as these, that for these two men who had gone on a foray, it was as if the dead had suddenly risen from the ground, as blind as before, no doubt, but much more dangerous, for almost certainly filled by a spirit of revenge. They prudently backed away in silence towards the entrance to their wing, perhaps the blind internees were beginning to take care of the corpses as charity and respect decreed, or, if not, they might leave behind without noticing one of the containers, however small, in fact there were not all that many contaminated internees there, perhaps the best solution would be to ask them, Please, take pity on us, at least leave a small container for us, after what has happened it is most likely that no more food will be delivered today. The blind moved as one would expect of the blind, groping their way, stumbling, dragging their feet, yet as if organised, they knew how to distribute tasks efficiently, some of them splashing about in the sticky blood and milk, began at once to withdraw and transport the corpses to the yard, others dealt with the eight containers, one by one, that had been dumped by the soldiers. Among the blind internees there was a woman who gave the impression of being everywhere at the same time, helping to load, acting as if she were guiding the men, some-

thing that was obviously impossible for a blind woman, and,
whether by chance or intentionally, more than once she turned
her head towards the wing where the contaminated were interned, as if she could see them or sense their presence. In a
short time the hallway was empty, with no other traces than the
huge bloodstain, and another small one alongside, white, from
the milk that had spilled, apart from these only crisscrossing
footprints in red or simply wet. Resigned, the contaminated
internees closed the door and went in search of crumbs, they
were so downhearted that one of them was on the point of saying, and this shows just how desperate they were, If we really
have to end up blind, if that is our fate, we might as well move
over into the other wing now, there at least we'll have something to eat, Perhaps the soldiers will still bring our rations,
someone suggested, Have you ever been in the army, another
asked him, No, Just as I thought.

Bearing in mind that the dead belonged to the one as much
as the other, the occupants of the first and second wards gathered together in order to decide whether they should eat first
and then bury the corpses, or the other way round. No one
seemed interested in knowing who had died. Five of them had
installed themselves in the second ward, difficult to say if they
had already known each other, or if they did not, if they had the
time and inclination to introduce themselves to each other and
unburden their hearts. The doctor's wife could not remember
having seen them when they arrived. The remaining four, yes,
these she recognised, they had slept with her, in a manner of
speaking, under the same roof, although this was all she knew
about one of them, and how could she know more, a man with
any self-respect does not go around discussing his private affairs with the first person he meets, such as having been in a
hotel room where he made love to a girl with dark glasses, who,
in her turn, if we mean her, has no idea that he has been in-

terned here and that she is still so close to the man who was the
cause of her seeing everything white. The taxi-driver and the
two policemen were the other casualties, three robust fellows
who could take care of themselves, whose professions meant, in
different ways, looking after others, and in the end there they
lie, cruelly mowed down in their prime and waiting for others
to decide their fate. They will have to wait until those who survived have finished eating, not because of the usual egoism of
the living, but because someone sensibly remembered that to
bury nine corpses in that hard soil and with only one spade was
a chore that would take until dinner-time at least. And since
it would not be admissible that the volunteers endowed with
good will should work while the others stuffed their bellies, it
was decided to leave the corpses until later. The food arrived
in individual portions, therefore easy to share out, that's yours,
and yours, until there was no more. But the anxiety of some of
the less fair-minded blind internees came to complicate what in
normal circumstances would have been so straightforward, and
although a serene and impartial judgment cautions us to admit that the excesses that took place had some justification, we
need only remember, for example, that no one could know, at
the outset, whether there would be enough food for everyone.
In fact, it is fairly clear that it is not easy to count blind people
or to distribute rations without eyes capable of seeing either the
rations or the people. Moreover, some of the inmates from the
second ward, with more than reprehensible dishonesty, tried to
give the impression that there were more of them than there
actually were. As always, this is where the presence of the doctor's wife proved to be useful. A few timely words have always
managed to resolve problems that a verbose speech would only
make worse. No less ill-intentioned and perverse were those
who not only tried, but actually succeeded in receiving double
rations. The doctor's wife was aware of this abuse, but thought

it wise to say nothing. She could not even bear to think of the consequences that would ensue if it were to be discovered that she was not blind, at the very least she would find herself at the beck and call of everyone, at worst, she might become the slave of some of them. The idea, aired at the outset, that someone should assume responsibility for each ward, might have helped, who knows? to solve these difficulties and others, alas, more serious, on condition however, that the authority of the person in charge, undeniably fragile, undeniably precarious, undeniably called into question at every moment, should be clearly exercised for the benefit of all and as such be acknowledged by the majority. Unless we succeed in this, she thought, we shall end up murdering one another in here. She promised herself that she would discuss these delicate matters with her husband and went on sharing out the rations.

Some out of indolence, others because they had a delicate stomach, had no inclination to go and practise grave-digging just after they had eaten. Because of his profession, the doctor felt more responsible than the others, and when he said without much enthusiasm, Let's go and bury the corpses, there was not a single volunteer. Stretched out on their beds, the blind internees were interested only in being left in peace to digest their food, some fell asleep immediately, hardly surprising, after the frightening experience they had been through, the body, even though poorly nourished, abandoned itself to the slow workings of digestive chemistry. Later, as evening was drawing in, when, because of the progressive waning of natural light, the dim lamps appeared to gain some strength, showing at the same time, weak as they were, the little purpose they served, the doctor, accompanied by his wife, persuaded two men from his ward to accompany them to the compound, even if only to balance out the work that had to be done and separate the corpses that were already stiff, once it had been decided that

each ward would bury its own dead. The advantage enjoyed by
these blind men was what might be called the illusion of light.
In fact, it made no difference to them whether it was day or
night, the first light of dawn or the evening twilight, the silent
hours of early morning or the bustling din of noon, these blind
people were forever surrounded by a resplendent whiteness,
like the sun shining through mist. For the latter, blindness did
not mean being plunged into banal darkness, but living inside
a luminous halo. When the doctor let slip that they were going
to separate the corpses, the first blind man, who was one of
those who had agreed to help him, wanted to know how they
would be able to recognise them, a logical question on the part
of a blind man which left the doctor in some confusion. This
time his wife thought it would be unwise to come to his assistance for fear of giving the game away. The doctor got out of
the difficulty gracefully by the radical method of coming clean,
that is to say, by acknowledging his mistake, People, he said, in
the tone of voice of someone amused at his own expense, get so
used to having eyes that they think they can use them when
they no longer serve for anything, in fact, all we know is that
there are four from our ward here, the taxi-driver, the two policemen, and one other who was with us, therefore the solution
is to pick up four of these corpses at random, bury them with
due respect, and in this way we fulfill our obligation. The first
blind man agreed, his companion likewise, and once again, taking it in turn, they began digging graves. These helpers would
never come to know, blind as they were, that, without exception, the corpses buried were precisely those of whom they had
been speaking, nor need we mention the work done, seemingly
at random, by the doctor, his hand guided by that of his wife,
she would grab a leg or arm, and all he had to say was, This
one. When they had already buried two corpses, there finally
emerged from the ward, three men disposed to help, most

likely they would have been less willing had someone told them
that it was already the dead of night. Psychologically, even
when a man is blind, we must acknowledge that there is a considerable difference between digging graves by the light of day
and after the sun has gone down. The moment they were back
in the ward, sweating, covered in earth, the sickly smell of de-
composed flesh still in their nostrils, the voice over the loudspeaker repeated the usual instructions. There was no reference whatsoever to what had happened, no mention of gunfire
or casualties shot at point-blank range. Warnings such as, To
abandon the building without any authorisation will mean immediate death, or The internees will bury the corpses in the
grounds without any formalities, now, thanks to the harsh experience of life, supreme mistress of all disciplines, these warnings took on real meaning, while the announcement that promised containers of food three times a day seemed grotesquely
ironic or, worse, contemptuous. When the voice fell silent, the
doctor, on his own, because he was getting to know every nook
and cranny in the place, went to the door of the other ward to
inform the inmates, We have buried our dead, Well, if you've
buried some, you can bury the rest, replied a man's voice from
within, The agreement was that each ward would bury its own
dead, we counted four and buried them, That's fine, tomorrow
we'll deal with those from here, said another masculine voice,
and then in a different tone of voice, he asked, Has no more
food turned up, No, replied the doctor, But the loudspeaker
said three times a day, I doubt whether they are likely always to
keep their promise, Then we'll have to ration the food that
might arrive, said a woman's voice, That seems a good idea, if
you like, we can talk about it tomorrow, Agreed, said the woman.
The doctor was already on the point of leaving when the voice
of the first man to speak could be heard, Who's giving the orders here, He paused, expecting to be given an answer, and it

came from the same feminine voice, Unless we organise ourselves in earnest, hunger and fear will take over here, it is
shameful that we didn't go with the others to bury the dead,
Why don't you go and do the burying since you're so clever
and sure of yourself, I cannot go alone but I'm prepared to
help, There's no point in arguing, intervened another masculine voice, we'll settle this first thing in the morning. The doctor sighed, life together was going to be difficult. He was already heading back to his ward when he felt a pressing need to
relieve himself. At the spot where he found himself, he was not
sure that he would be able to find the lavatories, but he decided
to take a chance. He was hoping that someone would at least
have remembered to leave there the toilet paper which had
been delivered with the containers of food. He got lost twice
on the way and was in some distress because he was beginning
to feel desperate and just when he could hold back no longer,
he was finally able to take down his trousers and crouch over
the open latrine. The stench choked him. He had the impression of having stepped on some soft pulp, the excrement of
someone who had missed the hole of the latrine or who had decided to relieve himself without any consideration for others.
He tried to imagine what the place must look like, for him it
was all white, luminous, resplendent, he had no way of knowing whether the walls and ground were white and he came to
the absurd conclusion that the light and whiteness there were
giving off the awful stench. We shall go mad with horror, he
thought. Then he tried to clean himself but there was no paper.
He ran his hand over the wall behind him, where he expected
to find the rolls of toilet paper or nails, where in the absence of
anything better, any old scraps of paper had been stuck up.
Nothing. He felt unhappy, disconsolate, more unfortunate than
he could bear, crushed there, protecting his trousers which
were brushing against that disgusting floor, blind, blind, blind,

and, unable to control himself, he began to weep quietly. Fumbling, he took a few steps and bumped into the opposite wall. He stretched out one arm, then the other, and finally found a door. He could hear the shuffling footsteps of someone who must also have been looking for the lavatories, and who kept tripping, Where the hell are they? the person was muttering in a neutral voice, as if deep down, he was not all that interested in finding out. He passed close to the toilets without realising there was someone there, but no matter, the situation did not degenerate into indecency, if it could be called that, a man caught in an embarrassing situation, his clothes in disarray, at the last minute, moved by a disconcerting sense of shame, the doctor had pulled up his trousers. Then he lowered them, when he thought he was alone, but not in time, he knew he was dirty, dirtier than he could ever remember having been in his life. There are many ways of becoming an animal, he thought, this is just the first of them. However, he could not really complain, he still had someone who did not mind cleaning him.

Lying on their beds, the blind internees waited for sleep to take pity on their misery. Discreetly, as if there was some danger that others might see this distressing sight, the doctor's wife had helped her husband to clean himself as well as she could. There was now that sorrowful silence one finds in hospitals when the patients are asleep and suffer even as they sleep. Sitting up and alert, the doctor's wife looked at the beds, at the shadowy forms, the fixed pallor of a face, an arm that moved while dreaming. She wondered whether she would ever go blind like them, what inexplicable reasons had saved her from blindness so far. With a weary gesture, she raised her hands to draw back her hair, and thought, We're all going to stink to high heaven. At that moment sighs could be heard, moaning, tiny cries, muffled at first, sounds that seemed to be words, that ought to be words, but whose meaning got lost in the cres-

cendo that transformed them into shouts and grunts and finally
heavy, stertorous breathing. Someone protested at the far end
of the ward. Pigs, they're like pigs. They were not pigs, only
a blind man and a blind woman who probably knew nothing
more about each other than this.

A N EMPTY belly wakes up early. Some of the blind internees opened their eyes when morning was still some way off, and in their case it was not so much because of hunger, but because their biological clock, or whatever you call it, was no longer working properly, they assumed it was daylight, then thought, I've overslept and soon realised that they were wrong, their fellow inmates were snoring their heads off, there was no mistaking that. Now as we know from books, and even more so from personal experience, anyone who gets up early by inclination or has been forced to rise early out of necessity finds it intolerable that others should go on sleeping soundly, and with good reason in the case to which we are referring, for there is a marked difference between a blind person who is sleeping and a blind person who has opened his eyes to no purpose. These observations of a psychological nature, whose subtlety has no apparent relevance considering the extraordinary scale of the cataclysm which our narrative is struggling to relate, only serve to explain why all the blind internees were awake so early, some, as was said at the outset, were roused by the churning of their empty stomachs in need of food, others were dragged from their sleep by the nervous impatience of the

early risers, who did not hesitate to make more noise than the
inevitable and tolerable when people cohabit in barracks and
wards. Here there are not only persons of discretion and good
manners, but some real vulgarians who relieve themselves each
morning by coughing up phlegm and passing wind without regard for anyone who might be present, and if truth be told,
they behave just as badly for most of the day, making the atmosphere increasingly heavy, and there is nothing to be done,
the only opening is the door, the windows cannot be reached
they are so high.

Lying beside her husband, as close as possible given the narrowness of the bed, but also out of choice, how much it had cost
them in the middle of the night to maintain some decorum, not
to behave like those whom someone had referred to as pigs,
the doctor's wife looked at her watch. It was twenty-three minutes past two. She took a closer look, saw that the second hand
was not moving. She had forgotten to wind up the wretched
watch, or wretched her, wretched me, for not even this simple
task had she remembered to carry out after only three days of
isolation. Unable to control herself, she burst into convulsive
weeping, as if the worst of all disasters had suddenly befallen
her. The doctor thought his wife had gone blind, that what he
so greatly feared had finally happened, and, beside himself, was
on the point of asking, Have you gone blind, when at the last
minute he heard her whisper, No, no, it isn't that, it isn't that,
and then in a drawn-out whisper, almost inaudible, both their
heads under the blanket, How stupid of me, I forgot to wind
my watch, and she went on sobbing, inconsolable. Getting up
from her bed on the other side of the passageway, the girl with
dark glasses moved in the direction of the sobbing with arms
outstretched, You're upset, can I get you anything, she asked
as she advanced, and touched the two bodies on the bed with
her hands. Discretion demanded that she should withdraw im-

mediately, and this certainly was the order that came from her
brain, but her hands did not obey, they simply made more subtle contact, gently caressing the thick, warm blanket. Can I get
you anything, the girl asked once more, and, by now she had
removed her hands, raised them until they became lost in that
sterile whiteness, helpless. Still sobbing, the doctor's wife got
out of bed, embraced the girl and said, It's nothing, I just suddenly felt sad, If you who are so strong are becoming disheart-
ened, then there really is no salvation for us, complained the
girl. Calmer now, the doctor's wife thought, looking straight at
her, The signs of conjunctivitis have almost gone, what a pity I
cannot tell her, she would be pleased. Yes, in all probability she
would be pleased, although any such satisfaction would be absurd, not so much because the girl was blind, but since all the
others there were blind as well, what good would it do her to
have beautiful bright eyes such as these if there is no one to
see them. The doctor's wife said, We all have our moments of
weakness, just as well that we are still capable of weeping, tears
are often our salvation, there are times when we would die if
we did not weep, There is no salvation for us, the girl with dark
glasses repeated, Who can tell, this blindness is not like any
other, it might disappear as suddenly as it came, It will come
too late for those who have died, We all have to die, But not
to be killed and I have killed someone, Don't blame yourself, it
was a question of circumstances, here we are all guilty and innocent, much worse was the behaviour of the soldiers who are
here to protect us, and even they can invoke the greatest of all
excuses, fear, What if the wretched fellow did fondle me, he
would be alive right now, and my body would be no different
from what it is now, Think no more about it, rest, try to sleep.
She accompanied the girl to her bed, Come now, get into bed,
You're very kind, said the girl, then lowering her voice, I don't
know what to do, it's almost time for my period and I haven't

brought any sanitary napkins, Don't worry, I have some. The hands of the girl with dark glasses searched for somewhere to hold on to, but it was the doctor's wife who gently held them in her own hands, Rest, rest. The girl closed her eyes, remained like that for a minute, she might have fallen asleep were it not for the quarrel that suddenly erupted, someone had gone to the lavatory and on his return found his bed occupied, no harm was meant, the other fellow had got up for the same reason, they had passed each other on the way, and obviously it did not occur to either of them to say, Take care not to get into the wrong bed when you come back. Standing there, the doctor's wife watched the two blind men who were arguing, she noticed they made no gestures, that they barely moved their bodies, having quickly learned that only their voice and hearing now served any purpose, true, they had their arms, that they could fight, grapple, come to blows, as the saying goes, but a bed swapped by mistake was not worth so much fuss, if only all life's deceptions were like this one, and all they had to do was to come to some agreement, Number two is mine, yours is number three, let that be understood once and for all, Were it not for the fact that we're blind this mix-up would never have happened, You're right, our problem is that we're blind. The doctor's wife said to her husband, The whole world is right here.

Not quite all of it. The food, for example, was there on the outside and taking ages to arrive. From both wards, some men had gone to station themselves in the hallway, waiting for orders to come over the loudspeaker. They kept shuffling their feet, nervous and impatient. They knew that they would have to go out to the forecourt to fetch the containers which the soldiers, fulfilling their promise, would leave in the area between the main gate and the steps, and they feared that there might be some ploy or snare, How do we know that they won't start firing, After what they've done already, they're capable

of anything, They are not to be trusted, You won't get me going out there, Nor me, Someone has to go if we want to eat, I
don't know if it isn't better to die being shot than to die of hunger, I'm going, Me too, We don't all have to go, The soldiers
might not like it, Or get worried and think we're trying to escape, that's probably why they shot the man with the injured
leg, We've got to make up our minds, We can't be too careful,
remember what happened yesterday, nine casualties no more
no less, The soldiers were afraid of us, And I'm afraid of them,
What I'd like to know is if they too go blind, Who's they, The
soldiers, In my opinion they ought to be the first. They were
all in agreement, yet without asking themselves why, and there
was no one there to give them the one good reason, Because
then they would not be able to aim their rifles. The time passed
and passed, and the loudspeaker remained silent. Have you already tried to bury your dead, a blind man from the first ward
asked for the want of something to say, Not yet, They're beginning to smell and infect everything around, Well let them
infect everything and stink to high heaven, as far as I'm concerned, I've no intention of doing anything until I've eaten, as
someone once said, first you eat then you wash the pan, That
isn't the custom, your maxim is wrong, generally it is after
burying their dead that the mourners eat and drink, With me
it's the other way round. After a few minutes one of these blind
men said, There's one thing that bothers me, What's that, How
are we going to distribute the food, As we did before, we know
how many we are, the rations are counted, everyone receives
his share, it's the simplest and fairest way, But it didn't work,
some internees were left without any food, And there were also
those who got double rations, The distribution was badly organised, It will always be badly organised unless people show
some respect and discipline, If only we had someone here who
could see just a little, Well, he'd try coming up with some ruse

in order to make sure he got the lion's share, As the saying goes, in the country of the blind, the one-eyed man is king, Forget about sayings, But this is not the same, Here not even the cross-eyed would be saved, As I see it, the best solution would be to share the food out in equal parts throughout the wards, then each internee can be self-sufficient, Who spoke, It was me, Who's me, Me, which ward are you from, From ward two, Who would have believed such cunning, since ward two has fewer patients such an arrangement would be to their advantage and they would get more to eat than us, since our ward is full, I was only trying to be helpful, the proverb also says that if the one who does the sharing out fails to get the better part, he's either a fool or a dullard, Shit, that's quite enough of proverbs, these sayings get on my nerves, What we should do is to take all the food to the refectory, each ward elects three of its inmates to do the sharing out, so that with six people counting there would be little danger of abuse and deception, And how are we to know that they are telling the truth when the others say how many there are in their ward, We're dealing with honest people, Is that a proverb too, No, that's me saying it, My dear fellow, I don't know about honest but we're certainly hungry.

As if it had been waiting all this time for the code word, some cue, an open sesame, the voice finally came over the loudspeaker, Attention, attention, the internees may come and collect their food, but be careful, if anyone gets too close to the gate they will receive a preliminary warning, and unless they turn back immediately, the second warning will be a bullet. The blind internees advanced slowly, some, more confident, towards the right where they thought they would find the door, the others, less sure of their ability to get their bearings, preferred to slide along the wall, in this way there was no possibility of mistaking the way, when they reached the corner all they had to do

was to follow the wall at a right angle and there they would find
the door. The hectoring voice over the loudspeaker impatiently
repeated the summons. The change of tone, unmistakable even
for those who had no reason to be suspicious, terrified the blind
internees. One of them declared, I'm not budging from here,
what they want to do is to catch us outside and then kill us all,
I'm not moving either, said another, Nor me, chipped in a third.
They were frozen to the spot, undecided, some wanted to go,
but fear was getting the better of all of them. The voice came
again, Unless within the next three minutes someone appears
to collect the containers, we shall take them away. This threat
failed to overcome their fear, only pushed it into the innermost
caverns of their mind, like hunted animals that await an opportunity to attack. Each one trying to hide behind the other, the
blind internees moved fearfully out onto the landing at the top
of the steps. They could not see that the containers were not
alongside the guide rope where they expected to find them, for
they were not to know that the soldiers, out of fear of being
contaminated, had refused to go anywhere near the rope which
the blind internees were holding on to. The food containers
were stacked up together, more or less at the spot where the
doctor's wife had collected the spade. Come forward, come forward, ordered the sergeant. In some confusion, the blind internees tried to get into a line so as to advance in orderly fashion, but the sergeant bellowed at them, You won't find the
containers there, let go of the rope, let go of it, move over to
the right, *your* right, *your* right, fools, you don't need eyes to
know which side you have your right hand. The warning was
given just in time, some of the blind internees who were punctilious in these matters, had interpreted the order literally, if it
was on the right, logically that would mean on the right of the
person speaking, therefore they were trying to pass under the
rope to go in search of the containers which were God knows

where. In different circumstances, this grotesque spectacle
would have caused the most restrained spectator to burst into
howls of laughter, it was too funny for words, some of the blind
internees advancing on all fours, their faces practically touching the ground as if they were pigs, one arm outstretched in
mid-air, while others, perhaps afraid that the white space, without a roof to protect them, would swallow them up, clung desperately to the rope and listened attentively, expecting to hear
at any minute that first exclamation of triumph once the containers were discovered. The soldiers would have liked to aim
their weapons and, without compunction, shoot down those
imbeciles moving before their eyes like lame crabs, waving
their unsteady pincers in search of their missing leg. They knew
what had been said in the barracks that morning by the regi-
mental commander, that the problem of these blind internees
could be resolved only by physically wiping out the lot of them,
those already there and those still to come, without any phoney
humanitarian considerations, his very words, just as one ampu-
tates a gangrenous limb in order to save the rest of the body,
The rabies of a dead dog, he said, to illustrate the point, is cured
by nature. For some of the soldiers, less sensitive to the beau-
ties of figurative language, it was difficult to understand what a
dog with rabies had to do with the blind, but the word of a reg-
imental commander, once again figuratively speaking, is worth
its weight in gold, no man rises to so high a rank in the army
without being right in everything he thinks, says and does. A
blind man had finally bumped into the containers and called
out as he got hold of them, They're here, they're here, if this
man were to recover his eyesight one day, he would certainly
not announce the wonderful news with greater joy. Within seconds, the others had pounced on the containers, a confusion of
arms and legs, each man pulling a container towards his side
and claiming priority, I'll carry it, no, I will. Those who were

still holding on to the rope began to feel nervous, they now had
something else to fear, that they might be excluded on account
of their idleness or cowardice, when the food was shared out,
Ah, you men refused to get down on the ground with your arse
in the air and risk the danger of being shot, so nothing to eat
for you, remember the proverb, nothing ventured nothing
gained. Persuaded by these sententious words, one of the blind
men let go of the rope and went, with arms outstretched, in the
direction of the uproar, They're not going to leave me out, but
suddenly the voices fell silent and there was only the noise of
people crawling on the ground, muffled interjections, a dispersed and confused mass of sounds coming from everywhere
and nowhere. He paused, undecided, tried to go back to the security of the rope, but he had lost his sense of direction, there
are no stars in his white sky, and what could now be heard was
the sergeant's voice as it ordered those arguing over the containers to get back to the steps, for what he was saying could
have been meant only for them, to arrive where you want to be,
everything depends on where you are. There were no longer
any blind internees holding on to the rope, all they had to do
was to return the way they had come, and now they were waiting at the top of the steps for the others to arrive. The blind
man who had lost his way did not dare to move from where he
was. In a state of anguish, he let out a loud cry, Please, help me,
unaware that the soldiers had their rifles trained on him as they
waited for him to tread on that invisible line dividing life from
death. Are you going to stay there all day, you blind bat, asked
the sergeant, in a somewhat nervous voice, the truth being that
he did not share the opinion of his commander, Who can guarantee that the same fate won't come knocking at the door tomorrow, as for the soldiers it is well known that they need only
to be given an order and they kill, to be given another order
and they die, You will shoot only when I say so, the sergeant

shouted. These words made the blind man realise that his life
was in danger. He fell to his knees and beseeched them, Please
help me, tell me where I have to go, Keep on walking, blind
man, keep on walking this way, a soldier called from beyond in
a tone of false camaraderie, the blind man got up, took three
paces, then suddenly came to another halt, the tense of the verb
aroused his suspicion, keep on walking this way is not the same
as keep going, keep on walking this way tells you that this way,
this very way, in this direction, you will arrive where you are
being summoned, only to come up against the bullet that will
replace one form of blindness with another. This initiative,
which we might well describe as criminal, was taken by a soldier of disreputable character, whom the sergeant immediately
rebuked with two sharp commands given successively, Halt,
Half turn, followed by a severe call to order directed at this dis-
obedient fellow, who to all appearances belonged to that class
of people who are not to be trusted with a rifle. Encouraged by
the sergeant's kind intervention, the blind internees who had
reached the top of the steps suddenly made a tremendous racket
which served as a magnetic pole for the blind man who had lost
his way. Now more sure of himself, he advanced in a straight
line, Keep on shouting, keep on shouting, he beseeched them,
while the other blind internees applauded as if they were watching someone complete a long, dynamic but exhausting sprint.
He was given a rapturous welcome, the least they could do, in
the face of adversity, whether proven or foreseeable, you know
who your friends are.

   This camaraderie did not last long. Taking advantage of
the uproar, some of the blind internees had sneaked off with a
number of containers, as many as they could carry, a patently
disloyal way of forestalling any hypothetical injustices in the
distribution. Those of good faith, who are always to be found
no matter what people may say, protested with indignation,

that they couldn't live like this, If we cannot trust each other, where are we going to end up? some asked rhetorically, although with full justification, What these rogues are asking for is a good hiding, threatened others, they had not asked for any such thing, but everyone understood what those words meant, an inaccurate expression that can be tolerated only because it is so very apt. Already gathered in the hallway, the blind internees came to an agreement, this being the most practical way of resolving the first part of the difficult situation in which they found themselves, that they would distribute the remaining containers equally between the two wards, fortunately an even number, and set up a committee, also on an equal basis, to carry out an investigation with a view to recovering the missing, that is to say, stolen containers. They wasted some time in debate, as was becoming their habit, the before and the after, that is to say, whether they should eat first and then investigate, or the other way round, the prevailing opinion being that, taking into account all the hours of enforced fasting they had spent, it would be more convenient to start by satisfying their stomachs and then proceeding with their inquiries, And don't forget that you have to bury your dead, said someone from the first ward, We haven't killed them yet and you want us to bury them, replied one witty fellow, amusing himself with this play on words. Everyone laughed. However they were soon to discover that the culprits were not to be found in the wards. At the doors of both wards, waiting for their food to arrive, the blind internees claimed to have heard passing along the corridors people who seemed to be in a great hurry, but no one had entered the wards, much less carrying containers of food, that they could swear to. Someone remembered that the safest way of identifying these fellows would be if they were all to return to their respective beds, obviously those that remained unoccupied must belong to the thieves, so all they had to do was to wait until they returned from wherever they had been hiding and licking their chops and then pounce on them, so that they might learn to respect the sacred principle of collective property. To proceed with this plan, however opportune and in keeping with a deep-seated sense of justice, had one serious disadvantage insofar as it would mean postponing, no one could foresee for how long, that much desired breakfast, already gone cold. Let's eat first, suggested one of the blind men, and the majority agreed that it was better that they should eat first. Alas, only the little that had remained after that infamous theft. At this hour, in some hiding place amongst these old and dilapidated buildings, the thieves must be gorging themselves on double and triple rations that unexpectedly seemed to have improved, consisting of coffee with milk, cold in fact, biscuits and bread with margarine, while decent folk had to content themselves with two or three times less, and not even that. Outside the loudspeaker could be heard summoning the contagious to fetch their food rations, the sound also reached some of the internees in the first wing, as they were sadly chewing on water biscuits. One of the blind men, undoubtedly influenced by the unwholesome atmosphere left by the theft of food, had an idea, If we were to wait in the hallway, they would get the fright of their lives just to see us there, they might even drop the odd container, but the doctor said he did not think this would be right, it would be an injustice to punish those without blame. When they had all finished eating, the doctor's wife and the girl with dark glasses carried the cardboard containers into the yard, the empty flasks of milk and coffee, the paper cups, in a word, everything that could not be eaten. We must burn the rubbish, the doctor's wife then suggested, and get rid of these horrible flies.

Seated on their respective beds, the blind internees settled down to wait for the pack of thieves to return, Thieving dogs,

that's what they are, commented a rough voice, unaware that
he was responding to a reminiscence of someone who is not
to blame for not knowing how to say things in any other manner. But the scoundrels did not appear, they must have suspected something, suspicions no doubt raised by some astute
fellow amongst them like the one here who suggested giving
them a good hiding. The minutes went by, several of the blind
men had stretched out, some were already asleep. For this, my
friends, is what it means to eat and sleep. All things considered,
things could be worse. So long as they go on supplying us with
food, for we cannot live without it, this is like being in a hotel.
By contrast, what a torment it would be for a blind man out
there in the city, yes, a real torment. Stumbling through the
streets, everyone fleeing at the very sight of him, his family in
a panic, terrified of approaching him, a mother's love, a child's
love, a myth, they would probably treat me just as I am treated
in this place, lock me up in a room and, if I was very lucky, leave
a plate outside the door. Looking at the situation objectively,
without preconceptions or resentments which always cloud our
reasoning, it had to be acknowledged that the authorities had
shown great vision when they decided to unite the blind with
the blind, each with his own, which is a wise rule for those who
have to live together, like lepers, and there can be no doubt that
the doctor there at the far end of the ward is right when he says
that we must organise ourselves, the question, in fact, is one of
organisation, first the food, then the organisation, both are indispensable for life, to choose a number of reliable men and
women and put them in charge, to establish approved rules for
our co-existence here in the ward, simple things, like sweeping the floor, tidying up and washing, we've nothing to complain about there, they have even provided us with soap and detergent, making sure our beds are always made, the important
thing is not to lose our self-respect, to avoid any conflict with

the soldiers who are only doing their duty by keeping us under guard, we do not want any more casualties, asking around if
there is anyone willing to entertain us in the evening with stories, fables, anecdotes, whatever, just think how fortunate we
would be if someone knew the Bible by heart, we could repeat
everything since the creation of the world, the important thing
is that we should listen to one another, pity we haven't a radio,
music has always been a great distraction, and we could follow
the news bulletins, for example, if a cure were to be discovered
for our illness, how we should rejoice.

Then the inevitable happened. They heard shots being fired
in the street, They're coming to kill us, someone shouted, Calm
down, said the doctor, we must be logical, if they wanted to kill
us, they would come here to shoot us, not outside. The doctor
was right, it was the sergeant who had given the order to shoot
in the air, not some soldier who had suddenly been struck blind
when his finger was on the trigger, clearly there was no other
way of controlling and intimidating the new internees as they
stumbled from the vans, the Ministry of Health had informed
the Ministry of Defence, We're despatching four van-loads,
And how many does that make, About two hundred internees, Where are all these people going to be accommodated, the
wards reserved for the blind internees are the three in the wing
on the right, according to the information we've been given,
the total capacity is one hundred and twenty, and there are already some sixty to seventy internees inside, minus a dozen or
so whom we were obliged to kill, There is one solution, open
up all the wards, That would mean the contaminated coming
into direct contact with those who are blind, In all probability,
sooner or later, the former will also go blind, besides, the situation being as it is, I suppose we'll all be contaminated, there
cannot be a single person who has not been within sight of a
blind man, If a blind man cannot see, I ask myself, how can he

transmit this disease through his sight, General, this must be
the most logical illness in the world, the eye that is blind trans-
mits the blindness to the eye that sees, what could be simpler,
We have a colonel here who believes the solution would be
to shoot the blind as soon as they appear, Corpses instead of
blind men would scarcely improve the situation, To be blind is
not the same as being dead, Yes, but to be dead is to be blind,
So there are going to be about two hundred of them, Yes, And
what shall we do with the taxi-drivers, Put them inside as well.
That same day, in the late afternoon, the Ministry of Defence
contacted the Ministry of Health, Would you like to hear the
latest news, that colonel we mentioned earlier has gone blind,
It'll be interesting to see what he thinks of that bright idea of
his now, He already thought, he shot himself in the head, Now
that's what I call a consistent attitude, The army is always ready
to set an example.

The gate had been opened wide. In keeping with barracks
routine, the sergeant ordered that a column should be formed
five deep, but the blind internees were unable to get the numbers right, sometimes they were more than five, at other times
less, and they all ended up by crowding around the entrance,
like the civilians they were, without any sense of order, they did
not even remember to send the women and children ahead, as
in other shipwrecks. It has to be said before we forget, that not
all of the gunshots had been fired in the air, one of the van-
drivers had refused to go with the blind internees, he protested
that he could see perfectly well, the outcome, three seconds
later, was to prove the point made by the Ministry of Health
when it decreed that to be dead is to be blind. The sergeant
gave the aforementioned orders, Keep going, there's a stairway with six steps, when you get there, go slowly up the steps,
if anyone trips, who knows what will happen, the only recommendation overlooked was that they should follow the rope,

but clearly if they had used it they would have taken forever to enter, Listen, cautioned the sergeant, his mind at rest because all of them were already inside the gate, there are three wards on the right and three on the left, each ward has forty beds, families should stay together, avoid crowding, wait at the entrance and ask those who are already interned for assistance, everything is going to be all right, settle in and keep calm, keep calm, your food will be delivered later.

It would not be right to imagine that these blind people, in such great numbers, proceed like lambs to the slaughter, bleating as is their wont, somewhat crowded, it is true, yet that is how they had always existed, cheek by jowl, mingling breaths and smells, There are some here who cannot stop crying, others who are shouting in fear or rage, others who are cursing, someone uttered a terrible, futile threat, If I get my hands on you, presumably he was referring to the soldiers, I'll gouge your eyes out. Inevitably, the first internees to reach the stairway had to probe with one foot, the height and depth of the steps, the pressure of those coming from behind knocked two or three of those in front to the ground, fortunately nothing more serious occurred, nothing except a few grazed shins, the sergeant's advice had proved to be a blessing. A number of the new arrivals had already entered the hallway, but two hundred persons cannot be expected to sort themselves out all that easily, moreover blind and without a guide, this painful situation being made even worse by the fact that we are in an old building and badly designed at that, it is not enough for a sergeant who knows only about military affairs to say, there are three wards on each side, you have to know what it's like inside, doorways so narrow that they look more like bottlenecks, corridors as crazy as the other inmates of the asylum, opening for no clear reason and closing who knows where, and no one is ever likely to find out. Instinctively, the vanguard of blind intern-

ees had divided into two columns, moving on both sides along
the walls in search of a door they might enter, a safe method,
undoubtedly, assuming there are no items of furniture blocking the way. Sooner or later, with know-how and patience, the
new inmates will settle in, but not before the latest battle has
been won between the first lines of the column on the left and
the contaminated confined to that side. It was only to be expected. There was an agreement, there was even a regulation
drawn up by the Ministry of Health, that this wing would be
reserved for the contaminated, and if it was true that it could
be foreseen that in all likelihood, every one of them would end
up blind, it was also true, in terms of pure logic, that until they
became blind there was no guarantee that they were fated to
blindness. There is then a person sitting peacefully at home,
confident that at least in his case all will turn out well, when
suddenly he sees coming directly towards him a howling mob
of the people he most fears. At first, the contaminated thought
this was a group of inmates like themselves, only more numerous, but the deception was short-lived, these people were blind
all right, You can't come in here, this wing is ours, it isn't for
the blind, you belong to the wing on the other side, shouted
those on guard at the door. Some of the blind internees tried
to do a turnaround and find another entrance, they didn't care
if they went left or right, but the mass of those who continued
to flock in from outside, jostled them relentlessly. The contaminated defended the door with punches and kicks, the blind
retaliated as best they could, they could not see their adversaries, but knew where the blows were coming from. Two hundred people could not get into the hallway, or anything like
that number, so it was not long before the door leading to the
courtyard, despite being fairly wide, was completely blocked,
as if obstructed by a plug, they could go neither backwards nor
forwards, those who were inside, crushed and flattened, tried

to protect themselves by kicking and elbowing their neighbours, who were suffocating, cries could be heard, blind children were sobbing, blind mothers were fainting, while the vast
crowd that had been unable to enter pushed even harder, terrified by the bellowing of the soldiers, who could not understand why those idiots had not gone through. There was one
terrible moment of violent backsurge as people struggled to
extricate themselves from the confusion, from the imminent
danger of being crushed, let us put ourselves in the place of the
soldiers, suddenly they see a considerable number of those who
had entered come hurtling out, they immediately thought the
worst, that the new arrivals were about to turn back, let us remember the precedents, there might well have been a massacre. Fortunately, the sergeant was once more equal to the crisis, he himself fired into the air, simply to attract attention, and
shouted over the loudspeaker, Calm down, those on the steps
should draw back a little, clear the way, stop pushing and try
to help each other. That was asking too much, the struggle inside continued, but the hallway gradually emptied thanks to a
much greater number of blind internees moving to the door of
the right wing, there they were received by blind inmates who
were happy to direct them to the third ward, so far free, or to
the beds in the second ward which were still unoccupied. For
one moment it looked as if the battle would be resolved in favour of the contaminated, not because they were stronger and
had more sight, but because the blind internees, having perceived that the entrance on the other side was less encumbered,
broke off all contacts, as the sergeant would say in his discussions about strategy and basic military tactics. However, the triumph of the defenders was of short duration. From the door of
the right wing came voices announcing that there was no more
room, that all the wards were full, there were even some blind
internees still being pushed into the hallway, precisely at that

moment when, once the human stopper up until then blocking the main entrance dispersed, once the considerable number of blind internees who were outside, were able to advance
and take shelter under the roof where, safe from the threats of
the soldiers, they would live. The result of these two displace-
ments, practically simultaneous, was to rekindle the struggle
at the entrance of the wing on the left-hand side, once again
blows were exchanged, once more there were shouts, and, as
if this were not enough, in their confusion some of the bewildered blind internees, who had found and forced open the hallway door leading directly into the inner courtyard, cried out
that there were corpses out there. Imagine their horror. They
withdrew as best they could, There are corpses out there, they
repeated, as if they would be the next to die, and, within a second, the hallway was once more the raging whirlpool it had
been at its worst, then, in a sudden and desperate impulse, the
human mass swerved towards the wing on the left, carrying
all before it, the resistance of the contaminated broken, many
of them no longer merely contaminated, others, running like
madmen, were still trying to escape their black destiny. They
ran in vain. One after the other they were stricken with blindness, their eyes suddenly drowned in that hideous white tide
inundating the corridors, the wards, the entire space. Out there
in the hallway, in the yard, the blind internees, helpless, some
badly bruised from the blows, others from being trampled,
dragged themselves along, most of them were elderly, many
women and children, beings with few or no defences, and it was
nothing short of a miracle that there were not more corpses in
need of burial. Scattered on the ground, apart from some shoes
that had lost their feet, lie bags, suitcases, baskets, each individual's bit of wealth, lost forever, anyone coming across these objects will insist that what he is carrying is his.

An old man with a black patch over one eye, came in from

the yard. He, too, had either lost his luggage or had not brought any. He had been the first to stumble over the corpses, but he did not cry out. He remained beside them and waited for peace and silence to be restored. He waited for an hour. Now it is his turn to seek shelter. Slowly, with his arms outstretched, he searched for the way. He found the door of the first ward on the right-hand side, heard voices coming from within, then asked, Any chance of a bed here.

THE arrival of so many blind people appeared to have brought at least one advantage, or, rather, two advantages, the first of these being of a psychological nature, as it were, for there is a vast difference between waiting for new inmates to turn up at any minute, and realising that the building is completely full at last, that from now on it will be possible to establish and maintain stable and lasting relations with one's neighbours, without the disturbances there have been up until now, because of the constant interruptions and interventions by the new arrivals which obliged us to be forever reconstituting the channels of communication. The second advantage, of a practical, direct and substantial nature, was that the authorities outside, both civilian and military, had understood that it was one thing to provide food for two or three dozen people, more or less tolerant, more or less prepared, because of their small number, to resign themselves to occasional mistakes or delays in the delivery of food, and quite another to be faced with the sudden and complex responsibility of feeding two hundred and forty human beings of every type, background and temperament. Two hundred and forty, take note, and that is just a manner of speaking, for there are at least twenty blind internees who have not managed to find a bed and are sleeping on the floor. In any case, it has to be recognised that thirty persons being fed on rations meant for ten is not the same as sharing out to two hundred and sixty, food intended for two hundred and forty. The difference is almost imperceptible. Now then, it was the conscious assumption of this increased responsibility, and perhaps, a hypothesis not to be disregarded, the fear that further disturbances might break out, that determined a change of procedure on the part of the authorities, in the sense of giving orders that the food should be delivered on time and in the right quantity. Obviously, after the struggle, in every respect lamentable, that we had to witness, accommodating so many blind internees was not going to be easy or free of conflict, we need only remember those poor contaminated creatures who before could still see and now see nothing, of the separated couples and their lost children, of the discomfort of those who had been trampled and knocked down, some of them twice or three times, of those who are going around in search of their cherished possessions without finding them, one would have to be completely insensitive to forget, as if it were nothing, the misfortunes of these poor people. However, it cannot be denied that the announcement that lunch was about to be delivered was like a consoling balm for everyone. And if it is undeniable that, given the lack of adequate organisation for this operation or of any authority capable of imposing the necessary discipline, the collection of such large quantities of food and its distribution to feed so many mouths led to further misunderstandings, we must concede that the atmosphere changed considerably for the better, when throughout that ancient asylum there was nothing to be heard except the noise of two hundred and sixty mouths masticating. Who is going to clean up this mess afterwards is a question so far unanswered, only in the late afternoon will the voice on the loudspeaker repeat the rules of orderly conduct that must be observed for the good of all, and then it will become clear with what degree of respect the new arrivals treat these rules. It is no small thing that the inmates of the second ward in the right wing have decided, at long last, to bury their dead, at least we shall be rid of that particular stench, the smell of the living, however fetid, will be easier to get used to.

As for the first ward, perhaps because it was the oldest and therefore most established in the process and pursuit of adaptation to the state of blindness, a quarter of an hour after its inmates had finished eating, there was not so much as a scrap of dirty paper on the floor, a forgotten plate or dripping receptacle. Everything had been gathered up, the smaller objects placed inside the larger ones, the dirtiest of them placed inside those that were less dirty, as any rationalised regulation of hygiene would demand, as attentive to the greatest efficiency possible in gathering up leftovers and litter, as to the economy of effort needed to carry out this task. The state of mind which perforce will have to determine social conduct of this nature cannot be improvised nor does it come about spontaneously. In the case under scrutiny, the pedagogical approach of the blind woman at the far end of the ward seems to have had a decisive influence, that woman married to the ophthalmologist, who has never tired of telling us, If we cannot live entirely like human beings, at least let us do everything in our power not to live entirely like animals, words she repeated so often that the rest of the ward ended up by transforming her advice into a maxim, a dictum, into a doctrine, a rule of life, words which deep down were so simple and elementary, probably it was just that state of mind, propitious to any understanding of needs and circumstances, that contributed, even if only in a minor way to the warm welcome the old man with the black eyepatch found there when he peered through the door and asked those inside, Any chance of a bed here. By a happy coincidence, clearly indicative of future consequences, there was a bed, the only one, and it is anyone's guess how it survived, as it were, the invasion, in that bed the car-thief had suffered unspeakable pain, perhaps that is why it had retained an aura of suffering that kept people at a distance. These are the workings of destiny, arcane mysteries, and this coincidence was not the first, far from it, we need only observe that all the eye patients who happened to be in the surgery when the first blind man appeared there have ended up in this ward, and even then it was thought that the situation would go no further, In a low voice, as always, so that no one would suspect the secret of her presence there, the doctor's wife whispered into her husband's ear, Perhaps he was also one of your patients, he is an elderly man, bald, with white hair, and he has a black patch over one eye, I remember you telling me about him, Which eye, The left, It must be him. The doctor advanced to the passageway and said, slightly raising his voice, I'd like to touch the person who has just joined us, I would ask him to make his way in this direction and I shall make my way towards him. They bumped into each other midway, fingers touching fingers, like two ants that recognise each other from the manoeuvring of their antennae, but this won't be the case here, the doctor asked his permission, ran his hands over the old man's face, and quickly found the patch. There is no doubt, here is the one person who was missing here, the patient with the black patch, he exclaimed, What do you mean, who are you, asked the old man, I am, or rather I was your ophthalmologist, do you remember, we were agreeing on a date for your cataract operation, How did you recognise me, Above all, by your voice, the voice is the sight of the person who cannot see, Yes, the voice, I'm also beginning to recognise yours, who would have thought it, doctor, now there's no need for an operation, If there is a cure for this, we will both need it,

I remember you telling me, doctor, that after my operation I would no longer recognise the world in which I was living, we now know how right you were, When did you turn blind, Last night, And they've brought you here already, The panic out there is such that it won't be long before they start killing people off the moment they know they have gone blind, Here they have already eliminated ten, said a man's voice, I found them, the old man with the black eyepatch simply said, They were from the other ward, we buried our dead at once, added the same voice, as if concluding a report. The girl with dark glasses had approached, Do you remember me, I was wearing dark glasses, I remember you well, despite my cataract, I remember that you were very pretty, the girl smiled, Thank you, she said, and went back to her place. From there, she called out, The little boy is here too, I want my mummy, the boy's voice could be heard saying, as if worn out from some remote and useless weeping. And I was the first to go blind, said the first blind man, and I'm here with my wife, And I'm the girl from the surgery, said the girl from the surgery. The doctor's wife said, It only remains for me to introduce myself, and she said who she was. Then the old man, as if to repay the welcome, announced, I have a radio, A radio, exclaimed the girl with dark glasses as she clapped her hands, music, how nice, Yes, but it's a small radio, with batteries, and batteries do not last forever, the old man reminded her, Don't tell me we shall be cooped up here forever, said the first blind man, Forever, no, forever is always far too long a time, We'll be able to listen to the news, the doctor observed, And a little music, insisted the girl with dark glasses, Not everyone likes the same music, but we're all certainly interested in knowing what things are like outside, it would be better to save the radio for that, I agree, said the old man with the black eyepatch. He took the tiny radio from his jacket pocket and switched it on. He began searching for the different stations, but his hand was still too unsteady to tune into one wavelength, and to begin with all that could be heard were intermittent noises, fragments of music and words, at last his hand grew steadier, the music became recognisable, Leave it there for a bit, pleaded the girl with dark glasses, the words got clearer, That isn't the news, said the doctor's wife, and then, as if an idea had suddenly struck her, What time is it, she asked, but she knew that no one there could tell her. The tuning knob continued to extract noises from the tiny box, then it settled down, it was a song, a song of no significance, but the blind internees slowly began gathering round, without pushing, they stopped the moment they felt a presence before them and there they remained, listening, their eyes wide open turned in the direction of the voice that was singing, some were crying, as probably only the blind can cry, the tears simply flowing as from a fountain. The song came to an end, the announcer said, At the third stroke it will be four o'clock. One of the blind women asked, laughing, Four in the afternoon or four in the morning, and it was as if her laughter hurt her. Furtively, the doctor's wife adjusted her watch and wound it up, it was four in the afternoon, although, to tell the truth, a watch is unconcerned, it goes from one to twelve, the rest are just ideas in the human mind. What's that faint sound, asked the girl with dark glasses, it sounded like, It was me, I heard them say on the radio that it was four o'clock and I wound up my watch, it was one of those automatic movements we so often make, anticipated the doctor's wife. Then she thought that it had not been worth putting herself at risk like that, all she had to do was to glance at the wristwatches of the blind who had arrived that day, one of them must have a watch in working order. The old man with the black eyepatch had one, as she noticed just that moment, and the time on his watch was correct. Then the doctor asked, Tell us what the situation is like out there. The old man with the black eyepatch said, Of course, but I'd better sit, I'm dead on my feet. Three or four to a bed, keeping each other company on this occasion, the blind internees settled down as best they could, they fell silent, and then the old man with the black eyepatch told them what he knew, what he had seen with his own eyes when he could still see, what he had overheard during the few days that elapsed between the start of the epidemic and his own blindness.

In the first twenty-four hours, he said, if the rumour going round was true, there were hundreds of cases, all alike, all showing the same symptoms, all instantaneous, the disconcerting absence of lesions, the resplendent whiteness of their field of vision, no pain either before or after. On the second day there was talk of some reduction in the number of new cases, it went from hundreds to dozens and this led the Government to announce at once that it was reasonable to suppose that the situation would soon be under control. From this point onwards, apart from a few inevitable comments, the story of the old man with the black eyepatch will no longer be followed to the letter, being replaced by a reorganised version of his discourse, re-evaluated in the light of a correct and more appropriate vocabulary. The reason for this previously unforeseen change is the rather formal controlled language, used by the narrator, which almost disqualifies him as a complementary reporter, however important he may be, because without him we would have no way of knowing what happened in the outside world, as a complementary reporter, as we were saying, of these extraordinary events, when as we know the description of any facts can only gain with the rigour and suitability of the terms used. Returning to the matter in hand, the Government therefore ruled out the originally formulated hypothesis that the country was being swept by an epidemic without precedent, provoked by some morbid as yet unidentified agent that took effect instantaneously and was marked by a complete absence of any previous signs of incubation or latency. Instead, they said, that in accordance with the latest scientific opinion and the consequent and updated administrative interpretation, they were dealing with an accidental and unfortunate temporary concurrence of circumstances, also as yet unverified, in whose pathogenic development it was possible, the Government's communiqué emphasised, starting from the analysis of the available data, to detect the proximity of a clear curve of resolution and signs that it was on the wane. A television commentator came up with an apt metaphor when he compared the epidemic, or whatever it might be, to an arrow shot into the air, which upon reaching its highest point, pauses for a moment as if suspended, and then begins to trace its obligatory descending curve, which, God willing, and with this invocation the commentator returned to the triviality of human discourse and to the so-called epidemic, gravity tending to increase the speed of it, until this terrible nightmare tormenting us finally disappears, these were words that appeared constantly in the media, and always concluded by formulating the pious wish that the unfortunate people who had become blind might soon recover their sight, promising them meanwhile, the solidarity of society as a whole, both official and private. In some remote past, similar arguments and metaphors had been translated by the intrepid optimism of the common people into sayings such as, Nothing lasts forever, be it good or bad, the excellent maxims of one who has had time to learn from the ups and downs of life and fortune, and which, transported into the land of the blind, should be read as follows, Yesterday we could see, today we can't, tomorrow we shall see again, with a slight interrogatory note on the third and final line of the phrase, as if prudence, at the last moment, had decided, just in case, to add a touch of a doubt to the hopeful conclusion.

Sadly, the futility of such hopes soon became manifest, the Government's expectations and the predictions of the scientific community simply sank without trace. Blindness was spreading, not like a sudden tide flooding everything and carrying all before it, but like an insidious infiltration of a thousand and one turbulent rivulets which, having slowly drenched the earth, suddenly submerge it completely. Faced with this social catastrophe, already on the point of taking the bit between their teeth, the authorities hastily organised medical conferences, especially those bringing together ophthalmologists and neurologists. Because of the time it would inevitably take to organise, a congress that some had called for was never convened, but in compensation there were colloquia, seminars, round-table discussions, some open to the public, others held behind closed doors. The overall effect of the patent futility of the debates and the occurrence of certain cases of sudden blindness during the sessions, with the speaker calling out, I'm blind, I'm blind, prompted almost all the newspapers, the radio and television, to lose interest in such initiatives, apart from the discreet and, in every sense, laudable behaviour of certain organs of communication which, living off sensational stories of every kind, off the fortunes and misfortunes of others, were not prepared to miss an opportunity to report live, with all the drama the situation warranted, the sudden blindness, for example, of a professor of ophthalmology.

The proof of the progressive deterioration of morale in general was provided by the Government itself, its strategy changing twice within the space of some six days. To begin with, the Government was confident that it was possible to circumscribe the disease by confining the blind and the contaminated within specific areas, such as the asylum in which we find ourselves. Then the inexorable rise in the number of cases of blindness led some influential members of the Government, fearful that the official initiative would not suffice for the task in hand, and that it might result in heavy political costs, to defend the idea that it was up to families to keep their blind indoors, never allowing them to go out on the street, so as not to worsen the already difficult traffic situation or to offend the sensibility of persons who still had their eyesight and who, indifferent to more or less reassuring opinions, believed that the white disease was spreading by visual contact, like the evil eye. Indeed, it was not appropriate to expect any other reaction from someone who, preoccupied with his thoughts, be they sad, indifferent, or happy, if such thoughts still exist, suddenly saw the change in expression of a person heading in his direction, his face revealing all the signs of total horror, and then that inevitable cry, I'm blind, I'm blind. No one's nerves could withstand it. The worst thing is that whole families, especially the smaller ones, rapidly became families of blind people, leaving no one who could guide and look after them, nor protect sighted neighbours from them, and it was clear that these blind people, however caring a father, mother or child they might be, could not take care of each other, otherwise they would meet the same fate as the blind people in the painting, walking together, falling together and dying together.

Faced with this situation, the Government had no alternative but to go rapidly into reverse gear, broadening the criteria it had established about the places and spaces that could be requisitioned, resulting in the immediate and improvised utilisation of abandoned factories, disused churches, sports pavilions and empty warehouses. For the last two days there has been talk of setting up army tents, added the old man with the black eyepatch. At the beginning, the very beginning, several charitable organisations were still offering volunteers to assist the blind, to make their beds, clean out the lavatories, wash their clothes, prepare their food, the minimum of care without which life soon becomes unbearable, even for those who can see. These dear people went blind immediately but at least the generosity of their gesture would go down in history. Did any of them come here, asked the old man with the black eyepatch, No, replied the doctor's wife, no one has come, Perhaps it was a rumour, And what about the city and the traffic, asked the first blind man, remembering his own car and that of the taxi-driver who had driven him to the surgery and had helped him to dig the grave, Traffic is in a state of chaos, replied the old man with the black eyepatch, and gave details of specific cases and accidents. When, for the first time, a bus-driver was suddenly struck by blindness as he was driving his vehicle on a public road, despite the casualties and injuries resulting from the disaster, people did not pay much attention for the same reason, that is to say, out of force of habit, and the director of public relations of the transport company felt able to declare, without further ado, that the disaster had been caused by human error, regrettable no doubt, but, all things considered, as unforeseeable as a heart attack in the case of someone who had never suffered from a heart complaint. Our employees, explained the director, as well as the mechanical and electrical parts of our buses, are periodically subjected to rigorous checks, as can be seen, showing a direct and clear relation of cause and effect, in the extremely low percentage of accidents in which, generally speaking, our company's vehicles have been involved. This laboured explanation appeared in the newspapers, but people had more on their minds than worrying about a simple bus accident, after all, it would have been no worse if its brakes had failed. Moreover, two days later, this was precisely the cause of another accident, but the world being what it is, where the truth often has to masquerade as falsehood to achieve its ends, the rumour went round that the driver had gone blind. There was no way of convincing the public of what had in fact hap-

pened, and the outcome was soon evident, from one moment
to the next people stopped using buses, they said they would
rather go blind themselves than die because others had gone
blind. A third accident, soon afterwards and for the same reason, involving a vehicle that was carrying no passengers, gave
rise to comment such as the following, couched in a knowingly
popular tone, That could have been me. Nor could they imagine, those who spoke like this, how right they were. When two
pilots both went blind at once a commercial plane crashed and
burst into flames the moment it hit the ground, killing all the
passengers and crew, notwithstanding that in this case, the mechanical and electrical equipment were in perfect working order, as the black box, the only survivor, would later reveal. A
tragedy of these dimensions was not the same as an ordinary
bus accident, the result being that those who still had any illusions soon lost them, from then on engine noises were no
longer heard and no wheel, large or small, fast or slow, was ever
to turn again. Those people who were previously in the habit
of complaining about the ever-increasing traffic problems, pedestrians who, at first sight, appeared not to know where they
were going because the cars, stationary or moving, were constantly impeding their progress, drivers who having gone round
the block countless times before finally finding a place to park
their car, became pedestrians and started protesting for the
same reasons, after having first voiced their own complaints,
all of them must now be content, except for the obvious fact
that, since there was no one left who dared to drive a vehicle,
not even to get from A to B, the cars, trucks, motorbikes, even
the bicycles, were scattered chaotically throughout the entire
city, abandoned wherever fear had gained the upper hand over
any sense of propriety, as evidenced by the grotesque sight of
a tow-away vehicle with a car suspended from the front axle,
probably the first man to turn blind had been the truck-driver.

The situation was bad for everyone, but for those stricken with blindness it was catastrophic, since, according to the current expression, they could not see where they were putting their feet. It was pitiful to watch them bumping into the abandoned cars, one after the other, bruising their shins, some fell, pleading, Is there anyone who can help me to my feet, but there were also those who, naturally brutish or made so by despair, cursed and fought off any helping hand that came to their assistance, Leave me alone, your turn will come soon enough, then the compassionate person would take fright and make a quick escape, disappear into that dense white mist, suddenly conscious of the risk to which their kindness had exposed them, perhaps to go blind only a few steps further on.

That's how things are out there, the old man with the black eyepatch concluded his account, and I don't know everything, I can only speak of what I was able to see with my own eyes, here he broke off, paused and corrected himself, Not with my eyes, because I only had one, now not even that, well, I still have it but it's no use to me, I've never asked you why you didn't have a glass eye instead of wearing that patch, And why should I have wanted to, tell me that, asked the old man with the black eyepatch, It's normal because it looks better, besides it's much more hygienic, it can be removed, washed and replaced like dentures, Yes sir, but tell me what it would be like today if all those who now find themselves blind had lost, I say physically lost, both their eyes, what good would it do them now to be walking around with two glass eyes, You're right, no good at all, With all of us ending up blind, as appears to be happening, who's interested in aesthetics, and as for hygiene, tell me, doctor, what kind of hygiene could you hope for in this place, Perhaps only in a world of the blind will things be what they truly are, said the doctor, And what about people, asked the girl with dark glasses, People, too, no one will be there to see them, An idea has just occurred to me, said the old man with the black eyepatch, let's play a game to pass the time, How can we play a game if we cannot see what we are playing, asked the wife of the first blind man, Well, not a game exactly, each of us must say what we saw at the moment we went blind, That could be embarrassing, someone pointed out, Those who do not wish to take part in the game can remain silent, the important thing is that no one should try to invent anything, Give us an example, said the doctor, Certainly, replied the old man with the black eyepatch, I went blind when I was looking at my blind eye, What do you mean, It's very simple, I felt as if the inside of the empty orbit were inflamed and I removed the patch to satisfy my curiosity and just at that moment I went blind, It sounds like an allegory, said an unknown voice, the eye that refuses to acknowledge its own absence, As for me, said the doctor, I was at home consulting some reference books on ophthalmology, precisely because of what is happening, the last thing I saw were my hands resting on a book, My final image was different, said the doctor's wife, the inside of an ambulance as I was helping my husband to get in, I've already explained to the doctor what happened to me, said the first blind man, I had stopped at the lights, the signal was red, there were people crossing the street from one side to the other, at that very moment I turned blind, then that fellow who died the other day took me home, obviously I couldn't see his face, As for me, said the wife of the first blind man, the last thing I can remember seeing was my handkerchief, I was sitting at home and crying my heart out, I raised the handkerchief to my eyes and went blind that very moment, In my case, said the girl from the surgery, I had just gotten into the elevator, I stretched out my hand to press the button and suddenly stopped seeing, you can imagine my distress, trapped in there and all alone, I didn't know whether I would go up or down, and I couldn't find the button to open the door, My situation, said the pharmacist's assistant, was simpler, I heard that people were going blind, then I began to wonder what it would be like if I too were to go blind, I closed my eyes to try it and when I opened them I was blind, Sounds like another allegory, interrupted the unknown voice, if you want to be blind, then blind you will be. They remained silent. The other blind internees had gone back to their beds, no easy task, for while it is true that they knew their respective numbers, only by starting to count from one end of the ward, from one upwards or from twenty downwards, could they be certain of arriving where they wanted to be. When the murmur of their counting, as monotonous as a litany, died away, the girl with dark glasses related what had happened to her, I was in a hotel room with a man lying on top of me, at that point she fell silent, she felt too ashamed to say what she was doing there, that she had seen everything white, but the old man with the black eyepatch asked, And you saw everything white, Yes, she replied, Perhaps your blindness is different from ours, said the old man with the black eyepatch. The only person still to speak was the chambermaid, I was making a bed, a certain person had gone blind there, I held up the white sheet before me and spread it out, tucked it in at the sides as one does, and as I was smoothing it out with both hands, suddenly I could no longer see, I remember how I was smoothing the sheet out, very slowly, it was the bottom sheet, she added, as if this had some special significance. Has everyone told their story about the last time they could see, asked the old man with the black eyepatch, I'll tell you mine, if there's no one else, said the unknown voice, If there is, he can speak after you, so fire away, The last thing I saw was a painting, A painting, repeated the old man with the black eyepatch, and where was this painting, I had gone to the museum, it was a picture of a cornfield with crows and cypress trees and a sun that gave the impression of having been made up of the fragments of other suns, Sounds like a Dutch painter, I think it was, but there was a drowning dog in it, already half submerged, poor creature, In that case it must be by a Spanish painter, before him no one had ever painted a dog in that situation, after him no other painter had the courage to try. Probably, and there was a cart laden with hay, drawn by horses and crossing a stream, Was there a house on the left, Yes, Then it was by an English painter, Could be, but I don't think so, because there was a woman as well with a child in her arms, Mothers and children are all too common in paintings, True, I've noticed, What I don't understand is how in one painting there should be so many pictures and by such different painters, And there were some men eating, There have been so many lunches, afternoon snacks and suppers in the history of art, that this detail in itself is not enough to tell us who was eating, There were thirteen men altogether, Ah, then it's easy, go on, There was also a naked woman with fair hair, inside a conch that was floating on the sea, and masses of flowers around her, Obviously Italian, And there was a battle, As in those paintings depicting banquets and mothers with children in their arms, these details are not enough to reveal who painted the picture, There were corpses and wounded men, It's only natural, sooner or later, all children die, and soldiers too, And a horse stricken with terror, With its eyes about to pop out of their sockets, Exactly, Horses are like that, and what other pictures were there in your painting, Alas, I never managed to find out, I went blind just as I was looking at the horse. Fear can cause blindness, said the girl with dark glasses, Never a truer word, that could not be truer, we were already blind the moment we turned blind, fear struck us blind, fear will keep us blind, Who is speaking, asked the doctor, A blind man, replied a voice, just a blind man, for that is all we have here. Then the old man with the black eyepatch asked, How many blind persons are needed to make a blindness, No one could provide the answer. The girl with dark glasses asked him to switch on the radio, there might be some news. They gave the news later, meanwhile they listened to a little music. At a certain point some blind internees appeared in the doorway of the ward, one of them said, What a pity no one thought of bringing a guitar. The news was not very encouraging, a rumour was going round that the formation of a government of unity and national salvation was imminent.

WHEN, at the beginning, the blind internees in this ward could still be counted on ten fingers, when an exchange of two or three words was enough to convert strangers into companions in misfortune, and with another three or four words they could forgive each other all their faults, some of them really quite serious, and if a complete pardon was not forthcoming, it was simply a question of being patient and waiting for a few days, then it became all too clear how many absurd afflictions the poor wretches had to suffer, each time their bodies demanded to be urgently relieved or as we say, to satisfy their needs. Despite this, and although knowing that perfect manners are somewhat rare and that even the most discreet and modest natures have their weak points, it has to be conceded that the first blind people to be brought here under quarantine, were capable, more or less conscientiously, of bearing with dignity the cross imposed by the eminently scatological nature of the human species. Now, with all the beds occupied, all two hundred and forty, not counting the blind inmates who have to sleep on the floor, no imagination, however fertile and creative in making comparisons, images and metaphors, could aptly describe the filth here. It is not just the state to which the lavatories were soon reduced, fetid caverns such as the gutters in hell full of condemned souls must be, but also the lack of respect shown by some of the inmates or the sudden urgency of others that turned the corridors and other passageways into latrines, at first only occasionally but now as a matter of habit. The careless or impatient thought, It doesn't matter, no one can see me, and they went no further. When it became impossible in any sense, to reach the lavatories, the blind internees began using the yard as a place to relieve themselves and clear their bowels. Those who were delicate by nature or upbringing spent the whole day restraining themselves, they put up with it as best they could until nightfall, they presumed it would be night when most people were asleep in the wards, then off they would go, clutching their stomachs or squeezing their legs together, in search of a foot or two of clean ground, if there was any amidst that endless carpet of trampled excrement, and, to make matters worse, in danger of getting lost in the infinite space of the yard, where there were no guiding signs other than the few trees whose trunks had managed to survive the mania for exploration of the former inmates, and also the slight mounds, now almost flattened, that barely covered the dead. Once a day, always in the late afternoon, like an alarm clock set to go off at the same hour, the voice over the loudspeaker would repeat the familiar instructions and prohibitions, insist on the advantages of making regular use of cleansing products, remind the inmates that there was a telephone in each ward in order to request the necessary supplies whenever they ran out, but what was really needed there was a powerful jet from a hose to wash away all that shit, then an army of plumbers to repair the cisterns and get them working again, then water, lots of water, to wash the waste down the pipes where it belongs, then, we beseech you, eyes, a pair of eyes, a hand capable of leading and guiding us, a voice that will say to me, This way. These blind internees, unless we come to their assistance, will soon turn into animals, worse still, into blind animals. This was not spoken by the unknown voice that talked of the paintings and images of this world, the person saying it, though in other words, late at night, is the doctor's wife lying beside her husband, their heads under the same blanket, A solution has to be found for this awful mess, I can't stand it and I can't go on pretending that I can't see, Think of the consequences, they will almost certainly try to turn you into their slave, a general dogsbody, you will be at the beck and call of everyone, they will expect you to feed them, wash them, put them to bed and get them up in the morning and have you take them from here to there, blow their noses and dry their tears, they will call out for you when you are asleep, insult you if you keep them waiting, How can you of all people expect me to go on looking at these miseries, to have them permanently before my eyes, and not lift a finger to help, You're already doing more than enough, What use am I, when my main concern is that no one should find out that I can see, Some will hate you for seeing, don't think that blindness has made us better people, It hasn't made us any worse, We're on our way though, just look at what happens when it's time to share out the food, Precisely, someone who can see could supervise the distribution of food to all those who are here, share it out with impartiality, with common sense, there would be no more complaints, these constant arguments that are driving me mad would cease, you have no idea what it is like to watch two blind people fighting, Fighting has always been, more or less, a form of blindness, This is different, Do what you think best, but don't forget what we are here, blind, simply blind, blind people with no fine speeches or commiserations, the charitable, picturesque world of the little blind orphans is finished, we are now in the harsh, cruel, implacable kingdom of the blind, If only you could see what I am obliged to see, you would want to be blind, I believe you, but there's no need, because I'm already blind, Forgive me, my love, if you only knew, I know, I know, I've spent my life looking into people's eyes, it is the only part of the body where a soul might still exist and if those eyes are lost, Tomorrow I'm going to tell them I can see, Let's hope you won't live to regret it, Tomorrow I'll tell them, she paused then added, Unless by then I, too, have finally entered their world.

But it was not to be just yet. When she woke up next morning, very early as usual, her eyes could see as clearly as before. All the blind internees in the ward were asleep. She wondered how she should tell them, whether she should gather them all together and announce the news, perhaps it might be preferable to do it in a discreet manner, without ostentation, to say, for example, as if not wishing to treat the matter too seriously, Just imagine, who would have thought that I would keep my sight amongst so many who have turned blind, or whether, perhaps more wisely, pretend that she really had been blind and had suddenly regained her sight, it might even be a way of giving the others some hope. If she can see again, they would say to each other, perhaps we will, too, on the other hand, they might tell her, If that's the case, then get out, be off with you, whereupon she would reply that she could not leave the place without her husband, and since the army would not release any blind person from quarantine, there was nothing for it but to allow her to stay. Some of the blind internees were stirring in their beds and, as every morning, they were relieving themselves of wind, but this did not make the atmosphere any more nauseating, saturation point must already have been reached. It was not just the fetid smell that came from the lavatories in gusts that made you want to throw up, it was also the accumulated body odour of two hundred and fifty people, whose bodies were steeped in their own sweat, who were neither able nor knew how to wash themselves, who wore clothes that got filthier by the day, who slept in beds where they had frequently defecated. What use would soaps, bleach, detergents be, abandoned somewhere around the place, if many of the showers were blocked or had become detached from the pipes, if the drains overflowed with the dirty water that spread outside the washrooms, soaking the floorboards in the corridors, infiltrating the cracks in the flagstones. What madness is this to think of interfering, the doctor's wife began to reflect, even if they were not to demand that I should be at their service, and nothing is less certain, I myself would not be able to stand it without setting about washing and cleaning for as long as I had the strength, this is not a job for one person. Her courage which before had seemed so resolute, began to crumble, to gradually desert her when confronted with the abject reality that invaded her nostrils and offended her eyes, now that the moment had come to pass from words to actions. I'm a coward, she murmured in exasperation, it would have been better to be blind than go around like some fainthearted missionary. Three blind internees had got up, one of them was the pharmacist's assistant, they were about to take up their positions in the hallway to collect the allocation of food intended for the first ward. It could not be claimed, given their lack of eyesight, that the distribution was made by eye, one container more, one container less, on the contrary, it was pitiful to see how they got muddled over the counting and had to start all over again, someone with a more suspicious nature wanted to know exactly what the others were carrying, arguments always broke out in the end, the odd shove, a slap for the blind women, as was inevitable. In the ward everyone was now awake, ready to receive their ration, with experience they had devised a fairly easy system of distribution, they began by carrying all the food to the far end of the ward, where the doctor and his wife had their beds as well

as the girl with dark glasses and the boy who was calling for
his mummy, and that is where the inmates went to fetch their
food, two at a time, starting from the beds nearest the entrance,
number one on the right, number one on the left, number two
on the right, number two on the left, and so on and so forth,
without any ill-tempered exchanges or jostling, it took longer,
it is true, but keeping the peace made the waiting worthwhile.
The first, that is to say, those who had the food right there
within arm's reach, were the last to serve themselves, except for
the boy with the squint, of course, who always finished eating
before the girl with dark glasses received her portion, so that
part of what should have been hers invariably finished up in the
boy's stomach. All the blind internees had their heads turned
towards the door, hoping to hear the footsteps of their fellow
inmates, the faltering, unmistakable sound of someone carrying something, but this was not the noise that could suddenly
be heard but rather that of people running swiftly, were such
a feat possible for people who could not see where they were
putting their feet. Yet how else could you describe it when they
appeared panting for breath at the door. What could have happened out there to send them running in here, and there were
the three of them trying to get through the door at the same
time to give the unexpected news, They wouldn't allow us to
bring the food, said one of them, and the other two repeated
his words, They wouldn't allow us, Who, the soldiers, asked
some voice or other, No, the blind internees, What blind internees, we're all blind here, We don't know who they are, said
the pharmacist's assistant, but I think they must belong to the
group that all arrived together, the last group to arrive, And
what's this about not allowing you to bring the food, asked the
doctor, so far there has never been any problem, They say all
that's over, from now on anyone who wants to eat will have
to pay. Protests came from all sides of the ward, It cannot be,

They've taken away our food, The thieves, A disgrace, the blind against the blind, I never thought I'd live to see anything like this, Let's go and complain to the sergeant. Someone more resolute proposed that they should all go together to demand what was rightfully theirs, It won't be easy, said the pharmacist's assistant, there are lots of them, I had the clear impression they form a large group, and the worst is that they are armed, What do you mean by armed, At the very least they have cudgels, this arm of mine still hurts from the blow I received, said one of the others, Let's try and settle this peacefully, said the doctor, I'll go with you to speak to these people, there must be some misunderstanding, Of course, doctor, you have my support, said the pharmacist's assistant, but from the way they're behaving, I very much doubt that you will be able to persuade them, Be that as it may, we have to go there, we cannot leave things like this, I'm coming with you, said the doctor's wife. The tiny group left the ward except for the one who was complaining about his arm, he felt that he had done his duty and stayed behind to relate to the others his hazardous adventure, their food rations two paces away, and a human wall to defend them, With cudgels, he insisted.

Advancing together, like a platoon, they forced their way through the blind inmates from the other wards. When they reached the hallway, the doctor's wife realised at once that no diplomatic conversation would be possible, and probably never likely to be. In the middle of the hallway, surrounding the containers of food, a circle of blind inmates armed with sticks and metal rods from the beds, pointing outwards like bayonets or lances, confronted the desperation of the blind inmates who were surrounding them and making awkward attempts to force their way through the line of defence, some with the hope of finding an opening, a gap someone had been careless enough not to close properly, they warded off the blows with raised arms, others crawled along on all fours until they bumped into the legs of their adversaries who repelled them with a blow to their backs or a vigorous kick. Hitting out blindly, as the saying goes. These scenes were accompanied by indignant protests, furious cries, We demand our food, We have a right to eat, Rogues, This is outrageous, Incredible though it may seem, there was one ingenuous or distracted soul who said, Call the police, perhaps there were some policemen amongst them, blindness, as everyone knows, has no regard for professions or occupations, but a policeman struck blind is not the same as a blind policeman, and as for the two we knew, they are dead and, after a great deal of effort, buried. Driven by the foolish hope that some authority would restore to the mental asylum its former tranquillity, impose justice, bring back some peace of mind, a blind woman made her way as best she could to the main entrance and called out for all to hear, Help us, these rogues are trying to steal our food. The soldiers pretended not to hear, the orders the sergeant had received from a captain who had passed through on an official visit could not have been clearer, If they end up killing each other, so much the better, there will be fewer of them. The blind woman ranted and raved as mad women did in bygone days, she herself almost demented, but from sheer desperation. In the end, realising that her pleas were futile, she fell silent, went back inside to sob her heart out and, oblivious of where she was going, she received a blow on the head that sent her to the floor. The doctor's wife wanted to run and help her up, but there was such confusion that she could not move as much as two paces. The blind internees who had come to demand their food were already beginning to withdraw in disarray, their sense of direction completely lost, they tripped over one another, fell, got up, fell again, some did not even make any attempt, gave up, remained lying prostrate on the ground, exhausted, miserable, racked with pain, their faces pressed against the tiled floor. Then the doctor's wife, terrified, saw one of the blind hoodlums take a gun from his pocket and raise it brusquely into the air. The blast caused a large piece of stucco to come crashing down from the ceiling onto their un-protected heads, increasing the panic. The hoodlum shouted, Be quiet everyone and keep your mouths shut, if anyone dares to raise their voice, I'll shoot straight out, no matter who gets hit, then there will be no more complaints. The blind intern-ees did not move. The fellow with the gun continued, Let it be known and there is no turning back, that from today onwards we shall take charge of the food, you've all been warned, and let no one take it into their head to go out there to look for it, we shall put guards at the entrance, and anyone who tries to go against these orders will suffer the consequences, the food will now be sold, anyone who wants to eat must pay. How are we to pay, asked the doctor's wife, I said no one was to speak, bellowed the armed hoodlum, waving his weapon before him. Someone has to speak, we must know how we're to proceed, where are we going to fetch the food, do we all go together, or one at a time, This woman is up to something, commented one of the group, if you were to shoot her, there would be one mouth less to feed, If I could see her, she'd already have a bullet in her belly. Then addressing everyone, Go back to your wards immediately, this very minute, once we've carried the food in-side, we'll decide what is to be done, And what about payment, rejoined the doctor's wife, how much shall we be expected to pay for a coffee with milk and a biscuit, She's really asking for it, that one, said the same voice, Leave her to me, said the other fellow, and changing tone, Each ward will nominate two people to be in charge of collecting people's valuables, all their valu-ables of whatever kind, money, jewels, rings, bracelets, ear-rings, watches, everything they possess, and they will take the lot to the third ward on the left, where we are accommodated, and if you want some friendly advice, don't get any ideas about trying to cheat us, we know that there are those amongst you who will hide some of your valuables, but I warn you to think again, unless we feel that you have handed in enough, you will simply not get any food and be left to chew your banknotes and munch on your diamonds. A blind man from the second ward on the right asked, And what are we to do, do we hand over everything at once, or do we pay according to what we eat, It would seem I haven't explained things clearly enough, said the fellow with the gun, laughing, first you pay, then you eat and, as for the rest, to pay according to what you've eaten would make keeping accounts extremely complicated, best to hand over everything at one go and then we shall see how much food you deserve, but let me warn you again, don't try to conceal anything for it will cost you dear, and lest anyone accuses us of not proceeding honestly, note that after handing over whatever you possess we shall carry out an inspection, woe betide you if we find so much as a penny, and now I want everybody out of here as quickly as possible. He raised his arm and fired another shot. Some more stucco crashed to the ground. And as for you, said the hoodlum with the gun, I won't forget your voice, Nor I your face, replied the doctor's wife.

No one appeared to notice the absurdity of a blind woman saying that she won't forget a face she could not see. The blind internees had already withdrawn as quickly as they could, in search of the doors, and those from the first ward were soon informing their fellow inmates of the situation, From what we've heard, I don't believe that for the moment we can do anything other than obey, said the doctor, there must be quite a number of them, and worst of all, they have weapons. We can arm ourselves too, said the pharmacist's assistant, Yes, some sticks cut from the trees if there are any branches left within arm's reach, some metal rods removed from our beds that we shall scarcely have the strength to wield, while they have at least one firearm at their disposal, I refuse to hand over my belongings to these sons of a blind bitch, someone remarked, Nor I, joined in another, That's it, either we all hand over everything, or nobody gives anything, said the doctor, We have no alternative, said his wife, besides, the regime in here, must be the same as the one they imposed outside, anyone who doesn't want to pay can suit himself, that's his privilege, but he'll get nothing to eat and he cannot expect to be fed at the expense of the rest of us, We shall all give up what we've got and hand over everything, said the doctor, And what about those who have nothing to give, asked the pharmacist's assistant, They will eat whatever the others decide to give them, as the saying rightly goes, from each according to his abilities, to each according to his needs. There was a pause, and the old man with the black eyepatch asked, Well then, who are we going to ask to be in charge, I suggest the doctor, said the girl with the dark glasses. It was not necessary to proceed to a vote, the entire ward was in agreement. There have to be two of us, the doctor reminded them, is anyone willing to offer, he asked, I'm willing, if no one else comes forward, said the first blind man, Very well, let us start collecting, we need a sack, a bag, a small suitcase, any of these things will do, I can get rid of this, said the doctor's wife, and began at once to empty a bag in which she had gathered cosmetics and other odds and ends at a time when she could never have imagined the conditions in which she was now obliged to live. Amongst the bottles, boxes and tubes from another world, there was a pair of long, finely pointed scissors. She could not remember having put them there, but there they were. The doctor's wife raised her head. The blind internees were waiting, her husband had gone up to the bed of the first blind man, he was talking to him, the girl with the dark glasses was saying to the boy with the squint that the food would be arriving soon, on the floor, tucked behind the bedside table, was a bloodstained sanitary napkin, as if the girl with dark glasses were anxious, with maidenly and point-less modesty, to hide it from the eyes of those who could not see. The doctor's wife looked at the scissors, she tried to think why she should be staring at them in this way, in what way, like this, but she could think of no reason, frankly what reason could she hope to find in a simple pair of long scissors, lying in her open hands, with its two nickel-plated blades, the tips sharp and gleaming, Do you have it there, her husband asked her, Yes, here it is, she replied, and held out the arm holding the empty bag while she put the other arm behind her back to conceal the scissors, What's the matter, asked the doctor, Nothing, replied his wife, who could just as easily have answered, Nothing you can see, my voice must have sounded strange, that's all, noth-ing else. Accompanied by the first blind man, the doctor moved towards her, took the bag in his hesitant hands and said, Start getting your things ready, we're about to begin collecting. His wife unclasped her watch, did the same for her husband, re-moved her earrings, a tiny ring set with rubies, the gold chain she wore round her neck, her wedding ring, that of her hus-band, both of them easy to remove, Our fingers have got thin-ner, she thought, she began putting everything into the bag, then the money they had brought from home, a fair amount of notes varying in value, some coins, That's everything, she said, Are you sure, said the doctor, take a careful look, That's every-thing we have of any value. The girl with dark glasses had al-ready gathered together her belongings, they were not so very different, she had two bracelets instead of one, but no wedding ring. The doctor's wife waited until her husband and the first blind man had turned their backs and for the girl with dark glasses to bend down to the boy with the squint, Think of me as your mummy, she was saying, I'll pay for us both, and then she withdrew to the wall at the far end. There, as all along the other walls, there were large nails sticking out that must have been used by the mad to hang treasures and other baubles. She chose the highest nail she could reach, and hung the scissors there. Then she sat down on her bed. Slowly, her husband and the first blind man were heading in the direction of the door, they would stop to collect possessions on both sides from those who had something to offer, some protested that they were being robbed shamefully, and that was the honest truth, others divested themselves of their possessions with a kind of indifference, as if thinking that, all things considered, there is nothing in this world that belongs to us in an absolute sense, another all too transparent truth. When they reached the door of the ward, having finished their collection, the doctor asked, Have we handed over everything, a number of resigned voices answered yes, some chose to say nothing and in the fullness of time we shall know whether this was in order to avoid telling a lie. The doctor's wife looked up at the scissors. She was surprised to find them so far up, hanging from one of the nails, as if she herself had not put them there, then she reflected that it had been an excellent idea to bring them, now she could trim her husband's beard, make him look more presentable, since, as we know, living in these conditions, it is impossible for a man to shave as normal. When she looked again in the direction of the door, the two men had already disappeared into the shadows of the corridor and were making their way to the third ward on the left, where they had been instructed to go and pay for their food. Today's food, tomorrow's as well, and perhaps for the rest of the week, And then, the question had no answer, everything we possessed will have gone in payment.

Surprisingly enough, the corridors were not congested as usual, because normally as the internees left their wards they inevitably tripped, collided and fell, those assaulted swore, hurled obscenities, their assailants retaliated with further insults, but no one paid any attention, a person has to give vent to his feelings somehow, especially if he is blind. Ahead there was the sound of footsteps and voices, they must be the emissaries from the other wards who were complying with the same orders, What a situation we're in, doctor, said the first blind man, as if our blindness were not enough, we've fallen into the clutches of blind thieves, that seems to be my fate, first there was the car-thief, now this rabble who are stealing our food at gunpoint, That's the difference, they're armed, But cartridges don't last forever, Nothing lasts forever, but in this case it might be preferable if it did, Why, If the cartridges were to run out, then that would mean that someone had used them up, and we already have too many corpses, We're in an impossible situation, It has been impossible ever since we came into this place, yet we go on putting up with it, You're an optimist, doctor, No, I'm not an optimist, but I cannot imagine anything worse than our present existence, Well, I'm not entirely convinced that there are limits to misfortune and evil, You may be right, said the doctor, and then, as if he were talking to himself, Something has to happen here, a conclusion that contains a certain contradiction, either there is something worse than this, after all, or, from now on, things are going to get better, although all the indications suggest otherwise. Having steadily made their way and having turned several corners, they were approaching the third ward. Neither the doctor nor the first blind man had ever ventured here, but the construction of the two wings, logically enough, had strictly adhered to a symmetrical pattern, anyone familiar with the wing on the right would have no difficulty in getting their bearings in the wing on the left, and vice versa, you had only to turn to the left on the one side while on the other you had to turn right. They could hear voices, they must be of those ahead of them, We'll have to wait, said the doctor in a low voice, Why, Those inside will want to

know precisely what these inmates are carrying, for them it is
not all that important, since they have already eaten they're in
no hurry, It must be almost time for lunch, Even if they could
see, it would do this group no good to know it, they no longer
even have watches. A quarter of an hour later, give or take a
minute, the barter was over. Two men passed in front of the
doctor and the first blind man, from their conversation it was
apparent that they were carrying food, Careful, don't drop anything, said one of them, and the other was muttering, What I
don't know is whether there will be enough for everyone. We'll
have to tighten our belts. Sliding his hand along the wall, with
the first blind man right behind him, the doctor advanced until
his hands came into contact with the doorjamb, We're from
the first ward on the right, he shouted. He made as if to take a
step forward, but his leg came up against an obstacle. He realised it was a bed standing crosswise, placed there to serve as a
trading counter, They're organised, he thought to himself, this
has not suddenly been improvised, he heard voices, footsteps,
How many of them are there, his wife had mentioned ten, but
it was not inconceivable that there might be many more, certainly not all of them were there when they went to get the
food. The fellow with the gun was their leader, it was his jeer-
ing voice that was saying, Now, let's see what riches the first
ward on the right has brought us, and then, in a much lower
tone, addressing someone who must have been standing nearby,
Take note. The doctor remained puzzled, what could this mean,
the fellow had said, Take note, so there must be someone here
who can write, someone who is not blind, so that makes two,
We must be careful, he thought, tomorrow this rascal might be
standing right next to us and we wouldn't even know it, this
thought of the doctor's was scarcely any different from what
the first blind man was thinking, With a gun and a spy, we're
sunk, we shall never be able to raise our heads again. The blind

man inside, the leader of the thieves, had already opened the bag, with practised hands he was lifting out, stroking and identifying the objects and money, clearly he could make out by touch what was gold and what was not, by touch he could also tell the value of the notes and coins, easy when one is experienced, it was only after some minutes that the doctor began to hear the unmistakable sound of punching paper, which he immediately identified, there nearby was someone writing in the braille alphabet, also known as anaglyptography, the sound could be heard, at once quiet and clear, of the pointer as it punched the thick paper and hit the metallic plate underneath. So there was a normal blind person amongst these blind delinquents, a blind person just like all those people who were once referred to as being blind, the poor fellow had obviously been roped in with all the rest, but this was not the moment to pry and start asking, are you one of the recent blind men or have you been blind for some years, tell us how you came to lose your sight. They were certainly lucky, not only had they won a clerk in the raffle, they could also use him as a guide, a blind person with experience as a blind person is something else, he's worth his weight in gold. The inventory went on, now and then the thug with the gun consulted the accountant, What do you think of this, and he would interrupt his bookkeeping to give an opinion, A cheap imitation, he would say, in which case the fellow with the gun would comment, If there is a lot of this, they won't get any food, or Good stuff, and then the commentary would be, There's nothing like dealing with honest people. In the end, three containers of food were lifted onto the bed, Take this, said the armed leader. The doctor counted them, Three are not enough, we used to receive four when the food was only for us, at that same moment he felt the cold barrel of the gun against his neck, for a blind man his aim was not bad, I'll have a container removed every time you complain, now

beat it, take these and thank the Lord that you've still got something to eat. The doctor murmured, Very well, grabbed two of
the containers while the first blind man took charge of the
third one and, much slower now, because they were laden, they
retraced the route that had brought them to the ward. When
they arrived in the hallway, where there did not appear to be
anyone around, the doctor said, I'll never again have such an
opportunity, What do you mean, asked the first blind man, He
put his gun to my neck, I could have grabbed it from him, That
would be risky, Not as risky as it seems, I knew where the gun
was resting, he had no way of knowing where my hands were,
even so, at that moment I'm convinced that he was the blinder
of the two of us, what a pity I didn't think of it, or did think of
it but lacked the courage, And then what, asked the first blind
man, What do you mean, Let's assume you had managed to
grab his weapon, I don't believe you would have been capable
of using it, If I were certain it would resolve the situation, yes I
would, But you're not certain, No, in fact I'm not, Then better
that they should keep their arms, at least so long as they do not
use them against us. To threaten someone with a gun is the
same as attacking them, If you had taken his gun, the real war
would have started, and in all likelihood we would never have
got out of that place alive, You're right, said the doctor, I'll pretend I had thought all that through, You mustn't forget, doctor,
what you told me a little while ago, What did I say, That something has to happen, It has happened and I didn't make the
most of it, It has to be something else, not that.

When they entered the ward and had to present the meagre amount of food they had brought to put on the table, some
thought they were to blame for not having protested and demanded more, that's why they had been nominated as the representatives of the group. Then the doctor explained what had
happened, he told them about the blind clerk, about the in-

sulting behaviour of the blind man with the gun, also about
the gun itself. The malcontents lowered their voices, ended up
by agreeing that undoubtedly the ward's interests were in the
right hands. The food was finally distributed, there were those
who could not resist reminding the impatient that little is better than nothing, besides, by now it must be almost time for
lunch, The worst thing would be if we got to be like that famous horse that died when it had already got out of the habit
of eating, someone remarked. The others gave a wan smile and
one said, It wouldn't be so bad if it's true that when the horse
dies, it doesn't know it's going to die.

THE old man with the black eyepatch had understood that the portable radio, as much for the fragility of its structure as for the information known about the length of its useful life, was to be excluded from the list of valuables they had to hand over in payment for their food, in consideration of the fact that the usefulness of the set depended in the first place on whether there were or were not batteries inside and, in the second place, on how long they would last. Judging by the rather husky voices still coming from the tiny box, it was obvious that little more could be expected of it. Therefore the old man with the black eyepatch decided not to have any more general broadcasts, additionally because the blind internees in the third ward on the left might turn up and take a different view, not owing to the material value of the set, which is virtually negligible in the short term, as we have seen, but owing to its immediate utility, which is undoubtedly considerable, not to mention the feasible hypothesis that where there is at least one gun there might also be batteries. So the old man with the black eyepatch said that, from now on, he would listen to the news under the blanket, with his head completely covered, and that if there were any interesting news item, he would alert

the others at once. The girl with dark glasses asked him to allow her to listen to a little music from time to time, So as not
to forget, she argued, but he was inflexible, insisted that the
important thing was to know what was going on outside, anyone who wanted music could listen to it in their own head, after all our memory ought to be put to some good use. The old
man with the black eyepatch was right, the music on the radio
was already as grating as only a painful memory can be, so for
this reason he kept the volume as low as possible, waiting for
the news to come on. Then he turned the sound up a little and
listened attentively so as not to lose a single syllable. Then he
summarised the news items in his own words, and transmitted
them to his immediate neighbours. And so from bed to bed,
the news slowly circulated round the ward, increasingly distorted as it was passed on from one inmate to the next, in this
way diminishing or exaggerating the details, according to the
personal optimism or pessimism of those relaying the information. Until that moment when the words dried up and the
old man with the black eyepatch found he had nothing more
to say. And it was not because the radio had broken down or
the batteries were used up, experience of life and lives has convincingly shown that no one can govern time, it was unlikely
that this tiny set would last long, but finally someone fell silent before it went dead. Throughout this first day spent in the
clutches of those blind thugs, the old man with the black eyepatch had been listening to the radio and passing on the news,
rejecting the patent falseness of the optimistic prophecies being officially communicated and now, well into the night, with
his head out of the blanket at last, he was listening carefully
to the wheeze into which the waning power of the radio had
transformed the announcer's voice, when suddenly he heard
him call out, I'm blind, then the noise of something striking
the microphone, a hasty sequence of confused sounds, excla-

mations, then sudden silence. The only radio station he had been able to get on the set had gone silent. For some time to come, the old man with the black eyepatch kept his ear to the box that was now inert, as if waiting for the announcer's voice to return and for the news to continue. However, he sensed, or rather knew, that it would return no more. The white sickness had not only blinded the announcer. Like a line of gunpowder, it had quickly and successively reached all those who happened to be in the studio. Then the old man with the black eyepatch dropped the radio on the floor. The blind thugs, if they were to come sniffing out hidden jewels, would find justification, had such a thought crossed their mind, for the omission of portable radios from their list of valuables. The old man with the black eyepatch pulled the blanket up over his head so that he could weep freely.

Little by little, under the murky yellowish light of the dim lamps, the ward descended into a deep slumber, bodies comforted by the three meals consumed that day, as had rarely happened before. If things continue like this, we'll end up once more reaching the conclusion that even in the worst misfortunes it is possible to find enough good to be able to bear the aforesaid misfortunes with patience, which, applied to the present situation, means that contrary to the first disquieting predictions, the concentration of food supplies into a single entity for apportioning and distribution, had its positive aspects, after all, however much certain idealists might protest that they would have preferred to go on struggling for life by their own means, even if their stubbornness meant going hungry. Unconcerned about tomorrow, forgetful that he who pays in advance always ends up being badly served, the majority of the blind internees, in all the wards, slept soundly. The others, tired of searching in vain for an honourable way out of the vexations suffered, also fell asleep one by one, dreaming of better days than these,

days of greater freedom if not of greater abundance. In the first
ward on the right, only the doctor's wife was still awake. Lying
on her bed, she was thinking about what her husband had told
her, when for a moment he suspected that amongst the blind
thieves there was someone who could see, someone whom they
might use as a spy. It was curious that they had not touched on
the subject again, as if it had not occurred to the doctor, accustomed as he was to the fact, that his own wife could still see. It
crossed her mind, but she said nothing, she had no desire to utter the obvious words, What he is unable to do after all, I can
do. What is that, the doctor would ask, pretending not to understand. Now, with her eyes fixed on the scissors hanging on
the wall, the doctor's wife was asking herself, What use is my
eyesight, It had exposed her to greater horror than she could
ever have imagined, it had convinced her that she would rather
be blind, nothing else. Moving cautiously, she sat up in bed.
Opposite her, the girl with the dark glasses and the boy with
the squint were asleep. She noticed that the two beds were very
close together, the girl had pushed hers over, almost certainly
to be closer to the boy should he need to be comforted or have
someone to dry his tears in the absence of his mother. Why did
I not think of it before, I could have pushed our beds together
and we could have slept together, without this constant worry
that he might fall out of bed. She looked at her husband, who
was fast asleep, in a deep sleep from sheer exhaustion. She had
not got round to telling him that she had brought the scissors,
that one of these days she would have to trim his beard, a task
that even a blind man is capable of carrying out so long as he
does not bring the blades too close to his skin. She has found
a good excuse for not mentioning the scissors, Afterwards all
the men here would be pestering me and I'd find myself doing nothing except trimming beards. She swung her body outwards, rested her feet on the floor and searched for her shoes.

As she was about to slip them on, she held back, stared at them closely, then shook her head and, without making a noise, put them back. She passed along the aisle between the beds and slowly made her way towards the door of the ward. Her bare feet came into contact with the slimy excrement on the floor, but she knew that out there in the corridors it would be much worse. She kept looking from one side to the other, to see if any of the blind internees were awake, although whether several of them might be keeping vigil, or the entire ward, was of no importance so long as she did not make a noise, and even if she did, we know how pressing our bodily needs can be, they do not choose their hour, in a word, what she did not want was that her husband should wake up and sense her absence in time to ask her, Where are you going, which is probably the question husbands most frequently put to their wives, the other being Where have you been, One of the blind women was sitting up in bed, her shoulders resting against the low headrest, her empty gaze fixed on the wall opposite, but she could not see it. The doctor's wife paused for a moment, as if not sure whether to touch that invisible thread that hovered in the air, as if the slightest contact would irrevocably destroy it. The blind woman raised her arm, she must have perceived some gentle vibration in the atmosphere, then she let it drop, no longer interested, it was enough not to be able to sleep because of her neighbours' snoring. The doctor's wife continued walking in ever greater haste as she approached the door. Before heading for the hallway, she looked along the corridor that led to the other wards on this side, further ahead, to the lavatories, and ultimately to the kitchen and refectory. There were blind inmates lying up against the walls, those who on arrival had been unsuccessful in finding a bed, either because in the assault they had lagged behind, or because they lacked the strength to contest a bed and win their battle. Ten metres away, a blind man was lying on top

of a blind woman, the man caught between her legs, they were
being as discreet as they could, they were the discreet kind, but
you would not have needed very sharp hearing to know what
they were up to, especially when first one and then the other
could no longer repress their sighs and groans, some inartic-
ulate word, which are the signs that all that is about to end.
The doctor's wife stopped in her tracks to watch them, not out
of envy, she had her husband and the satisfaction he gave her,
but because of an impression of another order, for which she
could find no name, perhaps a feeling of sympathy, as if she
were thinking of saying to them, Don't mind my being here, I
also know what this means, continue, perhaps a feeling of compassion, Even if this instant of supreme pleasure should last
you a lifetime, you will never become united as one. The blind
man and the blind woman were now resting, apart, the one lying beside the other, but they were still holding hands, they
were young, perhaps even lovers who had gone to the cinema
and turned blind there, or perhaps some miraculous coincidence brought them together in this place, and, this being the
case, how did they recognise each other, good heavens, by their
voices, of course, it is not only the voice of blood that needs no
eyes, love, which people say is blind, also has a voice of its own.
In all probability, though, they were taken at the same time, in
which case those clasped hands are not something recent, they
have been clasped since the beginning.
      The doctor's wife sighed, raised her hands to her eyes, she
had to because she could barely see, but she was not alarmed,
she knew they were only tears. Then she continued on her way.
On reaching the hallway, she went up to the door leading to
the courtyard. She looked outside. Behind the gate there was
a light which outlined the black silhouette of a soldier. On the
other side of the street, the buildings were all in darkness. She
went out onto the top of the steps. There was no danger. Even

if the soldier were to become aware of her shadow, he would
only shoot if she, having descended the stairs, were to get
nearer, after being warned, from that other invisible line which
represented for him the frontier of his safety. Accustomed now
to the constant noises in the ward, the doctor's wife found the
silence strange, a silence that seemed to occupy the space of
an absence, as if humanity, the whole of humanity, had disappeared, leaving only a light and a soldier keeping watch over it.
She sat on the ground, her back resting against the doorjamb,
in the same position in which she had seen the blind woman
in the ward, and stared ahead like her. The night was cold, the
wind blew along the front of the building, it seemed impossible that there should still be wind in this world, that the night
should be black, she wasn't thinking of herself, she was thinking of the blind for whom the day was endless. Above the light,
another silhouette appeared, it was probably the guard's relief,
Nothing to report, the soldier would be saying before going
off to his tent to get some sleep, neither of them had any idea
what was happening behind that door, probably the noise of
the shots had not even been heard out here, an ordinary gun
does not make much noise. A pair of scissors even less, thought
the doctor's wife. She did not waste time asking herself where
such a thought had come from, she was only surprised at its
slowness, at how the first word had been so slow in appearing, the slowness of those to follow, and how she found that
the thought was already there before, somewhere or other, and
only the words were missing, like a body searching in the bed
for the hollow that had been prepared for it by the mere idea
of lying down. The soldier approached the gate, although he is
standing against the light, it is clear that he is looking in this direction, he must have noticed the motionless shadow, although,
for the moment, there is not enough light to see that it is only
a woman seated on the ground, her arms cradling her legs and

her chin resting on her knees, the soldier points the beam of a torch at her, now there can be no doubt, it is a woman who is about to get up with a movement as slow as her previous thought had been, but the soldier is not to know this, all he knows is that he is afraid of that figure of a woman who seems to be taking ages to get to her feet, in a flash he asks himself whether he should raise the alarm, the next moment he decides against it, after all, it is only a woman and she is some way away, in any case, as a precaution he points his weapon in her direction, but this means putting the torch aside and, with that movement, the luminous beam shone directly into his eyes, like a sudden burning, an impression of being dazzled remained in his retina. When he recovered his vision, the woman had disappeared, now this guard will be unable to say to the person who comes to relieve him, Nothing to report.

The doctor's wife is already in the left wing, in the corridor that will take her to the third ward. Here too there are blind inmates sleeping on the floor, more of them than in the right wing. She walks noiselessly, slowly, she can feel the slime on the ground sticking to her feet. She looks inside the first two wards, and sees what she expected to see, bodies lying under blankets, there is a blind man who is also unable to sleep and says so in a desperate voice, she can hear the staccato snoring of almost everyone else. As for the smell that all this gives off, it does not surprise her, there is no other smell in the entire building, it is the smell of her own body of the clothes she is wearing. On turning the corner into the corridor giving access to the third ward, she came to a halt. There is a man at the door, another guard. He has a stick in his hand, he is wielding it in slow motion, to one side then the next, as if blocking the passage of anyone who might try to approach. Here there are no blind inmates sleeping on the ground and the corridor is clear. The blind man at the door continues his uniform toing-

and-froing, he seems never to tire, but it is not so, after several minutes he takes his staff in the other hand and starts all over again. The doctor's wife advanced keeping close to the wall on the other side, taking care not to rub against it. The curve made by the stick does not even reach halfway across the wide corridor, one is tempted to say that this guard is on duty with an unloaded weapon. The doctor's wife is now directly opposite the blind man, she can see the ward behind him. Not all the beds are occupied. How many are there, she wondered. She advanced a little further, almost to the point where his stick could reach, and there she came to a halt, the blind man had turned his head to the side where she was standing, as if he had sensed something unusual, a sigh, a tremor in the air. He was a tall man, with large hands. First he stretched out before him the hand holding the stick and with rapid gestures swept the emptiness before him, then took a short step, for one second, the doctor's wife feared that he might be able to see her, that he was only looking for the best place to attack her, Those eyes are not blind, she thought with alarm. Yes, of course they were blind, as blind as those of all the inmates living under this roof, between these walls, all of them, all of them except her. In a low voice, almost in a whisper, the man asked, Who's there, he did not shout like a real guard, Who goes there, friend or foe, the appropriate reply would be, Friend, whereupon he would say, Pass, but keep your distance, however, things did not turn out this way, he merely shook his head as if he were saying to himself, What nonsense, how could anyone be there, at this hour everyone is asleep. Fumbling with his free hand, he retreated back towards the door, and, calmed by his own words, he let his arms hang. He felt sleepy, he had been waiting for ages for one of his comrades to come and relieve him, but for this to happen it was necessary that the other, on hearing the inner voice of duty, should wake up by himself, for there were no alarm clocks around nor any means of using them. Cautiously, the doctor's wife reached the other side of the door and looked inside. The ward was not full. She made a rapid calculation, decided there must be some nineteen or twenty occupants. At the far end, she saw a number of food containers piled up, others were lying on the empty beds. As was only to be expected, they don't distribute all the food they receive, she thought. The blind man seemed to be getting worried again, but made no attempt to investigate. The minutes passed. The sound of someone coughing loudly, obviously a heavy smoker, could be heard coming from inside. The blind man turned his head apprehensively, at last he would get some sleep. None of those lying in bed got up. Then the blind man, slowly, as if afraid that they might surprise him in the act of abandoning his post or infringing at one go all the rules guards are obliged to observe, sat down on the edge of the bed blocking the entrance. For a few moments, he nodded, then he succumbed to the river of sleep, and in all certainty as he went under he must have thought, It doesn't matter, no one can see me. The doctor's wife counted once more those who were asleep inside, Including him there are twenty of them, at least she had gathered some real information, her nocturnal excursion had not been in vain, But was this my only reason for coming here, she asked herself, and she preferred not to pursue the answer. The blind man was sleeping, his head resting against the doorjamb, his stick had slipped silently to the floor, there was a defenceless blind man and with no columns to bring crashing down around him. The doctor's wife consciously wanted to think that this man had stolen the food, had stolen what rightfully belonged to others, that he took food from the mouths of children, but despite these thoughts, she did not feel any contempt, not even the slightest irritation, nothing other than a strange compassion for that drooping body before her, the head lolling backwards, the long neck covered in swollen veins. For the first time since she had left the ward she felt a cold shiver run through her, it was as if the flagstones were turning her feet to ice, as if they were being scorched. Let's hope it isn't fever, she thought. It couldn't be, more likely some infinite weariness, a longing to curl up inside herself, her eyes, especially her eyes, turned inwards, more, more, more, until they could reach and observe inside her own brain, there where the difference between seeing and not seeing is invisible to the naked eye. Slowly, ever more slowly, dragging her body, she retraced her footsteps to the place where she belonged, she passed by blind internees who seemed like sleepwalkers, as she must have seemed to them, she did not even have to pretend that she was blind. The blind lovers were no longer holding hands, they were asleep and lying huddled beside each other, she in the curve made by his body to keep warm, and taking a closer look, they were holding hands, after all, his arm over her body, their fingers clasped. There inside the ward, the blind woman who had been unable to sleep was still sitting up in bed, waiting until she became so tired that her body would finally overcome the obstinate resistance of her mind. All the others appeared to be sleeping, some with their heads covered, as if they were still searching for some impossible darkness. On the bedside table of the girl with dark glasses stood the bottle of eye-drops. Her eyes were already better, but she was not to know.

I F, BECAUSE of a sudden illumination that might quell his suspicions, the blind man entrusted with keeping an account of the ill-gotten gains of the miscreants had decided to come over to this side with his writing board, his thick paper and puncher, he would now almost certainly be occupied in drafting the instructive and lamentable chronicle of the inadequate diet and the many other privations of these new fellow inmates who have been well and truly fleeced. He would begin by saying that from where he had come, the usurpers had not only expelled the respectable blind inmates from the ward in order to take possession of the entire space, but, furthermore, had forbidden the inmates of the other two wards on the left-hand side any access or use of the respective sanitary installations, as they are called. He would remark that the immediate outcome of this infamous tyranny was that all those poor people would flock to the lavatories on this side, with consequences easy to imagine for anyone who still remembers the earlier state of the place. He would point out that it is impossible to walk through the inner courtyard without tripping over blind inmates getting rid of their diarrhoea or in contortions from ineffectual straining that had promised much and in the end resolved nothing, and, being an observant soul, he would not fail, deliberately, to register the patent contradiction between the small amount the inmates consumed and the vast quantity they excreted, perhaps thus showing that the famous relationship between cause and effect, so often cited, is not, at least from a quantitative point of view, always to be trusted. He would also say that while at this hour the ward of this thieving rabble must be crammed with containers of food, here it will not be long before the poor wretches are reduced to gathering up crumbs from the filthy floors. Nor would the blind accountant forget to condemn, in his dual role as participant in the process and its chronicler, the criminal conduct of these blind oppressors, who prefer to allow the food to go bad rather than give it to those who are in such great need, for while it is true that some of this foodstuff can last for weeks without going off, the rest, especially the cooked food, unless eaten immediately, soon turns sour or becomes covered in mould, and is therefore no longer fit for human consumption, if this sorry lot can still be thought of as human beings. Changing the subject but not the theme, the chronicler would write, with much sorrow in his heart, that the illnesses here are not solely those of the digestive tract, whether from lack of food or because of poor digestion of what was eaten, most of the people arriving here, though blind, were not only healthy, but some to all appearances were positively bursting with health, now they are like the others, unable to raise themselves from their miserable beds, stricken by influenza that spread who knows how. And not a single aspirin is there to be found anywhere in these five wards to lower their temperatures and relieve the pain of their headaches, what little was left was soon gone, after one had rummaged even through the lining of the women's handbags. Out of discretion, the chronicler would abandon any idea of making a detailed report of all the other ills that are afflicting most of the nearly three hundred inmates being kept in this inhumane quarantine, but he could not fail to mention at least two cases of fairly advanced cancer, for the authorities had no humanitarian scruples when rounding up the blind and confining them here, they even stated that the law once made is the same for everyone and that democracy is incompatible with preferential treatment. As cruel fate would have it, amongst all these inmates there is only one doctor, and an ophthalmologist at that, the last thing we needed. Arriving at this point, the blind accountant, tired of describing so much misery and sorrow, would let his metal punch fall to the table, he would search with a trembling hand for the piece of stale bread he had put to one side while he fulfilled his obligations as chronicler of the end of time, but he would not find it, because another blind man, whose sense of smell had become very keen out of dire necessity, had filched it. Then, renouncing his fraternal gesture, the altruistic impulse that had brought him rushing to this side, the blind accountant would decide that the best course of action, if he was still in time, was to return to the third ward on the left, there, at least, however much the injustices of those hoodlums stirred up in him feelings of honest indignation, he would not go hungry.

This is really the crux of the matter. Each time those sent to fetch the food return to their ward with the meagre rations they have been given there is an outburst of angry protest. There is always someone who proposes collective action, a mass demonstration, using the forceful argument about the cumulative strength of their numbers, confirmed time and time again and sublimated in the dialectic affirmation that determined wills, in general merely capable of being added one to the other, are also very capable in certain circumstances of multiplying among themselves ad infinitum. However, it was not long before the inmates calmed down, it was enough that someone

more prudent, with the simple and objective intention of pondering the advantages and risks of the action proposed, should
remind the enthusiasts of the fatal effects handguns tend to
have, Those who went ahead, they would say, would know what
awaits them there, and as for those behind, best not to think
of what might happen in the likely event that we should take
fright at the first shot, more of us would be crushed to death
than shot down. As an intermediate decision, it was decided in
one of the wards, and word of this decision was passed on to
the others, that, for the collection of food, they would not send
the usual emissaries who had been subjected to derision but
a sizable group, some ten or twelve persons to be more precise, who would try to express as one voice, the general discontent. Volunteers were asked to come forward, but, perhaps
because of the aforementioned warnings of the more cautious,
few came forward for this mission in any of the wards. Fortunately, this patent show of moral weakness ceased to have any
importance, and even to be a cause for shame, when, proving
prudence to be the correct response, the outcome of the expedition organised by the ward that had thought up the idea
became known. The eight courageous souls who had been so
bold were immediately chased away with cudgels, and while it
is true that only one bullet was fired, it is also true that it was
not aimed as high as the first shots, the proof being that the
protesters claimed they had heard it whistle right past their
heads. Whether there had been any intent to kill we shall perhaps discover later, for the present we shall give the marksman
the benefit of the doubt, that is to say, either that the shot was
no more than a warning, although a more serious one, or the
leader of these rogues underestimated the height of the demonstrators whom he imagined to be shorter, or, a disconcerting
thought, his mistake was to imagine them taller than they really were, in which case an intent to kill would inevitably have

to be considered. Leaving aside these trifling questions for the moment and turning to issues of general concern, which are those that matter, it was truly providential, even if merely a co-incidence, that the protesters should have declared themselves the representatives of such and such a ward. In this way, only that ward had to fast for three days as a punishment, and fortunately for them, for they could have had their provisions cut off forever, as is only just when someone dares to bite the hand that feeds him. So, during these three days, there was no other solution for those from the rebellious ward than to go from door to door and beg a crust of bread, for pity's sake, if possible with a bit of meat or cheese, they did not die of hunger, to be sure, but they had to take an earful, With ideas like that, what do you expect, If we had listened to you, where would we be now, but worst of all was to be told, Be patient, be patient, there are no crueller words, better to be insulted. And when the three days of punishment were over and it was thought that a new day was about to dawn, it became clear that the punishment of that unhappy ward where the forty rebellious inmates were quartered, was not yet over after all, for the rations which up until now had barely been enough for twenty, were now reduced to the point where they would not satisfy the hunger of ten. You can imagine, therefore, their outrage and indignation, and also, let it hurt whom it may, facts are facts, the fear of the remaining wards, who already saw themselves being besieged by the needy, their reactions divided between the classic duties of human solidarity and the observance of the ancient and no less time-honoured precept that charity begins at home.

Things were at this stage when an order came from the hoodlums that more money and valuables should be handed over inasmuch as they considered that the food supplies had exceeded the value of the initial payment, which moreover, according to them, had generously been calculated to be on the high side. The wards replied in despair that not so much as a coin was left in their pockets, that all the valuables collected had been scrupulously handed in, and that, a truly shameful argument, no decision could be altogether equitable if it were to ignore the difference in value of the various contributions, that is to say, in simple language, it was not fair that the upright man should pay for the sinner, and therefore that they should not cut off the provisions from someone, who in all probability, still had a balance to their credit. Obviously, none of the wards knew the value of what had been handed over by the others, but each ward thought it had every right to go on eating when the rest had already used up their credit. Fortunately, thanks to the fact that these latent conflicts were nipped in the bud, the hoodlums were adamant, their order had to be obeyed by everyone, if there had been any differences in the evaluation these were known only to the blind accountant. In the wards the exchanges were heated and bitter, sometimes becoming violent. Some suspected that certain selfish and dishonest inmates had withheld some of their valuables when the collection took place, and therefore had been given food at the expense of those who had given away everything to benefit the community. Others alleged, adopting what up until that moment had been a collective argument, that what they had handed over, should in itself be enough for them to go on being fed for many days to come, instead of being forced to feed parasites. The threat made by the blind thugs at the outset, that they would carry out an inspection of the wards and punish those who had disobeyed their orders, ended up by being carried out inside each of the wards, the honest at loggerheads with the dishonest, and even the malicious. No great fortunes were discovered, but some watches and rings came to light, mostly belonging to men rather than women. As for the punishments exacted by internal justice, these were nothing more than a few random slaps, a few halfhearted and badly aimed punches, most of the exchanges were verbal insults, some accusing expression culled from the rhetoric of the past, for example, You'd steal from your own mother, just imagine, as if a similar ignominy, and others of even greater consideration would only be committed the day that everyone went blind, and, having lost the light of their eyes, even lost the guiding spirit of respect. The blind thugs received the payment with threats of harsh reprisals, which fortunately they did not carry out, the assumption being that they had forgotten, when the truth is that they already had another idea, as would soon be revealed. If they were to carry out their threats and further injustices, they would aggravate the situation, perhaps with immediate dramatic consequences, insofar as two of the wards, in order to conceal their crime of holding back valuables, presented themselves in the name of others, burdening the innocent wards with transgressions they had not committed, one of them so honest, in fact, that it had handed over everything on the first day. Fortunately, in order to spare himself more work, the blind accountant had decided to keep note of the various contributions that had just been made on a single and separate sheet of paper, and this was to everyone's advantage, both the innocent and the guilty, for the fiscal irregularity would almost certainly have caught his attention if he had entered them against the respective accounts.

After a week, the blind hoodlums sent a message saying that they wanted women. Just like that, Bring us women. This unexpected demand, although not altogether unusual, caused an outcry as one might have expected, the bewildered emissaries who had come with the order returned at once to communicate that the wards, the three on the right and the two on the left, not excepting the blind men and women who were sleeping on the floor, had decided unanimously to ignore this degrading imposition, arguing that human dignity, in this in-

stance feminine, could not be debased to this extent, and that
if the third ward on the left-hand side had no women, the responsibility, if any, could not be laid at their door. The reply
was curt and intransigent, Unless you bring us women, you
don't eat. Humiliated, the emissaries returned to the wards
with this order, Either you go there or they will give us nothing to eat. The women on their own, those without any partner, or at least any fixed partner, protested at once, they were
not prepared to pay for the food for other women's menfolk
with what they had between their legs, one of them was even so
bold as to say, forgetting the respect she owed her own sex, I'll
go there if I want to, but whatever I may earn is for me, and if
I so please, I'll move in with them, then I'll have a bed and my
keep assured. These were the unequivocal words she uttered,
but she did not put them into action, she remembered in time
the horrors she would experience if she had to cope on her own
with the erotic frenzy of twenty desperate men whose urgency
gave the impression they were blinded by lust. However, this
declaration made so lightly in the second ward on the right-
hand side, did not fall on stony ground, one of the emissaries, with a particular sense of occasion, supported her by proposing that women volunteers should come forward for this
service, taking into account that what one does on one's own
initiative is generally less arduous than if one has to do something under duress. Only one last scruple, one last reminder of
the need for caution, prevented him from ending his appeal by
quoting the well-known proverb, When the spirit is willing,
your feet are light. Even so, no sooner had he stopped speaking
than the protests erupted, anger broke out on all sides, without pity or compassion, the men were morally defeated, they
were accused of being yobs, pimps, parasites, vampires, exploiters, panderers, according to the culture, social background and
personal disposition of the women who were rightly indig-

nant. Some of them declared their remorse at having given in, out of sheer generosity and compassion, to the sexual overtures of their companions in misfortune who were now showing their ingratitude by trying to push them into the worst of fates. The men tried to justify themselves, that it was not quite like that, that they should not dramatise, what the hell, by talking things over, people can come to some understanding, it was only because custom demands that volunteers should be asked to come forward in difficult and dangerous situations, as this one undoubtedly is, We are all at risk of dying of hunger, both you and us. Some of the women calmed down by this reasoning, but one of the others, suddenly inspired, threw another log on the fire when she asked ironically, And what would you do if these rascals instead of asking for women had asked for men, what would you do then, speak up so that everyone can hear. The women were jubilant, Tell us, tell us, they chorused, delighted at having backed the men up against the wall, caught in the snares of their own reasoning from which there was no escape, now they wanted to see how far that much lauded masculine logic would go, There are no pansies here, one man dared to protest, And no whores either, retorted the woman who had asked the provocative question, and even if there were, they might not be prepared to prostitute themselves for you. Put out, the men shrugged their shoulders, aware that there was only one answer capable of satisfying these vindictive women. If they were to ask for men, we would go, but not one of them had the courage to utter these brief, explicit and uninhibited words, and they were so dismayed that they forgot that there was no great harm in saying this, since those sons of bitches were not interested in relieving themselves with men but with women.

Now what did not occur to any of the men appeared to have occurred to the women, there could be no other explanation

for the silence that gradually descended on the ward where
these confrontations took place, as if they had understood that
for them, victory in a verbal battle of wits was no different from
the defeat that would inevitably follow, perhaps in the other
wards the debate had been much the same, since we know that
human reason and unreason are the same everywhere. Here,
the person who passed the final judgment was a woman already in her fifties who had her old mother with her and no
other means of providing her with food, I'll go, she said, without knowing that these words echoed those spoken by the doctor's wife in the first ward on the right-hand side, I'll go, there
are few women in this ward, perhaps for that reason the protests were fewer or less vehement, there was the girl with dark
glasses, there was the wife of the first blind man, there was the
girl from the surgery, there was the chambermaid, there was
one woman nobody knew anything about, there was the woman
who could not sleep, but she was so unhappy and wretched that
it would be best to leave her in peace, for there was no reason
why only the men should benefit from the women's solidarity. The first blind man had begun by declaring that his wife
would not be subjected to the shame of giving her body to
strangers in exchange for whatever, she had no desire to do
so nor would he permit it, for dignity has no price, that when
someone starts making small concessions, in the end life loses
all meaning. The doctor then asked him what meaning he saw
in the situation in which all of them there found themselves,
starving, covered in filth up to their ears, ridden with lice, eaten
by bedbugs, bitten by fleas, I, too, would prefer my wife not to
go, but what I want serves no purpose, she has said she is prepared to go, that was her decision, I know that my manly pride,
this thing we call male pride, if after so many humiliations we
still preserve something worthy of that name, I know that it
will suffer, it already is, I cannot avoid it, but it is probably the

only solution, if we want to live, Each person proceeds according to whatever morals they have, that's how I see it and I have
no intention of changing my ideas, the first blind man retorted
aggressively. Then the girl with dark glasses said, The others
don't know how many women are here, therefore you can keep
yours for your exclusive use, we shall feed both you and her, I'd
be interested to see how you feel then about your dignity, how
the bread we bring you will taste, That's not the point, the first
blind man started to reply, the point is, but his words tailed off,
were left hanging in the air, in reality he did not know what
the point was, everything he had said earlier had been no more
than certain vague opinions, nothing more than opinions belonging to another world, not to this one, what he ought to
do, no doubt about it, was to raise his hands to heaven thank-
ing fortune that his shame might remain, as it were, at home,
rather than bear the vexation of knowing that he was being
kept alive by the wives of others. By the doctor's wife, to be absolutely precise, because as for the rest, apart from the girl with
dark glasses, unmarried and free, about whose dissipated life-
style we have more than enough information, if they had husbands they were not to be seen. The silence that followed the
interrupted phrase seemed to be waiting for someone to clar-
ify the situation once and for all, for this reason it was not long
before the person who had to speak spoke up, this was the wife
of the first blind man, who said without so much as a tremor
in her voice, I'm no different from the others, I'll do whatever they do, You'll do as I say, interrupted her husband, Stop
giving orders, they won't do much good here, you're as blind
as I am, It's indecent, It's up to you not to be indecent, from
now on you don't eat, this was her cruel reply, unexpected in
someone who until today had been so docile and respectful towards her husband. There was a short burst of laughter, it came
from the hotel maid, Ah, eat, eat, what is he to do, poor fellow,

suddenly her laughter turned to weeping, her words changed, What are we to do, she said, it was almost a question, an almost resigned question to which there was no answer, like a despondent shaking of the head, so much so that the girl from the surgery did nothing but repeat, What are we to do. The doctor's wife looked up at the scissors hanging on the wall, from the expression in her eyes you would say she was asking herself the same question, unless what she was looking for was an answer to the question she threw back at them, What do you want from me.

However, to everything its proper season, just because you rise early does not mean that you will die sooner. The blind inmates in the third ward on the left-hand side are well organised, they had already decided that they would begin with those closest, with the women from the wards in their wing. The application of this method of rotation, a more than apt expression, has all the advantages and no drawbacks, in the first place, because it will allow them to know, at any given moment, what has been done and what remains to be done, like looking at a clock and saying of the day that is passing, I've lived from here to here, I've so much or so little left, in the second place, because when the round of the wards has been completed, the return to the beginning will bring with it an undeniable air of renovation, especially for those with a very short sensory memory. So let the women in the wards in the right wing enjoy themselves, I can cope with the misfortunes of my neighbours, words that none of the women spoke but which they all thought, in truth, the human being to lack that second skin we call egoism has not yet been born, it lasts much longer than the other one, that bleeds so readily. It also has to be said that these women are enjoying themselves on two counts, such are the mysteries of the human soul, for the inescapable impending threat of the humiliation to which they are to be subjected,

aroused and exacerbated in each ward sensual appetites that increasing familiarity had jaded, it was as if the men were desperately putting their mark on the women before they were taken
off, it was as if the women wanted to fill their memory with sensations experienced voluntarily in order to be able better to defend themselves from the aggression of those sensations which,
if they could, they would reject. It is inevitable that we should
ask, taking as an example the first ward on the right-hand side,
how the question of the difference between the number of men
and women was resolved, even discounting the impotent of the
males in the group, as in the case of the old man with the black
eyepatch as well as others, unidentified, both old and young,
who for one reason or another, neither said nor did anything
worth bringing into our narrative. As has already been mentioned, there are seven women in this ward, including the blind
woman who suffers from insomnia and whom nobody knows,
and the so-called normal couples, are no more than two, which
would leave an unbalanced number of men, because the boy
with the squint does not yet count. Perhaps in the other wards
there are more women than men, but an unwritten law, that
soon gained acceptance here and subsequently became statutory decrees that all matters have to be resolved in the wards in
which they have surfaced in accordance with the precepts of
the ancients, whose wisdom we shall never tire of praising, if
you would be well served, serve yourself. Therefore the women
from the first ward on the right-hand side will give relief to the
men who live under the same roof, with the exception of the
doctor's wife, who, for some reason or other, no one dared to
solicit either with words or an extended hand. Already the wife
of the first blind man, after having made the first move with
that abrupt reply she had given her husband, did, albeit discreetly, what the other women had done, as she herself had announced. There are, however, certain resistances against which

neither reason nor sentiment can do anything, such as is the case of the girl with dark glasses, whom the pharmacist's assistant, however many arguments he offered, however many pleas he made, was unable to win over, thus paying for his lack of respect at the outset. This same girl, there's no understanding women, who is the prettiest of all the women here, the one with the shapeliest figure, the most attractive, the one whom all the men craved when the word about her exceptional looks got around, finally got into bed one night of her own free will with the old man with the black eyepatch, who received her like summer rain and satisfied her as best he could, pretty well given his age, thus proving once more, that appearances are deceptive, that it is not from someone's face and the litheness of their body that we can judge their strength of heart. Everyone in the ward thought that it was nothing more than an act of charity that the girl with dark glasses should have offered herself to the old man with the black eyepatch, but there were men there, sensitive and dreamers, who having already enjoyed her favours, began to allow their thoughts to wander, to think there could be no greater prize in this world than for a man to find himself stretched out on his bed, all alone, thinking the impossible, only to realise that a woman is gently lifting the covers and slipping under them, slowly rubbing her body against his body, and then lying still, waiting for the heat of their blood to calm the sudden tremor of their startled skin. And all this for no good reason, just because she wanted to. These are fortunes that do not go to waste, sometimes a man has to be old and wear a black eyepatch covering an eye socket that is definitively blind. And then there are certain things that are best left unexplained, it's best just to say what happened, not to probe people's inner thoughts and feelings, as on that occasion when the doctor's wife had got out of bed to go and cover up the boy with the squint whose blanket had slipped off. She did not go

back to bed at once. Leaning against the wall at the far end of
the ward, in the narrow space between the two rows of beds,
she was looking in desperation at the door at the other end,
that door through which they had entered on a day that seemed
so remote and that now led nowhere. She was standing there
when she saw her husband get up, and, staring straight ahead
as if he were sleepwalking, make his way to the bed of the girl
with dark glasses. She made no attempt to stop him. Standing
motionless, she saw him lift the covers and then lie down,
whereupon the girl woke up and received him without protest,
she saw how those two mouths searched until they found each
other, and then the inevitable happened, the pleasure of the
one, the pleasure of the other, the pleasure of both of them, the
muffled cries, she said, Oh, doctor, and these words could have
sounded so ridiculous but did not, he said, Forgive me, I don't
know what came over me, in fact, we were right, how could we,
who hardly see, know what even he does not know, Lying on
the narrow bed, they could not have imagined that they were
being watched, the doctor certainly could not, he was suddenly
worried, would his wife be asleep, he asked himself, or was she
wandering the corridors as she did every night, he made to go
back to his own bed, but a voice said, Don't get up, and a hand
rested on his chest with the lightness of a bird, he was about to
speak, perhaps about to repeat that he did not know what had
got into him, but the voice said, If you say nothing it will be
easier for me to understand. The girl with dark glasses began to
weep, What an unhappy lot we are, she murmured, and then, I
wanted it too, I wanted it too, you are not to blame, Be quiet,
the doctor's wife said gently, let's all keep quiet, there are times
when words serve no purpose, if only I, too, could weep, say
everything with tears, not have to speak in order to be understood. She sat on the edge of the bed, stretched her arm over
the two bodies, as if gathering them in the same embrace, and,

bending over the girl with dark glasses, she whispered in her ear, I can see. The girl remained still, serene, simply puzzled that she should feel no surprise, it was as if she had known from the very first day but had not wanted to say so aloud since this was a secret that did not belong to her. She turned her head ever so slightly and responded by whispering into the ear of the doctor's wife, I knew, at least, I'm not entirely sure, but I think I knew, It's a secret, you mustn't tell a soul, don't worry, I trust you, And so you should, I'd rather die than betray you, You must call me "tu," Oh, no, I couldn't, I simply couldn't do it. They went on whispering to each other, first one, then the other, touching each other's hair, the lobe of the ear, with their lips, it was an insignificant dialogue, it was a profoundly serious dialogue, if this contradiction can be reconciled, a brief conspiratorial conversation that appeared to ignore the man lying between the two of them, but involved him in a logic outside the world of commonplace ideas and realities. Then the doctor's wife said to her husband, Lie there for a little longer, if you wish, No, I'm going back to our bed, Then I'll help you. She sat up to give him greater freedom of movement, contemplated for an instant the two blind heads resting side by side on the soiled pillow, their faces dirty, their hair tangled, only their eyes shining to no purpose. He got up slowly, looking for support, then remained motionless at the side of the bed, undecided, as if he had suddenly lost all notion of the place where he found himself, then she, as she had always done, took him by one arm, but the gesture now had another meaning, never had he so badly needed someone to guide him as at this moment, although he would never know to what extent, only the two women really knew, when the doctor's wife stroked the girl's cheek with her other hand and the girl impulsively took it and raised it to her lips. The doctor thought he could hear sobbing, an almost inaudible sound that could have come only from

tears trickling slowly down to the corners of the mouth where
they disappear to recommence the eternal cycle of inexplicable
human joys and sorrows. The girl with dark glasses was about
to remain alone, she was the one who ought to be consoled, for
this reason the doctor's wife was slow to remove her hand.

Next day, at dinner-time, if a few miserable pieces of stale
bread and mouldy meat deserved such a name, there appeared
in the doorway of the ward three blind men from the other
side. How many women have you got in here, one of them
asked, Six, replied the doctor's wife, with the good intention
of leaving out the blind woman who suffered from insomnia,
but she corrected her in a subdued voice, There are seven of
us. The blind thugs laughed, Too bad, said one of them, you'll
just have to work all the harder tonight, and another suggested,
Perhaps we'd better go and look for reinforcements in the next
ward, It isn't worth it, said the third blind man who knew his
sums, it works out at three men for each woman, they can stand
it. This brought another burst of laughter, and the fellow who
had asked how many women there were, gave the order, When
you've finished, come over to us, and added, That's if you want
to eat tomorrow and suckle your menfolk. They said these
words in all the wards, and still laughed at the joke with as
much gusto as on the day they had invented it. They doubled
up with laughter, stamped their feet, beat their thick cudgels
on the ground, until one of them suddenly cautioned, Listen
here, if any of you has got the curse, we don't want you, we'll
leave it until the next time, No one's got the curse, the doctor's
wife calmly informed him, Then prepare yourselves and don't
be long, we're waiting for you. They turned and disappeared.
The ward remained in silence. A minute later, the wife of the
first blind man said, I cannot eat any more, she had precious
little in her hand, and she could not bear to eat it. Nor me, said
the blind woman who suffered from insomnia, Nor me, said

the woman whom nobody seems to know, I've already finished, said the hotel maid, Me too, said the girl from the surgery, I'll throw up in the face of the first man who comes near me, said the girl with dark glasses. They were all on their feet, shaking and resolute. Then the doctor's wife said, I'll go in front. The first blind man covered his head with the blanket as if this might serve some purpose, since he was already blind, the doctor drew his wife towards him and, without saying anything, gave her a quick kiss on the forehead, what more could he do, it wouldn't make much difference to the other men, they had neither the rights nor the obligations of a husband as far as any of these women were concerned, therefore no one could come up to them and say, A consenting cuckold is a cuckold twice over. The girl with dark glasses got in behind the doctor's wife, then came the hotel maid, the girl from the surgery, the wife of the first blind man, the woman no one knows and, finally, the blind woman suffering from insomnia, a grotesque lineup of foul-smelling women, their clothes filthy and in tatters, it seems impossible that the animal drive for sex should be so powerful, to the point of blinding a man's sense of smell, the most delicate of the senses, there are even some theologians who affirm, although not in these exact words, that the worst thing about trying to live a reasonable life in hell is getting used to the dreadful stench down there. Slowly, guided by the doctor's wife, each of them with her hand on the shoulder of the one in front, the women started walking. They were all barefoot because they did not want to lose their shoes amidst the trials and tribulations they were about to endure. When they arrived in the hallway of the main entrance, the doctor's wife headed for the outer door, no doubt anxious to know if the world still existed. When she felt the fresh air, the hotel maid remembered, frightened, We can't go out, the soldiers are out there, and the blind woman suffering from insomnia said, All the better for us, in less than a minute we'd be dead, that is how we ought to be, all dead, You mean us, asked the girl from the surgery, No, all of us, all the women in here, at least then we'd have the best of reasons for being blind. She had never had so much to say for herself since she'd been brought here. The doctor's wife said, Let's go, only those who have to die will die, death doesn't give any warning when it singles you out. They passed through the door that gave access to the left wing, they made their way down the long corridors, the women from the first two wards could, if they had wished, tell them what awaited them, but they were curled up in their beds like animals that had been given a good thrashing, the men did not dare to touch them, nor did they make any attempt to get close, because the women immediately started screaming.

In the last corridor, at the far end, the doctor's wife saw a blind man who was keeping a lookout, as usual. He must have heard their shuffling footsteps, and informed the others, They're coming, they're coming. From within came cries, whinnying, guffaws of laughter. Four blind men lost no time in removing the bed that was blocking the entrance, Quickly, girls, come in, come in, we're all here like studs in heat, you're going to get your bellies filled, said one of them. The blind thugs surrounded them, tried to fondle them, but fell back in disarray, when their leader, the one who had the gun, shouted, The first choice is mine as you well know. The eyes of all those men anxiously sought out the women, some extended avid hands, if in passing they happened to touch one of them they finally knew where to look. In the middle of the aisle, between the beds, the women stood like soldiers on parade waiting to be inspected. The leader of the blind hoodlums, gun in hand, came up to them, as agile and frisky as if he were able to see them. He placed his free hand on the woman suffering from insomnia, who was first in line, fondled her back and front, her

hips, her breasts, between her legs. The blind woman began
to scream and he pushed her away, You're a worthless whore.
He passed on to the next one, who happened to be the woman
that no one knew, now he was fondling her with both hands,
having put his gun into his trouser pocket, I say, this one isn't
at all bad, and then he moved on to the wife of the first blind
man, then the employee from the surgery, then the hotel maid,
and exclaimed, Listen, men, these fillies are pretty good. The
blind hoodlums whinnied, stamped their feet on the ground,
Let's get on with it, it's getting late, some yelled, Take it easy,
said the thug with the gun, let me first take a look at the others. He fondled the girl with dark glasses and gave a whistle,
Now then, here's a stroke of luck, no filly quite like this one has
turned up before. Excited, as he went on fondling the girl, he
passed on to the doctor's wife, gave another whistle, This one
is on the mature side, but could turn out to be quite a woman.
He drew the two women towards him, and almost drooled as
he said, I'll keep these two, when I've finished with them, I'll
pass them on to the rest of you. He dragged them to the end of
the ward, where the containers of food, packets, tins had been
piled up, enough supplies to feed a regiment. The women, all
of them, were already screaming their heads off, blows, slaps,
orders could be heard, Shut up, you whores, these bitches are
all the same, they always have to start yelling, Give it to her
good and hard and she'll soon be quiet, Just wait until it's my
turn and you'll see how they'll be asking for more, Hurry up
there, I can't wait another minute. The blind woman suffering
from insomnia wailed in desperation beneath an enormous fellow, the other four were surrounded by men with their trousers
down who were jostling each other like hyenas around a carcass. The doctor's wife found herself beside the bed where she
had been taken, she was standing, her trembling hands grip-
ping the railings of the bed, she watched how the blind leader

with the gun tugged and tore the skirt of the girl with dark glasses, how he took down his trousers and, guiding himself with his fingers, pointed his member at the girl's sex, how he pushed and forced, she could hear the grunts, the obscenities, the girl with dark glasses said nothing, she only opened her mouth to vomit, her head to one side, her eyes turned towards the other woman, he did not even notice what was happening, the smell of vomit is only noticed when the atmosphere and all the rest does not smell the same, at last the man shuddered from head to foot, gave three violent jolts as if he were riveting three girders, panted like a suffocating pig, he had finished. The girl with dark glasses wept in silence. The blind man with the gun withdrew his penis, still dripping and said in a hesitant voice, as he stretched out his arm to the doctor's wife, Don't get jealous, I'll be dealing with you next, and then raising his voice, I say, boys, you can come and get this one, but treat her nicely for I may need her again. Half a dozen blind men advanced unsteadily along the passageway, grabbed the girl with dark glasses and almost dragged her away. I'm first, I'm first, said all of them. The blind man with the gun had sat down on the bed, his flaccid penis was resting on the edge of the mattress, his trousers rolled down round his ankles. Kneel down here between my legs, he said. The doctor's wife got onto her knees. Suck me, he said, No, she replied, Either you suck me, or I'll give you a good thrashing, and you won't get any food, he told her, Aren't you afraid I might bite off your penis, she asked him, You can try, I have my hands on your neck, I'd strangle you first if you tried to draw blood, he replied menacingly. Then he said, I seem to recognise your voice, And I recognise your face, You're blind and cannot see me, No, I cannot see you, Then why do you say that you recognise my face, Because that voice can have only one face, Suck me, and forget the chitchat, No, Either you suck me, or your ward won't see another crumb of

bread, go back there and tell them that if they have nothing to
eat it's because you refused to suck me, and then come back to
tell me what happened. The doctor's wife leaned forward, with
the tips of two fingers on her right hand she held and raised the
man's sticky penis, her left hand resting on the floor, touched
his trousers, groped, felt the cold metallic hardness of the gun,
I can kill him, she thought. She could not. With his trousers
round his ankles, it was impossible to reach the pocket where
he had put his weapon. I cannot kill him now, she thought. She
moved her head forward, opened her mouth, closed it, closed
her eyes in order not to see and began sucking.

Day was breaking when the blind hoodlums allowed the
women to go. The blind woman suffering from insomnia had
to be carried away in the arms of her companions, who could
scarcely drag themselves along. For hours they had passed from
one man to another, from humiliation to humiliation, from
outrage to outrage, exposed to everything that can be done to
a woman while leaving her still alive. As you know, payment is
in kind, tell those pathetic men of yours that they have to come
and fetch the grub, the blind man with the gun said mockingly
as they left. And he added derisively, See you again, girls, so
prepare yourselves for the next session. The other blind hoodlums repeated more or less in chorus, See you again, some
called them fillies, others whores, but their waning libido was
obvious from the lack of conviction in their voices. Deaf, blind,
silent, tottering on their feet, with barely enough willpower
not to let go of the hand of the woman in front, the hand, not
the shoulder, as when they had come, certainly not one of them
would have known what to reply if they had been asked, Why
are you holding hands as you go, it simply came about, there
are gestures for which we cannot always find an easy explanation, sometimes not even a difficult one can be found. As they
crossed the hallway, the doctor's wife looked outside, the sol-

diers were there as well as a truck that was almost certainly being used to distribute the food to those in quarantine. Just at that moment, the blind woman suffering from insomnia lost the power of her legs, literally, as if they had been cut off with a single blow, her heart also gave up, it did not even finish the rhythmic contraction it had started, at last we know why this blind woman could not sleep, now she will sleep, let us not wake her. She's dead, said the doctor's wife, and her voice was expressionless, if it were possible for such a voice, as dead as the word it had spoken, to have come from a living mouth. She raised the suddenly dislocated body, the legs covered in blood, her abdomen bruised, her poor breasts uncovered, brutally scarred, teeth marks on her shoulder where she had been bitten. This is the image of my body, she thought, the image of the body of all the women here, between these outrages and our sorrows there is only one difference, we, for the present, are still alive. Where shall we take her, asked the girl with dark glasses, For the moment to the ward, later we shall bury her, said the doctor's wife.

The men were waiting at the door, only the first blind man was missing, he had covered his head with his blanket once more when he realised the women were coming back, and the boy with the squint, who was asleep. Without hesitation, without having to count the beds, the doctor's wife laid the blind woman who suffered from insomnia on the bed she had occupied. She was unconcerned that the others might find it strange, after all, everyone there knew that she was the blind woman who was most familiar with every nook and cranny in the place. She's dead, she repeated, What happened, asked the doctor, but his wife made no attempt to answer him, his question might be simply what it appeared to mean, How did she die, but it could also imply What did they do to you in there, now, neither for the one nor for the other of these questions could there be an answer, she simply died, from what scarcely matters, it is foolish for anyone to ask what someone died from, in time the cause will be forgotten, only two words remain, She died, and we are no longer the same women as when we left here, the words they would have spoken we can no longer speak, and as for the others, the unnameable exists, that is its name, nothing else. Go and fetch the food, said the doctor's wife. Chance, fate, fortune, destiny, or whatever is the precise term for that which has so many names, is made of pure irony, how else could we understand why it was precisely the husbands of two of the women who were chosen to represent the ward and collect their food, when no one could imagine that the price would be what had just been paid. It could have been other men, unmarried, free, with no conjugal honour to defend, but then it had to be these two, who certainly will not now wish to bear the shame of extending a hand to beg from these degenerate rogues who have violated their wives. The first blind man said it, with all the emphasis of a firm decision, Whoever wishes can go, but I'm not going, I'll go, said the doctor, I'll go with you, said the old man with the black eyepatch. There won't be much food, but I warn you it's quite a weight, I still have the strength to carry the bread I eat, What always weighs more is the bread of the others, I have no right to complain, the weight carried by the others will buy me my food. Let us try to imagine, not the dialogue for that is over and done with, but the men who took part in it, they are there, face to face, as if they could see each other, which in this case is impossible, it is enough that the memory of each of them should bring out from the dazzling whiteness of the world the mouth that is articulating the words, and then, like a slow irradiation coming from this centre, the rest of the faces will start to appear, one an old man, the other not so old, and anyone who can still see in this way cannot really be called blind. When they moved off to go and collect the wages of shame, as the first blind man protested with rhetorical indignation, the doctor's wife said to the other women, Stay here, I'll be right back. She knew what she wanted, she did not know if she would find it. She needed a bucket or something that would serve the purpose, she wanted to fill it with water, even if fetid, even if polluted, she wanted to wash the corpse of the woman who had suffered from insomnia, to wipe away her own blood and the sperm of others, to deliver her purified to the earth, if it still makes sense to speak of the purity of the body in this asylum where we are living, for purity of the soul, as we know, is beyond everyone's reach.

Blind men lay stretched out on the long tables in the refectory. From a dripping tap over a sink full of garbage, trickled a thread of water. The doctor's wife looked around her in search of a bucket or basin but could see nothing that might serve her purpose. One of the blind men was disturbed by this presence and asked, Who's there, She did not reply, she knew that she would not be welcome, that no one would say, You need water, then take it, and if it's to wash the corpse of a dead woman, take all the water you want. Scattered on the floor were plastic bags, those used for the food, some of them large. She thought they must be torn, then reflected that by using two or three, one inside the other, not much water would be lost. She acted quickly, the blind men were already getting down from the tables and asking, Who's there, even more alarmed when they heard the sound of running water, they headed in that direction, the doctor's wife got out of the way and pushed a table across their path so that they could not come near, she then retrieved her bag, the water was running slowly, in desperation she forced the tap, then, as if it had been released from some prison, the water spurted out, splashed all over the place and soaked her from head to foot. The blind men took fright and drew back, they thought a pipe must have burst, and they had all the more reason to think so when the flood reached their feet, they were not to know that it had been spilled by the stranger who had entered, as it happened the woman had realised that she would not be able to carry so much weight. She tied a knot in the bag, threw it over her shoulder, and, as best she could, fled.

When the doctor and the old man with the black eyepatch entered the ward with the food, they did not see, could not see, seven naked women and the corpse of the woman who suffered from insomnia stretched out on her bed, cleaner than she had ever been in all her life, while another woman was washing her companions, one by one, and then herself.

O N THE fourth day, the thugs reappeared. They had come to exact payment from the women in the second ward, but they paused for a moment at the door of the first ward to ask if the women there had yet recovered from the sexual orgy of the other night, A great night, yes sir, exclaimed one of them licking his chops and another confirmed, Those seven were worth fourteen, it's true that one of them was no great shakes, but in the middle of all that uproar who noticed, their men are lucky sods, if they're man enough for them. It would be better if they weren't, then they'd be more eager. From the far end of the ward, the doctor's wife said, There are no longer seven of us, Has one of you vamoosed, someone in the group asked, laughing, She didn't vamoose, she died, Oh, hell, then you lot will have to work all the harder next time, It wasn't much of a loss, she was no great shakes, said the doctor's wife. Disconcerted, the messengers did not know how to respond, what they had just heard struck them as indecent, some of them even came round to thinking that when all is said and done all women are bitches, such a lack of respect, to refer to a woman like that, just because her tits weren't in the right place and she had no arse to speak of. The doctor's wife was

looking at them, as they hovered there in the doorway, undecided, moving their bodies like mechanical dolls. She recognised them, she had been raped by all three of them. At last,
one of them tapped his stick on the ground, Let's go, he said.
Their tapping and their warning cries, Keep back, keep back,
it's us, died away as they made their way along the corridor,
then there was silence, vague sounds, the women from the second ward were receiving the order to present themselves after
dinner. Once more the tapping of sticks could be heard, Keep
back, keep back, the shadows of the three blind men passed
through the doorway and they were gone.

The doctor's wife who had been telling the boy with the
squint a story, raised her arm and, without a sound, took the
scissors from the nail. She said to the boy, Later I'll tell you
the rest of the story. No one in the ward had asked her why
she had spoken with such disdain of the blind woman who had
suffered from insomnia. After a while, she removed her shoes
and went to reassure her husband, I won't be long, I'm coming straight back. She headed for the door. There she paused
and remained waiting. Ten minutes later the women from the
second ward appeared in the corridor. There were fifteen of
them. Some were crying. They were not in line, but in groups,
tied to each other with strips of cloth that had clearly been
torn from their bedclothes. When they had passed, the doctor's wife followed them. Not one of them perceived that
they had company. They knew what awaited them, the news
of the abuses they would suffer was no secret, nor were these
abuses anything really new, for in all certainty this is how the
world began. What terrified them was not so much the rape,
but the orgy, the shame, the anticipation of the terrible night
ahead, fifteen women sprawled on the beds and on the floor,
the men going from one to the other, snorting like pigs, The
worst thing of all is that I might feel some pleasure, one of

the women thought to herself. When they entered the corridor giving access to the ward they were heading for, the blind
man on the lookout alerted the others, I can hear them, they'll
be here any minute. The bed being used as a gate was quickly
removed, one by one the women entered, Wow, so many of
them, exclaimed the blind accountant, as he counted them enthusiastically, Eleven, twelve, thirteen, fourteen, fifteen, fifteen,
there are fifteen of them. He went after the last one, put his
eager hands up her skirt, This one is game, she's mine, he was
saying. They had finished sizing up the women and making a
preliminary assessment of their physical attributes. In fact, if
all of them were condemned to endure the same fate, there
was no point in wasting time and cooling their desire as they
made their choice according to height and the measurement of
busts and hips. They were soon taking them off to bed, already
stripping them by force, and it was not long before the usual
weeping and pleas for mercy could be heard, but the replies
when they came, were always the same, If you want to eat, open
your legs. And they opened their legs, some were ordered to
use their mouth like the one who was crouched down between
the knees of the leader of these ruffians and this one was saying nothing. The doctor's wife entered the ward, slipped slowly
between the beds, but she need not even have taken these precautions, no one would have heard her had she been wearing
clogs, and if, in the middle of the fracas, some blind man were
to touch her and become aware that it was a woman, the worst
that could happen to her would be having to join the others,
not that anyone would notice, in a situation like this it is not
easy to tell the difference between fifteen and sixteen.

The leader of these hoodlums still had his bed at the far end
of the ward where the containers of food were stacked. The
beds near his had been removed, the fellow liked to move at
will without having to keep bumping into his neighbours. Kill-

ing him was going to be simple. As she slowly advanced along
the narrow aisle, the doctor's wife studied the movements of
the man she was about to kill, how he threw his head back as
he took his pleasure, as if he were offering her his neck. Slowly,
the doctor's wife approached, circled the bed and positioned
herself behind him. The blind woman went on doing what was
expected of her. The doctor's wife slowly raised the scissors, the
blades slightly apart so that they might penetrate like two dag-
gers. Just then, at the last minute, the blind man seemed to be
aware of someone's presence, but his orgasm had transported
him from the world of normal sensations, had deprived him of
any reflexes, You won't have time to come, the doctor's wife reflected as she brought her arm down with tremendous force.
The scissors dug deep into the blind man's throat, turning on
themselves they struggled with the cartilage and the membra-
neous tissues, then furiously went deeper until they came up
against the cervical vertebrae. His cry was barely audible, it
might have been the grunting of an animal about to ejaculate,
as was happening to some of the other men, and perhaps it was,
and at the same time as a spurt of blood splashed onto her face,
the blind woman received the discharge of semen in her mouth.
It was her cry that startled the blind men, they were more than
used to hearing cries, but this was quite unlike the others. The
blind woman was screaming, where had this blood come from,
probably, without knowing how, she had done what it had
crossed her mind to do and bitten off his penis. The blind men
left the women, approached groping their way, What's going
on, what's all this screaming, they asked, but the blind woman
now had a hand over her mouth, someone had whispered in
her ear, Be quiet, and then gently pulled her back, Say nothing, it was a woman's voice, and this calmed her, if that is possible in such distressing circumstances. The blind accountant
arrived ahead of the others, he was the first to touch the body

which had toppled across the bed, the first to run his hands over it, He's dead, he exclaimed almost immediately. The head was hanging down on the other side of the bed, the blood was still spurting out, They've killed him, he said. The blind men stopped in their tracks, they could not believe their ears, How could they have killed him, who killed him, They've made an enormous slit in his throat, it must have been that whore who was with him, we've got to get her. The blind men stirred once more, more slowly this time, as if they were afraid of coming up against the blade that had killed their leader. They could not see that the blind accountant was hastily rummaging through the dead man's pockets, that he was removing his gun and a small plastic bag with about ten cartridges. Everyone was suddenly distracted by an outcry from the women, already on their feet, in panic, anxious to get away from that place, but some had lost any notion of where the ward door was located, they went in the wrong direction and ran into the blind men who thought the women were about to attack them, whereupon the confusion of bodies reached new heights of delirium. At the far end of the ward, the doctor's wife quietly awaited the right moment to make her escape. She had a firm grip on the blind woman, in her other hand she held the scissors ready to land the first blow if any man should come near her. For the moment, the free space was in her favour, but she knew that she could not linger there. A number of women had finally found the door, others were struggling to free themselves from the hands holding them back, there was even the odd one still trying to throttle the enemy and deliver another corpse. The blind accountant called out with authority to his men, Keep calm, don't lose your nerve, we'll get to the bottom of this matter, and anxious to make his order all the more convincing he fired a shot into the air. The outcome was exactly the opposite of what he expected. Surprised to discover that the gun was already in other

hands and that they were about to have a new leader, the blind
hoodlums stopped struggling with the women, gave up trying
to dominate them, one of the men having given up the struggle
altogether because he had been strangled. It was at this point
that the doctor's wife decided to move. Striking blows left and
right, she opened a path. Now it was the blind thugs who were
calling out, who were being knocked over and climbing all over
each other, anyone there with eyes to see, would perceive that,
compared with this, the previous upheaval had been a joke.
The doctor's wife had no desire to kill, all she wanted was to
get out as quickly as possible and, above all, not to leave a single blind woman behind. This one probably won't survive, she
thought as she dug the scissors into a man's chest. Another shot
was heard, Let's go, let's go, said the doctor's wife, pushing any
blind women whom she encountered ahead of her. She helped
them to their feet, repeated, Quickly, quickly, and now it was
the blind accountant who was shouting from the far end of the
ward, Grab them, don't let them escape, but it was too late, the
women were already out in the corridor, they fled, stumbling
as they went, half dressed, holding on to their rags as best they
could. Standing still at the entrance to the ward, the doctor's
wife called out in a rage, Remember what I said the other day,
that I'd never forget his face, and from now on think about
what I am telling you, for I won't forget your faces either, You'll
pay dearly for this outrage, threatened the blind accountant,
you and your companions and those so-called men of yours,
You neither know who I am nor where I've come from, You're
from the first ward on the other side, volunteered one of the
men who had gone to summon the women, and the blind accountant added, Your voice is unmistakable, you need only utter one word in my presence and you're dead, The other fellow said the same thing and now he's a corpse, But I'm not a
blind man like him or you, when you lot turned blind, I al-

ready knew everything about this world, You know nothing
about my blindness. You're not blind, you can't fool me, Perhaps I'm the blindest of all, I've already killed and I'll kill again
if I have to, You'll die first of hunger, from today onwards there
will be no more food, even if you were all to come offering on
a tray the three holes you were born with. For each day that
we're deprived of food because of you, one of the men here
will die the moment he steps outside this door, You won't get
away with this, Oh, yes we will, from now on we shall be collecting the food, and you can eat what you've hoarded there,
Bitch, Bitches are neither men nor women, they're bitches, and
you know now what they're worth. Enraged, the blind accountant fired in the direction of the door. The bullet whizzed past
the heads of the blind men without hitting anyone and lodged
itself in the corridor wall. You didn't get me, said the doctor's
wife, and take care, if your ammunition runs out, there are others here who would like to be leader too.

She moved away, took a few steps, still firm, then advanced
along the wall of the corridor, almost fainting, suddenly her
legs gave way, and she fell to the ground. Her eyes clouded
over, I'm going blind, she thought, but then realised it would
not be just yet, these were only tears blurring her vision, tears
such as she had never shed in all her life, I've killed a man, she
said in a low voice, I wanted to kill him and I have. She turned
her head in the direction of the ward door, if the blind men
were to come now, she would be unable to defend herself. The
corridor was deserted. The woman had disappeared, the blind
men, still startled by the gunfire and even more by the corpses
of their own men, did not dare come out. Little by little she regained her strength. Her tears continued to flow, slower and
more serene, as if confronted by something irremediable. She
struggled to her feet. She had blood on her hands and clothes,
and suddenly her exhausted body told her that she was old, Old

and a murderess, she thought, but she knew that if it were necessary, she would kill again, And when is it necessary to kill, she
asked herself as she headed in the direction of the hallway, and
she herself answered the question, When what is still alive is
already dead. She shook her head and thought, And what does
that mean, words, nothing but words. She walked on alone. She
approached the door leading to the forecourt. Between the railings of the gate she could just make out the shadow of a soldier
who was keeping guard. There are still people out there, people
who can see. The sound of footsteps behind her caused her to
tremble, It's them, she thought and turned round rapidly with
her scissors at the ready. It was her husband. As they went past,
the women from the second ward had been shouting out what
had happened on the other side, that a woman had stabbed and
killed the leader of the thugs, that there had been shooting, the
doctor did not ask them to identify the woman, it could only
be his wife, she had told the boy with the squint that she would
tell him the rest of the story later, and what would have become
of her now, probably dead as well, I'm here, she said, and went
up to him and embraced him, not noticing that she was smear-
ing him with blood, or noticing but unconcerned, for until now
they had shared everything. What happened, the doctor asked,
they said a man was killed, Yes, I killed him, Why, Someone had
to do it, and there was no one else, And now, Now we're free,
they know what awaits them if they ever try to abuse us again,
There's likely to be a battle, a war, The blind are always at war,
always have been at war, Will you kill again, If I have to, I shall
never be free from this blindness, And what about the food, We
shall fetch it, I doubt whether they'll dare to come here, at least
for the next few days they'll be afraid the same might happen
to them, that a pair of scissors will slit their throat, We failed to
put up resistance as we should have done when they first came
making demands, Of course, we were afraid and fear isn't al-

ways a wise counsellor, let's get back, for our greater safety we ought to barricade the door of the wards by putting beds on top of beds, as they do, if some of us have to sleep on the floor, too bad, better that than to die of hunger.

In the days that followed, they asked themselves if that was not what was about to happen to them. At first they were not surprised, from the outset they had become used to it, there had always been delays in the delivery of food, the blind thugs were right when they said the soldiers were sometimes late, but then they perverted this reasoning when, in a playful tone of voice, they affirmed that for this reason they had no choice but to impose rationing, these are the painful obligations of those who have to govern. On the third day when there was no longer as much as a rind or crumb, the doctor's wife with some companions, went out into the forecourt and asked, Hey, why the delay, whatever happened to our food, we haven't eaten for the last two days. Another sergeant, not the one from the time before, came up to the railing to declare that the army was not responsible, that no one there was trying to take the bread from their mouths, that military honour would never allow it, if there was no food it was because there was no food, and all of you stay where you are, the first one to advance knows the fate that waits for him, the orders have not changed. This warning was enough to send them back inside, and they conferred amongst themselves, And now what do we do if they won't bring us any food, They might bring some tomorrow, Or the day after tomorrow, Or when we no longer have the strength to move, We ought to go out, We wouldn't even get as far as the gate, If only we had our sight, If we had our sight we wouldn't have landed in this hell, I wonder what life is like out there, Perhaps those bastards might give us something to eat if we went there to ask, after all if there's a shortage for us, they must be running short too, That's why they're unlikely to give us anything they've got,

And before their food runs out we will have died of starvation, What are we to do then, They were seated on the floor, under the yellowish light of the only lamp in the hallway, more or less in a circle, the doctor and the doctor's wife, the old man with the black eyepatch, amongst the other men and women, one or two from each ward, from the wing on the left as well as from the one on the right, and then, this world of the blind being what it is, there occurred what always occurs, one of the men said, All I know is that we would never have found ourselves in this situation if their leader hadn't been killed, what did it matter if the women had to go there twice a month to give these men what nature gave them to give, I ask myself. Some found this amusing, some forced a smile, those inclined to protest were deterred by an empty stomach, and the same man insisted, What I'd like to know is who did the stabbing, The women who were there at the time swear it was none of them, What we ought to do is to take the law into our own hands and bring the culprit to justice, If we knew who was responsible, we'd say this is the person you're looking for, now give us the food, If we knew who was responsible. The doctor's wife lowered her head and thought, He's right, if anyone here should die of hunger it will be my fault, but then, giving voice to the rage she could feel welling up inside her contradicting any acceptance of responsibility, But let these men be the first to die so that my guilt may pay for their guilt. Then she thought, raising her eyes, And if I were now to tell them that it was I who killed him, they would hand me over, knowing that they would be delivering me to certain death. Whether it was the effect of hunger or because the thought suddenly seduced her like some abyss, her head spun as if she were in a daze, her body moved despite herself, her mouth opened to speak, but just at that moment someone grabbed and squeezed her arm, she looked, it was the old man with the black eyepatch, who said, Anyone who gave himself up, I'd kill him with my own hands, Why, people in the circle asked, Because if shame still has any meaning in this hell where we're expected to live and which we've turned into the hell of hells, it is thanks to that person who had the courage to go and kill the hyena in its lair, Agreed, but shame won't fill our plates, Whoever you may be, you're right in what you say, there have always been those who have filled their bellies because they had no sense of shame, but we, who have nothing, apart from this last shred of undeserved dignity, let us at least show that we are still capable of fighting for what is rightfully ours, What are you trying to say, That having started off by sending in the women and eaten at their expense like low-life pimps, the time has now come for sending in the men, if there are any, Explain yourself, but first tell us where you are from, I'm from the first ward on the right-hand side, Go on then, It's very simple, let's go and collect the food with our own hands, Those men are armed, As far as we know, they have only one gun and the ammunition will run out sooner or later, They have enough to make sure that some of us will die, Others have died for less, I'm not prepared to lose my life so that the rest can enjoy themselves. Would you also be prepared to starve, if someone should lose his life so that you might have food, the old man with the black eyepatch asked sarcastically, and the other man gave no reply.

In the entrance of the door leading to the wards in the right-hand wing, appeared a woman who had been listening out of sight. She was the one who had received the spurt of blood in her face, the one into whose mouth the dead man had ejaculated, the one in whose ear the doctor's wife had whispered, Be quiet, and now the doctor's wife is thinking, From here where I'm sitting in the midst of others, I cannot tell you to be quiet, don't give me away, but no doubt you recognise my voice, it's impossible that you could have forgotten it, my hand covered

your mouth, your body against mine, and I said, Be quiet, and
the moment has come to know whom I really saved, to know
who you are, that is why I am about to speak, that is why I am
about to say in a loud, clear voice so that you might accuse me,
if this is your destiny and mine, I am now saying, Not only the
men will go, but also the women, we shall return to that place
where they humiliated us so that none of that humiliation may
remain, so that we might rid ourselves of it in the same way that
we spat out what they ejaculated into our mouths. She uttered
these words and waited, until the woman replied, Wherever
you go, I shall go, that was what she said. The old man with the
black eyepatch smiled, it seemed a happy smile, and perhaps it
was, this is not the moment to ask him, it is much more interesting to observe the expression of surprise on the faces of the
other blind men, as if something had passed over their heads, a
bird, a cloud, a first hesitant glimmer of light. The doctor took
his wife's hand, then asked, Are there still people here intent
on discovering who killed that fellow, or are we agreed that
the hand that stabbed him was the hand of all of us, or to be
more precise, the hand of each one of us. No one replied. The
doctor's wife said, Let's give them a little longer, if, by tomorrow, the soldiers have not brought our food, then we advance.
They got up, went their separate ways, some to the right, others to the left, imprudently they had not reflected that some
blind man from the ward of the thugs might have been listening, fortunately the devil is not always behind the door, a saying that could not have been more appropriate. Somewhat less
appropriate was the blast that came from the loudspeaker, recently it had spoken on certain days, on others not at all, but always at the same time, as had been promised, clearly there was
a timer in the transmitter which at the precise moment started
up the recorded tape, the reason why it should have broken
down from time to time we are never likely to know, these are

matters for the outside world, it is in any case serious enough, insofar as it muddled up the calendar, the so-called counting of the days, which some blind men, natural obsessives, or lovers of order, which is a moderate form of obsession, had tried scrupulously to follow by making little knots in a piece of string, this was done by those who did not trust their memory, as if they were writing a diary. Now it was the time that was out of phase, the mechanism must have broken down, a twisted relay, some loose soldering, let's hope the recording will not keep going back forever to the beginning, that was all we needed as well as being blind and mad. Along the corridors, through the wards, like some final and futile warning, boomed an authoritarian voice, the Government regrets having been forced to exercise with all urgency what it considers to be its rightful duty, to protect the population by all possible means in this present crisis, when something with all the appearance of an epidemic of blindness has broken out, provisionally known as the white sickness, and we are relying on the public spirit and cooperation of all citizens to stem any further contagion, assuming that we are dealing with a contagious disease and that we are not simply witnessing a series of as yet inexplicable coincidences. The decision to gather together in one place all those infected, and, in adjacent but separate quarters all those who have had any kind of contact with them, was not taken without careful consideration. The Government is fully aware of its responsibilities and hopes that those to whom this message is directed will, as the upright citizens they doubtless are, also assume their responsibilities, bearing in mind that the isolation in which they now find themselves will represent, above any personal considerations, an act of solidarity with the rest of the nation's community. That said, we ask everyone to listen attentively to the following instructions, first, the lights will be kept on at all times, any attempt to tamper with the switches will be useless, they

don't work, second, leaving the building without authorisation
will mean instant death, third, in each ward there is a telephone
that can be used only to requisition from outside fresh supplies
for purposes of hygiene and cleanliness, fourth, the internees
will be responsible for washing their own clothes by hand, fifth,
it is recommended that ward representatives should be elected,
this is a recommendation rather than an order, the internees
must organise themselves as they see fit, provided they comply
with the aforesaid rules and those we are about to announce,
sixth, three times daily containers with food will be deposited
at the main door, on the right and on the left, destined respectively for the patients and those suspected of being contaminated, seventh, all the leftovers must be burnt, and this includes not only any food, but also the containers, plates and
cutlery which are all made of combustible material, eighth, the
burning should be done in the inner courtyards of the building or in the exercise yard, ninth, the internees are responsible
for any damage caused by these fires, tenth, in the event of a
fire getting out of control, whether accidentally or on purpose,
the firemen will not intervene, eleventh, equally, the internees
cannot count on any outside intervention should there be any
outbreaks of illnesses, nor in the event of any disorder or aggression, twelfth, in the case of death, whatever the cause, the
internees will bury the corpse in the yard without any formalities, thirteenth, contact between the wing of the patients and
that of the people suspected of being contagious must be made
in the central hall of the building by which they entered, fourteenth, should those suspected of being infected suddenly go
blind, they will be transferred immediately to the other wing,
fifteenth, this communication will be relayed daily at the same
time for the benefit of all new arrivals. The Government, but
at that very moment the lights went out and the loudspeaker
fell silent. Unconcerned, a blind man tied a knot in the piece of

string he was holding in his hands, then he tried to count them, the knots, the days, but he gave up, there were knots overlapping, blind knots in a manner of speaking. The doctor's wife said to her husband, The lights have gone out, Some lamp that had fused, and little wonder when they have been switched on for all this time, They've all gone out, the problem must have been outside, Now you're as blind as the rest of us, I'll wait until the sun comes up. She went out of the ward, crossed the hallway, looked outside. This part of the city was in darkness, the army's searchlight was not working, it must have been connected to the general network, and now, to all appearances, the power was off.

The following day, some earlier, others later, because the sun does not rise at the same time for all those who are blind, it often depends on the keenness of hearing of each of them, men and women from the various wards began gathering on the outer steps of the building with the exception, needless to say, of the ward occupied by the hoodlums, who at this hour must be having their breakfast. They were waiting for the thud of the gate being opened, the loud screeching of hinges that needed to be greased, the sounds that announced the arrival of their food, then the voice of the sergeant on duty, Don't move from where you are, let no one approach, the dragging of soldiers' feet, the dull sound of the containers being dumped on the ground, the hasty retreat, once more the creaking of the gate, and finally the authorisation, Now you can come out. They waited until it was almost midday and midday became the afternoon. No one, not even the doctor's wife, wanted to ask about the food. So long as they did not ask the question they would not hear the dreaded no, and so long as it was not spoken they would go on hoping to hear words like these, It's coming, it's coming, be patient, put up with your hunger for just a little longer. Some, however much they wanted, could not stand it any longer, they

fainted there and then as if they had suddenly fallen asleep, fortunately the doctor's wife was there to come to the rescue, it
was incredible how this woman managed to notice everything
that was happening, she must be endowed with a sixth sense,
some sort of a vision without eyes, thanks to which those miserable wretches did not remain there to broil in the sun, they
were carried indoors at once, and with time, water and gentle
slaps on the face, all of them eventually came round. But there
was no point in counting on the latter for the war, they would
not even be able to grab a she-cat by the tail, an old-fashioned
expression which never explained for what extraordinary reason a she-cat should be easier to deal with than a tom-cat. Finally the old man with the black eyepatch said, The food hasn't
come, the food won't come, let's go and get our food. They got
up, God knows how, and went to assemble in the ward furthest
away from the stronghold of the hoodlums, rather than have
any repetition of the imprudence of the other day. From there
they sent spies to the other wing, blind inmates who lived there
and were more familiar with the surroundings, At the first suspicious movement, come and warn us. The doctor's wife went
with them and came back with some disheartening information, They have barricaded the entrance with four beds stacked
one on top of the other, How did you know there were four,
someone asked, That wasn't difficult, I felt them, Did no one
realise you were there, I don't think so, What are we going to
do, Let's go, the old man with the black eyepatch suggested
once more, let's stick to what was decided, it's either that or
we're condemned to a slow death. Some will die sooner if we
go there, said the first blind man, Anyone who is going to die
is already dead and does not know it, That we're going to die
is something we know from the moment we are born, That's
why, in some ways, it's as if we were born dead, That's enough
of your foolish talk, said the girl with the dark glasses, I can-

not go there alone, but if we are now going to go back on what was agreed, then I'm simply going to lie on my bed and allow myself to die, Only those whose days are numbered will die, no one else, said the doctor, and raising his voice, he asked, Those who are determined to go, raise their hand, this is what happens to those who do not think twice before opening their mouth to speak, what was the point in asking them to raise their hands if there was no one there to count them, or so it was generally believed, and then say, Thirteen, in which case a new discussion would almost certainly start up to establish what, in the light of logic, would be more correct, whether to ask for another volunteer to avoid that unlucky number, or to avoid it by default, drawing lots to decide who should drop out. Some had raised their hand with little conviction, with a gesture that betrayed hesitation and doubt, whether because aware of the danger to which they were about to expose themselves, or because they realised the absurdity of the order. The doctor laughed, How ridiculous, to ask you to put up your hands, let's proceed in another manner, let those who cannot or do not wish to go withdraw, the rest stay behind to agree upon the action to be taken. There were stirrings, footsteps, murmurs, sighs, little by little, the weak and nervous dropped out, the doctor's idea had been as excellent as it was generous, in this way it will be less easy to know who had remained and who was no longer there. The doctor's wife counted those who had remained, they were seventeen, counting herself and her husband. From the first ward on the right-hand side, there was the old man with the black eyepatch, the pharmacist's assistant, the girl with dark glasses, and all the volunteers from the other wards were men with the exception of that woman who had said, Wherever you go, I shall go, she is here too. They lined up along the passageway, the doctor counted them, Seventeen, we're seventeen, That's not very many, remarked the pharmacist's assistant, we'll never manage. The front line of attack, if I may use a rather military term, will have to be a narrow one, said the old man with the black eyepatch, we have to be able to fit through a door, I'm convinced it would only complicate matters if there were more of us, They'd shoot the lot of us, agreed another, and everyone seemed pleased that in the end they were few.

Their arms we are already familiar with, bars taken from the beds, which might serve just as well as a crowbar or a lance, according to whether the sappers or assault troops were going into battle. The old man with the black eyepatch, who had clearly learned something about tactics in his youth, suggested that everyone should stay together, facing in the same direction, since this was the only way to avoid attacking each other, and that they should advance in absolute silence, so that the attack might benefit from the element of surprise, Let's take off our shoes, he suggested. Then it's going to be difficult for each of us to find our own shoes, someone said, and another commented, Any shoes left over will truly be dead men's shoes, with the difference that in this case, at least, there will always be someone to step into them, What is all this talk about dead men's shoes, It's a saying, to wait for dead men's shoes means to wait for nothing at all, Why, Because the shoes the dead were buried in were made of cardboard, they served their purpose, souls have no feet, as far as we know, And there's another point, interrupted the old man with the black eyepatch, when we get there, six of us, the six who are feeling bravest, will shove the beds inside as hard as they can, so that all of us may enter, In that case, we'll have to lay down our arms, I don't think that will be necessary, they might even help, if used upright. He paused, then said, with a sombre note in his voice, Above all, we must not split up, if we do we're as good as dead, And what about the women, said the girl with dark glasses, don't forget the women, Are you going as well, asked the old man with the black eyepatch, I'd rather you didn't, And why not, I'd like to know, You're very young, In this place, age is of no account, nor sex, therefore don't forget the women, No, I won't forget, the voice in which the old man with the black eyepatch spoke these words appeared to come from another dialogue, those that follow were already in their place, On the contrary, if only one of you women could see what we cannot see, take us along the right path, with the tip of our metal bars at the throats of these ruffians, as accurately as that other woman did, That would be asking too much, we can't easily repeat what we've done once already, besides, who's to say that she didn't die there and then, there has been no news of her, the doctor's wife reminded them, Women are born again in one another, the respectable are reborn as whores, whores are reborn as respectable women, said the girl with dark glasses. This was followed by a long silence, for the women everything had been said, the men would have to find the words, and they knew already that they would be incapable of doing so.

They filed out, the six braver ones in front as had been agreed, amongst them was the doctor and the pharmacist's assistant, then came the others, each armed with a metal rod from his bed, a brigade of squalid, ragged lancers, as they crossed the hallway one of them dropped his weapon, which made a deafening sound on the tiled floor like a blast of gunfire, if the hoodlums were to hear the noise and get wind of what we're up to, then we're lost. Without telling anyone, not even her husband, the doctor's wife ran ahead, looked along the corridor, then very slowly, keeping close to the wall, she gradually drew nearer to the entrance of the ward, there she listened attentively, the voices within did not sound alarmed. She brought back this information without delay and the advance recommenced. Apart from the slowness and the silence with which the army moved, the occupants of the two wards that were lo-

cated before the stronghold of the hoodlums, aware of what
was about to happen, gathered at the doors so as not to miss
the imminent clamour of battle, and some of those more on
edge, excited by the smell of gunpowder about to be lit, decided at the last minute to accompany the group, a few went
back to arm themselves, they were no longer seventeen, they
had at least doubled in number, the reinforcements would certainly displease the old man with the black eyepatch, but he
was never to know that he was commanding two regiments instead of one. Through the few windows that looked onto the
inner courtyard entered the last glimmer of light, grey, mori-
bund, as it rapidly faded, already slipping away into the deep
black well of the night ahead. Apart from the inconsolable sadness caused by the blindness from which they inexplicably continued to suffer, the blind internees, this at least was in their
favour, were spared any fits of depression produced by these
and other similar atmospheric changes, proven to be the cause
of innumerable acts of despair in the remote past when people
had eyes to see. When they reached the door of that cursed
ward, it was already so dark that the doctor's wife failed to notice that there were not four but eight beds forming a barrier,
doubled in number in the meantime like the assailants, however with more serious immediate consequences for the latter, as will soon be confirmed. The voice of the old man with
the black eyepatch let out a cry, it was the order, he did not remember the usual expression, Charge, or perhaps he did, but it
would have struck him as ridiculous to treat with such military
consideration, a barrier of filthy beds, full of fleas and bugs,
their mattresses rotted from sweat and urine, the blankets like
rags, no longer grey, but all the colours that disgust might wear,
this the doctor's wife already knew, not that she could see it
now, since she had not even noticed the reinforced barricade.
The blind inmates advanced like archangels surrounded by

their own splendour, they thudded into the obstacle with their
weapons upright as they had been instructed, but the beds did
not move, no doubt the strength of this brave vanguard was
not much greater than that of the weaklings who came behind
and by now could scarcely hold their lances, like someone who
carried a cross on his back and now has to wait to be raised up
on it. The silence had disappeared, those outside were shouting, those inside started shouting, probably no one has noticed
to this day how absolutely terrible are the cries of the blind,
they appear to be shouting for no good reason, we want to tell
them to be quiet and then end up shouting ourselves, all that's
wanting is for us to be blind too, but that day will come. This
then was the situation, some shouting as they attacked, others
shouting as they defended themselves, while those on the outside, desperate at not having been able to move the beds, flung
down their weapons willy-nilly and, all of them at once, at least
those who managed to squeeze into the space in the doorway,
and those who couldn't fit in pressed behind those in front, they
started pushing and pushing and it looked as if they might succeed, the beds had even moved a little, when suddenly, without
prior warning or threat, three shots rang out, it was the blind
accountant aiming low. Two of the assailants fell, wounded, the
others quickly retreated in disarray, they tripped on the metal
rods and fell, as if demented the walls of the corridor multiplied
their shouts, shouting was coming from the other wards too. It
was now almost pitch-black, it was impossible to know who
had been hit by the bullets, obviously one could ask from afar,
Who are you, but it did not seem appropriate, the wounded
must be treated with respect and consideration, we must approach them gently, place our hand on their forehead, unless
that is where the bullet unfortunately happened to strike, then
we must ask them in a low voice how they are feeling, assure
them it is not serious, the stretcher-bearers are already on the

way, and finally give them some water, but only if they are not
wounded in the stomach, as is expressly recommended in the
first-aid handbook. What shall we do now, asked the doctor's
wife, there are two casualties lying there on the ground. No
one asked her how she knew there were two of them, after all,
there had been three shots, without reckoning with the effect
of the ricochets, if there had been any. We must go and look
for them, said the doctor, The risk is great, observed the old
man with the black eyepatch despondently, who had seen that
his assault tactics had resulted in disaster, if they suspect there
are people here they'll start firing again, he paused and added
sighing, But we must go there, speaking for myself, I'm ready,
I'm going too, said the doctor's wife, there will be less danger
if we crawl, the important thing is to find them quickly, before
those inside there have time to react, I'm going too, said the
woman who had declared the other day, Wherever you go, I
go, of the many that were there no one thought to say that it
was very easy to check who was wounded, correction, wounded
or dead, for the moment no one yet knows, it was enough that
they should all start saying, I'm going, I'm not going, those
who remained silent were the latter.

And so the four volunteers began crawling, the two women
in the middle, a man on either side as it happened, they were
not acting out of male courtesy or some gentlemanly instinct
so that the women should be protected, the truth is that everything will depend on the angle of the shot, if the blind accountant should fire again. After all, perhaps nothing will happen,
the old man with the black eyepatch had come up with an idea
before they went, possibly better than the earlier ones, that
these companions here should start to talk at the top of their
voices, even to shout, besides they had every reason to do so,
so that they might drown the inevitable noise of their comings and goings, and also whatever might happen in the mean-

time, God knows what. In a few minutes, the rescuers reached their destination, they knew it before even coming into contact with the bodies, the blood over which they were crawling was like a messenger come to tell them, I was life, behind me there is nothing, My God, thought the doctor's wife, all this blood, and it was true, a thick pool, their hands and clothing stuck to the ground as if the floorboards and floor tiles were covered in glue. The doctor's wife raised herself on her elbows and continued to advance, the others had done the same. Stretching out their arms, they finally reached the corpses. Their companions back there continued to make as much noise as they could, and now sounded like professional mourners in a trance. The hands of the doctor's wife and of the old man with the black eyepatch grabbed the ankles of one of the casualties, in their turn the doctor and the other woman had grabbed an arm and leg of the other wounded man, now they were trying to drag them away out of the firing line. It was not easy, to achieve this they had to raise themselves up a little, to go on all fours, it was the only way of putting to good use the little strength they still possessed. The shot rang out, but this time did not hit anyone. The overwhelming terror did not make them flee, on the contrary, it helped them to summon that last ounce of energy that was needed. An instant later they were already out of danger, they got as close as they could to the wall on the side where the ward door was situated, only a stray bullet could possibly reach them, but it was doubtful that the blind accountant was skilled in ballistics, even elementary ones such as these. They tried to lift the bodies but gave up. Because of their weight they could only drag them, and with them, half congealed, trailed the blood already spilled as if spread by a roller, and the remaining blood, still fresh, that continued to flow from the wounds. Who are they, asked those who were waiting, How are we to know if we cannot see, said the old man with the black eyepatch, We can't stay here, said someone, if they decide to launch an attack we'll have more than two casualties, remarked another, Or corpses, said the doctor, at least I cannot feel their pulse. Like an army in retreat, they carried the corpses along the corridor, on reaching the hallway they came to a halt, and one would have said they had decided to camp there, but the truth of the matter was different, what had happened was that they were drained of all energy, I'm staying right here, I can't go any further. It is time to acknowledge that it must seem surprising that the blind hoodlums, previously so overbearing and aggressive, revelling in their own easy cruelty, now only defend themselves, raise barricades and fire from inside there at will, as if they were afraid to go out and fight in open territory, face to face, eye to eye. Like everything else in this life, this too, has its explanation, which is that after the tragic death of their first leader, all spirit of discipline or sense of obedience had gone in the ward, the serious error on the part of the blind accountant was to have thought that it was enough to take possession of the gun in order to usurp power, but the result was exactly the opposite, each time he fires, the shot backfires, in other words, with each shot fired, he loses a little more authority, so let's see what happens when he runs out of ammunition. Just as the habit does not make the monk, the sceptre does not make the king, this is a fact we should never forget, and if it is true that the royal sceptre is now held by the blind accountant, one is tempted to say that the king, although dead, although buried in his own ward, and badly, barely three feet under the ground, continues to be remembered, at least he makes his powerful presence felt by the stench. Meanwhile, the moon appeared. Through the door of the hallway that looks out onto the outer yard enters a diffused light that gradually becomes brighter, the bodies that are on the ground, two of them dead, the others still alive, slowly begin gaining volume, shape, characteristics, features, all the weight of a horror without a name, then the doctor's wife understood that there was no sense, if there ever had been any, in going on pretending to be blind, it is clear that here no one can be saved, blindness is also this, to live in a world where all hope is gone. She could tell in the meantime who was dead, this is the pharmacist's assistant, this is the fellow who said the blind hoodlums would shoot at random, they were both right after a fashion, and don't bother asking me how I know who they are, the answer is simple, I can see. Some of those who were present already knew as much and had remained silent, others had been suspicious for some time and now saw their suspicions confirmed, the surprise of the others was unexpected, and yet, on reflection, perhaps we should not be surprised, at another time the revelation would have caused much consternation, uncontrolled excitement, how fortunate for you, how did you manage to escape this universal disaster, what is the name of the drops you put in your eyes, give me your doctor's address, help me to get out of this prison, by now it came to the same thing, in death, blindness is the same for all. What they could not do was to remain there, defenceless, even the metal bars from their beds had been left behind, their fists would serve for nothing. Guided by the doctor's wife, they dragged the corpses out onto the forecourt, and there they left them in the moonlight, under the planet's milky whiteness, white on the outside, black at last on the inside. Let's return to the wards, said the old man with the black eyepatch, we'll see later on what can be organised. This is what he said, and they were mad words that no one heeded. They did not divide up according to where they had come from, they met up and recognised each other on the way, some heading for the wing on the left, others for the wing on the right, the doctor's wife had been accompanied this far by that woman who had said, Wherever you go, I go, this was not the idea she now carried in her

head, quite the contrary, but she did not want to discuss it, vows
are not always fulfilled, sometimes out of weakness, at other
times because of some superior force with which we had not
reckoned.

An hour passed, the moon came up, hunger and terror hold
sleep at bay, in the wards everyone is awake. But these are not
the only reasons. Whether because of the excitement of the
recent battle, even though so disastrously lost, or because of
something indefinable in the air, the blind internees are restless. No one dares go out into the corridors, but the interior of
each ward is like a beehive inhabited by drones, buzzing insects,
as everyone knows, little given to order and method, there is
no evidence that they have ever done anything in their lives or
preoccupied themselves in the slightest with the future, even
though in the case of the blind, unhappy creatures, it would
be unjust to accuse them of being exploiters and parasites, exploiters of what crumb, parasites of what refreshment, one has
to be careful with comparisons, in case they should turn out to
be frivolous. However, there is no rule without an exception,
and this was not lacking here, in the person of a woman who
entered the ward, the second one on the right-hand side, and at
once began rummaging through her rags until she found a tiny
object which she pressed in the palm of her hand, as if anxious
to conceal it from the prying eyes of others, old habits die hard,
even when that moment comes when we thought they were
lost forever. Here, where it ought to have been one for all and
all for one, we witnessed how the strong cruelly took the bread
from the mouths of the weak, and now this woman, remembering that she had brought a cigarette lighter in her hand-
luggage, unless she had lost it in all the upheaval, searched for
it anxiously and is now furtively hiding it, as if her survival depended on it, she does not think that perhaps one of these companions in misfortune might have one last cigarette on them,

and cannot smoke it because they do not have that tiny essential flame. Nor would there be time now to ask for a light. The woman has gone out without saying a word, no farewell, no goodbye, she makes her way along the deserted corridor, passes right by the door of the first ward, no one inside there noticed her pass, she crosses the hallway, the descending moon traced and painted a vat of milk on the floor tiles, now the woman is in the other wing, once more a corridor, her destination lies at the far end, in a straight line, she cannot go wrong. Besides, she can hear voices summoning her, figuratively speaking, what she can hear is the rumpus being made by the hoodlums in the last ward, they are celebrating their victory, eating and drinking to their heart's content, ignore the deliberate exaggeration, let us not forget that everything is relative in life, they eat and drink simply what is to hand, and long may it last, how the others would love to partake of the feast, but they cannot, between them and the plate there is a barricade of eight beds and a loaded gun. The woman is on her knees at the entrance to the ward, right up against the beds, she slowly pulls the covers off, then gets to her feet, she does the same with the bed on top, then with the third one, her arm cannot reach the fourth, no matter, the fuses are ready, now it is only a question of setting them alight. She can still remember how to regulate the lighter in order to produce a long flame, she got it, a tiny dagger of light, as bright as the sharp point of a pair of scissors. She starts with the bed on top, the flame laboriously licks the filthy bedclothes, then it finally catches fire, now the bed in the middle, now the bed below, the woman caught the smell of her own singed hair, she must be careful, she is the one who has to set the pyre alight, not the one who must die, she can hear the cries of the hoodlums within, at that moment it suddenly occurred to her, Suppose they have water and manage to put out the flames, in desperation she got under the first bed, ran

the lighter along the mattress, here, there, then suddenly the
flames multiplied, transformed themselves into one great curtain of fire, a spurt of water passed through them, splashed
onto the woman, but in vain, her own body was already feeding
the bonfire. What is it like in there, no one can risk entering,
but our imagination must serve for something, the fire quickly
spreads from bed to bed, as if wanting to set all of them alight at
the same time, and it succeeds, the hoodlums wasted indiscrim-
inately and to no avail the little water they still had, now they
are trying to reach the windows, unsteadily they climb onto
the headrests of the beds which the fire has still not reached,
but suddenly the fire is there, they slip, fall, with the intensity
of the heat the window-panes begin to crack, to shatter, the
fresh air comes whistling in and fans the flames, ah, yes, they
are not forgotten, the cries of rage and fear, the howls of pain
and agony, there they have been mentioned, note, in any case,
that they will gradually die away, the woman with the cigarette
lighter, for example, has been silent for some time.

By this time the other blind inmates are fleeing in terror towards the smoke-filled corridors, Fire, fire, they are shouting,
and here we may observe in the flesh how badly planned and
organised these human communities in orphanages, hospitals
and mental asylums have been, note how each bed, in itself,
with its framework of pointed metal bars, can be transformed
into a lethal trap, look at the terrible consequences of having
only one door to wards occupied by forty people, not counting
those asleep on the floor, if the fire gets there first and blocks
their exit, no one will escape. Fortunately, as human history
has shown, it is not unusual for good to come of evil, less is said
about the evil that can come out of good, such are the contra-
dictions of this world of ours, some warrant more consideration
than others, in this instance the good was precisely the fact that
the wards have only one door, thanks to this factor, the fire that

burnt the hoodlums tarried there for quite a while, if the confusion does not get any worse, perhaps we will not have to lament the loss of other lives. Obviously, many of these blind inmates are being trampled underfoot, pushed, jostled, this is the
effect of panic, a natural effect, you could say that animal nature is like this, plant life would behave in exactly the same way,
too, if it did not have all those roots to hold it in the ground,
and how nice it would be to see the trees of the forest fleeing
the flames. The protection afforded by the inner part of the
yard was fully exploited by the blind inmates who had the idea
of opening the existing windows in the corridors looking onto
it. They jumped, stumbled, fell, they weep and cry out, but for
now they are safe, let us hope that once the fire causes the roof
to cave in and launches a whirlwind of flames and burning embers into the sky and the wind, it will forget to spread to the
treetops. In the other wing the panic is much the same, a blind
man only has to smell smoke to imagine at once that the flames
are right by him, which does not happen to be true, soon the
corridor was crammed with people, unless someone imposes
some order here, the situation will be disastrous. At a certain
point, someone remembers that the doctor's wife still has her
eyesight, where is she, people ask, she can tell us what is happening, where we should go, where is she, I'm here, I've only
just managed to get out of the ward, the boy with the squint
was to blame because no one knew where he had got to, now
he's here with me and I'm holding him firmly by the hand, they
would have to pull off my arm before I'd let go of him, with my
other hand I'm holding my husband's hand, and then comes
the girl with dark glasses, and then the old man with the black
eyepatch, where there is the one there is the other, and then the
first blind man, and then his wife, all together, as compressed
as a pinecone, which, I very much hope, will not open even in
this heat. Meanwhile, a number of blind inmates from here had

followed the example of those in the other wing, they jumped into the inner yard, they cannot see that the greater part of the building on the other side is already one great bonfire, but they can feel on their faces and hands the blast of heat coming from there, for the moment the roof is still holding up, the leaves on the trees are slowly curling. Then someone shouted, What are we doing here, why don't we get out, the reply, coming from amidst this sea of heads, needed only four words, The soldiers are there, but the old man with the black eyepatch said, Better to be shot than burnt to death, it sounded like the voice of experience, therefore perhaps he was not really the person speaking, perhaps through his mouth the woman with the cigarette lighter had spoken, she who had not had the good fortune to be struck by the last bullet fired by the blind accountant. Then the doctor's wife said, Let me pass, I'll speak to the soldiers, they cannot leave us to die like this, soldiers too have feelings. Thanks to the hope that the soldiers might indeed have feelings, a narrow gap opened up, through which the doctor's wife advanced with considerable effort, taking her group with her. The smoke clouded her vision, soon she would be as blind as the others. It was almost impossible to enter the hallway. The doors opening onto the yard had been broken down, the blind inmates who had taken refuge there quickly realised the place was unsafe, they wanted to get out, pushed with all their might, but those on the other side resisted, held out as best they could, for the moment their greater fear was that the soldiers might suddenly appear, but as their strength gave out and the fire spread nearer, the old man with the black eyepatch was proved to be right, it would be preferable to die by a bullet. There was not long to wait, the doctor's wife had finally managed to get out onto the porch, she was practically half naked and with both her hands occupied she could scarcely fight off those who wanted to join her small group as it advanced, to

catch, in a manner of speaking, the moving train, the soldiers
would be goggle-eyed when they saw her appear before them
with her breasts half exposed. It was no longer the moonlight
that was illuminating the wide empty space that extended as far
as the gate, but the harsh glare of the blaze. The doctor's wife
shouted, Please, for your own peace of mind, let us out, do not
shoot. No reply came from over there. The searchlight was
still extinguished, nothing could be seen to move. Nervously,
the doctor's wife went down two steps, What's going on, asked
her husband, but she did not reply, could not believe her eyes.
She descended the remaining steps, walked in the direction of
the gate, still dragging behind her the boy with the squint, her
husband and company, there was no doubt about it, the soldiers
had gone, or been taken away, they too stricken by blindness,
everyone finally blind.

Then, to simplify matters, everything happened at once, the
doctor's wife announced in a loud voice that they were free, the
roof of the right wing collapsed with a terrifying crash, sending
out flames on all sides, the blind inmates rushed into the yard,
shouting at the top of their voices, some did not make it, they
remained inside, crushed against the walls, others were trampled underfoot and transformed into a formless, bloody mass,
the fire that has suddenly spread will soon reduce all of this to
ashes. The gate is wide open, the madmen escape.

S AY to a blind man, you're free, open the door that was separating him from the world, Go, you are free, we tell him once more, and he does not go, he has remained motionless there in the middle of the road, he and the others, they are terrified, they do not know where to go, the fact is that there is no comparison between living in a rational labyrinth, which is, by definition, a mental asylum and venturing forth, without a guiding hand or a dog leash, into the demented labyrinth of the city, where memory will serve no purpose, for it will merely be able to recall the images of places but not the paths whereby we might get there. Standing in front of the building which is already ablaze from end to end, the blind inmates can feel the living waves of heat from the fire on their faces, they receive them as something which in a way protects them, just as the walls did before, prison and refuge at once. They stay together, pressed up against each other, like a flock, no one there wants to be the lost sheep, for they know that no shepherd will come looking for them. The fire gradually begins to die down, the moon casts its light once more, the blind inmates begin to feel uneasy, they cannot remain there, For all eternity, as one of them said. Someone asked if it was day or night, the reason for this incongruous curiosity soon became apparent, Who knows, they might bring us some food, perhaps there has been some confusion, some delay, it has happened before, But the soldiers are no longer here. That doesn't mean a thing, they might have gone away because they're no longer needed, I don't understand, For example, because there is no longer any danger of infection, Or because a cure has been found for our illness, That would be good, it really would, What are we going to do, I'm staying here until daybreak, And how will you know it is daybreak, By the sun, by the heat of the sun, And what if the sky is overcast, There is only a limited number of hours and then it must be day at some point. Exhausted, many of the blind had sat down on the ground, others, weaker still, simply collapsed into a heap, some had fainted, it is possible that the cool night air will restore consciousness, but we can be certain that when it is time to break camp, some of these unfortunates will not get up, they have resisted until now, they are like that marathon runner who dropped dead three metres from the finish line, when all is said and done, what is clear is that all lives end before their time. Also seated or stretched out on the ground were those blind inmates who are still awaiting the soldiers, or others instead of them, the Red Cross is one hypothesis, they might bring them food and the other basic comforts, for these people disenchantment will come a little later, that is the only difference. And if anyone here believed that a cure had been discovered for our blindness, this does not appear to have made him any more contented.

For other reasons, the doctor's wife thought that it would be better to wait until night was over, as she told her group, The most urgent thing right now is to find some food and in the dark this would not be easy. Have you any idea where we are, her husband asked, More or less, Far from home, Quite a distance. The others also wanted to know how far they were from their homes, they told her their addresses, and the doctor's wife did her best to explain, the boy with the squint cannot remember, and little wonder, he has not asked for his mother for quite some time. If they were to go from house to house, from the one that is closest to the one furthest away, the first house will be that of the girl with dark glasses, the second one that of the old man with the black eyepatch, then that of the doctor's wife, and finally the house of the first blind man. They will undoubtedly follow this itinerary because the girl with dark glasses has already asked that she should be taken to her home as soon as possible, I can't imagine what state my parents will be in, she said, this sincere preoccupation shows how groundless are the preconceived ideas of those who deny the possibility of the existence of deep feelings, including filial ones, in the, alas, abundant cases of irregular conduct, especially in matters of public morality. The night turned cool, there is not much left for the fire to burn, the heat still coming from the embers is not enough to warm the blind inmates, numb with cold, who find themselves farthest away from the asylum gate, as is the case of the doctor's wife and her group. They are seated in a huddle, the three women and the boy in the middle, the three men around them, anyone seeing them there would say that they had been born like that, it is true that they give the impression of being but one body, one breath and one hunger. One after the other, they eventually fell asleep, a light sleep from which they were roused several times because blind inmates, emerging from their own torpor, got up and stumbled drowsily over this human obstacle, one of them actually stayed behind, there was no difference between sleeping there or in some other place. When day dawned, only a few thin columns of smoke rose from the embers, but not even these lasted for long, for it soon began to rain, a fine drizzle, a mere mist, it is true, but nevertheless persistent, to begin with it did not even touch the scorched earth, but transformed itself at once into vapour, but, as it continued to fall, as everybody knows, a soft water eats away hard stone, let someone else make it rhyme. It is not only the eyes of some of these inmates that are blind, their understanding is also clouded, for there can be no other explanation for the tortuous reasoning that led them to conclude that the much desired food would not arrive in this rain. There was no way of convincing them that the premise was wrong and that, therefore, the conclusion, too, had to be wrong, they simply would not be told that it was still too early for breakfast, in despair, they threw themselves to the ground in floods of tears. It won't come, it's raining, it won't come, they repeated, if that lamentable ruin were still fit for even the most primitive habitation, it would go back to being the madhouse it once was.

The blind man who, after tripping, had stayed behind that night, could not get to his feet. Curled up, as if anxious to protect the last of the heat in his belly, he did not stir despite the rain, which had started to get heavier. He's dead, said the doctor's wife, and the rest of us had better get away from here while we still have some strength. They struggled to their feet, tottering and dizzy, holding on to each other, then they got into line, in front the woman with eyes that can see, then those who though they have eyes cannot see, the girl with dark glasses, the old man with the black eyepatch, the boy with the squint, the wife of the first blind man, her husband, and the doctor last of all. The route they have taken leads to the city centre, but this is not the intention of the doctor's wife, what she wants is to find a place as soon as possible where she can leave those following behind in safety and then go in search of food on her own. The streets are deserted, either because it is still early, or because of the rain that is becoming increasingly heavy. There is litter everywhere, some shops have their doors open, but most of them are closed, with no sign of life inside, nor any light. The doctor's wife thought that it would be a good idea to leave her companions in one of these shops, taking care to make a mental note of the name of the street and the number on the door just in case she should lose them on the way back. She paused, said to the girl with dark glasses, Wait for me here, don't move, she went to peer through the glass-panelled door of a pharmacy, thought she could see the shadowy forms of people lying on the ground, she tapped on the glass, one of the shadows stirred, she knocked again, other human forms slowly began moving, one person got up turning his head in the direction where the noise had come from, They are all blind, the doctor's wife thought, but she could not fathom how they came to be here, perhaps they were members of the pharmacist's family, but if this was the case, why were they not in their own home, with greater comfort than a hard floor, unless they were guarding the premises, against whom, and for what purpose, this merchandise being what it is, can cure and kill equally well. She moved away, a little further ahead she looked inside another shop, saw more people lying down, women, men, children, some appeared to be preparing to leave, one of them came right up to the door, put his arm outside and said, It's raining, Is it raining much, was the question from inside, Yes, we'll have to wait until it eases off, the man, it was a man, was two paces from the doctor's wife, he had not noticed her presence, and was therefore startled when he heard her say, Good day, he had lost the habit of saying Good day, not only because the days of the blind, strictly speaking are never likely to be good, but also because no one could be entirely sure whether it was afternoon or night, and if now, in apparent contradiction to what has just been explained, these people are waking up more or less at the same time as morning, that is because some of them only went blind a few days ago and still have not entirely lost their sense of the succession of days and

nights, of sleep and wakefulness. The man said, It's raining, and
then asked, Who are you, I'm not from here, Are you out
searching for food, Yes, we haven't eaten for four days, And
how do you know it is four days, That's what I reckon, Are you
alone, I'm with my husband and some companions, How many
of them are there, Seven altogether, If you're thinking of staying here with us, forget it, there are far too many of us already,
We're only passing through, Where have you come from,
We've been interned ever since this epidemic of blindness began, Ah, yes, the quarantine, it didn't do any good, Why do you
say that, They allowed you to leave, There was a fire and, at
that moment, we realised that the soldiers who were guarding
us had disappeared, And you left, Yes, Your soldiers must have
been amongst the last to go blind, everyone is blind, the whole
city, the entire country, if anyone can still see, they say nothing,
keep it to themselves, Why don't you live in your own house,
Because I no longer know where it is, You don't know where it
is, And what about you, do you know where your house is, Me,
the doctor's wife was about to reply that that was precisely
where she was heading with her husband and companions, all
they needed was a quick bite to eat to recover their strength,
but at that very moment she saw the situation quite clearly,
somebody who was blind and had left their home would only
manage to find it again by some miracle, it was not the same as
before, when blind people could always count on the assistance
of some passerby, whether to cross the street, or to get back
onto the right path in the case of having inadvertently strayed
from the usual route, All I know is that it is far from here, she
said, But you'll never be able to get there, No, Now there you
have it, it's the same with me, it's the same with everyone, those
of you who have been in quarantine have a lot to learn, you
don't know how easy it is to find yourself without a home, I
don't understand, Those who go around in groups as we do, as

most people do, when we have to look for food, we are obliged
to go together, it's the only way of not losing each other, and
since we all go, since no one stays behind to guard the house,
assuming that we ever manage to find it again, the likelihood is
that it will already be occupied by another group also unable to
find their house, we're a kind of merry-go-round, at the outset
there was some conflict, but we soon became aware that we, the
blind, in a manner of speaking, have practically nothing we
may call our own, except for what we are wearing, The solution
would be to live in a shop selling food, at least so long as supplies lasted there would be no need to go out, Anyone who did
that, the least that might happen to them would be never to
have another moment's peace, I say the least, because I've heard
of the case of some who tried, shut themselves away, bolted the
door, but what they could not do was get rid of the smell of
food, those who wanted to eat gathered outside, and since those
inside refused to open the doors, the shop was set alight, it was
a blessed remedy, I didn't see it myself, others told me, in any
case it was a blessed remedy, and as far as I know no one else
dared to do the same, And do people no longer live in houses
and flats, Yes, they do, but it comes to the same thing, countless
people must have passed through my house, who knows if I'll
ever find it again, besides, in this situation, it's much more practical to sleep in the shops at ground level, in warehouses, it
saves us having to go up and down stairs, It's stopped raining,
said the doctor's wife, It's stopped raining, repeated the man to
those inside. On hearing these words, those who were still
stretched out got to their feet, gathered up their belongings,
haversacks, hand-luggage, bags made out of cloth and plastic,
as if they were setting off on an expedition, and it was true, they
were off in pursuit of food, one by one they began emerging
from the shop, the doctor's wife noticed that they were well
wrapped up even if the colours of their clothing scarcely har-

monised, their trousers either so short that they exposed their shins, or so long that the bottoms had to be turned up, but the cold would not get to this lot, some of the men wore a raincoat or an overcoat, two of the women wore long fur coats, not an umbrella to be seen, probably because they are so awkward to carry, and the spokes are always in danger of poking someone's eye out. The group, some fifteen people, moved off. Along the road, other groups appeared, as well as people on their own, up against the walls men were satisfying the urgent need felt each morning by their bladder, the women preferred the privacy of abandoned cars. Softened by the rain, the excrement, here and there, was spread all over the pavement.

The doctor's wife went back to her group, huddled together out of instinct under the awning of a cake shop that gave off a smell of soured cream and other rancid products. Let's go, she said, I've found a refuge, and she led them to the shop the others had just left. The stock in the shop was intact, there was nothing amongst the merchandise that could be eaten or worn, there were fridges, washing machines for both clothes and dishes, ordinary stoves as well as microwave ovens, food mixers, juicers, vacuum cleaners, the thousand and one elec-tro-domestic inventions destined to make life easier. The at-mosphere was charged with unpleasant odours, making the in-variable whiteness of the objects absurd. Rest here, said the doctor's wife, I'm going to look for some food, I have no idea where I'll find it, nearby, far away, I cannot say, wait patiently, there are groups out there, if anyone tries to come in, tell them the place is occupied, that ought to be enough to send them away, that's the custom now, I'm coming with you, said her hus-band, No, it's best I should go alone, we must find out how people are surviving now, from what I've heard everyone must have gone blind, In that case, quipped the old man with the black eyepatch, it's just as if we were still in the mental asylum,

There's no comparison, we can move about freely, and there must be a solution to the food problem, we won't die of hunger, I must also try to get some clothes, we're reduced to rags, she herself was in the greatest need, practically naked from the waist upwards. She kissed her husband, at that moment she felt something akin to a pain in her heart. Please, whatever happens, even if someone should try to come in, do not leave this place, and if you should be turned out, although I don't believe this will happen, but just to warn you of all the possibilities, stay together near the door until I arrive. She looked at them, her eyes filled with tears, there they were, as dependent on her as little children on their mother. If I should let them down—she thought. It did not occur to her that all around her the people were blind yet managed to live, she herself would also have to turn blind in order to understand that people get used to anything, especially if they have ceased to be people, and even if they have not quite reached that point, take the boy with the squint there, for example, who no longer even asks for his mother. She went out to the street, looked and made a mental note of the door number, the name of the shop, now she had to check out the name of the street on that corner, she had no idea where this search for food might take her, or what food, it might be only three doors away or three hundred, she could not afford to get lost, there would be no one from whom to ask the way, those who could see before were blind, and she, who could see, would not know where she was. The sun had broken through, it shone on the pools of water that had formed amidst the litter and it was easier to see the weeds that were sprouting up between the paving stones. There were more people outside. How do they find their way around, the doctor's wife asked herself. They did not find their way around, they kept very close to the buildings with their arms stretched out before them, they were constantly bumping into each other like ants on the trail, but when this happened no one protested, nor did they have to say anything, one of the families moved away from the wall, advanced along the wall opposite in the other direction, and thus they proceeded and carried on until the next encounter. Now and then they stopped, sniffed in the doorways of the shops in the hope of catching the smell of food, whatever it might be, then continued on their way, they turned a corner, disappeared from sight, soon another group turned up, they did not seem to have found what they were looking for. The doctor's wife could move with greater speed, she did not waste any time entering the shops to find out if there were any edible goods, but it soon became clear that it would not be easy to stock up in any quantity, the few grocers' shops she found seemed to have been devoured from inside and were like empty shells.

She had already travelled far from where she had left her husband and companions, crossing and re-crossing streets, avenues, squares, when she found herself in front of a supermarket. Inside it was no different, empty shelves, overturned displays, in the middle wandered the blind, most of them on all fours, sweeping up the filth on the floor with their hands, hoping to find something they might be able to use, a can of preserves that had withstood the pounding of those who had desperately tried to open it, some packet or other, whatever the contents, a potato, even if trampled, a crust of bread, even if as hard as stone. The doctor's wife thought, Despite everything, there must be something, the place is vast. A blind man got to his feet and complained that a bit of glass had got lodged in his knee, the blood was already trickling down one leg. The blind persons in the group gathered round him, What happened, what's the matter, and he told them, A glass splinter in my knee, Which one, The left one, one of the blind women crouched down. Take care, there might be other pieces of glass around, she probed and fumbled to distinguish one leg from the other, Here it is, she said, and it's still pricking in the flesh, one of the blind men started laughing, Well if it's pricking, make the most of it, and the others, both men and women, joined in the laughter. Bringing her thumb and forefinger together, a natural gesture that requires no training, the blind woman removed the piece of glass, then bandaged the knee with a rag she found in the bag over her shoulder, finally she cracked her own little joke to the amusement of all, Nothing to be done, no more pricking, everyone laughed, and the wounded man retorted, Whenever you feel the urge, we can have a go and find out what pricks most, there certainly are no married men and women in this group, since no one appeared to be shocked, they must all be people with lax morals who enter into casual relationships, unless the latter happen to be indeed husband and wife, hence the liberties they take with each other, but they really do not give that impression, and no married couple would say these things in public. The doctor's wife looked around her, whatever was still usable was being disputed amidst punches that nearly always missed and much jostling that made no distinction between friend and foe, and it sometimes happened that the object provoking the struggle escaped from their hands and ended up on the ground, waiting for someone to trip over it, Hell, I'll never get out of here, she thought, using an expression that formed no part of her usual vocabulary, once more showing that the force and nature of circumstances have considerable influence over language, remember that soldier who said shit when ordered to surrender, thereby absolving future expletives from the crime of bad manners in less dangerous situations. Hell, I'll never get out of here, she thought again, and just as she was preparing to leave, another thought came to her like a happy inspiration, In an establishment like this there must be a storeroom, not necessarily a large deposit, for that would be located elsewhere, probably some distance away, but backup supplies of certain products in constant demand. Excited at the idea, she began looking for a closed door that might lead her to the cave of treasures, but they were all open, and there inside, she found the same devastation, the same blind people rummaging through the same litter. Finally, in a dark corridor, where the light of day scarcely penetrated, she saw what looked like a cargo lift. The metal doors were closed and at the side there was another door, smooth, of the kind that slide on a track, The basement, she thought, the blind people who got this far found their path impeded, they must have realised there was an elevator, but it didn't occur to anyone that it was also normal for there to be a staircase in the event of there being a power cut, for example, as was now the case. She pushed the sliding door and received, almost simultaneously, two overwhelming impressions, first, that of the total darkness she would have to penetrate in order to reach the basement, and then the unmistakable smell of food, even when stored in jars and containers we call sealed, the fact is that hunger has always had a keen sense of smell, the kind that penetrates through all barriers, just as dogs do. She quickly turned back to rescue from the litter the plastic bags she would need to transport the food, at the same time asking herself, Without light, how am I to know what to take, she shrugged her shoulders, what a stupid thing to worry about, her concern now, given the state of weakness in which she found herself, ought to be whether she would have the strength to carry the bags once they were full, retrace her steps back from where she had come, at that moment, she was gripped by the most awful fear, that of not being able to return to the spot where her husband was waiting for her, she knew the name of the street, this she had not forgotten, but she had taken so many turnings, despair paralysed her, then slowly, as if her arrested brain had finally started to move, she saw herself bent over a map of the city, searching with the tip of her finger for the shortest route, as if she had two sets of eyes, one set watching her consult the map, another perusing the map and working out the route. The corridor remained deserted, a stroke of luck, given her nervous state because of the discovery she had made, she had forgotten to close the door. She now closed it carefully behind her only to find herself plunged into total darkness, as sightless as those blind people out there, the only difference was in the colour, if black and white can, strictly speaking, be thought of as colours. Keeping close to the wall, she began to descend the stairs, if this place should turn out not to be a secret, after all, and someone were to rise from the depths, they would have to proceed as she had seen on the street, one of them would have to abandon the safety of having somewhere to lean against, brushing against the vague presence of the other, perhaps for an instant foolishly fearing that the wall did not continue on the other side, I'm going mad, she thought, and with good reason, making this descent into a dark pit, without light or any hope of seeing any, how far would it be, these underground stores are usually never very deep, first flight of steps, Now I know what it means to be blind, second flight of steps, I'm going to scream, I'm going to scream, third set of steps, the darkness is like a thick paste that sticks to her face, her eyes transformed into balls of pitch, What is this before me, and then another thought, even more terrifying, And how shall I find the stairs again, a sudden unsteadiness obliged her to crouch down in order to avoid simply falling over, almost fainting, she stammered, It's clean, she was referring to the floor, it seemed remarkable to her, a clean floor. Little by little she recovered her senses, she felt dull pains in her stomach, not that this was anything new, but at this moment it was as if there were no other living organ in her body, there had to be others, but they gave no sign of be-

ing there, her heart, yes, her heart was pounding like a great
drum, forever working blindly in the dark, from the first of all
darknesses, the womb in which it was formed, to the last where
it would cease. She was still clutching the plastic bags, she had
not let go of them, now all she had to do was to fill them, calmly,
a storeroom is not a place for ghosts and dragons, here there is
nothing but darkness, and darkness neither bites nor offends,
as for the stairway I'm bound to find it, even if it means walking all the way round this awful place. Her mind made up, she
was about to get to her feet, but then remembered she was as
blind as all the others, better to do as they did, to advance on all
fours until she came across something, shelves laden with food,
whatever it might be, so long as it can be eaten as it is, without
having to be cooked or specially prepared, since there is no
time for fancy cooking.

Her fear crept surreptitiously back, she had scarcely gone a
few metres, perhaps she was mistaken, perhaps right there before her, invisible, a dragon was waiting for her with its mouth
open. Or a ghost with outstretched hand, to carry her off to
the dreadful world of the dead who never cease to die, because someone always comes to resuscitate them. Then, pro-
saically, with an infinite, resigned sadness, it occurred to her
that the place where she found herself was not a store for food,
but a garage, she actually thought she could smell the gaso-
line, the mind suffers delusions when it succumbs to the monsters it has itself created. Then her hand touched something,
not the ghost's viscous fingers, not the fiery tongue and fangs
of the dragon, what she felt was the contact of cold metal, a
smooth vertical surface, she guessed, without knowing what it
was called, that this was the upright of a set of shelves, She
calculated there must be others just like this, standing parallel
to this one, as was the custom, it was now a question of finding out where the food products were, not here, for this smell

is unmistakable, it is the smell of detergent. Without giving another thought to the difficulties she would have in finding the stairs, she began investigating the shelves, groping, sniffing, shaking. There were cardboard containers, glass and plastic bottles, jars of all sizes, tins that were probably preserves, various cartons, packets, bags, tubes. She filled one of the bags at random, Could all this be for eating, she thought to herself with some disquiet. The doctor's wife passed on to the next set of shelves, and the unexpected happened, her blind hand that could not see where it was going, came up against and knocked over some tiny boxes. The noise they made on hitting the floor almost made her heart stop beating, Matches, she thought. Trembling with excitement, she stooped down, ran her hand over the ground, found what she was looking for, this is a smell one never confuses with any other, and the noise of the little matchsticks when we shake the box, the sliding of the lid, the roughness of the sandpaper on the outside, which is where the phosphorus is, the scraping of the match head, finally the sparking of the tiny flame, the surrounding space a diffuse sphere as luminous as a star glimmering through the mist, dear God, light exists and I have eyes to see, praised be light. From now on, the harvest would be easy. She began with the boxes of matches, and almost filled a bag. No need to take all of them, the voice of common sense told her, then the flickering flames of the matches lit up the shelves, over here, then over there, soon the bags were full, the first had to be emptied because it contained nothing useful, the others already held enough riches to buy the city, nor need we be surprised at this difference of values, we need only recall that there was once a king who wanted to exchange his kingdom for a horse, what would he not give were he dying of hunger and was tempted by these plastic bags full of food. The stairway is there, the way out to the right. But first, the doctor's wife sits on the ground,

opens a packet of chorizo sausage, another with slices of black
bread, a bottle of water, and, without remorse, starts eating. If
she were not to eat now she would not have the strength to
carry the provisions where they were needed, she being the
provider. When she had finished, she slipped the bags over her
arms, three on each side, and with her hands raised before her,
she went on striking matches until she reached the stairs, then
she climbed them with some effort, she still had not digested
her food, which needs time to pass from the stomach to the
muscles and nerves, and, in her case, to what had shown the
greatest resistance, her head. The door slid noiselessly open,
And what if there is someone in the corridor, thought the doctor's wife, what shall I do. There was no one, but she started
asking herself again, What shall I do. When she reached the
exit, she could turn round and shout inside, There is food at the
end of the corridor, stairs lead to the store in the cellar, make
the most of it, I have left the door open. She could have done
it, but decided not to. Using her shoulder, she closed the door,
she told herself that it was better to say nothing, just imagine what would happen, the blind inmates running all over the
place like madmen, a repetition of what happened in the mental asylum when fire broke out, they would roll down the stairs,
be trampled and crushed by those coming behind, who would
also stumble and fall, it is not the same thing to put one's foot
on a firm step as to put it on a slippery body. And when the
food is finished, I shall be able to come back for more, she
thought. She now gripped the bags with her hands, took a deep
breath, and proceeded along the corridor. They would not be
able to see her, but there was the smell of what she had eaten,
The sausage, what a fool I was, it would be like a living trail.
She gritted her teeth, clutched the bags with all her strength,
I must run, she said. She remembered the blind man whose
knee had been cut by a splinter of glass, If the same thing hap-

pens to me, if I don't look out and step on broken glass, we may have forgotten that this woman is wearing no shoes, she still has not had time to go to a shoeshop like blind people in the city, who despite being unfortunates without sight, can at least choose footwear by touch. She had to run, and she did. At first, she had tried to slip through the groups of blind people, trying not to touch them, but this obliged her to go slowly, to stop several times in order to ascertain the way, enough to give off the smell of food, for auras are not only perfumed and ethereal ones, in no time a blind man was shouting, Who's eating sausage around here, no sooner were those words spoken than the doctor's wife threw caution to the wind and broke into reckless flight, colliding, jostling, knocking people over, with a devil-may-care attitude that was wholly reprehensible, for this is not the way to treat blind people who have more than enough reasons to be unhappy.

When she reached the street, it was raining buckets, All the better, she thought, panting for breath, her legs shaking, in this rain the smell will be less noticeable. Someone had grabbed the last rag that had barely covered her from the waist up, she was now going around with her breasts exposed and glistening, a refined expression, with the water from heaven, this was not liberty leading the people, the bags, fortunately full, are too heavy for her to carry them aloft like a flag. This is somewhat inconvenient, since these tantalising odours are travelling at a height that brings dogs on the scent, of course without masters to look after them and feed them, there is virtually a pack of them following the doctor's wife, let's hope none of these hounds remembers to take a bite to test the resistance of the plastic. In a downpour like this, which is almost becoming a deluge, you would expect people to be taking shelter, waiting for the weather to improve. But this is not the case, there are blind people everywhere gaping up at the heavens, slaking their thirst, storing up water in every nook and cranny of their bodies, and others, who are somewhat more far-sighted, and above all sensible, hold up buckets, bowls and pans, and raise them to the generous sky, clearly God provides the cloud according to the thirst. The possibility had not occurred to the doctor's wife that not so much as a drop of the precious liquid was coming from the taps in the houses, this is the drawback of civilisation, we are so used to the convenience of piped water brought into our homes, and forget that for this to happen there have to be people to open and close distribution valves, water towers and pumps that require electrical energy, computers to regulate the deficits and administer the reserves, and all of these operations require the use of one's eyes. Eyes are also needed to see this picture, a woman laden with plastic bags, going along a rain-drenched street, amidst rotting litter and human and animal excrement, cars and trucks abandoned any old way, blocking the main thoroughfare, some of the vehicles with their tyres already surrounded by grass, and the blind, the blind, open-mouthed and staring up at the white sky, it seems incredible that rain should fall from such a sky. The doctor's wife reads the street signs as she goes along, she remembers some of them, others not at all, and there comes a moment when she realises that she has lost her way. There is no doubt, she is lost. She took a turning, then another, she no longer remembers the streets or their names, then in her distress, she sat down on the filthy ground, thick with black mud, and, drained of any strength, of all strength, she burst into tears. The dogs gathered round her, sniffed at the bags, but without much conviction, as if their hour for eating had passed, one of them licks her face, perhaps it had been used to drying tears ever since it was a puppy. The woman strokes its head, runs her hand down its drenched back, and she weeps the rest of her tears embracing the dog. When she finally raised her eyes, the god of crossroads be praised a thousand times, she saw a great map before her, of the kind that town councils set up throughout city centres, especially for the benefit and reassurance of visitors, who are just as anxious to say where they have been as to know precisely where they are. Now that everyone is blind, you might be tempted to think that the money has been ill-spent, but it is a question of being patient, of letting time take its course, we should have learnt this once and for all, that destiny has to make many turnings before arriving anywhere, destiny alone knows what it has cost to bring this map here in order to let this woman know where she is. She was not as far away as she thought, she had simply made a detour in the other direction, all you have to do is to follow this street until you come to the square, there you count two streets to the left, then you take the first street on the right, that is the one you are looking for, the number you have not forgotten. The dogs gradually left her, something distracted them on the way, or they are familiar with the district and are reluctant to stray too far, only the dog that has dried her tears accompanied the person who had wept them, probably this encounter of the woman and the map, so well prepared by destiny, included the dog as well. The fact is that they entered the shop together, the dog of tears was not surprised to see people lying on the ground, so still that they might have been dead, the dog was used to this, sometimes they let him sleep amongst them, and when it was time to get up, they were nearly always alive. Wake up, if you're asleep, I've brought food, said the doctor's wife, but first she had closed the door, in case anyone passing in the street should hear her. The boy with the squint was the first to raise his head, weakness prevented him from doing any more, the others took a little longer, they were dreaming they were stones, and we all know how deeply stones sleep, a simple stroll in the countryside shows it to be so, there they lie sleeping, half buried, await-

ing who knows what awakening. The word food, however, has
magic powers, especially when hunger is pressing, even the
dog of tears, who knows no language, began wagging its tail,
this instinctive movement reminded it that it still had not done
what is expected of wet dogs, to shake themselves vigorously,
splashing everything around, for them it is easy, they wear their
pelt as if it were a coat. Holy water of the most efficacious variety, descended directly from heaven, the splashes helped the
stones to transform themselves into persons, while the doctor's
wife participated in this process of metamorphosis by opening
the plastic bags one after the other. Not everything smelled
of what it contained, but the aroma of a chunk of stale bread
would be as good, speaking in exalted terms, as the essence of
life itself. They are all awake at last, their hands are shaking,
their faces anxious, it is then that the doctor, as had happened
before to the dog of tears, remembers who he is, Careful, it's
not a good idea to eat too much, it could be harmful, What's
doing us harm is hunger, said the first blind man, Take heed
of what the doctor is saying, his wife rebuked him, and her
husband fell silent, thinking with faint resentment, He doesn't
even know anything about eyes, unjust words these, especially
if we take into account that the doctor is no less blind than the
others, the proof being that he was unaware that his wife was
naked from the waist up, it was she who asked him for his jacket
to cover herself, the other blind inmates looked in her direction, but it was much too late, if only they had looked before.

As they were eating, the woman told them of her adventures, of everything that had happened to her and everything
that she had done, without mentioning that she had left the
door to the storeroom closed, she was not entirely sure of the
humanitarian motives she had given to herself, to compensate
she told them about the blind man who got a piece of glass
stuck in his knee, they all laughed heartily, well, not all of them,

the old man with the black eyepatch only reacted with a weary smile, and the boy with the squint had ears only for the noise he made as he chewed his food. The dog of tears received his share, which he quickly repaid by barking furiously when anyone outside shook the door hard. Whoever it was, they did not persist, there was talk of mad dogs going around, not knowing where I'm putting my feet makes me quite mad enough. Calm was restored, and it was then, when everyone's initial hunger had been assuaged, that the doctor's wife related the conversation she had had with the man who had come out of this same shop to see if it was raining. Then she concluded, If what he told me is true, we cannot be certain of finding our homes as we left them, we don't even know whether we shall be able to get into them, I'm speaking of those who forgot to take the keys when they left, or lost them, we, for example, do not have them, they disappeared in the fire, it would be impossible to find them now amongst the ashes, she uttered that word and it was as if she were seeing the flames devouring her scissors, first burning the congealed blood that remained on them, then licking at the edges the sharp points, blunting them, and gradually making them dull, pliable, soft, formless, no one would believe that this instrument could have perforated someone's throat, once the fire has done its work it will be impossible in this unified mass of molten metal, to distinguish which are the scissors and which the keys, I've got the keys, said the doctor, and awkwardly introducing three fingers into a small pocket near the waistband of his tattered trousers, he brought out a tiny ring with three keys, How do you happen to have them when I had put them in my handbag which got left behind, I removed them, I was afraid they might get lost, I felt they were safer if they were always with me, and it was also a way of convincing myself that one day we would go back home, It's a relief to have the keys, but we might find the house with the door smashed in, They may not even have tried. For some moments, they had forgotten the others, but now it was important to know, from all of them, what had happened to their keys, the first to speak was the girl with dark glasses, My parents remained at home when the ambulance came to fetch me, I don't know what became of them afterwards, then the old man with the black eyepatch spoke up, I was at home when I went blind, they knocked at the door, the owner of the house came to tell me there were some male nurses looking for me, it wasn't the moment to be thinking about keys, that left only the wife of the first blind man, but she said, I cannot say, I've forgotten, she knew and remembered, but what she did not wish to confess is that when she suddenly saw that she was blind, an absurd expression, but so deeply rooted in the language that we've been unable to avoid it, she had run from the house screaming, calling out to her neighbours, those who were still in the building thought twice about going to her assistance, and she, who had shown herself so steadfast and capable when her husband had been struck by this misfortune, now went to pieces, abandoning her home with the door wide open, it did not even occur to her to ask that they should allow her to turn back, just for a minute, the time to close the door and say I'll be right back. No one asked the boy with the squint about the key to his house, since he cannot even remember where he lives. Then the doctor's wife gently touched the hand of the girl with dark glasses, Let's start with your house which is nearest, but first we must find some clothes and shoes, we can't go around like this, unwashed and in rags. She started to get up, but noticed that the boy with the squint, consoled by now and his hunger satisfied, had gone back to sleep. She said, let's rest then, let's sleep a little, then later we can go and see what awaits us. She took off her drenched skirt, then, to find some warmth, she snuggled up to her husband, and the first blind man and his wife did the same.

Is that you, he had asked, she remembered their home and it pained her, she did not say, Console me, but it was as if she had thought it, what we do not know is what feeling could have led the girl with dark glasses to put her arm round the shoulder of the old man with the black eyepatch, but there is no doubt that she did so, and there they remained, she sleeping, but not him. The dog went to lie down at the door, blocking the entrance, he is a gruff, ill-tempered animal when he does not have to dry someone's tears.

THEY dressed and put their shoes on, what they still had not solved was some way of washing themselves, but they already looked quite different from the other blind people, the colours of their clothes, notwithstanding the relative scarcity of the range on offer, for, as people often say, the fruit is handpicked, go well with each other, that is the advantage of having someone on the spot to advise us, You wear this, it goes better with those trousers, the stripes don't clash with the spots, details like that, to the men, of course, these matters do not make a blind bit of difference, but both the girl with dark glasses and the wife of the first blind man insisted on knowing what colours and styles they were wearing, so that, with the help of their imaginations they have some idea of how they look. As for footwear, everyone agreed that comfort should come before beauty, no fancy lacing and high heels, no calf or patent leather, given the state of the roads such refinements would be absurd, what they want here are rubber boots, completely waterproof and coming halfway up the leg, easy to slip into and out of, there is nothing better for walking through mud. Unfortunately, boots of this kind could not be found for everyone, there were no boots to fit the boy with the squint, for example, the larger sizes were like boats on him, so he had to settle for a pair of sports shoes with no clearly defined purpose, What a coincidence, his mother would say, wherever she might be, when someone told her what had happened, those are exactly the shoes my son would have chosen had he been able to see. The old man with the black eyepatch, whose feet were on the large side, solved the problem by wearing basketball shoes, specially made for players six foot tall and with extremities to match. It is true that he looks somewhat comical, as if he were wearing white slippers, but he will look ridiculous only for a while, within ten minutes the shoes will be filthy, just like everything else in life, let time take its course and it will find a solution.

It has stopped raining, there are no blind people standing about gaping. They go around not knowing what to do, they wander through the streets, but never for very long, walking or standing still is all the same to them, they have no other objective than the search for food, the music has stopped, never has there been so much silence in the world, the cinemas and theatres are only frequented by the homeless who have given up searching, some theatres, the larger ones, had been used to keep the blind in quarantine when the Government, or the few survivors, still believed that the white sickness could be remedied with devices and certain strategies that had been so ineffectual in the past against yellow fever and other infectious plagues, but this came to an end, not even a fire was needed here. As for the museums, it is truly heartbreaking, all those people, and I do mean people, all those paintings, all those sculptures, without a single visitor standing before them. What are the blind in this city waiting for, who knows, they might be awaiting a cure if they still believed in it, but they lost that hope when it became public knowledge that the epidemic of blindness had spared no one, that not a single person had been left with the

eyesight to look through the lens of a microscope, that the lab-
oratories had been abandoned, where there was no other solution for the bacteria but to feed on each other if they hoped to
survive. In the beginning, many of the blind, accompanied by
relatives who so far had maintained some sense of family solidarity, still rushed to the hospitals, but there they found only
blind doctors feeling the pulse of patients they could not see,
listening to them back and front, this was all they could do,
since they still had their hearing. Then, feeling the pangs of
hunger, those patients who could still walk began to flee the
hospitals, they ended up dying unprotected on the streets, their
families, if they still had them, could be anywhere, and then, so
that they might be buried, it was not enough for someone to
trip over them accidentally, their corpses had to start to smell,
and even then, only if they had died in some main thoroughfare. Little wonder that there are so many dogs, some of them
already resemble hyenas, the spots on their pelt are like those
of putrefaction, they run around with their hindquarters drawn
in, as if afraid that the dead and devoured might come back to
life in order to make them pay for the shame of biting those
who could not defend themselves. What's the world like these
days, the old man with the black eyepatch had asked, and the
doctor's wife replied, There's no difference between inside and
outside, between here and there, between the many and the
few, between what we're living through and what we shall have
to live through, And the people, how are they coping, asked the
girl with dark glasses, They go around like ghosts, this must be
what it means to be a ghost, being certain that life exists, because your four senses say so, and yet unable to see it, Are there
lots of cars out there, asked the first blind man, who was unable
to forget that his had been stolen, It's like a cemetery. Neither
the doctor nor the wife of the first blind man asked any questions, what was the point, when the replies were such as these.

As for the little boy with the squint, he has the satisfaction of wearing the shoes he had always dreamt of having and he is not even saddened by the fact that he cannot see them. This is probably the reason why he does not look like a ghost. And the dog of tears, who trails after the doctor's wife, would scarcely deserve to be called a hyena, he does not follow the scent of dead meat, he accompanies a pair of eyes that he knows are alive and well.

The home of the girl with dark glasses is not far away, but after being starved for a week, it is only now that the members of this group begin to recover their strength, that is why they walk so slowly, in order to rest they have no option but to sit on the ground, it had not been worthwhile taking so much trouble to choose colours and styles, when in such a short time their clothes are filthy. The street where the girl with dark glasses lives is not only short but narrow which explains why there are no cars to be seen here, they could pass in one direction only, but there was no place to park, it was prohibited. That there were also no people was not surprising, in streets like these there are many moments throughout the day when there is not a living soul to be seen, What's the number of your house, asked the doctor's wife, number seven, I live on the second floor in the flat on the left. One of the windows was open, at any other time that would be a sign that there was almost certainly someone at home, now everything was uncertain. The doctor's wife said, No need for all of us to go up, we two shall go on our own, the rest of you wait below. She realised the front door leading onto the street had been forced, the mortice lock was clearly twisted, a long splinter of wood had almost come away from the doorpost. The doctor's wife mentioned none of this. She let the girl go ahead since she knew the way, she did not mind the shadows into which the stairway was plunged. In her nervous haste, the girl with dark glasses stumbled twice, but laughed it off, Just imagine, stairs that I used to be able to go up and down with my eyes closed, clichés are like that, they are insensitive to the thousand subtleties of meaning, this one, for example, does not know the difference between closing one's eyes and being blind. On the landing of the second floor, the door they were looking for was closed. The girl with dark glasses ran her hand over the moulding until she found the bell, There's no light, the doctor's wife reminded her, and the girl received these four words that only repeated what everyone knew like a message bringing bad news. She knocked at the door, once, twice, three times, the third time loudly, using her fists and calling out, Mummy, daddy, and no one came to open, these terms of endearment did not affect the reality, no one came to say to her, Dearest daughter, you've come at last, we had given up hope of ever seeing you again, come in, come in, and let this lady who is your friend come in too, the house is a little untidy, pay no attention, the door remained closed. There is no one here, said the girl with dark glasses, and burst into tears leaning against the door, her head on her crossed forearms, as if with her whole body she were desperately imploring pity, if we did not have enough experience of how complicated the human spirit can be we would be surprised that she should be so fond of her parents as to indulge in these demonstrations of sorrow, a girl so free in her behaviour, but not far away is someone who has already affirmed that there does not exist nor ever has existed any contradiction between the one and the other. The doctor's wife tried to console her, but had little to say, it is well known that it is practically impossible for people to remain for a long time in their houses, We could ask the neighbours, she suggested, if there are any, Yes, let's go and ask, said the girl with dark glasses, but there was no hope in her voice. They began by knocking on the door on the other side of the landing, where once again no one replied. On the floor above the two doors were open. The flats had been ransacked, the wardrobes were empty, in the cupboards where food had been stored there was nothing to be found. There were signs that someone had been here recently, no doubt a group of vagrants, as they were all more or less by now, wandering from house to house, from absence to absence.

They went down to the first floor, the doctor's wife rapped on the nearest door, there was an expectant silence, then a gruff voice asked suspiciously, Who's there, the girl with dark glasses stepped forward, It's me, your upstairs neighbour, I'm looking for my parents, do you know where I can find them, what happened to them, she asked. They could hear shuffling footsteps, the door opened and a gaunt old woman appeared, nothing but skin and bone, emaciated, her long white hair dishevelled. A nauseating smell of mustiness and an indefinable putrefaction caused the two women to step back. The old woman opened her eyes wide, they were almost white, I know nothing about your parents, they came to fetch them the day after they took you away, at that time I could still see, Is there anyone else in the building, Now and then I can hear people climbing up or going down the stairs, but they are from outside and only come here to sleep, And what about my parents, I've already told you I know nothing about them, And what about your husband, your son and daughter-in-law, They took them away too, But left you behind, why, Because I was hiding, Where, Just imagine, in your flat, How did you manage to get in, Through the back and up the fire escape, I smashed a window-pane and opened the door from inside, the key was in the lock, And how have you managed since then to live all alone in your flat, asked the doctor's wife, Who else is here, asked the startled old woman turning her head, She's a friend of mine, she's with my group, the girl with dark glasses reassured her, And it's not just a question of being alone, what about food, how have you managed to get food during all this time, insisted the doctor's wife, The fact is that I'm no fool and I'm perfectly capable of looking after myself, If you'd rather not say, don't, I'm simply curious, Then I'll tell you, the first thing I did was to go round all the flats and gather up any food I could find, whatever might go bad I ate at once, the rest I kept, Do you still have some left, asked the girl with dark glasses, No, it's finished, replied the old woman with a sudden expression of mistrust in her sightless eyes, a way of speaking that is always used in similar situations, but it has no basis in fact, because the eyes, the eyes strictly speaking, have no expression, not even when they have been plucked out, they are two round objects that remain inert, it is the eyelids, the eyelashes and the eyebrows, that have to take on board the different visual eloquences and rhetorics, notwithstanding that this is normally attributed to the eyes, So what are you living on now, asked the doctor's wife, Death stalks the streets, but in the back gardens life goes on, the old woman said mysteriously, What do you mean, The back gardens have cabbages, rabbits, hens, they also have flowers, but they're not for eating, And how do you cope, It depends, sometimes I pick some cabbages, at other times I kill a rabbit or chicken, And eat them raw, At first I used to light a fire, then I got used to raw meat, and the stalks of the cabbages are sweet, don't you worry yourselves, my mother's daughter will not die of hunger. She stepped back two paces, almost disappeared into the darkness of the house, only her white eyes shone, and she said from within, If you want to go into your flat, go ahead, I won't stop you. The girl with dark glasses was about to say no, many thanks, it isn't worth it, to what purpose, if my parents aren't there, but suddenly she felt the desire to see her room, to see my room, how foolish, if I'm blind, at least to touch the walls, the bedcover, the pillow where I used to rest my crazy head, over the furniture, perhaps on the chest of drawers there might still be the flowers in the vase she remembered, unless the old woman had thrown them on the floor, annoyed that they could not be eaten. She said, Well, if you don't mind, I'll accept your offer, it's very kind of you, Come in, come in, but don't expect to find any food, what I have is barely enough for me, besides it would be no good to you unless you like raw meat, Don't worry, we have food, Ah, so you have food, in that case you can repay the favour and leave me some, We'll give you some food, don't worry, said the doctor's wife. They had already walked down the corridor, the stench had become unbearable. In the kitchen, dimly lit by the waning light outside, there were rabbit skins on the floor, chicken feathers, bones, and on the table, in a dirty plate covered in dried blood, unrecognisable pieces of meat, as if they had been chewed over and over again, And the rabbits and hens, what do they eat, asked the doctor's wife, Cabbages, weeds, any scraps left over, said the old woman, Don't tell us the hens and rabbits eat meat, The rabbits don't yet, but the hens love it, animals are like people, they get used to everything in the end. The old woman moved steadily, without tottering, she moved a chair out of the way as if she could see, then pointed to the door that led onto the emergency stairs, Through here, be careful not to slip, the handrail is not very secure. And what about the door, asked the girl with dark glasses, You only have to push the door, I have the key, it's somewhere around, It's mine, the girl was about to say, but at that same instant reflected that this key would be no good to her if her parents, or someone acting on their behalf, had taken away the others, the ones for the front door, she could not ask this neighbour to allow her to pass every time she wanted to come in or go out. She felt her heart contract slightly, probably because she was about to enter her own home and discover that her parents were not there, or for whatever reason.

The kitchen was clean and tidy, the dust on the furniture

was not excessive, another advantage of this rainy weather, as
well as having made the cabbages and greens grow, in fact, the
back gardens, seen from above, had struck the doctor's wife
as being jungles in miniature, Could the rabbits be running
around freely, she asked herself, most unlikely, they would still
be housed in the rabbit-hutches waiting for that blind hand
to bring them cabbage leaves then grab them by the ears and
pull them out kicking, while the other hand prepares the blind
blow that will break the vertebrae near the skull. The memory
of the girl with dark glasses had guided her into the flat, just
as the old woman on the floor below neither tripped nor fal-
tered, her parents' bed was unmade, they must have come to
detain them in the early hours of morning, she sat down there
and wept, the doctor's wife came to sit beside her, and told her,
Don't cry, what else could she say, what meaning do tears have
when the world has lost all meaning, In the girl's room on the
chest of drawers stood the glass vase with the withered flowers, the water had evaporated, it was there that her blind hands
directed themselves, her fingers brushed against the dead pet-
als, how fragile life is when it is abandoned. The doctor's wife
opened the window, she looked down into the street, there
they all were, seated on the ground, patiently waiting, the dog
of tears was the only creature to raise his head, alerted by his
keen hearing. The sky, once more overcast, began to darken,
night was approaching. She thought that today they would
not need to go and search for some refuge where they might
sleep, they would stay here. The old woman is not going to be
at all pleased if everyone starts tramping through her house,
she murmured. Just at that moment, the girl with dark glasses
touched her on the shoulder, saying, The keys were in the lock,
they did not take them. The problem, if there was one, was
therefore resolved, they would not have to put up with the ill-
humour of the old woman on the first floor, I'm going down

to call them, it will soon be night, how good, at least today we shall be able to sleep in a proper home with a roof over our heads, said the doctor's wife, You and your husband can sleep in my parents' bed, We'll see about that later, I'm the one who gives the orders here, I'm in my own home, You're right, just as you wish, the doctor's wife embraced the girl, then went down to look for the others. Climbing the stairs, chattering with excitement, now and then tripping on the stairs despite having been told by their guide, There are ten steps to each flight, it was as if they had come on a visit. The dog of tears followed them quietly, as if this were an everyday occurrence. From the landing, the girl with dark glasses looked down, it is the custom when someone is coming up, whether it be to find out who it is, if the person is a stranger, or to greet someone with words of welcome if they are friends, in this case no eyes were needed to know who was arriving. Come in, come in, make yourselves comfortable. The old woman on the first floor had come to her door to pry, she thought this lot was one of those mobs who turned up to sleep, in this she was not wrong, she asked, Who's there, and the girl with dark glasses replied from above, It's my group, the old woman was puzzled, how had she been able to reach the landing, then it dawned on her and she was annoyed with herself for having forgotten to retrieve the keys from the front door, it was as if she were losing her proprietorial rights over this building in which she had been the sole occupant for many months. She could find no better way of compensating for her sudden frustration than to say, opening the door, Remember you said you'd give me some food, don't go forgetting your promise. And since neither the doctor's wife nor the girl with dark glasses, the one busy guiding those who were arriving, the other in receiving them, made any reply, she shouted hysterically, Did you hear me, a mistake on her part, because the dog of tears, who at that precise moment was passing her, leapt at her and started barking furiously, the entire stairway echoed with the uproar, it was perfect, the old woman shrieked in terror and rushed back into her flat, slamming the door behind her, Who is that witch, asked the old man with the black eyepatch, these are things we say when we do not know how to take a good look at ourselves, had he lived as she had lived, we should like to see how long his civilised ways would last.

There was no food apart from what they had brought in the bags, they had to be sparing with it down to the very last drop, and, as for lighting, they had been most fortunate to find two candles in the kitchen cupboard, kept there to be used whenever there happened to be a power cut and which the doctor's wife lit for her own benefit, the others did not need them, they already had a light inside their heads, so strong it had blinded them. Though meagre rations were all this little group had, yet it ended up as a family feast, one of those rare feasts where what belongs to one, belongs to everybody. Before seating themselves at the table, the girl with dark glasses and the doctor's wife went down to the floor below, they went to fulfill their promise, were it not more exact to say that they went to satisfy a demand, payment with food for their passage through that customs house. The old woman received them, whining and surly, that cursed dog that only by some miracle did not devour her, You must have a lot of food to be able to feed such a beast, she insinuated, as if expecting, by means of this accusing observation, to arouse in the two emissaries what we call remorse, what they were really saying to each other, it would be inhumane to leave a poor old woman to die of starvation while a dumb animal gorges itself on scraps. The two women did not turn back to get more food, what they were carrying was already a generous ration, if we take into account the difficult circumstances of life at present, and this strangely enough, was how the old lady on the floor below appraised the situation, when all is said and done, less mean-hearted than she seemed, and she went back inside to find the keys for the back door, saying to the girl with dark glasses, Take it, this key is yours, and, as if this were not enough, she was still muttering as she closed her door, Many thanks. Amazed, the two women returned upstairs, so the old witch had feelings after all, She was not a bad person, living all that time alone must have unhinged her, commented the girl with dark glasses without appearing to think what she was saying. The doctor's wife did not reply, she decided to keep any conversation for later, and once all the others were in bed, some of them asleep, and the two women were sitting in the kitchen like mother and daughter trying to gather strength for the other chores to be done around the house, the doctor's wife asked, And you, what are you going to do now, Nothing, I'll wait here until my parents return, Alone and blind, I've got used to being blind, And what about solitude, I'll have to accept it, the old woman below also lives alone, You don't want to become like her, feeding on cabbages and raw meat, while they last, in these buildings around here there appears to be no one else living, you would be two women hating each other for fear that the food might come to an end, each stalk you gathered would be like taking it from the other's mouth, you didn't see that poor woman, you only caught the stench coming from her flat, I can assure you that not even where we were living before were things so repugnant, Sooner or later, we shall all be like her, and then it will all be over, there will be no more life, Meanwhile, we're still alive, Listen, you know much more than I do, compared with you I'm simply an ignorant girl, but in my opinion we're already dead, we're blind because we're dead, or if you would prefer me to put it another way, we're dead because we're blind, it comes to the same thing, I can still see, Lucky for you, lucky for your husband, for me, for the others, but you don't know how long you will go on seeing, should you become blind you will be like the rest of us, we'll all end up like the neighbour below, Today is today, tomorrow will bring what tomorrow brings, today is my responsibility, not tomorrow if I should turn blind, What do you mean by responsibility, The responsibility of having my eyesight when others have lost theirs, You cannot hope to guide or provide food for all the blind people in this world, I ought to, But you cannot, I shall do whatever I can to help, Of course you will, had it not been for you I might not be alive today, And I don't want you to die now, I must stay, it's my duty, I want my parents to find me if they should return, If they should return, you yourself said it, and we have no way of knowing whether they will still be your parents, I don't understand, You said that the neighbour below was a good person at heart, Poor woman, Your poor parents, poor you, when you meet up, blind in eyes and blind in feelings, because the feelings with which we have lived and which allowed us to live as we were, depended on our having the eyes we were born with, without eyes feelings become something different, we do not know how, we do not know what, you say we're dead because we're blind, there you have it, Do you love your husband, Yes, as I love myself, but should I turn blind, if after turning blind I should no longer be the person I was, how would I then be able to go on loving him, and with what love, Before, when we could still see, there were also blind people, Few in comparison, the feelings in use were those of someone who could see, therefore blind people felt with the feelings of others, not as the blind people they were, now, certainly, what is emerging are the real feelings of the blind, and we're still only at the beginning, for the moment we still live on the memory of what we felt, you don't need eyes to know what life has become today, if anyone were to tell me that one day I should kill, I'd take it as an insult, and yet I've killed, What then would you have me do, Come with me, come to our house, And what about the others, The same goes for them, but it's you I most care about, Why, I ask myself that question, perhaps because you have become almost like a sister, perhaps because my husband slept with you, Forgive me, It's not a crime that calls for pardon, We would suck your blood and be like parasites, There were plenty of them when we could see, and as for blood, it has to serve some purpose besides sustaining the body that carries it, and now let's try to get some sleep for tomorrow is another day.

Another day, or the same one. When he woke up, the boy with the squint wanted to go to the lavatory, he had diarrhoea, something that had disagreed with him in his weak condition, but it soon became obvious that it was impossible to go in there, the old woman on the floor below had clearly taken advantage of all the lavatories in the building until they could no longer be used, only by some extraordinary stroke of luck none of the seven, before going to bed last night, had needed to satisfy the urge to relieve their bowels, otherwise they would already know just how disgusting those lavatories were. Now they all felt the need to relieve themselves, especially the poor boy who could not hold it in any longer, in fact, however reluctant we might be to admit it, these distasteful realities of life also have to be considered, when the bowels function normally, anyone can have ideas, debate, for example, whether there exists a direct relationship between the eyes and feelings, or whether the sense of responsibility is the natural consequence of clear vision, but when we are in great distress and plagued by pain and anguish that is when the animal side of our nature becomes most apparent. The garden, exclaimed the doctor's wife, and she was right, were it not so early, we would find the neighbour from the flat below already there, it's time we stopped calling her the old woman, as we have disrespectfully done so far, she would already be there, as we were saying, crouched down, surrounded by hens, because the person who might ask the question almost certainly does not know what hens are like. Clutching his belly, protected by the doctor's wife, the boy with the squint went down the stairs in agony, worse still, by the time he reached the last steps, his sphincter had given up trying to resist the internal pressure, so you can imagine the consequences. Meanwhile, the other five were making their way as best they could down the emergency stairs, a most suitable name, if they have any inhibitions left since the time they lived in quarantine, this was the moment to lose them. Scattered throughout the back garden, groaning with the effort, suffering whatever remained of futile shame, they did what had to be done, even the doctor's wife who wept as she looked at them, she wept for all of them, which they seemed no longer to be able to do, her own husband, the first blind man and his wife, the girl with dark glasses, the old man with the black eyepatch, the boy, she saw them squatting on the weeds, between the knotty cabbage stalks, with the hens watching, the dog of tears had also come down to make one more. They cleaned themselves as best they could, superficially and in haste, with some handfuls of grass or broken bits of brick, wherever the arm could reach, in some cases the attempt to tidy up only made matters worse. They went back up the emergency stairs in silence, the neighbour on the first floor did not appear to ask them who they were, where they had come from, where they were going, she must still be sleeping off her supper, and when they got into the flat, first they did not know what to say, then the girl with dark glasses pointed out that they could not remain in that state, it is true that there was no water with which to wash themselves, pity there was no torrential rain like that of yesterday, they would go out once more into the garden, but now naked and without shame, they would receive on their head and shoulders the generous water from the sky above, they would feel it running

down their back and chest, down their legs, they could gather it
in their hands, clean at last and in this cup offer it to someone
to quench their thirst, no matter who, perhaps their lips would
gently touch their skin before finding the water, and desperately thirsty as they were, they would eagerly gather the last
drops from that shell, thus arousing, who knows, another thirst.
What leads the girl with dark glasses astray, as we have seen on
other occasions, is her imagination, what would she have to remember in a situation like this, tragic, grotesque, desperate as
it was. Despite everything, she is not without some sense of the
practical, the proof being that she went to open the wardrobe
in her room, then that of her parents, where she gathered up
sheets and towels, Let's clean ourselves up with these, she said,
it's better than nothing, and there is no doubt that it was a good
idea, when they sat down to eat they felt quite different.

It was at the table that the doctor's wife told them what was
on her mind. The time has come to decide what we want to
do, I'm convinced the entire population is blind, at least that
is my impression from observing the behaviour of the people I
have seen so far, there is no water, there is no electricity, there
are no supplies of any kind, this must be what chaos is, this is
what is really meant by chaos. There must be a government,
said the first blind man, I'm not so sure, but if there is, it will
be a government of the blind trying to rule the blind, that is to
say, nothingness trying to organise nothingness, Then there is
no future, said the old man with the black eyepatch, I cannot
say whether there will be a future, what matters for the moment is to see how we can live in the present, Without a future,
the present serves no purpose, it's as if it did not exist, Perhaps humanity will manage to live without eyes, but then it will
cease to be humanity, the result is obvious, which of us think
of ourselves as being as human as we believed ourselves to be
before, I, for example, killed a man, You killed a man, asked

the first blind man in alarm, Yes, the one who gave orders on the other side, I stabbed him in the throat with a pair of scissors, You killed him to avenge us, only a woman could avenge the women, said the girl with dark glasses, and revenge, being just, is something human, if the victim has no rights over the wrongdoer then there can be no justice, Nor humanity, added the wife of the first blind man, Let's get back to the matter we were discussing, said the doctor's wife, if we stay together we might manage to survive, if we separate we shall be swallowed up by the masses and destroyed, You mentioned that there are organised groups of blind people, observed the doctor, this means that new ways of living are being invented and there is no reason why we should finish up by being destroyed, as you predict, I don't know to what extent they are really organised, I only see them going around in search of food and somewhere to sleep, nothing more, We're going back to being primitive hordes, said the old man with the black eyepatch, with the difference that we are not a few thousand men and women in an immense, unspoiled nature, but thousands of millions in an uprooted, exhausted world, And blind, added the doctor's wife, When it starts to become difficult to find water and food, these groups will almost certainly disband, each person will think they have a better chance of surviving on their own, they will not have to share anything with others, whatever they can grab belongs to them and to no one else, The groups going around must have leaders, someone who gives orders and organises things, the first blind man reminded them, Perhaps, but in this case those who give the orders are just as blind as those who receive them, You're not blind, said the girl with dark glasses, that's why you were the obvious person to give orders and organise the rest of us, I don't give orders, I organise things as best I can, I am simply the eyes that the rest of you no longer possess, A kind of natural leader, a king with eyes in the land

of the blind, said the old man with the black eyepatch, If this
is so, then allow yourselves to be guided by my eyes so long as
they last, therefore what I propose is that instead of dispersing,
her in her house, you in yours, let us continue to live together,
We can stay here, said the girl with dark glasses, Our house is
bigger, Assuming it has not been occupied, the wife of the first
blind man pointed out, When we get there we'll find out, and if
it should be occupied we can come back here, or go and take a
look at your house, or yours, she added, addressing the old man
with the black eyepatch, and he replied, I have no home of my
own, I lived alone in a room, Have you no family, asked the girl
with dark glasses, No family whatsoever, Not even a wife, children, brothers and sisters, No one, Unless my parents turn up,
I shall be alone just like you. I'll stay with you, said the boy with
the squint, but did not add, Unless my mother turns up, he did
not lay down this condition, strange behaviour, or perhaps not
so strange, the young quickly adapt, they have their whole life
before them. What do you think, asked the doctor's wife, I'm
going with you, said the girl with dark glasses, all I ask is that
you should bring me here once a week just in case my parents should happen to return, Will you leave the keys with the
neighbour below, There's no alternative, she cannot take more
than she has taken already, She might destroy things, Now that
I've been here, perhaps not, We're coming with you too, said
the first blind man, although we should like, as soon as possible, to pass by our home and find out what has happened, Of
course, No point in passing by my house, I've already told you
it was just a room. But you'll come with us, Yes, on one condition, at first sight it must seem scandalous for someone to lay
down conditions when he is being done a favour, but some old
people are like that, they make up in pride for the little time
remaining to them, What condition is that, asked the doctor,
When I start becoming an impossible burden, you must tell

me, and if, out of friendship or pity, you should decide to say nothing, I hope I'll still have enough judgment to do the necessary, And what might that be, I'd like to know, asked the girl with dark glasses, Withdraw, take myself off, disappear, as elephants used to do, I've heard it said that recently things have been different, none of these animals reach old age, You're not exactly an elephant, Nor am I exactly a man, Especially if you start giving childish replies, retorted the girl with dark glasses, and the conversation went no further.

The plastic bags are now much lighter than when they were brought here, not surprisingly, the neighbour on the first floor also ate from them, she ate twice, first last night, and today they left her some more food when they asked her to take the keys and look after them until the rightful owners turned up, a question of keeping the old girl sweet, because as for her character we have learned more than enough, and the dog of tears also had to be fed, only a heart of stone would have been capable of feigning indifference before those pleading eyes, and while we are on the subject, where has the dog disappeared to, he is not in the flat, he did not go out the door, he can only be in the back garden, the doctor's wife went off to take a good look, and this was, in fact, where he was, the dog of tears was devouring a hen, the attack had been so quick that there was not even time to raise the alarm, but if the old woman on the first floor had eyes and kept a count on her hens, who can tell, out of anger, what fate might befall the keys, Between the awareness of having committed a crime and the perception that the human being whom he was protecting was going away, the dog of tears hesitated only for an instant, then began at once to scratch the soft earth, and before the old woman on the first floor appeared on the landing of the fire escape to sniff out the sounds that were coming into her flat, the hen's carcass was buried, the crime covered up, remorse reserved for some other

occasion. The dog of tears sidled upstairs, brushed like a breath
of air past the skirts of the old woman, who had no idea of the
danger she had just faced, and went to settle beside the doctor's wife, where he announced to the heavens the feat he had
just achieved. The old woman on the first floor, hearing him
bark so ferociously, feared, but as we know all too late, for the
safety of her larder, and, craning her neck upwards, called, This
dog must be kept under control before he kills one of my hens,
Don't worry, replied the doctor's wife, the dog isn't hungry, he
has already eaten, and we're leaving right away, Right away, repeated the old woman, and there was a break in her voice as if
of pain, as if she wanted to be understood in a quite different
way, for example, You're going to leave me here all alone, but
she did not utter another word, only that Right away which
asked for no reply, the hard of heart also have their sorrows,
this woman's heart was such that later she refused to open her
door to bid farewell to these ingrates to whom she had given
free access to her house. She heard them go downstairs, they
were talking amongst themselves, saying, Watch you don't
stumble, Put your hand on my shoulder, Hold on to the ban-
nister, the usual words, but now much more common in this
world of blind people, what did surprise her was to hear one of
the women say, It's so dark in this place that I can't see a thing,
that this woman's blindness should not be white was already
surprising in itself, but that she could not see because it was so
dark, what could this mean, She wanted to think, tried hard,
but her weak head did not help, soon she was saying to herself,
I must have misheard, whatever it was. In the street, the doctor's wife remembered what she had said, she must watch what
she was saying, she could move like someone who has eyes, But
my words must be those of a blind person, she thought.

Assembled on the pavement, she arranged her companions
in two rows of three, in the first one she placed her husband

and the girl with dark glasses, with the boy with the squint in the middle, in the second row the old man with the black eyepatch and the first blind man, one on either side of the other woman. She wanted to keep all of them close to her, not in the usual fragile Indian file, which can be broken at any moment, they only needed to encounter a more numerous or more aggressive group, and it would be like a steamer at sea cutting in two a sailboat that happened to cross its path, we know the consequences of such accidents, shipwrecks, disasters, people drowned, futile cries for help in that vast expanse of water, the steamer already sailing on ahead, not even aware of the collision, this is what would happen to this group, a blind person here, another there, lost in the disordered currents of the other blind people, like the waves of the sea that never stop and do not know where they are going, and the doctor's wife, too, not knowing to whose assistance she should hasten first, placing her hand on her husband's arm, perhaps on that of the boy with the squint, but losing the girl with dark glasses, the other two, the old man with the black eyepatch, far away, heading for the elephants' graveyard. What she is doing now is to pass around herself and all the others a cord made from strips of cloth knotted together while the rest were asleep, Don't hold on to me, she said, but hold on to the rope with all your strength, do not let go under any circumstances, whatever may happen. They were careful not to walk too closely to avoid tripping each other, but they needed to feel the proximity of their neighbours, a direct contact if possible, only one of them did not have to worry himself with these new questions of overland tactics, this was the boy with the squint who walked in the middle, protected on all sides. None of our blind friends thought to ask how the other groups navigate, if they too are advancing tied to each other by this or other processes, but the reply should be easy from what we have been able to observe,

groups in general, except in the case of a more cohesive group
for good reasons unknown to us, gradually gain and lose ad-
herents throughout the day, there is always one blind man who
strays and is lost, another who was caught by the force of gravity and tags along, he might be accepted, he might be expelled,
depending on what he is carrying with him. The old woman
on the first floor slowly opened the window, she does not want
anyone to know that she has this sentimental weakness, but no
noise can be heard coming from the street, they have already
gone, they have left this place where almost no one ever passes,
the old woman ought to be pleased, in this way she will not
have to share her hens and rabbits with the others, she should
be pleased but is not, in her blind eyes appear two tears, for
the first time she asked herself if she had some good reason for
wanting to go on living. She could find no reply, replies do not
always come when needed, and it often happens that the only
possible reply is to wait for them.

Along the route they were taking they would pass two blocks
away from the house where the old man with the black eyepatch had his bachelor room, but they had already decided
that they would travel on, there was no food to be found there,
clothing they do not need, books they cannot read. The streets
are full of blind people out searching for food. They go in and
out of shops, enter empty-handed and nearly always come out
empty-handed, then they debate among themselves the need
or advantage of leaving this district and going to forage elsewhere in the city, the big problem is that, things being as they
are, without running water, the gas cylinders empty, as well as
the danger of lighting fires inside the houses, no cooking can
be done, assuming that we would know where to look for the
salt, the oil and seasoning, were we to try and prepare a few
dishes with some hint of the flavours from the past, if there
were some greens, simply having them boiled would leave us

satisfied, the same being true of meat, apart from the usual rabbits and hens, dogs and cats could be cooked if they could be
caught, but since experience is truly the mistress of life, even
these animals, previously domesticated, learned to mistrust ca-
resses, they now hunt in packs and in packs they defend themselves from being hunted down, and since, thanks be to God,
they still have eyes, they are better equipped to avoid danger,
and to attack if necessary. All these circumstances and reasons
have led us to conclude that the best food for humans is what is
preserved in cans and jars, not only because it is often already
cooked, ready to be eaten, but also because it is so much easier
to transport and handy for immediate use. It is true that on all
these cans, jars and different packets in which these products
are sold there is a date beyond which it could be risky to con-
sume them and even dangerous in certain cases, but popular
wisdom was quick to put into circulation a saying to which in
a sense there is no answer, symmetrical with another saying no
longer much used, what the eyes do not see the heart does not
grieve over, people would now often say, eyes that do not see
have a cast-iron stomach, which explains why they eat so much
rubbish. Heading the group, the doctor's wife makes a mental calculation of the food she still has in reserve, there will be
enough, if that, for one meal, without counting the dog, but let
him sort himself out with the means at his disposal, the same
means that served him so well to grab the hen by the neck and
cut off its voice and life. She will have at home, as you may remember, and provided that no one has broken in, a reasonable quantity of preserves, enough for a couple, but there are
seven persons here who have to be fed, her reserves will not last
long, even if she were to enforce strict rationing. Tomorrow, or
within the next few days, she will have to return to the underground storeroom of the supermarket, she will have to decide
whether to go alone or to ask her husband to accompany her, or

the first blind man who is younger and more agile, the choice
is between the possibility of carrying a larger quantity of food
and acting speedily, without forgetting the conditions of the
retreat. The rubbish on the streets, which appears to be twice
as much since yesterday, the human excrement, that from before semi-liquified by the torrential downpour of rain, mushy
or runny, the excrement being evacuated at this very minute by
these men and women as we pass, fills the air with the most awful stench, like a dense mist through which it is only possible to
advance with enormous effort. In a square surrounded by trees,
with a statue in the middle, a pack of dogs is devouring a man's
corpse. He must have died a short while ago, his limbs are not
rigid, as can be seen when the dogs shake them to tear from the
bone the flesh caught between their teeth. A crow hops around
in search of an opening to get close to the feast. The doctor's
wife averted her eyes, but it was too late, the vomit rising from
her entrails was irresistible, twice, three times, as if her own
still-living body were being shaken by other dogs, the pack of
absolute despair, this is as far as I go, I want to die here. Her
husband asked, What's the matter, the others bound together
by the cord, drew closer, suddenly alarmed, What happened,
Did the food upset you, Something that was off, I don't feel a
thing, Nor me, All the better for them, all they could hear was
the uproar from the dogs, the sudden and unexpected cawing
of a crow, in the upheaval one of the dogs had bitten its wing
in passing, quite unintentionally, then the doctor's wife said, I
couldn't stop myself, forgive me, but some of the dogs here are
eating another dog. Are they eating our dog, asked the boy with
the squint, No, our dog as you call him, is alive, and prowling
around them but he keeps his distance. After eating that hen,
he can't be very hungry, said the first blind man. Are you feeling better, asked the doctor, Yes, let's be on our way, The dog
isn't ours, it simply latched on to us, it will probably stay be-

hind now with these other dogs, it may have stayed with them
before, but it has refound its friends, I want to do a poo, Here,
I've got stomachache, it hurts, complained the boy. He relieved
himself on the spot as best he could, the doctor's wife vomited
once more, but for other reasons. Then they crossed the vast
square and when they reached the shade of the trees, the doctor's wife looked back. More dogs had appeared and they were
already contesting what remained of the corpse. The dog of
tears arrived with its snout touching the ground as if it were
following some trail, a question of habit, for this time a simple
glance was enough to find the woman he was looking for.

The march continued, the house of the old man with the
black eyepatch was already some way behind them, now they
are making their way along a broad avenue with tall imposing buildings on either side. The cars here are expensive, ca-
pacious and comfortable, which explains why so many blind
people are to be seen sleeping in them, and from all appearances, an enormous limousine has actually been transformed
into a permanent home, probably because it was much easier to
return to a car than to a house, the occupants of this one must
do what was done back there in quarantine to find their bed,
groping their way along and counting the cars from the corner, twenty-seven, right-hand side, I'm back home. The building at whose door the limousine is parked is a bank. The car
had brought the chairman of the board to the weekly plenary
meeting, the first to be held since the epidemic of white sickness had been declared, and there had been no time to park it
in the underground garage until the meeting was over. The
driver went blind just as the chairman was about to enter the
building by the main entrance as usual, he let out a cry, we
are referring to the driver, but he, meaning the chairman, did
not hear it. Moreover, attendance at the plenary board meeting would not be as complete as its designation suggested, for

during the last few days some of the directors had gone blind. The chairman did not get round to opening the session, the agenda of which had provided for a discussion of measures to be taken in the event that all the directors and their deputies went blind, and he was not even able to enter the boardroom for when the elevator was taking him up to the fifteenth floor, between the ninth and the tenth floors to be exact, the electric power was cut off, never to be restored. And since disasters never come singly, at that same moment the electricians went blind who were responsible for maintaining the internal power supply and consequently that also of the generator, an old model, not automatic, that had long been awaiting replacement, this resulted, as we said before, in the elevator coming to a halt between the ninth and tenth floors. The chairman saw the attendant who was accompanying him go blind, he himself lost his sight an hour later, and since the power did not come back and the cases of blindness inside the bank multiplied that day, in all probability the two are still there, dead, needless to say, shut up in a coffin of steel, and therefore happily safe from voracious dogs.

There being no witnesses, and if there were there is no evidence that they were summoned to the postmortems to tell us what happened, it is understandable that someone should ask how it was possible to know that these things happened so and not in some other manner, the reply to be given is that all stories are like those about the creation of the universe, no one was there, no one witnessed anything, yet everyone knows what happened. The doctor's wife had asked, What will have happened to the banks, not that she was much concerned, despite having entrusted her savings to one of them, she raised the question out of simple curiosity, simply because she thought of it, nothing more, nor did she expect anyone to make a reply such as, for example, In the beginning, God created heaven and earth, the earth was without form and empty, and darkness was upon the face of the deep, and the spirit of God moved upon the face of the waters, instead of this what really happened was that the old man with the black eyepatch said as they were proceeding down the avenue, As far as I could judge when I still had an eye to see, at first, it was pandemonium, the people, afraid of ending up blind and unprovided for, raced to the banks to withdraw their money, feeling that they ought to safeguard their future, and this is understandable, if someone knows they will no longer be able to work, the only remedy, for as long as they might last, is to have recourse to the savings made in times of prosperity when long-term provisions were made, assuming in fact that the people were prudent enough to build up their savings little by little, the outcome of this precipitous run on the banks was that within twenty-four hours some of the main banks were facing ruin, the Government intervened to plead for calm and to appeal to the civic conscience of citizens, ending the proclamation with the solemn declaration that it would assume all the responsibilities and duties resulting from this public calamity they were facing, but this calming measure did not succeed in alleviating the crisis, not only because people continued to go blind but also because those who could still see were interested only in saving their precious money, in the end, it was inevitable, the banks, bankrupt or otherwise, closed their doors and sought police protection, it did them no good, between the noisy crowds that gathered in front of the banks there were also policemen in plain clothes who demanded what they had saved with so much effort, and some, in order to demonstrate at will, had even advised their command that they were blind and were therefore dismissed, and the others, still in uniform and on active service, their weapons trained on the dissatisfied masses, suddenly lost sight of their target, the latter, if they had money in the bank, lost all hope and, as if that were not enough, they were accused of having entered into a pact with the established authority, but there was worse to come when the banks found themselves attacked by furious hordes of whom some were blind and others not, but all of them desperate, here it was no longer a question of calmly handing in a cheque to be cashed at the counter and saying to the teller, I wish to withdraw my savings, but to lay hands on everything possible, on the cash in the till, whatever had been left in some drawer or other, in some safe-deposit box carelessly left open, in some old-fashioned moneybag as used by the grandparents of an older generation, you cannot imagine what it was like, the vast and sumptuous halls of the head office, the smaller branch offices in various districts witnessed truly terrifying scenes, nor should we forget the automatic tills, forced open and stripped of the very last note, on the screen of some of them appeared an enigmatic message of thanks for having chosen this bank. Machines are really very stupid, it might be more precise to say that these machines had betrayed their owners, in a word, the whole banking system collapsed, blown over like a house of cards, and not because the possession of money had ceased to be appreciated, the proof being that anyone who has it does not want to let go of it, the latter allege that no one can foresee what will happen tomorrow, this no doubt also being in the thoughts of the blind people who installed themselves in the vaults of the banks, where the strongboxes are kept, waiting for some miracle to open wide those heavy metal doors that separate them from this wealth, they leave the place only to go in search of food and water or to satisfy the body's other needs, and then return to their post, they have passwords and hand signs so that no stranger may penetrate their stronghold, needless to say they live in total darkness, not that it matters, in this particular blindness everything is white. The old man with the black eyepatch related these tremendous happenings

about banks and finance as they slowly crossed the city, with
the odd stop so that the boy with the squint might pacify the
unbearable turmoil in his intestines, and, despite the persuasive
tone he gave to this impassioned description, it is logical to suspect that there was some exaggeration in his account, the story
about the blind people who live in the bank vaults, for example,
how could he have known if he does not know the password
or the hand signal, in any case it was enough to give us some
idea.

The light was fading when they finally arrived in the street
where the doctor and his wife live. It is no different from the
others, there is squalor everywhere, groups of blind people
wandering aimlessly about, and, for the first time, but it was
mere chance that they had not encountered them before, two
huge rats, even the cats avoid them as they go on the prowl,
for they are almost as big as they are and in all certainty much
more ferocious. The dog of tears looked at both the rats and
the cats with the indifference of someone who lives in another
sphere of emotions, this we might say, were it not for the fact
that the dog continues to be the dog that he is, an animal of the
human type. At the sight of familiar places, the doctor's wife did
not make the usual melancholy reflection, that consists in saying, How time passes, only the other day we were happy here,
what shocked her was the disappointment, she had unwittingly
believed that, being hers, she would find the street clean, swept,
tidy, that her neighbours would be blind in their eyes, but not
in their understanding, How stupid of me, she said aloud, Why,
what is wrong, asked her husband, Nothing, daydreams, How
time passes, what will the flat be like, he wondered, We'll soon
find out. They did not have much strength, and so climbed the
stairs very slowly, pausing for breath on each landing, It's on
the fifth floor, the doctor's wife had said. They went up as best
they could, each under his or her own steam, the dog of tears

now in front, now behind, as if it had been born to guide a
flock, under orders not to lose a single sheep. There were open
doors, voices within, the usual foul odour wafting out, twice
blind people appeared on the threshold and looked with vacant eyes, Who's there, they asked, the doctor's wife recognised
one of the voices, the other voice was not that of someone who
lived in the building. We used to live here, was all she said. A
flicker of recognition also showed on her neighbour's face, but
she did not ask, Are you the doctor's wife, perhaps she might
say once back inside, The people from the fifth floor are back.
On reaching the last flight of stairs, even before setting foot
on the landing, the doctor's wife was already announcing, The
door is locked. There were signs of an attempt at a forced entry but the door had withstood the assault. The doctor put his
hand into the inside pocket of his new jacket and brought out
the keys. He held them in mid-air, waiting, but his wife gently
guided his hand towards the keyhole.

LEAVING aside the household dust that takes advantage of a family's absence to leave a subtle film on the surface of the furniture, it may be stated in this connection that these are the only occasions the dust has to rest, without being disturbed by a duster or vacuum cleaner, without children running back and forth unleashing an atmospheric whirlwind as they pass, the flat was clean, any untidiness was only what might be expected when one leaves in a hurry. Even so, while on that day they were expecting a summons from the Ministry and the hospital, the doctor's wife with the kind of foresight that leads sensible people to settle their affairs while alive, so that after their death, the tiresome need for a frantic putting of things in order does not arise, washed the dishes, made the bed, tidied the bathroom, the result was not exactly perfect, but truly it would have been cruel to ask any more of her with those trembling hands and tear-filled eyes. It was nevertheless a kind of paradise that the seven pilgrims had reached and this impression was so overwhelming, with no great disrespect for the strict meaning of the term, we could call it transcendental, that they stopped in their tracks in the entrance as if paralysed by the unexpected smell in the flat and it was simply that of a flat in need of a good airing, at any other time we would have rushed to open all the windows, To air the place, we would say, today the best thing to do would be to have them sealed up so that the putrefaction outside would be unable to come in. The wife of the first blind man said, We're going to dirty the whole place, and she was right, if they were to come in with these shoes covered in mud and excrement, paradise would in a flash become hell, the latter being the second place, according to the competent authorities where the putrid, fetid, nauseating, pestilential stench is the worst thing condemned souls have to bear, not the burning tongs, the cauldrons of boiling pitch and other artefacts of the foundry and the kitchen. From time immemorial it has been the custom of housewives to say, Come in, come in, really, it doesn't matter, I can clean up any dirt later, but this one, like her guests, knows where they have come from, she knows that in the world she lives in what is dirty will get dirtier still, therefore she asks them if they would be so kind as to remove their shoes on the landing, it is true that their feet are not clean either, but there is no comparison, the towels and sheets of the girl with dark glasses had some effect, they've got rid of most of the muck. So they went in without their shoes, the doctor's wife searched for and found a large plastic bag into which she put all the shoes intent upon giving them a good scrub, she had no idea when or how, then she carried them out onto the balcony, the air outside would not get any worse on this account. The sky began to darken, there were heavy clouds, If only it would rain, she thought. With a clear idea of what had to be done, she returned to her companions. They were in the sitting-room, silent, on their feet, for, despite their exhaustion, they had not dared to find themselves a chair, only the doctor vaguely ran his hands over the furniture leaving marks on the surface, the first dusting was under way, some of this dust is already stuck to his fingertips. The doctor's wife said, Take your clothes off, we can't remain in this state, our clothes are almost as dirty as our shoes, Take off our clothes, asked the first blind man, here, in front of each other, I don't think it's right, If you wish, I can put each of you in a different part of the flat, the doctor's wife replied ironically, then there will be no need to feel embarrassed, I'll take off my clothes right here, said the wife of the first blind man, only you can see me, and even were that not the case, I haven't forgotten that you have seen me worse than being naked, it's my husband who has the poor memory, I can't see what possible interest there can be in recalling disagreeable matters long since forgotten, muttered the first blind man, If you were a woman and had been where we have been, you would change your tune, said the girl with dark glasses, starting to undress the boy with the squint. The doctor and the old man with the black eyepatch were already naked from the waist up, now they were removing their trousers, the old man with the black eyepatch said to the doctor who was at his side, Let me lean on you while I get out of these trousers. They looked so ridiculous the poor fellows as they jumped about, it almost made you want to weep. The doctor lost his balance, dragged the old man with the black eyepatch with him as he fell, fortunately they both found the situation amusing, and it was pitiful to watch them, their bodies covered with every kind of filth imaginable, their private parts all besmeared, white hairs, black hairs, this was what the respectability of old age and a worthy profession had come to. The doctor's wife went to help them get to their feet, shortly there would be darkness all around and no one will have any cause to feel embarrassed, Are there any candles in the house, she wondered, the answer was that she recalled having seen two ancient lamps, an old oil lamp, with three nozzles, and an old paraffin lamp of the kind with a glass funnel, for the present, the oil lamp will be good enough, I have oil, a wick can be improvised, tomorrow I'll go in search

of some paraffin in one of those stores, it will be much easier to find than a can of food, Especially if I don't look for
it in the grocer's, she thought, surprising herself that she was
still capable of joking even in this situation. The girl with the
dark glasses was slowly undressing, in a way that gave the impression that there would always be something more no matter how many clothes she removed, one last article of clothing
to cover her nakedness, she cannot explain this sudden modesty, but had the doctor's wife been closer, she would have seen
the girl blushing, even though her face was so dirty, let those
who can, try to understand women, one of them suddenly assailed by shame after having gone around sleeping with men
she scarcely knew, the other perfectly capable of whispering in
her ear perfectly calmly, Don't be embarrassed, he cannot see
you, she would be referring to her own husband, of course, for
we must not forget how the shameless girl tempted him into
bed, well, as everyone knows, with women it is always a case of
buyer beware. Perhaps, in the meantime, the reason is something else, there are two other naked men here, and one of
them has slept with her.

The doctor's wife gathered up the clothes lying scattered
on the floor, trousers, shirts, a jacket, petticoats and blouses,
some soiled underwear, the latter would take at least a month's
soaking before she got them clean again, she bundled them up
into an armload, Stay here, she told them, I'm coming straight
back, She took the clothes out onto the balcony, as she had
done with the shoes, there she in turn undressed, looking at
the black city under the heavy sky. Not so much as a pale light
in the windows, nor a waning reflection on the house fronts,
what was there was not a city, it was a great mass of pitch which,
on cooling, had hardened in the shape of buildings, rooftops,
chimneys, all dead, all faded. The dog of tears appeared on the
balcony, it was restless, but now there were no tears to lick up,

the despair was all inside her, eyes were dry. The doctor's wife
felt cold, she remembered the others, standing naked in the
middle of the room, waiting for who knows what. She entered.
They had turned into simple, sexless forms, vague shapes, shadows losing themselves in the half-light, But this does not affect
them, she thought, they fade into the surrounding light, and it
is the light which does not allow them to see. I'm going to put a
light on, she said, At the moment I'm almost as blind as the rest
of you, Has the electricity come back on, asked the boy with
the squint, No, I'm going to light an oil lamp, What's that, the
boy asked again, I'll show you later. She rummaged for a box
of matches in one of the plastic bags, went to the kitchen, she
knew where she had stored the oil, she did not need much, she
tore a strip from a dish towel in order to make wicks, then returned to the room where the lamp stood, it was going to be
useful for the first time since it was manufactured, at first this
did not appear to be its destiny, but none of us, lamps, dogs
or humans, knows at the outset, why we have come into this
world. One after the other, over the nozzles of the lamp, three
tiny almonds of light lit up, from time to time they flicker until they give the impression that the upper part of the flames
is lost in mid-air, then they settle down again as if they were
becoming dense, solid, tiny pebbles of light. The doctor's wife
said, Now that I can see, I'm going to get clean clothes, But
we're dirty, the girl with the dark glasses said. Both she and the
wife of the first blind man were covering their breasts and their
sex with their hands, This is not for my sake, the doctor's wife
thought, but because the light of the lamp is looking at them.
Then she said, It is better to have clean clothes on a dirty body,
than to have dirty clothes on a clean body. She took the lamp
and went to search in the drawers of the chest, in the wardrobe,
after a few minutes she returned, she brought pyjamas, dress-
ing-gowns, skirts, blouses, dresses, trousers, underwear, every-

thing necessary for dressing seven people decently, it is true
that the people were not all the same size, but in their gaunt-
ness they were like so many twins. The doctor's wife helped
them to dress, the boy with the squint finished up with a pair of
the doctor's trousers, the kind you wear to the beach or in the
countryside, and which turn us all into children. Now we can
sit down, sighed the wife of the first blind man, Please guide us,
we do not know where to put ourselves.

    The room is like all sitting-rooms, it has a low table in
the middle, all around there are sofas that can accommodate
everyone, on this one here sit the doctor and his wife along
with the old man with the black eyepatch, on the other the first
blind man and his wife. They are exhausted. The boy fell asleep
at once, with his head on the lap of the girl with dark glasses,
having forgotten all about the lamp. An hour passed, this was
akin to happiness, under the softest of lights their grimy faces
looked washed, the eyes of those who were not asleep shone,
the first blind man reached out for his wife's hand and pressed
it, from this gesture we can see how a rested body can contribute to the harmony of the mind. Then the doctor's wife said,
Shortly we'll have something to eat, but first we should decide how we are going to live here, don't worry, I am not about
to repeat the speech that came over the loudspeaker, there's
enough room to accommodate everyone, we have two bedrooms that can be used by the couples, the others can sleep in
this room, each on his own sofa, tomorrow I must go in search
of some food, our supplies are running out, it would be helpful if one of you were to come with me to help me carry the
food, but also so that you can start to learn the way home, to
recognise the street corners, one of these days I might fall ill,
or go blind, I am always waiting for it to happen, in which case
I'll have to learn from you, on another matter, there will be a
bucket on the balcony for our physical needs, I know that it is

not pleasant to go out there, what with all the rain we've had and the cold, but it is, in any case, better than having the house smelling to high heaven, let us not forget that that was our life during the time when we were interned, we went down all the steps of indignity, all of them, until we reached total degradation, the same might happen here albeit in a different way, there we still had the excuse that the degradation belonged to someone else, not now, now we are all equal regarding good and evil, please, don't ask me what good and what evil are, we knew what it was each time we had to act when blindness was an exception, what is right and what is wrong are simply different ways of understanding our relationships with the others, not that which we have with ourselves, one should not trust the latter, forgive this moralising speech, you do not know, you cannot know, what it means to have eyes in a world in which everyone else is blind, I am not a queen, no, I am simply the one who was born to see this horror, you can feel it, I both feel and see it, and that's enough of this dissertation, Let's go and eat. No one asked any questions, the doctor simply said, If I ever regain my sight, I shall look carefully at the eyes of others, as if I were looking into their souls, Their souls, asked the old man with the eyepatch, Or their minds, the name does not matter, it was then that, surprisingly, if we consider that we are dealing with a person without much education, the girl with the dark glasses said, Inside us there is something that has no name, that something is what we are.

The doctor's wife had already put on the table some of the little food that was left over, then she helped them to sit down and said, Chew slowly, that helps to deceive your stomach. The dog of tears did not come to beg for food, it was used to fasting, moreover it must have thought that, after the banquet that morning, it had no right to take even a little food from the mouth of the woman who had wept, the others appeared not to interest him. In the middle of the table, the lamp with three flames was waiting for the doctor's wife to give the promised explanation, it finally happened after they had eaten, Give me your hands, she said to the boy with the squint, then guided his fingers slowly, saying, This is the base, round as you can see, and this the column that sustains the upper part with the oil container, here, watch you don't burn yourself, these are the nozzles, one, two, three, from these emerge twisted strips of material that suck up the oil from inside, a match is put to them and they start burning until the oil is finished, they give off a weak light but it's good enough to see each other, I can't see, One day you will see and on that day I'll give you the lamp as a present. What colour is it, Have you ever seen anything made of brass, I don't know, I don't remember, what is brass, Brass is yellow, Ah. The boy with the squint pondered for a moment, Now he is going to ask for his mother, thought the doctor's wife, but she was wrong, the boy simply said that he wanted water, that he was very thirsty, You will have to wait till tomorrow, we have no water in the house, at this very moment she remembered that there was water, some five litres or more of precious water, the whole contents of the toilet cistern, it could not be worse than what they had been drinking during the quarantine. Blind in the darkness, she went to the bathroom, feeling her way along, she raised the lid of the cistern, she really could not see if there was water, there was, her fingers told her, she searched for a glass, plunged it in with great care and filled it, civilisation had returned to the primitive sources of slime. When she entered the room everyone remained seated where they were. The lamp lit up their faces which turned towards her, it was as if she had said, I am back, as you can see, take advantage, remember this light won't last forever. The doctor's wife brought the glass to the boy with the squint's lips and said, Here is your water, drink slowly, slowly, and savour

it, a glass of water is a marvellous thing, she was not talking to
him, she was not talking to anyone, simply communicating to
the world what a marvellous thing a glass of water is. Where
did you get it, is it rain water, asked the husband, No, it's from
the cistern. Didn't we have a large bottle of water when we left
this place, he asked again, the wife said, Of course, why didn't
I think of it, a half-full bottle and another that had not even
been started, what luck, don't drink, don't drink anymore, she
said to the boy, we are all going to drink fresh water, I'll put our
best glasses on the table and we are going to drink fresh water.
This time she took the lamp and went to the kitchen, she returned with the bottle, the light shone through it, it made the
treasure inside sparkle. She put it on the table, went to fetch
the glasses, the best they had, of finest crystal, then, slowly, as
if she were performing a rite, she filled them. At last, she said,
Let's drink. The blind hands groped and found the glasses, they
raised them trembling. Let's drink, the doctor's wife said again.
In the middle of the table, the lamp was like a sun surrounded
by shining stars. When they had put the glasses back on the
table, the girl with the dark glasses and the old man with the
eyepatch were crying.

It was a restless night. Vague in the beginning, and impre-
cise, the dreams went from sleeper to sleeper, they lingered
here, they lingered there, they brought with them new memories, new secrets, new desires, that is why the sleepers sighed
and murmured, This dream is not mine, they said, but the
dream replied, You do not yet know your dreams, in this way
the girl with the dark glasses came to find out who the old man
with the black eyepatch was, lying there asleep two paces away,
in this way he thought he knew who she was, he merely thought
he did, it is not enough for dreams to be reciprocal in order to
be the same. As dawn broke it began to rain. The wind beating
fiercely against the windows sounded like the cracking of a

thousand whiplashes. The doctor's wife woke up, opened her eyes and murmured, Listen to that rain, then she closed them again, in the room it was still black night, now she could sleep. She barely managed a minute, she woke abruptly with the idea that she had something to do, but without yet understanding what it might be, the rain was saying to her, Get up, what did the rain want, Slowly, so as not to disturb her husband, she left the bedroom, crossed the sitting-room, paused for an instant to make sure they were all sleeping on the sofas, then she proceeded along the corridor as far as the kitchen, it was over this part of the building that the rain fell with the greatest force, driven by the wind. With the sleeve of her dressing-gown she cleaned the steamed-up glass panel of the door and looked outside. The entire sky was one great cloud, the rain poured down in torrents. Piled up on the balcony-floor were the dirty clothes they had taken off, there was the plastic bag with the shoes waiting to be washed. Wash. The last veil of sleep was suddenly torn, this was what she had to do. She opened the door, took one step, immediately the rain drenched her from head to foot, as if she were beneath a waterfall. I must take advantage of this water, she thought. She went back into the kitchen and, making as little noise as possible, began gathering together bowls, pots and pans, anything in which she could collect some of the rain that was falling from heaven in sheets, harried about by the wind, sweeping over the roofs of the city like a large and noisy broom. She took them outside, arranged them along the balcony up against the railing, now there would be water to wash the dirty clothes and filthy shoes, Don't let it stop, she murmured as she searched in the kitchen for soap and detergents, scrubbing brushes, anything that might be used to clean a little, at least a little, of this unbearable filth of the soul. Of the body, she said, as if to correct this metaphysical thought, then she added, It's all the same. Then, as if this had to be the inevitable

conclusion, the harmonious conciliation between what she had
said and what she thought, she quickly took off her drenched
dressing-gown, and, now, receiving on her body, sometimes a
caress, sometimes the whiplash of the rain, she began to wash
the clothes and herself at the same time. The sound of water
that surrounded her prevented her from noticing right away
that she was no longer alone. At the door to the balcony stood
the girl with dark glasses and the wife of the first blind man, we
cannot tell what presentiments, what intuition, what inner
voices might have roused them, nor do we know how they
found their way here, there is no point searching for explanations for the moment, conjectures are free. Help me, said the
doctor's wife when she saw them, How, since we cannot see,
asked the wife of the first blind man. Take off your clothes, the
less we have to dry afterwards, the better, But we can't see, the
wife of the first blind man repeated, It does not matter, said
the girl with the dark glasses, We shall do what we can, And I
shall finish off later, said the doctor's wife, I shall clean whatever is still dirty, and now to work, let's go, we are the only
woman in the world with two eyes and six hands. Perhaps in
the building opposite, behind those closed windows some blind
people, men, women, roused by the noise of the constant beating of the rain, with their head pressed against the cold window-panes covering with their breath on the glass the dullness
of the night, remember the time when, like now, they last saw
rain falling from the sky. They cannot imagine that there are
moreover three naked women out there, as naked as when they
came into the world, they seem to be mad, they must be mad,
people in their right mind do not start washing on a balcony
exposed to the view of the neighbourhood, even less looking
like that, what does it matter that we are all blind, these are
things one must not do, my God, how the rain is pouring down
on them, how it trickles between their breasts, how it lingers

and disappears into the darkness of the pubis, how it finally
drenches and flows over the thighs, perhaps we have judged
them wrongly, or perhaps we are unable to see this the most
beautiful and glorious thing that has happened in the history of
the city, a sheet of foam flows from the floor of the balcony, if
only I could go with it, falling interminably, clean, purified, naked. Only God sees us, said the wife of the first blind man, who,
despite disappointments and setbacks, clings to the belief that
God is not blind, to which the doctor's wife replies, Not even
he, the sky is clouded over, Only I can see you, Am I ugly, asked
the girl with the dark glasses, You are skinny and dirty, you will
never be ugly, And I, asked the wife of the first blind man, You
are dirty and skinny like her, not as pretty, but more than I,
You are beautiful, said the girl with the dark glasses, How do
you know, since you have never seen me, I have dreamt of you
twice, When, The second time was last night, You were dreaming about the house because you felt safe and calm, it's only
natural after all we've been through, in your dream I was the
home, and in order to see me you needed a face, so you invented it, I too see you as beautiful, and I never dreamt of you,
said the wife of the first blind man, Which only goes to show
that blindness is the good fortune of the ugly, You are not ugly,
No, as a matter of fact I am not, but at my age, How old are
you, asked the girl with the dark glasses, Getting on for fifty,
Like my mother, And her, Her, what, Is she still beautiful, She
was more beautiful once, that's what happens to all of us, we
were all more beautiful once, You were never more beautiful,
said the wife of the first blind man. Words are like that, they
deceive, they pile up, it seems they do not know where to go,
and, suddenly, because of two or three or four that suddenly
come out, simple in themselves, a personal pronoun, an adverb,
a verb, an adjective, we have the excitement of seeing them
coming irresistibly to the surface through the skin and the eyes

and upsetting the composure of our feelings, sometimes the nerves that cannot bear it any longer, they put up with a great deal, they put up with everything, it was as if they were wearing armour, we might say. The doctor's wife has nerves of steel, and yet the doctor's wife is reduced to tears because of a personal pronoun, an adverb, a verb, an adjective, mere grammatical categories, mere labels, just like the two women, the others, indefinite pronouns, they too are crying, they embrace the woman of the whole sentence, three graces beneath the falling rain. These are moments that cannot last forever, these women have been here for more than an hour, it is time they felt cold, I'm cold, said the girl with the dark glasses. We cannot do anything more with the clothes, the shoes are spick and span, now it is time for these women to wash themselves, they soak their hair and wash each other's backs and they laugh as only little girls laugh when they play blind man's buff in the garden before becoming blind. Day broke, the first rays of sun peered over the shoulder of the world before hiding once more behind the clouds. It continues to rain but with less force. The washerwomen went back to the kitchen, they dried themselves and rubbed themselves with the towels the doctor's wife had gone to fetch from the bathroom cupboard, their skins smell strongly of detergent, but such is life, if you haven't got a dog to hunt with use a cat, the soap disappeared in a twinkling of the eye, even though this house seems to have everything or is it just that they know how to make the best use of what they have got, at last, they covered themselves, paradise was out there, the dressing-gown of the doctor's wife is soaking wet, but she put on a flowered dress that she had not worn for years and which made her the prettiest of the three.

When they entered the sitting-room, the doctor's wife saw that the old man with the black eyepatch was sitting up on the sofa where he had slept. He held his head between his hands, his fingers plunged into the thatch of white hair which still grew from his forehead to the back of his neck, and he was calm, tense, as if he wanted to hold on to his thoughts, or, on the contrary, to stop them altogether. He heard them come in, he knew where they came from, and what they had been doing, that they had been naked, and if he knew all this it was not because he had suddenly regained his sight and, like the other old men, crept up to spy on not one Susanna in her bath, but on three, he was blind, he stayed blind, he had only got to the kitchen door from where he heard what they were saying on the balcony, the laughter, the noise of the rain and the beating of the water, he breathed in the smell of the soap, then he returned to the sofa, thinking that there was still life in this world, to ask whether there was still any part of it left for him. The doctor's wife said, The women have already washed, Now it is the men's turn, and the old man with the black eyepatch asked, Is it still raining, Yes, it is raining and there is water in the basins on the balcony, Then I prefer to wash in the bathroom, in the tub, he pronounced the word as if he were showing his birth certificate, as if he were explaining, I am of the generation in which people did not speak of baths but of tubs, and added, If you don't mind, of course, I do not want to dirty the house, I promise that I shall not spill any water on the floor, at least, I shall do my best, In that case I shall bring you some water into the bathroom, I'll help, I can manage on my own, I have to be of some use, I am not an invalid, Come, then. On the balcony, the doctor's wife pulled an almost full basin of water inside. Take a hold here, she said to the old man with the black eyepatch, guiding his hands, Now, they lifted the basin at one go. Just as well that you came to help me, I could not have managed alone, Do you know the saying, What saying, Old people cannot do much but their work is not to be despised, That's not the way it goes, All right, instead of old people, it should

be children, and instead of despise, it should be disdain, but if
sayings are to retain any meaning and to continue to be used
they have to adapt to the times. You are a philosopher, What
an idea, I am just an old man. They emptied the basin into the
bath, then the doctor's wife opened a drawer, she remembered
that she still had one new bar of soap. She put it into the hand
of the old man with the black eyepatch, You are going to smell
nice, better than us, use it all, do not worry, there may not be
any food, but there is bound to be soap in these supermarkets,
Thank you, Watch you don't slip, if you want I'll call my husband to help you, Thanks, I prefer to wash by myself, As you
like, and here, wait, give me your hand, there's a razor and a
brush, if you want to shave off that beard, Thanks. The doctor's
wife left. The old man with the eyepatch took off the pyjamas
which had been allotted to him in the distribution of clothes,
then, carefully, he got into the bath. The water was cold and
there was little of it, less than a foot, how different is this sad
puddle from receiving it in buckets from heaven as the three
women had. He knelt on the bottom of the bath, took a deep
breath, with both hands together he suddenly splashed water
against his chest which almost took his breath away. He rapidly
splashed water all over himself so as not to have time to shiver,
then, step by step, systematically, he started to soap himself, to
rub heavily starting from the shoulders, arms, chest and stomach, his groin, his penis, between his legs, I am worse than an
animal, he thought, then the thin thighs down to the layer of
grime that covered his feet. He made lather so that the cleaning process should be extended, he said, I have to wash my hair
and moved his hands back to untie the eyepatch, You too need
a bath, he loosened it and dropped it into the water, now he felt
warm, he wet and soaped his hair, he was a man of foam, white
in the middle of an immense white blindness where nobody
could find him, if that was what he thought, he was deceiving

himself, at that moment he felt hands touching his back, gathering the foam from his arms, and from his chest and spreading it over his back, slowly, as if, being unable to see what they were doing, they had to pay closer attention to the job. He wanted to ask, Who are you, but he couldn't speak, now he was shivering, not from the cold, the hands continued to wash him gently, the woman did not say, I am the doctor's wife, I am the wife of the first blind man, I am the girl with dark glasses, the hands finished their task, withdrew, in the silence one could hear the gentle noise of the bathroom door closing, the old man with the eyepatch was alone, kneeling in the bath as if imploring a favour from heaven, trembling, trembling, Who could it have been, he asked himself, his reason told him that it could only have been the doctor's wife, she is the one who can see, she is the one who has protected us, cared for us and fed us, it would not be surprising that she should have given me this discreet attention, it is what his reason told him, but he did not believe in reason. He continued to shiver, he did not know whether it was from excitement or from cold. He found the eyepatch at the bottom of the bath, rubbed it hard, wrung it dry and put it back, with it he felt less naked. When he entered the sitting-room, dry, perfumed, the doctor's wife said, We already have one man who is clean and shaven, and then, in the tone of voice of someone who has just remembered something that should have been done and was not, You had no one to wash your back, what a pity. The old man with the black eyepatch did not reply, he merely thought that he had been right not to believe in reason.

They gave what little food there was to the boy with the squint, the others would have to wait for fresh supplies. In the larder there were some jars of preserves, some dried fruit, sugar, some leftover biscuits, some dry toast, but they would use these reserves and others added to them only in case of extreme necessity, the food from day to day would have to be earned, just in case by some misfortune the expedition returned empty-handed, meanwhile two biscuits per person with a spoonful of jam, There is strawberry and peach, which do you prefer, three walnut halves, a glass of water, a luxury while it lasts. The wife of the first blind man said that she too wanted to look for food, three would *not* go amiss, even being blind, two of them could help to carry the food and besides, were it possible, bearing in mind that they were not that far away, she would like to go and see what state her home was in, if it had been occupied, if the people were known to her, for example neighbours from the building whose family had grown because some relatives from the provinces had arrived with the idea of saving themselves from the epidemic of blindness that had attacked their village, the city always enjoys better resources. Therefore the three of them left, dressed in what dry clothes they could find in the house, the others, those that have been washed, have to wait for better weather. The sky remained overcast but there was no threat of rain. Swept along by the water, especially in the steeper streets, the rubbish had piled up in small heaps leaving wide stretches of pavement clean. If only the rain would last, in this situation sunshine would be the worst that could happen to us, said the doctor's wife, we've got enough filth and bad smells already, We notice it more because we are washed, said the wife of the first blind man and her husband agreed, although he suspected that the cold bath had given him a cold. There were crowds of blind people in the streets, they took advantage of the break in the weather to search for food and to satisfy there and then their need to defecate which they still had despite the little food and drink they took in. Dogs sniffed everywhere, they scrabbled in the rubbish, the odd one carried a drowned rat in its mouth, a very rare occurrence that could only be explained by the extraordinary abundance of the re-

cent downpours, the flood caught him in the wrong place, being a good swimmer was of no use to him. The dog of tears
did not mix with his former companions in the pack and the
hunt, his choice is made, but he does not wait to be fed, he is
already chewing heaven knows what, these mountains of rubbish hide unimaginable treasures, it is all a matter of searching, scratching and finding. The blind man and his wife will
also have to search and scratch in their memory when the occasion arises, now they had memorised the four corners, not of
the house where they live, which has many more, but of their
street, the four street corners which will serve them as cardi-
nal points, the blind are not interested where east and west lie,
or north or south, all they want is that their groping hands tell
them that they are on the right road, formerly, when they were
still few, they used to carry white sticks, the sound of the continuous taps on the ground and the walls was a sort of code
which allowed them to identify and recognise their route, but
today, since everybody is blind, a white stick, in the middle of
the general clamour, is less than helpful, quite apart from the
fact that, immersed in his own whiteness, the blind man may
come to doubt whether he is actually carrying anything in his
hand. Dogs, as everyone knows, have, in addition to what we
call instinct, other means of orientation, it is certain that because of their shortsightedness they do not rely much on their
sight, however, since their nose is well ahead of their eyes, they
always get to where they want, in this case, just to be sure, the
dog of tears lifted its leg to the four corners of the wind, the
breeze will take on the task of guiding it home if it were to
get lost one day. As they went along the doctor's wife looked
up and down the streets in search of food shops where she
could build up their much reduced larder. The looting had not
been complete because in old-fashioned groceries there were
still some beans or some chickpeas in the storerooms, they are

dried pulses which take a long time to cook, one thing is water, another thing is fuel, therefore they are not much appreciated these days. The doctor's wife was not particularly keen on the tendency of proverbs to preach, nevertheless something of this ancient lore must have remained in her memory, the proof being that she filled two of the bags they had brought with beans and chickpeas, Keep what is of no use at the moment, and later you will find what you need, one of her grandmothers had told her, the water in which you soak them will also serve to cook them, and whatever remains from the cooking will cease to be water, but will have become broth. It is not only in nature that from time to time not everything is lost and something is gained.

Why they were loaded with bags of beans and peas and anything else they happened to pick up when they were still some distance away from the street where the first blind man and his wife lived, for that is where they are going, is a question that could only occur to someone who has never in his life suffered shortages. Take it home, even if it's a stone, that same grandmother had said, but she forgot to add, Even if you have to go around the earth, this was the feat they were now embarked upon, they were going home by the longest route. Where are we, the first blind man asked, he addressed the doctor's wife, that is what she had eyes for, and he said, This is where I went blind, on this corner with the traffic lights, Right here, on this corner, Precisely on this spot. I do not want to remember what happened, trapped in the car without being able to see, people shouting outside, and me shouting desperately that I was blind, until that man turned up and took me home, Poor man, the wife of the first blind man said, he will never steal a car again, We are so afraid of the idea of having to die, said the doctor's wife, that we always try to find excuses for the dead, as if we were asking beforehand to be excused when it is our turn, All this still seems like a dream, the wife of the first blind man said, it is as if I were dreaming that I am blind, When I was at home, waiting for you, I also thought so, said her husband. They had left the square where it had happened, now they climbed some narrow labyrinthine streets, the doctor's wife hardly knows these places but the first blind man does not get lost, he knows the way, she says the names of the streets and he says, Let's turn to the left, Let's turn to the right, finally he says, This is our street, the building is on the left-hand side, roughly in the middle, What is the number, asked the doctor's wife, he can't remember, Now then, it's not that I cannot remember, it's gone from my head, he said, that was a bad omen, if we do not even know where we live, if the dream has replaced our memory, where will that road take us, All right, this time it is not serious, it was lucky that the first blind man's wife had the idea of coming on the excursion, there we already have her saying the house number, this helped her to avoid having to have recourse to the first blind man, who was priding himself on the fact that he can recognise the door by the magic of touch, as if he were carrying a magic wand, one touch, metal, one touch, wood, with three or four more he would arrive at the full pattern, I'm sure it is this one. They entered, the doctor's wife first, What floor is it, she asked, The third, answered the first blind man, his memory was not as bad as had appeared, some things we forget, that's life, others we remember, for example, to remember when, already blind, he had entered this door, On what floor do you live, asked the man who had not yet stolen the car, Third, he replied, the difference being that this time they are not going up in the elevator, they walk up the invisible staircase which is at once dark and luminous, how people who are not blind miss electric light, or sunlight, or the light of a candle, now the doctor's wife has got used to the semi-darkness, half-way up they run into two blind women from the upper floors

coming down, perhaps from the third, nobody asked, it is true
the neighbours are not, in fact, the same.

The door was closed. What are we going to do, asked the
doctor's wife, Leave it to me, said the first blind man. They
knocked once, twice, three times. There's nobody in, one of
them said at exactly the moment when the door opened, the
delay was not surprising, a blind person at the back of the flat
cannot come running to answer the door. Who is it, what do
you want, asked the man who opened the door, he had a serious
look on his face, he was polite, he must be someone we can talk
to. The first blind man said, I used to live in this flat, Ah, the
other replied, Is there anybody with you, My wife, and also a
friend of ours, How can I be sure that this was your flat, That's
easy, the wife of the first blind man said, I can tell you everything there is inside. The other man paused a few seconds, then
he said, Come in. The doctor's wife went in last, here nobody
needed a guide. The blind man said, I am alone, my family
went to look for food, perhaps I should have said the women,
but I do not think it would be proper, he paused and then
added, Yet you may think that I should know, What do you
mean, asked the doctor's wife, The women I referred to are my
wife and my two daughters, and I should know when it is proper
to use the expression "women." I am a writer, we are supposed
to know such things. The first blind man felt flattered, imagine,
a writer living in my flat, then a doubt rose in him, was it good
manners to ask him his name, he might even have heard of his
name, it was even possible that he had read him, he was still
hesitating between curiosity and discretion, when his wife put
the question directly, What is your name, Blind people do not
need a name, I am my voice, nothing else matters, But you
wrote books and those books carry your name, said the doctor's
wife, Now nobody can read them, it is as if they did not exist.
The first blind man felt that the conversation was moving too

far from the topic which he was most interested in, And how do you come to be in my flat, he asked, Like many others who no longer live where they used to live, I found my house occupied by people who did not want to listen to reason, one might say that we were kicked down the stairs, Is your house far away, No, Did you try to get it back, asked the doctor's wife, it is now quite common for people to move from house to house, I have already tried twice, And are they still there, Yes. And what are you going to do now that you know that this is our flat, the first blind man wanted to know, are you going to throw us out as they did to you, No, I have neither the age nor the strength for that, and even if I did, I do not believe that I would be capable of such a speedy procedure, a writer manages to acquire in life the patience he needs to write. You will leave us the flat, though, Yes, if we cannot find another solution, I cannot see what other solution could be found. The doctor's wife had already guessed what the writer's reply would be, You and your wife, like the friend who is with you, live in a flat, I imagine, Yes, in her flat in fact, Is it far away, Not really, Then, if you'll permit me, I have a proposal to make, Go on, That we carry on as we are, at this moment we both have a place where we can live, I shall continue to keep a watchful eye on what is happening to mine, if one day I find it free, I shall move in immediately, you will do the same, Come here at regular intervals and when you find it empty, move in, I am not sure I like the idea, I didn't expect you to like it but I doubt whether you would prefer the only remaining alternative, What is that, For you to recover this flat which is yours, But, in that case, Precisely, in that case we shall have to find somewhere else to live, No, don't even think about it, intervened the wife of the first blind man, Let's leave things as they are, and see what happens, It occurred to me that there is another solution, said the writer, And what might that be, asked the first blind man, We shall live here as your guests, the flat is big enough for all of us, No, said the wife of the first blind man, We shall carry on as before, living with our friend, there is no need to ask if you agree, she added, addressing the doctor's wife, And there is no need for me to reply, I am obliged to all of you, said the writer, all this time I have been waiting for someone to reclaim the flat, To accept what one has is the most natural thing when one is blind, said the doctor's wife, How have you managed since the outbreak of the epidemic, We came out of internment only three days ago, Ah, you were in quarantine, Yes, Was it hard, Worse than that, How horrible, You are a writer, you have, as you said a moment ago, an obligation to know words, therefore you know that adjectives are of no use to us, if a person kills another, for example, it would be better to state this fact openly, directly, and to trust that the horror of the act, in itself, is so shocking that there is no need for us to say it was horrible, Do you mean that we have more words than we need, I mean that we have too few feelings, Or that we have them but have ceased to use the words they express, And so we lose them, I'd like you to tell me how you lived during quarantine, Why, I am a writer, You would have to have been there, A writer is just like anyone else, he cannot know everything, nor can he experience everything, he must ask and imagine, One day I may tell you what it was like, then you can write a book, Yes, I am writing it, How, if you are blind, The blind too can write, You mean that you had time to learn the braille alphabet, I do not know braille, How can you write, then, asked the first blind man, Let me show you. He got up from his chair, left the room and after a minute returned, he was holding a sheet of paper in his hand and a ball-point pen, this is the last complete page I have written, We cannot see it, said the wife of the first blind man, Nor I, said the writer, Then how can you write, asked the doctor's wife, looking at the sheet of paper where in the half-light of the room she could make

out tightly compressed lines, occasionally superimposed, By
touch, the writer answered smiling, it is easy, you place the
sheet over a soft surface, for example some sheets of paper, then
it's just a question of writing, But if you cannot see anything,
said the first blind man, A ball-point pen is an excellent tool for
blind writers, it does not permit them to read what they have
written, but it tells them where they have written, they only
have to follow with their fingers the impression left by the last
written line, then you write as far as the edge of the paper, and
calculating the distance to the next line is very easy, I notice
that some lines overlap, said the doctor's wife, gently taking the
sheet out of his hand, How do you know, I can see, You can see,
have you recovered your sight, how, when, the writer asked excitedly, I suppose I am the only person who has never lost it,
And why, what is the explanation for this, I have no explanation, there may not be one, That means that you saw everything that has happened, I saw what I saw, I had no option,
How many people were in the quarantine, Nearly three hundred, From when, From the beginning, we only came out three
days ago, as I said, I believe that I was the first person to go
blind, said the first blind man, That must have been horrible,
That word again, said the doctor's wife, Forgive me, suddenly
everything I have been writing about since we turned blind, my
family and I, strikes me as being ridiculous, About what, About
what we suffered, about our life, Everyone has to speak of what
they know, and what they do not know they should ask, That's
why I ask you, And I will answer, I don't know when, someday.
The doctor's wife brushed the writer's hand with the paper.
Would you mind showing me where you work and what you
are writing, Not at all, come with me, Can we come too, asked
the wife of the first blind man, The flat is yours, said the writer,
I am only passing through. In the bedroom there was a tiny
table with an unlit lamp. The dim light entering through the

window, allowed one to see to the left some blank sheets, others on the right-hand side had been written on, in the middle there was one half written. There were two new ball-point pens next to the lamp. Here it is, said the writer. The doctor's wife asked, May I? without waiting for a reply she picked up the written pages, there must have been about twenty, she passed her eye over the tiny handwriting, over the lines which went up and down, over the words inscribed on the whiteness of the page, recorded in blindness, I am only passing through, the writer had said, and these were the signs he had left in passing. The doctor's wife placed her hand on his shoulder, and with both hands he reached out for it and raised it slowly to his lips, Don't lose yourself, don't let yourself be lost, he said, and these were unexpected, enigmatic words that did not seem to fit the occasion.

When they returned home, carrying enough food for three days, the doctor's wife, interrupted by the excited interjections from the first blind man and his wife, told what had happened. And that night, as was only right, she read to all of them a few pages from a book she had gone to fetch from the study. The boy with the squint was not interested in the story, and after a little while he fell asleep with his head on the lap of the girl with the dark glasses and his feet resting on the legs of the old man with the eyepatch.

TWO days later the doctor said, I'd like to know what has happened to the surgery, at this stage we are no use for anything, neither it nor I, but perhaps one day people will recover their sight, the instruments must still be there waiting, We can go whenever you want, said his wife, Right now, And we could take advantage of this walk to pass by my home, if you don't mind, said the girl with the dark glasses, Not that I believe that my parents have returned, it's only to ease my conscience, We can go to your house too, said the doctor's wife. Nobody else wanted to join this reconnoitre of homes, not the first blind man and his wife, for they already knew what they could count on, the old man with the black eyepatch also knew, but not for the same reasons, and the boy with the squint because he still could not remember the name of the street where he had lived. The weather was bright, it seemed that the rain had stopped and the sun, though pale, could already be felt on their skin, I don't know how we can continue to live if the heat gets any worse, said the doctor, all this rubbish rotting all over the place, the dead animals, perhaps even people, there must be dead people inside the houses, the worst thing is that we are not organised, there should be an organisation in each building, in each street, in each district, A government, said the wife, An organisation, the human body is also an organised system, it lives as long as it keeps organised, and death is only the effect of a disorganisation, And how can a society of blind people organise itself in order to survive, By organising itself, to organise oneself is, in a way, to begin to have eyes, Perhaps you're right, but the experience of this blindness has brought us only death and misery, my eyes, just like your surgery, were useless, Thanks to your eyes we are still alive, said the girl with the dark glasses, We would also be alive if I were blind as well, the world is full of blind people, I think we are all going to die, it's just a matter of time, Dying has always been a matter of time, said the doctor, But to die just because you're blind, there can be no worse way of dying, We die of illnesses, accidents, chance events, And now we shall also die of blindness, I mean, we shall die of blindness and cancer, of blindness and tuberculosis, of blindness and AIDS, of blindness and heart attacks, illnesses may differ from one person to another but what is really killing us now is blindness, We are not immortal, we cannot escape death, but at least we should not be blind, said the doctor's wife, How, if this blindness is concrete and real, said the doctor, I am not sure, said the wife, Nor I, said the girl with the dark glasses.

They did not have to force the door, it opened normally, the key was on the doctor's key ring which had remained in the house when they had been taken off for quarantine. This is the waiting-room, said the doctor's wife, The room I was in, said the girl with the dark glasses, the dream continues, but I don't know what dream it is, whether it is the dream of dreaming which I experienced that day when I dreamt that I was going blind, or the dream of always having been blind and coming, still dreaming, to the surgery in order to be cured of an inflammation of the eyes in which there was no danger of

becoming blind, The quarantine was no dream, said the doctor's wife, Certainly not, nor was it a dream that we were raped,
Nor that I stabbed a man, Take me to my office, I can get there
on my own but you take me, said the doctor. The door was
open. The doctor's wife said, The place has been turned upside down, papers on the floor, the drawers of the file cabinet have been taken, It must have been the people from the
Ministry, not to waste time looking, Probably, And the instruments, At first sight, they seem to be in good order, That, at
least, is something, said the doctor, he advanced alone with his
arms outstretched, he touched the box with the lenses, his ophthalmoscope, the desk, then, addressing the girl with the dark
glasses, he said, I know what you are trying to say, when you
say that you are living a dream. He sat down at the desk, placed
his hands on the dusty top, then with a sad, ironic smile, as if he
were talking to someone sitting opposite him, he said, No, my
dear doctor, I am very sorry, but your condition has no known
cure, if you want me to give you one last piece of advice, cling
to the old saying, they were right when they said that patience
is good for the eyes. Don't make us suffer, said the woman,
Forgive me, both of you, we are in the place where miracles
used to be performed, now I don't even have the evidence of
my magic powers, they have taken it all away, The only miracle
we can perform is to go on living, said the woman, to preserve
the fragility of life from day to day, as if it were blind and did
not know where to go, and perhaps it is like that, perhaps it really does not know, it placed itself in our hands, after giving us
intelligence, and this is what we have made of it, You speak as
if you too were blind, said the girl with the dark glasses, In a
way I am, I am blind with your blindness, perhaps I might be
able to see better if there were more of us who could see, I am
afraid you are like the witness in search of a court to which
he has been summoned by who knows who, in order to make

a statement about who knows what, said the doctor, Time is coming to an end, putrescence is spreading, diseases find the doors open, water is running out, food has become poison, that would be my first statement, said the doctor's wife, And the second, asked the girl with dark glasses, Let's open our eyes, We can't, we are blind, said the doctor, It is a great truth that says that the worst blind person was the one who did not want to see, But I do want to see, said the girl with dark glasses, That won't be the reason you will see, the only difference would be that you would no longer be the worst blind person, and now, let's go, there is nothing more to be seen here, the doctor said.

On their way to the home of the girl with dark glasses, they crossed a large square with groups of blind people who were listening to speeches from other blind people, at first sight, neither one nor the other group seemed blind, the speakers turned their heads excitedly towards their listeners, the listeners turned their heads attentively to the speakers. They were proclaiming the end of the world, redemption through penitence, the visions of the seventh day, the advent of the angel, cosmic collisions, the death of the sun, the tribal spirit, the sap of the mandrake, tiger ointment, the virtue of the sign, the discipline of the wind, the perfume of the moon, the revindication of darkness, the power of exorcism, the sign of the heel, the crucifixion of the rose, the purity of the lymph, the blood of the black cat, the sleep of the shadow, the rising of the seas, the logic of anthropophagy, painless castration, divine tattoos, voluntary blindness, convex thoughts, or concave, or horizontal or vertical, or sloping, or concentrated, or dispersed, or fleeting, the weakening of the vocal cords, the death of the word, Here nobody is speaking of organisation, said the doctor's wife, Perhaps organisation is in another square, he replied. They continued on their way. A bit further on, the doctor's wife said, There are more dead in the road than usual, Our resistance is reaching its end, time is running out, the water is running out, disease is on the increase, food is becoming poison, you said so before, the doctor reminded her, Who knows whether my parents are not among these dead, said the girl with dark glasses, and here, I am passing by without seeing them, It's a time-honoured custom to pass by the dead without seeing them, said the doctor's wife.

The street where the girl with dark glasses lived, seemed even more deserted than usual. At the door to the building there was the body of a woman. Dead, half devoured by stray animals, luckily the dog of tears had not wanted to come to-day, it would have been necessary to keep him from digging his teeth into this corpse. It is the neighbour from the first floor, said the doctor's wife, Who, where, asked her husband, Right here, the first-floor neighbour, you can smell her, Poor woman, said the girl with dark glasses, why did she have to go out into the street, she never went out, Perhaps she felt that her death was near, perhaps she could not stand the idea of staying alone in the flat to rot, said the doctor. And now we can't go in, I don't have the keys, Perhaps your parents have returned and are inside waiting for you, said the doctor, I don't believe it, You are right not to believe it, said the doctor's wife, here are the keys. In the palm of the dead woman's half-open hand resting on the ground there was a set of keys, shining, sparkling. Perhaps they are hers, said the girl with dark glasses, I don't think so, she had no reason to bring her keys to where she was thinking of dying, But being blind, I would not be able to see them, if she thought of bringing them down so that I would be able to get into the flat, We don't know what she was thinking of when she decided to take the keys, perhaps she thought that you would regain your eyesight, perhaps she suspected that there was something unnatural, too easy, about the way we moved around when we were here, perhaps she heard me say that the stair was dark, that I could barely see, or perhaps it was none of that, delirium, dementia, as if, having lost her mind, she had got it into her head to give you the keys, the only thing we know is that her life ended when she set foot outside the door. The doctor's wife picked up the keys, handed them to the girl with dark glasses and then asked, And now, what do we do, are we going to leave her here, We cannot bury her in the street, we have no tools to lift the stones, said the doctor, There is the garden in the back, In that case we'll have to take her up to the second floor and then down by the emergency stairs, That's the only way, Do we have enough strength for this task, asked the girl with dark glasses, The question is not whether we have enough strength, the question is whether we can allow ourselves to leave this woman here, Certainly not, said the doctor, Then the strength must be found. They did manage, but it was hard work dragging the body upstairs, not because of what it weighed, little enough, and less still since the cats and dogs had been at it, but because the body was rigid, stiff, they had trouble turning the corners of the narrow staircase, during the short climb they had to rest four times. Neither the noise, nor the voices, nor the smell of putrefaction brought any other of the inhabitants of the building onto the landings, Just as I thought, my parents are not here, said the girl with dark glasses. When they finally got to the door they were exhausted and they still had to cross to the back of the building and go down the emergency stairs, but there with the help of the saints, they get down the stairs, the burden is lighter, the bends easier to manoeuvre because the stairs were out in the open, one only had to be careful not to let the poor creature's body slip from one's hands, a tumble would leave it beyond repair, not to mention the pain which, after death, is worse.

The garden was like an unexplored jungle, the recent rains had caused the grass and the weeds carried on the wind to grow in abundance, there would be no lack of fresh food for the rabbits which jumped about, and chickens manage even in hard times. They were sitting on the ground, panting, the effort had exhausted them, by their side the corpse rested like them, guarded by the doctor's wife who chased off the hens and rabbits, the rabbits only curious, their noses twitching, the chickens with their beaks like bayonets, ready for anything. The doctor's wife said, Before leaving, she remembered to open the doors of the rabbit hutches, she did not want the rabbits to die of hunger, The difficult thing isn't living with other people, it's understanding them, said the doctor. The girl with dark glasses cleaned her dirty hands on a clump of grass that she had pulled up, it was her own fault, she had grasped the corpse where she should not have, that's what happens when you're blind. The doctor said, What we need is a spade or a shovel, here one can see that the true eternal return is that of words, which now return, spoken for the same reasons, first for the man who stole the car, now for the old woman who returned the keys, once buried nobody will know the difference, unless somebody remembers them. The doctor's wife had gone up to the flat of the girl with dark glasses in order to find a clean sheet, she had to choose the least dirty of them, when she came down the hens were at it, the rabbits were merely chewing the fresh grass. Having covered and wrapped the body, the wife went in search of a spade or shovel. She found both in a garden shed along with other tools. I'll deal with this, she said, the ground is damp, it is easy to dig, you take a rest. She chose a spot where there were no roots of the type that have to be cut with an axe, and don't imagine that this is an easy job, roots have their own little ways, they know how to take advantage of the softness of the soil in order to avoid the blow and weaken the deadly effect of the guillotine. Neither the doctor's wife nor her husband nor the girl with dark glasses, the former because she was digging,

the latter two because their eyes were of no use to them, noticed the appearance of blind people on the surrounding balconies, not many, not on all of them, they must have been attracted by the noise of the digging, even in soft soil there is
noise, not forgetting that there is always some hidden stone
that responds loudly to the blow. There were men and women
who appeared as fluid as ghosts, they could have been ghosts
attending a burial out of curiosity, merely to recall how it had
been when they were buried. The doctor's wife finally saw them
when she had finished digging the grave, she straightened her
aching back and raised her arm to her forehead to wipe away
the sweat. Then, carried away by an irresistible impulse, without thinking, she called out to those blind people and to all the
blind of this world, She will rise again, note that she did not say
She will live again, the matter was not quite that important, although the dictionary is there to confirm, reassure or suggest
that we are dealing with complete and absolute synonyms. The
blind people took fright and went back inside their flats, they
could not understand why such words had been said, besides
they could not have been prepared for such a revelation, it was
clear that they did not go to the square where the magic ut-
terances were made, in respect of which all that was needed to
complete the picture was the addition of the head of the praying mantis and the suicide of the scorpion. The doctor said,
Why did you say she will rise again, to whom were you talking, To a few blind people who appeared on the balconies, I
was startled and I must have frightened them, And why those
words rather than any others, I don't know, they came into my
head and I said them, The next we know you'll be preaching
in the square we passed along the way, Yes, a sermon about the
rabbit's tooth and the hen's beak, come and help me now, over
here, that's right, take her by the feet, I'll raise her from this
end, careful, don't slip into the grave, that's it, just so, lower her

slowly, more, more, I made the grave a little deeper because of the hens, once they start scratching, you never know where they'll finish up, that's it. She used the shovel to fill the grave, stamped the earth firmly down, made the little mound that always remains of the earth that is returned to the earth, as if she had never done anything else in her life. Finally, she picked a branch from a rosebush growing in the corner of the yard and planted it at the head of the grave. Will she rise again, asked the girl with the dark glasses, Not her, no, replied the doctor's wife, those who are still alive have a greater need to rise again by themselves and they don't, We are already half dead, said the doctor, We are still half alive too, answered his wife. She put the shovel and the spade back in the shed, took a good look around the yard to check that everything was in order, What order, she asked herself and provided her own answer, The order that wants the dead where they should be among the dead, and the living among the living, while the hens and rabbits feed some and feed off others, I'd like to leave a small sign for my parents, said the girl with dark glasses, just to let them know that I am alive, I don't want to destroy your hopes, said the doctor, but first they would have to find the house and that is most unlikely. Just remember that we wouldn't have got there without someone to guide us, You're right, and I don't even know if they are still alive, but unless I leave them some sign, anything, I shall feel as if I had abandoned them. What's it to be then, asked the doctor's wife, Something they might recognise by touch, said the girl with the dark glasses, the sad thing is that I no longer have anything on me from the old days. The doctor's wife looked at her, she was sitting on the first step of the emergency stairs, with her hands limp on her knees, her lovely face anguished, her hair spread over her shoulders, I know what sign you can leave them, she said. She went rapidly up the stairs, back into the house and returned with a pair of scis-

sors and a piece of string, What are you thinking of, asked the
girl with dark glasses, worried when she heard the snipping of
the scissors cutting off her hair, If your parents were to return,
they would find hanging from the door handle a lock of hair,
who else could it possibly belong to but their daughter, asked
the doctor's wife, You make me want to weep, said the girl with
the dark glasses, and she had no sooner said it, than she lowered her head over the folded arms on her knees and gave in to
her sorrows, her sadness, to the emotions aroused by the suggestion made by the doctor's wife, then she noticed, without
knowing by what emotional route she had arrived there, that
she was also crying for the old woman on the first floor, the
eater of raw meat, the horrible witch, who with her dead hand
had restored to her the keys to the flat. And then the doctor's
wife said, What times we live in, we find the order of things inverted, a symbol that nearly always signified death has become
a sign of life, There are hands capable of these and greater
wonders, said the doctor, Necessity is a powerful weapon, my
dear, said the woman, and now that's enough of philosophy and
witchcraft, let's hold hands and get on with life. It was the girl
with dark glasses herself who tied the lock of hair to the door
handle, Do you think my parents will notice it, she asked, The
door handle is like the outstretched hand of a house, said the
doctor's wife, and with this commonplace expression, as one
might say, they concluded the visit.

That night once again they had a reading, there was no other
way of distracting themselves, what a pity, the doctor was not,
for example, an amateur violinist, what sweet serenades might
otherwise be heard on this fifth floor, their envious neighbours would say, Either they are doing very well or else they
are completely irresponsible and think they can escape misery by laughing at the misery of others. Now there is no music
other than that of words, and these, especially those in books,

are discreet, and even if curiosity should bring someone from
the building to listen at the door, they would hear only a soli-
tary murmur, that long thread of sound that can last into in-
finity, because the books of this world, all together, are, as they
say the universe is, infinite. When the reading ended, late that
night, the old man with the eyepatch said, That's what we have
come to, listening to someone reading, I'm not complaining,
I could stay here forever, said the girl with dark glasses, I am
not complaining either, I only mean that this is all we are good
for, listening to someone reading us the story of a human man-
kind that existed before us, let's be glad of our good fortune at
still having a pair of seeing eyes with us here, the last pair left,
if they are extinguished one day, I don't even want to think
about it, then the thread which links us to that human man-
kind would be broken, it will be as if we were to separate from
each other in space, forever, all equally blind, As long as I can,
the girl with dark glasses said, I'll keep on hoping, hoping to
find my parents, hoping the boy's mother will turn up, You forgot to speak of the hope we all have, What's that, Regaining
our sight, It's mad to cling to such hopes, Well, I can tell you,
without such hopes I would already have given up, Give me an
example, Being able to see again, We've already had that one,
give me another, I won't, Why, You wouldn't be interested, And
how do you know that I wouldn't, what do you think you know
about me that you can by yourself decide what interests me
and what doesn't, Don't get angry, I didn't mean to hurt you,
Men are all the same, they think because they came out of the
belly of a woman they know all there is to know about women,
I know very little about women, and about you I know nothing, as for men, in my opinion, by modern criteria I am now an
old man and one-eyed as well as being blind, Have you nothing else to say against yourself, A lot more, you can't imagine
how the list of self-recriminations grows with advancing age,
I am young and have my fair share already, You haven't done

anything really bad yet, How do you know, if you've never lived with me, You're right, I have never lived with you, Why do you repeat my words in that tone of voice, What tone of voice, That one, All I said was that I have never lived with you, Come on, come on, don't pretend that you don't understand, Don't insist, I beg you, I do insist, I want to know, Let's return to hopes, All right, The other example of hope which I refused to give was this, What, The last self-accusation on my list, Please, explain yourself, I never understand riddles, The monstrous wish of never regaining our sight, Why, So that we can go on living as we are, Do you mean all together, or just you and me, Don't make me answer, If you were only a man you could avoid answering, like all others, but you yourself said that you are an old man, and old men, if longevity has any sense at all, should not avert their face from the truth, answer me, With you, And why do you want to live with me, Do you want me to tell in front of everybody, We have done the dirtiest, ugliest, most repulsive things together, what you can tell me cannot possibly be worse, All right, if you insist, let it be, because the man I still am loves the woman you are, Was it so very difficult to make a declaration of love, At my age, people fear ridicule, You were not ridiculous, Let's forget it, please, I have no intention of forgetting it or of letting you forget it either, It's nonsense, you forced it out of me and now, And now it's my turn, Don't say anything you may regret later, remember the black list, If I'm sincere today, what does it matter if I regret it tomorrow, Please stop, You want to live with me and I want to live with you, You are mad, We'll start living together here, like a couple, and we shall continue living together if we have to separate from our friends, two blind people must be able to see more than one, It's madness, you don't love me, What's this about loving, I never loved anyone, I just went to bed with men. So you agree with me then, Not really, You spoke of sincerity, tell me then if it's true that you really love me, I love you enough to want to be with you, and that is the first time I've ever said that to anyone, You would not have said it to me either if you had met me somewhere before, an elderly man, half bald with white hair, with a patch over one eye and a cataract in the other, The woman I was then wouldn't have said it, I agree, the person who said it was the woman I am today, Let's see then what the woman you will be tomorrow will have to say, Are you testing me, What an idea, who am I to put you to the test, it's life that decides these things, It's already made one decision.

They had this conversation facing each other, blind eyes staring into blind eyes, their faces flushed and impassioned and when, because one of them had said it and because both of them wanted it, they agreed that life had decided that they should live together, the girl with dark glasses held out her hands, simply to give them, not in order to know where she was going, she touched the hands of the old man with the eyepatch, who gently pulled her towards him, and so they remained sitting side by side, it was not the first time, obviously, but now the words of engagement had been spoken. None of the others said anything, nobody congratulated them, nobody expressed wishes of eternal happiness, to tell the truth these are not the times for festivities and hopes, and when the decisions are so serious as these seem to have been, it is not even surprising that someone might think that one would have to be blind to behave in this way, silence is the best applause. What the doctor's wife did, however, was to put some sofa cushions out in the hallway, enough to make a comfortable bed, then she led the boy with the squint there and told him, From today you will sleep here. As to what happened in the living-room, there is every reason to believe that on that first night it finally became clear whose was the mysterious hand that washed the back of the old man with the black eyepatch on that morning when there was such an abundance of water, all of it purifying.

THE next day, while still in bed, the doctor's wife said to her husband, We have little food left, we'll have to go out again, I thought that today I would go back to the underground food store at the supermarket, the one I went to on the first day, if nobody else has found it, we can get supplies for a week or two, I'm coming with you and we'll ask one or two of the others to come along as well, I'd rather go with you alone, it's easier, and there is less danger of getting lost, How long will you be able to carry the burden of six helpless people, I'll manage as long as I can, but you are quite right, I'm beginning to get exhausted, sometimes I even wish I were blind as well, to be the same as the others, to have no more obligations than they have, We've got used to depending on you, If you weren't there, it would be like being struck with a second blindness, thanks to your eyes we are a little less blind, I'll carry on as long as I can, I can't promise you more than that, One day, when we realise that we can no longer do anything good and useful we ought to have the courage simply to leave this world, as he said, Who said that, The fortunate man we met yesterday, I am sure that he wouldn't say that today, there is nothing like real hope to change one's opinions, He has that all right, long may it last,

In your voice there is a tone which makes me think you are upset, Upset, why, As if something had been taken away from you,
Are you referring to what happened to the girl when we were
at that terrible place, Yes, Remember, it was she who wanted to
have sex with me, Memory is deceiving you, you wanted her,
Are you sure, I was not blind, Well, I would have sworn that,
You would only perjure yourself, Strange how memory can deceive us, In this case it is easy to see, something that is offered
to us is more ours than something we had to conquer, But she
didn't ever approach me again, and I never approached her, If
you wanted to, you could find each other's memories, that's
what memory is for, You are jealous, No, I'm not jealous, I was
not even jealous on that occasion, I felt sorry for her and for
you, and also for myself because I could not help you, How are
we fixed for water, Badly. After the extremely frugal breakfast,
lightened by some discreet, smiling hints at the events of the
previous night, the words appropriately veiled out of consideration for the presence of a minor, an odd precaution if we remember the terrible scenes that he witnessed during the quarantine, the doctor's wife and her husband set off, accompanied
this time only by the dog of tears, who did not want to stay at
home.

The state of the streets got worse with every passing hour.
The rubbish seemed to increase during the hours of darkness, it was as if from the outside, from some unknown country where there was still a normal life, they were coming in the
night to empty their trash cans, if we were not in the land of the
blind we would see through the middle of this white darkness
phantom carts and trucks loaded with refuse, debris, rubble,
chemical waste, ashes, burnt oil, bones, bottles, offal, flat batteries, plastic bags, mountains of paper, what they don't bring
is leftover food, not even bits of fruit peel with which we might
be able to allay our hunger, while waiting for those better days

that are always just around the corner. It is still early in the morning but the heat is already oppressive. The stench rises from the enormous refuse pile like a cloud of toxic gas, It won't be long before we have outbreaks of epidemics, said the doctor again, nobody will escape, we have no defences left, If it's not raining, it's blowing gales, said the woman, Not even that, the rain would at least quench our thirst, and the wind would blow away some of this stench. The dog of tears sniffs around restlessly, stops to investigate a particular heap of rubbish, perhaps there was a rare delicacy hidden underneath which it can no longer find, if it were alone it would not move an inch from this spot, but the woman who wept has already walked on, and it is his duty to follow her, one never knows when one might have to dry more tears. Walking is difficult, in some streets, especially the steep ones, the heavy rainwater, transformed into torrents, had thrown cars against other cars or against buildings, knocking down doors, smashing shop windows, the ground is covered with thick pieces of broken glass. Wedged in between two cars the body of a man is rotting away. The doctor's wife averts her eyes. The dog of tears moves closer, but death frightens it, it still takes two steps forward, suddenly its fur stands on end, a piercing howl escapes from its throat, the trouble with this dog is that it has grown too close to human beings, it will suffer as they do. They crossed a square where groups of blind people entertained themselves by listening to speeches from other blind people, at first sight neither group seemed to be blind, the speakers turned their heads excitedly towards the listeners and the listeners turned their heads attentively to the speakers. They were extolling the virtues of the fundamental principles of the great organised systems, private property, a free currency market, the market economy, the stock exchange, taxation, interest, expropriation and appropriation, production, distribution, consumption, supply and demand, poverty

and wealth, communication, repression and delinquency, lot-
teries, prisons, the penal code, the civil code, the highway code,
dictionaries, the telephone directory, networks of prostitution,
armaments factories, the armed forces, cemeteries, the police,
smuggling, drugs, permitted illegal traffic, pharmaceutical re-
search, gambling, the price of priests and funerals, justice, bor-
rowing, political parties, elections, parliaments, governments,
convex, concave, horizontal, vertical, slanted, concentrated,
diffuse, fleeting thoughts, the fraying of the vocal cords, the
death of the word. Here they are talking about organisation,
said the doctor's wife to her husband, I noticed, he answered,
and said no more. They continued walking, the doctor's wife
went to consult a street plan on a street corner, like an old
roadside cross pointing the way. We are very close to the supermarket, around here she had broken down and wept the day
that she had got lost, grotesquely weighed down by the plastic
bags which luckily were full to the brim, in her confusion and
anguish she had to depend on a dog to console her, the same
dog who is here snarling at the packs of other dogs who are
coming too close, as if it were telling them, You don't fool me,
keep away from here. A street to the left, another to the right
and there is the entrance to the supermarket. Only the door,
that's it, there is the door, there is the whole building, but what
cannot be seen are people going in and coming out, that ant-
heap of people which we find at all hours in these shops that
live on the comings and goings of vast crowds. The doctor's
wife feared the worst and said to her husband, We have arrived
too late, there won't be a crumb left in there, Why do you say
that, I don't see anybody going in or coming out, Perhaps they
have not yet discovered the basement storeroom, That's what I
am hoping for. They were standing on the pavement opposite
the supermarket when they spoke these words. Beside them, as
if they were waiting for the traffic lights to turn green, there

were three blind people. The doctor's wife did not notice the expression on their faces, which was of puzzled surprise, a kind of confused fear, she did not see that one of them opened his mouth to speak and then closed it again, she did not notice the sudden shrug of shoulders, You'll find out, we assume the blind man was thinking. As they were crossing the middle of the road, the doctor's wife and her husband were unable to hear the comment of the second blind person, Why did she say that she did not see, that she did not see anybody going in or coming out, and the third blind person answered, It's just a manner of speaking, a moment ago, when I stumbled you told me to watch where I was putting my feet, it's the same thing, we still haven't lost the habit of seeing, Oh God, how many times have I heard that before, exclaimed the first blind man.

The daylight illuminated the whole of the wide hall of the supermarket. Almost all the shelves were overturned, there was nothing but refuse, broken glass, empty wrappers, It is strange, said the doctor's wife, even if there is no food here, I don't understand why there is nobody around. The doctor said, You are right, it does not seem normal. The dog of tears whimpered softly. Its hair was standing on end again. The doctor's wife said to her husband, There is a bad smell in here, There's a bad smell everywhere, said the husband, It's not that, it's another smell, of rotting, There must be a dead body somewhere, I don't see anything, In which case you must be imagining it. The dog began to whine. What's the matter with the dog, asked the doctor, He's nervous, What are we going to do, Let's see, if there is a corpse we just give it a wide berth, at this stage the dead no longer frighten us, For me it's easier, I can't see them. They crossed the hall of the supermarket until they reached the door which opened onto the corridor leading to the basement store. The dog of tears followed them, but it stopped from time to time, howled to them, then duty obliged it to continue. When the doctor's wife opened the door, the stench grew stronger, It smells terrible, said her husband, You stay here, I'll be right back. She went down the corridor, it became darker with every step and the dog of tears followed her as if it were being dragged along. Filled with the stench of putrefaction, the air seemed thick. Halfway down, the woman vomited, What can have happened here, she thought between retchings and then she murmured these same words over and over again until she got to the metal door which went down into the basement. Confused by her nausea, she had not noticed before that there was a tenuous shimmer of light down there. Now she knew what it was. Small flames flickered around the edges of the two doors, that of the staircase and that of the goods lift. A new attack of vomiting gripped her stomach, it was so violent that it attracted the attention of the dog. The dog of tears gave a very long howl, it let out a wail that seemed never-ending, a lament which resounded through the corridor like the last voice of the dead down in the basement. The doctor heard the vomiting, the convulsions, the coughing, he ran as well as he could, he stumbled and fell, he got up and fell again, at last he held his wife in his arms, What happened, he asked, with a trembling voice she replied, Get me out of here, please, get me out of here, for the first time since the onset of blindness, it was the doctor who guided his wife, he guided her without knowing where, anywhere away from those doors, those flames that he could not see. When they had got out of the corridor, her nerves suddenly went to pieces, her sobbing became convulsive, there is no drying tears like these, only time and exhaustion can stop them, therefore the dog did not approach, it just looked for a hand to lick. What happened, the doctor asked again, what did you see, They are dead, she managed to say between sobs, Who is dead, They are, and she could not go on. Calm yourself, tell me when you can. A few minutes later

she said, They are dead, Did you see anything, did you open
the door, asked her husband, No, I only saw will-o'-the-wisps
around the doors, they clung there and danced around and did
not let go, I think it must have been phosphorised hydrogen as
a result of the decomposition of the bodies, What could have
happened, They must have found the basement, rushed down
the stairs looking for food, I remember how easy it was to slip
and fall on those steps, and if one fell, they would all fall, they
probably never reached where they wanted to go, or if they
did they could not return because of the obstruction on the
staircase, But you said that the door was closed, Most likely
other blind people closed it, converting the basement into an
enormous tomb and I am to blame for what happened, when I
came running out of there with my bags, they must have suspected that it was food and went in search of it, In a way, everything we eat has been stolen from the mouths of others and if
we rob them of too much we are responsible for their death,
one way or another we are all murderers, A small consolation,
I don't want you to start burdening yourself with imaginary
guilt, when you already have a hard enough time shouldering
the responsibility for six real and useless mouths, How could
I live without your useless mouth, You would live in order to
support the other five who are there, The question is, for how
long. It won't be for much longer, when everything is finished
we shall have to roam the fields in search of food, we'll pick
all the fruit from the trees, we'll kill all the animals we can lay
our hands on, if in the meantime dogs and cats do not start devouring us. The dog of tears did not react, this matter did not
concern it, its recent transformation into a dog of tears had not
been in vain.

The doctor's wife could hardly drag herself along. The shock
had robbed her of all her strength. When they left the supermarket, she fainting, he blind, neither would be able to say who

was assisting the other. Perhaps the intensity of the light had made her dizzy, she thought that she was losing her eyesight, but she was not afraid, it was only a fainting fit. She did not fall, nor even lose consciousness. She needed to lie down, close her eyes, breathe steadily, if she could just rest for a few minutes she was sure that she would regain her strength, she had to, her plastic bags were still empty. She did not want to lie down on the filth in the street, or return to the supermarket, not even dead. She looked around. On the other side of the street, a bit further on, was a church. There would be people inside, as everywhere, but it would be a good place to rest, at least it always had been. She said to her husband, I need to recover my strength, take me over there, There, where, I'm sorry, bear with me, and I'll tell you, What is it, A church, if I could only lie down for a while, I'd feel like new, Let's go. Six steps led up to the church, six steps, which the doctor's wife climbed with great difficulty, especially since she also had to guide her husband. The doors were wide open, which was a great help, a revolving door, even of the simplest type, would on this occasion have been a difficult obstacle to overcome. The dog of tears hesitated on the threshold. Despite the freedom of movement enjoyed by dogs in recent months, all of them had genetically programmed into their brains the prohibition which once, long ago, fell on the species, that on entering churches, probably because of that other genetic code which obliges them to mark their territory wherever they go. The good and faithful services rendered by the forebears of this dog of tears, when they licked the festering sores of saints before they were recognised and approved as such, nevertheless acts of compassion of the most selfless kind, because, as we well know, not just any beggar can become a saint, no matter how many wounds he may have on his body, and in his soul too where the tongues of dogs cannot reach. The dog now had the courage to enter the sacred space, the door was open, there was no doorkeeper, and the strongest reason of all, the woman who had wept had already gone in, I do not know how she manages to drag herself along, she murmurs but a single word to her husband, Hold me, the church is full, it is almost impossible to find even a foot of floor unoccupied, one might literally say that there is no stone upon which to rest one's head, again the dog of tears proved its usefulness, with two growls and a couple of charges, all without malice, it opened up a space where the doctor's wife let herself fall, giving in to the faint, at last fully closing her eyes. Her husband took her pulse, it is firm and regular, only a little faint, then he tried to lift her up, she's not in a good position, it is important to get the blood back into the brain quickly, to increase the cerebral irrigation, the best thing would be to sit her up, put her head between her knees and trust to nature and the force of gravity. At last, after some failed attempts, he managed to lift her up. A few minutes later, the doctor's wife gave a deep sigh, moved almost imperceptibly, and started to regain consciousness. Don't get up just yet, her husband told her, keep your head down for a while longer, but she felt fine, there was no sign of vertigo, her eyes could already distinguish the tiles on the floor which the dog of tears had left reasonably clean thanks to his energetic scrabbling before lying down himself. She raised her head to the slender pillars, to the high vaults, to confirm the security and stability of her blood circulation, then she said, I am feeling fine, but at that very moment she thought she had gone mad or that the lifting of the vertigo had given her hallucinations, it could not be true what her eyes revealed, that man nailed to the cross with a white bandage covering his eyes, and next to him a woman, her heart pierced by seven swords and her eyes also covered with a white bandage, and it was not only that man and that woman who were in that condition, all the images in the church had their eyes covered, statues with a

white cloth tied around the head, paintings with a thick brush-
stroke of white paint, and there was a woman teaching her
daughter how to read and both had their eyes covered, and a
man with an open book on which a little child was sitting, and
both had their eyes covered, and another man, his body spiked
with arrows, and he had his eyes covered, and a woman with a
lit lamp, and she had her eyes covered, and a man with wounds
on his hands and feet and his chest, and he had his eyes covered, and another man with a lion, and both had their eyes
covered, and another man with a lamb, and both had their eyes
covered, and another man with an eagle, and both had their
eyes covered, and another man with a spear standing over a
fallen man with horns and cloven feet, and both had their eyes
covered, and another man carrying a set of scales, and he had
his eyes covered, and an old bald man holding a white lily, and
he had his eyes covered, and another old man leaning on an un-
sheathed sword, and he had his eyes covered, and a woman
with a dove, and both had their eyes covered, and a man with
two ravens, and all three had their eyes covered, there was only
one woman who did not have her eyes covered, because she
carried her gouged-out eyes on a silver tray. The doctor's wife
said to her husband, You won't believe me if I tell you what I
have in front of my eyes, all the images in this church have
their eyes covered, How strange, I wonder why, How should I
know, perhaps it was the work of someone whose faith was
badly shaken when he realised that he would be blind like the
others, maybe it was even the local priest, perhaps he thought
that when the blind people could no longer see the images, the
images should not be able to see the blind either, Images don't
see, You're wrong, images see with the eyes of those who see
them, only that now blindness is the lot of everyone, You can
still see, I'll see less and less all the time, even though I may not
lose my eyesight I shall become more and more blind because

I shall have no one to see me, If the priest covered the eyes of the images, That's just my idea, It's the only hypothesis that makes any sense, it's the only one that can lend some dignity to our suffering, I imagine that man coming in here from the world of the blind, where he would have to return only to go blind himself, I imagine the closed doors, the deserted church, the silence, I imagine the statues, the paintings, I see him going from one to the other, climbing up to the altars and tying the bandages with a double knot so that they do not come undone and slip off, applying two coats of paint to the pictures in order to make the white night into which they are plunged still thicker, that priest must have committed the worst sacrilege of all times and all religions, the fairest and most radically human, coming here to declare that, ultimately, God does not deserve to see. The doctor's wife did not have a chance to reply, somebody beside her spoke first, What sort of talk is that, who are you, Blind like you, she said, But I heard you say that you could see, That's just a manner of speaking which is hard to give up, how many more times will I say it, And what's this about the images having their eyes covered, It's true, And how do you know when you are blind, You would know too if you did what I did, go and touch them with your hands, the hands are the eyes of the blind, And why did you do it, I thought that in order to have got to where we are someone else must have been blind, And that story about the parish priest covering the eyes of the images, I knew him very well, he would be incapable of doing such a thing, You never know beforehand what people are capable of, you have to wait, give it time, it's time that rules, time is our gambling partner on the other side of the table and it holds all the cards of the deck in its hand, we have to guess the winning cards of life, our lives, Speaking of gambling in a church is a sin, Get up, use your hands if you doubt my words, Do you swear it is true that the images have their eyes covered,

What do you want me to swear on, Swear on your eyes, I swear
twice on the eyes, on yours and mine. Is it true, It's true. The
conversation was overheard by the blind people in their immediate vicinity, and it goes without saying that there was no need
to wait for the confirmation by oath before the news started to
circulate, to pass from mouth to mouth, in a murmur which
shortly changed its tone, first incredulous, then alarmed, again
incredulous, it was unfortunate that there were several superstitious and imaginative people in the congregation, the idea
that the sacred images were blind, that their compassionate or
pitying eyes only stared out at their own blindness, became all
of a sudden unbearable, it was tantamount to having told them
that they were surrounded by the living dead, one scream was
enough, then another and another, then fear made all the
people rise up, panic drove them to the doors, here the inevitable repeated itself, since panic is much faster than the legs
which carry it, the feet of the fugitive trip up in their flight,
even more so when one is blind, and there he lies on the ground,
panic tells him, Get up, run, they are going to kill you, if only
he could get up, but others have already run and fallen too, you
have to be strong-minded not to burst out laughing at this grotesque entanglement of bodies looking for arms to free themselves and for feet to get away. Those six steps outside will be
like a precipice, but finally, the fall will not be very serious, the
habit of falling hardens the body, reaching the ground is, in itself, a relief, I'm staying where I am is the first thought, and
sometimes the last, in fatal cases. What does not change either
is that some take advantage of the misfortune of others, as is
well known, since the beginning of the world, the heirs and the
heirs of the heirs. The desperate flight of these people made
them leave their belongings behind, and when necessity con-
quers fear, they come back for them, then the difficult problem
will be to settle in a satisfactory manner what is mine and what

is yours, we shall see that some of the little food we had has vanished, probably this was a cynical ruse on the part of the woman who said that the images had their eyes covered, the depths some people will stoop to, they invent such tall tales merely to rob poor people of the few crumbs remaining to them. Now, the fault was the dog's, seeing the square empty it went foraging around, it rewarded itself for its efforts, as was only fair and natural, and it showed, in a manner of speaking, the entrance to the mine which meant that the doctor's wife and her husband left the church without remorse over the theft, with their bags half full. If they can use half of what they grabbed they can be content, regarding the other half they will say, I don't know how people can eat this, even when misfortune is common to all, there are always some who have a worse time than others.

The report of these events, each one of its kind, left the other members of the group aghast and confused, it has to be noted that the doctor's wife, perhaps because words failed her, did not even manage to convey to them the feelings of utter horror she experienced at the basement door, that rectangle of pale flickering lights at the top of the staircase which led to the other world. The description of the bandaged eyes of the images left a strong enough impression on their imaginations, though in quite different ways, the first blind man and his wife, for example, were rather uneasy, for them it was mainly an unpardonable lack of respect. The fact that all human beings were blind was a calamity for which they were not responsible, these are misfortunes nobody can avoid, and for that reason alone covering the eyes of the holy images struck them as an unpardonable offence, and if the parish priest had done it, even worse. The reaction of the old man with the black eyepatch was quite different, I can imagine the shock you must have had, I imagine a museum in which all the sculptures have their eyes covered, not because the sculptor did not want to carve the stone until he reached the eyes, but covered, as you say, with bandages, as if a single blindness were not enough, it's strange that a patch like mine does not create the same effect, sometimes it even gives people a romantic air, and he laughed at what he had said and at himself. As to the girl with the dark glasses, she said that she only hoped she would not have to see this cursed gallery in her dreams, she had enough nightmares already. They ate the rancid food at their disposal, it was the best they had, the doctor's wife said that it was becoming ever more difficult to find food, perhaps they should leave the city and go to live in the country, there at least the food they gathered would be healthier, And there must be goats and cows on the loose, we can milk them, we'll have milk, and there is water from the wells, we can cook what we want, the question is to find a good site, then everybody gave his opinion, some more enthusiastic than others, but for all of them it was obvious that the decision was pressing and urgent, the boy with the squint expressed his approval without any reservations, possibly because he retained pleasant memories from his holidays. After they had eaten, they stretched out to sleep, they always did, even during the quarantine, when experience taught them that a body in repose can put up with a lot of hunger. That evening they did not eat, only the boy with the squint got something to assuage his complaints and to allay his hunger, the others sat down to hear the reading, at least their minds would not be able to complain of lack of nourishment, the trouble is that the weakness of the body sometimes leads to a lack of attention of the mind, and it was not for lack of intellectual interest, no, what happened was that the brain slipped into a half sleep, like an animal settling down for hibernation, goodbye world, therefore it was not uncommon that the listeners gently lowered their eyelids, forced themselves to follow with the eyes of the soul the vicissitudes of the plot until

a more energetic passage shook them from their torpor, it was
not simply the noise of the book snapping shut, the doctor's
wife had these subtle touches, she did not want to let on that
she knew that the dreamer was drifting off to sleep.

The first blind man appeared to have entered into this soft
state, but this was not the case. True, his eyes were closed, and
he paid only scant attention to the reading, but the idea that
they would all go to live in the country kept him from falling
asleep, it seemed to him a serious error to go so far from his
home, however kind the writer was, it would be useful to keep
an eye on it, turn up from time to time. The first blind man was
therefore wide awake, if any other proof were needed it would
be the dazzling whiteness before his eyes, which probably only
sleep would darken, but one could not even be sure of that,
since nobody can be asleep and awake at the same time. The
first blind man thought that he had finally cleared up this doubt
when suddenly the inside of his eyelids turned dark, I've fallen
asleep, he thought, but no, he had not fallen asleep, he continued hearing the voice of the doctor's wife, the boy with the
squint coughed, then a great fear entered his soul, he thought
he had passed from one blindness to another, that having lived
in the blindness of light, he would now pass into a blindness
of darkness, the fear made him tremble, What's the matter, his
wife asked, and he replied stupidly, without opening his eyes,
I am blind, as if that were news, she tenderly held him in her
arms, Don't worry, we're all blind, there's nothing we can do
about it, I saw everything dark, I thought I had gone to sleep,
but I hadn't, I am awake, That's what you should do, sleep, don't
think about it. He was annoyed by this advice, here was a man
in great distress, and his wife could say nothing other than that
he should sleep. He was irritated and, about to utter a harsh
reply, he opened his eyes and saw. He saw and shouted, I can
see. His first shout was still one of incredulity, but with the sec-

ond and the third and many more the evidence grew stronger, I can see, I can see, he madly embraced his wife, then he ran to the doctor's wife and embraced her too, it was the first time he had seen her, but he knew who she was, and the doctor, and the girl with dark glasses and the old man with the black eyepatch, there was no mistaking him, and the boy with the squint, his wife came behind him, she did not want to let him go, and he interrupted his embraces to embrace her again, then he turned to the doctor, I can see, I can see, doctor, he addressed him by his title, something they had not done for a long time, and the doctor asked, Can you see clearly, as before, are there no traces of whiteness, Nothing at all, I even think that I can see better than before, and that's no small thing, I've never worn glasses. Then the doctor said what all of them were thinking without daring to say it, It is possible that we have come to the end of this blindness, it is possible that we will all recover our eyesight, hearing those words, the doctor's wife began to cry, she should have been happy yet she was crying, what strange reactions people have, of course she was happy, my God, it is easy to understand, she cried because all her mental resistance had suddenly drained away, she was like a newborn baby and this cry was her first and still-unconscious sound. The dog of tears went up to her, it always knows when it is needed, that's why the doctor's wife clung to him, it is not that she no longer loved her husband, it is not that she did not wish them all well, but at that moment her feeling of loneliness was so intense, so unbearable, that it seemed to her that it could be overcome only by the strange thirst with which the dog drank her tears.

The general joy turned into nervousness, And now, what are we going to do, asked the girl with dark glasses, after all that has happened I won't be able to sleep, Nobody will, I believe we should stay here, said the old man with the black eyepatch, he broke off as if he still had some doubts, then he concluded,

Waiting. They waited. The three flames of the lamp lit up the circle of faces. At first, they had talked animatedly, they wanted to know exactly what had happened, if the change had taken place only in the eyes or whether he had also felt something in his brain, then, little by little, their words grew despondent, at a certain moment it occurred to the first blind man to say to his wife that they would be going home the next day, But I am still blind, she replied, It doesn't matter, I'll guide you, only those present who heard it with their own ears could grasp how such simple words could contain such different feelings as protection, pride and authority. The second person to regain his eyesight, already late into the night, when the lamp, running out of oil, was flickering, was the girl with dark glasses. She had kept her eyes open as if sight had to enter through them rather than be rekindled from within, suddenly she said, I think I can see, it was best to be prudent, not all cases are the same, it even used to be said there is no such thing as blindness, only blind people, when the experience of time has taught us nothing other than that there are no blind people, but only blindness. Here we already have three who can see, one more and they would form a majority, but even though in the happiness of seeing again we might ignore the others, their lives will be very much easier, not the agony it was until today, look at the state of that woman, she is like a rope that has broken, like a spring that could no longer support the pressure it was constantly subjected to. Perhaps it was for this reason that the girl with dark glasses embraced her first, and the dog of tears did not know whose tears it should attend to first, both of them wept so much. Her second embrace was for the old man with the black eyepatch, now we shall know what words are really worth, the other day we were so moved by the dialogue which led to the splendid commitment by these two to live together, but the situation has changed, the girl with dark glasses has before her an old man whom she can now see in the flesh, the emotional idealisations, the false harmonies on the desert island are over, wrinkles are wrinkles, baldness is baldness, there is no difference between a black eyepatch and a blind eye, that is what, in other words, he is going to say to her, Look at me, I am the man you said you were going to live with, and she replied, I know you, you're the man I am living with, in the end these are words that are worth even more than those that wanted to surface, and this embrace as much as the words. The third one to regain his sight the next day at dawn was the doctor, now there could no longer be any doubt, it was only a question of time before the others would recover theirs. Leaving aside the natural and foreseeable expansive comments of which there has already been sufficient mention above, there is now no need for repetition, even concerning the chief characters of this narrative, the doctor asked the question which hung in the air, What is happening out there, the reply came from the very building in which they lived, on the floor below someone came out on the landing shouting, I can see, I can see, it looks like the sun will rise over a city in celebration.

The next morning's meal turned into a banquet. What was on the table, besides being very little, would repel any normal appetite, as happens at all moments of elation, the strength of feelings took the place of hunger and their happiness was the best nourishment, nobody complained, even those who were still blind laughed as if the eyes which could already see were theirs. When they had finished, the girl with dark glasses had an idea, What if I now went to the door of my own flat with a piece of paper saying that I'm here, my parents would know where to find me if they return, Let me come with you, I want to know what is happening out there, said the old man with the black eyepatch, And we will go out too, said he who had been the first blind man to his wife, Perhaps the writer can already see and is thinking about returning to his own place, on the way I shall try to find something to eat. I'll do the same, said the girl with dark glasses. Minutes later, alone now, the doctor sat down beside his wife, the boy with the squint was dozing in a corner of the sofa, the dog of tears, stretched out with his muzzle on its forepaws, opened and closed its eyes from time to time to show that it was still watchful, through the open window, despite the fact that they were so high up, the noise of excited voices could be heard, the streets must be full of people, the crowd shouting just three words, I can see, said those who had already recovered their eyesight and those who were just starting to see, I can see, I can see, the story in which people said, I am blind, truly appears to belong to another world. The boy with the squint murmured, he must be in the middle of a dream, perhaps he saw his mother and was asking her, Can you see me, can you see me, The doctor's wife asked, And the others, and the doctor answered, He will probably be cured by the time he wakes, it will be the same with the others, most likely they are already regaining their sight at this very moment, our man with the black eyepatch is in for a shock, Why, Because of the cataract, after all the time since I last examined him it must have deteriorated, Is he going to stay blind, No, when life gets back to normal, and everything is working again, I shall operate, it is a matter of weeks, Why did we become blind, I don't know, perhaps one day we'll find out, Do you want me to tell you what I think, Yes, do, I don't think we did go blind, I think we are blind, Blind but seeing, Blind people who can see, but do not see.

The doctor's wife got up and went to the window. She looked down at the street full of refuse, at the shouting, singing people. Then she lifted her head up to the sky and saw everything white, It is my turn, she thought. Fear made her quickly lower her eyes. The city was still there.

Seeing

For Pilar, every single day
For Manuel Vázquez Montalbán, who lives on

Let's howl, said the dog

—*The Book of Voices*

TERRIBLE voting weather, remarked the presiding officer of polling station fourteen as he snapped shut his soaked umbrella and took off the raincoat that had proved of little use to him during the breathless forty-meter dash from the place where he had parked his car to the door through which, heart pounding, he had just appeared. I hope I'm not the last, he said to the secretary, who was standing slightly away from the door, safe from the sheets of rain which, caught by the wind, were drenching the floor. Your deputy hasn't arrived yet, but we've still got plenty of time, said the secretary soothingly, With rain like this, it'll be a feat in itself if we all manage to get here, said the presiding officer as they went into the room where the voting would take place. He greeted, first, the poll clerks who would act as scrutineers and then the party representatives and their deputies. He was careful to address exactly the same words to all of them, not allowing his face or tone of voice to betray any political and ideological leanings of his own. A presiding officer, even of an ordinary polling station like this, should, in all circumstances, be guided by the strictest sense of independence, he should, in short, always observe decorum.

As well as the general dampness, which made an already oppressive atmosphere still muggier, for the room had only two
narrow windows that looked out onto a courtyard which was
gloomy even on sunny days, there was a sense of unease which,
to use the vernacular expression, you could have cut with a
knife. They should have postponed the elections, said the representative of the party in the middle, or the p.i.t.m., I mean,
it's been raining nonstop since yesterday, there are landslips
and floods everywhere, the abstention rate this time around
will go sky-high. The representative from the party on the
right, or the p.o.t.r., nodded in agreement, but felt that his con-
tribution to the conversation should be couched in the form of
a cautious comment, Obviously, I wouldn't want to underesti-
mate the risk of that, but I do feel that our fellow citizens' high
sense of civic duty, which they have demonstrated before on so
many occasions, is deserving of our every confidence, they are
aware, indeed, acutely so, of the vital importance of these municipal elections for the future of the capital. Having each said
their piece, the representative of the p.i.t.m. and the representative of the p.o.t.r. turned, with a half-sceptical, half-ironic air,
to the representative of the party on the left, the p.o.t.l., curious to know what opinion he would come up with. At that
precise moment, however, the presiding officer's deputy burst
into the room, dripping water everywhere, and, as one might
expect, now that the cast of polling station officers was complete, the welcome he received was more than just cordial, it
was positively enthusiastic. We therefore never heard the viewpoint of the representative of the p.o.t.l., although, on the basis of a few known antecedents, one can assume that he would,
without fail, have taken a line of bright historical optimism,
something like, The people who vote for my party are not the
sort to let themselves be put off by a minor obstacle like this,
they're not the kind to stay at home just because of a few mis-

erable drops of rain falling from the skies. It was not, however, a matter of a few miserable drops of rain, there were bucketfuls, jugfuls, whole niles, iguaçús and yangtses of the stuff, but faith, may it be eternally blessed, as well as removing mountains from the path of those who benefit from its influence, is capable of plunging into the most torrential of waters and emerging from them bone-dry.

With the table now complete, with each officer in his or her allotted place, the presiding officer signed the official edict and asked the secretary to affix it, as required by law, outside the building, but the secretary, demonstrating a degree of basic common sense, pointed out that the piece of paper would not last even one minute on the wall outside, in two ticks the ink would have run and in three the wind would have carried it off. Put it inside, then, out of the rain, the law doesn't say what to do in these circumstances, the main thing is that the edict should be pinned up where it can be seen. He asked his colleagues if they were in agreement, and they all said they were, with the proviso on the part of the representative of the p.o.t.r. that this decision should be recorded in the minutes in case they were ever challenged on the matter. When the secretary returned from his damp mission, the presiding officer asked him what it was like out there, and he replied with a wry shrug, Just the same, rain, rain, rain, Any voters out there, Not a sign. The presiding officer stood up and invited the poll clerks and the three party representatives to follow him into the voting chamber, which was found to be free of anything that might sully the purity of the political choices to be made there during the day. This formality completed, they returned to their places to examine the electoral roll, which they found to be equally free of irregularities, lacunae or anything else of a suspicious nature. The solemn moment had arrived when the presiding officer uncovers and displays the ballot box to the voters so that they can certify that it is empty, and tomorrow, if necessary, bear witness to the fact that no criminal act has introduced into it, at dead of night, the false votes that would corrupt the free and sovereign political will of the people, and so that there would be no electoral shenanigans, as they're so picturesquely known, and which, let us not forget, can be committed before, during or after the act, depending on the efficiency of the perpetrators and their accomplices and the opportunities available to them. The ballot box was empty, pure, immaculate, but there was not a single voter in the room to whom it could be shown. Perhaps one of them is lost out there, battling with the torrents, enduring the whipping winds, clutching to his bosom the document that proves he is a fully enfranchised citizen, but, judging by the look of the sky right now, he'll be a long time coming, if, that is, he doesn't end up simply going home and leaving the fate of the city to those with a black car to drop them off at the door and pick them up again once the person in the back seat has fulfilled his or her civic duty.

After the various materials have been inspected, the law of this country states that the presiding officer should immediately cast his vote, as should the poll clerks, the party representatives and their respective deputies, as long, of course, as they are registered at that particular polling station, as was the case here. Even by stretching things out, four minutes was more than enough time for the ballot box to receive its first eleven votes. And then, there was nothing else for it, the waiting began. Barely half an hour had passed when the presiding officer, who was getting anxious, suggested that one of the poll clerks should go and see if anyone was coming, voters might have turned up to find the door blown shut by the wind and gone off in a huff, grumbling that the government might at least have had the decency to inform people that the elections had been postponed, that, after all, was what the radio and television were for, to broadcast such information. The secretary said, But everyone knows that when a door blows shut it makes the devil of a noise, and we haven't heard a thing in here. The poll clerk hesitated, will I, won't I, but the presiding officer insisted. Go on, please, and be careful, don't get wet. The door was open, the wedge securely in place. The clerk stuck his head out, a moment was all it took to glance from one side to the other and then draw back, dripping, as if he had put his head under a shower. He wanted to proceed like a good poll clerk, to please the presiding officer, and, since it was the first time he had been called upon to perform this function, he also wanted to be appreciated for the speed and efficiency with which he had carried out his duties, who knows, with time and experience, he might one day be the person presiding over a polling station, higher flights of ambition than this have traversed the sky of providence and no one has so much as batted an eye. When he went back into the room, the presiding officer, half-rueful, half-amused, exclaimed, There was no need to get yourself soaked, man, Oh, it doesn't matter, sir, said the clerk, drying his cheek on the sleeve of his jacket, Did you spot anyone, As far as I could see, no one, it's like a desert of water out there. The presiding officer got up, took a few uncertain steps around the table, went into the voting chamber, looked inside and came back. The representative of the p.i.t.m. spoke up to remind the others of his prediction that the abstention rate would go sky-high, the representative of the p.o.t.r. once more played the role of pacifier, the voters had all day to vote, they were probably just waiting for the rain to let up. This time the representative of the p.o.t.l. chose to remain silent, thinking what a pathetic figure he would be cutting now if he had actually said what he was going to say when the presiding officer's deputy had come into the room, It would take more than a few miserable drops of rain to put off my party's voters. The secretary, on whom all

eyes were expectantly turned, opted for a practical suggestion,
You know, it might not be a bad idea to phone the ministry and
ask how the elections are going elsewhere in the city and in the
rest of the country too, that way we would find out if this civic
power cut was a general thing or if we're the only ones whom
the voters have declined to illumine with their votes. The representative of the p.o.t.r. sprang indignantly to his feet, I demand that it be set down in the minutes that, as representative
of the p.o.t.r., I strongly object to the disrespectful manner and
the unacceptably mocking tone in which the secretary has just
referred to the voters, who are the supreme defenders of democracy, and without whom tyranny, any of the many tyrannies
that exist in the world, would long ago have overwhelmed the
nation that bore us. The secretary shrugged and asked, Shall I
make a note of the representative of the p.o.t.r.'s comments, sir,
No, I don't think that will be necessary, it's just that we're all a
bit tense and perplexed and puzzled, and, as we all know, in that
state of mind, it's very easy to say things we don't really believe,
and I'm sure the secretary didn't mean to offend anyone, why,
he himself is a voter conscious of his responsibilities, the proof
being that he, as did all of us, braved the elements to answer
the call of duty, nevertheless, my feelings of gratitude, however
sincere, do not prevent me asking the secretary to keep rigorously to the task assigned to him and to abstain from any comments that might shock the personal or political sensibilities of
the other people here. The representative of the p.o.t.r. made a
brusque gesture which the presiding officer chose to interpret
as one of agreement, and the argument went no further, thanks,
in large measure, to the representative of the p.i.t.m., who took
up the secretary's proposal, It's true, he said, we're like ship-
wreck victims in the middle of the ocean, with no sails and no
compass, no mast and no oars, and with no diesel in the tank either, Yes, you're quite right, said the presiding officer, I'll phone

the ministry now. There was a telephone on another table and he walked over to it, carrying the instruction leaflet he had been given days before and on which were printed, amongst other useful things, the telephone numbers of the ministry of the interior.

The call was a brief one, It's the presiding officer of polling station number fourteen here, I'm very worried, there's something distinctly odd going on, so far, not a single voter has turned up to vote, we've been open for more than an hour, and not a soul, yes, sir, I know there's no way of stopping the storm, yes, sir, I know, rain, wind, floods, yes, sir, we'll be patient, we'll stick to our guns, after all, that's why we're here. From that point on the presiding officer contributed nothing to the dialogue apart from a few affirmative nods of the head, the occasional muted interjection and three or four phrases which he began but did not finish. When he replaced the receiver, he looked over at his colleagues, but without, in fact, seeing them, it was as if he had before him a landscape composed entirely of empty voting chambers, immaculate electoral rolls, with presiding officers and secretaries waiting, party representatives exchanging distrustful glances as they tried to work out who might gain and who might lose from this situation, and, in the distance, the occasional rain-soaked poll clerk returning from the door to announce that no one was coming. What did the people at the ministry say, asked the representative of the p.i.t.m., They don't know what to make of it either, after all, it's only natural that the bad weather would keep a lot of people at home, but apparently pretty much the same thing is happening all over the city, that's why they can't explain it, What do you mean pretty much, asked the representative of the p.o.t.r., Well, a few voters have turned up at some polling stations, but hardly any really, no one's ever known anything like it, And what about the rest of the country, asked the representative of

the p.o.t.l., after all, it's not only raining in the capital, That's
what's so odd, there are places where it's raining just as heavily as it is here and yet, despite that, people are still turning out
to vote, I mean, obviously there are more voters in areas where
the weather is good, speaking of which, the forecasters are saying that the weather should start to improve later on this morning, It might go from bad to worse, you know what they say,
rain at midday either gets much worse or clears away, warned
the second clerk, who had not, until then, opened his mouth.
There was a silence. Then the secretary put his hand into one
of his jacket pockets, produced a mobile phone and keyed in a
number. While he was waiting for someone to answer, he said,
It's a bit like the mountain and Mahomet, since we can't ask
the voters, whom we don't know, why they haven't come in to
vote, let's ask our own families, whom we do know, hi, it's me,
yes, how come you're still there, why haven't you been to vote,
I know it's raining, my trouser legs are still sopping wet, oh,
right, sorry, I forgot you'd told me you'd be over after lunch,
sure, I only phoned because things are a bit awkward here, oh,
you've no idea, if I told you that not a single voter has yet come
in to vote, you probably wouldn't believe me, right, fine, I'll
see you later then, take care. He turned off the phone and remarked ironically, Well, at least one vote is guaranteed, my wife
will be coming this afternoon. The presiding officer and the
clerks looked at each other, they were obviously supposed to
follow the secretary's example, but not one of them wanted to
be the first to do so, that would be tantamount to admitting
that when it came to quick thinking and self-confidence the
secretary won hands down. It did not take long for the clerk
who had gone over to the door to see if it was raining to conclude that he would have to eat a lot of bread and salt before
he could compete with the secretary we have here, capable of
casually pulling a vote out of a mobile phone like a magician

SEEING   351

pulling a rabbit out of a hat. Seeing that the presiding officer, in
one corner, was now calling home on his mobile, and that the
others, using their own phones, were discreetly, in whispers,
doing likewise, this same clerk privately applauded the honesty
of his colleagues who, by not using the phone provided in principle for official use only, were nobly saving the state money.
The only person who, for lack of a mobile phone, had to resign
himself to waiting for news from the others was the representative of the p.o.t.l., of whom it should be said that, living as he
did alone in the city, with his family in the provinces, the poor
man had no one to call. The conversations gradually came to
an end, one after the other, the longest being that of the presiding officer, who appears to be demanding that the person
he is talking to come immediately to the polling station, we'll
see if he has any luck with that, but the fact is he's the one who
should have spoken first, but, then, if the secretary decided to
get in ahead of him, too bad, he is, as we've already seen, a bit of
a smart aleck, if he had as much respect for hierarchy as we do,
he would have merely suggested the idea to his superior. The
presiding officer let out the sigh that had long been trapped
within his breast, put the phone away in his pocket and asked,
So, what did you find out. The question, as well as being superfluous, was, how can we put it, just the teensiest bit dishonest,
firstly, because, when it comes down to it, everyone would have
found out something, however irrelevant, secondly, because it
was obvious that the person asking the question was taking advantage of the authority inherent in his position to shirk his
duty, since it was up to him, in voice and person, to initiate any
exchange of information. If we bear in mind the sigh he uttered
and the rather querulous tone we thought we detected at one
point in the phone conversation, it would be logical to suppose
that the dialogue, presumably with a member of his family, had
not proved to be as placid and instructive as his perfectly jus-

tifiable interest as a citizen and as a presiding officer deserved, and that he does not feel sufficiently calm to launch into some hastily concocted extemporaneous comment, and is now side-stepping the difficulty by inviting his subordinates to have their say first, which, as we also know, is another, more modern way of being the boss. What the clerks and party representatives said, aside from the representative of the p.o.t.l., who, having no information of his own, is there in a purely listening capac-ity, was that their family members either didn't fancy getting a soaking and were waiting for the heavens to clear once and for all, or, like the secretary's wife, were intending to come and vote in the afternoon. Only the clerk who had gone over to the door earlier on seemed pleased with himself, his face bore the complacent expression of one who has reason to be proud of his own merits, which, translated into words, came down to this, No one answered at my house, which can only mean that they're on their way here now. The presiding officer resumed his seat and the waiting began again.

Nearly an hour later, the first voter arrived. Contrary to the general expectation, and much to the dismay of the clerk who had gone over to the door earlier on, it was a stranger. He left his dripping umbrella at the entrance to the room and, still wearing his plastic cape glistening with water and his plastic boots, went over to the table. The presiding officer looked up at him with a smile on his lips, for this voter, a man of advanced years, but still robust, signaled a return to normality, to the usual line of dutiful citizens moving slowly and patiently along, conscious, as the representative of the p.o.t.r. had put it, of the vital importance of these municipal elections. The man handed his identity card and voter's card to the presiding officer, the lat-ter then announced in a sonorous, almost joyful voice the num-ber on the card and its owner's name, the clerks in charge of the electoral roll leafed through it and, when they found both

name and number, repeated them out loud and drew a straight
line against the entry to indicate that the man had voted, then,
the man, still dripping, went into a voting booth clutching his
ballot paper, returned shortly afterward with the piece of paper
folded into four, handed it to the presiding officer, who slipped
it solemnly into the ballot box, retrieved his documents and left,
taking his umbrella with him. The second voter took another
ten minutes to appear, but from then on, albeit unenthusiastically, one by one, like autumn leaves slowly detaching themselves from the boughs of a tree, the ballot papers dropped into
the ballot box. However long the presiding officer and his colleagues took to scrutinize documents, a queue never formed,
there were, at most, at any one time, three or four people waiting, and three or four people, try as they might, can never make
a queue worthy of the name. I was quite right, commented the
representative of the p.i.t.m., the abstention rate will be enormous, massive, there'll be no possible agreement on the result
after this, the only solution will be to hold the elections again,
The storm might pass, said the presiding officer and, looking at
his watch, he murmured as if he were praying, It's nearly midday. Resolutely, the man to whom we have been referring as the
clerk who had gone over to the door earlier on got up and said
to the presiding officer, With your permission, sir, since there
are no voters here at present, I'll just pop out and see what the
weather's doing. It took only an instant, he was there and back
in a twinkling, this time with a smile on his face and bearing
good news, It's raining much less now, hardly at all really, and
the clouds are beginning to break up too. The poll clerks and
the party representatives very nearly embraced, but their happiness was not long-lived. The monotonous drip-drip of voters
did not change, one came, then another, the wife, mother and
aunt of the officer who had gone over to the door came, the
elder brother of the representative of the p.o.t.r. came, so did

the presiding officer's mother-in-law, who, showing a complete
lack of respect for the electoral process, informed her crest-
fallen son-in-law that her daughter would only be coming later
in the afternoon and added cruelly, She said she might go to
the cinema, the deputy presiding officer's parents came, as well
as other people who were members of none of their families,
they entered looking bored and left looking bored, the atmosphere only brightened somewhat when two politicians from
the p.o.t.r. arrived and, minutes later, one from the p.i.t.m.,
and, as if by magic, a television camera appeared out of nowhere, filmed a few images and returned into nowhere, a journalist asked if he could put a question, How's the voting going,
and the presiding officer replied, It could be better, but now
that the weather seems to be changing, we're sure the flow of
voters will increase, The impression we've been getting from
other polling stations in the city is that the abstention rate is
going to be very high this time, remarked the journalist, Well,
I prefer to take a more optimistic line, a more positive view of
the influence of meteorology on the way the electoral mecha-
nisms work, and as long as it doesn't rain this afternoon, we'll
soon make up for what this morning's storm tried to steal from
us. The journalist left feeling contented, it was a nice turn of
phrase, he could even use it as a subtitle to his article. And because the time had come to satisfy their stomachs, the electoral
officers and the party representatives organized themselves so
that, with one eye on the electoral roll and the other on their
sandwiches, they could take turns to eat right there.

It had stopped raining, but nothing seemed to indicate that
the civic hopes of the presiding officer would be satisfactorily
fulfilled by a ballot box in which, so far, the votes barely covered the bottom. All those present were thinking the same
thing, the election so far had been a terrible political failure.
Time was passing. The clock on the tower had struck half past

three when the secretary's wife came in to vote. Husband and wife exchanged discreet smiles, but there was also just a hint of an indefinable complicity, which provoked in the presiding officer an uncomfortable inner spasm, perhaps the pain of envy, knowing that he would never exchange such a smile with anyone. It was still hurting him in some fold of his flesh when, thirty minutes later, he glanced at the clock and wondered to himself if his wife had, in the end, gone to the cinema. She'll turn up, if she ever does, at the last possible moment, he thought. The ways of warding off fate are many and almost all are useless, and this one, forcing oneself to think the worst in the hope that the best will happen, is one of the most commonplace, and might even be worthy of further consideration, although not in this case, because we have it from an unimpeachable source that the presiding officer's wife really has gone to the cinema and, at least up until now, is still undecided as to whether to cast her vote or not. Fortunately, the oft-invoked need for balance which has kept the universe on track and the planets on course means that whenever something is taken from one side, it is replaced by something else on the other, something that more or less corresponds, something of the same quality and, if possible, the same proportions, so that there are not too many complaints about unfair treatment. How else can one explain why it was that, at four o'clock in the afternoon, an hour which is neither late nor early, neither fish nor fowl, those voters who had, until then, remained in the quiet of their homes, apparently blithely ignoring the election altogether, started to come out onto the streets, most of them under their own steam, but others thanks only to the worthy assistance of firemen and volunteers because the places where they lived were still flooded and impassable, and all of them, absolutely all of them, the healthy and the infirm, the former on foot, the latter in wheelchairs, on stretchers, in ambulances,

JOSÉ SARAMAGO

headed straight for their respective polling stations like rivers
which know no other course than that which flows to the sea.
It will probably seem to the sceptical or the merely suspicious,
the kind who are only prepared to believe in miracles from
which they hope to gain some advantage, that the present circumstance has shown the above-mentioned need for balance to
be utterly wrong, that the trumped-up question about whether
the presiding officer's wife will or will not vote is, anyway, far
too insignificant from the cosmic point of view to require compensation in one of Earth's many cities in the form of the unexpected mobilization of thousands and thousands of people of
all ages and social conditions who, without having come to any
prior agreement as to their political and ideological differences,
have decided, at last, to leave their homes in order to go and
vote. Those who argue thus are forgetting that not only does
the universe have its own laws, all of them indifferent to the
contradictory dreams and desires of humanity, and in the formulation of which we contribute not one iota, apart, that is,
from the words by which we clumsily name them, but everything seems to indicate that it uses these laws for aims and
objectives that transcend and always will transcend our understanding, and if, at this particular point, the scandalous dis-
proportion between something which might, but for now only
might, have seen the ballot box deprived of, in this case, the
vote cast by the presiding officer's supposedly unpleasant wife
and the tide of men and women now on the move, if we find
this difficult to accept in the light of the most elementary dis-
tributive justice, prudence warns us to suspend for the moment
any definitive judgement and to watch with unquestioning attention how events, which have only just begun to unfold, develop. Which is precisely what the newspaper, radio and television journalists, carried away by professional enthusiasm and
by an unquenchable thirst for news, are doing now, racing up

and down, thrusting tape-recorders and microphones into people's faces, asking What was it made you leave your house at
four o'clock to go and vote, doesn't it seem extraordinary to
you that everyone should have come out onto the street at the
same time, and receiving in return such abrupt or aggressive
replies as, It just happened to be the time I'd decided to go and
vote, As free citizens, we can come and go as we please, we
don't owe anyone an explanation, How much do they pay you
to ask these stupid questions, Who cares what time I leave or
don't leave my house, Is there some law that obliges me to answer that question, Sorry, I'm only prepared to speak with my
lawyer present. There were polite people too, who replied
without the reproachful acrimony of the examples given above,
but they were equally unable to satisfy the journalists' devouring curiosity, merely shrugging and saying, Look, I have the
greatest respect for the work you do and I'd love to help you
publish a bit of good news, but, alas, all I can tell you is that I
looked at my watch, saw it was four o'clock and said to the family Right, let's go, it's now or never, Why now or never, That's
the funny thing, you see, that's just how it came out, Try to
think, rack your brains, No, it's not worth it, ask someone else,
perhaps they'll know, But I've asked fifty people already, And,
No one could give me an answer, Exactly, But doesn't it strike
you as a strange coincidence that thousands of people should
all have left their houses at the same time to go and vote, It's
certainly a coincidence, but perhaps not that strange, Why not,
Ah, that I don't know. The commentators, who were following
the electoral process on the various television programmes
and, for lack of any firm facts on which to base their analyses,
were busily making educated guesses, inferring the will of the
gods from the flight and the song of birds, regretting that animal sacrifice was no longer legal and that they were thus prevented from poring over some creature's still twitching viscera

to decipher the secrets of chronos and of fate, these commentators woke suddenly from the torpor into which they had been plunged by the gloomy prospects of the count and, doubtless because it seemed unworthy of their educational mission to waste time discussing coincidences, hurled themselves like wolves upon the fine example of good citizenship that the population of the capital were, at that moment, setting the rest of the country by turning up en masse at polling stations just when the specter of an abstention on a scale unparalleled in the history of our democracy had seemed to be posing a grave threat to the stability not just of the regime but, even more seriously, of the system itself. The statement emanating from the ministry of the interior did not go quite that far, but the government's relief was evident in every line. As for the three parties involved in the election, the parties on the right, in the middle and on the left, they, having first made rapid calculations as to the losses and gains that would result from this unexpected influx of voters, issued congratulatory statements in which, along with other stylistic niceties, they affirmed that democracy had every reason to celebrate. With the national flag draped on the wall behind them, the president in his palace and the prime minister in his mansion both expressed themselves in similar terms, give or take a comma. At the polling stations, the lines of voters, standing three deep, went right round the block and as far as the eye could see.

Like all the other presiding officers in the city, the one at polling station number fourteen was all too aware that he was living through a unique moment in history. When, late that night, after the ministry of the interior had extended the deadline for voting by two hours, a period that had to be extended by a further half an hour so that the voters crammed inside the building could exercise their right to vote, when, at last, the poll clerks and the party representatives, exhausted and hungry, stood before the mountain of ballot papers that had been emptied out of the two ballot boxes, the second one had been an emergency requisition from the ministry, the immensity of the task that lay before them made them tremble with an emotion we would not hesitate to describe as epic or heroic, as if the nation's honored ghosts, brought back to life, had magically rematerialized in those ballot papers. One of the ballot papers belonged to the presiding officer's wife. She had been propelled out of the cinema by some strange impulse, she had then spent hours in a queue that advanced at a snail's pace, and when she finally found herself face to face with her husband, when she heard him speak her name, she felt in her heart something that was perhaps the shadow of a former happiness, only the shadow, but even so, she felt it had been worth going there just for that. It was gone midnight when the counting finished. The number of valid votes did not quite reach twenty-five percent, with the party on the right winning thirteen percent, the party in the middle nine percent and the party on the left two and a half percent. There were very few spoiled ballots and very few abstentions. All the others, more than seventy percent of the total votes cast, were blank.

FEELINGS of confusion and stupefaction, but also of mockery and scorn swept the country from north to south. The provincial town councils, where the elections had taken place without incident or upset, apart from the occasional delay caused by the bad weather, and which had obtained results that differed little from the norm, the usual number of straightforward voters, the usual number of inveterate abstainers, and no very significant number of spoiled or blank votes, these councils, who had felt humiliated by the display of centralist triumphalism that had been paraded before the rest of the country as an example of the purest electoral public spirit, could now return that slap in the face and laugh at the foolish presumption of those ladies and gentlemen who thought they were the cat's meow simply because they happened to live in the country's capital. The words Those ladies and gentlemen, pronounced with a curl of the lips that oozed disdain with every syllable, if not with every letter, were directed not at the people who had remained at home until four in the afternoon and then suddenly rushed out to vote as if they had received some irresistible order, but at the government who had hung out the flags too soon, at the political parties who had pounced

on the blank votes as if they were a vineyard to be harvested
and they were the harvesters, at the newspapers and the other
media for the ease with which they moved from applause on
the capitoline hill to having people hurled from the tarpeian
rock, as if they themselves did not play an active part in the
genesis of such disasters.

The provincial scoffers were right to some extent, but not
as right as they thought there were. Beneath the political agi-
tation that is racing through the capital like a gunpowder trail
in search of a bomb one can sense a disquiet that avoids being
spoken out loud, unless in a discussion amongst peers, or between individuals and their closest friends, members of a political party and the party machinery, or the government and
itself. What will happen when the election is held again, that
is the question everyone is asking in a quiet, controlled whisper, so as not to wake the sleeping dragon. There are those
who feel that the best plan would be to resist sticking the spear
between the creature's ribs and leave things as they are, with
the p.o.t.r. in government and the p.o.t.r. on the city council, to pretend that nothing has happened, to imagine, for example, that the government has declared a state of emergency
in the capital and that, consequently, all constitutional guarantees are suspended, and then, after a time, when the dust has
settled and the whole tragic incident has entered the list of
long-forgotten past events, to prepare for new elections, starting with a carefully planned electoral campaign, full of solemn
oaths and promises, at the same time trying to prevent, at all
costs, without worrying too much about any minor or major
illegalities, the possibility of the repetition of a phenomenon
which a celebrated expert on such matters has already rather
harshly dubbed sociopolitical teratology. There are also those
who take an entirely different view, they protest that the laws
are sacred, that what is written is there to be obeyed, regard-

less of who gets hurt in the process, and that if we follow the path of subterfuges and take the short-cut of under-the-table deals we will be heading straight for chaos and an end to conscience, in short, if the law stipulates that in the event of a natural disaster, the elections should be repeated eight days later, then they must be repeated eight days later, that is, on the following Sunday, and may god's will be done, since that is what he's there for. It should be noted, however, that when expressing their opinions, the political parties prefer not to take too many risks, in the spirit of trying to please everyone all the time, they say yes, but then again no. The leaders of the party on the right, which is in government and runs the city council, start by assuming that this undoubted trump card will hand them victory on a silver platter, and so they have adopted a tactic of serenity tinged with diplomacy, trusting to the judgement of the government upon whom it is incumbent to see that the law is respected, As is only logical and natural in a long-standing democracy like ours, they conclude. The leaders of the party in the middle also want the law to be obeyed, but are asking the government for something which they know to be totally impossible, that is, the establishment and application of rigorous measures to ensure that the next election takes place absolutely normally and, presumably, produces absolutely normal results, In order, they allege, that there will be no repetition in this city of the shameful spectacle it has just presented to the country and to the world. As for the party on the left, they have gathered together all their top people and, after a long debate, drawn up and published a statement in which they express their firm and genuine hope that the approaching election will bring into being the necessary political conditions for the advent of a new era of development and social progress. They don't actually say that they're hoping to win the next election and take over the city council, but the implication is there. That night, the prime minister went on television to announce to the people that, in accordance with the current legislation, the municipal elections would be held again on the following Sunday, and a new period of electoral campaigning, of four days only, would begin at midnight and end at midnight on Friday. Putting on a grave face and speaking with great emphasis, he added that the government was sure that the capital's population, when called upon to vote again, would exercise their civic duty with the dignity and decorum they had always shown in the past, thus declaring null and void the regrettable event during which, for reasons that have yet to be clarified, but into which investigations are already fairly well advanced, the usual clear judgement of the city's electorate had become unexpectedly confused and distorted. The message from the president will be kept back until the close of the campaign on Friday night, but its concluding phrase has already been chosen, Sunday, my dear compatriots, will be a fine day.

And it really was a fine day. From early morning on, with the protecting sky in all its splendor and the golden sun blazing forth against a backdrop of crystalline blue, to use the inspired words of a television reporter, the voters started leaving their homes and heading for their respective polling stations not in a blind mass as had appeared to happen a week before, but with each person setting out alone, and so conscientiously and diligently that even before the doors were opened there were already long, long queues of citizens awaiting their turn to vote. Not everything, alas, was pure and honest at these gatherings. There was not a single queue, not one amongst the more than forty that formed at various points of the city, that did not have amongst them one or more spies whose mission was to listen and record the comments of the people present, the police authorities being convinced that, as happens, for example, in doctors' waiting-rooms, a prolonged wait will always sooner or later loosen tongues, revealing, even if only by the merest slip, the secret intentions of the electorate. The great majority of the spies are professionals and belong to the secret service, but some are volunteers, patriotic amateurs of espionage who offered to help out of a desire to serve, without remuneration, as it said in the sworn declaration they signed, whilst others, quite a few, were attracted merely by the morbid pleasure of being able to denounce someone. The genetic code of what, somewhat unthinkingly, we have been content to call human nature, cannot be reduced to the organic helix of deoxyribonucleic acid, or dna, there is much more to be said about it and it has much more to tell us, but human nature is, figuratively speaking, the complementary spiral that we have not yet managed to prise out of kindergarten, despite the multitude of psychologists and analysts from the most diverse schools and with the most diverse abilities who have broken their nails trying to draw its bolts. These scientific considerations, whatever their value now or in the future, should not allow us to forget today's disquieting realities, like the one we have just seen, for not only are there spies in the queues, trying to look nonchalant as they listen and secretly record what people say, there are also cars that glide quietly past the queues, apparently looking for a place to park, but which carry inside them, invisible to our eyes, high-definition video cameras and state-of-the-art microphones capable of projecting onto a screen the emotions apparently hidden in the diverse murmurings of a group of people who believe, individually, that they are thinking of something else. The word has been recorded, as has the emotion behind it. No one is safe. Up until the moment when the doors of the polling stations were opened and the queues began to move, the recorders had captured only insignificant phrases, the most banal of comments on the beauty of the morning and the pleasant temperature or about the hurried breakfast they

had eaten, brief exchanges on the important subject of what to
do with the children while their mothers came to vote, Their
father is looking after them at the moment, we're just going to
have to take turns, first me, then him, I mean, obviously we'd
rather have come to vote together, but it was just impossible,
and, as the saying goes, what can't be cured must be endured,
We've left our youngest with his older sister, she's not reached
voting age yet, yes, this is my husband, Pleased to meet you,
Nice to meet you too, It's a lovely morning, isn't it, It's almost
as if it had been laid on deliberately, Well, I suppose it was
bound to happen sometime. Despite the auditory acuity of the
microphones passing and repassing, white car, blue car, green
car, red car, black car, with their aerials bobbing in the morning
breeze, nothing overtly suspicious raised its head from beneath
the skin of such innocent, ordinary expressions as these, or so,
at least, it appeared. However, one did not need to have a doc-
torate in suspicion or a degree in distrust to notice something
unusual about those last two phrases, about someone having
laid on the lovely morning deliberately, and especially the second phrase, about how it was bound to happen sometime, ambiguities which were perhaps unwitting, perhaps unconscious,
but, for that very reason, potentially even more dangerous and
therefore worth contrasting with a detailed analysis of the tone
of voice in which those words had been uttered, but, above
all, with the range of frequencies they generated, we are referring here to subtones, which, if recent theories are to be believed, must be taken into consideration, otherwise, the degree
of comprehension of any oral discourse will inevitably be in-
sufficient, incomplete and limited. The spy who happened to
be there had been given very precise instructions on what to
do in such cases, as had all his colleagues. He must not allow
himself to become separated from the suspect, he must place
himself in third or fourth position behind him in the queue of

voters, he must, as a double guarantee, and regardless of the sensitivity of his concealed recording equipment, commit to memory the voter's name and number when the presiding officer said them out loud, he must then pretend to have forgotten something and withdraw discreetly from the queue, go out into the street and phone headquarters to tell them what had happened, and, having done that, return to the hunting ground and take up another place in the queue. This activity cannot, strictly speaking, be compared to an exercise in target shooting, what they are hoping for here is that chance, destiny, luck, or whatever you want to call it, will place the target in front of the shot.

As the hours passed, information rained down upon the center of operations, but none of it revealed in a clear-cut and consequently irrefutable manner the intentions of the voter thus caught, all that appeared on the list were phrases of the kind described above, and even the phrase that seemed more suspicious than all the others, Well, I suppose it was bound to happen sometime, would lose much of its apparent slipperiness once restored to its context, a conversation between two men about the recent divorce of one of them, not that they spoke of it explicitly, in order not to arouse the curiosity of the people nearby, but which had concluded thus, with a touch of rancor, a touch of resignation, and with a tremulous sigh that came forth from the divorced man's breast and that should have led any sensitive spy, assuming, of course, that sensitivity is a spy's best attribute, to come down clearly on the side of resignation. The fact that the spy may not have considered this worthy of note, and that the recording equipment may not have captured it, can be put down to mere human failure and to technological blips which any good judge, knowing what men are like, and not unaware either of the nature of machines, would have to take into account, even if, and, although at first sight this may appear

shocking, it would, in fact, be magnificently just, even if in the
documents bearing on the case there was not the slightest indication of the accused's non-culpability. Were this innocent man
to be interrogated tomorrow, we tremble at the mere thought
of what could happen to him, Do you admit that you said to
the person you were with Well, I suppose it was bound to happen sometime, Yes, I do, Now, think carefully before answering, what were you talking about when you said that, About my
separation from my wife, Separation or divorce, Divorce, And
what were or are your feelings about that divorce, Half-angry,
half-resigned, More angry or more resigned, More resigned,
I guess, Don't you think, in that case, that the natural thing
would have been to utter a sigh, especially since you were talking to a friend, Well, I can't be sure I didn't sigh, I really don't
remember, Well, we know that you didn't, How can you know
that, you weren't there, Who told you we weren't there, Maybe
my friend remembers hearing me sigh, you'd have to ask him,
You obviously don't care much for your friend, What do you
mean, Summoning your friend and getting him into all kinds
of trouble, Oh, I wouldn't want that, Good, Can I go now, Certainly not, don't be in such a hurry, you still haven't answered
the question we asked you, What question, What were you really thinking about when you said those words to your friend,
But I've already told you, Give us another answer, that one
won't do, It's the only answer I can give because it's the true
one, That's what you think, Unless you want me to make one
up, Yes, do, we don't mind at all if you come up with answers
which, with time and patience, could be made to fit the proper
application of certain techniques, that way, you'll end up saying
what we want to hear, Tell me what the answer is then, and let's
be done with it, Oh, no, that wouldn't be any fun at all, who do
you think we are, sir, we have our scientific dignity to consider,
our professional conscience to defend, it's very important to us

that we should be able to demonstrate to our superiors that we deserve the money they pay us and the bread that we eat, Sorry, you've lost me, Don't be in such a hurry.

The impressive serenity of the voters in the streets and in the polling stations was not mirrored by an identical state of mind in ministerial offices and at party headquarters. The question that most worries them all is what the abstention rate will be this time, as if therein lay the way to salvation out of the tricky social and political situation in which the country has been plunged for over a week now. A reasonably high abstention rate, or even above the maximum recorded in the previous elections, as long as it wasn't too high, would signify a return to normality, to the known routine of those voters who had never seen the point of voting and are noticeable by virtue of their persistent absence, or those others who preferred to make the most of the good weather and go and spend the day at the beach or in the country with their family, or those who, for no other reason than invincible idleness, stayed at home. If the crowds outside the polling stations, which were as large as they had been for the previous election, showed, without any room for doubt, that the percentage of abstentions was going to be extremely low, possibly non-existent, what most confused the authorities, and was nearly driving them crazy, was the fact that the voters, with very few exceptions, responded with impenetrable silence to the questions asked by the people running exit polls on how they had voted, It's just for statistical purposes, you don't have to identify yourself, you don't have to give your name, they insisted, but even that did not convince the distrustful voters. A week earlier, journalists had at least managed to get answers out of them, although it's true that these had been given in impatient or ironic or scornful tones and were really another way of saying nothing at all, but at least there had been an exchange of words, one side had asked the question and the other had pretended to give an answer, but it was nothing like this dense wall of silence, as if it were built around a mystery shared by everyone and which everyone had sworn to defend. To many people it will seem astonishing, not to say impossible, this coincidence of behavior amongst so many thousands of people who do not know each other, who do not think the same, who belong to different social classes or strata, who, in short, despite being politically to the right or in the middle or to the left, or, indeed, nowhere at all, resolved individually to keep their mouth shut until the votes were counted, thus leaving the unveiling of the secret until later. This, with great hopes of being right, was what the interior minister wanted to tell the prime minister, this was what the prime minister hastened to pass on to the president, who, being older, more experienced and more case-hardened, who had, in brief, seen more of life, merely replied sardonically, If they're not prepared to talk now, give me one good reason why they should talk later. The only reason this bucket of cold water from the nation's supreme arbiter did not cause the prime minister or the interior minister to lose all hope and to fall into the grip of despair was because they had nothing else to cling to, even if only for a short time. The interior minister had preferred not to mention that, fearing possible irregularities in the electoral process, a concern which the facts themselves, meanwhile, proved to be entirely unfounded, he had ordered the posting at all polling stations of two plain-clothes policemen, each from a different police department, both being authorized to oversee the count, and each of whom was charged also with keeping an eye on his or her colleague, just in case there should be any kind of complicity between them, be it honorably political in nature or a deal struck at the market of petty treacheries. In this way, what with spies and vigilantes, recording devices and video cameras, they appeared to have everything under control, safe from any malign interference that might sully the purity of the electoral process, and now that the game was over, all that remained for them to do was to wait, arms folded, for the final verdict of the ballot boxes. When the presiding officer of polling station number fourteen, to whose workings we had the great pleasure of devoting, in homage to those dedicated citizens, an entire chapter, even down to the personal problems of certain of its members, and when the presiding officers of all the other polling stations, from number one to number thirteen, from number fifteen to number forty-four, at last emptied out the votes onto the long rows of benches that had served them as tables, the impetuous rumble of an avalanche was heard all over the city. It was a foreshadowing of the political earthquake that would soon follow. In homes, in cafés, in pubs and in bars, in all the public places where there was a television or a radio, the capital's inhabitants, some more calmly than others, awaited the final result of the count. No one confided in their nearest and dearest as to how they had voted, the closest of friends kept silent on the matter, and even the most talkative people seemed to have forgotten their words. Finally, at ten o'clock that night, the prime minister appeared on television. His face looked drawn, he had dark circles under his eyes, the result of a whole week of sleepless nights, and beneath the healthy glow of makeup he was pale. He was holding a piece of paper in his hand, but he didn't really read from it, he just glanced at it from time to time so as not to lose the thread of his speech, Dear fellow citizens, he said, the result of the elections carried out today in our country's capital was as follows, the party on the right, eight percent, the party in the middle, eight percent, the party on the left, one percent, abstentions, none, spoiled votes, none, blank votes, eighty-three percent. He paused to take a sip from the glass of water beside him, then went on, While we realize that today's vote is both a confirmation and an exacerbation of the trend established last Sunday and while we are in unanimous agreement as to the need for a serious investigation into the first and last causes of these troubling results, the government considers, after due consultation with his excellency the president, that its legitimacy in office was not called into question, not only because the election just held was merely a local election, but also because it declares and believes that its pressing and urgent duty is to carry out an in-depth investigation into the anomalous events of the last seven days, events in which we have all been both astonished witnesses and bold participants, and it is with profound sorrow that I say this, for those blank votes which have struck a brutal blow against the democratic normality of our personal and collective lives did not fall from the skies or rise up from the bowels of the earth, they were in the pockets of eighty-three out of every one hundred voters in this city, who placed them in the ballot boxes with their own unpatriotic hands. Another sip of water, this time more necessary, for his mouth had suddenly gone dry, There is still time to rectify this mistake, not by means of another election, which, given the current state of affairs, might prove not only useless but counter-productive, but through a rigorous examination of conscience, which, from this public platform, I urge on all the inhabitants of the capital, some so that they may better protect themselves from the terrible threat hanging over their heads, others, be they guilty or innocent in their intentions, so that they can either turn from the evil into which they have been dragged by who knows who or else risk becoming the direct target of the sanctions foreseen under the state of emergency whose declaration the government will be seeking from his excellency the president, after, of course, initial consultation with parliament, which has been convened tomorrow in extraordinary session, and from whom we expect to obtain unanimous approval. A change of tone, arms slightly spread, hands raised to shoulder height, The nation's government feels sure that in coming here, like a loving father, to remind that section of the capital's population who strayed from the straight and narrow of the sublime lesson to be learned from the parable of the prodigal son and by saying to them that there is no fault that cannot be forgiven a heart that is truly contrite and wholly repentant, the government is merely giving expression to the fraternal will of the rest of the country, of all those citizens who, with praiseworthy civic feeling, properly fulfilled their electoral duties. The prime minister's final flourish, Honor your country, for the eyes of the country are upon you, complete with drumrolls and bugle blasts, unearthed from the attics of the mustiest of nationalistic rhetoric, was ruined by a Good night that rang entirely false, but then that is the great thing about ordinary words, they are incapable of deceit.

In towns, houses, bars, pubs, cafés, restaurants, associations or party headquarters where voters from the party on the right, the party in the middle and even the party on the left were gathered together, the prime minister's message was much discussed, although, as is only natural, in different ways and from diverse points of view. Those most satisfied with his performance, and that barbaric term is theirs not the narrator's, were those of the p.o.t.r., who, with knowing looks and winks, congratulated themselves on their leader's excellent technique, an approach that is often rather curiously described as carrot-and-stick, and which, in olden times, was mainly applied to asses and mules, but which modernity, with notable success, has turned to human use. Some, however, the blustering, braggadocio types, felt that the prime minister should have finished his speech at the point where he announced the imminent declaration of a state of emergency, that everything he said afterward was entirely unnecessary, that the only thing the rabble understands is the big stick, start with half-measures and you'll get nowhere, never give your enemy so much as the time of day, and other outspoken expressions in the same vein. Their colleagues argued that it really wasn't like that, that their leader must have his reasons, but these pacifists, always so ingenuous, were unaware that the intemperate reaction of their intransigent colleagues was, in fact, a tactical maneuver, the aim of which was to keep alive the combative mood of the party members. Be prepared for everything, had been the slogan. Those in the p.i.t.m., as members of the principal opposition party, were in agreement with the main thrust of the speech, that is, the urgent need to find out who was responsible and to punish the culprits or conspirators, but they felt that the declaration of a state of emergency was entirely disproportionate, especially as they had no idea how long it would last, and besides, it was arrant nonsense to take away the rights of someone whose only crime had been to exercise one of those rights. What will happen, they wondered, if a citizen takes it into his head to go to the constitutional court, The truly intelligent and patriotic thing to do, they added, would be to form a government of national salvation consisting of representatives from all the parties, because, if this really is a collective emergency, declaring a state of siege isn't going to resolve it, the p.o.t.l. have just gone off at the deep end and will very likely drown. The members of the p.o.t.l. ridiculed any idea that they could possibly form part of a coalition government, what they were really concerned about was coming up with an interpretation of the election result that would disguise the disastrous drop in the party's percentage of the poll, for, having polled five percent in the last election and two and a half in the first round of this one, they now found themselves with a miserable one percent and a very bleak future. The results of their analysis culminated in the preparation of a statement which would suggest that, since there was no objective reason to think that the blank votes had constituted an attempt on the security of the state or on the stability of the system, the desire for change thus expressed could correctly be read as coinciding, quite by chance, with the progressive proposals contained in the p.o.t.l.'s manifesto. Nothing more and nothing less.

There were also people who just turned off the television as soon as the prime minister had finished speaking and, before going to bed, sat around talking about their lives, and there were others who spent the rest of the evening tearing up and burning papers. They weren't conspirators, they were simply afraid.

TO THE minister of defense, a civilian who had never even done his military service, the declaration of a state of emergency seemed pretty small beer, he had wanted a proper, full-blooded state of siege, a state of siege in the literal sense of the word, hard, implacable, like a moving wall capable of isolating the source of the sedition and then crushing it in one devastating counter-attack, Before the pestilence and the gangrene spread to the part of the country that's still healthy, he warned. The prime minister acknowledged the extreme seriousness of the situation, and that the country had been the victim of a vile assault on the very foundations of representative democracy, the minister of defense, however, begged to differ, I would compare it, rather, to a depth charge launched against the system, Quite so, but I think, and the president agrees with me on this, that, without losing sight of the dangers of the immediate situation, and in order to be able to vary the means and objectives of any action taken as and when it proves necessary, it would be preferable to begin by using methods which, while more discreet and less ostentatious, are possibly more effective than sending the army out onto the streets, closing the airport and setting up roadblocks at all routes out of the city, And what

375

methods would those be exactly, asked the minister of defense, making not the slightest attempt to disguise his annoyance, Nothing that you don't know about already, after all, the armed forces have their own espionage system, We call ours counter-espionage, Which comes to the same thing, Ah, I see what you're getting at, Good, I knew you'd understand, said the prime minister, at the same time gesturing to the interior minister, who spoke next, Without going into actual operational detail, which, as I'm sure you'll understand, is confidential, not to say top secret, the plan drawn up by my ministry is based, in general terms, on a broad and systematic infiltration of the population by specially trained agents, which may help us to uncover the reasons behind what has happened and equip us to take the necessary measures to destroy the evil ab ovo, Ab ovo, you say, as far as I can see, it's already hatched, remarked the justice minister, It was just a manner of speaking, replied the interior minister, sounding slightly irritated, then he went on, The time has come to inform this council of ministers, in complete and utter confidence, if you'll forgive the redundancy, that the espionage services under my orders, or rather, who answer to the ministry for which I am responsible, do not exclude the possibility that what happened may have its real roots abroad, and that what we are seeing may be only the tip of the iceberg of a gigantic, global destabilization plot, doubtless anarchist in inspiration, and which, for reasons we still do not comprehend, has chosen our country as its first guinea pig, Sounds a bit odd to me, said the minister of culture, to my knowledge, anarchists have never, even in the realm of theory, proposed committing acts of this nature and of this magnitude, That, said the minister of defense sarcastically, may be because my dear colleague's knowledge dates back to the idyllic world of his grandparents, and, strange though it may seem, things have changed quite a lot since then, there was a time when nihilism took a rather lyrical and not too bloody form, but what we are facing today is terrorism, pure and unadulterated, it may wear different faces and expressions, but it is, essentially, the same thing, You should be careful about making such wild claims and such facile extrapolations, commented the justice minister, it seems risky to me, not to say, outrageous, to label as terrorism, especially pure and unadulterated terrorism, the appearance in the ballot boxes of a few blank votes, A few votes, a few votes, spluttered the minister of defense, rendered almost speechless, how, I'd like to know, can you possibly call eighty-three out of every hundred votes a few votes, what we have to grasp, what we have to take on board, is that each one of those votes was like a torpedo striking below the water line, My knowledge of anarchism may be out of date, I don't deny it, said the minister of culture, but, as far as I'm aware, although I certainly don't consider myself an expert on naval battles either, torpedoes always strike below the water line, they don't have much option, that is what they were made to do. The interior minister suddenly sprang to his feet, perhaps to defend his colleague, the defense minister, from this sneering comment, perhaps to condemn the lack of political empathy evident at the meeting, but the prime minister brought his hand down hard on the table, demanding silence, The ministers of culture and of defense can continue elsewhere the academic debate in which they appear to be so hotly engaged, but I would just like to remind you that the reason we are gathered together in this room, which, even more than parliament, represents the heart of democratic power and authority, is in order to take decisions that will save the country from the gravest crisis it has faced in centuries, that is the challenge we face, I believe, therefore, that, confronted by this enormous task, we should call a halt to any further verbal poppycock or, indeed, to squabbles over interpretation, as being unworthy of our responsibilities. There was a pause, which no one dared to interrupt, then he continued, Meanwhile, I would like to make it perfectly clear to the minister of defense that the fact that, during this first stage of dealing with the crisis, the president has favored the application of the plan drawn up by the relevant staff at the ministry of the interior does not mean and never could mean that the possibility of declaring a state of siege has been entirely rejected, everything will depend on what direction events take, on the reactions of the population in the capital, on the response of the rest of the country, and on the not always predictable behavior of the opposition, especially, in this case, the p.o.t.l., who now have so little to lose that they won't mind betting the little that remains to them on some high-risk move, Oh, I don't think we need worry ourselves too much about a party that could only manage one percent of the votes, remarked the interior minister, with a scornful shrug, Did you read their statement, asked the prime minister, Of course I did, reading political statements is part of my job, one of my duties, it's true that there are those who pay assistants to chew their food for them first, but I belong to the old school, and I only trust my own head, even if I'm wrong, You're forgetting that ministers are, in the final analysis, the prime minister's advisors, And it's an honor to be one, sir, the difference, the vast difference, is that we bring you your food ready digested, That's all very fine, but let's leave gastronomy and the chemistry of the digestive processes for now and go back to the p.o.t.l.'s statement, give me your opinion, what did you think of it, It's a crude, naive version of the old saying that if you can't beat 'em, join 'em, And when applied to the present case, Applied to the present case, sir, it's a case of if they're not your votes, then try to make it look as if they are, Even so, it's as well to remain on the alert, their little trick just might work on the more left-leaning segment of the population, Although we have no idea at the moment which segment that is, said the justice minister, it seems to me that what we are refusing to face up to, frankly and openly, is that the vast majority of that eighty-three percent are our own voters or the p.i.t.m.'s voters, and that we should be asking ourselves why it is that they cast those blank votes, that's the crux of the matter, not whatever wise or naive arguments the p.o.t.l. might come up with, Yes, when you think about it, replied the prime minister, our tactic is not so very different from the one the p.o.t.l. is using, that is, if most of the votes aren't yours, then pretend they don't belong to your opponents either, In other words, piped up the minister of transport and communications from the corner of the table, we're all up to the same tricks, A somewhat flippant way of summing up the situation in which we find ourselves, and note that I am speaking here from a purely political viewpoint, but one not entirely lacking in sense, said the prime minister and drew the discussion to a close.

The rapid implementation of the state of emergency, like a kind of solomonic sentence dictated by providence, swiftly cut the gordian knot that the media, especially the newspapers, had, with more or less skill and with more or less delicacy, been trying to undo ever since the unhappy results of the first elections and, even more dramatically, of the second, although they always took great care not to draw too much attention to their efforts. On the one hand, it was their duty, as obvious as it was elementary, to condemn, with an energy tinged with civic indignation, in editorials and in specially commissioned opinion pieces, the unexpected and irresponsible behavior of an electorate who, apparently rendered blind to the superior interests of the nation as a whole by some strange and dangerous perversion, had complicated public life to an unprecedented degree, corralling it into a dark alleyway from which not even the brightest spark was able to see a way out. On the other hand, they had to weigh and measure every word they wrote, to ponder susceptibilities, to take, as it were, two steps forward and one step back, lest their readers should turn against a newspaper that had started calling them traitors and lunatics after years and years of perfect harmony and assiduous readership. The declaration of the state of emergency, by allowing the government to assume the relevant powers and to suspend at the stroke of a pen all constitutional guarantees, removed that uncomfortable weight, that threatening shadow hanging over the heads of editors and administrators. With freedom of expression and communication strictly regulated, with censorship always peering over the editor's shoulder, they had the very best of excuses and the most complete of justifications. We would really love, they would say, to provide our esteemed readers with the opportunity, which is also their right, to have access to news and opinions untrammeled by unreasonable interference and intolerable restrictions, especially during the extremely delicate times we are living through, but that is the way things are, and only someone who has worked in the honorable profession of journalism can know how painful it is having to work under virtual twenty-four-hour surveillance, but then, between you and me, the people who bear the greatest responsibility for what is happening are the voters in the capital, not the voters in the provinces, but, alas, to make matters worse, and despite all our pleading, the government will not allow us to produce a censored version for the capital and an uncensored one for the rest of the country, why, only yesterday, a high-up ministry official was telling us that censorship proper is like the sun, which, when it rises, rises for everyone, this is hardly news to us, we know the way the world works, and it is always the just who have to pay for the sinners. Despite all these precautions as regards both form and content, it soon became clear that the public's interest in reading newspapers had greatly declined.

Driven by an understandable urge to try and please everyone, some newspapers thought they could combat the absence of readers by plastering their pages with naked bodies, whether male or female, together or alone, singly or in pairs, at rest or in action, disporting themselves in modern gardens of delight, but the readers, grown impatient with images whose minimal and not particularly arousing variations in color and configuration had, even in remote antiquity, been considered banal commonplaces of man's exploration of the libido, continued, out of apathy, indifference and even nausea, to cause print runs and sales to plummet. Likewise, the search for and the exhibition of rather grubby intimacies, of all kinds of scandals and outrages, the old game of public virtues masking private vices, the jolly carousel of private vices elevated to the status of public virtues, which, until recently, had never lacked for spectators or for candidates willing to strut their stuff, failed to have a favorable impact on the day-to-day balance sheet of debit and credit, which was at an irremediably low ebb. It really seemed as if the majority of the city's inhabitants were determined to change their lives, their tastes and their style. Their great mistake, as they would soon begin to see, had been casting those blank votes. They wanted a cleanup and they would get one.

This was the firm view of the government and, in particular, of the ministry of the interior. The process of selecting the agents, some from the secret service, others from public bodies, who would surreptitiously infiltrate the bosom of the masses, had been swift and efficient. Having revealed, under oath, as evidence of their exemplary character as citizens, the name of the party for whom they had voted and the nature of that vote, having signed, again under oath, a document in which they expressed their active rejection of the moral plague that had infected a large part of the population, the first action of all agents, of both sexes, it must be said, so that it cannot be al-

leged, as it so often is, that all evil things are the work of man,
who were organized into groups of forty as if in a class and led
by teachers trained in the discrimination, recognition and interpretation of electronic recordings of both sound and image,
their first action, as we were saying, consisted in sifting through
the enormous quantity of material gathered by spies during the
second ballot, the material collected by those who had stood in
the queues listening and by those who, wielding video cameras
and microphones, had driven slowly past them in cars. By starting off with this operation of rummaging around in the infor-
mational intestines, the agents were given, before they launched
themselves with enthusiasm and the keen nose of a gun dog
into action and work in the field, an immediate taste of a be-
hind-closed-doors investigation the tone of which we had occasion to provide a brief but elucidatory example some pages
back. Simple, ordinary expressions, such as, I don't generally
bother to vote, but here I am, Do you think it'll turn out to
have been worth all the bother, The pitcher goes so often to
the well that, in the end, it leaves its handle there, I voted last
week too, but that day I could only leave home at four, This is
just like the lottery, I almost always draw a blank, Still, you've
got to keep trying, Hope is like salt, there's no nourishment in
it, but it gives the bread its savor, for hours and hours, these and
a thousand other equally innocuous, equally neutral, equally
innocent phrases were picked apart syllable by syllable, reduced
to mere crumbs, turned upside down, crushed in the mortar by
the pestle of the question, Explain to me again that business
about the pitcher, Why did the handle come off at the well and
not on the way there or back, If you don't normally vote, why
did you vote this time, If hope is like salt, what do you think
should be done to make salt like hope, How would you resolve
the difference in color between hope, which is green, and salt,
which is white, Do you really think that a ballot paper is the

same as a lottery ticket, What did you mean when you used the word blank, and then, What pitcher, Did you go to the well because you were thirsty or in order to meet someone, What does the handle of the pitcher symbolize, When you sprinkle salt on your food, are you thinking that you're actually sprinkling hope, Why are you wearing a white shirt, Tell me, was the pitcher a real pitcher or a metaphorical one, And what color was it, black, red, Was it plain or did it have a design on it, Was it inlaid with quartz, Do you know what quartz is, Have you ever won a prize in the lottery, Why is it that, during the first election, you only left home at four, when it had stopped raining two hours before, Who is that woman beside you in this photo, What are the two of you laughing about, Don't you think that an important act like voting requires all responsible voters to wear a grave, serious, earnest expression or do you consider democracy to be a laughing matter, Or perhaps you think it is a crying matter, Which do you think, a laughing matter or a crying matter, Tell me about that pitcher again, why didn't you consider gluing the handle back on, there are glues made specially for the purpose, Does that pause mean that you, too, are lacking a handle, Which one, Do you like the age in which you happen to live, or would you prefer to have lived in another, Let's go back to salt and hope again, how much would you have to add before the thing you were hoping for became inedible, Do you feel tired, Would you like to go home, I'm in no hurry, haste is a bad counselor, if a person doesn't think through the answers he or she is going to give, the consequences can be disastrous, No, you're not lost, the very idea, you obviously haven't yet quite grasped that, here, people don't lose themselves, they find themselves, Don't worry, we're not threatening you, we just don't want you to rush, that's all. At this point, with the prey cornered and exhausted, they would ask the fateful question, Now I want you to tell me how you voted, that is, which party you gave your vote to. Since five hundred suspects picked from the queues of voters had been summoned to be interrogated, a situation in which anyone could have found himself given the patent insubstantiality of an accusation based on the kind of phrases, of which we have just given a convincing example, captured by all those directional microphones and tape-recorders, the logical thing, bearing in mind the relative breadth of the statistical universe questioned, would be that the replies would be distributed, albeit with a small and natural margin of error, in the same proportion as the votes cast, that is, forty people declaring proudly that they had voted for the party on the right, the party in government, an equal number seasoning their reply with just a pinch of defiance by affirming that they had voted for the only opposition party worthy of the name, that is, the party in the middle, and five, no more than five, pinned down, backs to the wall, I voted for the party on the left, they would say firmly, but in the tone of someone apologizing for a stubborn streak which they are helpless to correct. The remainder, that enormous remainder of four hundred and fifteen replies should have said, in accordance with the modal logic of surveys, I cast a blank vote. That clear response, shorn of the ambiguities of presumption or prudence, would be the one given by a computer or a calculator and would be the only one that their inflexible, honest natures, that of the computer and the machine, would have allowed themselves, but we are dealing here with human beings, and human beings are known universally as the only animals capable of lying, and while it is true that they sometimes lie out of fear and sometimes out of self-interest, they also occasionally lie because they realize, just in time, that this is the only means available to them of defending the truth. To judge by appearances, therefore, the ministry of the interior's plan had failed, indeed, during those first few moments, the confusion amongst the advisors was both shameful and complete, there seemed no possible way round the unexpected obstacle, unless orders were given for all those people to be tortured, which, as everyone knows, is unacceptable in democratic but right-wing states skilful enough to achieve the same ends without resorting to such rudimentary, medieval methods. It was whilst embroiled in this complicated situation that the interior minister showed both political nous and a rare tactical and strategic flexibility, possibly, who knows, an indication of greater things to come. He took two decisions, both of them important. The first, which would later be denounced as perversely machiavellian, took the form of an official note from the ministry distributed to the mass media via the unofficial state agency and which, in the name of the whole government, offered heartfelt thanks to the five hundred exemplary citizens who, in recent days, had come forward of their own volition and presented themselves to the authorities, offering their loyal support and any help they could give that would advance the ongoing investigations into abnormal factors uncovered in the last two elections. As well as this elementary expression of gratitude, the ministry, anticipating questions, warned families that they should not be surprised or worried by the lack of news from their absent loved ones, because in that very silence lay the key that could guarantee their personal safety, given the maximum degree of secrecy, red/red, that had been accorded to this delicate operation. The second decision, for internal eyes and use only, was a complete inversion of the plan drawn up earlier, which, as you will recall, predicted that the mass infiltration of investigators into the bosom of the masses would be the means, par excellence, that would lead to the deciphering of the mystery, the enigma, the charade, the puzzle, or whatever you care to call it, of those blank ballot papers. From now on, the agents would work in two numerically unequal groups, the smaller group would work in the field, from which, if truth be told, they no longer expected great results, the larger group would continue with the interrogation of the five hundred people retained, not detained you notice, increasing, as and when, the physical and psychological pressure to which they were already being subjected. As the old saying has been telling us now for centuries, Five hundred birds in the hand are worth five hundred and one in the bush. Confirmation of this was not long in coming. When, after the application of great diplomatic skill, after many digressions and much testing of the water, the agent in the field, that is, in the city, managed to ask the first question, Would you mind telling me who you voted for, the reply he was given, like a message learned by heart, was, word for word, the one given in law, No one can, under any pretext, be forced to reveal his or her vote or be questioned about this by any authority. And when, in the nonchalant tone of someone who did not consider the subject to be of much importance, he asked the second question, Forgive my curiosity, but did you by any chance cast a blank vote, the reply he was given skilfully reduced the scope of the question to a simple academic matter, No, sir, I didn't, but if I had I would be just as much within the law as if I had voted for one of the parties listed or had made my vote void by drawing a caricature of the prime minister, casting a blank vote, mister questioner, is an unrestricted right, which the law had no option but to allow the electorate, it is clearly stated that no one can be persecuted for having cast a blank vote, but just to set your mind at rest, I repeat that I was not one of those who did so, I was just talking for talking's sake, it was merely an academic hypothesis, that's all. Normally speaking, hearing such a response twice or three times would be of no particular significance, all it would show was that there are a few people in the world who know the law of the land and make a point of telling you, but being forced to listen to it, unruffled, without so much as raising an eyebrow, a hundred times, a thousand times, like a litany learned by heart, was more than patience could bear for someone who, having been painstakingly prepared for this delicate task, found himself unable to carry it out. It is not, therefore, surprising that the electorate's systematically obstructive behavior caused some of the agents to lose control and to resort to insult and aggression, encounters from which, indeed, they did not always emerge unscathed, given that they were acting alone in order not to frighten off their prey and that it was not unusual, especially in so-called dodgy areas, for other voters to pitch in and help the aggrieved party, with easily imagined consequences. The reports that the agents sent back to the center of operations were discouragingly thin on content, not a single person, not one, had admitted to having cast a blank vote, some pretended not to understand, others said they'd talk another day when they had more time, but they had to rush off now, before the shops shut, but the worst of all were the old, devil take 'em, for it seemed that an epidemic of deafness had sealed them all inside a soundproof capsule, and when the agent, with disconcerting ingenuity, wrote the question down on a piece of paper, the cheeky so-and-sos would either say that their glasses were broken or that they couldn't make out the writing or, quite simply, that they didn't know how to read at all. There were other, wilier agents, however, who, taking the idea of infiltration seriously, in its literal sense, frequented bars, bought people drinks, lent money to penniless poker players, went to sports events, especially football and basketball, where people mingle more in the stands, and got chatting to their fellow spectators, and, in the case of football, if there was a goal-less draw, they would, with sublime cunning, refer to it knowingly as a blank result, just to see what happened. Pretty much nothing happened. Sooner or later, the moment would come to ask the questions, Would you mind telling me which party you voted for, Forgive my curiosity, but did you by any chance cast a blank vote, and then the familiar answers would be repeated, either solo or in chorus, Me, the very idea, Us, don't be silly, and they would immediately adduce the legal reasons, with all their articles and clauses, and so fluently that it was as if all the city's inhabitants of voting age had been through an intensive course in electoral law, both domestic and foreign.

As the days passed, it became noticeable, in a way that was, at first, imperceptible, that the word blank, as if it had suddenly become obscene or rude, was falling into disuse, that people would employ all kinds of evasions and periphrases to replace it. A blank piece of paper, for example, would be described instead as virgin, a blank on a form that had all its life been a blank became the space provided, blank looks all became vacant instead, students stopped saying that their minds had gone blank, and owned up to the fact that they simply knew nothing about the subject, but the most interesting case of all was the sudden disappearance of the riddle with which, for generations and generations, parents, grandparents, aunts, uncles and neighbors had sought to stimulate the intelligence and deductive powers of children, You can fill me in, draw me and fire me, what am I, and people, reluctant to elicit the word blank from innocent children, justified this by saying that the riddle was far too difficult for those with limited experience of the world. It seemed, therefore, that the high political office promised to the interior minister had been cut short at birth, that he was fated, after having come so close to touching the sun, to be drowned ignominiously in the hellespont, but another idea, as sudden as a lightning flash illuminating the night, made him rise again. All was not lost. He ordered back to base the agents confined to fieldwork, blithely dismissed those on short-term contracts, gave the secret police a thorough dressing-down and set to work.

It was clear that the city was a termites' nest of liars and that the five hundred he had in his power were also lying through all the teeth they had in their head, but there was one difference between these two groups, the former were free to enter and leave their homes, and, elusive and slippery as eels, could appear as easily as they could disappear, only to reappear later on and again vanish, whereas dealing with the latter was the easiest thing in the world, it was enough just to go down into the ministry cellars, all five hundred were not there, of course, there wasn't room, most were distributed around other investigatory units, but the fifty or so kept under permanent observation should be more than enough for an initial attempt. The reliability of the machine may have been called into question by certain sceptical experts and some courts may even have refused to admit as evidence the results obtained from the tests, but the interior minister was nonetheless hopeful that the use of the machine might at least give off a small spark that would help him find his way out of the dark tunnel into which the investigation had stuck its head. His plan, as you will no doubt have guessed, was to bring back into the fray the famous polygraph, also known as the lie detector, or, in more scientific terms, a machine that is used to record, simultaneously, various psychological and physiological functions, or, in more descriptive detail, an instrument for registering physiological phenomena of which an electrical recording is made on a sheet of damp paper impregnated with potassium iodide and starch. Connected to the machine by a tangle of wires, armbands and suction pads, the patient does not suffer, he simply has to tell the truth, the whole truth and nothing but the truth, and to cease to believe in the universal assertion, the old, old story, which, since the beginning of time, has been drummed into us, that the will can do anything, for you need look no further than the following example, which denies it outright, because that wonderful will of yours, however much you may trust it, however tenacious

it may have been up until now, cannot control twitching muscles, cannot staunch unwanted sweat or stop eyelids blinking or
regulate breathing. In the end, they'll say you lied, you'll deny
it, you'll swear you told the truth, the whole truth and nothing but the truth, and that might be true, you didn't lie, you
just happen to be a very nervous person, with a strong will, it's
true, but you are nevertheless a tremulous reed that shivers in
the slightest breeze, so they'll connect you up to the machine
again and it will be even worse, they'll ask if you're alive and
you'll say, of course I am, but your body will protest, will contradict you, the tremor in your chin will say no, you're dead,
and it might be right, perhaps your body knows before you do
that they are going to kill you. It would be unlikely that this
could happen in the cellars of the ministry of the interior, the
only crime these people have committed is to cast a blank vote,
and that would have been of no importance if they had merely
been the usual suspects, but there were a lot of them, too many,
almost everyone, who cares if it's your inalienable right when
they tell you it's to be used only in homeopathic doses, drop by
drop, you can't come here with a pitcher filled to overflowing
with blank votes, that's why the handle dropped off, we always
thought there was something suspicious about that handle, if
something that could always carry a lot was satisfied with carrying little, that shows a most praiseworthy modesty, what got
you into trouble was ambition, you thought you could fly up
to the sun and, instead, you fell headfirst into the dardanelles,
you will recall that we said the same about the interior minister,
but he belongs to a different race of men, the macho, the vir-
ile, the bristly-chinned, those who will not bow their head, let's
see now how you escape the hunter of lies, let's see what revealing lines your large and small transgressions will leave on that
strip of paper impregnated with potassium iodide and starch,
and you thought you were something special, this is what the

much-vaunted supreme dignity of the human being can be reduced to, a piece of damp paper.

Now the polygraph is not a machine equipped with a disc that goes backward and forward and tells us, depending on the case, He lied, He didn't lie, if that were the case, being a judge with the ability to condemn and absolve would be the easiest thing in the world, police stations would be replaced by departments of applied mechanical psychology, lawyers, for lack of clientele, would pull down the shutters, the courts would be abandoned to the flies until some other use had been found for them. A polygraph, as we were saying, cannot go anywhere without help, it needs to have by its side a trained technician who can interpret the lines on the paper, but this doesn't mean that the technician must be a connoisseur of the truth, all he has to know is what is there before his eyes, that the question asked of the patient under observation has produced what we might innovatively call an allergographic reaction, or in more literary but no less imaginative terms, the outline of a lie. Something, nevertheless, would have been gained. At least it would be possible to proceed to an initial selection, wheat on the one side, tares on the other, and restore to liberty and family life, thereby freeing up the detention centers, those people, finally vindicated, who, without being contradicted by the machine, responded No to the question Did you cast a blank vote. As for the rest, those who had the guilt of electoral transgressions weighing on their conscience, any mental reserves of the Jesuitical kind or spiritual introspection of the zen variety would prove useless to them, for the polygraph, implacable, unfeeling, would immediately sniff out a falsehood, whether they denied casting a blank vote or claimed to have voted for such and such a party. One can, if the circumstances are favorable, survive one lie, but not two. Just in case, the interior minister had given orders that whatever the result of the tests, for now, no one would be released, Leave them be, one never knows how far human malice will go, he said. And he was right, the wretched man. After many dozens of meters of squiggled-on, scribbled-on paper, on which had been recorded the tremors of the souls of everyone observed, after questions and answers repeated hundreds of times, always the same, always identical, one secret service agent, still a young lad, with little experience of temptation, fell with the innocence of a newborn lamb for the challenge thrown out to him by a pretty young woman who had just been submitted to the polygraph test and been declared to be deceitful and false. This mata hari said, That machine is useless, Useless, why, asked the agent, forgetting that dialogue did not form part of the task with which he had been entrusted, Because in a situation like this, when everyone is under suspicion, all you would have to do is to say the word Blank, nothing more, without even bothering to find out if the person had voted, to provoke negative reactions, turmoil, anxiety, even if the person being examined was the purest, most perfect personification of innocence, Oh, come off it, I don't believe that, retorted the agent confidently, anyone at peace with his conscience would simply tell the truth and pass the polygraph test easily, We're not robots or talking stones, mister agent, said the woman, and within every human truth there is always an element of anxiety or conflict, we are, and I am not referring simply to the fragility of life, we are a small, tremulous flame which threatens at any moment to go out, and we are afraid, above all, we are afraid, You're wrong there, I'm not afraid, I've been trained to overcome fear in all circumstances and, besides, I am not by nature a scaredy-cat, I wasn't even as a child, responded the agent, In that case, why don't we try a little experiment, suggested the woman, you let yourself be connected up to the machine and I'll ask the questions, You're mad, I'm the one with the authority here and, besides, you're

the suspect, not me, So you are afraid, No, I'm not, Then connect yourself up to that machine and show me what it means
to be a truthful man. The agent looked at the woman, who
was smiling, he looked at the technician, who was struggling
to conceal a smile, and said, All right, then, once won't hurt,
I agree to submit to the experiment. The technician attached
the wires, tightened the armbands, adjusted the suction pads,
I'm ready when you are. The woman took a deep breath, held
the breath in her lungs for three seconds and then, in a rush,
uttered one word, Blank. It wasn't a question, more of an exclamation, but the needles moved, leaving a mark on the paper.
In the pause that followed, the needles did not stop completely,
they continued moving, making tiny traces, like the ripples
made by a stone thrown into the water. The woman was looking at the needles, not at the bound man, but when she did turn
and look him in the eye, she asked in a gentle, almost tender
voice, Tell me, please, did you cast a blank vote, No, I didn't, I
never did and never will cast a blank vote, replied the man ve-
hemently. The needles moved rapidly, precipitately, violently.
Another pause. Well, asked the agent. The technician took a
while to respond, the agent repeated, Well, what does the machine say. The machine says that you lied, sir, said the embarrassed technician, That's impossible, cried the agent, I told the
truth, I didn't cast a blank vote, I'm a professional secret service agent, a patriot trying to defend the interests of the nation,
there must be something wrong with the machine, Don't waste
your energy, don't try to justify yourself, said the woman, I believe you told the truth, that you didn't cast a blank vote and
never will, but that, I must remind you, is not the point, I was
just trying to demonstrate to you, successfully as it turns out,
that we cannot entirely trust our bodies, It's all your fault, you
made me nervous, Of course it was my fault, it was the tempt-
ress eve's fault, but no one came to ask us if we were feeling

nervous when they hooked us up to that contraption, It's guilt that makes you feel nervous, Possibly, but go and ask your boss why it is that you, who are innocent of all our evils, behaved like a guilty man, There's nothing more to be said, replied the agent, it's as if what happened just now never happened at all. Then, addressing the technician, Give me that strip of paper, and remember, say nothing, if you do, you'll regret you were ever born, Yes, sir, don't worry, I'll keep my mouth shut, So will I, said the woman, but at least tell the minister that no amount of cunning will do any good, we will all continue to lie when we tell the truth, and to tell the truth when we lie, just like him, just like you, now just imagine if I had asked if you wanted to go to bed with me, what would you have said then, what would the machine have said.

THE defense minister's favorite expression, a depth charge launched against the system, partially inspired by the unforgettable experience of an historic trip he had made aboard a submarine, a trip that had lasted all of half an hour and had taken place in flat calm seas, began to gain in strength and to attract attention when the interior minister's plans, despite one or two minor successes of no appreciable significance to the situation as a whole, revealed themselves to be impotent when it came to achieving the main aim, namely, persuading the inhabitants of the city, or, more precisely, the degenerates, delinquents and subversives who had cast the blank votes, to acknowledge the error of their ways and to beg for the mercy and the penance of a new election to which, at the chosen moment, they would rush en masse to purge themselves of the sins of a folly which they would swear never to repeat. It had become clear to the whole government, with the exception of the ministers of justice and culture, who both had their doubts, that there was an urgent need to tighten the screw still further, especially given that the declaration of a state of emergency, for which they had both had such high hopes, had produced no perceptible shift in the desired direction, for, since the citizens of this country were not in the healthy habit of demanding the proper enforcement of the rights bestowed on them by the constitution, it was only logical, even natural, that they had failed even to notice that those rights had been suspended. As a consequence, a state of siege proper was declared, one not purely for show, but complete with a curfew, the closure of theaters and cinemas, constant army street patrols, a prohibition on gatherings of more than five people, and an absolute ban on anyone entering or leaving the city, along with a simultaneous lifting of the restrictive, although far less rigorous, measures still in force in the rest of the country, a clear difference in treatment that would make the humiliation of the capital all the more explicit and damning. What we are trying to tell them, said the minister of defense, and let's hope they finally get the message, is that, having shown themselves to be unworthy of trust, they will be treated accordingly. The interior minister, forced somehow to disguise the failure of his secret agents, thoroughly approved of the immediate declaration of a state of siege, and, to show that he still had a few cards in his hand and had not withdrawn from the game entirely, he informed the council of ministers that, after an exhaustive investigation, and in close collaboration with interpol, he had reached the conclusion that the international anarchist movement, If it exists to do anything more than to write a few jokes on walls, and he paused briefly for the knowing laughter of his colleagues, then, feeling equally pleased himself and with them, completed the sentence, Had absolutely nothing to do with the election boycott of which we have been the victims, and that this is, therefore, merely an internal matter, Forgive me saying so, said the minister of foreign affairs, merely does not seem to me the most appropriate of adverbs, and I must remind this council that a number of other states have expressed their concern to me that what is happening here could cross the border and spread like a modern-day black death, You mean blank death, don't you, said the prime minister with a placatory smile, In that case, the minister of foreign affairs went on unperturbed, we can, quite correctly, speak of depth charges launched against the stability of the democratic system, not simply, not merely, of one country, this country, but of the entire planet. The interior minister sensed that the role of major national figure to which recent events had elevated him was slipping from his grasp, and in order not entirely to lose his grip, having first thanked the minister of foreign affairs and, with great magnanimity, acknowledged the truth of what had been said, he was now keen to show that he, too, was capable of the most subtle of semiological interpretations, It is interesting to observe, he said, how the meanings of words change without our noticing, how we often use them to mean precisely the opposite of what they used to mean and which, in a way, like a fading echo, they still continue to mean, That's just a normal consequence of the semantic process, muttered the minister of culture, And what has that got to do with blank ballot papers, asked the minister for foreign affairs, Oh, it has nothing to do with blank ballot papers, but it has everything to do with the state of siege, declared the interior minister triumphantly, You've lost me, said the minister of defense, It's quite simple, It may be simple for you, but I don't understand, For example, what does the word siege mean, it's all right, that's a purely rhetorical question, I don't expect an answer, we all know that siege means blockade or encirclement, isn't that right, As sure as two and two are four, Therefore, declaring a state of siege is tantamount to saying that the country's capital is besieged, blockaded or encircled by an enemy, when the truth is that the enemy, if I may call it that, is not outside but inside. The other ministers looked at each other, the prime minister pretended not to be listening and started shuffling through some papers. But the minister of

defense was about to triumph in this semiological battle,
There's another way of looking at it too, What's that, That in
unleashing this rebellion, and I don't think I'm exaggerating
when I call what is happening a rebellion, the capital's inhabitants were, and quite right too, besieged or blockaded or encircled, the choice of term is, to be frank, a matter of complete indifference to me, May I remind our dear colleague and the
council as a whole, said the minister for justice, that, when they
decided to cast their blank votes, the citizens were only doing
what the law explicitly allows them to do, therefore, to speak of
rebellion in such a case is, as well as being, I imagine, a grave
semantic error, and you will forgive me, I hope, for venturing
into an area of which I know nothing, is also, from the legal
point of view, a complete nonsense, Rights are not abstractions,
retorted the minister of defense, people either deserve rights or
they don't, and these people certainly don't, anything else is
just so much empty talk, You're quite right, said the minister of
culture, rights aren't abstractions, they continue to exist even
when they're not respected, Now you're getting philosophical,
Has the minister of defense got anything against philosophy,
The only philosophy I'm interested in is military philosophy,
and then only if it leads us to victory, I am, gentlemen, a bar-
rack-room pragmatist, and my approach, whether you like it or
not, is to call a spade a spade, but now, just so that you don't
start looking down on me as someone of inferior intelligence, I
would appreciate it if you could explain to me, as long as it's not
a question of demonstrating that a circle can be transformed
into a square of an equal area, how a right, if it isn't respected,
can still continue to exist, Very simple, that right exists potentially in the duty of others to respect and comply with it, No
offence, but civic sermons and demagoguery will get us nowhere, slap a state of siege on them and see how they like it,
Unless it backfires on us, of course, said the minister of justice,

How exactly, That I don't know yet, we'll just have to wait, no one had even dared to imagine that what is happening in our country could ever happen anywhere, but there it is, like a tight knot we can't undo, here we are gathered round this table to make decisions which, despite all the proposals put forward as sure solutions to the crisis, have, until now, achieved nothing, let's just wait, we'll find out soon enough how people will react to the state of siege, Sorry, but I can't just let that comment pass unchallenged, spluttered the interior minister, the measures we took were unanimously approved by this council and, as far as I recall, no one present at that meeting brought to the debate any different or better proposals, the burden of the catastrophe, yes, I'll call it a catastrophe and I'll call it a burden, even though some of my fellow ministers may think I'm exaggerating, as that smug, ironic air of theirs so clearly demonstrates, the burden of the catastrophe, I say again, has fallen, firstly, as is only right, on his excellency the president and on the prime minister, and secondly, given the responsibilities inherent in the posts we occupy, on the minister of defense and on myself, as for the others, and I refer in particular to the minister of justice and the minister of culture, who have been so kind as to shine the light of their intellects upon us, I have yet to hear a single idea that was worth considering for longer than it took us to listen to it, The light with which, according to you, I was kind enough to illuminate this council, was not my own, but the light of the law and nothing but the law, replied the minister of justice, And as regards my own humble person and my part in this wholesale ticking-off, said the minister of culture, given the miserable budget I'm allotted, you can hardly expect more, Ah, now I understand those anarchist leanings of yours, said the interior minister tartly, sooner or later, you always come out with the same old gibes.

The prime minister had run out of papers to shuffle. He

tapped his pen lightly on his glass of water, calling for attention
and silence, I hate to interrupt this interesting debate of yours,
from which, although I may well have seemed somewhat distracted, I feel I have learned a great deal, because, as experience
should teach us, there is nothing like a good argument to release
accumulated tension, especially in a situation like this, which
is constantly reminding us that we have to do something, although quite what we don't know. He paused very deliberately,
pretended to consult some notes, then went on, So, now that
we are all calm and relaxed, with our spirits less inflamed, we
can, at last, approve the proposal put forward by the minister of
defense, namely, the declaration of a state of siege for an inde-
terminate period and with immediate effect from the moment
it is made public. There was a more or less general murmur of
assent, albeit with variations of tone whose origins were impossible to identify, despite the minister of defense taking his eyes
on a rapid panoramic excursion to catch any note of disagreement or muted enthusiasm. The prime minister went on, Experience, alas, has also taught us that when the time comes for
them to be acted upon even the most perfect and polished of
ideas can fail, whether because of some last-minute hiccup, or
because of a gap between expectation and reality, or because, at
some critical point, the situation got out of control, or because
of a thousand other possible reasons that it is not worth our
while going into right now and for which we would not have
time, it is therefore vital always to have at the ready a replacement or complementary idea, which would prevent, as might
well happen in this case, the emergence of a power vacuum,
or to use another more alarming expression, of street power,
either of which would have disastrous consequences. Accustomed to the prime minister's rhetoric, which took the form
of three steps forward and two steps back, or, put another way,
sitting firmly on the fence, his ministers were patiently await-

ing his final, concluding, definitive word, the one that would explain everything. It did not come. The prime minister took a sip of water, dabbed at his lips with a white handkerchief which he took from his inside jacket pocket, made as if to consult his notes, but instead, at the last moment, pushed them to one side and said, If the results of the state of siege fall below expectations, that is, if they prove incapable of restoring the citizens to democratic normality, to the balanced, sensible use of an electoral law which, due to an imprudent lack of attention by the legislators, left the door open to something which, without fear of paradox, it would be reasonable to classify as a legal abuse, then I would like to inform this council now that I, as prime minister, foresee the application of another measure which, as well as providing psychological reinforcement of the measure we have just taken, I am referring, of course, to the declaration of a state of siege, could, I feel sure, by itself reset the troubled needle of our country's political scales and put an end once and for all to the nightmare situation into which we have been plunged. Another pause, another sip of water, another dab with the handkerchief, then he went on, You might well ask why, in that case, we do not simply implement that measure now instead of wasting our time setting up a state of siege which, as we well know, will make every aspect of life very difficult for the capital's population, both the guilty and the innocent, and that question is not without relevance, there are, however, important factors that cannot be ignored, some purely logistical in nature, others not, the main one being the effect, which it would be no exaggeration to describe as traumatic, of the sudden introduction of this extreme measure, which is why I feel we should opt for a gradual sequence of actions, of which the state of siege will be the first. The prime minister again shuffled his papers, but did not, this time, touch his glass of water, I understand your curiosity on the subject, he said, but I will say nothing further about the matter now, except to inform you that I was received in audience this morning by his excellency the president of the republic, to whom I presented my idea, which received his entire and unconditional support. You will learn more later, now, before closing this productive meeting, I ask all of you, in particular the ministers of defense and of the interior, who will, together, shoulder responsibility for the complex actions required to impose and carry out the declaration of the state of siege, to work diligently and energetically toward the same desired end. The armed forces and the police, whether acting within the ambit of their specific areas of competence or in joint operations, always observing the most rigorous mutual respect and avoiding any arguments over precedence that would prove prejudicial to our aims, are charged with the patriotic task of leading the lost sheep back to the fold, if you will allow me to use an expression so beloved of our forefathers and so deeply rooted in our pastoral traditions. And remember, you must do everything possible to ensure that those who are, for the moment, only our opponents do not instead become the enemies of the nation. May god go with you and guide you on your sacred mission so that the sun of concord may once more light the consciences of our fellow citizens and so that peace may restore to their daily lives the harmony that has been lost.

While the prime minister was appearing on television to announce the establishment of a state of siege, invoking reasons of national security resulting from the current political and social instability, a consequence, in turn, of the action taken by organized subversive groups who had repeatedly obstructed the people's right to vote, units of infantry and military police, supported by tanks and other combat vehicles, were, at the same time, occupying train stations and setting up posts at all the roads leading out of the capital. The main airport, about

twenty-five kilometers to the north of the city, was outside the
army's specific area of control and would, therefore, continue
to function without any restrictions other than those foreseen
at times of amber alert, which meant that planes carrying tour-
ists would still be able to land and take off, although journeys
made by those native to the country, while not, strictly speaking, prohibited, would be strongly discouraged, except in special circumstances to be examined on a case-by-case basis. Images of these military operations invaded the houses of the
capital's bewildered inhabitants with, as the reporter put it, the
unstoppable force of a straight punch. Images of officers giving
orders, of sergeants yelling at their men to carry out these orders, of sappers erecting barriers, of ambulances and transmit-
ters, of spotlights lighting up the highway as far as the first
bend, of waves of soldiers, armed to the teeth, jumping out of
trucks and taking up positions, as well equipped for an immediate hard-fought battle as for a long war of attrition. Families
whose members worked or studied in the capital merely shook
their heads at this war-like display and murmured, They must
be mad, but others, who, every morning, despatched a father or
a son to a factory on one of the industrial estates that surround
the city and who waited every evening to welcome them back,
now asked themselves how and on what they were going to
live if they were not allowed to leave or enter the city. Perhaps
they'll issue safe-conduct passes to those with jobs outside, said
an old man, who had retired so many years ago that he still used
terminology from the days of the franco-prussian wars or other
ancient conflicts. Yet the wise old man was not so very wrong,
the proof being that, the following day, business associations
were quick to bring their well-founded anxieties to the government's notice, While we unreservedly and with an unwavering
sense of patriotism support the energetic measures taken by
the government, they said, as being a necessary campaign of

national salvation to oppose the harmful effects of thinly disguised subversive acts, allow us, nonetheless, and with the greatest respect, to ask the competent authorities for the urgent issue of passes to our employees and workers, at the risk, if such a provision is not made at once, of causing grave and irreversible damage to our industrial and commercial activities, with the subsequent, inevitable harm this would cause to the national economy as a whole. On the afternoon of that same day, a joint communiqué from the ministries of defense, the interior and finance, expressed the national government's understanding and sympathy for the employers' legitimate concerns, but explained that any such distribution of passes could never be carried out on the scale desired by businesses, moreover, such liberality on the part of the government would inevitably imperil the security and efficacy of the military units charged with guarding the new frontier around the capital. However, as a demonstration of their openness and readiness to avoid the very worst problems, the government was prepared to give such documents to any managers and technical teams who were judged to be vital to the regular running of the companies, who would then have to take full responsibility for the actions, criminal or otherwise, inside and outside the city, of the people chosen to benefit from this privilege. Assuming the plan was approved, these people would have to gather each workday morning at designated places in order to be transported in buses under police escort to the city's various exit points, where more buses would take them to the factories or other premises where they worked and whence they would have to return at the end of the day. The cost of these operations, from the hiring of buses to the remuneration paid to the police for providing the escorts, would have to be covered by the companies themselves, an outlay that might well be made tax-deductible, although a firm decision on this could only be taken after a feasibility study had been carried out by the ministry of finance. As you can imagine, the complaints did not stop there. It is a basic fact of life that people cannot live without food and drink, now, bearing in mind that the meat came from outside, that the fish came from outside, that the vegetables came from outside, that, everything, in short, came from outside, and that what this city could, on its own, produce or store away would not provide enough even for one week, it would be necessary to lay on supply systems very like those that would provide businesses with technicians and managers, only far more complex, given the perishable nature of certain products. Not to mention the hospitals and the pharmacies, the kilometers of ligatures, the mountains of cotton wool, the tons of pills, the hectoliters of injectable fluids, the many gross of condoms. And then there's the petrol and the diesel to think about, how to transport them to the service stations, unless someone in the government has had the machiavellian idea of punishing the inhabitants of the capital twice over by making them walk. It took only a few days for the government to realize that there is more to a state of siege than meets the eye, especially if there is no real intention of starving the besieged population to death as was the usual practice in the distant past, that a state of siege is not something that can be cobbled together in a moment, that you need to know exactly what your objectives are and how to achieve them, to weigh the consequences, to evaluate reactions, ponder the problems, calculate the gains and the losses, if only to avoid the vast mountain of work that suddenly faces the ministries, overwhelmed by an unstoppable flood of protests, complaints and requests for clarification, for almost none of which they can provide answers, because the instructions from on high had looked only at the general principles of the state of siege and had shown a complete disregard for the bureaucratic minutiae of its implementation, which is where chaos invariably finds a

way in. One interesting aspect of the situation, which the satir-
ical vein and sardonic eye of the capital's wits could not help
but notice, was the fact that the government, the de facto and
de jure besieger, was, at the same time, one of the besieged, not
just because its chambers and antechambers, its offices and corridors, its departments and archives, its filing cabinets and
stamps, were all in the very heart of the city, and, indeed, formed
an organic part of it, but also because some of its members,
at least three ministers, a few secretaries of state and under-
secretaries, as well as a couple of directors-general, lived on the
outskirts, not to mention the civil servants who, morning and
evening, in one way or another, had to use the train, metro or
bus if they did not have their own transport or did not want to
submit themselves to the complexities of urban traffic. The stories that were told, not always sotto voce, explored the well-
known theme of the hunter hunted or the biter bit, but did not
restrict themselves to such childishly innocent comments, to
the humor of a belle époque kindergarten, there was a whole
kaleidoscope of variations, some of them utterly obscene and,
from the point of view of the most elementary good taste, rep-
rehensibly scatological. Unfortunately, and here we have further proof of the limited range and structural weakness of all
sarcastic remarks, lampoons, burlesques, parodies, satires and
other such jokes with which people hope to wound a government, the state of siege was not lifted and the problems of supply remained unresolved.

The days passed, and the difficulties continued to increase,
they grew worse and multiplied, they sprang up underfoot like
mushrooms after rain, but the moral strength of the population
did not seem inclined to humble itself or to renounce what it
had considered to be a just stance and to which it had given expression through the ballot box, the simple right not to follow
any consensually established opinion. Some observers, usually

foreign correspondents hurriedly despatched to cover the
events, as they say in the jargon of the profession, and therefore
unfamiliar with local idiosyncrasies, commented with bemuse-
ment on the complete lack of conflict amongst the city's inhabitants, even though they had observed what later proved to be
agents provocateurs at work, trying to create the kind of unsta-
ble situations which might justify, in the eyes of the so-called
international community, the leap that had not yet been taken,
that is, the move from a state of siege to a state of war. One of
these commentators, in his desire to be original, went so far as
to describe this as a unique, never-before-seen example of ideological unanimity, which, if it were true, would make the capital's population a fascinating case, a political phenomenon
worthy of study. Whichever way you looked at it, the idea was
complete nonsense, and had nothing to do with the reality of
the situation, for here, as anywhere else on the planet, people
differ, they think differently, they are not all poor or all rich,
and, even amongst the reasonably well-off, some are more so
and some are less. The one subject on which they were all in
agreement, with no need for any prior discussion, is one with
which we are already familiar, and so there is no point going
over old ground. Nevertheless, it is only natural that one would
want to know, and the question was often asked, both by foreign journalists and by local ones, what singular reason lay behind the fact that there had, until now, been no incidents, no
fights, no shouting matches or fisticuffs or worse amongst those
who had cast blank votes and those who had not. The question
amply demonstrates how important a knowledge of the elements of arithmetic is for the proper exercise of the profession
of journalist, for they need only have recalled that the people
casting blank votes represented eighty-three percent of the
capital's population and that the remainder, all told, accounted
for no more than seventeen percent, and one must not forget

the debatable thesis put forward by the party on the left, according to which a blank vote and a vote for them were, metaphorically speaking, one bone and one flesh, and that if the supporters of the party on the left, and this is our own conclusion, did not all cast blank votes, although it is clear that many did in the second poll, it was simply because they had not been ordered to do so. No one would believe us if we were to say that seventeen people had decided to take on eighty-three, the days when battles were won with the help of god are long since gone. Natural curiosity would also lead one to ask two questions, what happened to the five hundred people plucked from the queues of voters by the ministry of the interior's spies and who subsequently underwent the torment of interrogation and the agony of seeing their most intimate secrets revealed by the lie detector and, the second question, what exactly are those specialist secret service agents and their less qualified assistants up to. On the first point, we have only doubts and no way of resolving them. There are those who say that the five hundred prisoners are, in accordance with that popular police euphemism, still helping the authorities with their inquiries in the hope of clarifying the facts, others say that they are gradually being freed, although only a few at a time so as not to attract too much attention, however, the more sceptical observers believe a third version, that they have all been removed from the city and are now in some unknown location and that, despite the dearth of results obtained hitherto, the interrogations continue. Who knows who is right. As for the second point, about what the secret service agents are up to, that we do know. Like all honest, worthy workers, they leave home every morning, tramp the city from end to end, and when they think the fish is about to bite, they try a new tactic, which consists of dropping all the circumlocutions and saying point-blank to the person they're with, Let's talk frankly now, like friends, I cast a blank vote, did you. At first, those questioned merely gave the answers described above, that no one was obliged to reveal how they voted, that no one can be questioned about it by any authority, and if one of them had the excellent idea of demanding that the impertinent questioner should identify himself and declare there and then on whose power and authority he was asking the question, then we would be treated to the pleasurable spectacle of seeing a secret service agent all in a fluster and scampering off with his tail between his legs, because, of course, it wouldn't occur to anyone that he would actually open his wallet and show them the card that would prove who he was, complete with photograph, official stamp and edged with the national colors. But, as we said, that was at the beginning. After a while, the general consensus deemed that, in such situations, the best attitude to take was to ignore the person asking the question and simply turn your back on them, or, if they proved extremely insistent, to say loudly and clearly Leave me alone, or, if preferred, and with more chance of success, to tell them, even more simply, to go to hell. Naturally, the reports sent by the secret service agents to their superiors camouflaged these rebuffs and disguised these setbacks, instead restating the stubborn and systematic absence of any collaborative spirit amongst the suspect sector of the population. You might think that things had reached a point very like that of two wrestlers endowed with equal strength, one pushing this way, the other pushing that, and while it was true that they had not moved from the spot where they had started, neither had they managed to advance even an inch, and, consequently, only the final exhaustion of one of them would give victory to the other. In the opinion of the person in charge of the secret services, this stalemate would be rapidly resolved if one of the wrestlers were to receive help from another wrestler, which, in this particular situation, would mean abandoning, as futile, the persuasive

techniques employed up until then and adopting, without reserve, dissuasive methods that did not exclude the use of brute
force. If the capital, for its own many faults, finds itself under a
state of siege, if it is up to the armed forces to impose discipline
and proceed accordingly in the case of any grave disruption of
the social order, if the high command take responsibility, on
their word of honor, not to hesitate when it comes to making
decisions, then the secret services will take it upon themselves
to create suitable focal points of unrest that would justify a pri-
ori the harsh crackdown which the government, very generously, has tried, by all peaceful and, let us repeat the word, persuasive means, to avoid. The insurrectionists would not be able
to come to them later with complaints, assuming they wanted
to and assuming they had any. When the interior minister took
this idea to the inner council, or emergency council, which had
been formed meanwhile, the prime minister reminded him
that he still had one weapon as yet undeployed in the resolution of the conflict and only in the unlikely event of that weapon
failing would he consider this new plan or any others that happened to arise. Whilst the interior minister expressed his disagreement laconically, in four words, We are wasting time, the
defense minister needed far more to guarantee that the armed
forces would do their duty, As they always have throughout our
long history, giving no thought to the sacrifice entailed. And
that was how the delicate matter was left, the fruit, it seemed,
was not yet ripe. Then it was that the other wrestler, grown
tired of waiting, decided to risk taking a step. One morning, the
streets of the capital were filled by people wearing stickers on
their chest bearing the words, in red letters on a black background, I cast a blank vote, huge placards hung from windows
declaring, in black letters on a red background, We cast blank
votes, but the most astonishing sight, waving above the heads
of the advancing demonstrators, was the endless stream of

blank, white flags, which would lead one unthinking correspondent to run to the telephone and inform his newspaper that the city had surrendered. The police loudspeakers bellowed and screamed that gatherings of more than five people were not allowed, but there were fifty, five hundred, five thousand, fifty thousand, and who, in such a situation, is going to bother counting in fives. The police commissioner wanted to know if he could use tear-gas and water cannon, the general in charge of the northern division if he was authorized to order the tanks to advance, the general of the southern airborne division if the conditions were right to send in paratroopers, or if, on the contrary, the risk of them landing on rooftops made this inadvisable. War was, however, about to break out.

Then it was that the prime minister revealed his plan to the government, who had been brought together in plenary session and with the president in the chair, The time has come to break the back of the resistance, he said, let's call a halt to all the psychological game-playing, to the espionage, the lie detectors and the other technological contraptions, since, despite the interior minister's worthy efforts, these methods have all proved incapable of solving the problem, I must add, by the way, that I also consider inappropriate any direct intervention by the armed forces, given the more than likely inconvenience of a mass slaughter which it is our duty to avoid at all costs, what I have to offer you instead is neither more nor less than a proposed multiple withdrawal, a series of actions which some may perhaps feel to be absurd, but which I am sure will lead us to total victory and a return to democratic normality, these actions are, namely, the immediate removal of the government to another city, which will become the country's new capital, the withdrawal of all the armed forces still in place, and the withdrawal of all police forces, this radical action will mean that the rebel city will be left entirely to its own devices and

will have all the time it needs to understand the price of being cut off from the sacrosanct unity of the nation, and when it
can no longer stand the isolation, the indignity, the contempt,
when life within the city becomes a chaos, then its guilty inhabitants will come to us hanging their heads and begging our
forgiveness. The prime minister looked about him, That is my
plan, he said, I submit it to you for your examination and discussion, but, needless to say, I am counting on your unanimous
approval, desperate diseases must have desperate remedies, and
if the remedy I am prescribing is painful to you, the disease afflicting us is, quite simply, fatal.

I N WORDS that can be grasped by the intelligence of those classes, who, though less educated, are nonetheless not entirely ignorant of the gravity and diversity of the many and various ailments that threaten the already precarious survival of the human race, what the prime minister had proposed was neither more nor less than a flight from the virus that had attacked the majority of the capital's inhabitants and which, given that the worst is always waiting just behind the door, might well end up infecting all the remaining inhabitants and even, who knows, the whole country. Not that he and his government were themselves afraid of being contaminated by the bite of this subversive insect, for apart from a few clashes between certain individuals and a few very minor differences of opinion, which were, anyway, more to do with means than ends, we have had ample proof of the unshakable institutional cohesion of the politicians responsible for the running of a country which, without a word of warning, had been plunged into a disaster never before seen in the long and always troubled history of the known world. Contrary to what certain ill-intentioned people doubtless thought or suggested, this was not the coward's way out, but rather a strategic move of the first order, unparalleled in its audacity, one whose future results can almost be touched with the hand, like ripe fruit on a tree. Now all that was needed for the task to be crowned with success was that the energy put into carrying out the plan should be up to the resolve of its aims. First, they will have to decide who will leave the city and who will stay. Obviously, his excellency the president and the whole of the government down to under-secretary level will leave, along with their closest advisors, the members of the national parliament will also leave so that the legislative process suffers no interruption, the army and the police will leave, including the traffic police, but all the members of the municipal council will remain, along with their leader, the fire fighters' organizations will stay too, so that the city does not burn down because of some act of carelessness or sabotage, just as the staff of the city cleansing department will stay in case of epidemic and, needless to say, the authorities will ensure continued supplies of water and electricity, those utilities so essential to life. As for food, a group of dieticians, or nutritionists, have already been charged with drawing up a list of basic dishes which, while not bringing the population to the brink of starvation, would make them aware that a state of siege taken to its ultimate consequences would certainly be no holiday. Not that the government believed things would go that far. It would not be many days before the usual delegations appeared at a military post on one of the roads out of the city, bearing the white flag, the flag of unconditional surrender not the flag of insurgency, the fact that both are the same color is a remarkable coincidence upon which we will not now pause to reflect, but there will be plenty of reasons to return to the matter later on.

After the plenary meeting of the government, to which we assume sufficient reference was made on the last page of the previous chapter, the inner ministerial cabinet or emergency council discussed and took a handful of decisions which will, in the fullness of time, be revealed, always assuming, as we believe we have warned on a previous occasion, that events do not develop in a way that renders those decisions null and void or requires them to be replaced by others, for, as it is always wise to remember, while it is true that man proposes, it is god who disposes, and there have been very few occasions, almost all of them tragic, when both man and god were in agreement and did all the disposing together. One of the most hotly disputed matters was the government's withdrawal from the city, when and how it should be done, with or without discretion, with or without television coverage, with or without military bands, with or without garlands on the cars, with or without the national flag draped over the bonnet, and an endless series of details which required repeated discussions about state protocol which had never, not since the founding of the nation itself, known such difficulties. The final plan for the withdrawal was a masterpiece of tactics, consisting basically of a meticulous distribution of different itineraries so as to make things as hard as possible for any large concentrations of demonstrators who might gather together to express the city's possible feelings of displeasure, discontent or indignation at being abandoned to its fate. There was one itinerary for the president, one for the prime minister and one for each member of the council of ministers, a total of twenty-seven different routes, all under the protection of the army and the police, with assault vehicles stationed at crossroads and with ambulances following behind the cortèges, ready for all eventualities. The map of the city, an enormous illuminated panel over which, with the help of military commanders and expert police trackers, they had labored for forty-eight hours, showed a red star with twenty-seven arms, fourteen turned toward the northern hemisphere, thirteen toward the southern hemisphere, with an equator dividing the capital

into two halves. Along these arms would file the black automobiles of the public institutions, surrounded by bodyguards and
walkie-talkies, antiquated contraptions still used in this country, but for which there was now an approved budget for mod-
ernization. All the people involved in the various phases of the
operation, whatever the degree of their participation, had to be
sworn to absolute secrecy, first with their right hand placed on
the gospels, then on a copy of the constitution bound in blue
morocco leather, and finally, completing this double commitment, by uttering a truly binding oath, drawn from popular
tradition, If I break this oath may the punishment fall upon my
head and upon that of my descendants unto the fourth generation. With secrecy thus sealed for any leaks, the date was set
for two days hence. The hour of departure, which would be simultaneous, that is, the same for everyone, was three o'clock in
the morning, a time when only the seriously insomniac are still
tossing and turning in their beds and saying prayers to the god
hypnos, the son of night and twin brother of thanatos, to help
them in their affliction by dropping on their poor, bruised eyelids the sweet balm of the poppy. During the remaining hours,
the spies, who had returned en masse to the field of operations, did nothing but pound, in more than one sense, the city's
squares, avenues, streets and sidestreets, surreptitiously taking
the population's pulse, probing ill-concealed intentions, con-
necting up words heard here and there, in order to find out
if there had been any leak of the decisions taken by the council of ministers, in particular the government's imminent withdrawal, because any spy worthy of the name must take it as a sacred principle, a golden rule, the letter of the law, that oaths are
never to be trusted, whoever made them, even an oath sworn
by the very mother who gave them life, still less when instead
of one oath there were two, and less still when instead of two
there were three. In this case, however, they had no alternative

but to recognize, with a certain degree of professional frustration, that the official secret had been well kept, an empirical truth that tallied with the ministry of the interior's central system of computation, which, after much squeezing, sieving and mixing, shuffling and reshuffling of the millions of fragments of recorded conversations, found not a single equivocal sign, not a single suspicious clue, not even the tiniest end of a thread which, if pulled, might have at its other end a nasty surprise. The messages despatched by the secret service to the ministry of the interior were wonderfully reassuring, as were the messages sent to the defense ministry's colonels of information and psychology by the highly efficient military intelligence, who, without the knowledge of their civilian competitors, were carrying out their own investigation, indeed, both camps could have used that expression which literature has made into a classic, All quiet on the western front, although not, of course, for the soldier who has just died. Everyone, from the president to the very least of government advisors, gave a sigh of relief. The withdrawal, thank god, would take place quietly, without any undue trauma to a population who had perhaps already, in part, repented their entirely inexplicable seditious behavior, but who, despite this, in a praiseworthy display of civic-mindedness, which augured well for the future, seemed to have no intention of harming, either in word or deed, their legitimate leaders and representatives at this moment of painful, but necessary, separation. This was the conclusion drawn from all the reports, and so it was.

At half past two in the morning everyone was ready to cut the ropes still attaching them to the president's palace, to the prime minister's mansion and to the various ministerial buildings. The gleaming black automobiles were lined up waiting, the trucks containing all the files were surrounded by security guards armed to the teeth and who were, incredible though it

may seem, capable of spitting poisoned darts, the police outriders were in position, the ambulances were ready, and inside, in the offices, the fugitive leaders, or deserters, whom we
should, in more elevated language, describe as tergiversators,
were still opening and closing the last cupboards and drawers, sadly gathering up a final few mementos, a group photograph, another bearing a dedication, a ring made out of human
hair, a statuette of the goddess of happiness, a pencil sharp-
ener from schooldays, a returned cheque, an anonymous letter, an embroidered handkerchief, a mysterious key, a redun-
dant pen with a name engraved on it, a compromising piece of
paper, another compromising piece of paper, but the latter is
only compromising for a colleague in the next department. A
few people were almost in tears, men and women barely able to
control their emotions, wondering if they would ever return to
the beloved places that witnessed their rise up the hierarchical
ladder, others, to whom the fates had proved less helpful, were
dreaming, despite previous disappointments and injustices, of
different worlds and new opportunities that would place them,
at last, where they deserved to be. At a quarter to three, when
the army and the police were already strategically stationed
along all twenty-seven routes, not forgetting the assault vehicles guarding all the major crossroads, the order was given to
dim the streetlights as a way of covering the retreat, however
harshly that last word may grate on the ear. In the streets along
which the cars and trucks would have to pass, there was not a
soul, not one, not even in plain clothes. As for the continual
flow of information from the rest of the city, this remained un-
changed, no groups were gathering, there was no suspicious
activity, and any nightbirds returning to their homes or leaving them did not seem a cause for concern, they were not carrying flags over their shoulders or concealing bottles of petrol
with bits of rag protruding from the neck, they weren't whirl-

ing clubs or bicycle chains above their heads, and if the occasional one appeared to stray from the straight and narrow,
there was no reason to attribute this to deviations of a political
nature, but to perfectly forgivable alcoholic excesses. At three
minutes to three, the engines of the cars in the convoys were
started up. At three o'clock on the dot, precisely as planned, the
retreat began.

Then, O surprise, O astonishment, O never-before-seen
prodigy, first confusion and perplexity, then disquiet, then fear,
dug their nails into the throats of the president and the prime
minister, of the ministers, secretaries of state and under-secretaries, of the deputies, security men and police outriders, and
even, although to a lesser degree, of the ambulance staff, who
were, by their profession, accustomed to the worst. As the cars
advanced along the streets, the façades of the buildings were lit
up, one by one, from top to bottom, by lanterns, lamps, spotlights, torches, candelabra when available, even perhaps by old
brass oil lamps, every window was wide open and aglow, letting
out a great river of light like a flood, a multiplication of crystals
made of white fire, marking the road, picking out the deserters'
escape route so that they would not get lost, so that they would
not wander off down any short-cuts. The first reaction of those
in charge of convoy security was to throw caution to the wind
and say put your foot down and drive like crazy, and that is
what began to happen, to the irrepressible joy of the official
drivers, who, as everyone knows, hate pootling along at a snail's
pace when they've got two hundred horsepower in their engine. The burst of speed did not last long. That brusque, precipitate decision, like all decisions born of fear, meant that, on
nearly every route, further ahead or further back, minor collisions took place, usually it was the vehicle behind bumping
into the one in front, fortunately without any very grave consequences for the passengers, a bit of a fright and that was all, a

bruise on the forehead, a scratch on the face, a ricked neck, nothing which, tomorrow, would justify the awarding of a medal for injuries sustained, a croix de guerre, a purple heart or some other such monstrosity. The ambulances raced ahead, the medical and nursing staff eager to help the wounded, there was terrible confusion, deplorable in every way, the convoys ground to a halt, telephone calls were made to find out what was happening on the other routes, someone was demanding loudly to be told exactly what the situation was, and then, on top of that, there were those lines of buildings lit up like Christmas trees, all that was missing were the fireworks and the merry-go-rounds, it was just as well that no one appeared at the windows to enjoy the free entertainment down in the street, to laugh, to mock, to point a finger at the colliding cars. Shortsighted sub-alterns, the sort who are only interested in the present moment, which is nearly all of them, would certainly think like that, as perhaps would a few under-secretaries and advisors with little future, but never a prime minister, certainly not one as far-sighted as this one has shown himself to be. While a doctor was dabbing at the prime minister's chin with some antiseptic and wondering to himself if it would be going too far to give the injured man an anti-tetanus injection, the prime minister kept thinking about the tremor of unease that had shaken his spirit as soon as the first lights in the buildings came on. It was, without a doubt, enough to upset even the most phlegmatic of politicians, it was, without a doubt, troubling, unsettling, but worse, much worse, was the fact that there was no one at those windows, as if the official convoys were foolishly fleeing from nothing, as if the army and the police, along with the assault vehicles and the water cannon, had been spurned by the enemy and been left with no one to fight. Still somewhat stunned by the collision, but with a plaster on his chin, and having refused with stoical impatience the anti-tetanus injection, the prime minister suddenly remembered that his first duty should have been to phone the president and ask him how he was, to inquire after the well-being of the presidential person, and that he should do this now, without more ado, lest the president, out of sheer mischief and political astuteness, should get in first, And catch me with my pants down, he muttered, not thinking about the literal meaning of the phrase. He asked his secretary to make the call, another secretary responded, the secretary at this end said that the prime minister wished to speak to the president, the secretary at the other end said one moment, please, the secretary at this end passed the phone to the prime minister and, he, as was only fitting, waited, How are things over there, asked the president, A few dents, but nothing serious, replied the prime minister, We've had no problems at all, Not even any collisions, Just a few bumps, Nothing grave, I hope, No, this armor plating is pretty much bombproof, Alas, sir, no armor-plated vehicle is bombproof, You don't need to tell me that, for every breastplate there's a spear and for every armor-plated vehicle a bomb, Are you hurt, Not a scratch. The face of a police officer appeared at the car window, indicating that they could drive on, We're on the move again, the prime minister told the president, Oh, we've barely had to stop at all, replied the president, May I say something, sir, Of course, Well, I must confess to feeling worried, much more so than on the day of the first election, Why, These lights that came on just as we were leaving and which will, in all probability, continue to light our way along the whole route, until we're out of the city, the complete absence of people, I mean, there isn't a soul to be seen at any of the windows or in the streets, it's odd, very odd, I'm beginning to think that I may have to consider something which, up until now, I have always rejected, that there is some purpose behind all this, an idea, a planned objective, because things are happening as if the population really were obeying some plan, as if there were some central co-ordination, Oh, I don't think so, prime minister, you know better than I do that the anarchist conspiracy theory doesn't hold water at all, and that the other theory positing an evil foreign state bent on destabilizing our country is equally invalid, We thought we had everything completely under control, that we were masters of the situation, and then they spring a surprise on us that no one could possibly have imagined, a real coup de théâtre, What do you think you'll do, For the moment, continue with our plan, if future circumstances require us to introduce any alterations, we will only do so after an exhaustive examination of the new data, whatever they may be, as for the fundamentals, though, I don't feel we need to make any changes, And in your opinion, the fundamentals are what, We discussed this and reached an agreement, sir, our aim is to isolate the population and then leave them to simmer, sooner or later there are bound to be fights, conflicts of interest, life will become increasingly difficult, the streets will fill up with rubbish, imagine, sir, what the place will be like when the rains come, and, as sure as I'm prime minister, there are bound to be serious problems with the supply and distribution of foodstuffs, problems which, if necessary, we will take care to create, So you don't think the city will be able to hold out for very long, No, I don't, besides, there's another important factor, possibly the most important of all, What's that, However hard people have tried and continue to try, it's impossible to get everyone to think the same way, It seems to have worked this time, It's too perfect to be real, sir, And what if there really is, as you have just admitted as a hypothesis, some secret organization, a mafia, a camorra, a cosa nostra, a cia or a kgb, The cia isn't a secret organization, sir, and the kgb no longer exists, Well, I shouldn't think that will make much difference, but let's just imagine something similar or, if that were possible, even worse, something more machiavellian, invented to create this near-unanimity around, well, to be perfectly honest, I don't know quite what, Around the blank ballot papers, sir, the blank ballot papers, That, prime minister, is a conclusion I could have reached on my own, what interests me is what I don't know, Of course, sir, But you were saying, Even if I were forced to accept, in theory and only in theory, the possible existence of a clandestine organization out to destroy state security and opposed to the legitimacy of the democratic system, these things can't be done without contacts, without meetings, without secret cells, without incentives, without documents, yes, without documents, you yourself know that it is impossible to do anything in this world without documents, and we, as well as having not a scrap of information about any of the activities I have just mentioned, have also failed to find even a page from a diary saying Onward, comrades, le jour de gloire est arrivé, Why would it be in French, Because of their revolutionary tradition, sir, What an extraordinary country we live in, a place where things happen that have never happened on any other part of the planet, But this is not the first time, as I'm sure I need not remind you, sir, That is precisely what I meant, prime minister, There is not the faintest possibility of a link between the two incidents, Of course not, one was a plague of white blindness and the other a plague of blank ballot papers, We still haven't found an explanation for the first plague, Or for this one either, We will, sir, we will, If we don't come up against a brick wall first, Let us remain confident, sir, confidence is fundamental, Confident in what, in whom, In the democratic institutions, My dear fellow, you can reserve that speech for the television, only our secretaries can hear us now, so we can speak plainly. The prime minister changed the subject, We're leaving the city now, sir, Yes, we are too over here, Would you mind just looking back for a moment, sir, Why, The lights, What about them, They're still on, no one has turned them off,

And what conclusions do you think I should draw from these illuminations, Well, I don't rightly know, sir, the natural thing would be for them to go out as we progressed, but, no, there they are, why, I imagine that, seen from the air, they must look like a huge star with twenty-seven arms, It would seem I have a poet for prime minister, Oh, I'm no poet, but a star is a star is a star, and no one can deny it, sir, So what next, The government isn't just going to sit around doing nothing, we haven't run out of munitions yet, we've still got some arrows in our quiver, Let's hope your aim is true, All I need is to have the enemy in my sights, But that is precisely the problem, we don't know where the enemy is, we don't even know who they are, They'll turn up, sir, it's just a matter of time, they can't stay hidden forever, As long as we don't run out of time, We'll find a solution, We're nearly at the frontier, we'll continue our conversation in my office, see you there later, at about six o'clock, Of course, sir, I'll be there.

The frontier was the same at all the exit points from the city, a heavy, movable barrier, a pair of tanks, one on either side of the road, a few huts, and armed soldiers in battledress and with daubed faces. Powerful spotlights lit up the scene. The president got out of his car, returned the commanding officer's impeccable salute with a polite though slightly disdainful gesture, and asked, How are things here, Nothing to report, sir, absolute calm, Has anyone tried to leave, No, sir, You are, I assume, referring to motorized vehicles, to bicycles, to carts, to skateboards, To motorized vehicles, sir, And people on foot, Not a single one, You will, of course, already have considered the possibility that any fugitives might not come by road, We have, sir, but they still wouldn't manage to get through, as well as the conventional patrols guarding the area between us and the two closest exit points on either side, we also have electronic sensors that would pick up a mouse if we had them adjusted to detect anything that small, Excellent, you're familiar, I'm sure, with what is always said on these occasions, the nation is watching you, Yes, sir, we are aware of the importance of our mission, You will, I assume, have received orders on what to do if there is any attempt at a mass exodus, Yes, sir, What are they, First, tell them to stop, That much is obvious, Yes, sir, And if they don't, If they don't, then we fire into the air, And if, despite that, they continue to advance, Then the squad of riot police assigned to us would take action, And what would they do, Well, sir, that depends, they would either use tear-gas or attack with water cannon, the army doesn't do that kind of thing, Do I note a hint of criticism in your words, It's just that I don't think that is any way to carry on a war, sir, An interesting observation, and if the people do not withdraw, They must withdraw, sir, no one can withstand tear-gas attacks and water cannon, Just imagine that they do withstand it, what are your orders in that situation, To shoot at their legs, Why their legs, We don't want to kill our compatriots, But that could well happen, Yes, sir, it could, Do you have family in the city, Yes, sir, What if you saw your wife and children at the head of the advancing multitude, A soldier's family knows how to behave in all situations, Yes, I'm sure, but just try to imagine, Orders must be obeyed, sir, All orders, Up until today, it has been my honor to have obeyed all the orders given to me, And tomorrow, Tomorrow, I very much hope not to have to come and tell you, sir, So do I. The president took two steps in the direction of his car, then asked suddenly, Are you sure your wife did not cast a blank vote, Yes, sir, I would put my hand in the fire, sir, Really, It's a manner of speaking, sir, I just meant that I'm sure she would have fulfilled her duty as a voter, By voting, Yes, But that doesn't answer my question, No, sir, Then answer it, No, sir, I can't, Why not, Because the law does not allow me to, Ah. The president stood looking at the officer for a long time, then said, Goodbye, captain, it is captain, isn't it, Yes, sir, Good night, captain, perhaps we'll see each other again sometime, Good night, sir, Did you notice that I didn't ask if you had cast a blank vote, Yes, sir, I did. The car sped away. The captain put his hands to his face. His forehead was dripping with sweat.

THE lights started to go out as the last army truck and the last police van left the city. One after the other, like someone saying goodbye, the twenty-seven arms of the star gradually disappeared, leaving the vague route map of deserted streets marked only by the dim street lamps that no one had thought to restore to their normal level of brightness. We will find out how alive the city is when the intense black of the sky begins to dissolve into the slow tide of deep blue which anyone with good eyesight would already be able to make out rising up from the horizon, then we will see if the men and women who inhabit the different floors of these buildings do, indeed, set off to work, if the first buses pick up the first passengers, if the metro trains race, thundering, through the tunnels, if the shops open their doors and remove the shutters, if newspapers are delivered to kiosks. At this early morning hour, while they wash, get dressed and drink their usual breakfast cup of coffee, people are listening to the radio which is announcing, in excited tones, that the president, the government and the parliament left the city in the early hours, that there are no police left in the city, and that the army has withdrawn too, then they turn on the television, which, in identical tones, gives them the same news, and both radio and television, with only the briefest of intervals, continue to report that, at seven o'clock precisely, an important message from the president will be broadcast to the whole country, and, in particular, of course, to the capital's obstinate inhabitants. Meanwhile, the kiosks have not yet opened, so there is no point in going out into the street to buy a newspaper, just as it is not worth searching the web, the worldwide web, although some more up-to-date citizens have already tried, for the president's predictable stream of invective. Official secrecy, while it may occasionally be plagued by leaks and disclosures, as demonstrated a few hours earlier by the synchronized switching on of lights in buildings, exercises extreme rigor when it comes to any higher authorities, who, as everyone knows, will, for the most frivolous of motives, not only demand swift and detailed explanations from those found wanting, they will, from time to time, also chop off their heads. It is ten minutes to seven, many of those people still lazing about should, by rights, be out in the street on their way to work, but not all days are alike, and it seems that public servants have been given permission to arrive late, and, as for private businesses, most of them will probably remain closed all day, just to see where all this leads. Caution and chicken soup never hurt anyone, in good health or bad. The world history of crowds shows us that, whether it's a specific breach of public order, or merely the threat of one, the best examples of prudence are generally given by those businesses and industries with premises on the streets, a nervous attitude which we have a duty to respect, given that they are the areas of professional activity who have most to lose, and who inevitably do lose, in terms of shattered shop windows, robberies, lootings and acts of sabotage. At two minutes to seven, with the lugubrious face and voice required by the circumstances, the television and radio presenters finally announce that the president is about to

address the nation. The image that follows, as a way of setting
the scene, shows the national flag flapping lazily, languidly, as
if it were, at any moment, about to slip helplessly down the
pole. There obviously wasn't much wind on the day they took
its picture, remarked one inhabitant. The symbolic insignia
seemed to revive with the opening chords of the national anthem, the gentle breeze had suddenly given way to a brisk wind
that must have blown in from the vast ocean or from some triumphant scene of battle, if it blows any harder, even just a little
bit harder, we're sure to see valkyries on horseback with heroes
riding pillion. Then, as it faded into the distance, the anthem
took the flag with it, or the flag took the anthem with it, the
order doesn't matter, and then the president appeared to the
people, seated behind a desk, his stern eyes fixed on the tele-
prompter. To his right, standing to attention, the flag, not the
one just mentioned, but an indoor flag, arranged in discreet
folds. The president interlaced his fingers, perhaps to disguise
some involuntary tic, He's nervous, said the man who had remarked upon the lack of wind, I want to see his expression
when he explains the low trick they've just played on us. The
people awaiting the president's imminent oratorical display
could not, for one moment, imagine the efforts expended on
preparing the speech by the president of the republic's literary
advisors, not so much as regards any actual statements made,
which would merely involve plucking a few strings on the stylistic lute, but the form of address with which, according to the
norm, the speech should begin, the standard words that usually
introduce tirades of this type. Indeed, given the delicate nature
of his message, it would be little short of insulting to say My
dear compatriots, or Esteemed fellow citizens, or even, were it
the moment for playing, with just the right amount of vibrato,
the bass string of patriotism, that simplest and noblest mode of
address, Men and women of Portugal, that last word, we hasten

to add, only appears due to the entirely gratuitous supposition, with no foundation in objective fact, that the scene of the dire events it has fallen to us to describe in such meticulous detail, could be, or perhaps could have been, the land of the afore-said Portuguese men and women. It was merely an illustrative example, nothing more, for which, despite all our good inten-tions, we apologize in advance, especially given that they are a people with a reputation around the world for having always exercised their electoral duties with praiseworthy civic disci-pline and religious devotion.

Now, returning to the home that we have made into our ob-servation post, we should say that, contrary to one's natural ex-pectations, not a single listener or viewer noticed that none of these usual forms of address issued from the president's mouth, neither this, that or the other, perhaps because the plangent drama of the first words tossed into the ether, I speak to you with my heart in my hands, had made the president's literary advisors realize that the introduction of any of the aforemen-tioned refrains would have been superfluous and inopportune. It would, indeed, have been quite incongruous to begin by say-ing affectionately, Esteemed fellow citizens or My dear com-patriots, as if he were about to announce that tomorrow the price of petrol will go down by fifty percent, only to proceed to present to the eyes of a horror-struck audience a bleeding, slippery, still pulsating internal organ. What the president was about to say, goodbye, goodbye, see you another day, was com-mon knowledge, but, understandably enough, people were cu-rious to see just how he was going to extricate himself. Here then is the whole speech, without, of course, given the impossi-bility of transcribing them into words, the tremor in the voice, the grief-stricken face, the occasional glimmer of a barely re-pressed tear, I speak to you with my heart in my hands, I speak to you as one torn asunder by the pain of an incomprehensible rift, like a father abandoned by his beloved children, all of us equally confused and perplexed by the extraordinary chain of events that has destroyed our sublime family harmony. And do not say that it was us, that it was me, that it was the government of the nation, along with its elected deputies, who were the ones to break away from the people. It is true that this morning we withdrew to another city which, from henceforth, will be the country's capital, it is true that we imposed on the city that was but no longer is the capital a rigorous state of siege, which will, inevitably, seriously hamper the smooth functioning of an urban area of such importance and of such large physical and social dimensions, it is true that you are currently besieged, surrounded, confined inside the perimeter of the city, that you cannot leave it, and that if you try, you will suffer the consequences of an immediate armed response, but what you will never be able to say is that it is the fault of those to whom the popular will, freely expressed in successive, peaceful, honest, democratic contests, entrusted the fate of the nation so that we could defend it from all dangers, internal and external. You are to blame, yes, you are the ones who have ignominiously rejected national concord in favor of the tortuous road of subversion and indiscipline and in favor of the most perverse and diabolical challenge to the legitimate power of the state ever known in the history of nations. Do not find fault with us, find fault rather with yourselves, not with those who spoke in my name, I am referring, of course, to the government, who again and again asked you, nay, begged and implored you to abandon your wicked obstinacy, whose ultimate meaning, despite the enormous investigatory efforts set in train by the state authorities, remains to this day impenetrable. For centuries and centuries, you were the head of the country and the pride of the nation, for centuries and centuries, in times of national crisis and collective anxiety, our people were accustomed to turn their eyes to this city, to these hills, knowing that thence would come the remedy, the consoling word, the correct path to the future. You have betrayed the memory of your ancestors, that is the harsh truth that will forever torment your consciences, yes, stone upon stone, they built the altar of the nation, and, shame on you, you chose to tear it down. With all my soul, I want to believe that your madness will prove a transitory one, that it will not last, I want to think that tomorrow, a tomorrow which I pray to heaven will not be long in coming, that tomorrow remorse will seep gently into your hearts and you will become reconciled with legality and with that root of roots, the national community, returning, like the prodigal son, to the paternal home. You are now a lawless city. You will not have a government to tell you what you should and should not do, how you should and should not behave, the streets will be yours, they belong to you, use them as you wish, there will be no authority to stop you in your tracks and offer you sound advice, but equally, and listen carefully to my words, there will be no authority to protect you from thieves, rapists and murderers, that will be your freedom, and may you enjoy it. You may mistakenly imagine that, guided by your free will and by your every whim, you will be able to organize and defend your lives better than we did using the old methods and the old laws. A very grave mistake on your part. Sooner or later, you will be obliged to find leaders to govern you, if they do not irrupt like beasts out of the inevitable chaos into which you will fall and impose their own laws upon you. Then you will realize the tragic nature of your self-deception. Perhaps you will rebel as you did in the days of authoritarian rule, as you did in the grim days of dictatorship, but do not delude yourselves, you will be put down with equal violence, and you will not be called upon to vote because there will be no elections, or if there are, they will not be free, open and honest like the elections you

scorned, and so it will be until the day when the armed forces
who, along with myself and the national government, today
decided to abandon you to your chosen fate, are obliged to return to liberate you from the monsters you yourselves have
engendered. All your suffering will have been futile, all your
stubbornness in vain, and then you will understand, too late,
that rights only exist fully in the words in which they are expressed and on the piece of paper on which they are recorded,
whether in the form of a constitution, a law or a regulation, you
will understand and, one hopes, be convinced, that their wrong
or unthinking application will convulse the most firmly established society, you will understand, at last, that simple common
sense tells us to take them as a mere symbol of what could be,
but never as a possible, concrete reality. Casting a blank vote
is your irrevocable right, and no one will ever deny you that
right, but, just as we tell children not to play with matches, so
we warn whole peoples of the dangers of playing with dyna-
mite. I will close now. Take the severity of my warnings not as
a threat, but as a cautery for the foul political suppuration that
you have generated in your own breast and in which you are
steeped. You will only see and hear from me again when you
deserve the forgiveness which, despite all, we still wish to bestow on you, I, your president, the government which, in happier times, you elected, and those of our people who remain
healthy and pure and of whom you are not at present worthy.
Until that day, goodbye, and may the lord protect you. The
grave, sad face of the president disappeared and in his place
stood the raised flag. The wind shook it furiously about as if
it were shaking a lunatic, while the anthem repeated the belli-
cose chords and the martial accents that had been composed in
times of unstoppable patriotic pride, but which now sounded
somewhat cracked. The man certainly talks well, said the oldest
member of the family, and of course he's quite right when he

says children shouldn't play with matches, because, as everyone
knows, they'll only pee their beds afterward.

The streets, which, up until then, had been almost deserted,
with most of the shops and businesses closed, filled up with
people within a matter of minutes. Those who had stayed at
home leaned out of the windows to watch the concourse, which
is not to say that everyone was heading in the same direction,
they resembled, rather, two rivers, one flowing up and one
flowing down, and they waved to each other from river to river,
as if the city were celebrating, as if it were a local holiday, and,
contrary to the fugitive president's ill-intentioned prognostica-
tions, there were no thieves or rapists or murderers. Here and
there, on some floors of some buildings, the windows remained
closed, and, where there were blinds, these were kept grimly
drawn, as if the families who lived there were the victims of
a painful bereavement. On those floors, no bright lights had
been lit in the early hours, at most, the inhabitants would have
peered out from behind their curtains, hearts tight with fear,
for the people who lived there had very firm political views,
they were the people who had voted, both in the first election and the second, for the parties they had always voted for,
the party on the right and the party in the middle, they had
no reason now to celebrate, on the contrary, they feared attack by the ignorant masses who were singing and shouting
in the streets, feared that the sacrosanct doors of their homes
would be kicked in, their family memories besmirched, their
silver stolen, Let them sing, they'll be crying soon enough,
they said to each other to give themselves courage. As for those
who voted for the party on the left, the only reason they are
not standing at their windows applauding is because they have
already joined the crowds, as evidenced in this very street by
the occasional flag which, now and then, as if testing the waters, rises above the fast-flowing river of heads. No one went to

work. The newspapers in the kiosks sold out, all of them carried the president's speech on the front page, along with a photograph taken while he was giving it, probably, to judge by the pained expression on his face, at the moment when he said he was speaking with his heart in his hands. Very few wasted time reading about something they knew already, most people were more interested in the views of the newspaper editors, the editorialists, the commentators, or some last-minute interview. The main headlines drew the attention of the curious, they were huge, enormous, others, on the inside pages, were normal size, but they all seemed to have sprung from the brain of the same genius of headline synthesis, allowing one blithely to dispense with reading the news item that followed. The headlines were by turns sentimental, Capital City Orphaned Overnight, ironic, Electoral Bombshell Blows Up In Voters' Faces or Blank Voters Blanked By Government, pedagogical, State Teaches Lesson To Insurrectionist Capital, vengeful, Time For A Settling Of Accounts, prophetic, Everything Will Be Different From Now On or Nothing Will Ever Be The Same Again, alarmist, Anarchy Just Around The Corner or Suspicious Maneuvers On Frontier, rhetorical, An Historic Speech For An Historic Moment, fawning, Dignified President Defies Irresponsible Capital, war-like, Army Surrounds City, objective, Withdrawal Of Government Agencies Takes Place Without Incident, radical, City Council Should Assume Total Control, and tactical, Solution Lies In Municipalist Tradition. There were only a few references to the marvellous star, the one with the twenty-seven arms of light, and these were stuck in willy-nilly amongst all the other news, not even graced with a headline, not even an ironic one, not even a sarcastic one, along the lines of And They Complain About The Price Of Electricity. Some of the editorials, while approving of the government's attitude, All Power To Them, urged one of them, dared

to express certain doubts about the alleged fairness of the prohibition on leaving the city that had been imposed on the inhabitants, Once again, as always, the just are going to have to
pay for the sinners, the honest for the criminals, the worthy
men and women of this city who, having scrupulously fulfilled
their duty as voters by voting for one of the legally constituted
parties that make up the framework of political and ideological options recognized and endorsed by society, now find their
freedom of movement restricted because of a freak majority of
troublemakers whose one characteristic, some say, is that they
don't know what they want, but who, in fact, as we understand
it, know perfectly well what they want and are now preparing for a final assault on power. Other editorials went further,
calling for the abolition, pure and simple, of the secret ballot and proposing that in future, when the situation returned
to normal, as, somehow or other, it was bound to do, every
voter should have a record card on which the presiding officer, having first ascertained before the ballot paper was put in
the box how the person had voted, would note down, for all
legal intents and purposes, both official and personal, that the
bearer had voted for this or that party, And which I, the under-
signed, hereby declare and confirm to be true. Had such a record card existed, had a legislator, aware of the possibility of the
dissolute use of the vote, dared to take that step, bringing together form and content of a totally transparent democratic
system, all the people who had voted for the party on the right
or the party in the middle would now be packing their bags
in order to emigrate to their true homeland, the one that always has its arms wide open to receive those it can most easily clasp to its bosom. Convoys of cars and buses, of minibuses
and removal vans, bearing the flags of the different parties and
honking rhythmically, p.o.t.r., p.i.t.m., would soon be following the government's example and heading toward the military

posts on the frontier, with girls and boys sticking their bottoms
out of the windows or yelling at the foot soldiers of the insurrection, You'd better watch your backs, you miserable traitors,
You'll get the beating of your life when we come back, you frig-
ging bandits, You rotten sons of bitches, or yelling the worst
possible insult in the vocabulary of democratic jargon, Illegals,
illegals, illegals, which would not, of course, be true, because
the people they were abusing would have at home or in their
pocket their very own voter's record card, where, ignominiously, as if branded with irons, would be written or stamped I
cast a blank vote. Only desperate remedies can cure desperate
diseases, concluded the editorialist seraphically.

The celebrations did not last long. It's true that no one actually got around to going to work, but an awareness of the
gravity of the situation soon muted the demonstrations of joy,
someone even asked, What have we got to be happy about,
when they've just put us in isolation as if we were plague victims in quarantine, with an army out there with their rifles
cocked, ready to fire at anyone who tries to leave the city, what
possible reason have we got to be happy. And others said, We
must organize ourselves, but they didn't know how or with
whom or why. Some suggested that a group should go and talk
to the leader of the city council to offer him their loyal support, to explain that the people who cast the blank votes had
not done so in order to bring down the system and to take
power, they wouldn't know what to do with it anyway, that they
had voted the way they voted because they were disillusioned
and could find no other way of making it clear just how disillusioned they were, that they could have staged a revolution,
but then many people would undoubtedly have died, something they would never have wanted, that all their lives they
had patiently placed their vote in the ballot box, and the results were there for all to see, This isn't democracy, sir, far from

it. Others were of the opinion that they should consider the facts more carefully, that it would be best to let the council have the first word, if we go to them with all these explanations and ideas, they'll think there's some political organization behind it, pulling the strings, and we're the only ones who know that isn't true, they're in a tricky situation too, mind, the government has left them holding a real hot potato, and we don't want to make it any hotter, one newspaper proposed that the council should assume full authority, but what authority, and how, the police have left, there isn't even anyone to direct the traffic, we certainly can't expect the councillors to go out into the streets and do the work of the very people they used to give orders to, there's already talk of the refuse collectors going on strike, if that's true, and we shouldn't be surprised if it is, it can only be seen as a provocation, either on the part of the council itself or, more likely, under orders from the government, they're going to do everything possible to make our lives more difficult, we have to be prepared for anything, including or, perhaps, especially, those things that now seem impossible to us, after all, they're holding the whole deck of cards, not to mention the cards up their sleeves. Others, of a pessimistic and fearful bent, felt that there was no way out of the situation, that they were doomed to failure, it'll all pan out the way it always does, with every man for himself and to hell with the others, the moral imperfection of the human race, as we have often said before, is hardly a novelty, it's historical fact, as old as the hills, it might seem now that we're all very supportive of each other, but tomorrow the bickering will start, and the next stage will be open war, discord, confrontation, while they sit back and enjoy it from their ringside seats, laying bets on how long we'll hold out, it'll be fine while it lasts, my friend, but defeat is certain and guaranteed, I mean, let's be reasonable, who could possibly have thought that something like this would get us what we wanted, people en masse casting blank votes and completely unprompted, it's madness, the government hasn't quite got over its surprise yet and is still trying to catch its breath, but the first victory has gone to them, they've turned their backs on us and told us we're nothing but a pile of shit, which, in their opinion, is what we are, and then there's the pressure from abroad to consider too, I bet you anything you like that right now governments and political parties all around the world are thinking of nothing else, they're not stupid, they can see how easily this could become a fuse, light it here and wait for the explosion over there, but then, if all we are to them is a pile of shit, then let's be shit all the way, shoulder to shoulder, because they're bound to get splattered with some of the shit that we supposedly are.

The next day, the rumor was confirmed, the refuse trucks did not go out onto the streets, the refuse collectors had announced an all-out strike and had made public a demand for more pay which a council spokesperson had immediately pronounced completely unacceptable, still less at a time like this, he said, when our city is grappling with an entirely unprecedented crisis from which it is difficult to see a way out. In the same alarmist vein, a newspaper which, from its inception, had specialized in acting as an amplifier of all governmental strategies and tactics, regardless of the government's party colors, whether from the middle, the right or any shade in between, published an editorial signed by the editor himself in which he stated that it was highly likely that the rebellion by the capital's inhabitants would end in a bloodbath if, as everything seemed to indicate, they refused to abandon their stubborn stance. No one, he said, could deny that the government's patience had been stretched to unthinkable limits, no one could expect them to do more, if they did, we would lose, possibly forever, that harmonious binomial authority-obedience in whose light the

happiest of human societies had always bloomed and without which, as history has amply shown, none of them would
have been feasible. The editorial was read, extracts were broadcast on the radio, the editor was interviewed on television, and
then, at midday exactly, while all this was going on, from every
house in the city there emerged women armed with brooms,
buckets and dustpans, and, without a word, they started sweeping their own patch of pavement and street, from the front
door as far as the middle of the road, where they encountered
other women who had emerged from the houses opposite with
exactly the same objective and armed with the same weapons.
Now, the dictionaries state that someone's patch is an area under their jurisdiction or control, in this case, the area outside
somebody's house, and this is quite true, but they also say, or at
least some of them do, that to sweep your own patch means to
look after your own interests. A great mistake on your part, O
absentminded philologists and lexicographers, to sweep your
own patch started out meaning precisely what these women
in the capital are doing now, just as their mothers and grandmothers before them used to do in their villages, and they, like
these women, were not just looking after their own interests,
but after the interests of the community as well. It was possibly
for this same reason that, on the third day, the refuse collectors
also came out onto the street. They were not in uniform, they
were wearing their own clothes. It was the uniforms that were
on strike, they said, not them.

THE interior minister, whose idea the strike had been, was not at all pleased to learn of the refuse collectors' spontaneous return to work, a stance which, in his ministerial understanding of the matter, was not a demonstration of solidarity with the admirable women who had made cleaning their streets a question of honor, a fact unhesitatingly recognized by any impartial observer, but bordered, rather, on criminal complicity. As soon as he received the bad news, he phoned the leader of the city council and commanded him to bring to book those responsible for disregarding orders and to force them to obey, which, in plain language, meant going back on strike, under penalty, if their insubordination continued, of all the punitive consequences foreseen by the laws and regulations, from suspension without pay to outright dismissal. The council leader replied that problems always seem much easier to resolve when seen from a distance, but the person on the ground, the person who actually has to deal with the workers, must listen to them closely before making any decisions, For example, minister, just imagine that I was to give that order to the men, I'm not going to imagine anything, I'm telling you to do it, Yes, minister, of course, but at least allow me to imagine it, for example, I can imagine giving them the order to go back on strike and them telling me to go and take a running jump, what would you do in that case, if you were in my position, how would you force them to do their duty, In the first place, no one would tell me to take a running jump, in the second place, I am not and never will be in your position, I am a minister, not a council leader, and while I'm on the subject, I would just like to say that I would expect from a council leader not only the official and institutional collaboration to which he is, by law, committed and which is my natural due, but also an esprit de corps which, it seems to me, is currently conspicuous by its absence, You can always count on my official and institutional collaboration, minister, I know my obligations, but as for esprit de corps, perhaps we'd better not talk about that just now, let's see how much of it is left when this crisis is over, You're running away from the problem, council leader, No, I'm not, minister, I simply need you to tell me how I am supposed to force the workers to go back on strike, That's your problem, not mine, Now it's my esteemed party colleague who is trying to run away from the problem, Never in my entire political career have I run away from a problem, Well, you're running away from this one, you're trying to run away from the obvious fact that I have no means at my disposal by which to carry out your order, unless you want me to call in the police, but, in that case, I would remind you that the police are not here, they left the city along with the army, both of them carried off by the government, besides, I'm sure we would agree that it would be a gross abnormality to use the police to persuade workers to go on strike, when, in the past, they have always been deployed to break strikes up, by infiltration or other less subtle means, Well, I'm astonished to hear a member of the party on the right talking like that, Minister, in a few hours' time it will be dark, and I will have to say that it is night, I would have to be either stu-

pid or blind to say then that it is day, What has that got to do
with the strike, Whether you like it or not, minister, it is night
now, pitch-black night, we know that something is happening
that goes far beyond our understanding, that exceeds our meagre experience, but we are behaving as if it were the same old
bread, made with the usual flour and cooked in the usual oven,
but it's simply not true, You know, I will seriously have to consider asking you to tender your resignation, If you do, it will be
a weight off my shoulders, and you can count on my profound
gratitude. The interior minister did not reply at once, he allowed a few seconds to pass in order to recover his composure,
then he asked, So what do you think we should do, Nothing,
My dear fellow, in a situation like this, you cannot ask a government to do nothing, Allow me to say that in a situation like this,
a government doesn't govern, it just looks as if it were govern-
ing, There I must disagree, we've managed to do a few things
since this whole thing began, Yes, we're like a fish on a hook, we
thrash about, we shake the line, we tug at it, but we cannot understand how a little piece of bent wire could be capable of
catching us and keeping us trapped, we might yet escape, I'm
not saying we won't, but we risk ending up with the hook stuck
in our gut, Frankly, I'm confused, There is only one thing to
do, What's that, didn't you just say there was no point in our
doing anything, Just pray that the prime minister's strategy
works, What strategy, Leave them to simmer, he said, but I'm
afraid even that could rebound against us, Why, Because they
are the ones doing the cooking, So we do nothing, Let's be serious, minister, would the government be prepared to put an
end to this farcical state of siege by ordering the army and the
air force in to attack the city, to wound and kill ten or twenty
thousand people just to set an example, and then put three or
four thousand more in prison, accused of no one quite knows
what because no real crime has been committed, This isn't a

civil war, all we want is to make people see reason, to show them the error into which they have fallen or were made to fall, that's what we need to do, to make them realize that the unfettered use of the blank ballot paper would make the democratic system unworkable, The results so far haven't, it would seem, been exactly brilliant, It will take time, but people will, in the end, see the light, Why, minister, I had no idea you had mystical tendencies, My dear fellow, when situations become as complicated and as desperate as this, we tend to grab hold of anything, I'm even convinced that some of my colleagues in government, if they thought it would do any good, wouldn't be averse to going on a pilgrimage to a shrine, candle in hand, to make a vow, While we're on the subject, I would appreciate you and your candle visiting a few shrines here of a rather different nature, Meaning, Can you please tell the newspapers and the television and radio people not to pour more petrol on the bonfire, if we don't act sensibly and intelligently, this whole thing could explode, you must have heard that the editor of the government newspaper was stupid enough to admit the possibility that this could all end in a bloodbath, It's not a government newspaper, If you'll allow me to say so, minister, I would have preferred to hear some other comment from you, The little man went too far, he overstepped the mark, it's what always happens when someone tries to do more than he was asked to do, Minister, Yes, What shall I do about the council refuse collectors, Let them work, that way the city council will look good in the eyes of the populace and that could prove useful to us in the future, besides, the strike was, of course, only one element in the strategy, and certainly not the most important, It wouldn't be good for the city, now or in the future, if the city council were to be used as a weapon of war against its citizens, In a situation like this, the council can't afford to remain on the sidelines, the council is, after all, part of this country and

no other, But I'm not asking you to let us remain on the sidelines, all I ask is that the government doesn't put any obstacles
in my way when it comes to exercising my responsibilities, that
it should, at no point, give the public the impression that the
city council is merely a tool, if you'll forgive the expression, of
its repressive policies, firstly, because it isn't true, and secondly,
because it never will be, Um, I'm afraid I don't quite understand or perhaps I understand all too well, One day, minister,
although when I don't know, this city will once again be the
country's capital, That's possible, but by no means certain, it
depends how far they want to take their rebellion, Be that as it
may, it is vital that this council, whether with me as leader or
with someone else, should never be seen, however indirectly, to
be an accomplice in or a co-author of a bloody repression, the
government that orders such a repression will have no alternative but to take the consequences, but the council, this council,
belongs to the city, the city does not belong to the council, I
hope I have made myself clear, minister, You've made yourself
so clear that I'm going to ask you a question, Feel free, minister, Did you cast a blank vote, Could you repeat the question,
please, I didn't quite hear, I asked if you cast a blank vote, I
asked if the ballot paper you put in the box was blank, Who can
say, minister, who can say, When all this is over, I hope we can
meet and have a long conversation, As you wish, minister,
Goodbye, Goodbye, What I'd really like to do is come over
there and give you a clip round the ear, Alas, I'm too old for
that, minister, If you ever become interior minister, you will
learn that clips round the ear and other such correctives have
no age limit, Don't let the devil hear you, minister, The devil
has such good hearing he doesn't need things to be spoken out
loud, Well, god help us then, There's no point asking him for
help either, he was born stone-deaf.

Thus ended this illuminating and prickly conversation be-

tween the interior minister and the council leader, with each
having bandied about points of view, arguments and opinions
which will, in all probability, have disoriented the reader, who
must now doubt that the two interlocutors do in fact belong,
as he or she thought, to the party on the right, the very party
which, as the administrative power, is carrying out a vile pol-
icy of repression, both on a collective level, with the capital
city submitted to the humiliation of a state of siege ordered by
the country's own government, and on an individual level, with
harsh interrogations, lie detectors, threats and, who knows, the
very worst kinds of torture, although the truth impels us to
say that if any such tortures were carried out, we could not
bear witness to them, we were not there, not, however, that
this means very much, for we were not present either at the
parting of the red sea, and yet everyone swears that it happened. As for the interior minister, you must already have noticed that in the armor of the indomitable fighter, which he
tries so hard to appear to be when locked in combat with the
defense minister, there is a subtle fault, or to put it more collo-
quially, a crack big enough to poke your finger through. Were
that not so, we would not have been witness to the successive
failures of his plans, and the speed and facility with which the
blade of his sword grows blunt, as this dialogue has just confirmed, for while he came in like a lion, he went out like a lamb,
if not something worse, one has only to look, for example, at
the lack of respect evident in his categorical statement that god
was born stone-deaf. As regards the council leader, we are, to
use the words of the interior minister, pleased to note that he
has seen the light, not the one the minister would like the capital's voters to see, but the light that those casters of blank votes
hope that someone will begin to see. The most common occurrence in this world of ours, in these days of stumbling blindly
forward, is to come across men and women mature in years

and ripe in prosperity, who, at eighteen, were not just beam-
ing beacons of style, but also, and perhaps above all, bold rev-
olutionaries determined to bring down the system supported
by their parents and to replace it, at last, with a fraternal paradise, but who are now equally firmly attached to convictions
and practices which, having warmed up and flexed their muscles on any of the many available versions of moderate con-
servatism, become, in time, pure egotism of the most obscene
and reactionary kind. Put less respectfully, these men and these
women, standing before the mirror of their life, spit every day
in the face of what they were with the sputum of what they
are. The fact that a politician belonging to the party on the
right, a man in his forties, who has spent his whole life under
the parasol of a tradition cooled by the air-conditioning of the
stock exchange and lulled by the steamy zephyr of the markets,
should have been open to the revelation, or, indeed, manifest
certainty, that there was some deeper meaning behind the gentle rebellion in the city he had been appointed to administer, is
something that is both worthy of record and deserving of our
gratitude, so unaccustomed have we become to such singular
phenomena.

It will not have gone unnoticed, by particularly exacting
readers and listeners, that the narrator of this fable has paid
scant, not to say non-existent, attention to the place in which
the action described, albeit in rather leisurely fashion, is taking
place. Apart from the first chapter, in which there were a few
careful brushstrokes applied to the area of the polling station,
although, even then, these were applied only to doors, windows
and tables, and with the exception of the polygraph, that machine for catching liars, everything else, which is quite a lot, has
passed as if the characters in the story inhabited an entirely in-
substantial world, were indifferent to the comfort or discomfort of the places in which they found themselves, and did noth-

ing but talk. In the room in which the government of the country has, more than once, and occasionally with the presence and participation of the president, gathered to debate the situation and take the necessary measures to pacify minds and restore peace to the streets, there would doubtless be a large table around which the ministers would sit on comfortable, upholstered chairs, and on which there were bound to be bottles of mineral water and glasses to match, pencils and pens in different colors, markers, reports, books on legislation, notebooks, microphones, telephones, and all the usual paraphernalia one finds in places of this calibre. There would be ceiling lights and wall lights, there would be padded doors and curtained windows, there would be rugs on the floor, there would be paintings on the walls and perhaps an antique or modern tapestry, there would, inevitably, be a portrait of the president, a bust representing the republic and the national flag. None of this has been mentioned, nor will it be mentioned in future. Even here, in the more modest, but nonetheless spacious office of the leader of the city council, with a balcony overlooking the square and a large aerial photograph of the city hanging on the main wall, there would be ample opportunity to fill a page or two with detailed descriptions, and to make the most of that generous pause in order to take a deep breath before confronting the disasters to come. It seems to us far more important to observe the anxious lines furrowing the brow of the council leader, perhaps he is thinking that he said too much, that he gave the interior minister the impression, if not the stark certainty, that he had joined the ranks of the enemy, and that, by his imprudence, he would, perhaps irremediably, have compromised his political career inside and outside the party. The other possibility, as remote as it is unimaginable, would be that his reasoning might have given the interior minister a push in the right direction and caused him to rethink entirely the strat-

egies and tactics with which the government hopes to put an
end to the sedition. We see him shake his head, a sure sign that,
having swiftly examined the possibility, he has discarded it as
being foolishly ingenuous and dangerously unrealistic. He got
up from the chair where he had remained seated throughout
his conversation with the minister and went over to the window. He did not open it, he merely drew back the curtain a
little and gazed out. The square looked as it always did, various
passers-by, three people sitting on a bench in the shade of a
tree, the café terraces and their customers, the flower-sellers, a
woman and a dog, the newspaper kiosks, buses, cars, the usual
scene. I need to go out, he thought. He went back to his desk
and phoned his chief administrative officer, I'm going out for a
while, he said, tell any councillors who are in the building, but
only if they ask for me, as for the rest, I leave you in charge,
Certainly, sir, I'll tell your driver to bring the car round to the
front door, Yes, if you would, but tell him that I won't be needing him, I'll drive myself, Will you be coming back to the town
hall today, Yes, I hope so, but I'll let you know if I decide otherwise, Very well, How are things in the city, Oh, nothing very
grave to report, the news we've received has been no more serious than usual, a few traffic accidents, the occasional bottle-
neck, a minor fire in which no one was hurt, a failed bank robbery, How did they manage, now that there are no police, The
robber was an amateur, and the gun, although it was a real one,
wasn't loaded, Where have they taken him, The people who
disarmed him took him to a fire station, Whatever for, they
haven't any facilities for detaining prisoners, Well, they had to
put him somewhere, So what happened next, Apparently, the
firemen spent an hour giving him a good talking-to and then
let him go, There wasn't much else they could do, I suppose,
No, sir, there wasn't, Tell my secretary to let me know when the
car arrives, Yes, sir. The council leader leaned back in his chair,

waiting, and his brow was again deeply furrowed. Contrary to the predictions of the gloom-mongers, there had been no more robberies, rapes or murders than before. It seemed that the police were, after all, not essential for the city's security, that the population itself, spontaneously and in a more or less organized manner, had taken over their work as vigilantes. The robbery at the bank was a case in point. No, the robbery at the bank, he thought, was irrelevant, the man had obviously been very nervous and unsure of himself, a mere novice, and the bank employees had seen that they were in no danger, but tomorrow it might be different, what am I saying, tomorrow, today, right now, over the last few days crimes will have been committed in the city that will obviously go unpunished, if we have no police, if the criminals aren't arrested, if there's no investigation and no trial, if the judges go home and the courts don't work, criminality will inevitably increase, it's as if everyone were expecting the council to take over the policing of the city, they're asking for it, demanding it, protesting that without some form of security, there can be no peace of mind, and I keep wondering how, by issuing a call for volunteers, for example, by creating urban militias, surely we're not going to go out into the street dressed like gendarmes straight out of a comic opera, with uniforms rented from the theater's costume department, and what about guns, where are we going to get those, and what about using them, not just knowing how to use them, but being capable of using them, taking out a gun and firing it, can anyone imagine me, the councillors, the town hall civil servants, engaged in a rooftop pursuit of the midnight murderer, the Tuesday rapist or the white-gloved cat burglar of high-society salons. The phone rang, it was his secretary, Sir, your car is here, Thank you, he said, I'm going out now and I'm not sure yet whether I'll be back today or not, but if there are any problems, just call me on my mobile, Take care, sir, Why do you say that, Given the way things are, sir, that's the least we can wish each other, May I ask you a question, Of course, as long as I have an answer for it, If you don't want to, don't answer, What's the question, Who did you vote for, No one, sir, Do you mean you abstained, No, I mean that I cast a blank vote, Blank, Yes, sir, blank, And you're telling me just like that, You asked me the question just like that, And that gave you the confidence to reply, Just about, sir, but only just, If I understand you rightly, you also thought it could be a risk, Well, I hoped that it wouldn't be, As you see, your confidence was rewarded, Does that mean that I won't be asked to hand in my notice, No, you can sleep easy on that score, It would be far better if we didn't need to sleep in order to feel at ease, sir, Well put, Anyone could have said the same, sir, it certainly wouldn't win any literary prizes, You will have to be satisfied with my applause, then, That's reward enough, sir, So let's leave it that if you need me, you can call me on my mobile, Yes, sir, Right, then, I'll see you tomorrow, if not later on today, Yes, see you later, or tomorrow, replied the secretary.

The council leader quickly tidied up the papers scattered about his desk, most of them might have been written about another country and another century, not about this capital now, under a state of siege, abandoned by its own government, surrounded by its own army. If he tore them up, if he burned them, if he threw them in the wastepaper basket, no one would come to him demanding an explanation for what he had done, people had far more important things to think about now, the city, after all, is no longer part of the known world, it's a pot full of putrefying food and maggots, an island set adrift in a sea not its own, a dangerous source of infection, a place which, as a precautionary measure, has been quarantined until the plague becomes less virulent or until it runs out of people to kill and ends up devouring itself. He asked his secretary to bring him his raincoat, picked up his briefcase containing papers to be studied at home and went downstairs. The driver, who was waiting for him, opened the car door, They said you won't be needing me, sir, No, I won't, you can go home, See you tomorrow, then, sir, See you tomorrow. It's odd how we spend every day of our life saying goodbye, saying and hearing others say see you tomorrow when, inevitably, on one of those days, which will be someone's last, either the person we said it to will no longer be here, or we who said it will not. We will see if on today's tomorrow, what we normally refer to as the following day, when the council leader and his chauffeur meet again, they will be capable of grasping what an extraordinary, near-miraculous thing it is to have said see you tomorrow and to find that what had been no more than a problematic possibility has come to pass as if it had been a certainty. The council leader got into his car. He was going for a drive around the city, to have a look at the people on the way, not in any hurry, but stopping now and then to get out and walk for a while, listening to what was being said, in short, taking the pulse of the city, assessing the strength of the incubating fever. From his childhood reading he remembered a king in some far eastern country, he wasn't sure now whether he had been a king or an emperor, he was, more than likely, the caliph of the time, who was in the habit of disguising himself and leaving his palace to go and mingle with the ordinary people, the lower orders, and to eavesdrop on what was said about him during frank exchanges in the squares and streets. The truth is that such exchanges would not have been as frank as all that, because in those days, as ever, there would have been no shortage of spies to take note of opinions, complaints and criticisms and of any embryonic conspiracies. It is an unvarying rule for those in power that, when it comes to heads, it is best to cut them off before they start to think, afterward, it might be too late. The council leader is not the king

of this besieged city, and as for the vizier of the interior, he has
exiled himself to the other side of the frontier and he will, at
this moment, doubtless be in some meeting with his collabora-
tors, we will find out who and why in a while. For this reason
the council leader does not need to disguise himself with a false
beard and moustache, the face he is wearing is the one he usually wears, except that it looks a little more preoccupied than
normal, as we have noticed before from the lines on his forehead. A few people recognize him, but few say hello. Do not assume, however, that the indifferent or the hostile are to be
found only amongst those who originally cast blank votes, and
who would, therefore, see him as an adversary, quite a few voters from his own party and from the party in the middle also
look at him with ill-disguised suspicion, not to say with clear
antipathy, What's he doing around here, they will think, what's
he doing mixing with this rabble of blankers, he should be at
work earning his salary, perhaps now that the majority has
changed hands, he's come looking for votes, well, if he has, he
hasn't got a hope in hell, there won't be any elections round
here for a while, if I was the government, I know what I would
do, I'd get rid of this whole council and instead appoint a decent administrative committee, who could be trusted politically. Before continuing this story, it would be as well to explain
that the use of the word blanker a few lines earlier was neither
accidental nor fortuitous, nor was it a slip of the fingers on the
computer keyboard, and it certainly isn't a neologism that the
narrator has hastily invented in order to fill a gap. The term exists, it really does, you can find it in any up-to-date dictionary,
the problem, if it is a problem, lies in the fact that people are
convinced that they know the meaning of the word blank and
of all its derivatives, and therefore won't waste their time going
back to the source to check, or else they suffer from chronic intellectual lazyitis and stay right where they are, refusing to take

even one step toward making a possibly beautiful discovery. No one knows who in the city first came up with it, which inquisitive researcher or chance discoverer, but one thing is certain, the word spread rapidly and immediately took on the pejorative meaning that its very appearance seems to provoke. Although we may not previously have mentioned the fact, which is in every way deplorable, even the media, especially the state television channels, are already using the word as if it were one of the very worst of obscenities. When you see it written down, you don't notice it so much, but as soon as you hear it spoken with that angry curl of the lips and in that snide tone of voice, you would have to have the moral armor of a knight of the round table not to put a noose around your neck, don a penitent's tunic and walk along beating your chest and renouncing all your old principles and precepts, A blanker I was, a blanker no more, forgive me, my country, forgive me, my lord. The council leader, who will have nothing to forgive, since he is no one's lord and never will be, who will not even be a candidate at the next elections, has stopped watching the passers-by, he is looking now for signs of shabbiness, neglect, decline, and, at least at a first glance, he can find none. The shops and department stores are all open, although they don't appear to be doing much business, the traffic is flowing, impeded only by the occasional minor jam, there are no queues of anxious customers at the doors of the banks, the kind of queue that always forms in time of crisis, everything seems to be normal, there are no violent muggings, no shoot-outs or knife fights, there is nothing but this luminous afternoon, neither too cold nor too hot, an afternoon that seems to have come into the world to satisfy all desires and to calm all anxieties. But not the council leader's unease or, to be more literary, his inner disquiet. What he feels, and he may be the only person amongst those passing by to feel this, is a kind of menace floating in the air, the kind

that sensitive temperaments feel when the thick clouds covering the sky grow tense with waiting for the thunderbolt to fall,
or as we might feel when a door creaked open in the darkness
and a current of icy air brushed our cheek, when an awful feeling of foreboding opened the gates of despair to us, when a diabolical laugh sundered the delicate veil of the soul. Nothing
concrete, nothing we could describe with any authority or ob-
jectivity, but the fact is that the council leader has to make a
real effort not to stop the first person who passes and say to
him, Be careful, don't ask me why or about what, just be careful, I've got a feeling that something bad is going to happen, If
you, the council leader, with all your responsibilities, don't
know, how do you expect me to, they would ask him, It doesn't
matter, what matters is that you should be very careful, Is it
some epidemic, No, I don't think so, An earthquake, This isn't
an area prone to earthquakes, there's never been one here, A
flood, then, a deluge, It's been years since the river broke its
banks, What then, Look, I don't know, Forgive me for asking,
You're forgiven before you've even asked, No offence, sir, but
have you perhaps had one drink too many, you know what they
say, the last one is always the worst, No, I only drink at meal-
times, and then only in moderation, I'm certainly not an alcoholic, Well, in that case, I don't understand, When it's happened, you will, When what has happened, The thing that is
going to happen. Bewildered, his interlocutor glanced around
him, If you're looking for a policeman to arrest me, said the
council leader, don't bother, they've all gone, No, I wasn't looking for a policeman, lied the other man, I'd arranged to meet a
friend here, oh, there he is, see you again, then, sir, and take
care, you know, to be perfectly frank, if I were you, I'd go
straight home to bed, when you sleep you forget everything,
But I never go to sleep at this hour, As my cat would say, all
hours are good for sleeping, May I ask you a question too, Of

course, sir, feel free, Did you cast a blank vote, Are you doing a
survey, No, I'm just curious, but if you'd rather not answer,
don't. The man hesitated for a second, then, very gravely, he replied, Yes, I did, it's not, as far as I know, forbidden to do so, No,
it's not forbidden, but look at the result. The man seemed to
have forgotten about his imaginary friend, Look, sir, I have
nothing against you personally, I'm even prepared to acknowledge that you've done a good job on the city council, but I'm
not to blame for what you call the result, I voted as I wanted to
vote, within the law, now it's up to you, the council, to respond,
if the potato's too hot, blow on it, Don't get upset, I just wanted
to warn you, You still haven't told me about what, Even if I
wanted to, I couldn't, Then I've been wasting my time here,
Forgive me, your friend's waiting for you, There isn't any friend
waiting, I was just using that as an excuse to get away, Then
thank you for having stayed a little longer, Sir, Please don't
stand on ceremony, From what I know about what goes on in
people's minds, I would say that it's your conscience that's troubling you, For something I didn't do, Some people say that's
the worst kind of remorse, for something you allowed to happen, Maybe you're right, I'll think about that, but, anyway, be
careful, I will, sir, and thank you for the warning, Even though
you still don't know what I'm warning you against, Some people
deserve our trust, You're the second person who's said that to
me today, Then you can safely say that you've had a very good
day indeed, Thank you, See you again, sir, Yes, see you again.

The council leader walked back to where he had parked his
car, he was pleased, at least he had managed to warn one person, if the man passed the word on, then in a matter of hours,
the whole city would be on the alert, ready for whatever might
happen, I'm clearly not in my right mind, he thought, the man
won't say anything to anyone, he's not a fool like me, well, it's
not foolishness exactly, the fact that I felt a threat I'm incapable

of defining is my problem, not his, I should just take his advice
and go home, any day during which we've been offered a piece
of good advice can never be considered to have been wasted.
He got into his car and phoned his office to say that he wouldn't
be going back to the town hall. He lived in a street in the center, not far from the overground metro station that served a
large part of the eastern sector of the city. His wife, who is a
surgeon, will not be at home, she's on night duty at the hospital, and as for their two children, the boy is in the army, he
might even be one of the men defending the frontier with a
heavy machine gun at the ready and a gas mask hanging round
his neck, and the girl works abroad as a secretary-cum-inter-
preter for an international organization, of the sort that always
build their vast, luxurious headquarters in the most important
cities, important politically speaking, of course. She, at least,
will have benefited from having a father well placed in the official system of favors received and paid back, made and returned. Since even the very best advice is, at best, only ever
half-obeyed, the council leader did not go to bed. He looked
through the papers he'd brought home with him, made decisions about some of them and put others aside for further examination. When supper time approached, he went into the
kitchen, opened the fridge, but found nothing that he fancied
eating. His wife had prepared something for him, she wouldn't
let him go hungry, but the effort of setting the table, heating up
the food and then washing the dishes seemed to him tonight a
superhuman one. He left the house and went to a restaurant.
When he had sat down at a table and while he was waiting for
his food to come, he phoned his wife. How's work, he asked
her, Oh, not too bad, how about you, Oh, I'm fine, just a bit
anxious, Well, in the current situation, I hardly need ask you
why, No, it's more than that, a kind of inner shudder, a shadow,
a bad omen, Hm, I had no idea you were superstitious, There's

a time for everything, Where are you, I can hear voices, In a
restaurant, I'll go home afterward, or perhaps I'll drop in and
see you first, being council leader opens many doors, But I
might be in the operating theater and I'm not sure how long
I'll be, All right, I'll think about it, lots of love, And to you too,
Loads, Tons. The waiter brought him his first course, Here you
are, sir, enjoy your meal. He was just raising his fork to his
mouth when an explosion shook the whole building, the glass
in the windows inside and out shattered, tables and chairs were
overturned, people were screaming and groaning, some were
injured, others were stunned by the blast, others were trembling with fright. The council leader was bleeding from a cut to
his face caused by a piece of glass. The restaurant had obviously
been hit by the shock wave from an explosion. It must have
been in the metro station, sobbed a woman struggling to get to
her feet. Pressing a napkin to his wound, the council leader ran
out into the street. Broken glass crunched beneath his feet, up
ahead rose a thick column of black smoke, he thought he could
even see the glow of flames, It happened, it's at the station, he
thought. He had discarded the napkin when he realized that
holding his hand to his head was slowing him down, now the
blood was running freely down his face and neck and soaking
into his shirt collar. Wondering if the service would still be
working, he stopped for a moment to dial the emergency number on his mobile phone, but the nervous-sounding voice that
answered told him that the incident had already been reported,
It's the council leader here, a bomb has exploded in the main
overground station in the eastern part of the city, send all the
help you can, firemen, civil defense people, scouts, if there are
any, nurses, ambulances, first-aid equipment, whatever you
have to hand, oh, and another thing, if there is some way of
finding out where any retired police officers live, call them too
and ask them to come and help, The firemen are already on

their way, sir, we're doing everything we can do. He rang off
and started running again. Other people were running alongside him, some overtook him, his legs felt like lead and it was as
if his lungs were refusing to breathe the thick, malodorous air,
and a pain, a pain that rapidly fixed itself in his trachea, kept
getting worse and worse. The station was about fifty meters
away now, the gray, grubby smoke, illuminated by the fire, rose
up in furious tangled skeins. How many dead will there be inside, who planted the bomb, the council leader was asking himself. The sirens of the fire engines could be heard getting closer
now, the mournful wailing, more like someone asking for help
than bringing it, grew shriller and shriller, at any moment now
they will come hurtling round one of these corners. The first
vehicle appeared as the council leader was pushing his way
through the crowd of people who had rushed to see the disaster, I'm the council leader, he said, I'm the leader of the city
council, let me through, please, and he felt painfully foolish
having to repeat this over and over, aware that the fact of being
council leader would not open all doors to him, indeed, inside,
there were people for whom the doors of life had closed once
and for all. Within minutes, great jets of water were being pro-
jected through openings that had once been doorways and
windows, or were aimed up into the air to soak the upper part
of the buildings in order to reduce the risk of the fire spreading. The council leader went over to the chief fire officer, What
do you make of it, he asked, It's the worst fire I've ever seen, in
fact, it has a distinct whiff of arson about it, Don't say that, it's
not possible, It may just be an impression, let's hope I'm wrong.
At that moment, a television recording van arrived, followed by
others from the press and the radio, now, surrounded by lights
and microphones, the council leader is answering questions,
How many lives do you think will have been lost, What information do you have so far, How many people have been in-

jured, How many people have suffered burns, When do you
think the station will be back to normal, Have you any idea
who might have been behind the attack, Was any warning received before the explosion, If so, who received it and what
measures were taken to evacuate the station in time, Do you
think it was a terrorist attack carried out by a group with links
to the subversive movement active in the city, Do you think
there will be more such attacks, As council leader and sole authority left in the city, what means do you have to carry out
the necessary investigations. When the rain of questions had
stopped, the council leader gave the only possible reply in the
circumstances, Some of these questions are outside my competence, and so I can't really answer them, I assume, however, that
the government will be making an official statement soon, as
for the other questions, all I can say is that we are doing everything humanly possible to help the victims, let's just hope we
get there in time, at least for some of them, But how many dead
are there, insisted a journalist, We'll only know that when we
go into that inferno, so, until then, please, spare me any more
stupid questions. The journalists protested that this was no way
to treat the media, who were, after all, only fulfilling their duty
to inform and therefore deserved to be treated with respect,
but the council leader cut short this corporate speech, One of
the newspapers today went so far as to call for a bloodbath, that
didn't happen this time, the burned don't bleed, they just get
fried to a crisp, now, please, let me through, I have nothing
more to add, we'll let you know when we have any concrete information. There was a general murmur of disapproval, and
further back a sneering voice said, Who does he think he is, but
the council leader made no attempt to find out who the dis-
senter was, during the last few hours, he, too, had done nothing
but ask, Who do I think I am.

Two hours later, the fire was declared to be under control,

the intense heat from the charred ruins took another two hours
to abate, but it was still impossible to know how many people
had died. About thirty or forty people were taken to hospital, suffering from injuries of varying degrees of severity, having escaped the worst of the blast because they had been in a
part of the ticket hall farthest from the place where the bomb
had exploded. The council leader remained there until the fire
had died down completely, and he only left when the fire chief
told him, Go and rest, sir, leave us to deal with things, and
do something about that cut on your face, I can't understand
why no one here noticed it, It's all right, they had more serious
things on their minds. Then he asked, And now, Now we have
to locate and remove the bodies, some will have been blown to
pieces, most will have been burned, Yes, I don't know if I could
bear that, In your present state, I don't think you could either,
I'm a coward, It's not cowardice, sir, even I passed out the first
time, Thank you, do what you can, All I can do is put out the
last burning ember, which is nothing, At least you'll be here.
Covered in soot, his cheek black with dried blood, he started
walking grimly back home. His whole body ached, from running, from nervous tension, from being on his feet for hours.
There was no point trying to phone his wife, the person who
answered would doubtless tell him, I'm sorry, sir, your wife is in
the operating theater, she can't come to the phone. On either
side of the road, people were looking out of their windows, but
no one recognized him. A real council leader travels in his official car, has a secretary with him to carry his briefcase, three
bodyguards to clear a path for him, but the man walking along
the street is a filthy, stinking tramp, a sad man on the verge of
tears, a ghost to whom no one would even lend a bucket of water in which to wash his sheet. The mirror in the lift revealed to
him the blackened face he would have had now if he had been
in the ticket hall when the bomb exploded, Horror, horror, he

murmured. He opened the door with tremulous hands and
went straight to the bathroom. He took the first-aid box out of
the cabinet, the packet of cotton wool, the hydrogen peroxide,
some liquid disinfectant containing iodine, some large sticking
plasters. He said to himself, It probably needs a few stitches.
His shirt was stained with blood all the way down to the waistband of his trousers, I bled more than I thought. He took off
his jacket, painfully undid the sticky knot of his tie and took
off his shirt. His vest was stained with blood too, I should have
a wash, get in the shower, no, don't be ridiculous, that would
just wash away the dried blood covering the wound and start it
bleeding again, he said softly, I should, yes, I should, I should
what. The word was like a dead body he had stumbled upon,
he had to find out what the word wanted, he had to remove the
body. The firemen and the civil defense people are going into
the station. They are carrying stretchers and wearing protec-
tive gloves, most of them have never before touched a burned
body, now they will know what it is like. I should. He went out
of the bathroom and into his study, where he sat down at his
desk. He picked up the phone and dialed a confidential number. It is almost three o'clock in the morning. A voice answers,
The interior minister's office, who's calling, It's the leader of
the city council in the capital, I'd like to speak to the minister, it's extremely urgent, if he's in, can you please put me
straight through to him, One moment, please. The moment
lasted two minutes, Hello, A few hours ago, minister, a bomb
exploded in the overground train station in the eastern sector
of the city, we don't yet know how many people have died, but
everything indicates that the death toll will be high, there are
already about forty or fifty wounded, Yes, I know, The reason
I'm phoning you now is that I've been at the scene of the explosion all this time, Very commendable. The council leader took
a deep breath, then asked, Haven't you anything to say to me,

minister, What do you mean, About who could have planted the bomb, Well, it seems fairly obvious, your friends who cast the blank votes have clearly decided to go in for a bit of direct action, Sorry, but I don't believe that, Whether you believe it or not, that is the truth, Is or will be, You can make up your own mind about that, What happened here, minister, was a heinous crime, Yes, I suppose you're right, that's what people usually call it, Who planted the bomb, minister, You seem upset, why don't you get some rest and call me when it gets light, but not before ten o'clock, Who planted the bomb, minister, What are you trying to insinuate, A question is not an insinuation, it would be an insinuation if I were to tell you what we are both thinking at this moment, There's no reason on earth why my thoughts should coincide with those of the leader of a municipal council. Well, they do this time, Careful now, you're going too far, Oh, I'm not just going too far, I've arrived, What do you mean, That I am speaking to the person directly responsible for the blast, You're mad, If only I was, How dare you cast aspersions on a member of the government, it's unheard of, From now on, minister, I am no longer the council leader of this besieged city, We'll talk tomorrow, but bear in mind that I have no intention of accepting your resignation, You'll have to accept it, just pretend that I died, In that case, I warn you, in the name of the government, that you will bitterly regret doing so, in fact, you won't even have time to regret it if you don't keep quiet about this whole affair, but that shouldn't prove too difficult, given that you say you're dead, Yes, I never imagined anyone could be so dead. The communication was cut at the other end. The man who had been the council leader got up and went into the bathroom. He took off his clothes and stood under the shower. The hot water quickly washed away the dried blood that had formed over the wound and the blood began to flow again. The firemen have just found the first charred body.

T WENTY-THREE deaths so far, and we've no idea how many more they'll find under the rubble, that's at least twenty-three deaths, interior minister, said the prime minister, bringing the flat of his hand down on the newspapers that lay open on his desk, The media are almost unanimous in attributing the attack to some terrorist group with links to the insurrection by the blankers, sir, Firstly, purely as a matter of good taste, please do me the great favor of not using the word blanker in my presence, secondly, please explain what you mean by the expression almost unanimous, It means that there are only two exceptions, two newspapers who do not accept the version that is doing the rounds and who are demanding a proper investigation, Interesting, Read what this one says, sir. The prime minister read out loud, We Demand To Know Who Gave The Order, And this one, sir, less direct, but along the same lines, We Want The Truth Whoever It May Hurt. The interior minister went on, It's nothing to get alarmed about, I don't think we need worry, in fact, it's rather a good thing that there should be a few doubts, that way people can't say they're all speaking with their master's voice, Do you mean that twenty-three or more deaths don't worry you, It was a calculated risk, sir, In the light of what happened, a very badly calculated one, Yes, I suppose you could see it like that, We assumed it would be a less powerful bomb, just something to give people a bit of a fright, There was clearly an unfortunate failure in the chain of command, If only I could be sure that was the only reason, The order was, I can assure you, correctly given, you have my word, sir, Your word, interior minister, For what it's worth, sir, Yes, for what it's worth, In either case, we knew there would be deaths, But not twenty-three, Even if there had been only three, they would have been no less dead than these twenty-three, it isn't a question of numbers, No, but it is also a question of numbers, May I remind you that he who wills the ends, wills the means, Oh, I've heard that refrain many times before, And this won't be the last time, even if, next time, you hear it from someone else's lips, Appoint a commission of inquiry at once, minister, To reach what conclusions, prime minister, Just set it to work, we'll sort that out later, Very good, sir, Give all necessary help to the families of the victims, both those who died and those who are currently in hospital, tell the council to take charge of the funerals, In the midst of all this confusion, I forgot to inform you that the council leader has resigned, Resigned, why, Well, to be more precise, he walked out, At this precise moment, I don't really care whether he resigned or walked out, my question is why, He arrived at the station immediately after the explosion took place and his nerve went, he couldn't cope with what he saw, No one could, I know I couldn't, indeed, I imagine even you couldn't, minister, so there must be some other reason for his abrupt departure, He thinks the government is responsible, and he didn't just hint at his suspicions either, he was quite explicit about it, Do you think he was the one who passed the idea on to those two newspapers, Frankly, prime minister, I don't, and, believe you me, I would love to be able to lay the blame at his door, What will the man do now,

His wife is a doctor, Yes, I know her, They'll have to get by until he finds a new job, And meanwhile, Meanwhile, prime minister, I will keep him under the strictest possible surveillance, if
that's what you mean, Whatever was the man thinking of, he
seemed so trustworthy, a loyal party member, with an excellent
political career, a future, The minds of human beings are not
always entirely at one with the world in which they live, some
people have trouble adjusting to reality, basically they're just
weak, confused spirits who use words, sometimes very skilfully,
to justify their cowardice, You're obviously something of an expert on the subject, did you glean all this from your own experiences, If I had, would I be in the post of interior minister, No,
I suppose not, but everything is possible in this world, no doubt
our finest torture specialists kiss their children when they get
home, and some may even cry at the cinema, And I sir, am no
exception, in fact, I'm just an old sentimentalist really, Glad to
hear it. The prime minister leafed slowly through the newspapers, he looked at the photographs one by one with a mix-
ture of repugnance and apprehension, and said, You probably
want to know why I don't sack you, Yes, sir, I'm curious to know
your reasons, Because if I did, people would think one of two
things, either that, independent of the nature and degree of
guilt, I considered you directly responsible for what had happened, or that I was quite simply punishing you for your supposed incompetence for not having foreseen the possibility of
such an act of violence in abandoning the capital to its fate, Yes,
knowing as I do the rules of the game, I thought those would
be your reasons, Obviously, there's a third reason, possible, as
all things are, but improbable, and therefore out of the question, What's that, That you might make public the truth behind
the attack, You know better than anyone that no interior minister, in any age or in any country in the world, has ever opened
his mouth to speak of the mean, dishonorable, treacherous,

criminal deeds committed in the course of his work, so you can rest easy on that score because I will prove no exception, If it becomes known that we ordered the bomb to be planted, we will give the people who cast the blank votes the final reason they needed, If you'll forgive me, prime minister, that way of thinking offends against logic, Why, And, if you'll allow me to say so, it does an injustice to the usual rigor of your thinking, Get to the point, Whether they find out or not, if they are then shown to be right, it's because they were right already. The prime minister pushed the newspapers away and said, This whole business reminds me of the story of the sorcerer's apprentice, the one who couldn't control the magical forces he had unleashed, Who, in your view, prime minister, is the sorcerer's apprentice in this case, them or us, Well, I very much fear that both of us are, they set off down a dead-end road with no thought for the consequences, And we followed them, Exactly, and now it's just a matter of waiting to see what the next step will be, As far as the government is concerned, we simply have to keep up the pressure, although after what has just happened, we obviously don't want to take any further action right now, And what about them, If the information I received before coming here is true, then they are preparing to hold a demonstration, What on earth do they hope to achieve by that, demonstrations never achieve anything, if they did, we wouldn't allow them, Presumably they want to protest against the attack, and as for getting authorization from the ministry of the interior, on this occasion, they won't even have to waste their time asking for it, Will we ever get out of this mess, That is not a matter for sorcerers, prime minister, the fully qualified or the apprentices, but, in the end, as always, the strongest side will win, The one who is strongest at the last moment will win, and we haven't yet reached that moment, the strength we have now may not be sufficient by then, Oh, I have every confidence, prime minister, an organized state cannot possibly lose a battle like this, it would be the end of the world, Or the beginning of another, Now I'm not quite sure what I should make of those words, prime minister, Well, don't go spreading it around that the prime minister is entertaining defeatist ideas, Such a thought would never even enter my head, Just as well, You were clearly speaking hypothetically, Of course, If you don't need me for anything else, I'll get back to work, The president tells me he's had a brilliant idea, What's that, He didn't want to go into detail, he is awaiting events, To some purpose one hopes, He is the president, That's what I meant, Keep me informed, Yes, prime minister, Goodbye, Goodbye, prime minister.

The information received by the ministry of the interior was correct, the city was preparing for a demonstration. The final death toll had risen to thirty-four. No one knows where or how the idea came about, but it was immediately taken up by everyone, the bodies were not to be buried in cemeteries like the ordinary dead, their graves were to remain per omnia sæcula sæculorum in the landscaped area opposite the station. However, a few families known for their right-wing allegiances and who were utterly convinced that the attack had been the work of a terrorist group with, as all the media affirmed, direct links to the conspiracy against the present government, refused to hand over their innocent dead to the community. Yes, they clamored, they truly were innocent of all guilt, because they had all their lives respected their own rights and those of others, because they had voted as their parents and their grandparents had, because they were orderly people and had now become the victims and martyrs of this murderous act of violence. They also alleged, in another tone entirely, perhaps so as not to scandalize anyone with such a lack of civic solidarity, that they had their own historical family vaults and it was a deep-rooted family tradition that those who had always been united in life should remain so after death, again per omnia sæcula sæculo-rum. The collective burial would not, therefore, be of thirty-four bodies, but twenty-seven. This was still a large number of people. Sent by who knows who, but certainly not by the council, which, as we know, will be without a leader until the interior minister approves the necessary appointment of a re-placement, anyway, as we were saying, sent by who knows who, there appeared in the garden a vast machine with many arms, one of those so-called multipurpose machines, like a gigantic quick-change artist, which can uproot a tree in the time it takes to utter a sigh and which would have been capable of digging twenty-seven graves in less time that it takes to say amen, if the gravediggers from the cemeteries, who were equally attached to tradition, had not turned up to carry out the work by hand, that is, using spade and shovel. What the machine had, in fact, come to do was to uproot half a dozen trees that were in the way, so that the area, once trodden down and leveled, looked as if it had been born to be a cemetery and a place of eternal rest, and then it, the machine that is, went off and planted the trees and the shade that they cast elsewhere.

Three days after the attack, in the early morning, people started to flood out into the streets. They were silent and grave-faced, many carried white flags, and all wore a white armband on their left arm, and don't let any experts in the et-iquette of funeral rites go telling you that white cannot be a sign of mourning, when we are reliably informed that it used to be so in this very country, and we know that it has always been so for the Chinese, not to mention the Japanese, who, if it was left up to them, would all be wearing blue. By eleven o'clock, the square was already full, but all that could be heard was the great breathing of the crowd, the dull whisper of air entering and leaving lungs, in and out, feeding with oxygen the blood of these living beings, in, out, in, out, until suddenly,

we will not finish the phrase, that moment, for those who have
come here, the survivors, has not yet come. There were innumerable white flowers, quantities of chrysanthemums, roses,
lilies, especially arum lilies, the occasional translucent white
cactus flower, and thousands of marguerites which were forgiven their black hearts. Lined up twenty paces apart, the cof-
fins were lifted onto the shoulders of the relatives and friends
of the deceased, those who had them, and carried in procession
to the graves, where, under the skilled guidance of the professional gravediggers, they were slowly lowered down on ropes
until, with a hollow thud, they touched bottom. The ruins of
the station still seemed to give off a smell of burned flesh. It
will seem incomprehensible to some that such a moving ceremony, such a poignant display of collective grief, was not
graced by the consolatory influence that would doubtless have
come from the ritual practices of the country's sundry religious
institutions, thus depriving the souls of the dead of their most
certain viaticum and depriving the community of the living of
a practical demonstration of ecumenicalism that might have
contributed to leading the straying population back to the fold.
The reason for this deplorable absence can only be explained
by the various churches' fear that they might become the focus
of suspicions, possibly tactical, or at worst strategic, of conniv-
ing with the blank-voting insurgency. This absence might also
have to do with a number of phone calls, with minimal variations on the same theme, made by the prime minister himself,
The nation's government would find it deeply regrettable if the
chance presence of your church at the funeral service, while,
of course, spiritually justified, should come to be considered,
and subsequently exploited, as evidence of your political, and
even ideological, support for the stubborn and systematic disrespect with which a large part of the capital's population continues to treat the legitimate and constitutional democratic au-

thority. The burials were, therefore, purely secular, which is
not to say that, here and there, a few private, silent prayers did
not rise up to the various heavens to be welcomed there with
benevolent sympathy. The graves were still open, when someone, doubtless with the best of intentions, stepped forward to
give a speech, but this was immediately repudiated by the other
people present, No speeches, we each have our own grief and
we all feel the same sorrow. And the person who came up with
this clear formulation of feelings was quite right. Besides, if
that were the intention of the frustrated orator, it would be
impossible to make a funeral oration for twenty-seven people,
both male and female, not to mention some small child with
no history at all. Unknown soldiers do not need the names that
they used in life in order to be showered with the right and
proper honors, and that's fine, if that's what we agree to do, but
if these dead, most of them unrecognizable, and two or three of
them still unidentified, want anything, it is to be left in peace.
To those punctilious readers, showing a praiseworthy concern
for the good ordering of the story, who want to know why the
usual, indispensable dna tests were not carried out, the only
honest answer we can give is our own total ignorance, allow us,
however, to imagine that the famous and much-abused expression, Our dead, so commonplace, so much part of the routine
patter of patriotic harangues, were to be taken literally in these
circumstances, that is, if these dead, all of them, belong to us,
we should not consider any of them exclusively ours, which
would mean that any dna analysis which took into account all
the factors, including, in particular, the non-biological ones,
and however hard it rummaged around inside the double helix,
would only succeed in confirming a collective ownership which
required no proof anyway. That man, or perhaps woman, had
more than enough reason to say, as we noted above, Here, we
each have our own grief and we all feel the same sorrow. Mean-

while, the earth was shoveled back into the graves, the flowers were shared out equally, those who had reasons to weep were embraced and consoled by the others, if such a thing is possible with such a recent grief. The loved one of each person, of each family, is here, although one does not know quite where, perhaps in this grave, perhaps in that, it would be best if we wept over all of them, as a shepherd once so rightly said, although heaven knows where he learned it, One can show no greater respect than to weep for a stranger.

The trouble with these narrative digressions, taken up as we have been with bothersome detours, is that one can find, too late, of course, almost without noticing, that events have moved on, have gone on ahead, and instead of us announcing what is about to happen, which is, after all, the elementary duty of any teller of tales worth his salt, all we can do is to confess contritely that it already has. Contrary to what we had supposed, the crowd has not dispersed, the demonstration continues and is now advancing en masse, filling the streets, in the direction, as the shouts are telling us, of the presidential palace. And on the way lies neither more nor less than the prime minister's official residence. The journalists from press, radio and television, who are at the head of the demonstration, take nervous notes, describe the events over the phone to the offices where they work, and excitedly unburden themselves of their professional and citizenly disquiets, No one seems to know quite what is going to happen, but we have reason to fear that the crowd is preparing to storm the presidential palace, which does not exclude, indeed we would say it remains highly likely, the possibility that they will also sack the prime minister's official residence and any ministerial buildings they pass on the way, this is not some apocalyptic vision, the mere fruit of our own fears, you have only to see the people's distraught faces, it would be no exaggeration to say that each of those faces is calling for blood and destruction, and thus, although it pains us to have to say this out loud and to the whole country, we reach the dreadful conclusion that the government, which has shown itself to be so efficient in other ways and was, for that very reason, applauded by all honest citizens, acted with a reprehensible lack of caution when it decided to abandon the city to the instincts of the angry mob, without the fatherly, dissuasive presence of the police on the streets, with no riot squads, with no tear-gas, no water cannon, no dogs, in a word, unchecked. This speech warning of certain disaster reached a peak of media hysteria when they came in sight of the prime minister's residence, a bourgeois mansion, late-eighteenth-century in style, where the journalists' shouts became screams, Now, now, anything could happen, may the holy virgin protect us all, may the glorious and revered spirits of our nation, up there in the empyrean into which they ascended, quell the wrathful hearts of these people. Anything could have happened, it's true, but, in the end, nothing did, apart from the demonstration, the small section of it that we can see, coming to a halt at the crossroads where the mansion, with its small surrounding park, occupies one corner, the rest of the crowd spilled over onto the pavements, into the adjoining squares and streets, if the police arithmeticians were here, they would say that, all in all, there were only about fifty thousand people, when the exact number, the real number, because we counted them all, one by one, was ten times higher.

It was here, where the demonstration had come to a halt and was standing in absolute silence, that a sharp-eyed television reporter discovered amidst that sea of heads a man whose face, despite half of it being covered by a dressing, he nonetheless recognized, especially since he had been lucky enough to catch a fleeting glimpse of his normal, healthy face, which, as is perfectly understandable, both confirms and is confirmed by the wounded half. Dragging his cameraman along behind him,

the reporter began pushing his way through the crowd, saying to the people on either side of him, Excuse me, excuse me,
may I come through, out of the way, please, this is very important, and then, when he was getting close, Sir, sir, excuse me,
although what he was thinking was less polite, What the hell
is this guy doing here. Reporters usually have good memories
and this particular reporter had not forgotten the public attack delivered by the council leader on the night of the bomb
blast and of which the news networks had been the entirely un-
deserving targets. Now the council leader would find out just
how wounded they had been. The reporter stuck the microphone in his face and made a kind of secret sign to the cameraman which could as easily have meant Start recording as
Beat him to a pulp, and which, in the present situation, probably meant both, Sir, may I say how astonished I am to see
you here, Astonished, why, For the reason I've just given, to
see you taking part in this demonstration, Well, I'm a citizen
like any other, I can demonstrate when and how I want to, especially now that there's no need to ask for authorization, But
you're not just any citizen, you're the council leader, No, I'm
not, I stopped being council leader three days ago, I'd have
thought that was common knowledge by now, It's the first I've
heard of it, we haven't received any official statement about it
as yet, from the council or from the government, You're surely
not expecting me to call a press conference, You resigned, No,
I walked out, Why, The only answer I have is a closed mouth,
mine, The city's population will want to know why their council leader, As I said, I'm no longer council leader, Why their
council leader has joined an anti-government demonstration,
This is not an anti-government demonstration, it's a demonstration of grief, the people here came to bury their dead, The
dead have been buried and yet the demonstration is continuing, how do you explain that, Ask these other people, At the

moment, it's your opinion I'm interested in, Well, I'm just going where they're going, Do you sympathize with the electors
who cast blank votes, with the blankers, They voted as they
wanted to vote, and whether I sympathize or not is irrelevant,
And what about your party, what will they say when they find
out you joined the demonstration, Ask them, You're not afraid
they'll impose sanctions on you, No, What makes you so sure,
For the simple reason that I no longer belong to the party, Did
they expel you, No, I left, just as I left the post of council leader,
What was the interior minister's reaction, Ask him, Who has
taken over from you or will take over, Find out for yourself,
Will we see you on more demonstrations, Turn up and you'll
find out, So you've left the party on the right, in which you've
spent your entire political career, and have gone over to the
left, One day, I hope to understand just where it is I have gone,
Sir, Don't call me that, Sorry, force of habit, and I have to confess to feeling confused, Careful, now, moral confusion, because
I'm assuming your confusion is moral, is the first step along the
path to disquiet and after that, as you yourselves are so fond
of saying, anything can happen, No, I really am baffled, sir, I
don't know what to think, Turn off the recording equipment,
your bosses might not like what you just said, and, please, don't
call me sir, The camera is already off, Just as well, that way you
won't get yourself into any trouble, They say that the demonstration is heading for the presidential palace, Ask the organ-
izers, Where are they, who are they, Everyone and no one, I
suppose, There must be a leader, movements like this don't organize themselves, spontaneous generation doesn't exist, still
less in the case of mass actions on this scale, Not until now,
no, Do you mean that you don't believe the blank vote movement was spontaneous, It's outrageous of you to make such an
inference, My impression is that you know much more about
this business than you're letting on, The time always comes

when we discover that we knew much more than we thought we did, now, leave me alone and get on with your job, find someone else to question, look, the sea of heads has started to move, What amazes me is that there isn't a single shout, a single long live or down with, not a single slogan saying what it is the people want, just this threatening silence that sends shivers down your spine, Forget the horror movie language, perhaps people are just tired of words, If people get tired of words, then I'll be out of a job, You won't say a truer word all day, Goodbye, sir, Once and for all, I'm not sir anymore. The leading front quarter of the demonstration had turned back on itself, now it was going up a steep slope toward a long, broad avenue at the end of which it would turn to the right and receive on its face the cool caress of the breeze from the river. The presidential palace was about two kilometers away, on the flat. The reporters had received orders to leave the demonstration and to run on to take up positions outside the palace, but the general idea, amongst both the professionals working on the ground and those back at the editorial desks, was that, from the point of view of news interest, the coverage had been a pure waste of time and money, or to put it more crudely, a real kick in the balls for the media, or, in more delicate and refined terms, an undeserved slight. These guys aren't even any good at demonstrations, they said, they might at least throw the odd stone, burn the president in effigy, break a few windows, sing one of the old revolutionary songs, anything to show the world that they're not as dead as the people they've just buried. The demonstration did not live up to their expectations. The people arrived and filled the square, they stood for half an hour staring in silence at the closed-up palace, then they dispersed, and, some walking, others in buses, still others cadging lifts from supportive strangers, they all went home.

This peaceful demonstration did what the bomb had failed

to do. Troubled and frightened, the loyal voters of the party
on the right and the party in the middle, or the p.o.t.r. and
the p.i.t.m., gathered together in their respective family councils and decided, each according to their own lights, but unanimous as regards their final decision, to leave the city. They felt
that the current situation, another bomb that might tomorrow
be aimed at them, the rabble taking over the streets with absolute impunity, should convince the government of the need to
revise the rigorous parameters they had established when imposing the state of siege, especially the scandalous injustice of
having the same harsh punishment fall, without distinction, on
the steadfast defenders of peace and on the declared fomenters
of disorder. So as not to embark on this venture blindly, some
of them, with friends in high places, set about sounding out by
telephone the government's likely position on giving authorization, explicitly or tacitly, that would allow those who, quite
rightly, were already beginning to describe themselves as prisoners in their own country, to enter free territory. The answers
received, generally vague and in some cases contradictory,
while not allowing them to draw hard and fast conclusions regarding the government's thinking on the matter, were, nevertheless, sufficient for them to admit as a valid hypothesis that, if
certain conditions were observed and certain material compen-
sations stipulated, the success of the escape, even though it was
relative, even though not all their requests could be met, was,
at least, conceivable, which meant that they could at least hold
out some hope. For a week, in absolute secrecy, the committee
responsible for organizing future convoys of cars, made up in
equal numbers of militants of different categories from both
parties and with the presence of consultants drawn from the
capital's various moral and religious institutions, debated and
finally approved an audacious plan of action which, in memory of the famous retreat of the ten thousand, received, on the

suggestion of a learned hellenist from the party in the middle, the name of xenophon. The families who were candidates for emigration were given three days and no more to decide, with pencil in hand and a tear in the eye, what they could take with them and what they would have to leave behind. Human nature being what we know it to be, there were, inevitably, examples of selfish fancies, feigned distractions, treacherous appeals to an all-too-easy sentimentality, deceptively seductive maneuverings, but there were also cases of admirable selflessness, of the kind that still allow us to believe that if we persevere in these and other such gestures of worthy abnegation, we will, in the end, more than fulfill our small part in the monumental project of creation. The withdrawal was set for the early hours of the fourth day, which would, as it turned out, be a night of wild rain, but that would not be a problem, on the contrary, it would give this collective migration a touch of heroism to be remembered and inscribed in the family annals as a clear demonstration that not all the virtues of the race had been lost. Now, having to transport one person in a car quietly and with the weather in repose is not the same as having to keep the windscreen wipers flailing back and forth like mad things just to keep at bay the sheets of water falling from the sky. One grave problem, which would be minutely debated by the committee, was the question placed on the table as to how the casters of blank votes, commonly known as blankers, would react to this mass flight. It is important to bear in mind that many of these anxious families live in buildings that are also inhabited by tenants who come from the other political shore and who might take a deplorably vengeful attitude and, to put it mildly, obstruct their departure or, more brutally, stop it altogether. They'll puncture our tyres, said one, They'll erect barricades on the landings, said another, They'll jam the lifts, offered a third, They'll put silicon in the locks of the cars, added the first,

They'll smash the windscreens, suggested the second, They'll attack us as soon as we step out of the front door, They'll hold grandpa hostage, sighed another in such a way that made one think that this was, unconsciously, precisely what he wanted. The discussion went on, becoming more and more impassioned, until someone reminded them that the behavior of all those thousands of people during the demonstration had, however you looked at it, been impeccable, I'd even say exemplary, and consequently there seemed little reason to fear that things would now be any different, In fact, I think they'll be relieved to be rid of us, That's all very well, intervened a sceptic, they may be lovely people, wonderfully gentle and responsible, but there is something we have, alas, forgotten, What's that, The bomb. As we said on a previous page, this committee, of public salvation, as it occurred to someone to call it, a name that was immediately rejected for more than justified ideological reasons, was broadly representative, which means that on this occasion there were over two dozen people sitting round the table. You should have seen the reaction. Everyone else present bowed their head, then an admonitory look reduced to silence, for the rest of the meeting, the rash person who appeared to be ignorant of a basic tenet of social behavior which teaches that in the house of the hanged man, one should never mention the word rope. The embarrassing incident had one virtue, it brought everyone together in agreement on the optimistic thesis they had formulated. What happened next would prove them right. At precisely three o'clock on the morning of the appointed day, just as the government had done, the families started leaving home with their suitcases large and small, their bags and their bundles, their cats and their dogs, the occasional tortoise roused from its sleep, the occasional Japanese fish in a bowl, the occasional cage of parakeets, the occasional macaw on a perch. But the doors of the other tenants did not open,

no one came out onto the landing to make fun of the spectacle, no one made jokes, no one insulted them, and it was not
just because it was raining that no one went and leaned out of
the windows to watch the convoys driving off in their different directions. Naturally, with all the noise, just imagine, going
down the stairs dragging all that junk, the lifts buzzing up and
down, the suggestions, the sudden alarms, Careful with the piano, careful with the tea service, careful with the silver platter,
careful with the painting, careful with grandpa, naturally, we
were saying, the tenants in the other apartments woke up, but
none of them got out of bed to go and peer through the spy
hole in the front door, they merely said to each other as they
snuggled down beneath the blankets, They're leaving.

THEY almost all came back. To echo the words used by the interior minister some days before when obliged by the prime minister to explain the discrepancy between the size of the bomb he had been ordered to plant and the bomb that had actually exploded, there was, in the case of this exodus, another grave failure in the chain of command. As experience has never tired of showing us, after long examination of many cases and their respective circumstances, victims not infrequently bear some responsibility for the misfortunes that befall them. Preoccupied as they were with political negotiations, none of which, as will soon become apparent, had been carried out at a high enough level to ensure the perfect execution of operation xenophon, the busy leaders of the committee had forgotten, or perhaps such a thing had simply never entered their heads, to check that the military would also be informed of their escape and, equally important, of the agreements they had reached. Some families, a half dozen at most, did manage to cross the line at one of the frontier posts, but this was because the young officer in charge had allowed himself to be convinced not just by the fugitives' repeated protestations of ideological purity and loyalty to the regime, but by their insistent declarations

that the government knew about their retreat and had approved it. Meanwhile, in order to free himself from the doubts
that soon assailed him, he phoned two other posts nearby, and
his colleagues there were kind enough to remind him that their
orders, since the beginning of the blockade, had been not to let
through a living soul, not even someone on their way to save
their father from the gallows or to give birth to a new baby in
their house in the country. Terrified that he had made the
wrong decision, which would doubtless be perceived as flagrant
and possibly premeditated disobedience of orders received,
with the consequent court-martial and more than likely loss of
rank, the officer gave orders for the barrier to be lowered at
once, thus blocking the kilometer-long caravan of cars and
vans, all packed to the gills, that stretched back along the road.
The rain continued to fall. Needless to say, brought face to face
with their responsibilities, the committee members did not
stand by waiting for the red sea to part. Mobile phone in hand,
they started waking up all the influential people whom they
felt could safely be wrenched from sleep without provoking
too angry a reaction, and it is quite possible that the whole
complicated affair could have been resolved in the best possible
way for the anxious fugitives had it not been for the fierce in-
transigence of the minister of defense, who decided to dig his
heels in, No one gets through without my say-so, he said. As
you will no doubt have guessed, the committee had forgotten
to consult him. You might say that a minister of defense is not
that important, that above a minister of defense there is a prime
minister to whom the former owes obedience and respect, that
higher still, is a president who is owed the same, if not greater,
obedience and respect, although, if truth be told, as far as this
particular president is concerned, this is mostly a matter of
show. And indeed, after a hard dialectical battle between the
prime minister and the minister of defense, in which the rea-

sons put up by both sides flashed and flickered like an exchange of tracer bullets, the minister finally surrendered. He was greatly put out, it's true, and in the blackest of moods, but he nevertheless gave in. You will naturally want to know what decisive, unanswerable argument the prime minister used to force his recalcitrant interlocutor into submission. It was simple and direct, My dear minister, he said, put that brain of yours to work and imagine the consequences tomorrow were we to shut the doors today on the very people who voted for us, As I recall, the order from the cabinet was to let no one pass, May I congratulate you on your excellent memory, but when it comes to orders, one has, from time to time, to be prepared to bend them, especially when it suits one to do so, which is precisely the case now, Sorry, I don't understand, Allow me to explain, tomorrow, once this problem has been resolved, with subversion crushed and spirits calmed, we will call new elections, isn't that right, It is, Do you think we could expect those we had turned away to vote for us again, No, they probably wouldn't, And we need those votes, remember, the party in the middle is hot on our heels, Yes, I understand, In that case, please give the order to allow the people to pass, Yes, sir. The prime minister put down the phone, looked at his watch and said to his wife, At this rate, I might be able to get another hour and a half or two hours' sleep, and added, I have a feeling that fellow will be sent packing at the next cabinet reshuffle, You shouldn't let people be so rude to you, said his other half, No one is ever rude to me, my love, they merely take advantage of my good nature, that's all, It comes to the same thing, she retorted, turning out the light. Before five minutes had passed, the telephone rang once more. It was the minister of defense again, Forgive me, prime minister, I'm sorry to interrupt your well-deserved rest, but unfortunately I have no option, What is it now, A detail we failed to notice, What detail, asked the prime minister, not

bothering to disguise the touch of irritation he felt at the other
man's use of we, It's quite simple, but very important, Get on
with it and don't waste my time, Well, I was just wondering
how we can be sure that all the people trying to leave the capital belong to our party, should we just take their word for it that
they voted in the elections, couldn't some of the hundreds of
vehicles queuing up along the roads be carrying subversive
agents ready to infect with the blank plague the parts of the
country that are as yet uncontaminated. The prime minister
felt his heart contract when he realized he had been caught out,
It's certainly a possibility to bear in mind, he murmured, That's
precisely why I phoned you again, said the minister of defense,
giving the screw another turn. The silence that followed these
words demonstrated once more that time has nothing to do
with the time told by clocks, those small machines made of
wheels that do not think and springs that do not feel, devoid of
a spirit that would allow them to imagine that five insignificant
seconds counted off, one, two, three, four, five, could be an agonizing torment for the person at one end of the phone and a
pool of sublime pleasure for the other. The prime minister
drew one striped pajama sleeve across his forehead, which was
now beaded with sweat, then, choosing his words carefully, he
said, The matter clearly requires a different approach, a careful
evaluation that looks at the problem in the round, cutting corners is always a mistake, My view precisely, How is the situation at the moment, asked the prime minister, Very tense on
both sides, at some posts, they've even had to fire shots in the
air, Do you have any suggestion to make as minister of defense,
In more maneuverable conditions, I would order them to
charge, but with all those cars blocking the roads, it's impossible, What do you mean charge, Well, I would get the tanks out,
And when the snouts of the tanks came into contact with the
first car, and I know tanks don't have snouts, it's just a manner

of speaking, what, in your opinion, would happen then, People normally take fright when they see a tank advancing on them, But, as I have just heard from your own lips, the roads are blocked, Yes, sir, So it wouldn't be easy for the car at the front to turn round, No, sir, it would be very difficult indeed, but then, one way or another, if we don't let them in, they're going to have to do that, But not in the state of panic that would inevitably be provoked by the sight of a phalanx of tanks with their guns pointing straight at them, No, sir, In short, you have no idea how to resolve the problem, said the prime minister, ramming the point home, sure now that he had taken back both control and the initiative, I'm afraid not, prime minister, Nevertheless, I am grateful to you for having drawn my attention to an aspect of the matter that had escaped me, It could have happened to anyone, Yes, to anyone, but it shouldn't have happened to me, You have so many things to think about, And now I have another, solving a problem for which the minister of defense has failed to find a solution, If that is how you feel, then I offer my resignation, Now I don't think I heard that and I don't think I want to, Yes, prime minister. There was another silence, shorter this time, barely three seconds, during which it was clear that the sublime pleasure and the agonizing torment had changed places. Another phone rang in the room. His wife answered it, she asked who was calling, then whispered to her husband, at the same time covering the mouthpiece of the phone, It's the interior minister. The prime minister gestured to her to wait, then issued his orders to the minister of defense, I want no more shots fired in the air and I want the situation stabilized until we can take the necessary measures, make it known to the people in the first few cars that the government is currently studying the situation and hopes to come up with proposals and directives shortly, and emphasize that everything will be resolved for the good of the country and of national security, May I remind you, prime minister, that there are hundreds of cars, So, We can't get the message to all of them, Don't worry, as long as the first cars at each post know, they'll make sure the information passes, like a powder trail, to the back of the queue, Yes, sir, Keep me informed, Yes, sir. The following conversation, with the interior minister, would be different, Don't waste any time telling me what's happened, I know already, They may not have told you that shots have been fired, It won't happen again, Ah, Now what we need to do is to get those people to turn round and go back, But if the army hasn't managed to do so, They haven't and they couldn't, you surely don't want the minister of defense to send in the tanks, Of course not, prime minister, From now on, the responsibility is yours, The police are no use in these situations and I have no authority over the army, Ah, but I wasn't thinking of the police, neither was I considering appointing you army chief of staff, Forgive me, prime minister, but I don't understand, Get your best speechwriter out of bed and put him straight to work, and meanwhile tell the media that the interior minister will speak on the radio at six o'clock, the television and the press can wait, it's the radio that matters now, It's almost five o'clock, prime minister, You don't have to tell me that, I have a watch, Sorry, I merely wanted to point out that there isn't much time, If your speechwriter can't come up with thirty lines in fifteen minutes, with or without syntax, then you'd better put him out in the street, And what should he write, Oh, any old line of argument that will convince these people to go home, that will inflame their patriotic feelings, tell them they're committing the crime of lèse-patrie by abandoning the capital to the subversive hordes, tell them that all those who voted for the parties who built the current political system, including, inevitably, the party in the middle, our direct competitor, constitute the first line of defense of all democratic institutions, tell them that the homes they have left behind them unprotected will be burgled and looted by insurrectionist gangs, but don't tell them that we will, if necessary, burgle them ourselves, We could add that any citizen who decides to return home, regardless of age or social class, will be considered by the government to be a loyal promoter of legality, Promoter doesn't seem to me quite the right word, it's too vulgar, too commercial, besides, legality is getting more than enough promotion, we spend all our time talking about it, All right, then, defenders, heralds or legionnaires, Legionnaires is better, it sounds strong, martial, defenders is a term that lacks pride, it would give a negative impression of passivity, and heralds has a whiff of the middle ages about it, whereas the word legionnaire immediately suggests combative action, an aggressive mindset, and is also, as we know, a word with solid traditions, Let's just hope that the people on the road hear the message, It would seem, my dear fellow, that waking up too early clouds your perceptive faculties, I would bet my post as prime minister that at this very moment every one of those car radios is turned on, what matters is that news of the broadcast to the nation is announced at once and the announcement repeated every minute, What I fear, prime minister, is that these people may not be in a frame of mind to be convinced, if we tell them there's going to be a statement from the government, they will more than likely think that we're going to authorize them to cross the frontier, and their subsequent disappointment could have very grave consequences, It's very simple, your speechwriter is going to have to justify both the bread that he eats and his salary, he's got the lexical and rhetorical skills, let him sort it out, If I may just give voice to an idea that has only this minute occurred to me, Feel free to give voice to anything you like, but may I just point out that we are wasting time, it's already five past five, The statement would carry much more force if you, as prime minister, were to make it, Oh,

I don't doubt it for a moment, In that case, why don't you, Because I am reserving myself for another occasion, one more suited to my station, Ah, I think I understand, It is, after all, merely a matter of common sense or, shall we say, hierarchical gradation, just as it would offend against the dignity of the nation's supreme court for the president to go on the radio to ask a few drivers to get off the roads, so must this prime minister be protected from everything that might trivialize his status as leader of the government, Hm, I see the idea, Good, it's a sign that you've finally managed to wake up, Yes, prime minister, And now to work, by eight o'clock at the latest, I want those roads cleared, and make sure the television companies get out there with all the terrestrial and aerial means at their disposal, I want the whole country to see the reports, Yes, sir, I'll do what I can, You won't do what you can, you will do what is necessary to obtain the results I have just demanded of you. The interior minister did not have time to respond, the prime minister had put the phone down. That's how I like to hear you talk, said his wife, Well, when someone gets my dander up, And what will he do if he can't solve the problem, He'll be given his marching orders and sent packing, Like the minister of defense, Exactly, You can't just dismiss ministers as if they were servants, They are servants, Yes, but you'll only have to find new ones, That is a subject that requires calm consideration, What do you mean, consideration, Look, I'd rather not talk about it at the moment, But I'm your wife, no one can hear us, your secrets are my secrets, All I mean is that, bearing in mind the gravity of the situation, it would come as no surprise to anyone if I myself were to take on the portfolios of defense and the interior, that way the state of national emergency would be reflected in the structures and workings of the government, that is, total co-ordination and total centralization, that could be our watchword, It would be a huge risk, you could win everything or lose every-

thing, Yes, but if I could triumph over a subversive action unparalleled anywhere, at any time, an action that attacked the
system's most sensitive organ, that of parliamentary represen-
tation, then I would be assured of a lasting place in history, a
unique place, as the savior of democracy, And I would be the
proudest of wives, whispered his wife, slithering closer to him,
as if touched by the magic wand of a rare brand of lust, a mix-
ture of carnal desire and political enthusiasm, but her husband,
conscious of the gravity of the hour and making his the harsh
words of the poet, Why do you grovel before my rough boots?
/ Why do you loosen your perfumed hair / and treacherously
open your soft arms? / I am nothing but a man with coarse
hands / and a cold heart / and if, in order to pass, / I had to
trample you underfoot / then, as you well know, I would trample you underfoot, abruptly threw off the bedclothes and said,
I'm going to my study to keep an eye on developments, you
go back to sleep, rest. The thought flashed through his wife's
mind that, in a critical situation like this, when moral support
would be worth its weight in gold, always supposing moral support had a weight, the widely accepted code of basic marital
obligations, in the chapter on mutual help, determined that she
should, without summoning the maid, immediately get up and
prepare with her own hands a comforting cup of tea with the
appropriate alimentary accompaniment of a few plain biscuits,
instead, annoyed, frustrated, with her nascent lust quite evaporated, she turned over in bed and firmly closed her eyes, in the
faint hope that sleep might still be able to make use of the rem-
nants of that lust to put on a brief, private, erotic fantasy for
her. Oblivious to the disappointments he had left behind him,
and wearing over his striped pajamas one of those silk dressing-
gowns adorned with exotic motifs, with Chinese pavilions and
golden elephants, the prime minister went into his study, turned
on all the lights, and switched on first the radio and then the

television. The television screen still showed only the test card, it was too early for broadcasting to begin, but all the radio stations were already talking animatedly about the monstrous traffic jams on the roads, and opinions were bandied about on what was clearly an attempt at a mass escape from the unhappy prison into which the capital, through its own stupid fault, had been transformed, although there were also comments to the effect that such an unusually large circulatory blockage would mean that the vast trucks that brought food into the city every day would be unable to get through. These commentators did not yet know that these same trucks were being held, on strict orders from the army, three kilometers from the frontier. Radio reporters, traveling on motorbikes, questioned people all along the lines of cars and vans and were able to confirm that this was, indeed, a properly organized collective action, bringing together whole families, in order to escape the tyranny and the suffocating atmosphere which the forces of subversion had imposed on the city. Some household heads complained about the delay, We've been here for nearly three hours and the queue hasn't moved a millimeter, while others protested that they had been betrayed, They promised us we'd be able to get through with no problem, and here you have the brilliant result, the government bolted, went on holiday and threw us to the lions, and now, when we had our chance to get out too, they have the nerve to slam the door in our face. There were hysterical outbursts, children crying, old people white-faced with fatigue, angry men who had run out of cigarettes, exhausted women trying to impose some order on the desperate family chaos. The occupants of one car tried to turn round and drive back into the city, but were forced to give up under the hail of insults and abuse that fell on them, Cowards, black sheep, blankers, bastards, spies, traitors, sons of bitches, now we know why you came, to demoralize us decent folk, but if you think we're going to let you go, you've got another think coming, if necessary, we'll let your tyres down and see if that teaches you some respect for other people's sufferings. The phone rang in the prime minister's study, it could be the minister of defense, or the interior minister, or the president. It was the president, What's going on, why wasn't I informed immediately about the general pandemonium along all the routes out of the capital, he asked, Sir, the government has the situation under control, the problem will soon be resolved, Yes, but I should have been informed, you owe me that courtesy at least, Well, I felt, and I take personal responsibility for the decision, that there was no reason to interrupt your sleep, but I was going to phone you in about twenty minutes or half an hour, but, as I say, I take full responsibility, president, Good, good, that was kind of you, but if my wife were not in the healthy habit of getting up early, I, the president, would still be sleeping while the country burns, It's not burning, president, all the appropriate measures have been taken, Don't tell me you're going to bomb the lines of vehicles, As you should know by now, president, that is not my style, It was, of course, just a manner of speaking, obviously I never thought you would commit such a barbaric act, The radio should soon announce that the interior minister will address the nation at six o'clock, there it is, they're giving the first announcement now, and there will, of course, be others, it's all organized, president, Well, at least, that's something, It's the beginning of success, president, I have complete confidence that we will be able to persuade these people to return to their homes in peace and good order, And if they don't, If they don't, the government will resign, Oh, don't play that old trick on me, you know as well as I do that, in the situation in which the country finds itself, I couldn't accept your resignation even if I wanted to, Yes, I know, but I had to say it, Fine, anyway, now that I'm awake, be sure to keep me up to date on what's hap-

pening. The radios kept insisting, We interrupt the programme
once again to inform our listeners that the interior minister
will, at six o'clock, be making a statement to the nation, we repeat, at six o'clock the interior minister will make a statement
to the nation, we repeat, a statement will be made to the nation
by the interior minister at six o'clock, we repeat, at six o'clock
the nation will be made a statement by the interior minister,
the ambiguity of this last reformulation did not go unnoticed
by the prime minister, who remained for a few seconds smiling
at his own thoughts, amusing himself by wondering how the
devil an interior minister could make the nation into a statement. He might have reached some conclusion that could have
proved of future use had the test card on the television screen
not vanished to give way to the usual image of the flag flapping
lazily on the flagpole, as if it, too, had just woken up, while the
national anthem blasted out with its trombones and drums,
with the odd clarinet trill in the middle and a few persuasive
belches from the bass tuba. The presenter who then appeared
had the knot in his tie all awry and a sour look on his face, as if
he had just been the victim of some insult that he would not
readily forgive or forget, Considering the gravity of the political and social situation, he said, and in accordance with the
population's sacred right to have access to a free and diverse
news media, we are starting our broadcast early today. Like
many of those listening, we have just learned that the interior
minister will be speaking on the radio at six o'clock, presumably to express the government's attitude to the attempted exodus from the city by many of its inhabitants. This television
company does not believe that it has been the object of any deliberate and intentional discrimination, but, rather, that through
some inexplicable misunderstanding, unexpected in highly experienced politicians such as those who form the present national government, this particular company was somehow for-

gotten. At least, apparently. There will be those who will point out the relatively early hour at which the statement is to be made, but the employees of this network, throughout its long history, have given more than sufficient proof of their self-sacrifice, their dedication to the public cause and their unalloyed patriotism, not to be relegated now to the humiliating condition of bearers of secondhand news. We are confident that, before the hour fixed for the promised statement, it may still be possible to reach a basis for agreement which, without wishing to take away what has been given to our colleagues in public radio, will restore to us that which, by merit, belongs to us, that is, our position and our responsibility as the country's prime news medium. While we await this agreement, and we hope to receive news of it at any moment, we wish to report that a television helicopter is lifting off even as I speak, in order to offer our viewers the first images of the vast queues of vehicles, whose planned withdrawal was, we have learned, given the evocative and historic name of xenophon, and which now stand immobilized all along the city's exit routes. Fortunately, the rain that has been beating down on the selfless convoys all night stopped over an hour ago. The sun will soon rise above the horizon and break through the dark clouds. Let us hope that its appearance will also remove the barriers which, for reasons we fail to understand, still prevent these our courageous compatriots from reaching freedom. May they, for the good of the nation, prove successful. The following images showed the helicopter in the air, then, looking down, the tiny heliport from which it had taken off, and, afterward, the first view of the nearby roofs and streets. The prime minister put his right hand on the phone. He did not have to wait long, Prime minister, began the interior minister, Yes, I know, no need to say anything, we made a mistake, We made a mistake, you say, Yes, we did, because if one of us was wrong and the other failed to correct

him, then the mistake belongs to both, But I don't have your
authority or your responsibility, prime minister, Ah, but you
had my trust, So what do you want me to do then, You will
speak live on television and there will be a simultaneous radio
broadcast, problem solved, And we don't bother to reply to the
impertinent terms and tone in which the gentlemen of the television station chose to refer to the government, In time, we
will, but not now, I'll deal with them later, Good, You've got the
statement with you, Yes, of course, do you want me to read it to
you, No, don't bother, I'll wait to hear it live, It's nearly time, I
must go, Are they expecting you, then, asked the prime minister, puzzled, Yes, I told my secretary of state to negotiate with
them, Without my knowledge, You know as well as I do that we
had no alternative, Without my approval, insisted the prime
minister, Let me remind you that I had your trust, those are
your words, besides, if one makes a mistake and the other cor-
rects it, then both are right, If this whole business isn't sorted
out by eight o'clock, I'll expect your immediate resignation,
Yes, prime minister. The helicopter was flying low over one of
the lines of cars, people were waving at it from the road, they
must have been saying to each other, It's the television people,
it's the television people, and the fact that the great gyratory
bird had, indeed, been sent by the television people seemed to
everyone a clear guarantee that the impasse was about to be resolved. If the television cameras are here, they said, that's a
good sign. It wasn't. At six o'clock prompt, when the horizon
was already becoming tinged with pink, the interior minister's
voice boomed out from all the car radios, Dear fellow countrymen and women, in the last few weeks, our nation has been
through what is, without doubt, the most serious crisis recorded in the history of our people since the very dawn of na-
tionhood, never before has there been a more urgent need to
defend national cohesion to the hilt, the behavior of certain

people, a tiny, ill-advised minority of the country's population
as a whole, under the influence of ideas entirely at odds with
the correct functioning of our current democratic institutions
and with the respect that is due to them, has made them the
mortal enemies of that cohesion, which is why, today, a terrible
threat hovers over our normally peaceable society, the threat of
a civil conflict with unforeseeable consequences for the future
of the nation, the government was, needless to say, the first to
understand the thirst for freedom that lay behind the attempted
exodus from the capital carried out by those whom we have always known to be patriots of the first water, people who, in the
most adverse of circumstances, have shown themselves, either
by voting or by the simple example of their day-to-day lives, to
be genuinely incorruptible defenders of legality, restoring and
renewing the very best of the old legionnaire spirit and honor-
ing its traditions by placing themselves at the service of the
public good, the government was also the first to see that, by
firmly turning their backs on the capital, the sodom and gomorrah of our day, these patriots were demonstrating a most
praiseworthy combative spirit which the government does, of
course, recognize, however, taking into consideration the national interest as a whole, it is the government's belief, and, to
this end, we appeal to the minds of those men and women who
have spent so many anxious hours waiting for a clear message
from those responsible for the country's fate, it is, I repeat, the
government's belief, that the most appropriate militant action
to be taken in the present circumstances is for those thousands
of people to reintegrate themselves back into the life of the
capital city, to return to their homes, those bastions of legality,
those centers of resistance, those bulwarks where the unsullied
memory of their ancestors watches over the works of their descendants, it is, I say again, the government's belief that these
sincere and objective reasons, brought to you heart in hands,

should be weighed by those people in their cars listening to this official statement, and although the material aspects of the situation should, of course, count for little in a calculation in which spiritual values are paramount, the government would like to take this opportunity to reveal that it has received information concerning the existence of a plan to burgle and plunder your abandoned homes, a plan which, according to our latest information, has already been set in motion, as I must conclude from the note I have just been handed, for, according to our sources, a total of seventeen apartments have so far been burgled and plundered, as you see, dear countrymen and women, your enemies are wasting no time, only a few hours have passed since your departure, and yet already the vandals are breaking down the doors of your homes, already the barbarians and savages are stealing your possessions, it lies, therefore, in your hands to avoid a still greater disaster, consult your consciences, know that the nation's government is on your side, it is up to you now to decide whether you are for us or against us. Before disappearing from the screen, the interior minister just had time to shoot a look at the camera, and in his face there was self-confidence, but also something that looked very like a challenge, although you would have to be privy to the secrets of the gods to interpret that rapid glance with total accuracy, the prime minister, however, was not fooled, for him it was just as if the interior minister had thrown in his face the words, You who pride yourself on your tactics and your strategies, could not have done better. And he had to agree that he could not, although they would have to wait and see just what the results would be. The helicopter reappeared, and there, once again, was the city, there again were the endless lines of cars. For a good ten minutes, nothing moved. The reporter was struggling to fill in time, he imagined the family councils that would be taking place inside the cars, he praised the minister's statement, he railed against the burglars, demanded that they be treated with all the rigor of the law, but it was obvious that unease was gradually seeping into him, it was plain as plain that the government's words had fallen on stony ground, not that he, still waiting for some last-minute miracle, dared to say so, but any viewer with a reasonable degree of experience in deciphering audiovisuals would have noticed the poor journalist's distress. Then the much-desired, much-longed-for marvel occurred, just when the helicopter was flying over the tail end of one of the queues, the last car in the line turned round, followed by the car ahead, and then by another and another and another. The reporter gave an excited yelp, We are, dear viewers, witnessing a truly historic moment, for, responding with exemplary discipline to the government's appeal, in a display of civic duty that will be inscribed in letters of gold in the annals of the capital, the people are beginning their return home, thus bringing to a peaceful close what could have been a catastrophe with, as the interior minister so rightly said, unforeseeable consequences for the future of our nation. From this point on, for some minutes more, the report took on a decidedly epic tone, transforming the retreat of these ten thousand defeated people into a victorious ride of the valkyries, replacing xenophon with wagner, transmuting into odoriferous sacrifices wafting up to the gods of olympus and valhalla the foul-smelling fumes belching forth from the car exhausts. There were now brigades of reporters on the streets, from the radio and the press, and all were trying to hold the cars back for a moment so as to glean from the passengers, live and from the source itself, some description of the emotions filling them as they set off on their forced return home. As was to be expected, they encountered all sorts, frustration, disappointment, anger, a desire for revenge, we may not have got out this time, but we will the next, edifying affirmations of patriotism, exalted declarations of party loyalty, long live the party of the center, long live the party in the middle, unpleasant odors, annoyance at not having slept a wink all night, take that camera away, will you, we don't want any photographs, agreement or disagreement as to the reasons given by the government, some scepticism about what would happen tomorrow, fear of reprisals, criticism of the authorities' shameful apathy, But there are no authorities, the reporter remarked, That's precisely the problem, there are no authorities, but mainly there was a great concern for the fate of the possessions left behind in the homes to which the occupants of the cars had only expected to return once the revolt of the blankers had been finally crushed, the number of burgled houses will doubtless now be more than seventeen, who knows how many will have been stripped of even their last rug, their last vase. The helicopter was now showing an aerial shot of how the lines of cars and vans, in which those who had been last were now first, branched off as they entered the areas near the center and how, from a certain point onward, it was no longer possible to distinguish amongst the confusion of traffic those who were returning from those who were already there. The prime minister phoned the president, a very brief conversation, an exchange of congratulations, These people must have lukewarm water running in their veins, the president said scornfully, if it had been me in one of those cars, I promise you I would have driven through however many barriers they put in front of me, It's lucky you're the president then, it's lucky you weren't there, said the prime minister, smiling, Yes, but if things start to get difficult again, that will be the moment to implement my idea, About which I still know nothing, One of these days, I'll tell you about it, And you will have my undivided attention, by the way, I'm calling a cabinet meeting for today in order to discuss the situation, it would be very useful if you could be there too, if, that is, you have no more pressing

duties to perform, Don't worry, it's just a matter of re-arranging
things, all I have to do today is go and cut a ribbon somewhere
or other, Very good, sir, I will inform the cabinet. The prime
minister decided that it was high time he said a kind word to
the interior minister and congratulated him on the effective-
ness of his statement, why not, after all, just because he didn't
like the man didn't mean he couldn't recognize that this time
he had coped very well with the problem to be resolved. His
hand was just reaching for the phone when a sudden change in
the voice of the television reporter made him look at the screen.
The helicopter was flying so low now that it was almost touching the rooftops, you could see quite clearly various people
coming out of the buildings, men and women standing on the
pavement, as if they were waiting for someone, We have just
been informed, said the reporter in great alarm, that the images
our viewers are seeing of people leaving the buildings and waiting on the pavement are being repeated at this moment all over
the city, we don't want to think the worst, but everything indicates that the inhabitants of these buildings, who are clearly insurrectionists, are preparing to prevent the people, who yesterday were their neighbors and whose homes they have doubtless
just plundered, from entering the building, if that is so, then,
much as it pains us to say so, the government who ordered the
withdrawal of the police force from the capital must be brought
to book, it is with a heavy heart that we ask ourselves how, or
indeed if, the bloody physical confrontation which is clearly
about to take place can possibly be avoided, president, prime
minister, where are the police who should be defending innocent people from the barbarous treatment these others are preparing to mete out to them, oh, dear god, dear god, whatever is
going to happen next, said the reporter, almost sobbing now.
The helicopter hung motionless in the air, and there was a clear
view of everything that was happening in the street. Two cars

stopped outside the building. The doors opened and the occupants got out. Then the people on the pavement went over to them, This is it, this is it, we must prepare ourselves for the worst, screamed the reporter, hoarse with excitement, then the people exchanged a few inaudible words and, without more ado, began unloading the cars and carrying into the buildings in broad daylight what had been carried out under cover of a dark and rainy night. Shit, exclaimed the prime minister, and thumped the table.

THIS brief scatological interjection, with the expressive potential of an entire speech on the state of the nation, summed up and distilled the depth of disappointment that had gradually been gnawing away at the government's mental energies, in particular the energies of those ministers who, given the nature of their respective posts, had been most closely linked to the different phases of the political and repressive processes brought into play against the forces of sedition, in short, the ministers responsible for defense and the interior, who, from one moment to the next, each in his own field, had lost all the prestige gained from the good services they had rendered to the country during the crisis. Throughout the day, until it was time for the cabinet meeting to start, and, indeed, during it too, that grubby word was frequently muttered in the silence of thought, and, if there were no witnesses close by, even uttered out loud or murmured like some irrepressible unburdening of the soul, shit, shit, shit. It had occurred to neither of those ministers, of defense or the interior, or, which is truly unforgivable, to the prime minister either, to ponder briefly, even in a strict, disinterested academic sense, what might happen to the frustrated fugitives when they returned to their homes, however, if they had bothered to do so, they would probably have got no further than the horrific prophecy of the reporter in the helicopter which we failed to record earlier, Poor things, he was saying, almost in tears, they're going to be massacred, I'm sure of it. In the end, and it was not in that street alone that the marvel occurred, rivaling the most noble historical examples, both religious and profane, of love for one's neighbor, the slandered and insulted blankers went to the aid of the vanquished members of the opposing faction, and each person made this decision entirely on his or her own and in consultation with his or her own conscience, there was no evidence of any order issued from above or of a password to be learned by heart, the fact is that they all came to offer whatever help their strength permitted, and then they were the ones to say, careful with the piano, careful with the tea service, careful with the silver platter, careful with grandpa. It is understandable, therefore, that there should be so many frowning faces around the great cabinet table, so many beetling brows, so many eyes red with anger or from lack of sleep, probably nearly all of these men would have preferred some blood to have been spilt, they would not have wanted the massacre announced by the television reporter, but some incident that would have shocked the sensibilities of the population outside the capital, something that would set the whole country talking for the next few weeks, an argument, a pretext, another reason to demonize these wretched rebels. Which is why one can also understand why the minister of defense has just whispered, out of the corner of his mouth, to his colleague the interior minister, What the hell are we going to do now. If anyone else overheard the question, they were intelligent enough to pretend otherwise, because that was precisely why they were gathered there, to find out what the hell they were going to do now, and they would doubtless not leave the room empty-handed.

The first person to speak was the president of the republic, Gentlemen, he said, in my opinion, and as I think we would all agree, we are living through the most difficult and complex moment since the first election revealed the existence of a vast subversive movement hitherto undetected by the security services, not that we were the ones to make the discovery, for it chose, instead, to reveal itself, the interior minister, whose actions have otherwise always had my personal and institutional support, will, I am sure, agree with me when I say that the worst thing is that we have not, up until now, taken a single effective step toward solving the problem, and, perhaps graver still, we have been forced to watch, powerless, the rebels' brilliant tactic of helping our voters to move all their useless junk back into their apartments, that, gentlemen, could only be the brainchild of some machiavellian mastermind, someone who remains hidden behind the curtain and makes the puppets do exactly as he wants, we all know that we sent those people back out of sheer painful necessity, but now we must prepare ourselves for a more than likely chain reaction that will lead to new escape attempts, not this time of whole families, nor of spectacular convoys of cars, but of isolated individuals or small groups, and not by road, but across country, the minister of defense will assure me that these areas are regularly patrolled, that there are electronic sensors installed all along the frontier, and I could not bring myself to doubt the efficacy of such measures, however, in my view, complete containment can only be achieved by the construction of a wall around the capital, an impassable wall made out of concrete slabs, and, I would say, about eight meters high, using, of course, the system of electronic sensors already in existence and backed up by as many barbed-wire fences as are judged to be necessary, I am firmly convinced that no one would manage to get past that, not even, I would say, a fly, if you'll allow me my little joke, but not so much because

flies couldn't get through it, as because, as far as one can judge
from their normal behavior, they have no reason to fly that
high. The president of the republic paused to clear his throat
and ended by saying, The prime minister already knows about
this proposal of mine and, shortly, he will doubtless submit it
for discussion by the government, who will then, as is their
duty, decide upon the appropriateness and practicability of carrying it out, as for me, I am content in the knowledge that you
will bring all your experience to bear on the matter. A diplomatic murmur went round the table, which the president of the
republic interpreted as one of tacit approval, an idea he would
have had to correct had he heard the minister of finance's muttered remark, And where would we find the money for a crazy
scheme like that.

Having shuffled the documents in front of him from one
side to the other, as was his custom, the prime minister was the
next to speak, The president of the republic, with the brilliance
and rigor we have come to expect, has just given us a clear picture of the difficult and complex situation in which we find
ourselves, and there is, therefore, no point in my adding to his
exposition any details of my own, which would, after all, serve
only to lend further shading to his original sketch, however,
having said that, and in view of recent events, I believe that
what we need is a radical change of strategy, which would pay
special attention, along with all the other factors, to the possibility of the birth and growth in the capital of an atmosphere of
social harmony purely as a consequence of this gesture of unequivocal solidarity, doubtless machiavellian, doubtless politically motivated, to which the whole country has borne witness
in the last few hours, you have only to read the unanimously
complimentary comments in the special editions brought out
by the newspapers, consequently, we have no option but to recognize that all our attempts to make the rebels listen to rea-

son have, each and every one, been a resounding failure, and that the cause of that failure, at least in my opinion, could well have been the severity of the repressive measures we chose to use, and secondly, if we continue with the strategy we have followed up until now, if we continue with the escalation of coercive methods, and if the response of the rebels also continues to be what it has been up until now, which is to say no response at all, we will be forced to resort to drastic measures of a dictatorial nature, such as the indefinite withdrawal of civil rights from the city's population, which, to avoid ideological favoritism, would have to include our own voters too, or, with the aim of preventing the spread of the epidemic, the passing of an emergency electoral law that would apply to the whole country and would make blank votes void, and so on. The prime minister paused to take a sip of water, then went on, I spoke of the need for a change of strategy, however, I did not say that I had such a strategy drawn up and prepared for immediate implementation, we need to bide our time, to allow the fruit to ripen and for brave resolutions to rot, I must confess that I myself would actually prefer a period of slight relaxation during which we could work to gain as much advantage as possible from the few signs of concord that seem to be emerging. He paused again and seemed to be about to continue speaking, but then said only, Now let me hear your opinions.

The interior minister raised his hand, I notice that you are confident of the persuasive influence our voters may have on the minds of those to whom I must confess I was somewhat astonished to hear you refer merely as rebels, but you did not, I believe, speak of the contrary possibility, that the subversives might use their harmful theories to confuse those citizens who are still respecters of the law, You're quite right, I don't think I did mention that possibility, said the prime minister in response, because I imagined that were that to happen, it would

not bring about any fundamental change, the worst possible
consequence would be that the current eighty percent of people
who cast blank votes would become one hundred percent, and
the quantitative change introduced into the problem would
have no qualitative impact, apart, obviously, from creating unanimity. What shall we do then, asked the minister of defense,
That is precisely why we are here, to analyze, consider and decide, Including, I assume, the proposal made by the president
of the republic, which, of course, has my wholehearted support,
The president's proposal, given the scale of the work involved
and its many implications, requires an in-depth study to be un-
dertaken by an ad hoc commission that will have to be set up
for that purpose, on the other hand, it is, I think, fairly obvious
that the building of a wall of partition would not immediately
resolve any of our difficulties and would inevitably create others, the president knows my views on the subject, and the personal and institutional loyalty I owe him would not allow me to
remain silent about it here at this cabinet meeting, but this
does not, I repeat, mean that the commission's work should not
begin as early as possible, as soon as it has been appointed,
within the next few days. The president of the republic was vis-
ibly put out, I am the president, of course, and not the pope,
and I do not, therefore, presume to any kind of infallibility, but
I would like my proposal to be discussed with some urgency, As
I said before, sir, came the prime minister's prompt reply, I give
you my word that you will receive news of the commission's
findings sooner than you might imagine, Meanwhile, I suppose
we'll just have to continue groping our way blindly forward,
said the president. The silence that fell was thick enough to
blunt the blade of even the sharpest of knives. Yes, blindly, he
repeated, unaware of the general embarrassment. From the
back of the room came the minister of culture's calm voice, Just
as we did four years ago. The minister of defense rose, red-

faced, to his feet, as if he had been the object of a brutal, unforgivable obscenity, and, pointing an accusing finger, he said, You have just shamefully broken a national pact of silence to which we all agreed, As far as I know, there was no pact, far less a national one, I was a grown man four years ago, and I have no recollection of the population being summoned to sign a piece of parchment promising never to utter one word about the fact that for several weeks we were all of us blind, You're right, there was no formal pact, said the prime minister, intervening, but we all thought, without any need for any agreement on paper, that the dreadful test we had been through would, for the sake of our mental health, be best thought of as a terrible nightmare, something that existed as a dream rather than as a reality, In public maybe, but you are surely not telling me that you have never spoken about what happened in the privacy of your own home, Whether we have or not is of no importance, a lot of things happen in the privacy of one's home that never go beyond its four walls, and, if I may say so, your allusion to the as yet unexplained tragedy that occurred amongst us four years ago shows a degree of bad taste that I would not have expected in a minister of culture, The study of bad taste, prime minister, must be one of the longest and juiciest chapters in the history of culture, Oh, I didn't mean that kind of bad taste, but the other sort, otherwise known as a lack of tact, It would seem, prime minister, that you share the belief that death exists only because it has a name, that things have no real existence if we have no name to give them, There are endless things for which I don't know the name, animals, vegetables, tools and machines of every shape and size and for all conceivable purposes, But you know that they have names, and that puts your mind at rest, We're getting off the subject, Yes, prime minister, we are getting off the subject, all I said was that four years ago we were blind and what I'm saying now is that we probably still are. The

indignation was general, or almost so, cries of protest leapt up
and jostled for position, everyone wanted to speak, even the
transport minister, who, being possessed of a strident voice,
usually spoke very little, but was now setting his vocal cords to
work, May I speak, may I speak. The prime minister looked at
the president of the republic as if asking his advice, but this
was pure theater, the president's diffident attempt at a gesture,
whatever it was intended to mean, was quashed by the raised
hand of his prime minister, Bearing in mind the emotive and
passionate tone of the interpolations, it is clear that a debate
would get us nowhere, which is why I will let none of you speak,
especially since, possibly without realizing it, the minister of
culture was spot on when he compared the plague currently afflicting us to a new form of blindness, That is not a comparison
of my making, prime minister, I merely remarked that we were
blind and that we very probably continue to be blind, any ex-
trapolation not logically contained in my initial proposition is
not allowable, Changing the position of words often changes
their meaning, but they, the words, when weighed one by one,
continue physically, if I may put it like that, to be exactly what
they were and, therefore, In that case, allow me to interrupt
you, prime minister, I want to make it quite clear that responsibility for any changes in the position or meaning of my words
lies entirely with you and that I had nothing whatsoever to do
with it, Let's say that you provided the nothing and I contributed the whatsoever and that the nothing and the whatsoever
together authorize me to state that the blank vote is as destruc-
tive a form of blindness as the first one, Either that or a form of
clear-sightedness, said the minister of justice, What, asked the
interior minister, who thought he must have misheard, I said
that the blank vote could be seen as a sign of clear-sightedness
on the part of those who used it, How dare you, in the middle
of a cabinet meeting, utter such antidemocratic garbage, you

ought to be ashamed of yourself, no one would think you were the minister of justice, cried the minister of defense, Actually, I wonder if I've ever been more of a minister of justice or for justice than I am at this moment, Soon you'll have me believing that you, too, cast a blank vote, said the interior minister drily, No, I didn't cast a blank vote, but I'll certainly consider doing so next time. When the scandalized clamor of voices resulting from this last statement had begun to die away, a question from the prime minister brought it to a complete halt, Do you realize what you have just said, Yes, so much so that I place in your hands the post with which you entrusted me, I am tendering my resignation, replied the man who was now no longer either minister for or minister of justice. The president of the republic turned pale, he looked like an old rag that someone had distractedly left behind on the back of the chair, I never thought I would live to see the face of treachery, he said, and felt that history was sure to record the phrase, and should there be any risk of history forgetting, he would make a point of reminding it. The man who had up until now been the minister of justice got to his feet, bowed in the direction of the president and the prime minister and left the room. The silence was interrupted by the sudden scraping of a chair, the minister of culture had got up and, from the bottom of the table, in a strong, clear voice, was announcing, I wish to resign too, Oh, come on, don't tell me that, as your friend promised us just now in a moment of commendable frankness, you're considering casting a blank vote next time as well, the prime minister said, trying to be ironic, I doubt that will be necessary, I did so last time, Meaning, Exactly what you heard, nothing more, Kindly leave the room, Yes, prime minister, I was about to, the only reason I turned back was to say goodbye. The door opened, then closed, leaving two empty chairs at the table. Well, exclaimed the president of the republic, we hardly had time to get over the first shock when we got another slap in the face, That was no slap in the face, president, ministers come and ministers go, it's the most common thing in the world, said the prime minister, anyway, the government entered this room with a full complement of ministers and will leave with a full complement, I'll take over the post of justice minister and the minister for public works will take care of cultural affairs, But I don't have the necessary qualifications, remarked the latter, Yes, you do, culture, as certain people in the know are always telling me, is also a public work, it will, therefore, be perfectly safe in your hands. He rang the bell and ordered the clerk who appeared at the door, Take those chairs away, then, addressing the meeting, Let's have a short break of fifteen or twenty minutes, the president and I will be in the next room.

Half an hour later, the ministers resumed their places round the table. The absences went unnoticed. The president of the republic came in looking utterly perplexed, as if he had just been given a piece of news whose meaning was completely beyond his comprehension. The prime minister, on the other hand, seemed very pleased with himself. The reason would soon become clear. When, earlier on, I brought to your attention the urgent need for a change of strategy, given the failure of all the actions drawn up and executed since the beginning of this crisis, he began, I never for one moment expected that an idea capable of carrying us forward to victory would come precisely from a minister who is no longer with us, I refer, as you will doubtless have surmised, to the ex–minister of culture, who has shown once again how important it is to examine the ideas of your adversary in order to discover which aspects of those ideas can be used to your advantage. The ministers of defense and of the interior exchanged indignant glances, that was all they needed, to hear the intelligence of a despised traitor being praised to the skies. The interior minister scribbled a few rapid

words on a piece of paper and passed it to his colleague, My
instinct was right, I distrusted those guys right from the start,
to which the minister of defense replied by the same means
and with the same emotion, There we were trying to infiltrate
them, and it turns out they had infiltrated us. The prime minister was continuing to discuss the conclusions he had reached
based on the ex–minister of culture's sibylline statement about
how we had all been blind yesterday and continued to be blind
today, Our mistake, our great mistake, for which we are paying
right now, lay in that attempt at obliteration, not of our memories, since we would all of us be capable of recalling what happened four years ago, but of the word, the name, as if, as our
ex-colleague remarked, in order for death to cease to exist, we
would simply have to stop saying the word we use to describe it,
Aren't we getting away from the main problem, asked the president of the republic, we need concrete proposals, objectives,
the cabinet is going to have to take some important decisions,
On the contrary, president, this is the main problem, and if I'm
right, this is the idea that will give us, on a plate, the possibility
of resolving once and for all a problem which we have, at most,
managed only to patch up here and there, but those patches
quickly come unstitched and leave everything exactly as it was,
What are you getting at, explain yourself, please, President,
gentlemen, let us dare to take a step forward, let us replace silence with words, let us put an end to this stupid, pointless pretence that nothing happened four years ago, let us talk openly
about what life, if it can be called a life, was like during the
time that we were blind, let the newspapers report it, let writers write about it, let the television show us images of the city
taken immediately after we recovered our sight, let's encourage
people to talk about the many and various evils we had to endure, let them talk about the dead, the disappeared, the ruins,
the fires, the rubbish, the putrefaction, and then, when we have

torn off the rags of false normality with which we have tried
to bind up the wound, we will say that the blindness of those
days has returned in a new guise, we will draw people's attention to the parallel between the blankness of that blindness of
four years ago and the blind casting of blank ballot papers now,
the comparison is crude and fallacious, as I would be the first to
recognize, and there will be those who will reject it at once as
an offence to intelligence, to logic and to common sense, but it
is just possible that many people, and I hope they will soon become the overwhelming majority, will be convinced, will stand
before the mirror and ask themselves if they are, again, blind, if
this blindness, more shameful than the other blindness, is not
leading them from the straight and narrow, propelling them
toward the ultimate disaster which would be the possibly definitive collapse of a political system which, without our even
noticing the threat, carried within it, right from the start, in its
vital nucleus, in the voting process itself, the seeds of its own
destruction or, a no less disquieting hypothesis, of a transition
to something entirely new and unknown, so different that we
would probably have no place in it, raised as we were in the
shelter of an electoral routine which, for generations and generations, managed to conceal what we now realize was one of
its great trump cards. I firmly believe, the prime minister continued, that the strategic change we needed is in sight, yes, the
restoration of the system to the status quo ante is within our
grasp, however, I am the prime minister of this country and not
some vulgar snake-oil salesman promising miracles, but I will
say that, while we may not get results in twenty-four hours, I
am sure we will begin to see them within twenty-four days, the
struggle, though, will be long and hard, because sapping the
energy of this new blank plague will take time and much effort, not forgetting, ah, not forgetting the dreaded head of the
tapeworm, which can hide itself away anywhere, for until we
can locate it in the foul innards of the conspiracy, until we can

drag it out into the light of day to be given the punishment it deserves, that fatal parasite will continue to produce its rings and to undermine the strength of the nation, but we will win the final battle, my word and your word, now and until the final victory, will be the guarantee of that promise. Pushing back their chairs, the ministers rose as one man and stood applauding enthusiastically. Purged of its troublesome members, the cabinet was, at last, a cohesive whole, one leader, one will, one plan, one path. Seated in his armchair, as befitted the dignity of his office, the president of the republic was clapping too, but only with the tips of his fingers, thus letting it be known, as well as by the stern look on his face, how piqued he was not to have been the object of some reference, however minimal, in the prime minister's speech. He should have known better who he was dealing with. When the clamorous crackle of applause was beginning to subside, the prime minister raised his right hand to call for silence and said, Every voyage needs a captain, and during the dangerous voyage on which the country is now embarked, that captain is and must be your prime minister, but woe betide the ship that does not carry a compass to guide it over the vast ocean and through the storms, well, gentlemen, the compass that guides me and the ship, the compass, in short, that guides us all, is here, by our side, always keeping us on course with his vast experience, always encouraging us with his wise advice, always instructing us with his peerless example, a thousand rounds of applause, then, and a thousand thanks to his excellency the president of the republic. The ovation was even warmer than the first and seemed as if it would never end, nor would it end as long as the prime minister continued to clap his hands or until the clock in his head said, Enough, stop there, he's won. Just two minutes more to confirm that victory and, at the end of those two minutes, the president of the republic, with tears in his eyes, was embracing the prime minister. Perfect, nay, even sublime moments can occur in the life of a politician, he said afterward, his voice choked with emotion, but whatever tomorrow may hold for me, I assure you that this moment will never be erased from my memory, it will be my crowning glory in happy times, my consolation in sad ones, I thank you with all my heart, with all my heart, I embrace you. More applause.

Perfect moments, especially when they verge on the sublime, have the grave disadvantage of being very short-lived, which fact, being obvious, we would not need to mention were it not that they have a still greater disadvantage, which is that we do not know what to do once they are over. This awkward pause, however, reduces down to almost nothing when there is an interior minister present. As soon as the cabinet had resumed their usual places, with the minister of public works and culture still wiping away a furtive tear, the interior minister raised his hand to ask permission to speak, Carry on, said the prime minister, As the president of the republic so touchingly pointed out, there are perfect, truly sublime moments in life, and we have had the great privilege of experiencing two such moments here, with the president's speech of thanks and the prime minister's new strategy, which has, of course, received our unanimous approval and to which I will refer in this intervention, not in order to withdraw my applause, nothing could be further from my mind, but, if I may be so immodest, to amplify and facilitate the effects of that strategy, I am referring to what the prime minister said about not being able to guarantee results in twenty-four hours, but being sure of getting them before twenty-four days were up, now, with respect, I do not believe that we can afford to wait twenty-four days, or twenty or fifteen or even ten, cracks are beginning to appear in the social edifice, the walls are shaking, the foundations are trembling, it could all come crashing down at any moment, Do you have any real proposal to make, asked the prime minister, apart from describing the imminent collapse of a building, Oh, yes,

replied the interior minister, unperturbed, as if he had not noticed the prime minister's sarcastic tone, Be so kind as to en-
lighten us, then, First of all, prime minister, I must make it
clear that my proposal is merely intended to complement the
proposal you presented to us and which we approved, it does
not seek to amend, correct or perfect, it is simply another suggestion which is, I hope, deserving of everyone's attention, Oh,
get on with it and stop beating about the bush, get to the point,
What I propose, prime minister, is a rapid action, a shock of-
fensive, with helicopters, You're surely not thinking of bom-
barding the city, Yes, sir, I am, but with paper, With paper, Exactly, prime minister, with paper, first, in order of importance,
we would have a proclamation signed by the president of the
republic and addressed to the population of the capital, second,
a series of brief, punchy messages intended to pave the way and
prepare people's minds for the doubtless slower actions advo-
cated by the prime minister, that is, newspaper articles, television programmes, memories of the time when we were blind,
stories by writers, etc., by the way, I would just mention that
my ministry has its own team of writers, people highly trained
in the art of persuasion, which, as I understand it, writers normally achieve only briefly and after much effort, It seems an
excellent idea to me, said the president of the republic, but obviously the text would have to be submitted to me for my approval so that I could make any changes I deem appropriate,
but, on the whole, I like it, it's a splendid idea, which, above all,
has the enormous political advantage of placing the figure of
the president of the republic in the front line of battle, oh, yes,
a fine idea. The murmur of approval in the room indicated to
the prime minister that this last move had been won by the interior minister, So be it, then, take all the necessary steps, he
said, and on the appropriate page in the government's school
progress report he mentally added another black mark against
the minister's name.

THE reassuring idea that, later or sooner, and, more likely, sooner than later, fate will always strike down pride, was roundly confirmed by the humiliating opprobrium suffered by the interior minister, who, believing that he had, in extremis, won the latest round in the pugilistic battle in which he and the prime minister had been engaged, saw his plans fizzle out after an unexpected intervention from the skies, which, at the last moment, decided to change sides and join the enemy. However, in the final analysis and, indeed, in the first, the blame for this, in the view of the most attentive and competent of observers, lay entirely with the president of the republic for having delayed his approval of the manifesto which, bearing his signature and intended for the moral edification of the city's inhabitants, should have been distributed by the helicopters. During the three days that followed the cabinet meeting the celestial vault revealed itself to the world in its magnificent suit of seamless blue, perfect weather, smooth and faultless, and above all with no wind, ideal for hurling papers out into the air and watching them float down, dancing the dance of the elves, to be picked up by anyone who happened to be passing or who had come out into the street curious to learn what news or orders were drifting down from above. During those three days, the much-thumbed text traipsed back and forth between the presidential palace and the ministry of the interior, sometimes more profuse in arguments, sometimes more concise in ideas, with words crossed out and replaced by others that would immediately suffer the same fate, with phrases which, shorn of what went before, no longer fitted what came after, so much wasted ink, so much torn-up paper, this, we will have you know, is what is meant by the torment of writing, the torture of creation. On the fourth day, the sky, grown tired of waiting, and seeing that things down below still kept chopping and changing, decided to start off the morning covered by a layer of low, dark clouds, of the sort that usually bring the rain they promise. By late morning, a few sparse droplets had begun to fall, stopping now and then and starting up again, an irritating drizzle which, despite threatening more, seemed unlikely to get much worse. This on-off state of affairs continued until midafternoon, and then, suddenly, without warning, like someone who has grown weary of hiding his true feelings, the heavens opened to give way to a continuous, steady, monotonous rain, intense but not violent, the kind of rain that can continue falling for a whole week and for which farmers are generally grateful. Not so the ministry of the interior. Even assuming that the air force's supreme command would authorize the helicopters to take off, which, would, in itself, be highly problematic, hurling papers down from above in weather like this would be utterly ridiculous, and not just because there would be hardly any people in the streets, and the main concern of the few who were would be to remain as dry as possible, even worse was the thought that the presidential manifesto might land in the mud, be swallowed up by the devouring drains, might crumble and dissolve in the puddles that the wheels of cars splash rudely through, throwing up fountains of grubby water as they go, in

truth, in truth I say to you, only a fanatical believer in legality and the respect one owes to one's superiors would bother
to stoop down and rescue from the ignominious slime an explanation about the relationship between the general blindness
of four years ago and this majority blindness now. To the interior minister's vexation, he had to stand by and watch, powerless, as, on the pretext of the ongoing and unpostponable
national emergency, the prime minister, with, moreover, the
reluctant agreement of the president of the republic, set in motion the media machinery, encompassing press, radio, television and all the other written, aural and visual submedia available, both current and concurrent, whose task it would be to
persuade the capital's population that it was, alas, once more
blind. When, days later, the rain stopped and the upper air had
once more clothed itself in azure, only the stubborn and ultimately angry insistence of the president of the republic managed to get the postponed first part of the plan put into action,
My dear prime minister, said the president, do not think for a
moment that I have reneged on or am even considering reneg-
ing on the decision taken by the cabinet, I continue to believe
that it is my duty to address the nation personally, But, sir, it really isn't worth it, the clarification process is already underway
and I'm sure we'll soon be getting results, Those results could
be about to appear around the corner the day after tomorrow,
but I want my manifesto to be launched first, The day after tomorrow is, of course, just a manner of speaking, All the better, get that manifesto distributed now, Believe me, sir, A word
of warning, if you don't do it, I'll blame you for the inevitable
loss of personal and political trust between us, Allow me to remind you, sir, that I still have an absolute majority in parliament, any threatened loss of trust would be merely personal in
nature and would have no political repercussions, It would if I
made a statement to parliament declaring that the word of the

president of the republic had been hijacked by the prime minister, Please, sir, that isn't true, It's true enough for me to say
so, in parliament or out of it, Distributing the manifesto now,
The manifesto and the other papers, Distributing the manifesto now would be pointless, That's your opinion, not mine,
But president, The fact that you call me president means that
you recognize me as such, so do as I say, Well, if you put it like
that, Oh, I do, and another thing, I'm tired of watching your
battles with the interior minister, if you think he's no good,
then sack him, but if you don't want to sack him or can't, then
put up with it, if you yourself had come up with the idea of a
manifesto signed by the president, you would probably have
issued orders for it to be delivered door to door, Now that's
unfair, sir, Maybe it is, I don't deny it, but people get upset and
lose their temper and end up saying things they didn't intend
to or hadn't even thought, Let's consider the matter closed, All
right, the matter is closed, but tomorrow morning I want those
helicopters in the air, Yes, president.

　　If this acerbic exchange had not taken place, if the presidential manifesto and the other leaflets had, because unnecessary, ended their brief life in the rubbish, the story we are telling would have developed quite differently from this point on.
We can't imagine exactly how or in what way, we just know it
would have been different. Obviously, any reader who has been
paying close attention to the meanderings of the plot, one of
those analytical readers who expects a proper explanation for
everything, would be sure to ask whether the conversation between the prime minister and the president of the republic was
simply added at the last moment to justify such a change of
direction, or if it simply had to happen because that was its
destiny, from which would spring soon-to-be-revealed consequences, forcing the narrator to set aside the story he was intending to write and to follow the new course that had sud-

denly appeared on his navigation chart. It is difficult to give
such an either-or question an answer likely to satisfy such a
reader totally. Unless, of course, the narrator were to be unusually frank and confess that he had never been quite sure how
to bring to a successful conclusion this extraordinary tale of a
city which, en masse, decided to return blank ballot papers, in
which case this violent exchange of words between the prime
minister and the president of the republic, which ended so happily, would have been as welcome to him as flowers in May.
What other explanation is there for his abrupt abandonment
of the complex narrative thread he had been developing merely
in order to set off on gratuitous digressions not about what-
did-not-happen-but-might-have, but about what-did-happen-
but-might-not-have. We are referring, to put it plainly, to the
letter which the president of the republic received three days
after the helicopters had showered the capital's streets, squares,
parks and avenues with the colored leaflets in which the ministry of the interior's writers set out their conclusions about
the likely connection between the tragic collective blindness
of four years ago and the present-day electoral madness. The
signatory was fortunate in that his letter fell into the hands of
a particularly scrupulous clerk, the sort who looks at the small
print before he starts reading the large, the sort who is capable of discerning amongst the untidy scrawl of words the tiny
seed that requires immediate watering, if only to find out what
it might grow into. This is what the letter said, Your excellency,
Having read, with due and deserved attention, the manifesto
addressed by you to the people and, in particular, to the inhabitants of the capital, and being keenly aware both of my duty as
a citizen of this country and of the need, during the crisis into
which the nation is currently plunged, for every one of us to
maintain a close, constant, zealous watch for anything strange
that we might see now or might have seen in the past, I wish to

bring to the attention of your excellency's renowned powers of judgement a few unknown facts which may help toward a better understanding of the nature of the plague that befell us. I say this because, although I am just an ordinary man, I believe, as you do, that there must be some link between the recent blindness of casting blank ballot papers and that other blindness which, for weeks that none of us will ever forget, made us all outcasts from the world. What I am suggesting, your excellency, is that the first blindness might perhaps help to explain this blindness now, and that both might be explained by the existence, and possibly by the actions, of one person. Before going on, however, impelled as I am by a sense of civic duty upon which I would challenge anyone to cast doubt, I wish to make it clear that I am not an informer or a sneak or a grass, I am simply trying to be of service to my country in the distressing situation in which it currently finds itself, without so much as a lantern with which to illumine the path to salvation. I do not know, how could I, if the letter I am writing will be enough to light that lantern, but I repeat, duty is duty, and at this moment, I see myself as a soldier taking a step forward and presenting myself as a volunteer for a mission, and this mission, your excellency, consists in revealing, and I use the word reveal because this is the first time I have spoken of this matter to anyone, that four years ago, together with my wife, I fell in with a group of people who, like so many others, were struggling desperately to survive. It will seem that I am not telling you anything that you, through your own experiences, do not know already, but what no one knows is that one of the people in our group, the wife of an ophthalmologist, did not go blind, her husband went blind like the rest of us, but she did not. At the time, we made a solemn vow never to speak about the matter, she said that she did not want to be seen afterward as a rare phenomenon, to be subjected to questions and submitted to

examinations once we had all recovered our sight, that it would
be best just to forget and pretend it had never happened. I have
respected that vow until today, but can no longer remain silent. Your excellency, allow me to say that I would feel deeply
offended if this letter were seen as a denunciation, although,
on the other hand, perhaps it should be seen as such, because,
and this is something else you do not know, during that time,
a murder was committed by the person I am telling you about,
but that is a matter for the courts, I content myself with the
thought that I have done my duty as a patriot by drawing your
lofty attention to a fact which has, until now, remained a secret
and which, once examined, might perhaps produce an explanation for the merciless attack of which the present political
system has been the target, this new blindness which, if I may
humbly reproduce your excellency's own words, strikes at the
very foundations of democracy in a way in which no totalitar-
ian system ever succeeded in doing. Needless to say, sir, I am
at your disposal, or at the disposal of whichever institution is
charged with carrying out what is clearly a necessary investigation, to amplify, develop and elaborate on the information contained in this letter. I assure you that I feel no animosity toward
the person in question, however, what counts above all else is
this our nation, which has found in you the most worthy of
representatives, that is my one law, the only one I hold to with
the serenity of a man who has done his duty. Yours faithfully.
There followed the signature and below that, on the left, the
signatory's full name, address and telephone number, as well as
his identity card number and e-mail address.

The president of the republic slowly placed the piece of paper on his desk and, after a brief silence, asked his cabinet secretary, How many people know about this, No one apart from
the clerk who opened it and recorded the letter in the register,
Can he be trusted, Yes, I suppose so, president, he's a party

member, but it might be a good idea to let him know that the slightest hint of disloyalty on his part could cost him very dear, and, if I may make a suggestion, that warning should be delivered directly, By me, No, sir, by the police, it's more effective that way, the man is summoned to the main police station where the toughest policeman they have takes him into an interrogation room and puts the fear of god into him, Oh, I don't doubt the results would be excellent, but I see one grave difficulty, What's that, sir, It will be a few days before the case reaches the police and, meanwhile, the fellow's tongue will start to wag, he'll tell his wife, his friends, he might even talk to a journalist, in short, he'll drop us in the soup, You're quite right, sir, the solution would be to have an urgent word with the chief of police, if you like, sir, I'll happily do that myself, Short-circuit the hierarchical chain of government, go over the prime minister's head, is that your idea, Obviously I wouldn't dare to do so if the case were not so serious, sir, My friend, in this world, and, as far as we know, there is no other, everything gets out in the end, now while I believe you when you say that the clerk is to be trusted, I couldn't say the same of the chief of police, what if, as is more than likely, he's in cahoots with the interior minister, imagine the fuss there would be, the interior minister demanding an explanation from the prime minister because he can't demand one from me, the prime minister wanting to know if I'm trying to by-pass his authority and his responsibilities, in a matter of hours, the thing we are trying so hard to keep secret will be out in the open, Once again, sir, you are right, Well, I wouldn't go so far as to say, as a certain fellow politician once did, that I'm always right and rarely have any doubts, but I'm not far off, So what shall we do, sir, Send the man in, The clerk, Yes, the one who read the letter, Now, In another hour it might be too late. The cabinet secretary used the internal phone to summon the clerk, Come to the president's office immediately and be quick about it. Walking down the various corridors and through the various rooms usually took at least five minutes, but the clerk appeared at the door after only three. He was breathing hard and his legs were shaking. There was no need to run, said the president, smiling kindly, The cabinet secretary said I should be quick, sir, said the clerk, panting, Good, now the reason I wanted to see you was this letter, Yes, sir, You read it, of course, Yes, sir, Do you remember what was in it, More or less, sir, Don't use such expressions with me, answer my question, Yes, sir, I remember it as if I had read it this minute, Do you think you could try to forget its contents, Yes, sir, Think carefully now, you know, of course, that trying to forget and actually forgetting are not the same thing, No, sir, they're not, So mere effort won't be enough, you'll need to do something more, You have my word of honor, sir, You know, I was almost tempted to tell you again not to use such expressions, but I'd prefer you to explain precisely what you so romantically call your word of honor means to you in the present situation, It means, sir, a solemn declaration that, whatever happens, I will in no way divulge the contents of the letter, Are you married, Yes, sir, Right, I'm going to ask you a question, And I will answer it, sir, Supposing you were to reveal the nature of the letter to your wife and only to your wife, do you think you would, in the strict sense of the term, be divulging anything, I refer, of course, to the letter, not to your wife, No, sir, because divulge, strictly speaking, means to broadcast, to make public, Correct, I am pleased to see that you know your etymologies, But I wouldn't even tell my wife, Do you mean that you will tell her nothing, Nor anyone else, sir, Give me your word of honor, Forgive me, sir, but I already have, Imagine that, I had forgotten already, if the fact escapes me again, the cabinet secretary here will remind me, Yes, sir, said the two voices in unison. The president fell silent for a few seconds, then asked, What if I were to look in the letter register and see what you had written, can you save me the bother of getting out of my chair and tell me what I would find there, Just one word, sir, You must have a remarkable capacity for synthesis if you can sum up such a long letter in one word, Petition, sir, What, Petition, that's the word in the register, Nothing more, Nothing more, But that way no one will know what the letter is about, That was exactly my thinking, sir, that it would be best if no one knew, the word petition covers everything. The president leaned contentedly back and gave the prudent clerk a broad, toothy smile, then he said, Well, if you had said that in the first place you wouldn't have had to give away something as serious as your word of honor, One precaution guarantees the other, sir, Not bad, not bad at all, but have a look at the register from time to time, just in case someone should think to add something else to the word petition, I've already blocked the line, sir, so that nothing can be added, You can go now, As you wish, sir. When the door had closed, the cabinet secretary said, I must confess I hadn't thought him capable of showing such initiative, I believe we have just satisfactorily proved to ourselves that he deserves our trust, He might deserve yours, said the president, but not mine, But I thought, You thought rightly, my friend, but, at the same time, wrongly, the safest way of categorizing people is not by dividing them up into the stupid and the clever, but into the clever and the too clever, with the stupid, we can do what we like, with the clever, the trick is to get them on our side, whereas the too clever, even when they're on our side, are still intrinsically dangerous, they can't help it, the oddest thing is that in everything they do, they are constantly warning us to be wary of them, but, generally speaking, we pay no attention to the warnings and then have to face the consequences, Do you mean to say, sir, Yes, I mean that our prudent clerk, that prestidigitator of the letter register, capable of transforming a troubling letter like that into a mere petition, will soon be getting a call from the police so that they can give him the fright that you and I, between ourselves, had promised him, he himself said as much, though without quite realizing it, one precaution guarantees the other, You're right as usual, sir, you're always so far-sighted, Yes, but the biggest mistake I made in my political life was letting them sit me down in this chair, I didn't realize at the time that the arms of this chair had handcuffs on them, That's because it's not a presidentialist regime, Exactly, and that's why all they allow me to do is cut ribbons and kiss babies, Now, though, you're holding a trump card, As soon as I hand it to the prime minister, it will be his trump card, and I will simply have acted as postman, And the moment he hands it to the interior minister, it will belong to the police, since the police are at the end of the assembly line, You've learned a lot, I'm at a good school, sir, Do you know something, I'm all ears, sir, Let's leave the poor devil alone, who knows, tonight, when I get home, or later on, in bed, I might tell my own wife what the letter said, and you, my dear cabinet secretary, will probably do the same, your wife will look at you as if you were a hero, her own sweet husband privy to all the secrets and webs that the state weaves, who's in the know, who inhales, without benefit of a mask, the putrid stench of the gutters of power, Please, sir, Oh, take no notice, I don't think I'm as bad as the worst, but sometimes I'm suddenly very conscious that that isn't enough, and my soul aches more than I can say, Sir, my mouth is and will remain closed, As will mine, as will mine, but there are times when I imagine what the world would be like if we all opened our mouths and didn't stop talking until, Until what, sir, Oh, nothing, nothing, leave me alone now.

Less than an hour had passed when the prime minister, summoned urgently to the palace, entered the office. The president gestured to him to sit down and, as he handed him the letter, said, Read this and tell me what you think. The prime minister sat down in the chair and started to read. He must have been about halfway through the letter when he looked up with an interrogative expression on his face, like someone who has not quite grasped what someone has just said to him, then he went on and, without further interruptions or other gestural manifestations, read to the end. A patriot full of good intentions, he said, and, at the same time, a complete swine, Why a swine, asked the president, If what he says here is true, if this woman, always assuming she did exist, really didn't go blind and helped these six other people to survive that terrible time, it is not beyond the bounds of possibility that the writer of this letter owes her the good fortune of being alive today, my parents might be alive too if they had had the good fortune to meet her, He says that she murdered someone, No one knows for certain how many people were killed during that period, president, it was decided that all the bodies found had died accidentally or from natural causes and the matter was laid to rest, Even things laid to rest can be woken, That's true, president, but, in this case, I don't feel it would be for the best, it's highly unlikely there were any witnesses to the crime and, even if there were, they were just the blind amongst the blind, it would be absurd, a complete nonsense, to bring that woman to trial for a murder no one saw her commit and where the corpus delicti does not exist, The writer of the letter states that she killed someone, Yes, but he doesn't say that he was a witness to the murder, besides, sir, as I said before, the person who wrote this letter is a complete swine, Moral judgements are beside the point, As I well know, sir, but it does one good sometimes to say what one feels. The president took the letter back, looked at it as if it wasn't there and asked, What do you think you'll do, Me, nothing, replied the prime minister, there isn't a thread of evidence to go on, You noticed, of course, that the writer of the letter suggests

the possibility of a link between the fact that this woman didn't
go blind and the massive casting of blank votes that got us into
this mess in the first place, Sir, we haven't always agreed with
each other, That's only natural, Yes it is, as natural as it is for me
not to have the slightest doubt that your intelligence and your
common sense, which I greatly respect, will reject out of hand
the idea that a woman, simply because she did not go blind four
years ago, should today be deemed responsible for the fact that
a few hundred thousand people, who had never even heard of
her, chose to cast blank ballot papers when summoned to vote
in an election, Well, put like that, There is no other way to put
it, sir, my advice is to file the letter under correspondence from
crazies and let the matter drop, while we continue the search
for a solution to our problems, real solutions, not the fantasies
or grudges of an imbecile, You're quite right, I was taking a lot
of inconsequential twaddle far too seriously and I've wasted
your time by asking you to come over here to see me, Oh, that
doesn't matter, sir, my wasted time, if you want to call it that,
has been more than made up for by our having reached agreement, Thank you, I'm glad you see it like that, Right, then, I'll
leave you to get on with your work and I'll return to mine. The
president of the republic was about to hold out his hand to
say goodbye when the phone rang. He picked up the receiver
and heard his secretary say, The interior minister would like
to speak to you, sir, Put him through. The conversation was a
long one, the president listened and, as the seconds passed, the
expression on his face altered, sometimes he murmured Yes,
on one occasion he said It's certainly worth looking into, and
he ended with the words Speak to the prime minister about
it. He put the receiver down, That was the interior minister,
And what did that delightful man want, He's received a letter
along the same lines and he's decided to begin an investigation, Bad news, But I told him to talk to you first, So I heard,

but it's still bad news, Why, If I know the interior minister, and I'm sure few can know him as well as I do, he will have already spoken to the chief of police by now, Stop him, Oh, I'll try, but I'm afraid it might be useless, Use your authority, What, and be accused of blocking an investigation into facts that affect the nation's security, at a moment when everyone knows that the nation is in grave danger, asked the prime minister, adding, You would be the first to withdraw your support from me, the agreement we've just reached would be a mere illusion, it already is, since it serves no purpose. The president nodded, then said, A little while ago, in connection with this letter, my cabinet secretary came out with a very illuminating phrase, What was that, He said that the police were at the end of the assembly line, Let me congratulate you, sir, on having such an excellent cabinet secretary, meanwhile, you had better warn him that there are some truths that should not be spoken out loud, This room is soundproof, That doesn't mean there aren't a few microphones hidden about the place, Perhaps I'd better have the room searched, Please believe me when I say that, if you do find any microphones, I was not the one who ordered them to be placed here, Very funny, Very sad, May I say how sorry I am, my friend, that circumstances have left you in this blind alley, Oh, there'll be some way out, although, I confess, I can't see one at the moment, and going back is impossible. The president accompanied the prime minister to the door, It's odd, he said, that the man who wrote the letter didn't write to you as well, He probably did, but your secretariat and that of the interior minister are clearly more diligent than mine, Very funny, No, sir, very sad.

THE letter addressed to the prime minister, because there was a letter, took two days to reach his hands. He realized at once that the clerk in charge of recording the letter had been less discreet than the president's clerk, how else explain the rumors that had been flying around for the last two days, rumors which, in turn, were either the result of a leak by mid-level civil servants eager to demonstrate that they were au courant or in the know, or else had been deliberately started by the ministry of the interior as a way of stopping in its tracks any attempt by the prime minister to oppose the police investigation or, however symbolically, obstruct it. There remained the possibility, which we will describe as the conspiracy theory, that the supposedly secret conversation between the prime minister and his interior minister that took place after the former had been summoned to the presidential palace, had been far less private than one might have thought, given the padded walls, which, who knows, may have concealed a few latest-generation microphones, of the kind that only an electronic gun dog with the finest pedigree could sniff out and find. Whatever the truth of the matter, there was nothing to be done about it, it is a sad moment for state secrets, which have no one to defend them.

The prime minister is so conscious of this deplorable certainty, so convinced of the pointlessness of secrets, especially when they have ceased to be so, that, with the look of someone observing the world from a very high vantage point, as if he were saying Don't say a word, I know everything, he slowly folded the letter up and put it in one of his inside jacket pockets, It came straight from the blindness of four years ago, I'll keep it with me, he said. The air of shocked surprise on his cabinet secretary's face made him smile, Don't worry, my friend, there are at least two other letters identical to this, not to mention the many photocopies that are doubtless already doing the rounds. His cabinet secretary's face suddenly assumed a look of feigned innocence or abstraction, as if he had not quite understood what he had heard, or as if his conscience had suddenly leapt out at him along the road, accusing him of some ancient, or else very recent, misdeed. You can go now, I'll call you if I need you, said the prime minister, getting up from his chair and going over to one of the windows. The noise he made in opening it concealed the sound of the door closing. From there, he could see little more than a succession of low roofs. He felt a nostalgia for the capital city, for the happy times when voters did as they were told, for the monotonous passing of the hours and days spent either at his petit-bourgeois official residence or at the national parliament, for the agitated and not infrequently jolly and amusing political crises, which were like sudden eruptions of foreseeable duration and controlled intensity, almost always put on, and through which one learned not only not to tell the truth, but, when necessary, to make it correspond, point by point, with the lie, just as the wrong side and the right side of things are, quite naturally, always found together. He wondered if the investigation would already have begun, he paused to speculate upon whether the agents taking part in the police action would be those who had fruitlessly remained behind in

the capital charged with obtaining information and submitting
reports, or if the interior minister would have preferred, for
this new mission, people whom he knew and trusted, who were
to hand and within easy reach, and, who knows, were seduced
by the glamorous movie adventure element of a clandestine
breaking of the blockade, crawling, with a knife tucked in their
belt, underneath barbed-wire fences, outwitting the dreaded
electronic sensors with magnetic desensitizers, and emerging
on the other side in enemy territory, heading for their objective, like moles endowed with the agility of a cat and with night-
vision glasses. Knowing the interior minister as he did, only
slightly less bloodthirsty than dracula, and even more theatri-
cal than rambo, this was sure to be the mode of action he would
order them to adopt. He was absolutely right. Hidden in the
small area of forest that almost borders the perimeter of the
besieged city, three men are waiting for night to become early
dawn. However, not everything that the prime minister imagined from his office window corresponds to the reality we see
before us. For example, these men are dressed in plain clothes,
there are no knives tucked into belts, and the weapon they have
in their holster is the gun which is always so reassuringly described as regulation. As for the dreaded magnetic desensitizers, there is, amongst the various bits of apparatus the men are
carrying, nothing that looks as if it fulfilled that function, which,
when one thinks about it, could mean merely that magnetic desensitizers are quite simply and deliberately made not to look
like magnetic desensitizers. We will soon learn, however, that,
at a pre-arranged time, the electronic sensors in this section of
the border will be turned off for five minutes, which was considered more than enough time for three men, one by one,
without undue haste or hurry, to cross the barbed-wire barrier,
part of which was cut today precisely for the purpose of avoiding torn trousers and lacerated skin. The army's sappers will be

back to repair it before the rosy fingers of dawn return to reveal the threatening barbs rendered harmless only very briefly, as well as the enormous rolls of wire stretching out along both sides of the frontier. The three men are already through, in front goes the leader, who is the tallest, and they cross, in indian file, a field whose wet grass oozes and squeaks beneath their shoes. On a minor road on the outskirts of the city, about five hundred meters from there, a car is waiting to carry them through the silence of the night to their destination in the capital, a bogus insurance and reinsurance company which a complete dearth of clients, whether local or foreign, had not as yet managed to bankrupt. The orders that these men received directly from the lips of the interior minister are clear and categorical, Bring me results and I won't ask by what means you obtained them. They have no written instructions with them, no safe-conduct pass to cover them or which they could show as a defense or as a justification if things should turn out worse than they expect, and there is, of course, always the possibility that the ministry would simply abandon them to their fate if they committed some action that might prejudice the state's reputation and the immaculate purity of its objectives and processes. These three men are like a commando group entering enemy territory, there seems no reason to think that they will risk their lives there, but they are all aware of the delicate nature of a mission that demands a talent for interrogation, flexibility in drawing up strategy and swiftness in carrying it out. All to the maximum degree. I don't think you'll need to kill anyone, the interior minister had said, but if, in an extreme situation, you consider that there's no other option, then don't hesitate, I'll sort things out with the minister for justice, Whose post has just been taken over by the prime minister, remarked the leader of the group. The interior minister pretended not to hear, he merely glared at the importunate speaker, who had no alternative but to look away. The car drove into the city, stopped in a square so that they could change drivers, and finally, after going round various blocks thirty or so times in order to throw off any unlikely pursuer, deposited them at the door of the building where the insurance and reinsurance office has its base. The porter did not come out to see who was arriving at what was a most unusual hour for an office building, one assumes he had received a visit from someone the previous afternoon who had persuaded him gently to go to bed early and advised him not to slip out from between the sheets, even if insomnia kept him from closing his eyes. The three men took the lift up to the fourteenth floor, went down a corridor to the left, another to the right, a third to the left, and finally reached the office of providential ltd, insurance and reinsurance, as anyone can read on the notice on the door, in black letters on a tarnished, rectangular brass plate, affixed with nails that have brass heads in the shape of truncated pyramids. They went in, one of the subordinates turned on the light, the other closed the door and put the security chain on. Meanwhile the leader of the group walked through the various rooms, checked phone lines, plugged in machines, went into the kitchen, into the bedrooms and bathrooms, opened the door to what was intended to be the filing room and had a quick look at the various armaments stored in there, at the same time breathing in the familiar smell of metal and lubricant, he will inspect it all properly tomorrow, piece by piece, weapon by weapon. He summoned his assistants, sat down and told them to sit down too, Later this morning, at seven o'clock, he said, we will begin the work of following the suspect, notice that I call him the suspect, even though, as far as we know he has committed no crime, I do so not only to simplify communication between ourselves, but also because, for security reasons, it is best that his name is not mentioned, at least not during these first few days, I would add that with this operation, which I hope will last no longer than a week, our first objective is to get an idea of the suspect's movements around the city, where he works, where he goes, who he meets, the usual routine for a basic investigation, reconnoitring the terrain before making a direct approach, Should he be aware that he's being followed, asked the first assistant, Not for the first four days, but after that, yes, I want him to feel worried, uneasy, Having written that letter, he must surely be expecting someone to come looking for him, We'll do that when the moment comes, what I want, and it's up to you to achieve this effect, is to frighten him into thinking that he's being followed by the people he denounced, By the doctor's wife, No, not by her, but by her accomplices, the people who cast the blank votes, Aren't we taking things a bit fast, asked the second assistant, we haven't even started work yet, and here we are talking about accomplices, All we're doing is making a preliminary sketch, a simple sketch, that's all, I want to put myself in the shoes of the guy who wrote that letter and, from there, try to see what he sees, Well, a week spent tailing the guy seems far too long to me, said the first assistant, it should take us three days at most to bring him to boiling point. The leader frowned, he was going to say, Look, I said one week and it will be one week, but then he remembered the interior minister, he didn't recall him having expressly asked for rapid results, but since that is the demand most often heard from the lips of those in charge, and since there was no reason to think that the present case would be any exception, quite the contrary, he showed no more reluctance in agreeing to the period of three days than that considered normal between a superior and a subordinate, on the rare occasions when the person issuing the orders is forced to give in to the reasoning of the person receiving them. We have photographs of all the adults who live in the building, I mean, of course, those of the male sex, said the leader, adding unnecessarily, One of them is that of the man we are looking for, We can't start following him until we've identified him, said the first assistant, True, replied the leader, but nevertheless, at seven o'clock, I want you to be strategically positioned in the street where he lives and to follow the two men you think most closely resemble the kind of person who would have written that letter, that's where we'll start, intuition and a good police nose must have their uses, Can I say something, asked the second assistant, Of course, To judge by the tone of the letter, the guy must be a total bastard, Does that mean, asked the first assistant, that we should only follow the ones who look like bastards, then he added, Although in my experience, the worst bastards are precisely the ones who don't look like they're bastards, It would have made much more sense to have gone straight to the identity card people and asked for a copy of the guy's photograph, it would have saved time and work. Their leader decided to cut this discussion short, I presume you're not intending to teach the priest to say the our father or the mother superior the hail mary, if they didn't tell us to do that it must be because they didn't want to arouse any curiosity that could have caused the operation to be aborted, With respect, sir, I disagree, said the first assistant, everything indicates that the guy is dying to spill the beans, in fact, I think if he knew we were here, he'd be banging on our door right now, You may be right, said the group leader, struggling to control the irritation he felt at what had every appearance of being a devastating critique of his plan of action, but we want to know as much as we can about him before we make direct contact, How's this for an idea, piped up the second assistant, Not another one, said his chief sourly, This is a good one, I guarantee it, one of us disguises himself as an encyclopedia salesman, that way we'll be able to see who opens the door, That encyclopedia salesman trick went out with the ark, said the first assistant, besides, it's usually the wives who come to open the door, I mean, it would be a great idea if our man lived on his own, but, as I recall from what he says in the letter, he's married, Oh, rats, exclaimed the second assistant. They sat in silence, looking at each other, the two assistants knowing that the best thing now would be to wait for their superior to have an idea of his own. They would, in principle, be prepared to applaud it even if it was as leaky as an old boat. The leader of the group was weighing up everything that had been said, trying to fit the various suggestions together in the hope that two pieces of the puzzle might just slot into place and that something would emerge, something so holmesian, so poirotesque, that it would make these two men under orders from him open their mouths wide in amazement. And suddenly, as if the scales had fallen from his eyes, he saw the way forward, Most people, he said, unless, of course, they're physically incapacitated, don't spend all their time stuck at home, they go out to work, go shopping or for a walk, so my idea is that we should wait until there's no one in the apartment and then break in, the guy's address is on the letter, we've got plenty of skeleton keys, and there are bound to be photos around, it wouldn't be hard to identify him from the various photographs and that way we'd have no problem following him, and if we want to find out when the place is empty, we'll use the phone, we'll get his number tomorrow from directory inquiries, or we could look it up in the telephone book, one or the other, it doesn't really matter. As he uttered this rather lame conclusion, he realized that the pieces of the puzzle really didn't fit. Although, as explained before, the two assistants' attitude toward the results of their leader's cogitations was one of total benevolence, the first assistant, trying to find a tone of voice that would not wound his chief's susceptibilities, felt obliged to observe, Correct me if I'm wrong, but wouldn't it be best, since we know the guy's address, just to go and knock on his door and ask whoever answers Does So-and-so live here, if it's him, he'll say Yes, that's me, if it's his wife, she'll probably say I'll just go and call my husband, that way we would have the bird in our hand without having to beat about the bush. The leader raised his clenched fist like someone about to give the desk an almighty thump, but, at the last moment, he checked the violence of that gesture, slowly lowered his arm and said in a voice that seemed to fade with every syllable, We'll examine that possibility tomorrow, I'm going to bed now, good night. He was just going over to the door of the bedroom he would occupy during the time the investigation lasted when he heard the second assistant ask, So do we still start the operation at seven o'clock as planned. Without turning round, the group leader replied, That plan of action is suspended until further orders, you will receive your instructions tomorrow, once I have read through any messages from the ministry, and, if necessary, so as to speed up the work, I will make any changes I see fit. He said good night again, Good night, sir, replied his two subordinates, and then he went into his room. As soon as the door had closed, the second assistant prepared to continue the conversation, but the other man quickly put a forefinger to his lips and shook his head, indicating to him not to speak. He was the first one to push back his chair and say, Right, I'm off to bed, if you're staying up, be careful not to wake me when you come in. Unlike their leader, these two men, as the subordinates they are, do not have the right to a room of their own, they are both going to sleep in a large room with three beds, a kind of small dormitory which is rarely fully occupied. The bed in the middle is always the one least used. When, as in this case, there were two agents, they invariably used the beds on either side, and if only one policeman was sleeping there, he was also sure to prefer to sleep in one of those, never in the middle bed, perhaps because sleeping there would make him feel as if he were under siege or a prisoner under arrest. Even the hardest, most thick-skinned of policemen, and these two have not yet had the opportunity to prove that they are, need to feel protected by the proximity of a wall. The second assistant, who had understood the message, got to his feet and said, No, no, I'm not sitting up, I'm going to bed too. According to rank, first one, then the other, made use of the bathroom which was, as it should be, equipped with everything necessary for their ablutions, for we have not at any point in this report mentioned that the three policemen each brought with them only a small suitcase or a simple rucksack with a change of clothing, a toothbrush and a razor. It would be surprising if an enterprise christened with the fortunate name of providential did not take care to provide those to whom it gave temporary shelter with the various articles and products essential for their comfort and for the successful fulfillment of the mission with which they had been charged. Half an hour later, the two assistants were in their respective beds, wearing their official pajamas, with the police emblem over their heart. So the plan from the ministry of the interior's planning department was useless, said the second assistant, It's always the same when they don't take the elementary precaution of consulting the people who've got the experience, replied the first assistant, Our leader's got plenty of experience, said the second assistant, if he hadn't, he wouldn't be where he is today, Sometimes, being too close to the centers of decision-making brings on myopia, makes you shortsighted, replied the first assistant sagely, Do you mean to say that if we ever get to a position of real power, like the chief, the same thing will happen to us, asked the second assistant, There's no reason why, in this particular case, the future should be any different from the present, replied the first assistant wisely. Fifteen minutes later, both were asleep. One was snoring, the other wasn't.

It was not yet eight o'clock in the morning, when the group

leader, already washed, shaved and dressed, came into the room
where the ministry's plan of action, or, to be more precise, the
interior minister's plan of action that had been so rudely loaded
onto the patient shoulders of the police authorities, had been
torn to shreds by his two assistants, albeit with praiseworthy
discretion and considerable respect, and even a slight touch of
dialectical elegance. He had no problem in acknowledging this
and bore them no rancor, on the contrary, he was clearly very
relieved. With the same energetic strength of will with which
he had overcome the incipient insomnia that had caused him
to toss and turn for a while in bed, he took total control of
operations, generously rendering unto caesar what could not
be denied to caesar, but making it quite clear that, in the end,
all benefits will sooner or later revert to god and to authority,
god's other name. It was, therefore, a serene, confident man
whom the two sleepy assistants found when, minutes later,
they, in turn, shuffled into the living-room, still in their dress-
ing-gowns, which were also adorned with the police emblem,
and in their pajamas and bedroom slippers. Their chief had calculated as much, he had foreseen that the first point of the day
would go to him, and he had already noted it on the blackboard.
Good morning, boys, he said in a cordial tone, I hope you slept
well. Yes, sir, said one. Yes, sir, said the other, Let's have breakfast, then get yourselves washed and dressed, who knows, we
might catch him still in his bed, that would be fun, by the way,
what day is it today, Saturday, today is Saturday, no one gets up
early on Saturday, you wait, he'll open the door looking just the
way you do now, in dressing-gown and pajamas, shuffling down
the corridor in his slippers, and consequently with his defenses
down, psychologically at a low ebb, come on, come on, who's
the brave man who's going to volunteer to make breakfast, Me,
said the second assistant, knowing full well that there was no
third assistant to do the job. In a different situation, that is, if,

instead of being thrown out, the ministry's plan had been accepted without further discussion, the first assistant would have
stayed behind with his chief to agree and fine-tune, however
unnecessarily, some detail of the investigation they were about
to embark upon, but, in the circumstances, especially now that
he, too, had been reduced to the inferiority of bedroom slippers, he decided to make a great gesture of camaraderie and
say, I'll help you. Their leader agreed, it seemed a good idea,
and he sat down to go over some notes he had made before going to sleep. Barely fifteen minutes had passed when the two
assistants reappeared carrying a tray each, bearing the coffee
pot, the milk jug, a packet of plain biscuits, orange juice, yo-
ghurt and jam, no doubt about it, the catering corps of the
political police had once again done honor to their hard-won
reputation. Resigned to drinking their coffee with cold milk or
having to reheat it, the assistants said that they were going to
get washed and dressed and would be back in a moment, We'll
be as quick as we can. In fact, it seemed to them a grave lack of
respect, with their superior there in suit and tie, to join him in
their disheveled state, unshaven, eyes blinking, and emanating
the thick, nocturnal smell of unwashed bodies. There was no
need for them to explain, what was left unspoken was, for once,
more than eloquent. Naturally, given this new atmosphere of
peace, and with his assistants put firmly back in their places,
it cost their chief nothing to urge them to sit down and share
bread and salt with him, We're colleagues, we're in the same
boat, a fine boss I'd be if I had to keep flaunting my stripes in
order to get people to obey me, anyone who knows me knows
I'm not like that, sit down, sit down. Slightly embarrassed, the
assistants sat down, conscious that, whatever anyone said, there
was something improper about the situation, two down-and-
outs having breakfast with a person who, in comparison, looked
like a dandy, they were the ones who should have got their

asses out of bed early, more than that, they should have had the table set and ready for when their chief came out of his room, in dressing-gown and pajamas if he so wished, but us, no, we should have been properly dressed and with our hair combed, it is these small cracks in the varnish of behavior, rather than noisy revolutions, which, slowly, through repetition and persistence, finally bring down the most solid of social edifices. It is a wise dictum that says, If you want to be respected, don't encourage familiarity, let us hope, for the good of the job, that this particular chief does not have reason to regret this moment. In the meantime, he seems confident of his authority, we have only to hear him, This operation has two objectives, a main one and a secondary one, the secondary objective, which I'll deal with now so as not to waste time, is to find out as much as possible, but without, in theory, too much outlay of energy, about the supposed murder committed by the woman who led the group of six blind people mentioned in the letter, the main objective, to which we will apply all our efforts and abilities and for which we will use all reasonable means, whatever they may be, is to establish whether or not there is any connection between this woman, who is said to have retained her sight while the rest of us were all staggering around blind, and this new epidemic of blank ballot papers, It won't be easy to find her, said the first assistant, That's why we're here, all attempts to unearth the roots of the boycott have failed up until now and it might well be that this guy's letter won't get us very far either, but it at least opens a new line of inquiry, It seems pretty unbelievable to me that this woman could be behind a movement that involves some hundreds of thousands of people and that, tomorrow, if we don't stamp the whole business out now, she might gather together millions and millions more, said the second assistant, Both things are equally impossible, but if one of them happened, so could the other one, replied the chief, and concluded, with the look of someone who knows more than he is authorized to say, never imagining how true his words will prove to be, Impossibilities never come singly. With this happy concluding phrase, the perfect close to a sonnet, breakfast also came to an end. The assistants cleared the table and carried the crockery and what remained of the food into the kitchen, We'll go and get washed and dressed now, we won't be a moment, they said, Wait, said the chief, then, addressing himself to the first assistant, You'd better use my bathroom, otherwise we'll never get out of here. The lucky assistant blushed with contentment, his career had just taken a great leap forward, he was going to pee in his chief's toilet.

In the underground garage a car was waiting for them, the keys of which had been deposited the day before on the chief's bedside table, along with a brief explanatory note indicating its make, color, registration number and the parking place where the vehicle had been left. Avoiding the foyer, they took the lift straight down to the garage and had no difficulty in finding the car. It was nearly ten o'clock. The chief said to the second assistant as the latter was opening the back door for him, You drive. The first assistant sat in the front, next to the driver. It was a pleasant, very sunny morning, which shows yet again that the punishments of which the sky was such a prodigal source in the past, have, with the passing of the centuries, lost their force, those were good and just times, when any failure to obey the divine diktat was enough for several biblical cities to be annihilated and razed to the ground with all their inhabitants inside. Yet here is a city that cast blank votes against the lord and not a single bolt of lightning has fallen upon it, reducing it to ashes, as happened, in response to far less exemplary vices, to sodom and gomorrah, as well as to admah and to zeboyim, burned down to their very foundations, although the last two cities are mentioned less often than the first, whose names, per-

haps because of their irresistible musicality, have remained forever in people's ears. Nowadays, having abandoned their blind
obedience to the lord's orders, lightning bolts fall only where
they want to, and, as has become manifest, one can clearly not
count on them to lead this sinful city and caster of blank votes
back to the path of righteousness. In their place, the ministry
of the interior has sent three of its archangels, these three policemen, chief and subalterns, who, from now on, we will des-
ignate by their corresponding ranks, which are, following the
hierarchical scale, superintendent, inspector and sergeant. The
first two sit watching the people walking along, none of them
innocent, all of them guilty of something, and they wonder if
that venerable-looking old gentleman, for example, is not perhaps the grand master of outer darkness, if that girl with her
arms about her boyfriend is not the incarnation of the undy-
ing serpent of evil, if that man walking along, head down, is
not going to some unknown cave where the potions that poisoned the spirit of the city are distilled. The sergeant, whose
lowly condition means that he is under no obligation to think
elevated thoughts or to harbor suspicions about what lies beneath the surface of things, has rather homelier concerns, like
this one with which he is about to dare to interrupt his superiors' meditations, With weather like this, the man might have
gone to spend the day in the country, What country, asked the
inspector in an ironic tone, What do you mean what country,
The real country is on the other side of the frontier, on this
side, it's all city. It was true. The sergeant had missed a golden
opportunity to remain silent, but he had learned a lesson, asking such questions would get him nowhere. He concentrated
on his driving and swore to himself that he would only open his
mouth if asked to. That was when the superintendent spoke,
We will be hard and implacable, we won't resort to any of the
classic tricks, like that old, outmoded hard cop, soft cop rou-

tine, we are a commando of operatives, feelings don't count here, we will imagine that we are machines made to perform a specific task and we will simply carry out that task without so much as a backward glance, Yes, sir, said the inspector, Yes, sir, said the sergeant, breaking his own oath. The car turned into the street where the man who wrote the letter lives, over in that building, on the third floor. They parked the car a little further on, the sergeant opened the door for the superintendent, the inspector got out the other side, the commando is complete, on the firing line, fists clenched, action.

Now we see them on the landing. The superintendent gestures to the sergeant, who rings the doorbell. Total silence inside. The sergeant thinks, You see, I was right, he has gone to spend the day in the country. Another gesture, another ring on the doorbell. A few seconds later, they hear someone, a man, ask from behind the door, Who is it. The superintendent looks at his immediate subordinate, who says in a loud voice, Police, One moment, please, said the man, I have to get dressed. Four minutes passed. The superintendent made the same gesture, the sergeant again rang the doorbell, this time keeping his finger pressed down. One moment, one moment, please, I'm coming, I've only just got up, these last words were spoken with the door open by a man wearing shirt and trousers and still in his slippers, Today is the day of the slipper, thought the sergeant. The man did not seem alarmed, he wore the look of someone finally seeing the arrival of the visitors he has been waiting for, any hint of surprise was probably due only to the fact that there were so many of them. The inspector asked him his name and he told them, adding, Do come in, and I apologize for the state the place is in, I never imagined you would come so early, besides, I thought you would call me in to make a statement, but you've come to me instead, it's about the letter, I assume, Yes, it's about the letter, said the inspector bluntly, Come in, come in. The sergeant went in first, sometimes the hierarchy works in reverse, followed by the inspector, with the superintendent bringing up the rear. The man shuffled down the corridor, Follow me, this way, he opened a door that gave onto a small sitting-room and said, Sit down, please, and if you don't mind, I'll just go and put some shoes on, this is no way to receive visitors, We're not exactly what you would call visitors, remarked the inspector, No, of course not, it was just a manner of speaking, Go and put some shoes on, then, and be quick about it, we're in a hurry, No, we're not, we're not in any hurry at all, said the superintendent, who had not until then said a word. The man looked at him, and this time he did so with an air of slight alarm, as if the tone in which the superintendent had spoken was not what had been agreed, and all he could think of to say was, You can, I assure you, count on my entire cooperation, sir, Superintendent, said the sergeant, Superintendent, repeated the man, and you, sir, Don't worry, I'm just a sergeant. The man turned to the third member of the group, replacing his question with an interrogative lift of the eyebrows, but the answer came from the superintendent, This gentleman is an inspector and my chief officer, then he added, Now go and put some shoes on, we'll wait for you. The man left the room. I can't hear anyone else in the apartment, it looks as if he lives alone, whispered the sergeant, His wife's probably gone to spend the day in the country, said the inspector with a smile. The superintendent signaled to them to be quiet, I'll ask the first questions, he said, lowering his voice. The man came back in and, as he sat down, said May I, as if he were not in his own house, and then, Here I am, now how can I help you. The superintendent nodded kindly, then began, Your letter, or, rather, your three letters, because there were three of them, Yes, I thought it was safer that way, because you never know, one of them might have got lost, the man began, Don't interrupt, just

answer any questions I ask you, Yes, superintendent, Your letters, I repeat, were read with great interest by their recipients,
especially as regards what you say about a certain unidentified
woman who committed a murder four years ago. There was no
question in these words, it was a simple reiteration of facts, and
so the man said nothing. There was an expression of confusion
and perplexity on his face, he could not understand why the
superintendent did not get straight to the heart of the matter
instead of wasting time on an episode which he had only mentioned in order to cast a still darker light on an already disquieting portrait. The superintendent pretended not to notice,
Tell us what you know about that murder, he asked. The man
suppressed an urge to remind the superintendent that this had
not been the most important part of the letter, that, compared
with the country's current situation, the murder was the least of
it, but no, he wouldn't do that, prudence told him to follow the
music they were asking him to dance to, later on, they were
sure to change the record, I know that she killed a man, Did
you see her do it, were you there, asked the superintendent,
No, superintendent, but she herself confessed, To you, To me
and to other people, You do know, I assume, the technical
meaning of the word confession, More or less, superintendent,
More or less isn't enough, either you do or you don't, In the
sense that you mean, no, I don't, Confession means a declaration of one's own mistakes or faults, it can also mean an ac-
knowledgement of guilt or of the truth of an accusation by the
accused to someone in authority or in a court of law, now, can
these definitions be applied rigorously to this case, No, not rigorously, superintendent, Fine, continue, My wife was there, my
wife witnessed the man's death, What do you mean by there,
There, in the old insane asylum where we were quarantined,
Your wife, I assume, was also blind, As I said the only person
who didn't go blind was her, Who's her, The woman who com-

mitted the murder, Ah, We were in a dormitory, And the murder was committed there, No, superintendent, in another dormitory, So none of the people from your dormitory were
present when the murder was committed, Only the women,
Why only the women, It's difficult to explain, superintendent,
Don't worry, we've got plenty of time, There were some blind
men who took over and started terrorizing us, Terrorizing, Yes,
superintendent, terrorizing, How, They got hold of all the food
and if we wanted to eat, we had to pay, And they demanded
women as payment, Yes, superintendent, And that woman killed
a man, Yes, superintendent, Killed him how, With a pair of scissors, Who was this man, The one who was in charge of the
other blind men, She's obviously a brave woman, Yes, superintendent, Now tell us why you reported her, But I didn't, I only
mentioned it because it seemed relevant, Sorry, I don't understand, What I meant to say in the letter was that someone who
was capable of doing that was capable of doing the other thing.
The superintendent did not ask what other thing this was, he
merely looked at the person whom he had, using navy language, called his chief officer, inviting him to continue the interrogation. The inspector paused for a few seconds, Would
you mind asking your wife to join us, he asked, we'd like to talk
to her, My wife isn't here, When will she be back, She won't,
we're divorced, When did that happen, Three years ago, Would
you object to telling us why you got divorced, For personal
reasons, Naturally they would be personal, For private reasons
then, As with all divorces. The man looked at the inscrutable
faces before him and realized that they would not leave him in
peace until he had told them what they wanted to know. He
cleared his throat, crossed and uncrossed his legs, I'm a man of
principle, he began, Oh, we know that, said the sergeant, unable to contain himself, I mean, I know that, I had the privilege
of reading your letter. The superintendent and the inspector

smiled, it was a justifiable blow. The man looked at the sergeant, bewildered, as if he had not expected an attack from that quarter, and, lowering his eyes, he went on, It was to do with those blind men, I couldn't bear the fact that my wife had done it with those vile men, for a whole year I put up with the shame of it, but, in the end, it became unbearable, and so I left her, got a divorce, How odd, I thought you said that these other blind men gave you food in exchange for your women, said the inspector, That's right, And your principles, I assume, did not allow you to touch the food that your wife brought to you after she had, to use your expression, done it with those vile men. The man hung his head and did not reply. I understand your discretion, said the inspector, it really is too private a matter to be bandied about amongst strangers, oh, sorry, I didn't mean to wound your sensibilities. The man looked at the superintendent as if pleading for help, or at least asking him to replace the pincers with a spell on the rack. The superintendent obliged and applied the garrotte, In your letter, you referred to a group of seven people, Yes, superintendent, Who were they, Apart from the woman and her husband, Which woman, The one who didn't go blind, The one who acted as your guide, Yes, superintendent, The one who, in order to avenge her fellow women, stabbed the leader of the bandits with a pair of scissors, Yes, superintendent, Go on, Her husband was an ophthalmologist, We know that, There was a prostitute too, Did she tell you she was a prostitute, Not that I remember, no, superintendent, So how did you know she was a prostitute, By her manner, it was clear from her manner, And, of course, manners never deceive, go on, And there was an old man who was blind in one eye and wore a black eyepatch, and he and she lived together afterward, Who's she, The prostitute, Were they happy, I've no idea, You must have some idea, During the year that we still saw each other, yes, they seemed happy. The superintendent counted on his fingers, There's still one missing, he said, Yes, there was a boy with a squint who had lost his parents in all the confusion, Do you mean that you all met in the dormitory, No, superintendent, we had all met before, Where, At the ophthalmologist's where my then wife took me when I went blind, in fact, I think I was the first person to go blind, And you infected the others, the whole city, including your visitors today, It wasn't my fault, superintendent, Do you know the names of these people, Yes, superintendent, Of all of them, Apart from the boy, if I knew his name then, I've forgotten it now, But you remember the others, Yes, superintendent, And their addresses, Yes, unless they've moved in the last three years, Of course, unless they've moved in the last three years. The superintendent glanced round the small room, and his gaze lingered on the television as if he were hoping for some inspiration from it, then he said, Sergeant, pass your notebook to this gentleman and lend him your pen so that he can write down the names and the addresses of the people of whom he has spoken so warmly, apart from the boy with the squint, who wouldn't be of any use to us anyway. The man's hands trembled when he took the pen and the notebook, they continued to tremble as he wrote, he was telling himself that there was no reason to feel afraid, that the police were there because he had, in some way, summoned them himself, what he didn't understand was why they didn't talk about the blank ballot papers, the insurrection, the conspiracy against the state, about the only real reason he had written his letter. His hands were trembling so much that his writing was almost illegible, May I use another sheet, he asked, Use as many as you like, replied the sergeant. His writing began to grow steadier, it was no longer a motive for embarrassment. While the sergeant retrieved the pen and handed the notebook to the superintendent, the man was wondering what gesture, what word could win him, even if only belatedly, the sympathy of these policemen, their benevolence, their complicity. Suddenly, he remembered, I've got a photograph, he exclaimed, yes, I think I've still got it, What photograph, asked the inspector, Of the group, it was taken shortly after we had recovered our sight, my wife didn't want it, she said she'd get a copy, she said I should keep it so that I wouldn't forget, Were those her words, asked the inspector, but the man did not reply, he had stood up and was about to leave the room, when the superintendent ordered, Sergeant, go with this gentleman, if he has any trouble finding the photograph, help him, don't come back without it. They were absent for only a few minutes. Here it is, said the man. The superintendent went over to the window to be able to see better. In a line, side by side, the six adults stood in pairs, couple by couple. On the right, alongside his wife, stood the man himself, plainly recognizable, to the left there stood, without a shadow of a doubt, the old man with the black eyepatch and the prostitute, and in the middle, by a process of elimination, two people who could only be the doctor's wife and her husband. In front, kneeling down like a football player, was the boy with the squint. Next to the doctor's wife was a large dog looking straight at the camera. The superintendent beckoned to the man to join him, Is that her, he asked, pointing, Yes, superintendent, that's her, And the dog, If you like, I can tell you the story, superintendent, No, don't bother, she'll tell me. The superintendent left first, followed by the inspector and then the sergeant. The man who had written the letter watched them go down the stairs. The building has no lift and there is little hope that it ever will.

THE three policemen drove around the city for a while, filling in time until lunch, although they would not eat together. The plan was to park the car near an area where there were plenty of restaurants and then to go their separate ways, each to a different place, and meet exactly ninety minutes later in a square some way off, where the superintendent, this time at the wheel, would pick his subordinates up. Obviously, no one here knows who they are, besides, none of them has a capital P branded on his forehead, but common sense and prudence tell them not to wander around as a group through the center of a city which is, for many reasons, hostile to them. True, there are three men over there, and another three ahead of them, but a quick glance is enough to see that they are normal people, belonging to the common species of passer-by, ordinary folk, free of all suspicion of being representatives of the law or pursued by it. During the drive, the superintendent wanted to hear his two subordinates' impressions of the man who had written the letter, making it clear, however, that he was not interested in any moral judgements, We know he's a bastard of the first order, so there's no point wasting time coming up with other descriptions. The inspector was the first to speak, saying that he

had particularly admired the way in which the superintendent
had directed the interrogation, skilfully omitting any reference
to the malicious suggestion contained in the letter, that the
doctor's wife, given her exceptional personal circumstances
during the plague of blindness four years ago, could be the
cause of or in some way implicated in the conspiracy that led to
the capital's population casting blank votes. The guy was obviously completely thrown, he said, he was expecting that to be
the main and possibly the only subject the police would be interested in, but how wrong he was. I almost felt sorry for him,
he added. The sergeant agreed with what the inspector had
said, noting, too, how, by alternating the role of interrogator
between himself and the inspector, he had succeeded brilliantly
in breaking down the interrogatee's defenses. He paused and,
in a low voice, said, Superintendent, it is my duty to inform you
that when you told me to leave the room with him I used my
pistol on him, Used it, how, asked the superintendent, I stuck it
in his ribs, he's probably still got the mark, But why, Well, I
thought it would take a while to find the photo and that the guy
would take advantage of the interruption to come up with some
trick to hinder the investigation, something that would force
you, sir, to change the line of inquiry in the direction that best
suited him, And now what do you want me to do, pin a medal
on your chest, said the superintendent mockingly, We gained
time, sir, the photo appeared in an instant, And I'm sorely
tempted to make you disappear, Forgive me, sir, Oh, don't
worry, I'll tell you when you're forgiven, always assuming I remember, Yes, sir, One question, Yes, sir, Was the safety catch
on, Yes, sir, Why, because you'd forgotten to take it off, No, sir,
I really just wanted to frighten the guy, And you managed to do
that, Yes, sir, Well, it looks like I'll have to give you that medal
after all, but, please, don't get too excited, and mind you don't
run over that old lady or jump a red light, the last thing I want

is to have to explain myself to a policeman, But there are no
police in the city, sir, they were withdrawn when the state of
siege was declared, said the inspector, Ah, now I understand, I
was wondering why it was so quiet. They drove past a park
where children were playing. The superintendent looked at
them with an air that seemed distracted, absent, but the sigh
that suddenly emerged from his breast showed that he must
have been thinking about other times and other places. After
we've had lunch, he said, I'll be going back to base, Yes, sir, said
the sergeant, Do you have any orders for us, sir, asked the inspector, Go for a walk, stroll around the city, go into the cafés
and shops, keep your eyes and ears open, and come back in
time for supper, we won't be going out tonight, there's bound
to be some canned stuff in the kitchen, Yes, sir, said the sergeant, And tomorrow we'll be working on our own, our bold
driver, the policeman with the gun, will go and talk to the ex-
wife of the man who wrote the letter, the inspector here, sitting
in the dead man's seat, will visit the old man with the black eyepatch and his prostitute, and I'll reserve the doctor's wife and
the doctor for myself, as for tactics, we'll stick strictly to those
we used today, no mention of blank votes, no getting involved
in political debates, restrict your questions to the circumstances
surrounding the murder, to the personality of the presumed
murderer, get them to talk about the group, how it was formed,
if they had met before, what their relationship is like today,
they're probably friends and will want to protect each other,
but they're bound to make mistakes if they haven't reached
some prior agreement about what they should say and what it
would be best to stay quiet about, our job is to help them make
those mistakes, and, to cut this rather long speech short, remember the most important fact of all, tomorrow morning, we
must arrive at the houses of these people at exactly half past
ten, I'm not telling you to synchronize watches, because that

only happens in action movies, but we mustn't give any of the
suspects the chance to pass on the message, to warn the others,
but now let's go and have lunch, ah, yes, and when you come
back, come in through the garage, on Monday, I'll have to find
out whether or not the porter can be trusted. Rather more than
the stipulated ninety minutes later, the superintendent picked
up his assistants, who were waiting for him in the square, then
dropped them off in turn, first the sergeant, then the inspector,
in different parts of the city, where they would carry out the
orders they had been given, to walk about, go into cafés and
shops, keep their eyes and ears open, in short, to sniff out any
crime. They will return to base for the promised canned supper
and to sleep, and when the superintendent asks them if they
have anything to report, they will confess that they have absolutely nothing to tell him, that while the inhabitants of this city
aren't any less talkative than those in any other, they certainly
don't talk about the subject of most interest. That's a good sign,
he will say, the proof that there is a conspiracy lies precisely in
the fact that no one talks about it, silence, in this case, does not
contradict, it confirms. The phrase was not his, it had been spoken by the interior minister, with whom, when he got back to
providential ltd, he'd had a brief phone conversation, which,
even though the line was extremely safe, complied with all the
precepts of the law of basic official secrecy. Here is a summary
of their conversation, Hello, puffin speaking, Hello, puffin, replied albatross, First contact made with local bird life, friendly
reception, useful interrogation with the participation of hawk
and gull, good results, Substantial, puffin, Very substantial, albatross, we got an excellent photograph of the whole flock, tomorrow we'll start identifying the different species, Well done,
puffin, Thank you, albatross, Listen, puffin, I'm listening, albatross, Don't be fooled by occasional silences, puffin, when birds
are quiet, it doesn't necessarily mean that they're on their nests,

it's the calm that conceals the storm, not the other way round, the same thing happens with human conspiracies, the fact that no one mentions them doesn't mean they don't exist, do you understand, puffin, Yes, albatross, I understand perfectly, What are you going to do tomorrow, puffin, I'm going to go for the osprey, Who is the osprey, puffin, explain yourself, It's the only one on the whole coast, albatross, indeed, as far as we know, there has never been another, Ah, now I understand, Do you have any orders for me, albatross, Just carry out rigorously those I gave you before you left, puffin, They will be rigorously carried out, albatross, Keep me posted, puffin, I will, albatross. Once he had checked that all microphones were switched off, the superintendent gave muttered vent to his feelings, Ye gods of the police and of espionage, what a farce, I'm puffin and he's albatross, the next thing you know we'll be communicating by squawks and screeches, there'd be a storm then, no fear. When his subordinates finally arrived back, tired from pounding the city streets, he asked them if they had any news, and they said no, they had strained eyes and ears watching and listening, but, alas, with no result. These people talk as if they had nothing to hide, they said. It was then that the superintendent, without giving his source, uttered the interior minister's words about conspiracies and the ways in which they disguise themselves.

The following day, after breakfast, they looked at the map and in the city guide for the streets they were interested in. The nearest one to the building where providential ltd is based is the street where the ex-wife of the man who wrote the letter, formerly known as the first blind man, has her apartment, the doctor's wife and her husband are a little further off, and furthest away are the old man with the black eyepatch and the prostitute. Let's just hope they're in. As on the previous day, they took the lift down to the garage, in fact, for those leading clandestine lives, this is not the best way of proceeding, because while it is true that, up until now, they have escaped the porter's busybodying, I wonder who those spooks are, I've never seen them around here before, he would think to himself, but they will not escape the curiosity of the garage attendant, and we will soon find out with what consequences. This time, the inspector will drive, since he has the longest journey. The sergeant asked the superintendent if he had any special instructions to give him and was told that he had no special instructions, only general ones, I just hope you don't do anything stupid and that you keep your gun firmly in its holster, But I would never threaten a woman with a gun, sir, Oh, yeah, anyway, don't forget, you are forbidden to knock on her door before half past ten, Yes, sir, Go for a walk, have a coffee if you can find somewhere, buy a newspaper, look in the shop windows, you can't have forgotten everything you were taught at police college, No, sir, Good, this is your street, out you get, Where will we meet when we've finished, asked the sergeant, we need to arrange a meeting place, that's the trouble with only having one key to the office, I mean, if I, for example, was to finish my interrogation first, I wouldn't be able to go back to base, Nor would I, said the inspector, That's what comes of them not providing us with mobile phones, insisted the sergeant, sure of his reasoning and trusting that the beauty of the morning would dispose his superior to be kind. The superintendent agreed, Meanwhile, we'll have to make do with what we've got, but if the investigation calls for it, then I'll requisition more equipment, as for keys, if the ministry authorizes the expense, tomorrow, you'll each have a key of your own, And what if they refuse, Then I'll sort something out, But what are we going to do about fixing a meeting place, asked the inspector, From what we know of this story already, everything indicates that my investigation is going to take the longest, so why don't you meet me there, make a note of the address, we'll see then how the people being interrogated react to the arrival of two more police officers, An excellent idea, sir, said the inspector. The sergeant merely nodded, since he could not say out loud what he was thinking, that any praise for the idea belonged to him, even if only indirectly and by a very tortuous route. He made a note of the address in his investigator's notebook and got out of the car. The inspector drove off and, as he did so, said, To be fair, he really tries, poor boy, I can remember being just like him when I was starting out, so eager to do something right that I made nothing but blunders, in fact, I sometimes ask myself how I ever came to be promoted to inspector, Or how I came to be what I am today, You too, sir, Me too, me too, my friend, all policemen start out much the same, everything else is just a question of luck, Luck and knowledge, Knowledge on its own isn't always enough, whereas with luck and time you can achieve almost anything, but don't ask me what luck is because I wouldn't be able to tell you, all I can say is that often you can get what you want just by having friends in the right places or some favor to call in, Not everyone was born to be a superintendent, True, Besides, a police force made up entirely of superintendents wouldn't work, Nor would an army made up entirely of generals. They turned into the street where the ophthalmologist lives. Drop me here, said the superintendent, I'll walk the rest of the way, Good luck, sir, And to you, Let's hope we can resolve this matter quickly, to be perfectly honest I feel as if I was lost in the middle of a minefield, Calm down, man, there's no reason to be worried, look at these streets, see how peaceful and quiet the city is, That's exactly what worries me, sir, a city like this, with no one in charge, with no government, no security, no police, and no one seems to care, there's something very mysterious going on here which I can't quite understand, That's what we were sent here to do, to understand, we have the knowledge and I just hope the rest comes with it,

Luck, you mean, Yes, luck, Well, good luck, then, sir, Good luck, inspector, and if the woman who's supposed to be a prostitute shoots you a seductive look or gives you a glimpse of thigh, just pretend you haven't noticed, concentrate on the interests of the investigation, think of the eminent dignity of the organization that we serve, The old man with the black eyepatch is sure to be there too, and old men, I'm reliably informed, are real terrors, said the inspector. The superintendent smiled, Old age is catching up with me as well, I wonder if I'll live long enough to turn into a real terror. Then he glanced at his watch, It's a quarter past ten already, I hope you manage to get there on time, As long as you and the sergeant keep to the timetable, it doesn't really matter if I'm a bit late, said the inspector. The superintendent said goodbye, See you later, and got out of the car and, as soon as he set foot on the pavement, as if he had made an appointment to meet his own flawed reasoning right there, he realized that it made no sense to have been so rigorous about the time when they should knock on the suspects' respective doors, since, with a policeman in their home, they would have neither the sangfroid nor the opportunity to phone their friends to warn them of the imagined danger, always assuming they were that astute, astute enough for them to work out that if they were the object of police attention, then their friends would be too, Besides, thought the superintendent, irritated with himself, they obviously won't be their only friends, and in that case, how many of their friends would each of them have to ring, how many. He was not just thinking these thoughts to himself now, he was muttering accusations, abuse, insults, How did such an imbecile ever manage to become superintendent, how could the government have given an imbecile like me full responsibility for an investigation on which the fate of the whole country might hang, and how did this imbecile come up with that stupid order to his subordinates, I just hope they're not both laughing at me at this very moment, I shouldn't think the sergeant is, but the inspector is bright, too bright really, even though, at first sight, he doesn't seem to be, or perhaps he's just good at hiding it, which, of course, makes him doubly dangerous, no, I'd better be very careful with him, treat him with caution, I wouldn't want this to get out, others have found themselves in similar situations and with catastrophic results, someone once said, I can't remember who, that a moment's folly can ruin a whole career. This implacable bout of self-flagellation did the superintendent good. Seeing him crushed and ground into the mud, it was the turn of cool reflection to speak and to show him that the order had not been foolish at all, Imagine what would have happened if you hadn't given those instructions and the inspector and the sergeant had turned up at whatever time they fancied, one of them in the morning, the other in the afternoon, then you really would have been an imbecile, an out-and-out imbecile, not to see what would inevitably happen, the people who had been interrogated in the morning would rush to warn those who were to be interrogated in the afternoon, and when, that afternoon, the investigator knocked on the door of the suspects he'd been allocated he would find himself confronted by a line of defense he might not be able to break down, that's why you're a superintendent and will continue to be, not just because you know your job, but also because you're lucky enough to have me here, cool reflection, to put things in perspective, starting with the inspector, whom you won't now have to start treating with kid gloves, as was your intention, a rather cowardly one if you don't mind my saying. The superintendent didn't mind. With all this coming and going, thinking and rethinking, he was late in carrying out his own order, and it was already a quarter to eleven when he raised his hand to press the doorbell. The lift had carried him up to the fourth floor, this is the door.

The superintendent was waiting for someone inside to ask Who is it, but the door simply opened and a woman appeared and said, Yes. The superintendent put his hand in his pocket and produced his identification, Police, he said, And what do the police want with the people who live in this apartment, asked the woman, The answers to a few questions, About what, Look, I hardly think the landing is the best place to begin an interrogation, Oh, so it's an interrogation, is it, asked the woman, Madam, even if I only had two questions to ask you, it would still be an interrogation, You appreciate precision in language I see, Especially in the answers I am given, Now that's a good answer, It wasn't difficult, you served it up to me on a plate, And I'll serve you up some others if what you're after is the truth, Looking for the truth is the fundamental aim of any policeman, Well, I'm very glad to hear you say that so emphatically, you'd better come in, my husband has just popped out to buy the newspapers, he won't be long, If you prefer, if you think it would be more proper, I can wait outside, Nonsense, come in, in what safer hands could anyone be than in those of the police, said the woman. The superintendent went in, the woman walked ahead of him and opened the door to a welcoming living-room in which one sensed a friendly, lived-in atmosphere, Please, superintendent, sit down, she said, and asked, Would you like a cup of coffee, No, thank you, we don't accept anything when we're on duty, Naturally, that's how all the great corruptions begin, a cup of coffee today, a cup of coffee tomorrow, and by the third cup, it's too late, It's one of our rules, madam, May I ask you to satisfy one little curiosity of mine, What's that, You told me that you were from the police, you showed me an identity card that says you're a superintendent, but, as far as I know, the police withdrew from the capital some weeks ago, leaving us to fall into the clutches of the violence and crime that is rife everywhere, am I to under-

stand from your presence here today that our policemen have
come home, No, madam, we have not, to use your expression,
come home, we are still on the other side of the dividing line,
You must have strong reasons, then, to cross the frontier, Yes,
very strong, And the questions you have come to ask are, naturally, to do with those reasons, Naturally, So I'd better wait until you ask them, Exactly. Three minutes later, they heard the
front door open. The woman left the room and said to the person who had come in, Guess what, we've got a visitor, a police
superintendent no less, And since when have police superintendents been interested in innocent people. These last words
were spoken in the room itself, the doctor preceding his wife
and addressing the superintendent, who answered, getting up
out of the chair in which he had been sitting, There are no innocent people, even when not guilty of an actual crime, we are
all unfailingly guilty of some fault, And what crime or fault are
we being blamed for or accused of, There's no rush, doctor, let's
make ourselves comfortable first, that way we can talk more
easily. The doctor and his wife sat down on a sofa and waited.
The superintendent remained silent for a few seconds, he was
suddenly unsure which was the best tactic to adopt. It was one
thing for the inspector and the sergeant, in order not to start
the hare too early, to limit themselves, in accordance with the
instructions they had been given, to asking questions about the
murder of the blind man, but he, the superintendent, had his
eyes fixed on a more ambitious goal, to find out if the woman
before him, sitting beside her husband as calmly as if, owing
nothing, she had nothing to fear, was, as well as being a murderer, also part of the diabolical plot that had caused the government's current state of humiliation, having forced it to bow
its head and kneel. It is not known who in the official department of cryptography decided to bestow on the superintendent the grotesque code-name of puffin, doubtless some per-

sonal enemy, for a more fitting and justifiable nickname would
be alekhine, the grand master of chess, who has, sadly, now
left the ranks of the living. The doubt that had arisen dissipated like smoke and a solid certainty took its place. Observe
with what sublime, combinatorial art he is about to develop
the moves that will lead him, or so he thinks, to the final check-
mate. With a sly smile, he said, Actually I wouldn't mind that
cup of coffee you were kind enough to offer me, It's my duty to
remind you that the police accept nothing while on duty, the
doctor's wife replied, enjoying the game, Superintendents are
authorized to infringe the rules whenever they think it appropriate, You mean when useful to the interests of the investigation, You could put it like that, And you're not afraid that the
coffee I'm about to bring you will be a step along the road to
corruption, Ah, I seem to remember you saying that that only
happens with the third cup of coffee, No, what I said was that
the third cup of coffee completed the corrupting process, the
first opened the door, the second held it open so that the as-
pirant to corruption could enter without stumbling, the third
slammed the door shut, Thank you for the warning, which I
take as a piece of advice, and so I'll stop at the first cup, Which
will be served at once, said the woman, and with that she left
the room. The superintendent glanced at his watch. Are you
in a hurry, asked the doctor pointedly, No, doctor, I'm not in
a hurry, I was just wondering if I'm keeping you from your
lunch, It's too early yet for lunch, And I was also wondering
how long it will take before I can leave here with the answers
I want, Does that mean that you know the answers you want
or that you want answers to your questions, asked the doctor,
adding, they are not the same thing, You're quite right, they're
not, during the brief conversation I had alone with your wife,
she had occasion to remark that I admire precision in language,
and I see that is also the case with you, In my profession, it's not

unusual for diagnostic errors to occur simply because of some linguistic imprecision, You know, I've been calling you doctor and you haven't yet asked me how I know you're a doctor, Because it seems to me a waste of time asking a policeman how he knows what he knows or claims to know, A good answer, just as one would not ask god how he became omniscient, omnipresent and omnipotent, You're not saying that the police are god, are you, We are merely his modest representatives on earth, doctor, Oh, I thought they were the churches and the priests, The churches and the priests are only second in the ranks.

The woman came back with the coffee, three cups on a tray and a few plain biscuits. It seems that everything in this world is doomed to repeat itself, thought the superintendent, while his palate relived the tastes of breakfast at providential ltd, Thank you very much, but I'll just have the coffee, he said. When he replaced the cup on the tray, he thanked her again and added with a knowing smile, Excellent coffee, madam, I might even reconsider my decision not to have a second cup. The doctor and his wife had already finished theirs. None of them had touched the biscuits. The superintendent produced a notebook from his jacket pocket, prepared his pen, and allowed his voice to emerge in a neutral, expressionless tone, as if he were not really interested in the answer, What explanation would you give, madam, for the fact that during the epidemic four years ago you did not go blind. The doctor and his wife looked at each other, surprised, and she asked, How do you know that I didn't go blind four years ago, Just now, said the superintendent, your husband, with great perspicacity, remarked that he considered it a waste of time asking a policeman how he knows what he knows or claims to know, Yes, but I'm not my husband, And I do not have to reveal, either to you or to him, the secrets of my profession, it's enough that I know you did not go blind. The doctor made as if to intervene, but his wife placed her hand on his arm, All right, then, tell me, and I assume that this is not a secret, of what possible interest can it be to the police that I did or did not go blind four years ago, If you had gone blind like everyone else, if you had gone blind as I myself did, you can be quite sure that I would not be here now, Was it a crime not to go blind, she asked, No, not going blind wasn't and never could be a crime, although, now that you mention it, you were able to commit a crime precisely because you weren't blind, A crime, A murder. The woman glanced at her husband as if asking his advice, then turned rapidly back to the superintendent and said, Yes, it's true, I did kill a man. She did not go on, she kept her eyes fixed on him, waiting. The superintendent pretended to be writing something down in his notebook, but all he was doing was playing for time, trying to think what his next move would be. The woman's response had surprised him less because she had confessed to a murder than because of the way she had immediately fallen silent again afterward, as if there were nothing more to be said on the subject. And the truth is, he thought, it isn't the crime that interests me. I assume you had a good reason, he ventured, For what, asked the woman, For committing the crime, It wasn't a crime, What was it then, An act of justice, That's what the courts are for, to administer justice, But I could hardly have gone and complained to the police, for as you yourself said, at the time, you were blind, like everyone else, Apart from you, Yes, apart from me, Who did you kill, A rapist, a vile creature, Are you telling me that you killed someone who was raping you, No, not me, a friend, Was she blind, Yes, she was, And the man was blind too, Yes, How did you kill him, With a pair of scissors, Did you stab him in the heart, No, in the throat, You don't have the face of a murderer, I'm not a murderer, You killed a man, He wasn't a man, superintendent, he was a bedbug. The superintendent wrote something else down and turned to the doctor,

And where were you, sir, while your wife was busy killing this bedbug, In the dormitory of the former lunatic asylum where they had put us when they still thought that by isolating the first people to go blind they could stop the spread of the blindness, You are, I believe, an ophthalmologist, Yes, I had the privilege, if I can call it that, of dealing with the first person to go blind, A man or a woman, A man, Did he end up in the same dormitory, Yes, along with a few other people who were in my surgery at the time, Did it seem to you a good thing that your wife had murdered the rapist, It seemed necessary, Why, You wouldn't ask that question if you had been there, Possibly, but I wasn't, and so I'll ask you again why it seemed necessary to you that your wife should have killed the bedbug, that is, the man raping her friend, Someone had to do it, and she was the only one who could see, Just because the bedbug was a rapist, It wasn't just him, all the others in the same dormitory were demanding women in exchange for food, he was the ringleader, Your wife was also raped, Yes, Before or after her friend, Before. The superintendent made another note in his book, then asked, In your view, as an ophthalmologist, what explanation could there be for the fact that your wife did not go blind, In my view as an ophthalmologist, there is no explanation, You have a remarkable wife, sir, Yes, I do, but not just because of that, What happened afterward to the people who had been interned in that old lunatic asylum, There was a fire, most of them must have been burned alive or crushed by falling masonry, How do you know there was falling masonry, Very simple, because we could hear it once we were outside, And how did you and your wife escape, We got out in time, You were lucky, Yes, she guided us, Who do you mean by us, Myself and a few other people, the ones who had been in my surgery, Who were they, The first blind man, to whom I referred earlier, and his wife, a young woman with conjunctivitis, an older

man with a cataract, and a young boy with a squint who was
with his mother, And your wife helped them all escape from the
fire, Yes, all of them, apart from the boy's mother, she wasn't in
the asylum, she had got separated from her son, and they only
found each other again weeks after we had recovered our sight,
Who took care of the boy during that time, We did, Your wife
and yourself, Yes, well, she did, because she could see, and the
rest of us helped as best we could, Do you mean to say that you
lived together as a group, with your wife as guide, As guide and
provider, You were very lucky, said the superintendent again,
You could call it that, Did you stay in touch with the people in
the group once things had got back to normal, Yes, of course,
And you still do, Apart from the first blind man, yes, Why that
one exception, He wasn't a very nice person, In what sense, In
all senses, That's too vague, Yes, I know, And you don't want to
be more specific, Speak to him yourself and make up your own
mind, Do you know where they live, Who, The first blind man
and his wife, They split up, they're divorced, Do you still see
her, Yes, we do, But not him, No, not him, Why, As I said, he's
not a nice person. The superintendent went back to his notebook and wrote down his own name so that it would not look
as if he had learned nothing from such a long interrogation. He
was about to make his next move, the most problematic and
risky of the whole game. He raised his head, looked at the doctor's wife, opened his mouth to speak, but she anticipated him,
You're a police superintendent, you came and identified yourself as such and have been asking us all kinds of questions, but
aside from the matter of the premeditated murder which I
committed and to which I have confessed, but for which there
were no witnesses, some because they died, and all of them because they were blind, not to mention the fact that no one
wants to know now what happened four years ago when everything was in chaos and the law was a mere dead letter, we are

still waiting for you to tell us what brought you here, I think it's time you put your cards on the table, stopped beating about the bush and got straight down to what really interests the person who sent you here. Up until that moment, the superintendent had had a very clear idea of the aim of the mission with which he had been charged by the interior minister, neither more nor less than finding out if there was some relationship between the phenomenon of the blank votes and the woman sitting there before him, but her interpolation, blunt and to the point, had disarmed him, and, worse than that, had made him suddenly aware of how ridiculous it would seem if he were to ask her, with his eyes cast down because he would not have the courage to look at her, You wouldn't by any chance be the organizer, the leader, the head of the subversive movement that came into being in order to place democracy in a situation which it would be no exaggeration to describe as perilous, if not fatal, What subversive movement, she would ask, The one behind the blank votes, Are you telling me that casting a blank vote is a subversive act, she would ask again, If it happens in large numbers, yes, And where does it say that, in the constitution, in the electoral law, in the ten commandments, in the highway code, on the cough medicine bottle, she would insist, Well, it's not written down exactly, but anyone can see that it's a simple matter of a hierarchy of values and of common sense, first there are the valid votes, then the blank votes, then the void votes, and, finally, the abstentions, I mean, obviously, democracy will be imperiled if one of those secondary categories overtakes the primary one, the votes are there so that we can make prudent use of them, And I'm the person to blame for what happened, That's what I'm trying to find out, And just how did I manage to get the majority of the population to cast blank votes, by slipping pamphlets under their doors, offering up midnight prayers and conjurations, adding a special chemical to the water supply, promising first prize in the lottery to everyone, or buying votes with the money my husband earns at his surgery, You kept your sight when everyone else was blind and you have been unable or unwilling to explain why, And that makes me guilty of a plot against world democracy, That's what I'm trying to find out, Well, go and find out, and when you've completed your investigation, come and tell me about it, until then you won't get another word out of me. And that, above all else, was what the superintendent did not want. He was just preparing to say that he had no further questions, but would return the following day, when the doorbell rang. The doctor got up and went to see who it was. He returned to the living-room accompanied by the inspector. This gentleman says he's a police inspector and that you gave him orders to come here, Yes, I did, said the superintendent, but I've finished my work for the day, we'll continue tomorrow at the same hour, Sir, you told me and the sergeant, the inspector broke in, but the super-intendent cut him off, What I did or did not tell you is of no interest now, So, tomorrow, will all three of us come, Inspector, that question is impertinent, any decisions I make are made in the proper place and at the proper time, and you will find out what they are in due course, replied the superintendent angrily. He turned to the doctor's wife and said, Tomorrow, as you re-quested, I won't waste time with circumlocutions, I'll come straight to the point, and you'll find what I have to ask you no less extraordinary than I find the fact that you kept your sight during the general epidemic of blindness four years ago, I went blind, the inspector went blind, your husband went blind, but you did not, we'll find out if, in this case, the old dictum holds true, she that made the saucepan made the lid, So it's to do with saucepans, then, superintendent, asked the doctor's wife in a wry tone, No, it's to do with lids, madam, lids, replied the su-perintendent as he withdrew, relieved that his adversary had supplied him with a reasonably nimble exit line. He had a faint headache.

THEY did not have lunch together. Sticking to his tactic of controlled dispersal, the superintendent reminded the inspector and the sergeant, when they went their separate ways, that they should not go to the same restaurants they had gone to yesterday, and, just as he would have done had he been his own subordinate, he himself scrupulously carried out the orders he had given. He did so in a spirit of self-sacrifice too, for he ended up choosing a restaurant which, despite the three stars promised on the menu, only put one on his plate. This time, there was not one meeting point, but two, the sergeant was waiting at the first, and the inspector at the second. They both saw at once that their superior was not in the mood for conversation, the encounter with the ophthalmologist and his wife had clearly not gone well. And since they, in turn, had gleaned no useful results from their investigations, the planned exchange and study of information back at providential ltd, insurance and reinsurance, did not promise to be the smoothest of rides. This professional tension was only heightened by the unexpected and troubling question put to them by the garage attendant when they arrived in their car, Where are you gentlemen from. It is true that the superintendent, all honor to him

his experience in the job, did not lose his cool, We're
from providential ltd, he replied sharply, and then, even more
sharply, We're going to park where we always park, in the company's designated space, so your question is not just impertinent, it's rude, It may well be impertinent and rude, but I really
don't remember seeing you here before, That, said the superintendent, is because not only are you rude, you also have a very
poor memory, my colleagues here are new to the company and
this is their first visit, but I've certainly been here before, now
get out of our way will you, the driver's a little nervous and he
might accidentally run you over. They parked the car and got
into the lift. Not even considering that it might be a rash thing
to say, the sergeant was eager to explain that he wasn't in the
least nervous, that in the aptitude tests he'd done before joining
the police, he had been described as very calm, but the superintendent silenced him with a brusque gesture. And now, protected by the reinforced walls and soundproof floor and ceiling of providential ltd, he launched a pitiless attack, Did it not
even occur to you, you idiot, that there might be microphones
installed in the lift, I'm sorry, sir, really I am, I wasn't thinking, spluttered the poor man, Tomorrow, you can stay here and
keep watch over the place and use the time to write out five
hundred times I am an idiot, Sir, please, Oh, leave it, take no
notice, I know I'm exaggerating, but that man annoyed me,
we've been carefully avoiding using the front door so as not to
draw attention to ourselves and then that creep shows up, Perhaps we should get our people to write him a note, the way they
did with the porter before we arrived, suggested the inspector,
That would be counter-productive, we don't want anyone to
notice us at all, It may be too late for that, sir, perhaps if the service has another place in the city, it would be best if we moved
in there, Oh, they have, they have, but as far as I know, none
of them is currently in operation, We could try, No, there's

no time, and, besides, the ministry wouldn't like the idea, this
business has got to be sorted out quickly, urgently, May I speak
frankly, sir, asked the inspector, Go ahead, Well, it seems to me
we're up a blind alley or, worse still, trapped inside a poisoned
wasps' nest, What makes you think that, It's hard to explain really, but the fact is that I feel as if we were sitting on a barrel
of gunpowder with the fuse lit, and that it's going to blow up
at any moment. The superintendent could have been listening
to his own thoughts, but his position and the responsibility he
bore to the mission he had been charged with allowed for no
swerving from the straight road of duty, I disagree, he said, and
with those two words brought the matter to a close.

  Now they were sitting round the table where they had eaten
breakfast that morning, with their notebooks open, ready for a
brainstorming session. You start, the superintendent told the
sergeant, As soon as I went into the apartment, he said, I could
tell no one had tipped the woman off, Of course they hadn't,
we had agreed that we would all arrive at half past ten, Yes, but
I was a bit late, it was actually ten thirty-seven when I knocked
on the door, confessed the sergeant, That doesn't matter now,
carry on, let's not waste any more time, She told me to come in
and asked if I would like a coffee, and I said I would, well, I
didn't see why not, I felt almost like a visitor, then I told her
that I was investigating what happened four years ago in the insane asylum, but then I thought it would be best not to broach
the subject of the blind murder victim immediately, which is
why I decided to ask instead about the cause of the fire, she
found it odd that after four years we should want to revisit the
very thing that everyone had been trying to forget, and I said
that the idea now was to record as many facts as possible because the weeks when those events took place could no longer
remain a blank in the nation's history, but she was no fool, she
immediately pointed out the incongruity, that was the word she

used, of us being in the situation in which we now find ourselves, with the city isolated and under a state of siege because of the blank votes, and someone having the idea of investigating what had happened during the plague of blindness, I have to admit, sir, that, at first, I was completely thrown and didn't know what to say in response, but I managed to come up with an explanation, which was that the investigation had been decided upon before the blank votes business, but that it had got delayed by bureaucratic red tape and that it had only been possible to implement it now, then she said that she had no idea what had caused the fire, it must have been mere coincidence, something that could easily have happened at any time, then I asked her how she had managed to get out, and she started telling me about the doctor's wife and praising her to the skies, saying what a remarkable person she was, completely unlike anyone she had met in her entire life, utterly remarkable, I'm sure, she said, that if it hadn't been for her, I wouldn't be here talking to you today, she saved us all, and it isn't just that she saved us, she did more than that, she protected us, fed us, looked after us, then I asked her who she meant when she used the personal pronoun us, and she listed, one by one, the people we already know about, and finally, she said that her then husband had also been part of the group, but that she didn't want to talk about him because they'd been divorced for three years, and that was all I learned from the conversation, sir, the impression I came away with was that the doctor's wife must be some kind of heroine, a truly noble soul. The superintendent pretended not to have heard those last few words. By doing so, he would not have to reprehend the sergeant for describing as a heroine and a truly noble soul a woman who was currently under suspicion of being involved in the worst crime that could, in the present circumstances, be committed against the nation. He felt tired. And in a quiet, flat voice, he asked the inspector to report on what he had learned at the house of the prostitute and the old man with the black eyepatch, Well, if she was a prostitute, I don't think she is anymore, Why, asked the superintendent, Because she doesn't have the manners or gestures or words or style of a prostitute, You seem to know a lot about prostitutes, Not really, sir, only the usual things, plus a bit of personal experience, but mainly preconceived ideas, Go on, They received me politely enough, but they didn't offer me any coffee, Are they married, Well, they were both wearing wedding rings, And what did you make of the old man, He's old, and that's about all there is to be said about him, There you're wrong, there is everything to be said about the old, it's just that no one asks them anything, and so they keep quiet, Well, he didn't, Good for him, carry on, Anyway, I started talking about the fire, as my colleague here did, but then realized that I wouldn't get anywhere doing that, and so I decided to make a head-on attack, I mentioned a letter that the police had received and which described certain criminal acts committed in the asylum before the fire, amongst them a murder, and I asked them if they knew anything about it, and she said that she did, that no one could possibly know more, since she herself was the murderer, And did she say what the murder weapon was, asked the superintendent, Yes, a pair of scissors, And did she stab the man in the heart, No, sir, in the throat, And what else, To be honest, I was completely taken aback, Yes, I can imagine, Suddenly we had two perpetrators for the same crime, Go on, What comes next is pure horror, The fire, you mean, No, sir, she started describing in shocking, almost brutal detail what happened to the women who were raped in the dormitory occupied by the blind men, And what did he do while his wife was describing all this, He just looked straight at me, with his one eye, as if he could see inside me, That's just your imagination, No, sir, I learned then that one eye can see better than two, because, not having the other eye to help it, it has to do all the work itself, Perhaps that's why they say that in the country of the blind, the one-eyed man is king, Perhaps it is, sir, Go on, continue, When she had stopped talking, he began by saying that he didn't believe that the motive for my visit, that was the expression he used, had anything to do with ascertaining the causes of a fire of which nothing now remained or of clearing up the circumstances surrounding a murder that could never be proved, and that, if I had nothing more of any value to add, would I please leave, And what did you say, I invoked my authority as a policeman, said that I'd gone there with a mission to carry out and that I'd take whatever steps were necessary to do so, And what did he say, He replied that, in that case, I must be the only policeman on duty in the entire capital, since the police force had disappeared weeks ago, and that he therefore thanked me for my concern for their safety and, he hoped, my concern for the safely of a few other people too, since he couldn't quite believe that a policeman had been sent solely for the benefit of the two people in that room, And then, The situation had become difficult and I couldn't really do much more, the only way I could find of covering my retreat was by saying that they should prepare themselves for a confrontation in court because, according to the information we had, which was absolutely reliable, it was not she who had killed the leader of the blind criminals, but another person, a woman who had already been identified, And how did they react, At first, I thought I had frightened them, but the old man recovered at once and said that, there in their home, or wherever it might be, they would be accompanied by a lawyer who knew more about the law than the police, Do you think you really did frighten them, asked the superintendent, Yes, I think so, but obviously I can't be sure, They might have been afraid, but certainly not for themselves, Who for, then, sir, For the real murderer, the doc-

tor's wife, But the prostitute, Look, I don't know that we have
the right to continue calling her that, inspector, All right, the
wife of the man with the black eyepatch said that she was the
killer, even though it's true that the man doesn't accuse her in
his letter, but the doctor's wife, Who was, in fact, the real per-
petrator of the crime, she herself confessed and confirmed as
much to me. At this point, it was logical for the inspector and
the sergeant to assume that their superior, now that he had
touched on the subject of his own investigations, would give
them a more or less complete report of what he had found out
from his visit, but the superintendent merely said that he would
be going back to the suspects' apartment the next day to interrogate them further and only then would he decide what to do
next, And what about us, what should we do tomorrow, asked
the inspector, Surveillance operations, nothing more, you take
care of the ex-wife of the man who wrote the letter, she doesn't
know you, so you shouldn't have any problem, Which means,
automatically and by a process of elimination, said the sergeant,
that I'll be taking care of the old man and the prostitute, Unless
you can prove that she really is a prostitute, or continues to be
one if she ever was, the use of the word prostitute is henceforth
banned from our conversations, Yes, sir, And even if she is, find
some other way of referring to her, Yes, sir, I'll use her name,
The names were all transcribed into my notebook, they are no
longer in yours, If you'd just tell me what her name is, sir, then
there'd be no more of this prostitute business, Sorry, I can't, I
consider that information to be, for the moment, confidential,
Her name, or all the names, asked the sergeant, All of them,
Well, then, I don't know what to call her, You can call her, for
example, the girl with the dark glasses, But she wasn't wearing
dark glasses, I can swear to that, Everyone has worn dark glasses
at least once in their life, replied the superintendent, getting
up. Shoulders hunched, he made his way over to the part of the

office where he had his bedroom and closed the door behind him. I bet you he's going to get in touch with the ministry, said the inspector, What's up with him, asked the sergeant, He feels as bewildered as we do, It's as if he doesn't believe in what he's doing, Do you, No, but I'm just following orders, he's in charge, he shouldn't be giving off these confusing signals, because we'll be the ones to suffer the consequences, when the wave hits the rock, it's always the mussels that pay, Hm, I'm not sure how accurate a comparison that is, Why, Because it always seems to me that the mussels are really glad when the water rushes over them, Search me, but I've certainly never heard mussels laugh, Oh, they not only laugh, they positively chuckle, it's just that the sound of the waves drowns them out, and you have to put your ear really close, That's not true, you're having fun now at the expense of a lowly sergeant, Don't get annoyed with me, it's simply a harmless way of passing the time, There's a better way than that, What, Sleep, I'm tired, I'm going to bed, The superintendent might need you, What, to go and bang my head against a brick wall again, I don't think so, You're probably right, said the inspector, I'll follow your example and go and have a lie-down too, but I'll leave a note here to tell him to call us if he needs us, Good idea.

The superintendent had taken off his shoes and lain down on the bed. He was lying on his back, with his hands clasped behind his head, looking up at the ceiling, as if hoping for some advice from there or, if not that, at least what we usually call a disinterested opinion. Perhaps because it was soundproof, and therefore deaf, the ceiling had nothing to say to him, and, since it spent most of its time alone, it had practically lost the power of speech. The superintendent was going over in his mind the conversation he'd had with the doctor's wife and her husband, her face and his face, the dog that had got to its feet, growling, when he came in, only to lie down again at a word from his mistress, the old brass oil lamp which reminded him of an identical one that had been in his parents' house, but which had disappeared no one knew how, he was mixing these memories with what he had just heard from the mouths of the inspector and the sergeant and he was wondering what the hell he was doing there. He had crossed the frontier in pure movie detective style, he had convinced himself that he had come to rescue his country from mortal danger, and, in the name of that conviction, had given his subordinates ridiculous orders for which they had been kind enough to forgive him, he had tried to hold together a precarious framework of suspicions that was gradually falling apart with each minute that passed, and now he was wondering, surprised by a vague anxiety that made his diaphragm tighten, what reasonably credible information could he, the puffin, invent to transmit to an albatross who would, at this moment, be asking impatiently why he was so late in sending him news. What am I going to say to him, he wondered, that our suspicions about the osprey have been confirmed, that the husband and the others are part of the conspiracy, then he'll ask who these others are, and I'll say there's an old man with a black eyepatch who would really suit the code-name wolf-fish, and a girl with dark glasses whom we could call cat-fish, and the ex-wife of the guy who wrote the letter, and she could be called needle-fish, always assuming you agree with these designations, albatross. The superintendent had already got up from the bed and was talking now on the red phone, he was saying, Yes, albatross, the people I've just mentioned are not really big fish, they were just lucky enough to meet the osprey, who protected them, And what did you make of the osprey, puffin, She seemed a decent woman, normal, intelligent, and, if everything the others said about her is true, albatross, and I'm inclined to think it is, then she is clearly a quite extraordinary person, So out of the ordinary, puffin, that she was capable of killing a man with a pair of scissors, According to the witnesses, albatross, the man was a vile rapist, a totally repellent creature, Let's not delude ourselves, puffin, it's clear to me that these people have cooked up a single version of events just in case anyone should ever come and interrogate them, they've had four years to do so, and the way I see it, from the information you've given me and from my own deductions and intuitions, I would bet anything you like that these five people constitute an organized cell, probably, even, the head of that tapeworm we talked about a while ago, Neither I nor my colleagues had that impression, albatross, Well, puffin, you're going to have no option but to change your mind, We would need proof, without proof, we can do nothing, albatross, Find it, then, puffin, make a rigorous search of all their homes, But we can't make house searches without the authorization of a judge, albatross, I would remind you, puffin, that the city is under a state of siege and that all the inhabitants' rights and guarantees have been suspended, And what if we can't find any proof, albatross, I refuse to admit that possibility, puffin, you strike me as rather too ingenuous for a superintendent, as long as I've been interior minister, any proofs that weren't there always turned up in the end, What you're asking me to do is neither easy nor pleasant, albatross, I'm not asking, puffin, I'm ordering you, Yes, albatross, but I would just like to point out that we have found no evidence of any crime, there's no proof that the person whom it was decided to consider as a suspect is, in fact, a suspect, indeed, all the contacts we have made, all the interrogations we have carried out, point to the innocence of that person, The photograph taken of a detainee, puffin, is always that of someone presumed to be innocent, only afterward does one learn that the criminal was there all the time, May I ask a question, albatross, Ask and I will answer, puffin, I've always been good at giving answers, What will happen if no proof of

guilt is found, The same as would happen if no proof of innocence were found, How should I understand that, albatross,
That there are cases when the sentence has been handed down
before the crime has even been committed, In that case, if I understand you rightly, albatross, I ask to be withdrawn from this
mission, You will be withdrawn, puffin, I promise you, but not
now, nor at your request, you will be withdrawn when this case
is closed, and this case will only be closed thanks to the praiseworthy efforts of you and your assistants, now listen carefully,
I'll give you five days, is that clear, five days, not a day longer, to
hand over the whole cell to me, bound hand and foot, your osprey and her husband, to whom, poor thing, we didn't ever get
round to giving a name, and the three little fishes who have just
surfaced, the wolf, the cat and the needle, I want them crushed
beneath a weight of evidence impossible to deny, slide out of,
contradict or refute, that is what I want, puffin, All right, albatross, I'll do what I can, You will do exactly what I have just said,
meanwhile, so that you don't think badly of me, and being, as I
am, a reasonable person, I realize that you will need some help
to bring your work to a successful conclusion, Are you going to
send me another inspector, albatross, No, puffin, my help will
be of a different nature, but just as effective, or possibly more
so, than if I were to despatch all the police at my command, I
don't understand, albatross, You will be the first to understand
when the bell sounds, The bell, The bell for the last round,
puffin. The line went dead.

The superintendent left the room when it was twenty minutes past six by the clock. He read the message that the inspector had left on the table and wrote underneath it, I have something to sort out, wait for me. He went down to the garage, got
into the car, started it and headed for the exit ramp. There he
stopped and beckoned to the attendant. Still smarting from the
angry exchange of words and the ill-treatment he had received

from the tenant of providential ltd, the man came reluctantly
over to the car window and uttered the customary phrase, Can
I help you, A while ago, I was rather rough with you, Oh, that's
all right, we're used to it here, Yes, but I didn't mean to offend
you, No, I'm sure you didn't, sir, Superintendent, I'm a police
superintendent, here's my identification, Forgive me, superintendent, I would never have imagined, and the other gentlemen, The youngest is a sergeant and the other one is an inspector, I understand, superintendent, and I promise I won't bother
you again, but I had the very best of intentions, We've been
carrying out an investigation here, but that's finished now, and
so we're just like anyone else, it's as if we were on holiday, although, for your own sake, I nevertheless recommend great
discretion, remember that, even when he's on holiday, a policeman is still a policeman, it is, if you like, in his blood, Oh, I understand perfectly, superintendent, but, in that case, if you don't
mind me speaking frankly, it would have been better not to
have told me anything, what the eye doesn't see, the heart
doesn't grieve over, he that knows nothing sees nothing, Yes,
but I needed to tell someone, and you were the person nearest
to hand. The car was already going up the ramp, but the superintendent had one further piece of advice, Keep your mouth
shut, I wouldn't want to have to regret what I told you. He certainly would have regretted it if he had turned round, for he
would have found the man muttering secretively into the
phone, perhaps telling his wife that he had just met a police superintendent, perhaps informing the porter of the identity of
the three men in dark suits who always go straight up from the
garage to providential ltd, insurance and reinsurance, perhaps
this, perhaps that, we will probably never know the truth about
this phone call. A few meters further on, the superintendent
drew up by the kerb, took his notebook out of his jacket pocket,
leafed through it until he reached the page where he had tran-

scribed the names and addresses of the treacherous letter writer's former companions, then consulted the map and the city guide to check again where the traitor's ex-wife lived, since she was closest. He also made a note of the route he would have to follow to the house of the man with the black eyepatch and the girl with the dark glasses. He smiled to remember the sergeant's confusion when he told him that this would be the perfect name for the wife of the old man with the black eyepatch, But she wasn't wearing dark glasses, the poor sergeant had replied, bewildered. That was unfair of me, thought the superintendent, I should have shown him the group photo, in which the girl is standing with her arms by her side and in her right hand is holding a pair of dark glasses, elementary, my dear watson, but one had to have a superintendent's eyes to notice such things. He started the car. An impulse had made him leave providential ltd, an impulse had made him tell the garage attendant who he was, an impulse is taking him now to the home of the divorcee, an impulse will take him to the home of the old man with the black eyepatch, and the same impulse would have driven him afterward to the home of the doctor's wife had he not told them, both wife and husband, that he would be back tomorrow, at the same time, to continue the interrogation. What interrogation, he thought, would he say to her, for example, you are suspected of being the organizer, the leader, the kingpin of the subversive movement that has placed democracy in such grave danger, I am referring to the blank vote movement, and don't play the innocent with me, don't waste my time asking me if I have proof of what I'm saying, you, madam, are the one who will have to prove her innocence, because you can be quite sure, madam, that the proof will appear when it's needed, it's just a matter of inventing one or two irrefutable ones, and even if they're not completely irrefutable, the circumstantial evidence, however remote in time, will be enough for us, as will the incomprehensible fact that you did not go blind four years ago when everyone else in the city was stumbling around and bumping into lampposts, and before you say that one thing has nothing to do with the other, let me just say, she that made the saucepan made the lid, that, at least, albeit expressed in different words, is the opinion of my minister, whom I have to obey even if it makes my heart ache, now you will say, a superintendent's heart can't ache, well, that's what you think, you may know a lot about superintendents, but I can guarantee you know nothing about this one, it's true I didn't come here with the honest aim of finding out the truth, it's true that you will have been condemned before even being judged, but the heart of this puffin, which is what my minister calls me, is aching and I don't know how to make it stop, take my advice, confess, confess even if you're not guilty, the government will tell the people that they have been the victims of an unparalleled case of mass hypnosis, that you are a genius in the art, people might even be amused and life will get back on track, you'll spend a few years in prison, your friends will end up there too if we so choose, and meanwhile, of course, there'll be a reform of the electoral law and an end to blank votes, or else they'll be distributed equally amongst all the parties as valid votes, so that the percentages will not be affected, after all, dear lady, it's the percentages that count, as for the voters who abstain and fail to produce a medical certificate, why not publish their names in the newspapers just as, in the olden days, criminals were pilloried in the public square, the reason I'm speaking to you in this way is because I like you, and just so that you can see how much I like you, I will tell you that the greatest happiness life could have given me four years ago, apart from not having lost part of my family in that tragedy, which, alas, I did, would have been to be a member of the group that you protected, I wasn't a superintendent then, I was a blind inspector, just a blind inspector who, after recovering his sight, would be there in the photo along with the others whom you saved from the fire, and your dog would not have growled when he saw me, and if all that and more had happened, I would be able to declare on my word of honor to the interior minister that he is wrong, that an experience like that and four years of friendship are enough for anyone to say that they know a person well, and to think that I entered your house as an enemy and now don't know how to leave it, whether alone, in order to confess to the minister that I have failed in my mission, or accompanied by you, taking you to prison. These last thoughts did not come from the superintendent, he was now more concerned with finding somewhere to park than with anticipating decisions on the fate of a suspect and on his own fate. He once more consulted his notebook and rang the bell of the apartment block where the ex-wife of the man who wrote the letter lives. He rang again and again, but the door did not open. He was reaching out his hand to make a fresh attempt, when he saw a ground-floor window open and an elderly woman in rollers and a housecoat poke her head out, Who are you looking for, she asked, The lady who lives in the first-floor apartment on the right, replied the superintendent, She's not in, in fact, I saw her go out, Do you know when she'll be back, No idea, but I'll be glad to give her a message, said the woman, Thank you, but it doesn't really matter, I'll come back another day. It didn't even occur to him that the woman with the rollers might be thinking that the divorcee on the first floor on the right had apparently taken to receiving male visitors, the one who came this morning and this one now, who was old enough to be her father. The superintendent glanced at the map open on the seat beside him, started the car and set off for his second objective. This time, no neighbors appeared at the windows. The street door was open and so he could go straight up to the second floor, this is where the old man with the black eyepatch and the girl with the dark glasses live, what a strange couple, it's understandable that their helplessness when blind would have brought them together, but four years had passed, and while, for a young woman, four years are nothing, for an old man, it's more like eight. And yet they're still together, thought the superintendent. He rang the bell and waited. No one answered. He pressed his ear to the door and listened. Silence from the other side. He rang again out of habit, not because he expected anyone to come. He went down the stairs, got into the car and murmured, I know where they are. If he had had a direct line in his car and could have phoned the minister to tell him where he was going, he was sure the minister would reply in more or less these words, Bravo, puffin, that's the way to do it, catch those guys red-handed, but be careful, you should take reinforcements with you really, a man alone against five desperate villains, that's the kind of thing you only see in movies, besides, you don't know karate, that's after your time, Don't worry, albatross, I may not know karate, but I know what I'm doing, Go in there with your gun in your hand, terrify them, scare the shit out of them, Yes, albatross, Good, I'll start sorting out your medal now, There's no hurry, albatross, we don't yet know if I'll get out of this enterprise alive, It's a dead cert, puffin, I have every confidence in you, oh, I certainly knew what I was doing when I appointed you to this mission, Yes, albatross.

The streetlights come on, the evening is creeping up the ramp of the sky, soon night will begin. The superintendent rang the bell, no reason for surprise, policemen mostly do ring the bell, they don't always kick the door down. The doctor's wife appeared, I was expecting you tomorrow, superintendent, I'm afraid I can't talk to you right now, she said, we have visitors, Yes, I know them, that is, I don't know them personally, but I know who they are, That doesn't seem reason enough for me to let you in, Please, My friends have nothing to do with what brought you here, Not even you know what brought me here, and it's high time you did, Come in.

THERE is an idea abroad that, generally speaking, the conscience of a police superintendent tends, on professional grounds and on principle, to be fairly accommodating, not to say resigned to the incontrovertible fact, theoretically and practically proven, that what must be must be and that there's nothing to be done about it. The truth is, however, that, although it may not be the most common of spectacles, it has been known for one of these valuable public servants, by chance and when least expected, to find himself caught between the devil and the deep blue sea, that is, between what he should be and what he would prefer not to be. For the superintendent of providential ltd, insurance and reinsurance, that day has come. He had spent at most half an hour at the home of the doctor's wife, but that short time was enough to reveal to the astonished group gathered there the murky depths of his mission. He said he would do everything possible to divert from that place and those people the more than disquieting attentions of his superiors, but that he could not guarantee success, he told them he had been given the extremely tight deadline of five days to conclude the investigation and knew that the only acceptable verdict would be one of guilty, and, addressing the doctor's wife, he said The person they want to make the scapegoat, if you'll forgive the obvious impropriety of the expression, is you, madam, and, possibly indirectly, your husband, as for the others, I don't think you're in any real danger, your crime, madam, wasn't murdering that man, your great crime was not going blind when the rest of us did, the incomprehensible can be merely an object of scorn, but not if there is always a way of using it as a pretext. It is three o'clock in the morning, and the superintendent is tossing and turning in bed, unable to get to sleep. He is mentally making plans for the next day, he repeats them obsessively and then starts all over again, telling the inspector and the sergeant that, as arranged, he will go to the doctor's house to continue the interrogation of the wife, reminding them of the task he had charged them with, following the other members of the group, but, given the present situation, none of this makes sense anymore, now what he needs to do is to impede, to hinder events, to invent for the investigation advances and delays that will, without making it too obvious, simultaneously feed and hamper the minister's plans, in short, he needs to wait and see what the minister's promised help involves. It was nearly half past three when the red telephone rang. The superintendent leapt out of bed, put on the slippers bearing the police insignia and, half-ran, half-stumbled over to the desk on which the phone stood. Even before he had sat down, he was putting the receiver to his ear and saying, Hello, It's albatross here, said the voice at the other end, Hello, albatross, puffin here, Now pay attention, puffin, I have some instructions for you, Yes, albatross, Today, at nine o'clock, this morning, not tonight, a person will be waiting for you at post six-north on the frontier, the army has been warned, so there'll be no problem, Am I to understand that this person is coming to replace me, albatross, There's no reason for you to think that, puffin, you have done well so far and will, I hope, continue

to do so until this affair is closed, Thank you, albatross, and
what are your orders, As I said, a person will be waiting for you
at nine o'clock this morning at post six-north on the frontier,
Yes, albatross, I've already made a note of that, You will give
this person the photograph you mentioned, the one of the
group in which the main suspect appears, you will also give him
the list of names and addresses you obtained and which you
have in your possession. The superintendent felt a shiver run
down his spine, But that photograph is necessary for my ongoing investigations, he said, Well, I don't think it's as necessary as you say it is, puffin, indeed, I would go so far as to say
that you don't need it at all, given that, either personally or
through your subordinates, you have already made contact
with all the members of the gang, You mean group, don't you,
albatross, A gang is a group, Yes, albatross, but not all groups
are gangs, Why, puffin, I had no idea you were so concerned
about correct definitions, you obviously make good use of dictionaries, Forgive me for correcting you, albatross, my mind's
still a bit fuzzy, Were you asleep, No, albatross, I was thinking
about what I have to do tomorrow, Well, now you know, the
person who will be waiting for you at post six-north is a man
about your age and he will be wearing a blue tie with white
spots, I shouldn't think there will be many other ties like that at
military posts on the frontier, Do I know him, albatross, No,
you don't, he's not from our department, Ah, He will respond
to your password with the phrase No, there's never enough,
And what's mine, There's always plenty of time, Very good, albatross, your orders will be carried out, I'll be there on the
frontier at nine o'clock to meet him, Now go back to bed and
sleep well for the rest of the night, puffin, I myself have been
working up until now, so I'm going to do the same, May I ask
you a question, albatross, Of course, but keep it short, Does the
photograph have anything to do with the help you promised

me, Very sharp of you, puffin, nothing gets past you, does it, So it does have something to do with it, Yes, it has everything to do with it, but don't expect me to tell you how, if I told you that, it would ruin the element of surprise, Even though I'm the person directly responsible for the investigations, Exactly, Does that mean you don't trust me, albatross, Draw a square on the ground, puffin, and put yourself inside it, within the space delineated by the lines of that square I trust you, but outside of it, I trust only myself, your investigation is that square, be content with the square and with your investigation, Yes, albatross, Sleep well, puffin, you'll hear from me before the week is out, I'll be here waiting, albatross, Good night, puffin, Good night, albatross. Despite the minister's conventional wishes for a good night's sleep, what little remained of the night did not prove of much use to the superintendent. Sleep refused to come, the doors and passageways of the brain were all closed, and inside ruled insomnia, queen and absolute mistress. Why does he want the photo, he asked himself over and over again, what did he mean by that threat that I would hear from him before the week was out, there was no threat contained in the individual words, but the tone, yes, the tone was threatening, if the superintendent, after a lifetime of interrogating all kinds of people, has learned to distinguish in amongst the tangled labyrinth of syllables the path he must follow to get out, he is also perfectly capable of noticing the shadowy zones that each word produces and trails behind it whenever it is pronounced. Say out loud the words You'll hear from me before the week is out, and you will see how easy it is to introduce into them a drop of insidious dread, the putrid stench of fear, the authoritarian timbre of a paternal ghost. The superintendent would prefer to think such soothing thoughts as these, But I have no reason to feel afraid, I do my work, I carry out the orders I'm given, and yet, in the depths of his conscience, he knew this was not true, he wasn't carrying out those orders for the simple reason that he did not believe that because the doctor's wife had not gone blind four years she was therefore to blame for eighty-three percent of the capital's voting population having cast blank votes, as if the first odd fact were automatically responsible for the second. Even he doesn't believe it, he thought, he just wants a target to aim at, if this one fails, he'll find another, and another, and another, as many as it takes until he finally gets it right, or until, by dint of sheer repetition, the people he is trying to persuade of his merits grow indifferent to the methods and processes he adopts. In either case, the party will have won. Thanks to the skeleton key of digression, sleep had managed to open a door, escape down one of the corridors and immediately set the superintendent dreaming that the interior minister had asked him for the photograph so that he could stick a pin through the eyes of the doctor's wife, all the while singing a wizard's spell, Blind you were not, blind you will be, white you wore, black you will see, with this pin I prick you, from behind and before. Terrified, drenched in sweat, his heart pounding, the superintendent woke to the screams of the doctor's wife and the loud laughter of the minister, What an awful dream, he muttered as he turned on the light, what monstrous things the brain can generate. According to the clock, it was half past seven. He calculated how much time he would need to reach post six-north and was almost tempted to thank the nightmare for having been so kind as to wake him. He dragged himself out of bed, his head weighed heavy as lead, his legs weighed even more than his head, and he staggered uncertainly to the bathroom. He emerged twenty minutes later, slightly reinvigorated by the shower, newly shaved and ready for work. He put on a clean shirt and finished dressing, He'll be wearing a blue tie with white spots, he thought, and went into the kitchen to heat up a cup of coffee left over from the previous evening. The inspec-

tor and the sergeant must still have been sleeping, at least, they
gave no sign of life. He munched his way unenthusiastically
through a biscuit, and even bit into another one, then returned
to the bathroom to clean his teeth. He went into the bedroom,
placed in a medium-sized envelope the photograph and the list
of names and addresses, having first copied the latter onto another piece of paper, and when he went back into the sitting-
room, he heard noises coming from the room in the apartment
where his subordinates were sleeping. He didn't wait for them,
nor did he knock on their door. He scribbled a note, I had to go
out early, I'm taking the car, do as I told you yesterday and concentrate on following the women, the wife of the man with
the black eyepatch and the ex-wife of the man who wrote the
letter, have lunch out if you can manage it, I'll be back here
later this afternoon, I expect results. Clear orders, precise instructions, if only everything could be like that in this superintendent's difficult life. He left providential ltd and took the lift
down to the garage. The attendant was already there, the superintendent said good morning, received a greeting in return,
and wondered, in passing, if the man actually slept in the garage too, There don't seem to be any specific hours of work in
this place. It was nearly half past eight, I've got time, he thought,
I'll be there in less than half an hour, besides, I shouldn't be the
first to arrive, albatross was quite explicit, quite clear about
that, the man will be waiting for me at nine o'clock, so I can arrive a minute later, or two or three, at midday if I want. He
knew this wasn't true, that he must simply not arrive before the
man he was going to meet, Perhaps it's because the soldiers on
guard at post six-north would get nervous seeing someone
parked on this side of the dividing line, he thought, as he put
his foot down on the accelerator to go up the ramp. Monday
morning, but there wasn't much traffic, the superintendent
would take twenty minutes at most to reach post six-north. But

where the devil is post six-north, he suddenly asked out loud. In the north, of course, but six, where the hell was that. The minister had said six-north as if it were the most natural thing in the world, as if it were one of the capital's most famous monuments or else the metro station that had been destroyed by a bomb, the kind of place that everyone was sure to know, and, foolishly, it had not occurred to him to ask, Just where exactly is that, albatross. In a matter of a moment the amount of sand in the upper part of the hour-glass had dwindled dramatically, the tiny grains were rushing through the opening, each grain more eager to leave than the last, time is just like people, sometimes it's all it can do to drag itself along, but at others, it runs like a deer and leaps like a young goat, which, when you think about it, is not saying much, since the cheetah is the fastest of all the animals, and yet it has never occurred to anyone to say of another person He runs and jumps like a cheetah, perhaps because that first comparison comes from the magical late middle ages, when gentlemen went deer hunting and no one had ever seen a cheetah running or even heard of its existence. Languages are conservative, they always carry their archives with them and hate having to be updated. The superintendent, having managed to park the car somewhere, had unfolded the map of the city and was now resting it on the steering-wheel, anxiously searching for post six-north on the northern periphery of the capital. It would be relatively easy to locate if the city were shaped like a rhombus or a lozenge or formed a parallelogram, a space whose four lines circumscribed, as albatross had so coolly put it, the amount of trust he deserved, but the city's outline is irregular and, on the fringes, on either side, it is impossible to tell where the north ends and where the east or the west begins. The superintendent looks at his watch and feels as afraid as a sergeant expecting a reprimand from his superior. He won't arrive on time, it's simply impossible. He tries to reason calmly, Logic would say, but since when has logic ruled human decisions, that the various military posts would have been numbered in a clockwise direction from the westernmost point of the northern sector, hour-glasses are clearly of no use in this instance. Perhaps this reasoning is wrong, but then since when has reason ruled human decisions, not an easy question to answer, but it's always better to have one oar than none, and, besides, it is written that a moored boat goes nowhere, and so the superintendent put a cross where it seemed to him post number six should be and set off. Since the traffic was light and there wasn't so much as the shadow of a policeman on the streets, he was sorely tempted to jump every red light he came to, a temptation he did not resist. He was not speeding, he was flying, he barely took his foot off the accelerator, and when he had to brake, he performed a controlled skid, as those acrobats of the steering-wheel do in car chases in the movies, making the more nervous spectators jump in their seats. The superintendent had never driven like this in his life and he never would again. It was already gone nine o'clock when he finally reached post six-north, and the soldier who came to find out what this agitated driver wanted told him that this was, in fact, five-north. The superintendent swore out loud and was about to turn round, but stopped this precipitate gesture just in time and asked in which direction he would find six-north. The soldier pointed east and, just in case there was any doubt, uttered two brief words, That way. Fortunately, there was a road running more or less parallel to the frontier, it was only a matter of three kilometers, the way is clear, there aren't even any traffic lights, the car started, accelerated, braked, took a bend at breathtaking speed and screeched to a halt, almost touching the yellow line painted across the street, there it is, post six-north. Next to the barrier, about thirty meters away, a middle-aged man was waiting, So he's quite a bit younger than me, thought the superintendent. He picked up the envelope and got out of the car. He couldn't see a single soldier, they must have had orders to keep out of sight or to look the other way while this ceremony of meeting and handing-over took place. The superintendent walked toward the man. He was holding the envelope in his hand and thinking, I mustn't make any excuses about being late, if I were to say Hello, good morning, sorry about the delay, I had a bit of trouble finding the place, and, do you know what, albatross forgot to tell me where post six-north was, you didn't have to be a genius to realize that this long, rambling sentence could be understood by the other man as a false password, and then one of two things would happen, the man would either summon the soldiers to arrest this liar and provocateur, or he would take out his gun and with a cry of Down with blank ballot papers, down with sedition, death to all traitors, would carry out a summary execution. The superintendent had reached the barrier. The man did not move, he just looked at him. He had his left thumb hooked in his belt, his right hand in his raincoat pocket, all far too natural to be real. He's armed, he's carrying a gun, thought the superintendent, and said, There's always plenty of time. The man did not smile or even blink, he said, No, there's never enough, and then the superintendent gave him the envelope, perhaps now they could say good morning to each other, perhaps chat for a few moments about what a pleasant Monday morning it was, but the other man merely said, Fine, you can leave now, I'll make sure this finds its way to the right person. The superintendent got into his car, reversed and drove back to the city. Feeling embittered and utterly frustrated, he tried to console himself by imagining what a good joke it would have been to hand the man an empty envelope and then wait to see what happened. The minister, ablaze with anger and incandescent with rage, would immediately phone him to demand an explanation and he, the superintendent, would then swear by all the saints in the court of heaven, including those on earth still awaiting canonization, that the envelope had contained the photograph and the list of names and addresses, just as he had ordered, My responsibility, albatross, ended the moment that your messenger, having put down the gun he was holding, yes, I could see he was carrying a gun, took his right hand out of his raincoat pocket to receive the envelope, But the envelope was empty, I opened it myself, the minister would scream, That's nothing to do with me, albatross, he would reply with the serenity of someone at perfect peace with his conscience, Oh, I know what you're up to, the minister would bawl, you don't want me to touch so much as a hair on the head of your fancy woman, She's not my fancy woman, she's a person who is entirely innocent of the crime she's been accused of, albatross, Don't call me albatross, your father was an albatross, your mother was an albatross, but I'm the interior minister, If the interior minister has ceased to be an albatross, then the police superintendent will cease to be a puffin, At this precise moment, the puffin is very likely to cease being a superintendent, Well, anything's possible, Anyway, send me another copy of the photo today, do you hear, But I haven't got one, Oh, but you will have, more than one if necessary, How, Very easy, by going to where you'll find one, in your fancy woman's apartment or in the other two apartments, you don't expect me to believe that the photo that disappeared was the only copy, do you. The superintendent shook his head, The minister's no fool, there would be no point handing him an empty envelope. He was almost in the center of the city now, where things were, of course, livelier, although not in any exaggerated or noisy way. He could see that the people he passed had their worries, but, at the same time, they seemed quite calm. The superintendent ignored the obvious contradiction, the fact that he could not explain in words what

he saw did not mean that he couldn't feel it, that he could not
sense it with his feelings. The man and woman over there, for
example, you can see that they like each other, that they're fond
of each other, that they love each other, you can see that they're
happy, look, they just smiled, and yet, not only are they worried, they are, if I may put it like this, calmly and clearly aware
of that. You can see that the superintendent is worried too, perhaps, well, what does one more contradiction matter, perhaps
that is why he has gone into this café to have a proper breakfast
that will distract him and make him forget the warmed-up coffee and the stale biscuits of providential ltd, insurance and reinsurance, he has just ordered some freshly squeezed orange
juice, some toast and a cup of real coffee with milk. God bless
whoever invented you, he murmured piously to the toast when
the waiter set it down before him, wrapped in a napkin in the
old-fashioned way, so that it would not get cold. He asked for a
newspaper, the front page carried only foreign news, there was
nothing of local interest, apart from a statement from the minister of foreign affairs announcing that the government was
preparing to consult various international bodies about the
former capital's anomalous situation, starting with the united
nations and ending with the court in the hague, passing through
the european union, the organization for economic cooperation and development, the organization of petroleum-export-
ing countries, the north atlantic treaty organization, the world
bank, the international monetary fund, the world trade organization, the world organization for atomic energy, the world
organization for labor, the world meteorological organization,
and a few other bodies, which were only secondary or still under discussion, and therefore not mentioned. Albatross will be
most put out, it seems they're trying to steal his sweets, thought
the superintendent. He looked up from the newspaper like
someone who feels a sudden need to gaze into the distance and

said to himself that perhaps this news was the reason behind that unexpected and urgent demand for the photograph, He never was one to allow people to get one over on him, he's obviously preparing his next trick, and it'll probably be a dirty trick, the dirtiest of the dirty, he murmured. Then it occurred to him that he had the whole day to himself, that he could do whatever he wanted. He had set the inspector and the sergeant their task, and a useless task it was, they would, at this moment, be lurking in some doorway or behind a tree, they would already be waiting to see who left the house first, the inspector doubtless hoping it would be the girl with dark glasses, while the sergeant, because there was no one else, would have to content himself with the ex-wife of the man who wrote the letter. The worst thing that could happen to the inspector would be for the old man with the black eyepatch to appear, not so much for the reason you are thinking, that following a pretty, young woman is obviously a more attractive prospect than trailing after an old man, but because people with only one eye see twice as much, they don't have their other eye to distract them or to insist on looking at something else, we've said as much before, but truths need to be repeated many times so that they don't, poor things, lapse into oblivion. And what shall I do, wondered the superintendent. He summoned the waiter, returned the newspaper, paid the bill and left. As he was sitting down behind the wheel again, he glanced at his watch, Half past ten, he thought, a good time, precisely the hour I set for the second interrogation. A good time, he had thought, but he would not have been able to say why or for what. He could, if he chose, go back to providential ltd and rest until lunchtime, perhaps even sleep a little and make up for the sleep he had lost during the wretched night he had had to endure, the painful conversation with the minister, the nightmare, the screams of the doctor's wife when the albatross stuck the pin through her eyes, but the idea of shutting himself up between those gloomy walls seemed repulsive to him, he had nothing to do there, he certainly didn't want to spend his time reviewing the store of arms and munitions, as he had thought he would do when he first arrived, and as was his duty as superintendent, as surely as if it had been set down in writing. The morning still retained some of the luminous quality of dawn, the air was cool, the ideal weather for a walk. He got out of the car and started walking. He went to the end of the street, turned left and found himself in a square, he crossed it, set off down another street and reached another square, he had a memory of having been here four years ago, one blind man amongst other blind men, listening to speakers who were also blind, the last echoes, if one could but hear them, would be from the most recent political meetings to have been held in those places, the p.o.t.r. in the first square, the p.i.t.m. in the second, and as for the p.o.t.l., as if this were its historical fate, it had had to make do with a bit of waste ground right on the edge of the city. The superintendent walked and walked, and suddenly, how he didn't know, found himself in the street where the doctor and his wife lived, he did not, however, think, This is the street where the doctor lives. He slackened his pace, continuing along on the other side, and he was perhaps twenty meters away when the door of the building opened and the doctor's wife appeared with the dog. The superintendent immediately swung round, went over to a shop window and stood there looking in and waiting, if she crossed over, she would see him reflected in the glass. She didn't. The superintendent stared studiously in the opposite direction, the doctor's wife was moving away from him, the dog, with no lead, was walking along beside her. Then it occurred to the superintendent that he should follow her, that it wouldn't go amiss if he were to do what the sergeant and the inspector were doing at that very moment, if they were trudging the streets behind the other

suspects, then he had a duty to do the same even if he was a superintendent, now where's that woman going, the dog is probably just a cover, or perhaps she uses the dog's collar for trans-
porting secret messages, ah, what happy times they were when
St Bernard dogs used to carry little barrels of brandy around
their neck and with that small amount how many lives feared
lost in the snowy alps were saved. His pursuit of the suspect, if
we want to continue calling her that, did not last long. In a se-
cluded spot, rather like a village forgotten in the middle of the
city, there was a slightly neglected park, with large shady trees,
sandy walks and flower beds, rustic, green-painted benches,
and, in the middle, a lake in which a statue, representing a female figure, bent over the water with her empty water jar. The
doctor's wife sat down, opened the bag she had brought with
her and took out a book. Until she had opened the book and
started reading, the dog would not move from there. She looked
up from the page and said, Off you go, and he ran off to do, as
people used to say in more euphemistic days, what no one else
could do for him. The superintendent watched from a distance
and remembered his question to himself after breakfast, And
what shall I do. For about five minutes he lurked behind the
bushes, it was lucky the dog hadn't come this way, he might
have recognized him and this time done more than just growl
at him. The doctor's wife wasn't waiting for anyone, she had, as
so many other people do, simply taken her dog for a walk. The
superintendent went straight over to her, making the sand
crunch underfoot, and stopped a few feet away. Slowly, as if she
found it hard to tear herself away from her reading, the doctor's wife raised her head and looked at him. She did not appear
to recognize him at first, probably because she wasn't expecting
to see him there, then she said, We were waiting for you, but
when you didn't come and the dog was getting impatient for
his walk, I decided to bring him here, but my husband's at

home, he'll look after you until I get back, unless, of course, you're in a hurry, No, I'm not in a hurry, You go ahead, then, I'll be right there, once the dog has had a bit of a run, after all, it's not his fault people decided to cast blank ballot papers, If you don't mind, and since chance seems to have arranged it this way, I'd prefer to talk to you here, without witnesses, And I assumed that this interrogation, to continue calling it by that name, would take place with my husband present, like the first one, It wouldn't be an interrogation, my notebook won't leave my pocket, and I haven't got a tape-recorder concealed about my person either, besides, I have to say that my memory isn't what it was, it forgets easily, especially when I don't tell it to record what it hears, Oh, I had no idea the memory could hear, It's our second set of ears, those on the outside only serve to carry the sound inside, What do you want then, Like I said, I want to talk to you, About what, About what's happening in this city, Superintendent, I'm very grateful to you for coming to my house yesterday evening and for telling us, and my friends too, that there are people in the government interested in the strange phenomenon of the doctor's wife who failed to go blind four years ago and who now, it seems, is the organizer of a conspiracy against the state, but, to be perfectly frank, unless you have something more to say to me on the subject, I really don't think there's much point in our talking about anything else, The interior minister made me hand over the group photograph of you, your husband and your friends, this very morning I went to a military post on the frontier to do so, So you did have something to tell me, but there really wasn't any need for you to follow me, you could have gone straight to my house, you know the way, But I didn't follow you, I wasn't hiding behind a tree or pretending to read a newspaper while I waited for you to leave your house so that I could follow you, as the inspector and the sergeant engaged with me on this investiga-

tion will be doing with your friends right now, although the
only reason I ordered them to do so was to keep them occupied, that's all, Do you mean to tell me you're here by chance,
Yes, I happened to be walking down the street and I saw you
leaving your house, It's hard to believe that it was pure chance
that brought you to the street where I live, Call it what you
like, But it was, at any rate, a happy coincidence, if you prefer
to call it that, without it I wouldn't have found out that the
photograph is now in the hands of your minister, Oh, that I
would have told you on another occasion, And what, may I ask,
does he want with it, I've no idea, he didn't tell me, but I'm sure
it won't be for any good purpose, So you didn't come to submit
me to a second interrogation, said the doctor's wife, No, not today, not tomorrow, never, as far as I'm concerned, I know all I
need to know about this story, You'll have to explain yourself
better, sit down, don't just stand there like that woman with the
empty water jar. The dog suddenly appeared and came bound-
ing out from behind some bushes heading straight for the superintendent, who instinctively drew back, Don't be frightened, said the doctor's wife, grabbing the dog by the collar, he
won't bite you, How did you know I was afraid of dogs, Oh, I'm
no witch, I just observed you when you were in our apartment,
Is it that obvious, It is rather, steady, this last word was addressed to the dog, who had stopped barking and was instead
producing a low, continuous noise in its throat, far more intimidating than a growl, the sound of an organ the bass notes of
which have been badly tuned. You'd better sit down, that way
he'll know you mean me no harm. The superintendent gin-
gerly sat down, keeping his distance, Is his name Steady, No,
it's Constant, but for us and for my friends he's the dog of tears,
we called him Constant for short, Why the dog of tears, Because four years ago I was crying and this creature came and
licked my face, During the time of the white blindness, Yes,

during the time of the white blindness, this dog is the second
marvel from those wretched days, first the woman who did not
go blind when it seems it was her duty to do so, then this compassionate dog who came and drank her tears, Did that really
happen, or was I dreaming, What we dream also happens, superintendent, Hopefully not everything, Do you have some
reason for saying that, No, not really, I was just talking for the
sake of it. The superintendent was lying, the sentence he had
refused to allow his mouth to utter would have been quite different, Hopefully the albatross will not come and poke out
your eyes. The dog had come closer and was almost touching
the superintendent's knees with its nose. It was looking at him
and its eyes were saying, I won't hurt you, don't be afraid, she
wasn't when I found her on that other day. Then the superintendent slowly reached out his hand and touched the dog's
head. He felt like crying and letting the tears course down his
face, perhaps the marvel would be repeated. The doctor's wife
put her book away in her bag and said, Let's go, Where, asked
the superintendent, You'll have lunch with us, won't you, if
you've nothing more important to do, Are you sure, About
what, That you want to have me sitting at your table, Yes, I'm
sure, And you're not afraid I might be tricking you, Not with
those tears in your eyes, no.

WHEN the superintendent arrived back at providential ltd, it was after seven o'clock in the evening, and he found his subordinates waiting for him. They were clearly not happy. How was your day, any news to report, he asked them in a bright, almost jovial tone, pretending an interest which, as we know better than anyone, he did not feel, As for the day, awful, as for news to report, even worse, replied the inspector, We would have been better off staying in bed and sleeping, said the sergeant, What do you mean, In my entire life, I cannot remember ever having been involved in such a stupid, pointless investigation, began the inspector. The superintendent would gladly have chimed in with You don't know the half of it, but he chose to remain silent. The inspector went on, It was ten o'clock by the time I reached the street where the guy who wrote the letter's ex lives, Sorry, said the sergeant, but you can't say ex, Why not, Because that could mean she was just his ex-girlfriend, Does it matter, asked the inspector, Yes, she wasn't his girlfriend, she was his spouse, All right, what I should have said was that at ten o'clock I reached the street where the guy who wrote the letter's ex-spouse lives, That's better, But spouse sounds ridiculous and pretentious, when you

introduce your wife to someone, I bet you don't say and this is
my spouse. The superintendent cut short the discussion, Keep
that for another time, let's get to what's important, What's important, went on the inspector, is that I was there until nearly
midday, and she still hadn't left her apartment, not that this really surprised me, the city's all topsy-turvy, some companies
have closed and others are only working half-time, people don't
necessarily have to get up early, Lucky them, said the sergeant,
So did she go out or didn't she, asked the superintendent, who
was beginning to get impatient, She went out at precisely a
quarter past twelve, Is there some reason why you say precisely,
No, sir, I naturally looked at my watch and there it was, a quarter past twelve, Go on, Well, keeping an eye on any taxis that
passed, in case she should get into one of them and leave me
stranded in the middle of the street looking like a complete
fool, I followed her, but it didn't take me long to realize that
wherever it was she was going, she would be going there on
foot, And where did she go, You're going to laugh, sir, I doubt
it, She walked for more than half an hour, so fast I could hardly
keep up, just as if she was doing it for the exercise, and suddenly, unexpectedly, I found myself in the street where the old
man with the black eyepatch and the girl with the dark glasses,
you know, the prostitute, live, She's not a prostitute, inspector,
She may not be one now, but she was once, it's all the same, It's
all the same in your mind, but not in mine, and since it's me
you're talking to and I'm your superior, kindly use words in a
way that I can understand, In that case, I'll say ex-prostitute,
Say the man with the black eyepatch's spouse just as, a few minutes ago, you said the guy who wrote the letter's ex-spouse, as
you see, I'm using your terms, Hm, Anyway, you found yourself
in their street and then what happened, She went into the
building where they live and stayed there, And what did you
do, the superintendent asked the sergeant, I was hiding, but

when she went inside, I joined the inspector to work out a strategy, And then, We decided to work together while we could, said the inspector, and agreed on how we would proceed if we had to split up again, And then, Since it was lunchtime, we took advantage of the break, So you went and had lunch, No, sir, he'd bought two sandwiches and he gave me one, and that was our lunch. The superintendent finally smiled, You deserve a medal, he said to the sergeant, who, emboldened, responded, People have won one for less, sir, You don't know how right you are, Put my name down on the list, then. The three of them smiled, but only briefly, the superintendent's face soon darkened again, What happened next, he asked, It was half past two when they all came out, they must have had lunch together there, said the inspector, we were immediately on the alert because we didn't know if the old man had a car or not, but he didn't use it, perhaps he's saving petrol, anyway, we followed them and if it was an easy job for one, imagine what it was like for two, And where did all this end, In a cinema, they went to the cinema, Did you check to see if there was another door they could have left by without you realizing, There was one, but it was closed, just in case, though, I told him to keep an eye on it for half an hour, No one left, the sergeant confirmed. The superintendent felt weary of this comedy, What else, just summarize the rest, he said in a tense voice. The inspector looked at him in surprise, The rest, sir, well, there isn't much else, they left together when the film ended, they took a taxi, and we took another, we gave the driver the classic order We're the police, follow that car, it was just another straightforward trip, the wife of the guy who wrote the letter was the first to get out, Where, In the street where she lives, as we said, sir, we don't have any news to report, then the taxi took the others to their house, And what did you do, Well, I stayed behind in the first street, said the sergeant, And I stayed in the second, said the inspector,

And then, Then, nothing, none of them went out again, and I
was there for nearly another hour, in the end, I caught a taxi,
passed by the other street to pick up my colleague and we came
back together, in fact, we've just got in, A pointless task then,
said the superintendent, It certainly seems like it, said the inspector, the most interesting thing about this whole business is
that it started out fairly well, the interrogation of the guy who
wrote the letter, for example, was worthwhile, even amusing,
the poor devil didn't know what to do with himself and ended
up with his tail between his legs, but after that, I don't know
how, we got stuck, I mean, we got ourselves stuck, you must
know a bit more, sir, since you got to interrogate the real suspects twice, Who are the real suspects, asked the superintendent, Well, first, the doctor's wife and then the husband, it
seems quite clear to me that if they share a bed, they must share
the blame too, What blame, You know as well as I do, sir, Imagine that I don't, explain it to me, The blame for the situation
we're in, What situation, The blank ballot papers, the city under a state of siege, the bomb in the metro station, Do you
really believe what you're saying, asked the superintendent,
That's why we came here, to investigate and capture the guilty
party, You mean the doctor's wife, Yes, sir, as far as I'm concerned the interior minister's orders were pretty clear on that
front, The interior minister didn't say the doctor's wife was to
blame, Sir, I may only be a police inspector who may never
make it as far as superintendent, but I've learned from my experience in this job that things half-spoken exist in order to say
what can't be fully expressed, When the next post for superintendent comes up, I'll support your promotion, but until then,
the truth requires me to inform you that, as regards the doctor's wife, the word, not half-spoken, but fully expressed, is innocence. The inspector shot the sergeant a sideways glance, a
plea for help, but the sergeant had the absorbed look of someone who has just been hypnotized, so he could expect no help

from him. Cautiously, the inspector asked, Are you saying that we're going to leave here empty-handed, Or we could, if you prefer, leave here with our hands in our pockets, And that's how we should present ourselves to the minister, If there's no guilty party, we can't invent one, Are those your words or the minister's, Oh, I doubt they're the minister's words, at least, I don't remember having heard him say them, Well, sir, I've never heard them all the time I've been in the police, but I'll say no more, I won't open my mouth again. The superintendent got up, looked at his watch and said, Go and have supper in a restaurant somewhere, you hardly had any lunch at all, you must be hungry, but don't forget to bring me the bill so that I can stamp it, And what about you, sir, asked the sergeant, No, I had a good lunch, and if I do feel peckish, there's always tea and biscuits to keep hunger at bay. The inspector said, The respect I feel for you, sir, obliges me to say how concerned I am about you, Why, We're just subordinates, the worst thing that can happen to us is a reprimand, but you're responsible for the success of this mission and you seem determined to declare it a failure, Does declaring an accused person innocent mean that a mission has failed, It does if the mission was designed to put the blame on an innocent party, A short while ago, you stated categorically that the doctor's wife was to blame, now you're almost on the point of swearing on the holy gospel that she's innocent, Sir, I might well swear it on the gospel, but not in the presence of the interior minister, Of course, I understand, you have your family, your career, your life, That's right, sir, you might also add, my lack of courage, We're both human beings, and I would never go that far, my only advice to you is that, from now on, you take our sergeant here under your wing, I've a feeling you're going to need each other. The inspector and the sergeant said, See you later, sir, and the superintendent replied, Have a nice meal, and don't rush. The door closed.

The superintendent went into the kitchen for a drink of wa-

ter, then he went into his room. The bed was still unmade, a pair
of dirty socks lay on the floor, one here, one over there, a dirty
shirt was draped untidily over a chair, not to mention the state
the bathroom was in, this is a matter which providential ltd, insurance and reinsurance, will have to resolve sooner or later,
i.e. whether or not it is compatible with the natural discretion
surrounding the work of the secret service to place at the disposal of the agents who stay here a woman who would act as
housekeeper, cook and chambermaid. The superintendent gave
the sheet and bedspread a quick tug, punched the pillow a couple of times, rolled up the shirt and the socks and stuffed them
in a drawer, and the desolate appearance of the room improved
a little, although, naturally, any female hand would have done
it better. He looked at the clock, it was a good time, although
he would soon find out whether the result would be equally
good. He sat down, switched on the desk lamp and dialed the
number. On the fourth ring, a voice answered, Hello, It's puffin
here, Albatross speaking, Just calling in to report on the day's
operations, albatross, Well, I hope you have some satisfactory
results to give me, puffin, That depends on what you call satisfactory, albatross, Look, I have neither the time nor the patience for the finer shades of meaning, puffin, get to the point,
May I ask you first, albatross, if the package reached its destination, What package, The nine o'clock package, at post six-
north, Oh, yes, it arrived perfectly, it's going to be very useful,
you'll find out just how useful in due course, puffin, but now
tell me what you and your men have been up to today, There's
really not much to tell, albatross, a couple of surveillance operations and an interrogation, Let's take things one at a time,
puffin, what was the result of the surveillance operations, Practically nil, albatross, Why, Throughout the time they were being followed, the people we would term the number two suspects behaved absolutely normally, albatross, And what about

the interrogation of the number one suspects, which, I seem
to recall, was your responsibility, puffin, To be perfectly honest, What did you say, To be perfectly honest, albatross, What's
all this about honesty, puffin, It's just a way of beginning a sentence, albatross, Then will you please stop being perfectly honest and tell me, simply, whether or not you are in a position
to confirm, without beating about the bush and without any
further circumlocutions, that the doctor's wife, whose photo I
have before me, is guilty, She admitted she was guilty of a murder, albatross, You know that for many reasons, amongst them
the lack of a corpus delicti, this is not what interests us, Yes,
albatross, So get straight to the point and tell me whether or
not you can confirm that the doctor's wife is part of the movement behind the blank votes and that she may even be the head
of the whole organization, No, albatross, I can't confirm that,
Why, puffin, Because no policeman in the world, albatross, and
I consider myself to be the last of them, would find a scrap of
evidence to support such an accusation, You appear to have forgotten, puffin, that we had agreed that you would provide the
necessary proof, And what proof would that be in a case like
this, albatross, if you don't mind my asking, That neither was
nor is my affair, I left that to your judgement, puffin, when I
was still confident that you would be capable of bringing your
mission to a successful conclusion, With respect, albatross, deciding that a suspect is innocent of the crime he or she is accused of seems to me the most successful of conclusions, Let's
drop this code-name comedy, you're a police superintendent
and I'm the interior minister, Yes, minister, Now, in order to
see if we can finally come to some understanding, I'm going to
put the question I asked you just now in a different way, Yes,
minister, Setting aside your personal beliefs, are you prepared
to confirm that the doctor's wife is guilty, yes or no, No, minister, And you have weighed the consequences of what you have

just said, Yes, minister, Very well, then, take a note of the decisions I have just taken, I'm listening, minister, You will tell the inspector and the sergeant that they have orders to return tomorrow morning, that at nine o'clock they must be at post six-north on the frontier where they will be met by the person who will bring them here, a man more or less your age and wearing a blue tie with white spots, tell them to bring the car you've been using and which will, of course, no longer be necessary, Yes, minister, And as for you, As for me, minister, You will remain in the capital until you receive further orders, which will doubtless not be long in coming, And the investigation, You yourself said that there is nothing to investigate, that the suspect is innocent, That is my sincere belief, minister, Then you certainly can't complain, your case is solved, But what shall I do while I'm here, Nothing, do nothing, go for walks, enjoy yourself, go to the cinema, the theater, visit the museums, and, if you like, invite your new friends out to supper, charge it to the ministry, Minister, I don't understand, The five days I gave you for the investigation are still not yet up, perhaps in the time that remains a different light will go on in your head, I doubt it, minister, Nevertheless, five days are five days, and I'm a man of my word, Yes, minister, Good night, sleep well, superintendent, Good night, minister.

The superintendent put down the phone. He got up from the chair and went to the bathroom. He needed to see the face of the man who had just been summarily dismissed. The actual words had not been spoken, but could be clearly seen, letter by letter, in all the other words, even those wishing him a good night's sleep. He wasn't surprised, he knew exactly what his interior minister was like and knew that he would be made to pay for not having obeyed the instructions he had received, the explicit and, above all, the implied instructions, the latter had, after all, been as clear as the former, but he was surprised by the serenity of the face he saw in the mirror, a face from which the lines seemed to have vanished, a face in which the eyes had become limpid and luminous, the face of a man of fifty-seven, a police superintendent by profession, who had just been through the fire and had emerged from it as if from a purifying bath. Yes, a bath would be a good idea. He got undressed and stepped into the shower. He allowed the water to flow freely, after all, what did he care, the ministry would foot the bill, he slowly soaped himself and again the water washed away any remaining dirt from his body, then his memory carried him on its back to a time four years ago, when they were all blind and wandering, filthy and starving, about the city, ready to do anything for a crust of stale, mouldy bread, for anything that could be eaten, or at least chewed, as a way of staving off hunger with their own juices, he imagined the doctor's wife guiding through the streets, beneath the rain, her little flock of unfortunates, her six lost sheep, her six fledglings fallen from the nest, her six newborn blind kittens, perhaps one day, in some street or other, he had bumped into them, perhaps they, out of fear, had repelled him, perhaps, out of fear, he had repelled them, it was every man for himself at the time, steal before they steal from you, hit out before they hit you, your worst enemy, according to the law of the blind, is always the person nearest you, But it's not only when we have no eyes that we don't know where we're going, he thought. The hot water fell clamorously upon his head and shoulders, it coursed over his body and disappeared, clean and gurgling, down the drain. He got out of the shower, dried himself on the bath towel bearing the police emblem, picked up the clothes he had left hanging on the hook and went into the bedroom. He put on clean underwear, his last, and it would have to be his last, for he hadn't thought of packing any more for a mission lasting only five days. He looked at his watch, it was nearly nine o'clock. He went into the kitchen, boiled some water for tea, dunked one sad teabag in the water and waited for the recommended number of minutes. The biscuits were like sugary granite. He bit into them hard, reduced them to smaller pieces that were easier to chew, then slowly crumbled them up. He sipped his tea, he preferred the green variety, but had to content himself with this black stuff, so old it hardly tasted of anything, providential ltd, insurance and reinsurance, really should stop lavishing such luxuries on its temporary guests. The minister's words echoed sarcastically in his ears, The five days I gave you for the investigation are still not yet up, until they are, go for walks, enjoy yourself, go to the cinema, charge it to the ministry, and he wondered what would happen then, would they send him back to headquarters, alleging that he was incapable of active service, would they sit him down at a desk to shuffle papers, a superintendent demoted to the lowly condition of pen-pusher, that would be his future, unless they made him take early retirement and forgot about him and only mentioned his name again when he died and they could strike him from the staff records. He finished eating, he threw the cold, damp teabag into the rubbish bin, washed the cup and scooped the crumbs off the table with the edge of his hand. He did all this with great concentration in order to keep his thoughts at bay, in order to let them in only one at a time, having first asked them what they contained, because you can't be too careful with thoughts, some present themselves to us with a cloying air of false innocence and then, when it's too late, reveal their true wicked selves. He again looked at his watch, a quarter to ten, how time passes. He left the kitchen and went into the living-room, sat down on a sofa and waited. He woke to the sound of the key in the door. The inspector and the sergeant came in, they had clearly had plenty to eat and drink, not, however, to any reprehensible extent. They said their good evenings, then the inspector, on behalf of them both,

apologized for coming in a little late. The superintendent
looked at his watch, it was past eleven, It's not that late, he said,
but I'm afraid you're going to have to get up rather earlier than
you perhaps expected, Another mission, asked the inspector,
placing a package on the table, Yes, if you can call it that. The
superintendent paused, glanced again at his watch and went on,
At nine o'clock tomorrow morning you are to be at military
post six-north with all your belongings, Why, asked the sergeant, You've been taken off the investigation that brought you
here, Was that your decision, sir, asked the inspector, grave-
faced, No, it was the minister's decision, But why, He didn't tell
me, but don't worry, I'm sure he's got nothing against you personally, he'll ask you a lot of questions, but you'll know what to
say, Does that mean you're not coming with us, sir, asked the
sergeant, No, I'm staying here, Are you going to continue the
investigation on your own, The investigation is over, With no
concrete results, Neither concrete nor abstract, Then I don't
understand why you're not coming with us, said the inspector,
Orders from the minister, I'll stay here until the end of the five-
day period he originally set, which means until Thursday, And
what then, Perhaps he'll tell you when he questions you, Questions us about what, About how the investigation went, about
how I ran it, But you just said that the investigation was over,
Yes, but it's possible he may want to continue it in other ways,
although not with me, Well, I can't make head nor tail of it, said
the sergeant. The superintendent got up, went into the study
and returned with a map, which he spread out on the table,
pushing the package a little to one side to make room. Post six-
north is here, he said, placing his finger on it, don't go to the
wrong one, waiting for you will be a man whom the minister
describes as more or less my age, but he's actually quite a lot
younger, you'll recognize him by the tie he'll be wearing, blue
with white spots, when I met him, we had to exchange pass-

words, but I don't think that will be necessary this time, at least
the minister didn't say anything to me about it, I don't understand, said the inspector, It seems pretty clear, said the sergeant, we just go to post six-north, No, what I don't understand
is why we're leaving and the superintendent is staying, The
minister must have his reasons, Ministers always do, But they
never say what they are. The superintendent intervened, There's
no point talking about it, your best bet is not to ask for any explanations and to distrust any explanations they offer you, in
the unlikely event that they do, because they're nearly always
lies. He carefully folded up the map and, as if the thought had
just occurred to him, said, You take the car, You're not even
keeping the car, asked the inspector, There are plenty of buses
and taxis in the city, besides, walking is good for the health,
This whole thing is just getting harder and harder to understand, There's nothing to understand, my friend, I was given
my orders and I'm carrying them out, and you must do the
same, you can analyse and ponder all you like, but it doesn't
change the reality one millimeter. The inspector pushed the
package toward him, We brought this, he said, What is it, Well,
the stuff they left for our breakfast here is so awful, we decided
to buy some different biscuits, a bit of cheese, some decent butter, ham and a sandwich loaf, Are you going to take it with you
or leave it here, said the superintendent, smiling, Well, if you're
in agreement, sir, tomorrow we'll have breakfast together and
whatever's left stays, said the inspector, smiling too. They had
all smiled, the sergeant keeping the others company, but now
all three were serious again, not knowing what to say. In the
end, the superintendent said, I'm off to bed, I slept badly last
night and it's been a busy day, starting with that business at post
six-north, What business, sir, asked the superintendent, we
don't yet know why you went to post six-north, No, that's true,
I didn't get a chance to tell you, well, on orders from the min-

ister I went and handed over the group photograph to that man wearing the blue tie with white spots, the same man you're going to meet tomorrow, What would the minister want with that photo, To use his words, we'll find out in due course, It smells very fishy to me. The superintendent nodded and went on, Then, by pure coincidence, I bumped into the doctor's wife, joined them for lunch at their apartment, and then, to top it all, had the conversation with the minister I told you about, We have the greatest respect for you, sir, said the inspector, but there's one thing we'll never forgive you, and I know I'm speaking for both of us here because we've already talked about it, What's that, You never let us go to that woman's apartment, You went there, inspector, Only to be shooed straight out again, Yes, that's true, agreed the superintendent, Why, Because I was afraid, Afraid of what, we're not monsters, Afraid that the need to find a guilty party at all costs would stop you seeing the person who was there before you, Did you trust us so little, sir, It wasn't a question of trust, of whether I did or didn't trust you, it was more as if I had found a treasure and wanted to keep it all to myself, no, that's not it, it wasn't a question of feelings, that wasn't what I was thinking, I simply feared for that woman's safety, I thought that the fewer people who questioned her, the safer she would be, So put in plain and simple language, and forgive my boldness, sir, said the sergeant, you didn't trust us, No, you're right, I admit it, I didn't, Well, don't bother asking our forgiveness, said the inspector, you're forgiven already, especially since you may well have been right to be afraid, we could have ruined everything, we could have gone in there like a couple of bulls in a china shop. The superintendent opened the package, took out two slices of bread, put two slices of ham in between and gave an apologetic smile, I must confess I'm hungry, all I had was a cup of tea and I nearly broke my teeth on those bloody biscuits. The sergeant went into the kitchen and brought him a can of beer and a glass, Here you are, sir, this will help the bread slide down more easily. The superintendent sat down and munched his way through the ham sandwich, savoring every mouthful, then drank down the beer as if he were washing clean his soul, and when he had finished, he said, Right, now I will go to bed, sleep well, you two, and thanks for supper. He went over to the door that led to his bedroom, stopped and turned round, I'm going to miss you, he said. He paused and added, Don't forget what I told you earlier, What do you mean, sir, asked the inspector, That I have the feeling you're really going to need each other, don't be taken in by any sweet talk or promises of rapid promotion, I'm responsible for the conclusions reached by this investigation and no one else, you won't be betraying me as long as you tell the truth, but refuse to accept any lies in the name of a truth that is not your own, Yes, sir, promised the inspector, Help each other, said the superintendent, and then, That's all I wish for you, all I ask of you.

THE superintendent did not wish to take advantage of the interior minister's prodigal munificence. He did not seek distraction in theaters and cinemas, he did not visit the museums, he only left providential ltd, insurance and reinsurance, to have lunch and supper, and when he paid the bill at the restaurant, instead of taking the bill with him, he left it on the table along with the tip. He did not go back to the doctor's house and had no reason to return to the garden where he had made his peace with the dog of tears or, as he was officially known, Constant, and where, eye to eye, spirit with spirit, he had spoken with the dog's mistress about guilt and innocence. Nor did he go and spy on what the girl with dark glasses and the old man with the black eyepatch might be doing, or the divorced wife of the man who had been the first to go blind. As for the latter, the author of the vile letter of denunciation and author, too, of many misfortunes, the superintendent had no doubt that, if he saw him, he would cross over to the other side of the road. The rest of the time, for hours on end, morning and evening, he spent sitting by the phone, waiting, and even when he was sleeping, his ears were listening. He was sure that the interior minister would phone in the end, he could not oth-

erwise understand why the minister had wanted to drain to the
very last minute, or more accurately, to the final dregs, the five
days he had allocated for the investigation. The most natural
thing would be for the minister to order him back to headquarters to settle all outstanding accounts, whether by enforced retirement or by resignation, but experience had shown him that
anything natural was far too simple for the interior minister's
tortuous mind. He remembered the inspector's words, banal
but expressive, It smells very fishy to me, he had said when the
superintendent had told him about handing over the photograph to the man wearing the blue tie with white spots at military post six-north, and it seemed to him that the heart of the
matter must lie there, in the photograph, although he could
not imagine how or why. It was in this slow waiting, which had
an end in sight and which would not, as people say when they
want to embellish a story, be interminable, and in thoughts
such as these, which were often nothing but a continuous, irrepressible somnolence from which his half-watchful consciousness occasionally startled him awake, that he would spend the
three remaining days, Tuesday, Wednesday, Thursday, three
leaves from the calendar which resisted being torn from midnight's stitching and which then remained stuck to his fingers,
transformed into a shapeless, glutinous mass of time, into a soft
wall that both resisted and sucked him in. Finally, on Wednesday, at half past eleven at night, the minister phoned. He did
not say hello or good evening, he did not ask the superintendent if he was well or how he was coping with being alone, he
did not mention whether he had questioned the inspector and
the sergeant, together or separately, in friendly conversation or
by issuing harsh threats, he merely said in passing, as if apropos
of nothing, I think you'll find something in tomorrow's newspapers to interest you, I read the papers every day, minister,
Congratulations, you're obviously very well-informed, never-

theless I urge you most strongly not to miss tomorrow's editions, you'll find them most interesting, I'll be sure to read them, minister, And watch the television news too, don't miss it whatever you do, We have no television set at providential ltd, minister, What a shame, although, on second thought, I rather approve, it's better like that, it might distract you from the arduous investigatory problems we set you, besides, you could always go and visit one of your new friends and suggest you all get together and enjoy the show. The superintendent did not respond. He could have asked what his disciplinary situation would be after Thursday, but he preferred to say nothing, it was clear that his fate lay in the minister's hands, and so it was up to him to pronounce sentence, if he did ask, he was sure to receive some sharp riposte, along the lines of, Don't be in such a hurry, you'll find out tomorrow. Suddenly, the superintendent became aware that the silence had lasted longer than is considered normal in a telephone conversation, a mode of communication in which the pauses or rests between phrases are, generally speaking, either brief or even briefer. He had not reacted to the interior minister's spiteful suggestion and this had not appeared to trouble him, he had remained silent as if he were leaving time for his interlocutor to think of a response. The superintendent said cautiously, Minister. The electrical impulses carried the word down the line, but there was no sign of life at the other end. The albatross had hung up. The superintendent put the phone back on its rest and left the room. He went into the kitchen and drank a glass of water, it was not the first time he had noticed that talking to the interior minister created in him an almost desperate thirst, as if throughout the conversation he had been burning up inside and now had to hurry to put out his own fire. He went and sat down on the sofa in the sitting-room, but did not stay there long, the state of semi-lethargy in which he had lived for the past two days had disappeared, as if it had vanished at the minister's first word, for things, that vague agglomeration to which we usually give the generic and lazy label of things when it would take too much time and too much space to explain or merely define it, had begun to move very fast and they would not stop now until the end, but what end, and when, and how, and where. Of one thing he was sure, he did not need to be a maigret, a poirot or a sherlock holmes to know what the newspapers would publish the following day. The waiting was over, the interior minister would not phone him again, any order still to be issued would arrive through the intermediary of a secretary or directly from the police commissioner, a mere five days and five nights had been enough for him to go from being a superintendent in charge of a difficult investigation to a wind-up toy whose spring had gone and which was to be thrown out with the rubbish. It was then that it occurred to him that he still had one duty to perform. He looked up a name in the telephone book, mentally confirmed the address and dialed the number. The doctor's wife answered, Hello, Oh, good evening, it's me, the superintendent, forgive me for phoning you at this hour of the night, That's all right, we never go to bed early, Do you remember me telling you, when we were talking in the park, that the interior minister had ordered me to hand over that group photograph, Yes, I remember, Well, I have every reason to believe that the photograph will be published in tomorrow's newspapers and broadcast on television, Well, I won't ask you why, but I do remember you telling me that the minister wouldn't have wanted it for any good purpose, Exactly, but I never expected him to use it like this, What's he up to, We'll see tomorrow what the newspapers do apart from printing the photograph, but I imagine that they'll try to stigmatize you in the mind of the public, Because I didn't go blind four years ago, You know very well that the minister finds it highly suspicious that you didn't go blind when everyone else was losing their sight, and now that fact has become more than sufficient, from his point of view, for him to find you responsible, either wholly or in part, for what is happening now, Do you mean the blank votes, Yes, the blank votes, But that's absurd, utterly absurd, As I've learned in this job, not only are the people in government never put off by what we judge to be absurd, they make use of absurdities to dull consciences and to destroy reason, What do you think we should do, Hide, disappear, but don't go to your friends' apartments, you wouldn't be safe there, they'll be putting them under surveillance soon as well, if they haven't already, You're right, but, in any case, we would never put at risk the safety of someone who had chosen to protect us, right now, for example, I'm wondering if you haven't been foolish in phoning us, Don't worry, the line is secure, in fact, there aren't many lines much securer than this, Superintendent, Yes, There's a question I'd like to ask, but I'm not sure I dare, Ask it, please, Why are you doing this for us, why are you helping us, Because of something I read in a book, years ago now, and which I had forgotten, but which has come back to me in the last few days, What was that, We are born, and at that moment, it is as if we had signed a pact for the rest of our life, but a day may come when we will ask ourselves Who signed this on my behalf, Fine, thought-provoking words, what's the book called, You know I'm ashamed to say it, but I can't remember, Never mind, even if you can't remember anything else, not even the title, Not even the name of the author, Those words, which probably no one else, at least not in that precise form, would ever have said before, had the good fortune not to have lost each other, they had someone to bring them together, and who knows, perhaps the world would be a slightly better place if we were able to gather up a few of the words that are out there wandering around alone, Oh, I doubt the poor despised creatures would ever find each other,

No, probably not, but dreaming is cheap, it doesn't cost any money, Let's see what the papers say tomorrow, Yes, let's see, I'm prepared for the worst, Whatever the immediate results, think about what I said, hide, disappear, All right, I'll talk to my husband, Let's hope he manages to persuade you, Good night, and thank you for everything, There's nothing to thank me for, Take care. After he had hung up, the superintendent wondered if he hadn't been rather stupid to declare, as if it were his property, that the line was secure, that there wouldn't be many lines in the country much more secure. He shrugged and murmured, What does it matter, nothing is secure, no one is secure.

He did not sleep well, he dreamed of a cloud of words that fled and scattered as he chased after them with a butterfly net, pleading, Stop, please, don't move, wait for me. Then, suddenly, the words stopped and gathered together in a clump, one on top of the other, like a swarm of bees waiting for a hive they could swoop down on, and he, with a cry of joy, lunged forward with his net. What he had caught was a newspaper. It had been a bad dream, but it would have been worse if the albatross had returned to prick out the eyes of the doctor's wife. He woke early. He pulled on some clothes and went downstairs. He no longer went out via the garage, through the tradesmen's entrance, now he went out through the main door, what one might call the pedestrian entrance, he greeted the porter with a nod of his head if he happened to see him in his lodge or exchanged a word or two with him if he was outside, but it wasn't necessary, he—the superintendent, not the porter—was, in a way, merely there on loan. The streetlights were still on, the shops wouldn't open for another two hours. He looked for and found a newspaper kiosk, one of the larger ones that receives all the papers, and he stood there waiting. Fortunately, it wasn't raining. The streetlights went out, leaving the city plunged for a few moments in a last, brief darkness, which vanished as soon as his eyes grew accustomed to the change, and the bluish light of early morning descended upon the streets. The delivery van arrived, unloaded the bundles of papers and continued on its way. The newsagent started opening the bundles and arranging the newspapers according to the number of copies received, from left to right, from large to small. The superintendent went over to him, Good morning, he said, I'll have a copy of all of them. While the man was putting his purchases into a plastic bag, the superintendent looked at the rows of newspapers and saw that, with the exception of the last two, they all carried the photograph on the front page under banner headlines. The arrival of this keen customer with sufficient means to pay has got the newspaper kiosk off to good start this morning, indeed, we can safely say that the rest of the day will be no different, for every one of the newspapers will be snapped up, apart from those two piles on the right, of which only the usual number of copies will be sold. The superintendent was no longer there, he had run to catch a taxi he had spotted on the nearby corner, and having given the driver the address of providential ltd, and apologized for the shortness of the journey, he was now nervously taking the papers out of the bag and opening them. Alongside the group photo, with an arrow indicating the doctor's wife, was an enlargement of her face in a circle. And the headlines were, in red and in black, Revealed At Last—The Face Behind The Conspiracy, Four Years Ago This Woman Escaped Blindness, Mystery Of The Blank Ballot Papers Solved, Police Investigation Yields First Results. The still faint morning light and the swaying of the car as it bumped over the cobbled surface prevented him from reading the smaller print of the articles beneath. In less than five minutes the taxi had deposited him outside the door of the building. The superintendent paid, left the change in the driver's hand and rushed in. He raced past the porter without bothering to greet him and got into the lift, his state of excitement almost making him tap his toes with impatience, come on, come on, but the machinery, which had spent its whole life carrying people up and down, listening to conversations, unfinished monologues, tuneless fragments of songs, the occasional irrepressible sigh, the occasional troubled murmur, pretended that this was none of its business, it took a certain amount of time to go up and a certain amount of time to come down, like fate, if you're in that much of a hurry, take the stairs. The superintendent finally put the key in the door of providential ltd, insurance and reinsurance, turned on the light and made straight for the table on which he had spread out the map of the city and where he had eaten a last breakfast with his now absent assistants. His hands were shaking. Forcing himself to slow down and not to skip any lines, he read, word by word, the articles in the four newspapers that had published the photograph. With a few small changes in style, with slight differences in vocabulary, the information was the same in all of them and one could sense a kind of arithmetic mean calculated by the editorial consultants at the ministry of the interior to fit the original font. The primitive prose read more or less like this, Just when we were thinking that the government had decided to leave it to time, to that same time by which everything is worn away and transformed, the job of isolating and shrinking the malignant tumor that so unexpectedly grew in this nation's capital, taking the abstruse and aberrant form of the mass casting of blank ballot papers, which, as our readers know, vastly exceeded the number of votes cast for all the democratic political parties put together, our editorial desk has just received the most surprising and gratifying news. The investigatory genius and persistence of the police, in the persons of a superintendent, an inspector and a sergeant, whose names, for security reasons, we are not authorized to reveal, have managed to uncover the individual who is, in all probability, the head of the tapeworm whose coils have kept the civic conscience of the majority of the city's inhabitants of voting age entirely paralyzed and in a state of dangerous atrophy. A certain woman, married to an ophthalmologist, and who, wonder of wonders, was, according to reliable witnesses, the only person to escape the terrible epidemic four years ago that made of our homeland a country of the blind, this woman is now considered by the police to be the person responsible for the current blindness, limited this time, fortunately, to what used to be the capital city, and which has introduced into political life and into our democratic system the dangerous germ of perversion and corruption. Only a diabolical mind, like those of the greatest criminals in the history of humankind, could have conceived what, according to reliable sources, his excellency the president of the republic has so eloquently described as a torpedo fired below the water line of the majestic ship of democracy. For that is what it is. If it is proved, beyond a shadow of a doubt, as everything indicates it will be, that this doctor's wife is guilty, then all those citizens who still respect order and the law will demand that the full rigor of justice falls upon her head. How strange life is. Given the singularity of her case four years ago, this woman could have become an invaluable subject of study for our scientific community, and, as such, would have deserved a prominent place in the clinical history of ophthalmology, but she will now be singled out for public execration as an enemy of her country and of her people. One is tempted to say that it would have been better if she had gone blind.

That last sentence, clearly threatening in tone, sounded like a judicial sentence, just as if it had said It would have been better if you had never been born. The superintendent's first impulse was to phone the doctor's wife, to ask if she had read the newspapers, to comfort her as best as he could, but he was prevented by the thought that, overnight, the probability of her phone being tapped had become one hundred percent. As for the phones of providential ltd, the red and the gray ones, they, of course, were linked directly to the state's private network. He leafed through the other two newspapers, which had not printed a single word on the subject. What should I do now, he asked out loud. He went back to the article, re-read it, and found it strange that they had not identified the people in the photograph, in particular, the doctor's wife and the doctor. It was then that he noticed the caption, which read thus, The suspect is indicated by an arrow. It seems, although there is no solid confirmation of this fact, that the doctor's wife took this group under her wing during the epidemic of blindness. According to official sources, identification of these people is at an advanced stage and will be made public tomorrow. The superintendent murmured, They're probably trying to find out where the boy lives, as if that would help them. Then, after some thought, At first sight, the publication of the photograph, unaccompanied by any other measures, appears to make no sense, since all the people in the photo, as I myself advised, could seize the opportunity and vanish, but then the minister loves a spectacle, a successful manhunt would give him greater political weight and more influence in both the government and the party, and as for other measures, the homes of these people are almost certainly already under round-the-clock surveillance, the ministry has had more than enough time to get agents into the city and to set up such a programme. While all of this was true, none of it answered his question What should I do now. He could phone the ministry of the interior on the pretext that, since it was now Thursday, he wanted to know what decision had been taken about his disciplinary situation, but there was no point, he was sure the minister would not speak to him, some secretary would merely come on the line, telling him to get in touch with the police commissioner, the days of conversations between albatross and puffin are over, superintendent. What shall I do now, he asked again, just sit here rotting away until someone finally remembers me and sends orders for the corpse to be removed, try to leave the city when it's more than likely that strict orders have been given at the frontier posts not to let me pass, what shall I do. He looked at the photograph again, the doctor and his wife in the middle, the girl with the dark glasses and the old man with the black eyepatch to the left, the guy who wrote the letter and his wife to the right, the boy with the squint kneeling down in front like a football player, the dog sitting at its mistress's feet. He re-read the caption, Full identification will be made public tomorrow, will be made public, tomorrow, tomorrow, tomorrow. At that moment, he was suddenly gripped by an idea for a plan of action, but the following moment, caution was immediately protesting that it would be utter madness, The sensible thing, it said, would be not to wake the sleeping dragon, the stupid thing would be to approach while it's awake. The superintendent got out of his chair, paced twice around the room, returned to the table on which the newspapers lay, and looked again at the head of the doctor's wife surrounded by a white ring that looked already like a hangman's noose, at this hour, half the city is reading the newspapers and the other half is sitting in front of the television to hear what the newsreader on the first news bulletin is going to say or listening to the voice of the radio announcing that the woman's name will be made public tomorrow, and not only her name, but her address too, so that the whole population will know where evil has made its nest. The superintendent went to fetch the typewriter and brought it over to the table. He folded up the newspapers, pushed them to one side and sat down to work. The paper he was using bore the heading providential ltd, insurance and reinsurance, and could, if

not tomorrow, certainly the day after tomorrow, be used by
the state prosecution as proof of a second crime, that of using civil service stationery for his own purposes, an aggravat-
ing factor being the confidential nature of that correspondence
and the conspiratorial use to which it was put. What the superintendent was typing was neither more nor less than a detailed
account of the events of the last five days, from early Saturday morning when he and his two assistants had clandestinely
breached the city blockade, until today, and this very moment
of writing. Providential ltd does, of course, have a photocopier,
but it seems to the superintendent impolite to give the original letter to one person and a mere copy to the other, however
convincingly the very latest reprographic techniques may assure us that not even the eyes of a hawk could tell them apart.
The superintendent belongs to the second oldest generation
of those who still eat bread in this world, which is why he re-
tains a respect for form, which means that, having finished the
first letter, he started carefully copying it out onto a clean sheet
of paper. It is, to be sure, still a copy, but not in the same way.
When he had completed this task, he folded up the letters and
placed each one in an envelope bearing the company name,
sealed the envelopes and wrote the respective addresses. While
it is true that the letters will be delivered by hand, the addressees will understand, if only by the discreet elegance of the gesture, that these letters from providential ltd, insurance and reinsurance, deal with important matters deserving of the news
media's attention.

   The superintendent is about to go out again. He placed the
two letters in one of his inside jacket pockets and put on his
raincoat, even though the weather is as mild as one could hope
for at this time of year, as, indeed, he could ascertain for himself by opening the window and looking up at the slow, sparse,
white clouds passing by overhead. It is possible that there may

have been another strong reason, for the raincoat, especially of
the belted trench-coat variety, is a kind of identifying feature
of detectives from the classic era, at least ever since raymond
chandler first created the character of marlowe, so much so
that seeing a man walk by, a slouch hat on his head and his raincoat collar turned up, and immediately proclaiming there goes
humphrey bogart with his piercing eyes gazing out between the
edge of his collar and the brim of his hat, is the kind of knowledge that is within easy grasp of any reader of detective fiction,
p.o. box death. This superintendent is not wearing a hat, his
head is bare, as determined by the fashion of a modern world
that loathes the picturesque and, as they say, shoots to kill without even asking if you're still alive. He has got out of the lift,
walked past the porter's lodge, from where the porter waved to
him, and now he is in the street ready to carry out his three objectives for that morning, namely, to eat a belated breakfast, to
take a walk down the street where the doctor's wife lives, and
to deliver the letters to their addressees. He achieves the first
in this café, a cup of milky coffee, a couple of slices of buttered
toast, not as tender and succulent as those he ate the other day,
but there's no surprise there, life is like that, you win some, you
lose some, and there are very few cultivators of buttered toast
left, both amongst those who prepare it and those who eat it.
Forgive these extremely banal gastronomic thoughts in a man
who is carrying a bomb in his pocket. He has eaten and paid,
now he is striding toward his second objective. It took him almost twenty minutes to get there. He slowed his pace when
he reached the street and adopted the air of one just out for a
stroll, he knows that if there are any surveillance police about
they will probably recognize him, but he doesn't care. If one
of them sees him and informs his immediate boss of what he
saw, and if the boss passes on the information to his immediate superior, who then tells the police commissioner, who then

tells the interior minister, you can guarantee that the albatross
will croak out in his harshest tones, Don't come bothering me
with things I already know, tell me what I don't know, namely,
what that wretched superintendent is up to. The street is more
crowded than usual. There are small knots of people standing around outside the building where the doctor's wife lives,
they are locals moved by a curiosity which is in some cases innocent and in other cases morbid, and who have come, newspaper in hand, to the place where the accused woman lives, a
woman they know more or less by sight or from an occasional
exchange of words, and there is the inevitable coincidence that
the eyes of some have benefited from the expertise of her ophthalmologist husband. The superintendent has already spotted
the surveillance policemen, the first has positioned himself next
to one of the larger groups, the second, leaning with feigned
idleness against a wall, is reading a sports magazine as if, in the
world of letters, nothing more important could possibly exist.
The fact that he is reading a magazine and not a newspaper
can be easily explained, a magazine, while affording sufficient
protection, takes up much less of the watcher's visual field and
can be quickly stuffed into a pocket should it become necessary
to follow someone. Policemen know these things, they learn
them in kindergarten. It happens that the men here have no in-
kling of the stormy relations between the superintendent walking along and the ministry they all work for, which is why they
assume he is just part of the operation and has come to make
sure that everything is going to plan. Nothing odd about that.
Although at certain levels in the organization, there are already
mutterings that the minister is dissatisfied with the superintendent's work, the proof of which is that he has ordered his
two assistants to come back, leaving the superintendent to lie
fallow, or, as others say, on standby, these mutterings have not
yet reached the lower levels to which these officers belong. We

should point out, however, before we forget, that the said mut-
terers have no very clear idea what the superintendent came
to do in the capital, which just goes to show that the inspector and the sergeant, wherever they are now, have kept their
mouths shut. The interesting thing, although not in the least
amusing, was to see how the policemen went over to the superintendent and whispered conspiratorially out of the corner
of their mouth, Nothing to report. The superintendent nodded, looked up at the windows on the fourth floor and walked
away, thinking, Tomorrow, when the names and addresses are
published, there will be far more people here. Further on, he
saw a taxi and hailed it. He got in, said good morning and,
taking the envelopes out of his pocket, read the addresses and
asked the driver, Which of these is closest, The second one,
Take me there, then, please. On the seat next to the driver lay
a folded newspaper, the one that bore the striking headline, in
letters the color of blood, Revealed At Last—The Face Behind
The Conspiracy. The superintendent was tempted to ask the
driver his opinion of the sensational news published in today's
newspapers, but abandoned the idea for fear that an overly inquisitive tone in his voice might betray his profession, One
of the hazards of being a policeman, he thought. It was the
driver who brought the subject up, I don't know about you,
but I reckon this story about the woman they claim didn't go
blind is just one of those whoppers they dream up to sell newspapers, I mean, I went blind, we all went blind, how was it that
this one woman kept her sight, you'd have to be a fool to believe that, And what about them saying that she was behind all
those people casting blank votes, That's another load of old
nonsense, a woman is a woman, she wouldn't get involved in
things like that, I mean, if it was a man, possibly, he could be,
but a woman, pfff, Yes, it'll be interesting to see how it all turns
out, Once they've squeezed the juice out of this story, they'll

invent another one, it's always the same, oh, you'd be surprised the things you learn behind the wheel, and I'll tell you something else too, Go on, Contrary to what everyone thinks, the rear-view mirror isn't just for checking on the cars behind, you can use it to look into the souls of your passengers too, I bet you'd never thought of that, No, I certainly hadn't, you astonish me, Like I say, this steering-wheel teaches you a lot. After such a revelation, the superintendent thought it best to allow the conversation to lapse. Only when the driver stopped the car and said, Here we are, did he dare to ask if that business about the rear-view mirror and the soul applied to all cars and all drivers, but the driver was quite clear about it, No, only taxis, sir, only taxis.

The superintendent entered the building, went over to the reception desk and said, Good morning, I represent providential ltd, insurance and reinsurance, and I'd like to speak to the director, If you're here about insurance, perhaps it would be better to speak to the administrator, In principle, yes, you're quite right, but what brings me to your newspaper is not a mere technical matter, and it's vital, therefore, that I speak to the director himself, The director isn't here right now, and I don't imagine he'll be in until the afternoon, Who do you think I should speak to then, who would be the best person, Probably the editor-in-chief, In that case, I would be grateful if you could tell him I'm here, providential ltd, insurance and reinsurance, Could you tell me your name, Providential will do fine, Oh, I see, the firm bears your name, Exactly. The receptionist made the phone call, explained the situation and, when she had hung up, said, Someone will be right down, mister providential. A few minutes later, a woman appeared, I'm the editor-in-chief's secretary, would you care to come with me. He followed her down a corridor, feeling quite calm and serene, then, suddenly, without warning, a realization of the bold step he was about to take took his breath away as if he had been punched in the solar plexus. There was still time to go back, to make some excuse, Oh, no, what a nuisance, I've forgotten a really important document which I really must have if I'm to talk to the editor-in-chief, but it wasn't true, the document was there, in his inside jacket pocket, the wine has been poured, superintendent, you have no option now but to drink it. The secretary showed him into a small, modestly furnished room, a couple of battered sofas that had fetched up here in order to live out the rest of their long lives in reasonable peace, a table in the middle with a few newspapers on it, a jumbled bookshelf. Sit down, please, the editor-in-chief asked if you wouldn't mind waiting for a moment, he's busy right now, That's fine, I'll wait, said the superintendent. This was his second chance. If he walked out of here and retraced the path that had led him into this trap, he would be safe, like someone who, having glimpsed his own soul in a rear-view mirror, had decided it was a fool, and that souls should not go around dragging people into the most terrible of disasters, but should, on the contrary, keep them safe from such things and behave themselves, because souls, if ever they do leave the body, almost always get lost, they simply don't know where to go, and it is not just behind the wheel of a taxi that one learns such things. The superintendent did not leave, not now that the wine has been poured, etc. etc. The editor-in-chief came in, I do apologize for keeping you waiting for so long, but I was in the middle of doing something and I couldn't leave it half-finished, There's no need to apologize, it's very good of you to see me at all, So, mister providential, what can I do for you, although from what I've been told, this does seem to be more a matter for the administrative office. The superintendent raised his hand to his pocket and took out the first envelope, I'd be grateful if you would read the letter inside this envelope, Now, asked the editor-in-chief, Yes, if you wouldn't mind, but I must tell you first that my name is not Providential, So what is your name, You'll understand when you've read the letter. The editor-in-chief tore open the envelope, unfolded the piece of paper and started to read. He stopped after the first few lines and looked, perplexed, at the man before him, as if asking if it wouldn't be more prudent to stop right there. The superintendent made a gesture urging him to continue. The editor did not look up again until he had finished reading, on the contrary, it seemed as if, with each word, he were plunging deeper and deeper in, and as if he could not possibly return to the surface wearing his usual editor-in-chief's face once he had seen the fearful creatures inhabiting the lower depths. It was a deeply troubled man who finally looked up at the superintendent and said, Forgive the blunt question, but who are you, My name is there in the signature, Yes, I can see the name, but a name is just a word, it doesn't explain anything about who the person is, I'd prefer not to have to tell you, but I understand perfectly your need to know, In that case, tell me, Not unless you give me your word of honor that the letter will be published, In the absence of the director, I'm not authorized to make that commitment, They told me in reception that the director will only be in this afternoon, Yes, that's true, at around four o'clock, Right, I'll come back later then, but I just want you to know now that I have an identical letter with me and that if you're not interested in the matter, I'll deliver it to that other addressee, The letter is, I assume, addressed to another newspaper, Yes, but not to any of the papers that published the photograph, Of course, but you can't be sure that the other newspaper would be prepared to take the inevitable risks involved in publishing the facts you describe, No, I can't be sure, I'm betting on two horses and I risk losing on both, My feeling is that you risk much more if you win, Just as you do if you decide to publish. The superin-

tendent got to his feet, I'll be here at a quarter past four, Here's
your letter, since we haven't yet come to an agreement, I can't
and shouldn't hold on to it, Thank you for not making me ask
you for it. The editor-in-chief used the telephone in the room
to call the secretary, Show this gentleman out, will you, he said,
and make a note that he will be back at a quarter past four, and
you'll be there to receive him and take him to the director's office, Yes, sir. The superintendent said, See you later, then, Yes,
see you later, and they shook hands. The secretary opened the
door for the superintendent, If you'd like to follow me, mister
providential, she said, and once they were out in the corridor, If
you don't mind my saying, this is the first time I've ever come
across someone with that surname, it didn't even occur to me
that it could exist, Well, now you know, It must be nice to be
called Providential, Why, Well, because it's providential, That's
the best possible answer. They had reached reception, I'll be
here at the time agreed, said the secretary, Thank you, Goodbye, mister providential, Goodbye.

The superintendent looked at his watch, it wasn't yet one
o'clock, too early to have lunch, besides, he wasn't hungry, the
buttered toast and coffee were still there in his stomach. He
hailed a taxi and asked to be taken to the park where, on Monday, he had met the doctor's wife, there's no reason why one
should always do the thing one first decided to do. He had not
thought of going back to the park, but here he is. He will then
continue on foot, like a police superintendent quietly carrying
out his patrol, he will see how crowded the street is and may
even exchange professional notes with the two guards. He
walked through the garden and stopped for a moment to study
the statue of the woman with the empty water jar, They left me
here, she seemed to be saying, and now all I'm good for is staring into this grubby water, there was a time when the stone I'm
made from was white, when a fountain flowed day and night

from this jar, they never told me where all that water came from, I was just here to tip up the jar, but now not a drop falls from it, and no one has come to tell me why it stopped. The superintendent murmured, It's like life, my dear, we don't know why it starts or why it ends. He dipped the fingers of his right hand into the water and raised them to his lips. It did not occur to him that the gesture could have any meaning, however, anyone watching him from afar would have sworn that he had kissed that murky water, which was green with slime and came from a muddy pond, as impure as life itself. The clock had not advanced very much, he would have had time to sit down in the shade somewhere, but he did not. He repeated the route he had taken with the doctor's wife, he went into the street, where the scene had changed completely, now he could barely push his way through, there weren't just small knots of people, but a huge crowd that blocked the traffic, it was as if everyone from the neighboring area had left their houses to come and witness some promised apparition. The superintendent beckoned the two policemen over to the doorway of a building and asked them if anything had happened in his absence. They said that no one had left, that the windows had remained closed at all times, and they reported that two people unknown to them, a man and a woman, had gone up to the fourth floor to ask if the people in the apartment needed anything, but that the latter had replied in the negative and thanked them for their kindness. Is that all, asked the superintendent, As far as we know, replied one of the policemen, it's certainly going to be an easy report to write. He said this just in time, clipping the wings of the superintendent's imagination, which had unfurled and were already carrying him up the stairs, where he would ring the bell and announce, It's me, and then go in and tell them about the latest events, about the letters he had written, his conversation with the editor-in-chief, and then the doctor's wife would say

Stay and have lunch with us, and he would, and the world would be at peace. Yes, at peace, and the policemen would write in their report, A superintendent who joined us went up to the fourth floor and only came down again an hour later, he did not say anything about what happened up there, but we both got the impression that he had had a good lunch. The superintendent went to have lunch somewhere else, but he did not eat much and showed no interest in the dish they set before him, at three o'clock, he was sitting in the park again looking at the statue of the woman with her pitcher inclined like someone still expecting the miraculous restoration of the waters. At half past three, he got up from the bench where he had sat down and walked back to the newspaper offices. He had time, he didn't need to take a taxi in which, however reluctantly, he would have been unable to keep himself from looking in the rear-view mirror, he knew quite enough about his soul already and he might see something in the mirror that he didn't like. It was not quite a quarter past four when he arrived back at the newspaper offices. The secretary was already in reception, The director is expecting you, she said. She did not add the words mister providential, perhaps she had been told that it was not his real name and perhaps she felt offended by the trap into which she had, in all good faith, fallen. They walked down the same corridor, but this time they continued to the end, where they turned the corner, on the second door on the right there is a small notice which says Director. The secretary knocked discreetly, and someone inside answered, Come in. She went in first and held the door open for the superintendent. Thank you, we won't be needing you for the moment, said the editor-in-chief to the secretary, who left immediately. I'm most grateful to you for agreeing to talk to me, sir, began the superintendent, Let me be perfectly frank with you, I foresee enormous difficulties in our publishing the material that the editor-in-chief here has described to me, although I would, of course, be delighted to read the entire document, Here it is, sir, said the superintendent, handing him the envelope, Sit down, said the director, and just give me a couple of minutes, will you. The reading of the document did not make him bow his head as it had the editor-in-chief, but he was clearly a confused and worried man when he looked up, Who are you, he asked, unaware that the editor-in-chief had asked the same question, If your newspaper agrees to make public the contents of that document, then you will find out who I am, if you don't, then I will take back my letter and leave without another word, except to thank you for letting me take up so much of your time, The director knows that you have an identical letter which you intend to give to another newspaper, said the editor-in-chief, Exactly, said the superintendent, I have it here, and if we don't reach an agreement, I will deliver it today, because it's vital that this is published tomorrow, Why, Because tomorrow there may still be time to prevent an injustice being committed, You mean to the doctor's wife, Yes, sir, they are doing all they can to make her the scapegoat for the country's current political situation, But that's ridiculous, Don't tell me that, tell the government, tell the interior minister, tell your colleagues who write what they're told to. The director exchanged a look with the editor-in-chief and said, As you can imagine, it would be impossible for us to publish your statement as it stands, with all these details, Why, Don't forget, we are still living under a state of siege, the censors have their eyes trained on the press, especially on a newspaper like ours, Publishing this would get the newspaper shut down immediately, said the editor-in-chief, So is there nothing to be done, asked the superintendent, We can try, but we can't be sure it will succeed, How, said the superintendent. After another brief exchange of glances with the editor-in-chief, the director said, It's time you told us, once and for all, who you are, there's a name on the letter, it's true, but we have no way of knowing that it's not a false name, you could, quite simply, be an agent provocateur sent here by the police to put us to the test and to compromise us, we're not saying that you are, of course, but I have to make it quite clear that we cannot take this conversation any further unless you identify yourself right now. The superintendent reached into a pocket and pulled out his wallet, Here you are, he said, and handed the director his police identification. The expression on the director's face changed at once from mistrust to stupefaction, What, you're a police superintendent, he said, A police superintendent, repeated the editor-in-chief dully when the director passed the document to him, Yes, came the calm response, and now I think we can continue the conversation, If you'll forgive my curiosity, said the director, what made you take a step like this, Personal reasons, Tell me one of those reasons, so that I can persuade myself that I'm not dreaming, When we are born, when we enter this world, it is as if we signed a pact for the rest of our life, but a day may come when we will ask ourselves Who signed this on my behalf, well, I asked myself that question and the answer is this bit of paper, You do know what might happen to you, don't you, Yes, I've had time enough to think about that. There was a silence, which the superintendent broke, You said you could try, We've thought of a little trick, said the director, and indicated to the editor-in-chief that he should continue, The idea, the editor said, would be to publish, albeit in very different terms and without the tasteless rhetoric, what was published elsewhere today, and then, in the final section, weave in some of the information you've given us today, it won't be easy, but it doesn't strike me as impossible, it's just a matter of skill and luck, We're relying on the boredom or even laziness of the civil servant in the censor's office, added the director, praying that he will think that since he knows this bit of news already, there's no point reading to the end, What's the probability that we'll succeed, asked the superintendent, To be perfectly frank, pretty low, admitted the editor-in-chief, we'll have to content ourselves with possibilities, And what if the ministry of the interior want to know where you got your information, To begin with we'll take refuge in insisting on the confidentiality of our sources, but that isn't going to be much use in a state of siege situation, And if they press you, if they threaten you, Then, much against our will, we will have no option but to reveal our source, we'll be punished, of course, but you will suffer the worst consequences, said the director, Fine, said the superintendent, now that we all know what to expect, let's do it, and if praying serves any purpose, I'll pray that the readers don't do as we're hoping the censor will do, that is, I'll pray that the readers do read the article through to the end, Amen, chorused the director and the editor-in-chief.

It was shortly after five o'clock when the superintendent left. He could have taken advantage of the taxi that someone else had just left at the door of the newspaper offices, but he preferred to walk. Oddly enough, he felt light and serene, as if someone had removed from some vital organ the foreign body that had been gradually gnawing away at him, a bone in the throat, a nail in the stomach, poison in the liver. Tomorrow all the cards in the deck would be on the table, the game of hide-and-seek would be over, and so he has not the slightest doubt that the minister, always assuming that the article does see the light of day, and, even if it doesn't, that news of it reaches his ears, will know immediately at whom to point the accusing finger. Imagination seemed prepared to go further, it even took a first, troubling step, but the superintendent grabbed it by the throat, Today is today, madam, and tomorrow will come soon enough, he said. He had decided to go back to providential ltd, his legs felt suddenly heavy, his nerves as lax as if they were an elastic band that had been kept fully stretched for far too long, he experienced an urgent need to close his eyes and sleep. I'll hail the first taxi that appears, he thought. He still had to walk for quite a way, all the taxis that passed were occupied, one didn't even hear him call, and finally, when he could barely drag his feet along, a small lifeboat picked up the shipwrecked man just before he drowned. The lift hoisted him charitably up to the fourteenth floor, the door opened unresistingly, the sofa received him like a dear friend, and a few minutes later, the superintendent was lying, legs outstretched, fast asleep, or sleeping the sleep of the just, as people used to say in the days when they believed that the just existed. Snuggled up in the maternal lap of providential ltd, insurance and reinsurance, whose peaceful atmosphere did full justice to the names and attributes conferred upon it, the superintendent slept for a good hour, at the end of which he awoke with renewed energy, or so at least it seemed to him. When he stretched, he felt the second envelope in his inside jacket pocket, the one he had not delivered, Perhaps I was wrong to bet everything on one horse, he thought, then quickly realized that he could not possibly have had the same conversation twice, that he could not have gone straight from one newspaper to the next and told the same story, and by repetition, worn away at its veracity, What's done is done, he thought, there's no point thinking about it anymore. He went into his bedroom and saw the light on the answering machine flashing. Someone had phoned and left a message. He pressed the button, the telephonist's voice spoke first, then that of the police commissioner, Please note that tomorrow, at nine o'clock, I repeat, at nine o'clock, not at twenty-one hundred hours, your colleagues, the inspector and the sergeant, will be waiting for you at post six-north, I should tell you that, not only has your mission failed due to the technical and scientific incompetence of the person in charge, your presence in the capital has now also come to be considered inappropriate both by the interior minister and by myself, I need only add that the inspector and the sergeant are officially responsible for escorting you to my presence and have orders to arrest you if you resist. The superintendent stood staring at the answering machine, and then, slowly, like a person saying goodbye to someone setting off on a long trip, reached out his hand and pressed the erase button. Then he went into the kitchen, took the envelope out of his pocket, soaked it in alcohol and, folding it to form an inverted V in the sink, set fire to it. A gush of water carried the ashes down the drain. Having done that, he went back into the living-room, turned on all the lights, and devoted himself to a leisurely perusal of the newspapers, paying special attention to the paper to which or to whom, in some way, he had handed his fate. When it was time, he went and looked in the fridge to see if he could prepare something resembling supper from whatever was in there, but soon gave up, scarcity was not, in this case, a synonym for either freshness or quality. They should install a new fridge here, he thought, this one has given all it had to give. He went out, ate quickly in the first restaurant he came across and returned to providential ltd. He had to get up early the following day.

THE superintendent was awake when the telephone rang. He did not get up to answer it, he was sure that it would be someone from the police commissioner's office reminding him of the order he had received to appear at nine o'clock, note, at nine o'clock, not at twenty-one hundred hours, at military post six-north. They probably won't phone again, and one can easily understand why, for in their professional lives and, who knows, possibly in their private lives too, policemen make great use of the mental process we call deduction, also known as logical inference. If he doesn't answer, they would say, it's because he's already on his way. How wrong they were. It's true that the superintendent has now got out of bed, it's true that he has entered the bathroom to perform the appropriate actions to relieve and cleanse his body, it is true that he has got dressed and is about to leave, but not in order to hail the first taxi that appears and say to the driver, who is looking at him expectantly in the rear-view mirror, Take me to post six-north, Post six-north, I'm sorry, but I've no idea where that is, it must be a new street, No, it's a military post, I can show you where it is if you have a map. No, this dialogue will never take place, not now or ever, the superintendent is going out to buy the newspapers, that was why he went to bed early yesterday, not in order to get enough rest and arrive promptly for the meeting at post six-north. The street lamps are still on, the man at the newspaper kiosk has just raised the shutters, he is starting to set out the week's magazines, and when he finishes this work, as if it were a sign, the street lamps go out and the distribution truck arrives. The superintendent approaches while the man is still sorting out the newspapers into the order with which we are already familiar, but, this time, there are almost as many copies of one of the less popular newspapers as there are of the papers with a larger circulation. The superintendent felt this was a good omen, but this pleasant feeling of hope was immediately succeeded by a violent shock, the headlines on the first newspapers in the row were sinister, troubling, and all in intense red ink, Murderess, This Woman Killed, Woman Suspect's Other Crime, A Murder Committed Four Years Ago. At the other end of the row, the newspaper whose offices the superintendent had visited yesterday asked, What Haven't We Been Told. The headline was ambiguous, it could mean this or that, or the opposite, but the superintendent preferred to see it as a small lantern placed there to guide his stumbling steps out of the valley of shadows. A copy of each, he said. The newsagent smiled, thinking that he seemed to have acquired a good customer for the future, and handed him the plastic bag containing the newspapers. The superintendent looked around for a taxi, he waited in vain for nearly five minutes, then decided to walk back to providential ltd, which is not, as we know, very far from here, but he is carrying a heavy load, a plastic bag bursting with words, it would be easier to carry the world on one's back. As luck would have it, though, he took a short-cut down a narrow street and came upon a modest, old-style café, the sort that opens early because the owner has nothing else to do and which the customers visit in order to make sure that everything is there in its usual place and where the taste of the breakfast muffin speaks of eternity. He sat down at a table, ordered a white coffee, asked if they served toast, with butter, of course, no margarine, please. The coffee, when it arrived, was merely passable, but the toast had come direct from the hands of an alchemist who had only failed to discover the philosopher's stone because he had never managed to get beyond the putrefaction stage. The superintendent had opened the newspaper that most interested him today, he did so as soon as he sat down, and a quick glance was enough for him to see that the trick had worked, the censor had allowed himself to be taken in by the confirmation of what he already knew, and the thought had clearly never even crossed his mind that one must always take great care with what one thinks one knows, because behind it one finds concealed an endless chain of unknowns, the last of which will probably prove insoluble. Nevertheless, there was no point in harboring any great illusions, the newspaper would not be on sale at the kiosks all day, he could already imagine the enraged interior minister brandishing a copy and yelling, Get this garbage impounded at once and find out who leaked this information, the last part of the phrase had attached itself automatically, for the minister would know perfectly well that there was only one possible source for this act of treachery and betrayal. It was then that the superintendent decided that he would visit as many newspaper kiosks as his strength would allow in order to find out if the newspaper was selling in large or small numbers, to see the faces of the people who were buying it and to find out if they turned straight to the article or were distracted by frivolities. He glanced quickly at the four biggest-selling newspapers. Crudely elementary, but effective, the work of poisoning the public was continuing, two and two are four and always will be four, if that's what you did yesterday, then you must have done the same today, and anyone who has the

temerity to doubt that one thing inevitably leads to another is
an enemy of legality and order. Pleased, he paid the bill and
left. He started with the kiosk where he himself had bought the
newspapers and had the satisfaction of seeing that the relevant
pile had gone down quite a bit. Interesting, isn't it, he said to
the newsagent, it's selling really well, Apparently some radio
station mentioned an article they published, One hand washes
the other and both hands wash the face, said the superintendent mysteriously, Yes, you're right, replied the man, although
he had no idea what the superintendent meant. So as not to
waste time looking for other kiosks, the superintendent asked
each newsagent where the next one was, and, perhaps because
of his respectable appearance, they always gave him the information, but it was clear that every one of those newsagents
would like to have asked him What have they got that I haven't.
The hours passed, the inspector and the sergeant, over there at
post six-north, had grown weary of waiting and had asked for
instructions from the police commissioner's office, the commissioner had informed the minister, the minister had explained
the situation to the prime minister, and the prime minister had
replied, It's not my problem, it's yours, you sort it out. Then the
expected happened, when he reached the tenth kiosk, the superintendent could not find the newspaper. He asked for it,
pretending he was going to buy a copy, but the newsagent said,
You're too late, they took them all away less than five minutes
ago, They took them, why, They're collecting them from all
the kiosks, Collecting them, That's another way of saying im-
pounding them, But why, what was in the newspaper to make
them do that, It was something about that woman and the conspiracy, you know, it's been in all the other papers, well, now it
seems she killed a man, Couldn't you get me a copy, you'd be
doing me a great favor, No, I haven't got one, and even if I had,
I wouldn't sell it to you, Why not, How do I know you're not a

police officer on the prowl to see if I take the bait, You're quite right, you can't be too careful, said the superintendent and walked off. He didn't want to go back to providential ltd, insurance and reinsurance, to listen to that morning's phone call and doubtless others demanding to know where he was, why he wasn't answering the phone, why he had disobeyed the order to be at post six-north at nine o'clock, but the fact is he has nowhere to go, by now, there must be a sea of people outside the house of the doctor's wife, all shouting, some in favor, some against, although they're probably all in favor, the others would be in the minority, they probably don't want to risk being insulted or worse. Nor can he go to the offices of the newspaper that published the article, if there aren't any plain-clothes policemen at the entrance, they'll be around somewhere, he can't even phone because all the lines will doubtless be tapped, and when he thought this, he understood, at last, that providential ltd, insurance and reinsurance, would be under surveillance too, that all the hotels would have been forewarned, that there is not a single soul in the city who could take him in, even if he or she wanted to. He imagines that the newspaper will have received a visit from the police, he imagines that the director will have been forced, willingly or not, to reveal the identity of the person who provided him with the subversive information they had published, he might even have been reduced to showing them the letter bearing the name providential ltd, and signed in the fugitive superintendent's own hand. He felt tired, his feet dragged, his body was bathed in sweat, although it wasn't even particularly hot. He couldn't wander these streets all day just pointlessly killing time, then, suddenly, he felt a great desire to go to the park with the statue of the woman and the water jar, to sit down by the edge of the pool, to stroke the green water with the tips of his fingers and raise them to his mouth. But then what will I do, he asked. Nothing, except plunge back into the labyrinth of streets, to get disoriented and lost and then turn back, walking and walking, eating even if he isn't hungry, just to keep his body going, spending a couple of hours in a cinema, distracting himself by watching the adventures of an expedition to mars in the days when it was still inhabited by little green men, and coming out, blinking in the bright afternoon light, considering going to another cinema to waste another two hours traveling twenty thousand leagues under the sea in captain nemo's submarine, and then entirely giving up the idea because there is clearly something strange happening in the city, men and women are handing out small sheets of paper that people stop to read and then immediately stuff into a pocket, they've just handed one to the superintendent, it's a photocopy of the article from the impounded newspaper, the one bearing the headline What Haven't We Been Told, the one which, between the lines, tells the true story of the last five days, the superintendent can control himself no longer, and right there, like a child, he bursts into convulsive sobs, a woman of about his age comes and asks if he's all right, if he needs help, and he can only shake his head, no, thank you, he's fine, don't worry, and since chance does occasionally do the right thing, someone from one of the top storeys of this building hurls out a handful of papers, and another and another, and down below the people hold up their arms to catch them, and the papers float down, they glide like doves, and one of them rests for a moment on the superintendent's shoulder before sliding to the ground. So, in the end, nothing is lost, the city has taken the matter into its own hands and set hundreds of photocopiers working, and now there are animated groups of boys and girls slipping the sheets of paper into mailboxes or delivering them to people's doors, someone asks if they're advertising something and they say, yes, sir, it's the very best of advertisements. These happy events gave the superintendent a new soul, and as if with a magic wave of the hand, white magic, not black, all his tiredness vanished, this is a different man walking these streets now, this is a different mind doing the thinking, seeing clearly what had been obscure before, amending conclusions that had seemed rock-solid and which now crumble between the fingers that touch them and decide, instead, that it is highly unlikely that providential ltd, insurance and reinsurance, since it is a secret base, would have been placed under surveillance, after all, posting police guards there could arouse suspicions as to its importance and significance, although that would not, on the other hand, be particularly grave, since they could simply take providential ltd somewhere else and the matter would be resolved. This new and negative conclusion cast stormy shadows over the superintendent's spirit, but his next conclusion, while not entirely reassuring, at least served to resolve the serious problem of accommodation or, in other words, not knowing where he would sleep that night. The matter can be explained in a few brief words. The fact that the ministry of the interior and the police commissioner's office viewed with more than justifiable displeasure the way that this public servant had unilaterally severed all contact with them did not mean that they had lost interest in where he was and where he could be found if needed urgently. If the superintendent had decided to lose himself in this city, if he had gone to ground in some gloomy backstreet, as outcasts and runaways usually do, they would have the devil's own job to find him, especially if he had established a network of contacts amongst other subversive elements, an operation which, on the other hand, given its complexity, is not something that can be set in motion in the space of six days or so, which is the time we have spent here. Therefore, far from guarding the two entrances to providential ltd, they would, on the contrary, leave the way free so that the homing instinct that is natural to all creatures would make the wolf return to its cave, the puffin to its hole in the cliffs. So the superintendent could still enjoy a familiar, welcoming bed, always assuming they don't come and wake him in the middle of the night, having opened the front door with delicate skeleton keys and forced him to surrender with the threat of three guns pointed straight at him. It is true, as we have said before, that there are times in life so grim that it's either raining on one side or blowing a gale on the other, and this is the situation in which the superintendent finds himself now, obliged to choose between spending an uncomfortable night under a tree in the park, like a tramp, within sight of the woman with the water jar, or comfortably ensconced between the stale blankets and crumpled sheets of providential ltd, insurance and reinsurance. This explanation did not prove to be quite as succinct as we promised, however, as we hope you will understand, we could not dismiss any of the possible variables without due consideration, detailing, impartially, the diverse and contradictory risk and safety factors, only to reach the conclusion we should have reached at the start, that there is no point running away to baghdad in order to avoid a meeting arranged for you in samarra. Having weighed and considered everything and decided to waste no further time on pondering the various weights down to the last milligram, the last possibility and the last hypothesis, the superintendent took a taxi to providential ltd, this was at the end of the evening, when the shadows cool the path ahead and the sound of water falling into pools grows bolder and, to the surprise of those who pass, becomes suddenly perceptible. There is not a single piece of paper left in the streets. Despite all this, it is clear that the superintendent feels slightly apprehensive and he has reason enough to do so. His own reasoning and the knowledge he has acquired over time regarding the wiles of the police have led him to conclude that no danger awaits him at providential ltd or will assail him later tonight, but this does not mean that samarra is not where it has to be. This thought caused the superintendent to place his hand on his gun and to think, Just in case, I'll use the time it takes to go up in the lift to leave the gun cocked. The taxi stopped, We're here, said the driver, and it was at that moment that the superintendent saw, stuck to the windscreen, a photocopy of the article. Despite his fear, all the anxiety and trepidation had been worthwhile. The lobby was deserted, the porter absent, the scene was set for the perfect crime, a stab wound in the heart, the dull thud of the body as it drops to the tiled floor, the door closing, the car with false number plates that draws up and leaves, bearing away the murderer, nothing simpler than killing and being killed. The lift was there, he did not need to summon it. Now it is going up in order to leave its cargo on the fourteenth floor, inside it a sequence of unmistakable clicks says that a gun has been made ready to fire. There isn't a soul to be seen in the corridor, the offices are all closed at this hour. The key slipped easily into the lock, almost noiselessly the door allowed itself to be opened. The superintendent leaned against it to close it, turned on the light and will now go into every room, open all the wardrobes where a person might hide, peer under the beds, draw back the curtains. No one. He felt vaguely ridiculous, a swashbuckling hero wielding a gun with nothing to point at, but, as the saying goes, slow but sure ensures a ripe old age, as providential ltd must well know, since it deals not only with insurance but with reinsurance. In the bedroom, the light on the answering machine is blinking, and the display indicates that there have been two calls, one might be from the inspector warning him to be careful, the other will be from one of albatross's under-secretaries, or they might both be from the police commissioner, in despair at the treachery of a man he had trusted and, at the same time, worried about his own future, even though he himself had not been responsible for appointing him. The superintendent took out the piece of paper with the names and addresses of the group, to which he had added the doctor's telephone number, which he dialed. No one answered. He dialed again. He dialed a third time, but this time, as if it were a signal, he let it ring three times and then hung up. He dialed a fourth time and, at last, someone answered, Yes, said the doctor's wife abruptly, It's me, the superintendent, Oh, hello, we've been expecting you to call, How have things been, Terrible, in a matter of twenty-four hours, they've managed to transform me into a kind of public enemy number one, Believe me, I'm really sorry for the part I've played in all this, You weren't the one who wrote what the newspapers published, No, I didn't go that far, Maybe the article that appeared in one of them today and the thousands of photocopies that were distributed will help to clear up this whole absurd situation, Maybe, You don't sound very hopeful, Oh, I have hopes, naturally, but it will take time, this business isn't going to resolve itself from one moment to the next, We can't go on living like this, shut up in this apartment, it's like being in prison, All I can say is that I did everything I could, You won't be visiting us again, then, The mission they gave me is over, and I've received orders to go back, Well, I hope we see each other again someday, in happier times than these, if there ever are any, They seem to have got lost en route, Who, Those happier times, You're going to leave me feeling more discouraged than I was, Some people manage to stay standing even when they've been knocked down, and you're one of them, Well, right now, I'd be very grateful for some help getting back on my feet, And I'm only sorry I can't give you that help, Oh, I think you've helped much more than you let on, That's just your impression, you're talking to a policeman, remember, Oh, I haven't forgotten, but the truth is that I no longer think of you as one, Thank you for that, now all that remains is to say goodbye, until the next time,

Until the next time, Take care, And you, Good night, Good night. The superintendent put the phone down. He had a long night ahead of him and no way of getting through it except by sleeping, unless insomnia got into bed with him. They would probably come for him tomorrow. He had not arrived at post six-north as he had been ordered to, and that is why they will come for him. Perhaps one of the messages he erased had said just that, perhaps they had called to warn him that the people sent to arrest him will be here at seven o'clock in the morning and that any attempt at resistance will only make matters worse. They will not, of course, need skeleton keys to get in, because they will bring a key of their own. The superintendent is fantasizing. He has an arsenal of weapons to hand, ready to be fired, he could fight to the last cartridge, or at least, let's say, to the first canister of tear-gas that they lob into the fortress. The superintendent is fantasizing. He sat down on the bed, then allowed himself to fall backward, he closed his eyes and pleaded for sleep to come soon, I know the night has barely begun, he was thinking, that there is still light in the sky, but I want to sleep the way a stone seems to sleep, without the traps set by dreams, but to be enclosed in a block of black stone, at least, please, at the very least, until morning, when they come to wake me at seven o'clock. Hearing his desolate cry, sleep came running and stayed there for a few moments, then withdrew while he undressed and got into bed, only to return at once, with hardly a second's delay, to remain by his side all night, chasing any dreams far away into the land of ghosts, the place where, mingling fire and water, they are born and multiply.

It was nine o'clock when the superintendent woke up. He wasn't crying, a sign that the invaders had not used tear-gas, he did not have handcuffs round his wrists or guns leveled at his head, how often fears come to sour our life and prove, in the end, to have no foundation, no reason to exist. He got up,

shaved, washed and dressed as usual, then went out intending to go to the café where he had eaten breakfast the previous day. On the way, he bought the newspapers, I thought you
weren't coming today, said the man at the kiosk with all the
familiarity of an old acquaintance, There's one missing, commented the superintendent, It didn't appear today, and the dis-
tributor doesn't know when it will be published again, possibly next week, apparently they've had a massive fine slapped
on them, But why, Because of that article, the one they made
all those photocopies of, Oh, I see, Here's your bag, there are
only five papers today, so you'll have less to read. The superintendent thanked him and went in search of the café. He could
no longer remember where the street was and his appetite was
growing with each step he took, the thought of toast made his
mouth water, we must forgive this man for what may appear,
at first sight, to be deplorable gluttony, inappropriate in a man
of his age and standing, but we must remember that yesterday he went to bed on an empty stomach. He finally found the
street and the café, now he is sitting at the table, and while he
waits, he glances through the papers, here are the headlines,
in black and red, so that we can get a rough idea of their respective contents, Another Subversive Act By The Enemies Of
Our Country, Who Set the Photocopiers Working, The Dangers Of Disinformation, Who Paid For Those Photocopies.
The superintendent ate slowly, savoring every mouthful down
to the last crumb, even the coffee tastes better than yesterday,
and when he had finished his meal, his body now refreshed, his
spirit which, ever since yesterday, had felt itself under an obligation to the park and the pond, to the green water and the
woman with the water jar, reminded him, You so wanted to go
there, but you didn't, Well, I'll go now, replied the superintendent. He paid, put all the papers back in the bag and set off. He
could have caught a taxi, but he preferred to go on foot. He had

nothing else to do and it was a way of passing the time. When he reached the park, he went and sat on the bench where he had talked to the doctor's wife and become properly acquainted with the dog of tears. From there he could see the pond and the woman with the water jar poised for pouring. Underneath the tree, it was still slightly cool. He drew his raincoat over his knees and, with a sigh of satisfaction, made himself comfortable. The man wearing the blue tie with white spots came up behind him and shot him in the head.

Two hours later, the interior minister was giving a press conference. He was wearing a white shirt and a black tie and, on his face, an expression of deep regret, of profound grief. The table was crowded with microphones and the only other ornament was a glass of water. As always, the national flag hung meditatively behind him. Good afternoon, ladies and gentlemen, said the minister, I have summoned you here today to give you the tragic news of the death of the superintendent who had been charged by me with investigating the conspiratorial web whose leader, as you know, has how been revealed. Unfortunately, his was not a natural death, but the result of a deliberate, premeditated murder, the work, no doubt, of a professional criminal of the worst kind if we bear in mind that a single bullet was enough to carry out the killing. Needless to say, all the indications are that this was a new criminal action by the subversive elements in our unhappy former capital, who continue to undermine the stability of the democratic system and its correct functioning, and to work cold-bloodedly against the political, social and moral integrity of our nation. I need hardly point out that the example of supreme dignity offered to us today by the murdered superintendent will, forever after, be the object not just of our utter respect, but also of our most profound veneration, for his sacrifice has, from this day forth, and a most unhappy day it is, bestowed on him a place of honor in the pantheon of our nation's martyrs who, up there in the beyond, have their eyes always upon us. The national government, which I am here to represent, shares the mourning and grief of all those who knew the extraordinary human being we have just lost, and, at the same time, assures all the citizens of this land that it will not be discouraged in this war we are waging against the evil of the conspirators and the irresponsibility of those who support them. Just two further points, the first to tell you that the inspector and the sergeant who were assisting the murdered superintendent in the investigation had been withdrawn from the mission at the latter's request so as to protect their lives, the second to inform you that, as regards this fine man, this exemplary servant of the nation, who, alas, we have just lost, the government will examine by what legal means he may, exceptionally and posthumously, and as quickly as possible, be awarded the highest honor with which the nation distinguishes those of its sons and daughters who bring honor upon it. Today, ladies and gentlemen, is a sad day for decent people, but duty requires us all to cry sursum corda, lift up your hearts. A journalist raised his hand to ask a question, but the interior minister was already leaving, on the table only the untouched glass of water remained, the microphones recorded the respectful silence due to the dead, and, behind them, the flag tirelessly continued its meditation. The following two hours were spent by the minister and his closest advisors in drawing up an immediate plan of action that would consist, basically, in arranging a surreptitious return to the capital city of a large number of policemen, who, for now, would work in plain clothes, with no outward sign that might indicate to which organization they belonged. This was an implicit admission that they had committed a very grave error indeed in leaving the former capital unsupervised. But it's not too late to correct that mistake, said the minister. At that precise moment, an under-secretary came in to tell the interior minister that the prime minister wished to speak to him immediately in his office. The minister made a muttered comment that the prime minister could have chosen a better time, but had no option but to obey the summons. He left his advisors to put the finishing logistical touches to the plan and set off. The car, with guards to front and rear, bore him to the building in which the cabinet offices had been installed, this took him ten minutes, and five minutes later, he was entering the prime minister's office, Good afternoon, prime minister, Good afternoon, do sit down, You phoned me just as I was working on a plan to rectify the decision we took to withdraw the police from the capital, I can probably bring it to you tomorrow, Don't bother, Why not, prime minister, Because you won't have time, The plan is almost finished, it just needs a few minor touches, You do not, I'm afraid, understand, when I say that you won't have time, I mean that by tomorrow you will no longer be interior minister, What, the question emerged just like that, explosive and somewhat disrespectful, You heard what I said, there's no need for me to repeat it, But, prime minister, Let's save ourselves a pointless conversation, your duties cease as of this moment, Such harshness is most unjust, prime minister, and is, if I may say so, a strange and arbitrary way of rewarding my services to the nation, there must be a reason, which I hope you will give me, for this brutal dismissal, yes, brutal, I won't withdraw the word, Your services during the crisis have been one long string of errors which I won't bother to enumerate, I can understand that necessity knows no law, that the ends justify the means, but always on condition that the ends are achieved and the law of necessity is obeyed, but you obeyed and achieved neither, and now there's the death of the superintendent, He was murdered by our enemies, Please, don't come to me with any operatic arias, I've been in this game too long to believe in fairy tales, the enemies of whom you speak had, on the contrary, every reason to make him their hero and no reason at all to kill him, There was no other way out, prime minister, the man had become a subversive influence, We would have settled our accounts with him later, not now, his death was an unforgivable blunder, and now, as if that weren't enough, we've got demonstrations in the streets, Insignificant, prime minister, my information, Your information is worthless, half the population is out on the street already and the other half will soon be joining them, The future, prime minister, will, I am sure, judge that I was right, And a fat lot of good it will do you if the present judges you to be wrong, and now, that's an end to it, please leave, this conversation is over, But I need to hand on any matters pending to my successor, Don't worry, I'll send someone over to deal with all that, But what about my successor, I'm your successor, after all, why shouldn't the prime-minister-cum-justice-minister also be the interior minister, that way we can keep it all in the family, so don't you worry, I'll take care of everything.

A T TEN o'clock in the morning on this same day, two plain-clothes policemen went up to the fourth floor and rang the bell. The doctor's wife answered and asked, Who are you, what do you want, We're policemen and we have orders to take your husband away to be questioned, and there's no point telling us he's gone out, the building is being watched, which is why we know he's here, You have absolutely no reason to question him, up until now, I've been the one accused of all the crimes, That's not our business, we've received strict orders to take the doctor and not the doctor's wife, so, unless you want us to force our way in, go and call him, and keep that dog under control too, we wouldn't want anything to happen to it. The woman closed the door. She opened it again shortly afterward, and this time her husband was with her, What do you want, To take you in for questioning, we've told your wife already, we're not going to stand here all day repeating it, Do you have any credentials with you, a warrant, We don't need a warrant, the city's under a state of siege, and as for credentials, here's our identification, will that do, Can I change my clothes first, One of us will go with you, Are you afraid I'll run away or commit suicide, We're just following orders, that's all. One of the policemen went inside, they did not take long. Wherever my husband's going, I'm going with him, said the woman, Like I said, you're not going anywhere, you're staying here, don't make me have to get nasty with you, You couldn't be any nastier than you already are, Oh, believe me, I could, you can't imagine how nasty I can be, and then to the doctor, You've got to be handcuffed, hold out your hands, Please, don't put those things on me, please, I give you my word of honor that I won't try to escape, Come on, put your hands out, and forget about words of honor, right, that's better, you're safer like that. The woman embraced her husband and kissed him, weeping, They won't let me come with you, Don't worry, I'll be back home tonight, you'll see, Come home soon, I will, my love, I will. The lift started to go down.

At eleven o'clock, the man in the blue tie with white spots went up onto the flat roof of the building almost opposite the back of the building where the doctor's wife and her husband live. He is carrying a box of varnished wood, rectangular in shape. Inside is a dismantled weapon, an automatic rifle with a telescopic sight, which he will not use because at such a short distance no good marksman could possibly miss his target. He will not use the silencer either, but, in this case, it is for reasons of an ethical order, the man in the blue tie with white spots feels that the use of such apparatus shows a gross disrespect for the victim. The weapon has been assembled now and loaded, with each piece in its place, a perfect instrument for the job it is intended to do. The man in the blue tie with white spots chooses the place from which he will fire and prepares himself to wait. He is a patient man, he has been doing this for years and always does his work well. Sooner or later, the doctor's wife will come out onto the balcony. Meanwhile, just in case the waiting should go on for too long, the man in the blue tie with white spots has brought with him another weapon, an ordinary cata-

pult, the sort that is used for hurling stones, especially for the
purpose of breaking windows. No one hears the glass breaking
and no one comes running to see who the childish vandal was.
An hour has passed, and the doctor's wife has still not appeared,
she has been crying, poor thing, but now she will go and get
some fresh air, she doesn't open one of the windows that give
onto the street because there are always people watching, she
prefers the back of the house, so much quieter since the advent of television. The woman goes over to the iron balustrade,
places her hands on it and feels the coolness of the metal. We
cannot ask her if she heard the two successive shots, she is lying dead on the ground and her blood is sliding and dripping
onto the balcony below. The dog comes running out, he sniffs
and licks his mistress's face, then he stretches out his neck and
unleashes a terrifying howl which another shot silences. Then
a blind man asked, Did you hear something, Three shots, replied another blind man, But there was a dog howling too, It's
stopped now, that must have been the third shot, Good, I hate
to hear dogs howl.